"A masterwork of political intrigue and suspense. There are very few times when I can't put a book down, but I had to read this twisting and gripping thriller late into the night."

—Patrick Robinson,
New York Times bestselling author of *To the Death*,
on *Banquo's Ghosts*

"An intelligent, supercharged thriller. Rich Lowry and Keith Korman have crafted a scenario so real, and so frightening, that readers (both inside and outside the CIA) will undoubtedly lose sleep over it. This is what the modern espionage novel is all about."

—Brad Thor,
New York Times bestselling author
of *The Last Patriot,* on *Banquo's Ghosts*

"Captivating . . . Engaging and memorable."
—*Publishers Weekly*
(starred review) on *Secret Dreams*

"A dazzling debut political thriller . . . A fast-paced and chilling wild ride."

—Robert K. Tanenbaum,
New York Times bestselling author of *Escape*,
on *Banquo's Ghosts*

ALSO BY KEITH KORMAN

Swan Dive

Archangel

Secret Dreams

Banquo's Ghosts
(with Rich Lowry)

END TIME

KEITH KORMAN

TOR

A TOM DOHERTY ASSOCIATES BOOK • NEW YORK

This is a work of fiction. All of the characters, organizations, and events portrayed in this novel are either products of the author's imagination or are used fictitiously.

END TIME

Line drawings of The Dancing Men, Cyclic Adenosine Monophosphate, and Lagrange Points by Jacqueline Koprowski

A Tor Book
Published by Tom Doherty Associates, LLC
175 Fifth Avenue
New York, NY 10010

www.tor-forge.com

Tor® is a registered trademark of Tom Doherty Associates, LLC.

ISBN 978-0-7653-7049-5

Our books may be purchased in bulk for promotional, educational, or business use. Please contact your local bookseller or the Macmillan Corporate and Premium Sales Department at 1-800-221-7945, extension 5442, or by e-mail at MacmillanSpecialMarkets@macmillan.com.

First Edition: August 2015
First Mass Market Edition: August 2016

Printed in the United States of America

0 9 8 7 6 5 4 3 2 1

For Maxine
My Tea House of the Hidden Moon

ACKNOWLEDGMENTS

We've got to live, no matter how many skies have fallen.
—D. H. Lawrence,
Lady Chatterley's Lover

The theater of life is a confusing and amusing drama. Just as on the stage, some players have greater roles than others. In the book's four male archetypes—the Scientist, Bhakti Singh; the Soldier, Billy Shadow; the Husband, Guy Poole; the Industrialist, Clem Lattimore—you can see the reflections of Bernard Korman, Sensei Masakazu Takahashi, Bert Wheeler, and the late Theron Raines. Men larger than life and deeper than any archetypes—*the best* humanity can offer. Men who can distinguish good from bad, right from wrong, and up from down. No matter how many skies have fallen.

In Granny Sparrow you can see my mother, Joan Raines, not 100 years old, as in the book—but presently in her mid-eighties, still hale and hearty—listening for the whoop of my wolf whistle ring coming out of the tall grass.

But if you ever meet Professor Guppy of the Ant Colony, droning away in some lecture hall, or the Pied Piper, lurking in some tenement of the mind—they're no relation of mine. Just people I've seen in the passing parade. Be warned and give them a wide berth.

As for the *Tea House of the Hidden Moon* . . . it dwells in all of us. Silently waiting for the time we need it most.

January 2015

CONTENTS

Part One
HORROR SHOW
1

Part Two
YELLOW JACK
251

Part Three
WEATHER
437

Epilogue
AMERICAN GOTHIC
571

PART ONE

Horror Show

Whatever the scientists may say, if we take the supernatural out of life, we leave only the unnatural.

—Nineteenth-century novelist Amelia Edith Barr,
author of *Remember the Alamo*, whose husband
and three of six children perished in the
Yellow Fever Epidemic of 1867

PART ONE

Horror Show

1

※

Fairfield

The New Haven Line Metro-North train from Manhattan was crowded as always, even at 3 p.m. The first carloads of commuters; the early risers home from the morning shift; union construction workers who finished early in the afternoon; middle-class moms—some with nannies, some without—their preschoolers in tow from a day in the city, a museum, a matinee play, or just Central Park. Fridays the cars often packed wall to wall with the weekender getaways. This Friday no exception.

Somewhere around Norwalk the fight started. A young man clad in a shimmering chartreuse Lycra cycling suit, complete with crème-de-menthe helmet that made him look like the love child of Froggy Long Legs and the Riddler, stood by the pneumatic doors, touring bicycle balanced on the rear wheel, hoping to minimize his own use of space. As the doors opened and the crush of commuters exited the train, one of the bike wheels accidentally touched a business man's head. The man, who looked like he'd never had an easy day in his life, turned on the Green Goblin, his face an evil dirty rag.

"You need a permit for that! You need a damn permit!"

The cyclist came back just as hard. "I have a *damn* permit. You want to see it? Here's my damn permit!" The wheel brushed the graying business man's shoulder. Other commuters were crowding the doors to exit, but the fight was on. The $800 touring bike thrown down half on the platform, half in the car. People trying to step over the damn thing while the two men tangled in a death grip.

A woman holding a folded baby stroller in one arm and her toddler in the other was pushed by the surging crowd onto the bike pedals, cutting her shin. She shrieked as the train doors closed and opened and opened and closed on the fallen bike. The two men were now on the Norwalk platform, wrestling on the ground, biting and kicking and strangling like two of the Three Stooges. Where was Moe? Hey Moe!

Guy Poole, one of a thousand daily commuters traveling north from the city, watched it all from a seat nearby; the thought entered his mind to interfere, break it up—but there were simply too many bodies between him and the two idiots. Better to let it play out.

In the end, the New Haven Line conductor finally noticed, the Norwalk police were called, the train delayed for an hour, and Guy Poole didn't get home to Lauren and the two sweet doggies in Fairfield till 6:30 p.m., just the same as if he'd left the office at five. Why bother leaving early? A simple enough reason: like half of everybody down in corporate Manhattan, the ad agency had fired him that week.

Farewell, Pequod Advertising Group.

Sorry, *downsized*, let him go. When the musical chairs stopped Guy was the one extra account executive looking for a seat, and closest to the door. The personal possessions in his office were cleaned out, boxed, and sent down to Shipping for UPS. They'd probably take it out of his severance. And nobody was giving farewell parties anymore. But that was the least of it, in a world gone mad.

On a brighter note, Poole's severance might last him a little over a year. And that was a blessing. Lauren worked at a local realtor, often bringing in a solid 75K, which would cover groceries, health care, and vet bills. Lauren's Auntie Whitcomb left her a small legacy. The house had been paid off a dozen years ago. And Poole had Lauren. Things could have been a lot worse.

Poole and Lauren owned one of the oldest clapboard houses in Fairfield, a short walk from the village, still listing for a little under a million even during the crash. The Henry Finn House, little brass historical plaque by the front door, almost 3000 square feet, a four-bedroom, three-bath, four-fireplace gem, with a picket fence, a nice hunk of yard. At the front of the house there was the Keeping Room, left over from colonial times. Back when houses were small and cold the Keeping Room was the center of the home with a large fireplace, connected to the kitchen; often where the Puritan adults slept, sending the children into the colder attic. The Keeping Room was a sort of parlor, a place to gather, to get warm, and even write when cold New England winters froze the ink in the inkwells. In more splendid homes there were larger keeping rooms where people even danced and drank and sang songs to pass the nights away. If they weren't Shakers or Quakers.

And when the power went out late last fall in the ice storm, Guy and Lauren actually used the Keeping Room. Four days without power, one night going down to 16 degrees outside. Huddled around the fireplace, with kerosene lamps and candles for light, Poole and Lauren played Parcheesi and went to bed early in their sleeping bags. Their faithful greyhounds, Corky and Peaches, found a spot much to their liking wedged on one of their cushy dog beds in between the two of them.

Some of the best fun they'd ever had, even if they didn't shower for four days. Looking at Lauren's clear face in the candlelight and flutter light of the fire, Poole could almost see her in wimple, apron, and buckled shoes like in Puritan times, and when he caught Lauren's eye it glistened back at him with a flicker of laughter.

"Are you planning to make us stand at dinner, my Husband?" she asked him.

"I'm partial to that custom," Poole answered her. "But I won't make you say 'Thee' or 'Thou,' but you can call me Sir Guy. And as the Parcheesi rules haven't changed, stop your female babbling and throw us the devil dice, Woman."

He'd had the presence of mind to dribble some antifreeze into the toilet tanks and bowls so the porcelain didn't burst in the freeze. Such forethought let him live as Sir Guy or Master Poole for quite some time thereafter.

On one of those powerless ice-storm nights Poole awoke to put more wood on the fire. He returned to his sleeping bag on the floor, touching it once to make sure it wasn't getting too hot. Before Poole's head fell to the pillow something caught his eye by the dark stairs to the upper bedrooms; a figure crouched in the flickering shadows.

A young lady.

She sat on the bottom step dressed in a little striped dress with puffed sleeves, and an apron with pockets like one of those Sir John Tenniel illustrations out of *Alice in Wonderland*. She held a sparrow in her cupped hands. The tiny bird hopped from one finger to another and then chirped once. Corky lifted his head from his dog bed and stared, but made no sound. Peaches did the same, looking along her long nose toward the stairs. Generally the two dogs liked chasing birds, and squirrels—but not this time. Boy dog and girl dog sniffed curiously, but didn't move from their warm spot by the fire.

Mildly alarmed, Poole had risen on one elbow in his bag and began to struggle out of the thing. "Hello," he said softly, trying not to wake Lauren or stir up the dogs. "Hello there—what's your na—"

The fire sputtered, a long jet hissing from a log, brighter than before.

The stairs were empty.

Lying back down on his pillow, Poole stared at the fire for a long time, occasionally glancing over to the stairs, as though waiting for the strange figure to return. Corky snuggled up against him, neither dog nor man saying a word. Corky breathed peacefully, and this helped settle his mind. Peaches crawled into a snuggly space on Lauren's sleeping bag, and Guy covered her lanky legs with an extra dog blanket. Neither of the animals made a noise or stirred for the rest of the night. The fire burned well, the Keeping Room stayed warm, and Guy finally fell asleep. When he woke in the morning the two dogs looked at him in that knowing way dogs seem to do, and this strange moment with the girl on the staircase became a secret between them.

A t last Poole got off the train at the Fairfield station and walked past a large white Leprechaun Charter bus without looking too closely at it or the passengers. The packed bus closed its door with a hydraulic hiss and rumbled out of town. Scrawled protest signs littered the ground about the station, along with a crowd's refuse, trash barrels overflowing with fast food wrappers and Starbucks coffee cups. Some of the discarded protest signs were hand-scrawled; others with some kind of union label, but Poole didn't pause to examine them. Whatever their complaint it didn't concern him. Probably a school board thing. But there seemed to be an awful lot of discarded stuff.

The walk home from the Fairfield station was a brisk ten minutes, the blue shadows of an early spring evening, punctuated by the welcoming lights from the village shops and streetlamps, dwindling to darker tree-lined streets. The village lights always seemed to comfort Poole, the reassuring normality of small town life.

But as the town lights began to give way to the quiet

residential houses, Poole sensed something wrong. He passed the village gazebo in the gathering dusk; the firehouse was lit up, the truck bay doors open, one truck on a call. And farther on he spotted fire truck lights under the trees. His pace quickened. He was coming up on his street. And his heart jumped.

More lights, a local sheriff cruiser, a Connecticut State Police vehicle, that town fire truck—the lights bounced off the houses like broken glass thrown in his eyes. Poole began to run, praying *Jesus please, Jesus please* without any coherent thought behind it; Lauren's face swam before his eyes.

In a wave of relief he saw the shadowed figures of his family, counting heads in a nanosecond, yes everyone there, Lauren holding Corky on a leash in one hand and Peaches in the other. The dogs' tails were wagging; always a good sign. Every one of his neighbors, all the families had come out into the street, standing on their patch of yard. The firemen were wrapping their hoses, but his house didn't seem burned.

Sheriff Mike was talking to Lauren; when she saw her husband, she ran to Poole hugging him. "We're okay." And she wrapped him in her sweet scent. Both dogs nosed for a good place under his hand, delighted to see him, doing the greyhound chattering thing which some thought meant doggie laughter. Lauren snuggled in his arm.

Relief washed through him, but what Guy saw at the house made him wonder even more. A ten-foot section of his white picket fence was flattened, like a buffalo had trampled through. The sidewalk around his house was littered with more discarded protest posters, cheap wooden handles, plastic water bottles, plastic deli bags, a scattered box of wet Cracker Jacks. A bag of candy corn scattered everywhere, and a mess of toffee buttons, like some kid had dropped his Halloween swag bag.

What the hell?

Then he saw the reason for the fire truck. A swath of lawn before his front door was burned. Three eight-foot letters scorched into the grass. P—I—G. And the word *bloodsuckr*—misspelled.

"Charcoal fluid," Sheriff Mike explained. "Don't worry about it lighting up again, and the Staties have some names and addresses if you want to press charges. There's a parade permit on file." The scorched grass, the soaked grass, the busted picket fence. Sheriff Mike frowned, baffled, almost ashamed. "I'm really sorry about this, Guy. It kinda got away from us. Then I just wanted them back on the bus and outta here. I don't have holding cells for a hundred ass-clowns."

"Who the hell are these people?" Poole demanded.

Sheriff Mike sighed. "They're some group from down in the city, going on a tour of the rich people's places. They were okay, right up until the end. Maybe the little brass historical plaque set them off," Sheriff Mike suggested. "Thought you were a town father or something." Scuff marks on the front steps; someone had pried off the brass plaque. It was nowhere in sight. Stolen? No, it lay bent on the damp ground. Finally, a message scrawled across his white-painted front door in purple indelible marker: *Felix says Hi!* Corky sniffed a little brown scruffy thing at the corner of the front steps. A dead sparrow. Then Peaches nosed it too.

"No, Corky, Peaches—keep away!" Lauren pulled the two dogs back from the dead feathers.

"P-I-G? Pig?" It dawned on Poole. "As in *Capitalist*? Oh yeah, that's right. The big moneybag outfits, banks and things everybody's mad at."

"Yeah, I guess so." That from Sheriff Mike.

"*Geez.*" Lauren shook her head in complete disbelief. "You didn't even work for a bank."

2

The Pied Piper

The Pied Piper always stood on the southeast corner of Washington Square Park in Manhattan, the "dark" corner because the tall buildings blocked the sunshine most of the day. Then only in late afternoon did the slants of light come in from the West Side. As usual he dressed in his signature top hat and tails, black trousers with the black satin ribbon down the seam.

He'd bought the outfit from a costume liquidator back in LA, oh maybe like *over 60 years ago* . . . in the safe, secure, and Playtex-living-girdled 1950s. The smarmy clerk told him at the time, "This is the exact outfit they used in *Tales of Manhattan*—last worn by Eddie Robinson. And I'll be damned and bite my tongue if it isn't true."

Ten minutes after the Pied Piper left with the jacket and pants tied in brown paper, the top hat in a "complimentary" hatbox for an extra four cents, the smarmy clerk caught his shoe on a creaky floorboard and banged his chin on the counter. Biting off a bit of his tongue. He lisped for the rest of his days, and damned if that wasn't true.

Today, in our present day—the Piper set up in his usual spot by a park bench, putting an open violin case on the pavement for coins, a battered boom box behind it, and his small black doctor's satchel on the bench. The satchel was pasted over with Felix the Cat stickers, smiling Felix at his "Howdy!" smiling best. The Pied Piper had two acts— the teaser and the pay-off—which he announced by way of a square slab of cardboard; on one side was scrawled the word MUSIC—at which point the boom box would flip on with Dvorak's *New World Symphony* while the Pied Piper synced along on his violin.

The violin a dented wreck with no strings; the strung bow with a wisp of bowstring flying about his face. The top hat, the tails, the trousers, the long, gaunt man sawing away—a goofy enough street act. Pure dumb-show, but funny enough to sometimes get a crowd.

When any manner of audience appeared, he'd leave off the music, flip the cardboard around, which now read MAGIC—and he'd go into his second bit. An old cassette tape in the boom box played the Ann Bennett rendition of Felix's theme song. But oftentimes the tape skipped or blurred rendering the lyrics nearly incoherent:

Felix the cat,
The funderful, funderful cat!
Whenever he gets hisself fixed,
He makes you gag on hiz bag of trix!

And that's when Felix's magic doctor satchel came in for a workout.

Last audience of the day was a lone scrawny kid of about thirteen in a dingy Hope T-shirt that looked like it hadn't been washed this month. The Pied Piper opened his bag of tricks and pulled out a box of candy. He showed them to the boy. Chocolate Babies.

"Hey kid," he whispered, "want an N-Word candy?"

The man's narrow, Satan's face peered down, waiting for a reply.

The boy didn't even blink. Maybe he'd never heard the fashionable euphemism actually spoken out loud—if that was possible—just the real N-Word from rappers wit attitudes on the radio or called out across the street in the 'hood. He looked at the creased, smudged candy box and shook his head. The Pied Piper spilled a few coco-babies into his open violin case, amongst a handful of coins and dollar bills. These chocolate babies were a little different: All their mouths were open and they were howling.

"Mama told me never take nuthin' from strangers."

Another dingy box of candy came out of the satchel. "How about some Jujubes? The kikes eat those; they make the Joos rich." Now the kid knew he was in the presence of a whack-a-doodle.

"Didja hear me, my mother said—"

The Pied Piper threw the box of Jujubes into the violin case, and some scattered across the pavement, little cylindrical candy drops of a thousand colors like tiny gems. The gaunt Piper leaned forward, his long face a few inches from the kid's. "Boy, your sainted mother is a crack whore who's standing on the corner of Avenue B right this second, tricking for dinner money and a fix. If there's any left over, she might remember to buy you a bologna sandwich and a carton of milk."

The kid took a step back. His dark face twisted in rage. Forget the N-Word; now this peckerwood brought Mama into it. "I'm getting my boys. My boys are coming back here for you. I'm gonna follow you, I'm gonna find out where you live."

The Piper stood to his full six-foot-five height, a human praying mantis. A creased smile crossed the sharp hatchet face; a pale tongue licked his thin lips. "I like it. You do that. You bring all your boys to me." He reached for his satchel again. "No Chocolate Babies, no Jujubes, how about a little dinner in case your mama forgets the milk and bologna?"

Out came a rather large, dead rat. It swung before the lad's face.

"You're fukked up."

"Really? I'm gratified you think so." The long, gaunt man dropped the rat into his violin case, and it fell with a leaden thump.

"And now for my last trick. . . ."

He reached inside the satchel and slowly drew out a bright children's book. It was large and flat and way too big for the satchel, like one of those endless scarves magicians pull from their sleeves that keep on coming. He placed it carefully on the park bench, upright. "This is for you and your *boys*. Maybe between the four of y'all, you can actually read a page, if you go slowly and mouth out the words."

"I don't need your fukkin' book."

"Why, look at that!" The Piper's eyes fell to the violin case; the dead rat had lifted its head and was sniffing the air. "Well, well, well. . . . Whattaya know, I guess Mr. Rat wasn't so dead after all."

The kid jumped away from the suddenly alert, sniffing rodent, then took a few steps back, retreating from the long man's presence; the waddling rat now scooted under the bench and onto the grass. "We're gonna find you, Slim."

"I'm counting on it."

Show over.

The tall man carefully packed his things: his satchel, violin case, and boom box; with his cardboard sign under his arm he left the park. He knew the kid was following him at a safe distance. Smart lad.

An hour later the kid passed the park bench again on his way back to Avenue B. The children's book was still there; no one had touched it. Gingerly he picked it up. The cover showed some sort of old castle town in sunset and in black silhouette a parade going over a bridge, led by a long, gaunt man. The title read *The Pied Piper of Hamelin*. And that long-legged honkie was right on the money. . . . This boy in the hopey T-shirt, son of the crack whore, couldn't read so well, but at least the book had pictures.

There were still a few cruddy apartments over in the West Village that weren't taken over by the gentrified, whitesy-cutesy, uppity-and-coming. They existed like the

eyes on a potato, a few here, a few there. The apartment
overlooking Sheridan Square was one. A three-story walk-
up, a dozen smelly habitats. And Number 4A, the long
gaunt man called home. He lived behind his closed door
like that very rat he'd dropped in Washington Square Park.
Paint peeling off the walls, cracked tiles in the bathroom,
no shower curtain around the leprous tub, yellow blinds
drawn. A porcelain stove and sink in one corner. The power
company had turned the electric and gas off years ago, but
that didn't bother Piper. And his was the only apartment
in the building that didn't have a dozen locks, jimmy bars,
or dead bolts on the door. Just another Felix the Cat poster
glued to the outside in the hallway—enough protection.
Everyone knew better than to bother him.

Some of his neighbors had seen him do his tricks in the
park, but he didn't go to the park every day, so they just
thought, *Hey, he works from home*. In any case, that's where
his most important business was done.

His creature comforts were simple. An old leather club
chair sat in front of an old Zenith TV with rabbit ear antennae. A large coffee table, with bowls of Fireballs; boxes
of animal crackers; circus peanuts; long strips of white
paper with candy buttons; a glass jar of Pixie Sticks; and a
few packages of wax Coke bottles filled with red, green,
blue, and yellow treacly syrup, Nik-L-Nips.

A Kenner Products Easy-Bake oven—the kind little girls
used to yearn for every Christmas Eve in the dark ages of
the 1960s—sat near the crusty, useless kitchen stove, along
with some open Betty Crocker Angel Food cupcake mix.
The Easy-Bake oven plug lay on the counter unplugged, as
did the Zenith television cord, snaking along the floor and
lying useless under the wall socket. As Leona Helmsley
once famously said, "Only the little people pay taxes."

In Mr. P.'s safe bubble only the little people needed electric current to make their lives work—while he could
short out a lamppost or turn it on again like an electric eel.

The man was a lanky humanoid lightning rod. No need for a power grid or Con Ed to make his appliances blink; the Piper always had plenty of juice on demand.

He sat in front of the TV and pointed. "On please." The old TV clicked and warmed up. . . . Then after a moment, "Cable Channel Guide."

The blue image of the channel guide filled the screen, with its little boxes.

"What to see . . . ? What to see . . . ?" The blue page scrolled down, pausing every so often. "A thousand channels and nothing to watch," the gaunt man sighed.

He paused over *Bridezillas*. Worth watching some little twat drink too many Jell-O shots and barf on her little $4,000 white gown? Or swing at the groom with a chainsaw? No, been there, done that.

What Not to Wear. There you go. That was always good for a laugh. Especially as a repeat. He'd seen the episode before. The classy Stacy London and dapper Clinton Kelly were trying to dress a brassy young lady with enormous bosoms who normally dressed like the Bride of Frankenstein and insisted on going to job interviews with her hair in a Kennedy Girl's Vegas beehive. In the original airing of the episode Stacy and Clinton had assisted her very well: some slimming dresses, plain open-collared shirts, the hair went from beehive to French twist. No more chartreuse nail polish.

And when the victim's friends and family finally saw her again, presenting herself in her new clothes on a fancy veranda of a seaside restaurant, they were astonished, pleased, and awed at the cool maturity of her new look.

Yeah, *now* she'd be somebody you'd want to hire.

But this time around, Mr. P. thought he'd have a little fun at the poor young woman's expense. Rewriting and directing the episode as he saw fit, a favorite game. Rewrite the Rerun. Every time the hussy went to a rack of clothes he murmured, "Nope, not that one. Nope. Try again." And dutifully she picked one lousy outfit after another, finally settling on a bright red gaucho vest with silver bangles and a black crepe skirt with a band of pleats about the hips that made her look like a gussied-up fighting bull ready for the sword.

"That's the ticket, darling."

While Stacy and Clinton gave each other a knowing glance—*What a hog*—but Stacy said sincerely, "I think we're getting somewhere." And Clinton, "Very somewhere."

At the conclusion of this rewritten power-of-mind episode the hosts led the calf to the slaughter, presenting her once more to friends and family on the stone patio of a swank local restaurant overlooking the ocean. But this time the admirers, the poor gal's thirty closest friends, shrieked in dismay, all in unison. A savage rejection. And the poor, distraught girl ran from the restaurant patio in tears, breaking a three-inch heel on the way.

From his seat in the battered leather club chair Mr. P. nodded in approval. "Save to file."

The Zenith went to commercial.

Now every time the cable company played the rerun it'd be as Mr. P. tweaked it. A mysterious glitch in the system. Would anyone notice the change? Who knew? But since everyone in sight, on or off the camera, had signed a full release all the fuss might go to the lawyers with nothing resolved. A job well done. Still, the gaunt man felt slightly deflated. This was all whoopee cushions and giving hotfoots to bums on park benches. Well, better times were right around the corner.

The Piper didn't know exactly what he wanted to do just yet, at this exact point in his extremely long life, but he knew he wanted to make a difference. Set the top to spinning, and that meant making the biggest mess of things he could. Not simply reconceptualize TV reruns, but rewrite the whole damn system. First things first: Make that grinning cat face famous all over again; plaster Felix from coast to coast, spread him like a pox across the fruited plain. High time people in this soft land of milk and honey learned that when Felix grinned, *a dog's breakfast of human scum was going to hit the whirring fan.*

His stomach rumbled. Hunger.

He picked up the telephone from the floor by the chair. He'd found it in a pawn shop, a stage prop, not a real phone, where the label claimed the item was: **Billy's Telephone**—*Twilight Zone Episode "Long Distance Call"—Talk to Grandma Collect.* He'd never bothered to call Grandma, though; he used it mostly for takeout. Tonight, a pizza night.

He dialed, it rang, the man at the other end answered, "Stromboli's."

"Yeah, you delivering yet?" Mr. P. rasped. "I'd like a pie. With everything."

3

Divorce American Style

How did it come to this? How did it all go wrong? It started so perfect. Cheryl "Chippy" Gibson had come up from the valley, parking her California Highway Patrol motorcycle on a lip of a canyon in Ladera Heights to think things through. She took off her CHiPs helmet and let the warm air rush across her face. She caught sight of herself in the bike's side-view mirror.

If you took away the uniform, the holster, the radio, the BMW copper chopper—just another black face in LA. Praline cocoa skin, a few shades lighter than fancy molasses, and glinting eyes that always looked warm, even in chilly weather, even in the shadows. But wearing the britches and 17-inch knee-high Chippewa boots, helmet, and shades she was bitchin' on wheels, deadly nightshade and nobody with whom you'd dare to mess.

LA at night, city of light. Long tracks of streetlights on a black pan leading to the Pacific, the moon silvering the waves. The cars coming and going, red and white, the occasional siren, racing to an eventuality, all so distant from this spot it almost seemed benign. She and Rachel used to come up here just to hold hands. From a swanky house down below, the sound of a radio playing faintly out an open window rose into the air. That Bob Seger song, *Hollywood Nights*; curiously, the music was right but the words sounded all wrong, the radio blatting out twisted lyrics from the famous oldie. . . .

Oh, how Hollywood Bites
Those cute Hollywood Jills
She was looking so dead
With her needles and pills

That wasn't how Cheryl remembered the song at all. The signal wavered in and out until the song finally ended. Then the announcer came on—nobody Cheryl had heard before, no gruff Wolfman Jack, but a silky voice, the kind that enchants the ear if only reciting the phone book.

The voice crept up the canyon walls.

"This is the Piper on Night to Night—" the announcer said. "Your favorite Oldies as Newbies, in ways you've never heard. . . ."

Down below someone killed the radio and the seductive voice died. The silence felt even creepier.

Her and Rachel.

How had it all gone so wrong? When it started so right? *I know your face better than my own*, Rachel once told her.

Going from lust to romance to building a life. Eyes and mind and heart for no one else. African-American lady cop and Hollywood Jewish lady lawyer; married on Nantucket not a year ago. Somebody even found a miniature California Highway Patrol chopper to put on the cake, a mini-Cheryl in uniform standing next to a mini-Rachel in a dark black suit. Blue and black. Good fit, good yin and yang. But then it somehow turned black and blue. The first time Cheryl slapped Rachel's face she wasn't even that drunk.

And what was so important about the argument that somebody needed a bitch-slapping? What color to make the window treatments? Spoiled milk in the fridge? An unpaid parking ticket? Did Rachel work herself into high Hollywood lawyer dudgeon, about Cheryl never paying attention and not caring? Bringing the job home at the end of her shift? What then was so provoking?

Well, actually a life-and-death thing. A creep died while Chippy Gibson lived.

And all Rachel had to ask was a simple question, an innocuous question—with the wrong choice of words. Nothing to get angry about. Nothing at all.

But all Cheryl could think about was what came before, life and death. A bad day on the job.

The Felix Kidz. It all came back to that.

For some time now a strange bit of graffiti had been popping up in all the hoods. Sometimes spray-painted in bubble-letter style, sometimes in chalk—Felix the Cat, grinning for all he was worth from alley wall or pavement.

And sometimes this bit of scribble wasn't simply limited to South Central or the weirder parts of West Hollywood. At first, like most things that suddenly appear out of nowhere, nobody really noticed it. Not like the President as the Joker that got noticed real quick. This one, just another bit of urban effluence, of questionable significance, easily overlooked in the general chaos of LA's freewheeling freeway culture.

Felix's goofy face appearing on walls in alleys strewn with empty crack vials, wine cooler bottles, and condom wrappers. Then his wild grin showed up on the crack vials themselves, and meth bags.

Surfacing again as a tattoo on a Jane Doe—some nameless young woman, her body dumped in a concrete spillway of the LA River. Like so many of the hopefuls coming to the City of Angels for a modeling job, for a bit part, to get away from Daddy who called her "the best kisser in the trailer park," to finally a waitress, then hostess in some strip dump, to finally get her big break in the movies—but this time bent over, ass up, and really acting like she meant it.

But not moaning up to snuff and tripping down to Hollywood Boulevard for a real spell of Stanislavski method acting. And failing at that, finding the needle or the powder. All ending somehow in a damp storm drain, missing a high-heeled pump with her skirt over her waist. Felix the Cat grinning at Chippy Gibson of the California Highway Patrol from the Jane Doe dead body, the DB's pale, cold rump. The uniformed cops who always found these innocent gals gave them a nickname, Sweet Jane. And the authorities finally started to notice these girls turning up dead in the general vicinity of a grinning cat face.

Three or four days before Rachel's face slap, Cheryl's sergeant chalked up a version of Felix's mug on the blackboard in the ready room for their shift briefing.

"I guess you've all noticed the new cat on the street. . . ."

He shrugged a little. "Puss 'n' Boots here. And I'd like to tell you we know what the hell it is. We can't. Gang Task Force tell us it's spread across territory lines, Crips, Bloods, over to the Spanish, M-13, La Surenos, Los Zetas, and even the Wah Chings—there just doesn't seem to be any locus we can put our finger on."

The sergeant shrugged again. "So what can I say today? What I say every day—you see one of these marks, in an alley, on the sidewalk, on a routine stop—exhibit extreme caution. Ladies and gentlemen, don't try to figure it out on your own, but take a picture on your cell, take some notes, and we'll shoot it all back to Intelligence for the big brains to cogitate."

Here, the sergeant wiped Felix's grinning puss from the board, swiping it into a faceless mush of chalk dust. "As the saying goes . . . *Exercise extreme caution*."

So later in her shift, Cheryl showed extreme etcetera when she flagged a smoking hot Lowrider on Interstate 10 out by Redlands, belching exhaust; but the pull-over didn't go down easy. The souped-up Impala ignored her, sped up, and ripped down the I-10 off-ramp, jamming a side street and blasting through the chained gate at Pharaoh's Lost Kingdom, a quarter mile away. Thirty seconds of tear-ass, Cheryl's legs turning to water as she clung to the bike. The defunct amusement and water park was dead as the great Sphinx of Giza. Lawyer carrion had been fighting over its carcass for years, one of LA's dead zones—and this was no good.

Cheryl heard her own voice, a trifle too urgent, talking to Dispatch: "Officer 62, I-10, WB, Pharaoh's Lost Kingdom Parking lot, reckless speed, ignoring instructions. Request other units or local PD."

Dispatch came back, "Pharaoh Parking."

"That's affirm."

The vehicle screeched to a halt with a smoke of rubber, but its engine still belched exhaust. Cheryl stopped her BMW copper chopper twenty feet behind.

"Mid-sixties bright orange Chevy Impala, California Vanity Plate, FLX22."

Dispatch came back again. "Local San Bernardino, black & white ETA three minutes."

Three minutes. A prompt response window, but still an ice age in real life real time. Cheryl dismounted the motorcycle, unclipped the safety strap from her Glock 9mm, held her right hand on the grip, ready to pull the gun from the holster. She always hated the way the thing felt in her hand. Always blood-warm, since she drove around in the sun all day, and then clammy at night.

"Please shut off your engine, sir." Her voice came out strongly now, no room for argument. The engine died with a last burp of exhaust. She approached the orange Chevy, five steps away. "Please put your hands on the wheel, sir."

But the driver's hands were *already* clamped on the steering wheel, yet something was decidedly wrong. Cheryl took in the man in the front seat. A Chicano, about age twenty, Laker's B-Ball Jersey, yellow, number 24, Bryant— with the wrong kind of hands on the wheel. A *woman's hands*; a pair of lady's hands sat at ten and two o'clock, normal driving position—but the driver's own hands— young-man hands—sat on his thighs, a finger going tap-tap-tap as if impatient with everything.

The young man was wearing an extra pair of arms.
Wearing.

It seared into the back of her skull in all of a second. The top section of a human body had been skinned, the shoulders and arms, specifically, cut from the torso; a large hole where the neck used to be, a broad flap from the spine, leaking blood. From inside the bloodstained Laker's Jersey, the dead arms protruded from the arm holes, gripping the wheel. The driver wore the skinned mantle like football shoulder pads, so he could steer from the 6 o'clock position with his real hands.

The rest of the body lay on the backseat. Head and trunk intact; only the arms and back flap of skin missing. Lovely, angelic face. Another Sweet Jane.

The young man looked around from his place at the wheel. "Buenos Dias, Officer." A small round tattoo of Felix the Cat grinned at Cheryl from the Chicano's forehead.

"Sir, please put your real hands on the steering wheel." Chippy felt her voice about to crack, but somehow it didn't. Flat, even, controlled.

"No problemo." But just before he placed his hands on the wheel, his finger flipped a switch on the dash, powering up the hop-and-dance feature of the hydraulics. The radio blasted to life at the same time, the tune from the funk band War way back in the 1970s. The late Charles Miller's black tar voice rumbled out the car window, the thumper "Low Rider." Perfect choice as the musician had been murdered in LA and the killer never found, perfect Hollywood.

Now that she thought back to it, she seemed to remember the words coming out of the radio were wrong here too. Was this the first time she'd heard the wrong words coming out of a radio? Cheryl couldn't quite remember—not with a dissected Sweet Jane in the back of the car, a guy wearing an extra pair of hands, and that hand over her Glock.

2 Mins 30 Seconds to Back Up—an ice age:

All my Frenz know the Low Slider
That Low Slider skins 'em always better
The Low Slider skins a little slower
Low Slider is a real goer.

The powerful thump of the jumping car hydraulics and the low beat of "Low Rider" caught her by surprise, and Cheryl stepped back. The other half of Sweet Jane lolled around in the backseat like an armless broken doll. The music kept rocking on, the grinning face of Felix staring at her from the kid's forehead.

Low Slider knows every street, yeah
Felix is the one to meet, yeah
That Cat don't use no mask now
Low Slider make Jane his bitch now

Then the Chicano boy did the second stupidest thing of his life. A gun appeared in his real hand and pointed out the window.

"I got something for you, chica."

Cheryl didn't think; she drew and fired. The kid's face exploded. Bye-bye grinning kitty. But the car kept pumping away, and the girl in the back rolled from side to side. As the hydraulics sapped the battery, the car jumped lower and lower, the song fading on the radio:

> *Take a little tip, Take a little tip*
> *Take a little tip from me*
> *Smack her on the lip,*
> *Smack her on the lip for me*

Cheryl's three minutes were up, and two San Bernardino black-and-whites screeched to a halt behind her. She sensed the officers at her back, guns drawn but pointing at the Chevy. The Chino car dead on the pavement.

One of the backup cops examined the orange Chevy. Glanced at Sweet Jane in the rear and had to turn away for a moment. Then mastered himself, slipped on a pair of latex gloves, and reached into the front seat. He showed Cheryl the young man's weapon. A fake gun from a magic store, the little red flag poking from the muzzle; the flag read: *Bang.*

And that's when Cheryl thought she would gag. But the spasm passed, just a spell of dry mouth, shortly washed away with a couple of gulps from a water bottle fetched from the black-and-white. The real gagging came a little later.

That first night was okay. Rachel held her in bed, the idea pretty clear: *I'm just so glad you're alive.* . . . She might have even said it out loud. But Cheryl was a little foggy on the details; it was a tequila and Mexican night. How friggin' appropriate. Finally curling up in bed with the TV droning and the blue light flickering against the walls. She thought she heard Rachel tell her, "You've got time coming. Take a tip from me. When this settles down, let's take a little trip." And for a fleeting second Cheryl shivered. Did Rachel really say, *Take a little tip*? God, she never wanted to hear "Low Rider" again.

The noose tightened about three days later; her departmental paperwork had been filed, time for the official Internal Affairs Q&A. The Inquisition. Her required taped statement with Internal Affairs didn't go smoothly. Lots of photos of the fake gun with the imbecilic bang flag sticking out the muzzle. The pictures looked more and more absurd as they were shoved across the table at her. The Internal Affairs officer stared at her with the face of a ferret, lean cheeks, pockmarked from an ancient bout of chicken pox. Didn't listen to Mother when she told him not to scratch.

"Whattaya mean you didn't see this?"

"Didn't notice anything wrong?"

"How many times have you discharged your weapon in the line of duty?"

Answer, obvious, just look at the record: first time. And now, maybe the last.

Worse than that there were two other jackals at the hearing: a division captain from the LAPD sat in, some politically connected friend of the mayor's, along with a suit from the Department of Justice, Los Angeles Civil Rights Division. This last sit-in probably because a local civil rights group was making ugly noises and planted a few protesters across the street from the crumbling Parker Center at the new HQ. The photos of the Bang-Flag-Gun had magically appeared, blown up as homemade protest signs. Not good. And every day the rent-a-mob left for the afternoon, Felix's face in chalk grinned up from the pavement. . . .

The light from the windows threw bars across the interrogation table, blinding white against black field; motes of dust stirred lazily in the air. Nothing was going to be settled that afternoon. Cheryl's eyes wandered from the men in front of her, and she stifled the urge to yawn. The urge came on by surprise, and it took all her will to stifle it. Yawning *very* bad. What every cop knew: yawning during an interrogation meant you were guilty.

But apparently she couldn't mask her glassy eyes.

"Are you sleepy, Officer Gibson? Are we boring you?" the pockmarked ferret asked her; and then out of the blue, a curveball: "Take a little tip from me, don't yawn." That damn "Low Rider" lyric, like he'd been listening to the same old tunes as Chico in the Chevy.

The police captain, the mayor's crony, a well-fed man, full of himself, played at being her friend. Telling the ferret, "Oh, I think we've covered what we can today, Felix. Let's let Officer Gibson off for the weekend."

Felix? The Internal Affairs agent's ID tag said, Frederick. A nickname? And he took his cue from the Captain, "Sure, whatever." Then to Cheryl, "Thanks for your cooperation."

The ride home seemed endless: miles of snaking traffic, of glinting chrome, and a cap of yellow smog over all. Rachel wasn't in from work yet. No surprise; she often worked late, lawyer's hours. Cheryl watched the sun go down from the patio; this time of year it always set between two yucca plants. The landscaper had planted their canyon backyard in Sonoran colors, sandy shale, rocks, cactus, and a large sitz pool with a horizon edge, water bubbling from a crack of boulders, running off the edge of sight seamlessly into the Pacific. A 100K in "pretty sand" Rachel called it. Hell, she was allowed—her Hollywood lawyer salary made it happen.

Too many times Cheryl felt like the spare tire in their jalopy, safely there in an emergency but not on the axle. Rachel's firm was A-Minus List, so for society's eyes

Cheryl had to buy a closet full of clothes to match. Things she'd never have bought on her own. Never mind afford. The curious aspect of people relations, the subtle way class still seemed to matter. Not so much race, but the right schools, the right opportunities, the thousand clubs and associations. And of course, the right clothes. Did people talk to her differently, look at her differently? Not really. If anything they bent over backward to bring her into the winners' circle. In LA cops were movie stars; she'd even been tapped for a profile on the latest police show, *Lady Blue*. But that stoked the coals too; a lower-middle-class insecurity lingering in the Big Box Store of her mind.

"Don't worry, Sugah," Cheryl always teased Rachel when they were getting dolled up for some function, whether it was the Media & Entertainment Counsel of the Year Awards or say the Southern California Paperclip Counting Conference, "I still have all my teeth. And they're all mine."

The tequila bottle came too easily off the shelf that night she got home alone. One pull after another as the sun did its sinking thing and the streetlights came on down below. Cheryl felt her eyes grow heavy and her chin nodding to her breast as she lay on the lounge chair. But still, she seemed to see out across the vast expanse beyond the canyon. Dark blue-and-gray clouds rushed in from the west, rolling over themselves, the sound of galloping hooves coming in wave after wave.

A figure stood at the edge of the patio. And Cheryl knew exactly who it was: Sweet Jane from the backseat of the Chevy without her shoulders or her arms. The young lady looked plaintively at her, begging her for something. To come earlier, to have found her before it all went bad, before she lost her arms to this crazy Chico. Now the scene shifted to an abandoned warehouse with pigeons cooing on the rafters, Sweet Jane tied to a metal cot, mewing behind a gagged mouth; now the knife was going in, now the arms were coming off. . . . And somebody was singing, *"Take a little Tip"*—

Sweet Jane stood over her, touching her shoulder, somehow touching her without arms. The pigeons flew into Cheryl's face and she woke with a shout of *Wait!*

No, it was *Rachel stood over her,* leaping backward in surprise. "Jesus!"

Rachel. Home at last.

They both paused for a moment. Rachel standing, hovering, Cheryl half up in the lounge chair. Rachel dragged its match over and sat on it, so their faces were level. Cheryl's heart still pounded in her ears. And she stared back; Rachel's eyes wide, lips a thin line. She glanced at the tequila bottle standing on the stone patio. "You gotta lay off that stuff. It's no good."

Cheryl's hand drifted to the bottle; she picked it up and contemplated it. About three shots gone, her mouth a wad of cotton. She nodded silently; you're *right as rain,* searching in vain for the bottle cap. Rachel's eyes glowed a little in approval; always a lot better when people knew they'd had more than enough. "Here." She found the cap, which had rolled away somewhere. Cheryl's heart was slowing to normal as Rachel's smooth and melodious voice came at her again with that same line, "When this is over; take a tip from me. When you're done, we should take a little trip—"

The rubber band inside Cheryl's gut finally snapped— and she smacked Rachel's face.

"Shut up! Shut up! Just shut up!"

Rachel started, tears leapt to her eyes, her face gone white and her hand went to her cheek.

When the doorbell rang.

Cheryl lurched from the lounge chair, finally stood, trying to mouth *I'm so sorry.* But Rachel was already marching through the house toward the front door, wiping her eyes on her suit sleeve.

The front door stood open, a nosy young man in a cheap suit and tie and bad black JCPenney shoes peered into the house, smiling insincerely. He held a sheaf of papers, bound in a blue folder.

"Cheryl Gibson?"

She came forward. "That's me." The blue folder with the papers came into her hand. "The family of Ricardo Montoya. Wrongful Death. You've been served." So the family was going after her, and the bloody house and unspecified damages. Christ, she couldn't even afford the bloody payments or the taxes, not on her yearly copper 40K. This was citizens' revenge, pure and simple. If she'd been a single occupancy renter, the family might not have bothered at all. Sued the PD and left her alone. But 100K in pretty sand was too attractive to pass up.

In a few short days things went from bad to worse. The Sweet Jane nightmare, the tequila bottle that seemed to slide off the shelf on its own. Cheryl just folded into herself, and Rachel's sullen eyes stared at her from the bathroom mirror in the morning when she thought Cheryl wasn't looking. But she was.

"You want a divorce? Will that fix it? I'll go back to living on my salary, move down the hill. Financial separation, something."

Rachel finished her eye makeup. After a breath, "Don't be an ass." But that pause, that tiny second, crushed Cheryl's heart. *Her gal'd thought about it already.* How to get out of this crap.

Have a nice day.

Herman, her union lawyer, met her at Canter's Deli so they could prep for the departmental hearing. The process had slid downward a couple of notches. Cleared by Internal Affairs with a personal reprimand that wouldn't go on her record, assigned to temporary desk duty—but the mayor's crony captain still wanted to show the people of Los Angeles his boss loved every stinking one of them. Even Chicano arm choppers. And Sweet Jane turned out to be nobody, a runaway, a Jane Doe. Not even a councilman's daughter. Not even a studio head's estranged trophy chick who put on shows for all his pals. So a departmental hearing open to the public would be held. A show trial. Star witness Officer Gibson and the Bang-Flag-Gun.

Herman and Cheryl sat along the wall of the delicatessen, her on the long black leather couch, him in the brown leather chair. Herman, a once-upon-a-time New Yorker, haunted Canter's like so many of his Manhattan and Brooklyn brothers transplanted to Gollywood. Too fat for pot roast anymore, he tried to satisfy himself with cottage cheese, a canned peach half, a maraschino cherry, and a pickle on the side. Good luck with that.

Cheryl felt no such compunction, shamelessly ordering corned beef and chopped liver with a slice of tomato and a slice of Bermuda onion. Plain, no sauce. Back in New York, one deli called it a Joan Rivers. A real "Joan Alexandra Molinsky" of a sandwich. That schmear of chopped liver made it slide down the gullet right proper. A cholesterol coma on rye.

Herman stared at it lovingly, smiling sadly. "Oh, those were the days."

Which made her laugh. But Herman sighed and went back to his cottage cheese plate in measured denial. Getting on with business.

"Look, this is where we stand. Let's start with the obvious. You're African American, you're a gal, you're gay, you're a friggin' rainbow Rambo—they can't touch you. You seen the news?" He slid a newspaper clipping across at her. A printout of the LA Times.

"I haven't turned on the television, no newspaper. Nothing."

Herman nodded in approval, "You're one in a million." Demonstrably true. And he wasn't kidding about the Rambo thing. The headline:

RAINBOW RAMBO—
FREEWAY CHiPs CHIPPY BANGS BANGER.

The item slanted her way, with bits about what a cocksucker the late and lamented Ricardo Montoya was. Doubtless some of the local Spanish papers were calling him a choirboy. But as it turned out the recently deceased Montoya was part of the VHG gang, the Varrio Hawaiian Gardens gang; a slew of them recently arrested by the Feds for targeting blacks, trying to "eliminate" persons of the African American persuasion from the Hawaiian Gardens suburb in Southeastern LA. As Cheryl and Jane Doe were both "persons of color"—albeit coffee and cream—some wretched bloggers were calling Jane Doe the *Hindu Princess*. In any case, Sweet Jane wasn't lily white—so this whole incident could be tagged on to the U.S. Attorney's spectacular indictment of sixty or so of Varrio's "Hate Gang" members.

Herman played with his cottage cheese. "This hearing is just for show so the undocumented community can wave the La Raza flag and go back home for another taco and trim. So, testify. Let the panel rumble a little. *This isn't going anywhere.* You got a house, you got a mortgage. You're a citizen."

"That's my problem," Chippy told him, and for a few long moments Rachel's sullen eyes in the bathroom mirror crept back into her head. The deeper message on Rachel's face as Cheryl's one-and-only came to the inescapable conclusion that she'd bit off more than she could swallow, much more than she bargained for, and a lot less than she could hope to salvage. Sure, if it meant honor and vows Rachel would fight thigh to thigh with her, but that single devastating look told of a thousand days of doubt, a thousand mute nights and morning regrets in the makeup mirror.

The worst of them, that standing thigh to thigh wasn't Rachel's first choice. Just mopping up the trail of mud Chippy had tracked inside their house, the litigation, the depositions, the liens, the writs and appeals—which *were fine* for somebody else—but God, you wouldn't want them on your own living room Bokhara. No cop's salary could possibly clean that rug up.

Cheryl came back to the delicatessen table and Herman's cottage cheese wondering if she'd been talking to herself in public.

"That's my problem," she repeated, leaving out what she'd been thinking. "Things that aren't going anywhere." And nevertheless finding the bottom line, "But this might just take everything, Herman. I killed a kid. The family of the bereaved served me. He was a worthless, macho slice-and-dice artist and now he's dead. His mamacita's crying and his name was on my bullet. I'm thinking of moving back east." She took a breath. "Besides, my father was Italian. I'm half an octamaroon or something."

"No you're a *complete* maroon if you don't do that hearing; the union can represent or co-represent on the civil suit." Herman sighed, but hardheaded cops were his specialty. "Like you have a choice. Look, if you were a cookie or a seventeenth-century gentlewoman, I'd name you Lorna Doone. You stood up. You did your job. And you're married to a lawyer, for crying out loud. The little crap-hat would have killed you stone cold if he could have and then bragged about it later. You know you're going to testify. Even if you move, you'll want another job. You'll need a recommendation from the department. You'll have to be cleared. Capping a perp out in LA won't look so bad back east either."

"I know, but that doesn't mean I have to like it."

Herman cut a chunk of peach with his spoon, found some cottage cheese for it. "Who says you do? And since when is Gibson an Italian name?"

"It isn't. But Gibone was. I think we were all lucky Great Grandpa Woppo G didn't change it to Gibbon."

"Well, look at the bright side," Herman told her. "Once you put all this behind you, leave CHiPs, take a little tip from me, take a little trip—someplace far away where nobody'll call you Chippy anymore."

Cheryl's angst dissolved like the sugar in her ice tea. "Low Rider" again. What was this, catching? Some kind of mental disease?

Herman pushed his messed-up plate of curds away from him. "So . . . you need a divorce lawyer too?"

That time she didn't bother answering. It wasn't like that between her and Rachel. Their thing wasn't about *things*. It was about them. Each other. The Big Trust, which a single look in the mirror had shattered. Everything deteriorating from there. . . . How pitiful, truly pathetic. And moving day had arrived.

A couple of weeks had passed, and now it was Rachel's turn to find the tequila bottle a little too often. She sat at the spectacular safety glass table in the dining room under the $2,000 chandelier she'd gotten half price at the Cherokee Iron Works. The chandelier ran the length of the thick glass like a pool table light, translucent parchment behind paper-thin iron silhouettes marching along its sides. The fancy lamp was called *Cattle Drive*: little doggies and longhorns wandering between cactus and cowboys on horseback. The lamps behind always made it look like sunset. Pure kitsch, but Cheryl loved it. No, not something she could unbolt from the ceiling and take away.

A cloying melancholy had descended on both of them. No shouting, no hair-pulling, no anger or recriminations.

No jealous love scenes. And maybe no divorce either, just a separation. It sort of depended on what the lawyers said. There had to be some kind of asset protection, but maybe not. If divorce meant Rachel's liability could be limited, they'd do it. If it didn't . . . well, Cheryl still had to get away.

"You can take what you want," Rachel told her.

"I know."

"We could fight it out here, together."

"I know." She took a sip from Rachel's shot glass. "Let's just see how things go, okay?"

But she knew she was lying. Moving back east pretty well broke it. Rachel wasn't about to give up her lawyer job and put the house up for sale. One of the movers rolled an overstuffed wardrobe box toward the front door, its sides bulging. All those party clothes.

Rachel pounded back the rest of the shot. "You're going to be the best-dressed lipstick lez in all of Dutchess County."

"That's not hard, Sugah."

"I know." Rachel reached for the bottle again. "I've been to Dutchess County."

One of the movers, a bald guy with bulging pecs, popped his head around a hallway corner. "Hey, there's somebody out here for you."

He meant Cheryl.

She stopped short as she came out the door. A man was waiting by the moving van, dark suit, open collar. Never seen him before. Broad, open face and scruffy graying beard; intelligent, sad, knowing eyes. The fellow seemed a cross between John Q. Citizen and a well-established foreign gentleman, originally from somewhere in northwestern India—now standing in her driveway in American clothes. A guy some people might have called a Dot Head or Sabu when he wasn't looking. He'd come in a rental full-size black SUV Ford Explorer, anonymity in four-wheel drive. And he spoke in a whisper-soft voice:

"Miss Gibson," the man asked. "May I come in?"

Something in his manner—the sincerity and gentleness—made it so she didn't want to refuse. But he could see she was a little apprehensive. "My name is Dr. Bhakti Singh." That meant nothing to her. He held out a photo of a young lady, smiling with daddy at a birthday party table. Daddy was wearing a silver cone hat. The girl was kissing him on the cheek, like she'd just got her first pony. Sweet Jane. Sweet Jane alive, before she became an armless Jane Doe torso in the back of a Chevy.

"Janet was my daughter."

"Oh my God, come in."

They sat at the long glass table; Rachel had magically pulled herself together, tequila bottle back on the shelf, water for green tea on the bright red Viking range. Boy, was she good. But this sudden appearance of Sweet Jane's father stopped Cheryl. How the hell had he found his way to her door? Maybe he read Officer Gibson's name in the papers. But that didn't come close to explaining how he made the leap between Sweet Jane and his *Janet*.

The man, apologetic, said, "I'm sorry for disturbing you. I can see you're busy. And I won't take much of your time. The coroner's office gave me your name, after . . ." He paused to breathe; then with some effort, ". . . after I identified Janet's body. I hope that was all right?"

"No, please—it's all right." Still, Cheryl remained confused. "Did you register Janet a missing person? We never got a CODIS hit, nothing. How did you know to come here?"

"Just lucky, I guess." He looked down at his large hands; they left faint sweat outlines on the safety glass table. "I'm from Texas," he said with the exhausted look of a man who'd just driven from Texas. "Three weeks ago, my Janet went down to a little border town on the Rio Grande with a friend for a local music festival. And neither of the girls ever came back. I've been looking for her since."

The green tea arrived; kind of pointless now. Bhakti stared at the steaming cup and nodded at it, as if finally recognizing the stuff. "I don't think Janet's DNA was properly entered into the system—so that's why there was no CODIS recognition. I just—" His eyes clouded over. "Some people have asked me, how it was possible for such a homely man like me to make such a beautiful daughter." He reached into his breast pocket for a handkerchief. His swarthy face pale and dry but he patted it anyway. "I just came by to say, I know it doesn't make any difference now—" He choked a moment, then regained his voice. "I just came by to say thank you."

4

The Sikh's Wife

That Felix face reached into peoples' lives in the most peculiar ways.

Hours after his daughter had failed to return from the Rio Grande border town music festival, Professor Bhakti Singh lost his only child, his wife, and a chunk of his mind all in the same day. Actually it took nearly two days, the longest of his life. Or maybe it was just Eleanor his wife who lost her mind—when they lost Janet. Or couldn't get her back or—it hurt just to think about it.

Amazing how quickly things could crumble, all in a few hours, making him wonder at everything he'd ever built, through years of struggle—gone in a matter of hours. His CV read like alphabet soup: MA in Applied Physics from the Rajiv Gandhi Technical University, a PhD from the California Institute of Technology, another from MIT in Materials Research.

Then onto real life.

Meeting Eleanor at NASA where he steadily rose with her help to head their radiation materials research team. The idea was to create a woven polyethylene fabric that could be molded around a spacecraft with two goals in mind: preventing punctures from micrometeoroids or space bullets, and attempting to solve the allied problem of solar radiation, capable of frying things flying beyond the Earth's safe atmospheric cloak.

Even though their blessed life didn't work out as planned, Bhakti and Eleanor pursued what they loved. Perhaps their private heaven started with the birth of Janet—but for twenty years Bhakti never quite saw it that way. Except for the night his daughter failed to come home.

Janet's birth wasn't an easy one. When Eleanor's time came, something with the epidural went wrong. The obstetrician called it a one-in-a-million spinal trauma. Maybe the nurses had left her lying on her side too long, Bhakti never really found out; Eleanor lost the use of her left leg, and her right one below the knee. Even with physical therapy, and hobbling around on prosthetic braces, she'd be sitting in a wheelchair for most of the day for the rest of her life. But somehow with each other and with baby Janet to raise, none of this destroyed them. Sure, living on braces or sitting in a wheelchair made things take longer, but Eleanor's sunny disposition helped make things easier.

Yet even as her condition deteriorated with the loss of more personal motor functions, his wife's will to live, to participate and overcome, seemed like a rock on which their family stood. The indignities of an adult in diapers faded to their proper place; another unremarkable aspect of life, no more, no less. So Janet—child, girl, adolescent—didn't think anything was strange in their house growing up: a miracle in and of itself.

Then came the Job. The move from Houston.

From NASA to space tourism, with the fledgling company Escape Velocity, founded by the eccentric but immensely wealthy media master Clem Lattimore—or Cowboy Clem as he was known to many. Besides owning a cable network, a publishing conglomerate, an online You-Buy-Mart, a few of the remaining profitable newspapers in America, and Lattimore Aerospace, none of this was nearly enough for Cowboy Clem—he still lusted after going where no man had gone before. And that meant booking suborbital and soon orbital flights for wannabe Buck Rogers with enough cash in the bank and a hankering for the weightless beyond. It also meant buying up nearly 100,000 acres in Somewhere Texas for his spaceport.

Actually it did have a name: Van Horn.

And as big a bit of nowhere you couldn't find if you were looking for it.

Endless acres of flats and rocky hills; a hunk of desert north of the Rio Grande and an hour east of Laredo. Nothing more than a bus stop of a town; with a traffic light, a Budget Motel, a Budget Rent-a-Car, and any number of Budget Bar-B-Qs. No doubt soon to have helicopter pads in everyone's backyard and airstrips for George Jetson's flying car.

The distance from Houston to Van Horn was six hundred or so miles, leaving a real city, with real hospitals, real universities, a real museum, and real restaurants—yet what smart ole Clem offered Bhakti beat all. The scientist's own budget, his pick of team, a blank check. Cowboy Clem built Bhakti and family a house to suit down to the last detail, wheelchair accessible, the counters, the beds, the bathrooms, wind and solar net metering, backup generator, swimming pool, the works. Not only that, the house was done in four months, before they moved in. Eleanor Singh couldn't say no. She even liked the color.

Since Eleanor still helped Bhakti with his work, even his lab at the skeletal spaceport hangar was designed around her. And that went for the rest of his team. They'd make as much in a two-year contract as they had slaving away in their respective cubicles and workstations for a decade, no matter how prestigious. Cal-Tech, Hewlett Packard, Boeing, Microsoft, Sun Microsystems all lost personnel. Better health insurance, a free house, the work they loved—it was like joining the Manhattan Project, except this time they weren't going to blow people up by government dictate and live in a Quonset hut; they were going to *send* people up on the private dime.

Then bring 'em down again in one piece to brag all about it.

A nd Van Horn, Texas, turned out a whole lot better than first impressions. *"The Town So Healthy We Had to Shoot a Man to Start a Cemetery."* Very small, yes, a few adobe mission-style buildings, the crossroads of West Texas, and tourists flocked through on their way to Carlsbad Caverns. The place was named after Jefferson Van Horne, a US Union Army major who discovered the nearby wells, allowing the place to fill bathtubs and irrigate crops—cotton, mostly. A stage stop on the San Diego–San Antonio Mail Route and later the Texas & Pacific Railroad.

They even had a modern ghost town south of nowhere—Lobo—that slowly died. Looking like something out of a US government atomic test site from the late 1940s, nearby Lobo sat in the dust while its nearby sister town thrived on tourists. Such were the inequities of location, water, fate, and chance, the ghost town of Lobo being where the wells finally ran dry.

While the town of Van Horn lost Major Van Horne's *"e"*;

got a Diesel Fried Chicken restaurant in compensation, along with the occasional lost tourist from Carlsbad Caverns a mere 100 miles north; and a trip to the stars. Suborbital for now. That is, if Bhakti and Eleanor could make themselves a good Spaceskin.

The night Janet failed to return Bhakti knew something was wrong the moment he opened his eyes.

He'd been dreaming of India; he sometimes dreamt of his eastern homeland, but mostly it came on floated scents, of gardenias and cow dung on the humid air, chattering monkeys climbing on a garden wall, a peacock's forlorn cry outside his family's gated compound. The place was almost an estate: where his father's Bombay wealth insulated them all from the crowded, dusty, sweaty, struggling humanity on all sides.

And also allowed him to study, to go to university, to make something of himself, even come to America.

But this dream of India was different.

A northern desert town—Jaipur or Udaipur—a broad open square flanked by dry, flaking concrete buildings. The sun beat down like a white hot cap on his head. Here stood the ruins of a temple to forgotten gods. A ruin older than Shiva and Vishnu: a simple square pancake ziggurat, layer upon layer of a hundred steps rising to a narrow platform. He stood looking about him, at the thin blue dome of the sky, the surrounding buildings, their windows like black empty eyes.

Far below he spotted a youth, a cripple dressed in rags. He looked down at his own clothes, finery by all comparison, khaki pants, pressed shirt, polished loafers. The trappings of a prince. This was before his time in America, before he trimmed his beard, cut his hair, and left his crimson turban at home. Not that these symbols of his faith embarrassed him, not at all. Bhakti still kept his turban at home and wore it for special occasions, or when he went back to Bombay to visit the family; the hair and full beard would always grow back. No, he had abandoned these things for the demands of science: Turbans got in the way; long hair dropped onto laboratory tables; beards could catch on fire.

But in the dream of the ancient temple steps, he felt the crimson turban on his head and the thick beard even as he stared down at the cripple in the square. He realized with sudden certitude, this was a cripple from his childhood in the 1960s, when they still wore terrible rags. Now the outcasts and their pimps used cell phones and cut up territories like little gangsters. But back in his childhood the awful savagery and destitution made the gangster pimps take certain babies from their mothers, the lowest of the low. They'd break their bones at the joints when they were infants and never let them set correctly—to make them more pitiable, to make them better beggars.

And this youth was one of them.

His rags hung on him like the wrappings of a starving monk streaked with dirt, wooden crutches. He limped. Putting one foot on the temple step, then a crutch, then another foot, then the crutch. Slowly climbing. His ankle had separated at the joint, so his twisted foot shifted up the calf, held together by a thick wad of flesh. Stump and climb, crutch and struggle—the youthful beggar toiled up the temple steps one at a time, closer and closer. Now Bhakti saw the clay bowl in his hand with a few miserable coins. And the youth's voice came up to greet him: "Rupee, rupee?"

At the high platform there was nowhere for Bhakti Singh to go, nowhere to flee. He stood, frozen—petrified as this twisted creature painfully crawled to his perch. He could see the youth's flesh-attached foot and ankle now so clearly, the little coins in the bowl, the boy's eye. "Rupee?"

* * *

And awoke with a shout: "Here!" Clawing the sheets; he grabbed his wallet off the nightstand, looking to pay the boy something. Anything. Sweat poured off his chest, the scent of dust and dirty rags still in his nostrils. No coins, no boy—just a dream, the fear showing him how western he'd become, how American. Had he grown soft inside? No, just sensitive; the comforts of American life had a way of doing that.

The space beside him was empty, rumpled. Eleanor? Had she gotten up and gone for a drink of water or to the bathroom without asking for help? No . . . her water glass was still on the end table and her braces by the headboard.

The luminous clock face by the bed read 3 a.m.

And somehow in a blinding second he knew Janet hadn't come home yet.

"Eleanor?"

The darkness of the bedroom seemed to cloak him.

The TV quietly droned on—it might have been an infomercial for six-pack abs or colon detox, no way to tell. But the flickering image arrested him; Bhakti stopped and stared at the TV for a moment, but the advertisement confounded reason, hawking abject lunacy instead.

The huckster was a lanky man, in black tie and tails, looking like a carny show magician; the set showed an open window and beyond that, a New York City skyline. The bony fellow ostentatiously took a live wriggling lobster out of his top hat, showed it around, and then unceremoniously flung it out the open window behind him. Some woman off-screen screamed as the lobster struck the pavement—while the ticker-crawl at the bottom of the screen proclaimed, *No Money Down! For an Unlimited Time Only! Buy! Buy! Buy!*

Too absurd. Never mind.

The bathroom light out, with just the illuminated switch glowing on the switch plate. No, she wasn't there.

He found his robe on the bedpost and slipped it on; then

crept from the bedroom. Eleanor stood at the plate-glass window looking into their front lawn and the houses on the subdivision. The white Western-style streetlights of their little spot of heaven in civilization shone across her body.

She was standing.

Standing without braces or the chair. Just staring out into the street. Eleanor pulled the drawstring, closing the curtains, but continued to stare blankly at the fabric.

"She's not home," Eleanor said to the curtained window. "Janet's not home. Go to the sheriff now."

Bhakti swallowed his surprise at her standing there. Eleanor hadn't stood on her own in twenty years.

"Stop staring at me and just do it. Go right now."

First to their neighbor's right across the street, the Chen's—Amy and Wen Chen had followed them from NASA. Janet and the Chen's daughter, Lila, friends for years; the girls did everything together. Wen met him at his own front door, dressed—Bhakti could see Amy down the hall, her eyes bright with fear. Wen's tough, round face was set and grim. One look and neither man had much to say.

Wen, sharp and to the point as always: "We'll take my car."

First to the sheriff's office at the courthouse.

Closed, naturally, but there was one light coming from an office down the hall. Bhakti and Chen banged on the courthouse door. For a few moments nothing. They banged again. Then from inside a door opened, throwing down a bar of light, and the dark figure of a man tromped out into the hall rubbing his eyes. Deputy Jimmy, who had no doubt been sleeping—with his feet on the desk, the radio humming softly. The police scanner and dispatch radio lit but silent. From dead snore to roused in all of three knocks. Now rubbing his face and peering through the glass front doors.

"Mr. Chen, Mr. Singh—what's the trouble, fellas? Why didn't you call?"

Deputy Jimmy sat and listened. The two girls went to a music festival near El Paso—our side of the border— earlier in the evening. They were supposed to be home by 2 a.m., understandable—the long drive. They'd never been late before. Neither girl was answering her cell phone. And that *never* happened. There was something wrong.

Mr. Chen was getting more and more irritated. He'd shoved over his wallet photos, slightly out of date, given a detailed description—height, weight, hair color, name, Social Security number. Bhakti too. Angry now, Chen was losing control. "I've given you everything here, why can't we—what do you call it, put out an Amber alert?"

Deputy Jimmy wasn't such a bad man, as lawmen went—but now tried to explain, the excuses ringing hollow in the concrete Sheriff's Office. "I'm sorry, Mr. Chen, Mr. Singh—the children have to be seventeen or younger. Neither girl is. And we have to know they've actually been abducted. And we don't know that for sure yet. There may be another explan—"

"We *know,*" both men said at once.

Didn't matter. What was worse; three days were required to elapse before Janet and Lila could be registered as missing persons. Still, as a matter of procedure, smart thinking, and an effort to mollify the fathers, Deputy Jimmy promised to notify the Texas Rangers, the Hudspeth County Sheriff's Department halfway to El Paso, and every church or mission they could find in the county phone book. In this empty part of the world, not that many.

And naturally if the girls phoned home they could use the cell phone service provider to trace the location. Provided there was an emergency. In a flash of foresight, Bhakti showed Chen his BlackBerry. "This has a recording feature somewhere. I'll have to look up how to activate it." Chen nodded silently, good idea.

That's when things got really ugly.

Bhakti returned home to find Eleanor still standing by the window, staring at the closed curtains.

She didn't have to ask him. "Well?" It was as though she already knew.

Without speaking to her he went to the bathroom to splash cold water on his face. Somehow Bhakti didn't want to do it in the kitchen in front of her. It seemed somehow irresolute, weak. And for the life of him he couldn't fathom why something as simple as that would feel that way.

The tap from the bathroom sink was warm, as always. Water was always warm in this part of the world. Funny, just like home too, India. Water always warm. That's when he noticed the graffiti. At some point during the night Eleanor had scrawled some lines on the bathroom wall in lipstick. A little ditty right by the toilet, frat rat stuff, as if in the time it took to sit down and then find her legs she had somehow lost her mind:

> *Here I sit, Muscles Flexin'*
> *Giving Birth to another Texan.*

Crazy talk.

That's when his BlackBerry rang; and things spiraled down.

The caller ID read JANET. At first Bhakti breathed a deep sigh of relief, a whoosh of sweat flushing his system of fear. But something about Eleanor standing in front of the curtains made him pause, even as he answered the call.

"Janet!"

Treacly sounds trickled out; he raised the volume, some sort of kiddies' song: *Felix the Cat, the funderful, funderful cat!* The cloying verse repeated again. "Janet!" No Janet. Just the idiotic verses. Eleanor's voice came at him from the window.

"She's not there."

Bhakti ignored his wife; rushing out the door, he met Wen Chen in the street between their houses. Chen's iPhone was blatting the same ditty. His oriental eyes were wide and round. "We've got a signal, we can locate them!" Chen cried.

But in a bitter crack of his mind Bhakti felt the hollow pit at the bottom of his stomach open like an abyss.

They were grasping at straws.

The two men roared off down Interstate 10, followed by Deputy Jimmy. A Texas Highway Patrol Ford Interceptor, bubble lights blazing, hooked up with them ten miles west of Van Horn, then took the lead.

They'd traced two cell phones about forty miles farther west around the border town of Sierra Blanca. Bhakti sat in the passenger's seat watching Chen—driving crash-dummy, expressionless, hands gripping the wheel, eyes dead ahead. Neither man talked. Bhakti cupped his Black-Berry in his hand, still connected. The kiddies' tune continued to whimper from the device, the charge bars shrinking from three to two to one. Only moments to go before the thing died. He had forgotten to bring the charge cable from his own car. Even though he hated the sugary tune the humming unit was a connection, a slim thread to Janet. And he clutched the thing, hoping against hope a human voice would come through. When the device finally lost all its juice, he let it quietly die.

Only thing Chen said to him the whole drive, "I didn't want Lila to go. Amy didn't like it either, but we thought it was okay because you didn't seem worried." Bhakti didn't reply. What was there to say? I'm your boss? You trusted me? I'm sorry you feel that way? Nothing good to say.

Chen fished in his pocket and opened his own cell phone. Again, the gritty tune filled the car. "Save your battery," Bhakti told him. But Chen ignored him.

The Ford Interceptor and Jimmy's cop car started to slow—they were reaching their destination.

He had been to this place once or twice before. The desert around Sierra Blanca was just that: white mountains. Sand, dust, scrub. Railroad tracks paralleled the interstate; once upon a time the town served the Texas & Pacific and Southern Pacific. Not much to write home about: a depot museum in a red caboose railroad car, the oldest working adobe courthouse in Texas. And the distinction of once being the largest sewage sludge dump in the nation, on the short end of the stick from places as far away as Detroit or New York City. Municipalities saying, *Here we sit, muscles flexin', giving our crud to another Texan. . . .* Was Eleanor trying to tell him something? Bhakti wondered. Was this the writing on the wall?

A cluster of streets and houses; an in-between border town, neither totally alive nor totally dead. Population 553. Five a.m.; the stars still shone hard and bright in the night sky like distant witnesses. But the horizon glowed purple in the east; dawn soon. The three cars came to a halt on the apron of an abandoned ruin of a truck stop. Square concrete building, spiky weeds had overtaken the place, paint peeled off the awning over the pumps. The plate-glass windows of the storefront were intact, but split with long cracks, the wind and heat taking their toll.

Deputy Jimmy and the Texas Highway Patrolman were already out of their cars; Bhakti and Chen followed the beams of their flashlights lancing over the ground. The patrolman held some sort of cell phone signal locator, and Deputy Jimmy seemed to skip along behind the man looking over his shoulder; their cowboy boots going *click-clack* on the paved surface, then swishing as they moved through the weeds.

The two policemen paused a moment looking down at the locator, and the spot on which they stood. Then pointed in different directions as if uncertain which way to go. An argument was bubbling between them—the service station? The road, the rail tracks? Deputy Jimmy complaining, "Look it's all over the place, first north then south, then north again." With the Texas Highway Patrolman arguing, "No it always swings south again." And the two men weren't getting anywhere.

Bhakti's BlackBerry buzzed in his shirt pocket. Really weird, as if the batt still possessed a drop of juice. The screen ID flashed ELEANOR, a Twitter feed: *Here I stand stupidly texting, thinking railroad tracks be Chen's last hope thing.*

"Up to the railroad tracks," Bhakti urged. "Don't ask me why. Eleanor seems to know already."

Chen gave him a weird, doubtful glance, but didn't challenge him. The fathers picked up speed, past the truck stop and onto a strip of desert. The two lawmen hustled to catch up. The banked gravel bed of the railroad tracks stood out like a low wall. The flashlights danced back and forth. They caught a bit of color and automatically homed in on it. What they found was very, very bad. Two cell phones discarded on the gravel and a pile of girls' clothes strewn on the tracks.

Bhakti had to restrain Chen from scooping them up; the man was in tears, frantic. "Don't touch them, no!" Bhakti hissed, and it took the two lawmen to shake some sense into the father, blocking Chen from the empty shreds of jeans and tops, torn undies.

"We'll get dogs. We'll start tracking first light, just as soon as they get here. Just don't touch a thing, you'll ruin the scent."

Chen collapsed to his knees. "No, no, God no. . . ."

How much worse could it get?

They found out soon enough.

The dogs didn't have much luck; they were good dogs, they snuffed around for a bit, but wound up mostly going in circles. Some of the clothes were shredded as if torn apart by a berserk animal.

The cell phones weren't much help either. No strange numbers in the memory, a confusion of sweaty prints. There should have been some kind of registry, cell IP address, a digital fingerprint on the Felix song—but there wasn't. The stupid song seemed to have come out of thin air, untraceable. And by the middle of the day, by the looks of the lawmen, neither believed Bhakti or Chen had actually heard it. DNA would take some extra time. But no footprints, no remains; the girls had simply been plucked naked from the earth, leaving only their rags behind.

The two fathers drove back to Van Horn, neither speaking a word. The gray interstate rolled under them; a gritty roar seeping into every crevice of their brains. A blinding, deadening sound; the yellow sun coming up, a blistering eye.

Bhakti could see his days stretching out before him like a path of broken glass on which he would crawl. There'd be trips down to every border patrol post five hundred miles east and west. A hundred meals in diners, another hundred in Motel 6s. Every other night, wondering how long his strength would last, how long he could keep on searching. Handing out the endless stack of flyers in every border town from New Orleans to San Diego, trying to get on "America's Most Wanted," and the thousand copies to every cop's office in the United States; there'd be the stapling up of the handmade handbills with Janet's picture on a dozen lampposts on every Main Street, and public notice boards that everyone walked by without looking. He'd walked by handbills like that himself a million times, just walked by with a touch of pity at the faces of children, the milk-carton kidz half covered by ads for landscapers, house painters, and goats for sale.

Then there'd be the telephone calls that rang in the middle of the night, heartbreakers of well-intentioned folk who thought they'd seen Janet, but had mistaken her for some-one else—and the dirtiest of all, people who hadn't seen her but worked some scam, preying on the desperate.

Then the calls home to Eleanor, calls he'd never want to make. Reduced at last to what? A hopeless wreck of a man ready to go into any seedy fortune-teller for a séance with one of Janet's stuffed animals she still kept on her bed? At least now that Eleanor could walk, it wouldn't be so hard for her to come along.

But that day wasn't through with them yet. Not with Chen at any rate. Chen stopped the car in his subdivision driveway. Amy, his wife, had turned on the lawn sprinklers and now knelt on the short, clipped grass soaked to the skin, her gleaming black hair in a glistening rope about her neck. As Chen and Bhakti got out of the car the water pressure in the sprinkler faded and died. It sometimes did that. Wait an hour, the water would come back.

"Amy?" Chen ran to his wife. Still staring at the two, Bhakti went to the side of Chen's house and punched off the sprinkler spigot on the control timer. Then walked carefully through the damp grass to where the two both knelt. Chen had put his arm over Amy's shoulders; they were staring at something on the wet lawn. An object, no, not an object—

A body part: *an ear with an earring.*

Bhakti recognized it immediately: one of Lila Chen's hematite earrings, a long pendant, with little polished knobs of tortoiseshell ending in a dangle of shiny gray metal.

He recognized it because his daughter Janet liked them so much and sometimes borrowed them. Eleanor had been talking about getting Janet her own pair of hematite dan-glers. It seemed fitting; the faintly magnetic iron oxide some thought encouraged healing, intuition, serenity, and balance. Magical iron. They'd even found hematite on Mars, yin-yang on a planetary scale.

Yes, Janet was always borrowing them—*but not this*

time. That wasn't Janet's ear. Yes, an ear, but not Janet's ear. You see, Janet had two piercings, this ear only one. *Not Janet. Thank God it wasn't Janet's ear*; that meant she might be alive—and Bhakti felt a twinge of guilt that he could think such a thing with Amy and Chen kneeling before him and so obviously torn in little pieces.

The guilt washed away in a rush of relief, then a clutch of dry-mouth. The fear came back; his little girl still missing. At least alive, but still missing. Amy shivered uncontrollably, inconsolable. Chen had picked up the ear and just stared at it, dumbfounded; the earring tinkled a little as it trembled in his hand.

"Wen, Amy," Bhakti tried to get through to them. "We have to give that to the police; they have to examine it. Wen!" But Wen and Amy ignored him. Wen pulled his wife from her kneeling position and slowly walked her back to the house, clutching the last bits of his child. The front door opened and closed, and Bhakti found himself alone on their green lawn. At his feet a scrap of paper, somehow forgotten. He picked it up. A handwritten note: *They've been real good. Thanks for everything.*

He glanced back at his own house across the street. Eleanor still stood behind the closed window, this time holding the curtain open by the sash. Had she seen who delivered the grisly bits of Lila? After a moment the curtain fell back in place and the figure of Eleanor disappeared from view.

Then Bhakti noticed something even stranger at every house in the subdivision, up one side and down their manicured street. The curtains were open a crack there too, people watching—all the nosy hausfraus? Mrs. Biedermeier in her blue housecoat, Mrs. Stanton in her tennis whites, all the wives standing at their plate-glass windows. He could see their eyes staring at him. One-two-three-four down the subdivision street. Simply staring. After a moment the curtains flicked shut.

Had anyone seen anything? Dammit! Knock on one door, wait, make the demand. What did you see? Who dropped off the things on Wen's lawn? Did you see something—a bicycle, a car, a license plate, *something*?

Mrs. Biedermeier didn't come to the door at all.

Bhakti knocked and hammered, called out hoarsely, "Mrs. Biedermeier!" Nothing. Then soft padding came to the closed door. "Mrs. Biedermeier, I'd just like to ask you—"

But a soft voice came through the blank door. "Go away, just go away."

"I'm going to have the police come and ask."

"That's fine, just go away."

The same thing happened at Mrs. Stanton's, and this time Bhakti nearly kicked the damn door in. But he stopped himself. *Forget 'em*—time for another police call. Oh, God, that's right, the BlackBerry was dead.

In a dumb rage Bhakti stumped heavily back to his own front door. Eleanor stood in the living room.

"I didn't see anything either."

Of course not—she'd been standing behind a closed curtain the whole day staring at the curtain fabric. Eleanor hadn't moved from her spot. Somehow this took all the wind out of Bhakti's sails. He made the police call from the house phone, and Deputy Jimmy said they'd be out shortly. But something had collapsed inside—an emptiness Bhakti had never felt before.

The fire at the Chen's house started four minutes later, burned hot and quick and couldn't be brought under control for fifteen minutes. Enough time to burn mostly everything. None of the neighbors came to watch, no kids, no nothing—and that was strange too. Fires bring people out: kids on their bikes, fathers watching in their trek shorts and sandals—but not this time.

Fire trucks, ambulances, nearly the whole Van Horn

Sheriff's Department, but Bhakti seemed to be Amy and Wen Chen's only witness from the subdivision. He watched the sheriff's men knocking on doors and talking to whoever opened them—Mrs. Stanton, Mrs. Biedermeier—but it felt only like show, like they were going through the motions for him alone.

Deputy Jimmy came back with his notepad. "You say there was some sort of evidence, body parts?"

"I told you, Jimmy. . . ." Harder to say than he thought. "An ear with a dangling earring."

"What kind of earring again?"

Bhakti went through it once more. Deputy Jimmy nodded, taking it all down. "Yeah, we found some burned"—he paused—"burned stuff. Flesh I mean. Just a lump, really, all mixed in with timber and plastic near one of the bodies. I'll get it processed."

The firemen rolled their hoses, the EMTs brought two bodies out of the Chen house on stretchers. Amy and Wen. Cause of death? They were pretty scorched up, but it looked like smoke inhalation. Deputy Jimmy halted at the mouth of the ambulance and unzipped the body bags for Bhakti to look. Bhakti made the final nod, heard the final zip of the zipper, and silently bowed his head in a wordless goodbye.

The afternoon passed, the sun went down, and still Bhakti hadn't gone indoors. He sat on his front stone steps staring at the rubble of the Chen house and smelling the rancid smell of burnt oil that comes from a lot of torched plastic. The streetlights came on, casting a nice, familiar glow up and down the subdivision. Televisions glowed in houses; the sounds of people making dinner, the clink of plates and utensils.

American normality.

But nothing came from Bhakti's house. Was Eleanor still standing at the window behind the curtain?

By some unknown impulse Bhakti rose and went across

the street to the damp ruins. Char and tar and crunchy wood crumbled under his feet. The open frame of the house, timbers and weight-bearing posts, moved by him like burned wraiths. The floorboards creaked ominously under his feet as though ready to break.

Drawn to Lila Chen's room he looked around.

The beam from his flashlight lanced about the charred walls.

In a corner sat a girl's dresser, white-painted, blistered and scorched. An item stared at him from the dresser top. A single hematite earring, a match for the one in Lila's ear. That happened to girls a lot; they lost earrings. They bought replacements. Could Deputy Jimmy have been that sloppy to miss this one? You'd think he would have bagged it out of thoroughness.

Gingerly he picked the earring off the dresser and for no reason at all put it carefully in his shirt pocket.

Why?

Again, maybe a connection to Janet, or Lila, their bodies or souls—wherever they were, wherever God had taken them. Deflated, defeated, Bhakti sighed and went back across the street. Tired, tired to the bone. Once inside, he barely glanced at Eleanor, who still stood by the drawn window curtain; the bed just as he'd left it hours ago looked up at him. And that's the last thing he remembered from that day.

E leanor was gone when he woke up. She took the extra car, a wad of bills from his wallet, some clothes, and left a note. *Taking a little trip to see my sister. I have my cell.*

Bhakti stared at the note. This was all so incomprehensible.

Leave? Now?

He simply stared at the scribbled scrap of paper. That

would be sister Lauren; who still lived back east, up in Connecticut. Once upon a time Lauren and Eleanor were close, but then came their aunt's will and the disposition of the Fairfield house, and Eleanor got into a bit of a huff over not even getting a penny of Auntie's estate. The will was clear enough and nobody was in a mind to contest it. . . . Still, the slight became like a canker, swelling up with emotional pus and dissipating as the years rolled by. Then swelling up again.

Sister Lauren even tried to make amends, offering some money from a recent real estate killing. But Eleanor quietly shrugged it away, a day late and a dollar short, saying, *Well, you and Guy may have kids someday, so keep the money. We're fine.* Still, Bhakti knew it quietly rancored; so the two sisters' relations were in an off-year right now. God, what would Lauren think when Eleanor climbed out of the car without her crutches?

And without Janet? What absurd tale would she tell? *Yeah, Sis, Punjab husband is looking for our kid, so what's new with you?*

After a two-thousand-mile trip, she might be back in the chair again. But the wheelchair stood in the living room near the front windows; damn, she hadn't even taken the wheelchair along.

Idly, Bhakti wondered when Eleanor would call and from where. He was so preoccupied with finding Janet he almost didn't notice that all the wives in the subdivision had hit the road for parts unknown. The Biedermeiers, the Stantons—every wife in every house. Vamoosed into thin air. And what was worse, nobody seemed to care. Bhakti watched all the men on the street come out of their respective front doors.

The husbands gathered on the asphalt for a moment in a rough circle, intermittently speaking as though each confirming to his neighbor the missing person in their lives. Then just as quietly they broke apart and went back to their houses, shutting the doors, the subdivision street empty again. This was Sunday morning, but no one came out to mow his lawn; no one played Frisbee or raced his kids' motorized toy cars in the street. No smell of backyard grilling, nothing.

A dismal quiet had descended over every house.

The next two weeks proceeded pretty much as Bhakti had feared in that fruitless car ride home from Sierra Blanca, leaving behind the girls' discarded clothes on the railroad tracks.

Endless days of handing out handbills, the trips to every border patrol post hundreds of miles east and west while the bitter sun stared back at him through his bug-splattered windshield. The calls to Eleanor on his cell that she ignored, choosing instead, distant perfunctory text message replies telling him not to worry—as if a stranger were pressing the keys. Exchanges with his wife raised more questions than they answered, but Bhakti couldn't be in two places at once. It was either look for his daughter or deal with a crazy wife, and the child came first.

The stale menus and meals in diners, the lonely motels with cheap bed coverlets and pillows that smelled faintly of mildew or even more faintly of some stranger's sleep from the night before. Always noticing the streak of dust where housekeeping missed a swipe across the TV screen, or that crooked Emmett Kelly clown oil over the bed.

Bhakti wore out faster than he thought he would. And it shamed him. A man was supposed to be relentless on the hunt, never tiring, never giving up. But two weeks in—he was worn to the bone.

So worn that when he came out of a local police department in Las Cruces, New Mexico, from yet another round of handbill handouts he almost walked right by Madame Zelda's. Dusk was still in the latter half of its magic phase, the sun down but not near night, the kind of blue that still had rose tips in its color, and touches of orange that always made Bhakti think of skies on alien worlds.

Of course, the astrology shop front wasn't called Madame Zelda's, but a little sign read: SENORA MALVEDOS. A narrow glass window, next to a narrower door lacquered up in dried and flaking robin's-egg blue paint. The window glass showed a decal of palmistry, and another old decal of a Tarot deck—cracked red and orange and purple decals, blistered from endless New Mexico suns.

The palmistry decal showed five fingers and different regions of the human hand: Love, Marriage, Life, Heart, Head. Then the fingers named after the ancients gods: Mercury, Apollo, Saturn, Jupiter. A dusty cactus sat at the base of the window, next to a crucifix with hanging Jesus dying for eternity.

A faint light shone through a crack in the velvet curtains behind the window: so somebody was home after all.

Bhakti pushed open the paint-flaked door and found himself in a front parlor: a couple of worn chairs, some magazines, a side table with perhaps two dozen icons of Catholic saints clustered together like a crowd of friends at a party. Bhakti, no expert in Catholic saints, couldn't tell one from the next. Maybe Saint Francis, because he held a bird in his palm.

Over the table an old flat-screen TV hung from the ceiling, playing to empty chairs. Another infomercial with that weirdo wearing the top hat and tails again—no, *a game show* this time; an enormous woman, naked to the waist, clutched her massive breasts and coyly exposed her back to the camera. The show's name: "Peer Pressure!"

The lanky creep in the tuxedo held a large mop and was swabbing off the woman's naked back with soapy water while the audience hooted and hollered.

Who the hell *was* this guy? The next "big thing"?

Then a midget in a tiny tuxedo came out throwing fistfuls

of rainbow-colored goose feathers in every direction, many of which stuck to the soapy wench, making her look like an enormous rainbow chicken. A huge graphic blazed out of the screen, demanding, *So Who's Next?*

The women in the audience clamored wildly, "Pick me! Pick me! Feather! Feather! Feather me next!"

Bhakti shook his head; people watched such crap.

The entranceway to the "inner sanctum" was a mere open door with thick ropes of dirty wooden beads. The beads clicked gently as Bhakti tore his eyes from the TV. A little Spanish girl of about nine stood there, thoughtfully biting the end of her thumb. She smiled coyly at him and twisted a lock of her black hair.

For the first time since he'd left the subdivision, Bhakti smiled back at someone. "Hello."

But the little girl didn't answer, just smiled in that pert *I've got a secret* way so endearing in children under ten before they change into quasi-adults with adolescent sensibilities and advanced human flaws. Not knowing how to keep on with her, Bhakti asked, "Is Senora Malvedos available?"

A woman's voice came out of the inner sanctum, raspy as a crow's with a subtle cough. A lifetime of cigarettes. "Pick a saint."

Bhakti hesitated, staring at the little girl, who hadn't moved from her spot at the beads. There was something different about her—not her looks, but beneath the skin. The words *child of the Magi* popped into his head. A child who walked before the Three Kings, an innocent brought into this world to see ahead, through cloud and storm, keeping those who searched, who sought redemption, on the true path—no matter how difficult or daunting. When Bhakti looked at her he could almost see her shining halo—that stylized golden circle in a thousand years of Christian art. And he had never felt or seen as much on any child before, even his own.

This blessed child was destined, fated for something. But what?

Could she mark his own path to Janet?

He had no clue.

Bhakti stared back down at the table covered with the little statuettes. There were so many saints, some with crowns, some holding little baby Jesus, some with rays of power emanating from their robes, some with wings and swords like angels, others with the globe of the world in their palms—how was he to pick? The voice cleared its throat again.

"You choose, you choose, and by your choice I can know."

Still he hesitated. His hand strayed to one and then another, then fluttered back again.

The raspy cigarette voice came one last time, "Or let the girl pick."

5

Frozen Smoke

The fortune-teller could tell a thousand things about people the moment she laid eyes on them. Whether they'd slept well the night before, whether they'd had sex in the last two months. Whether they were rich or poor. And whether they were faking about either. The first thing every palm reader learns is how to read the body, the clothes, the mannerisms. The way a person moved, crossed his legs, or sat down—you could always tell whether he was keeping a secret or trying to confess. Mostly it was both.

Senora Malvedos was good at reading people, always had been. And Little Maria was going to be very, very good. The saint statuette the girl brought in from the parlor wasn't Madonna of the Streets, or Saint Joseph—but Santa Judah. Saint Jude. The patron saint of lost causes. Little Maria's own reading of the tired, sad man before her—absolutely spot-on: a desperate human being, trapped in his own web perhaps, or crushed under an unbelievable burden. But Little Maria's choices were also warnings for the Senora, for these were not people with hopes, but people without hope, and they could turn on you in a flash. Harbor some crazy grudge. Come back later for revenge.

Yet the second she saw him, Senora Malvedos knew this man had no violence in him. Not for her, at any rate, not even if she told him he would die of cancer in six months. Or that his child was dead—

The hand touched the back of her neck. *Oh God, not now. Not the real thing.* She feared and despised *the hand*; how to know if it came from God or the Devil? Oh, God, not now. Little Maria saw the flash of fear in the old woman's eyes, placed the statuette of Saint Jude on the table, and slowly shrank into a corner.

The last one had been easy, a year ago at least. The last time *the hand* had touched the back of the Senora's neck the client had been a brassy middle-aged woman who pulled up in a Ford Torino muscle car like a character out of a 1970s cop show. She wore a curious combination of biker leather pants, denim jacket with a small Confederate flag patch on the shoulder, and reading glasses like Mr. Geppetto specs out of *Pinocchio*. The woman had limped into the parlor, stumping along on crutches, and sat heavily at Senora Malvedos' table without even being asked. She seemed to have been pretty banged up, a car wreck maybe, but a little red scar under her ear told a different story, a stab wound? Maybe . . . but that wasn't the insight.

Without waiting for Senora Malvedos to perceive all

manner of secrets, this strange gruff broad spilled her guts in bits and pieces. Wandering the deserts of New Mexico on a tourist visa from life she was trying to decide her future, lost as any stray. Whether to live out here in the clean wasteland until she healed up—or return to her saloon, Big Bea's Bar and Grill, where she polished beer mugs and fed her government disability into the business when things got tight.

Not to mention, she was worried sick over a wayward brother who had recently drifted away; an egghead, a bookworm—now they'd lost touch. But she was too beaten up, too bruised to go on the hunt for him.

On that day a year ago, Little Maria had brought in Saint Lucy, the blessed Virgin Lucy. A young woman in robes martyred by a Roman emperor; a gruesome image, the woman held a plate, and on the plate sat her plucked-out eyes. Yet for all that, a good saint to bring to the table, for Saint Lucy stood for virtue, zeal, and fidelity. The legend told of how when she rejected her pagan bridegroom, Roman centurions gouged out her eyes, and yet she still could see. So when the single finger touched the back of Senora's neck the vision had come like a welcome rain.

She saw the brother sitting in a darkened modern amphitheater, carefully tapping into his notebook. The lecturer, an egghead scientist, pointed at a light screen, his voice a nasal whine. There were no windows in the darkened amphitheater, but Senora could feel the weather outside. Rain lashed down across rolling hills. It had rained for many nights before; this had to be back east someplace, the Midwest maybe. Ohio . . .

New Job—that's where Younger Brother was hiding. Senora caught a fragment of the light screen images in the amphitheater: genetics, genetic engineering, rDNA— recombinant DNA.

"Not to worry," Senora Malvedos told Big Sis. "He got that job he wanted. Engineering people, tiny threads in people. That very research position with that very special laboratory—"

The relief washed over the gruff woman's face. "That's right," she said. Then with a smile, "Webster, that little brat told me it might be hush-hush. Believe it or not I helped him get that job—"

But the Senora had stopped listening; the hand gone. Her part done, now it was up to the both of them. Brother and Sister. Find each other or not. Money was shoved across the table, but Senora never took the money when the hand touched her. There was something grotesque and wrong about charging for her gift. So she just shook her head. "Not this time Senorita, maybe next."

Now, right now with this sad brown man, no such luck. Only bad news coming for him. The man stared quietly across the table over the statuette of Saint Jude, the patron of lost causes. . . . The hand touched Senora Malvedos and she knew the question to ask.

"Let me see what you brought."

At first he seemed confused, then slowly fished a trinkly thing out of his shirt pocket, and a scrap of paper. A hematite earring. A sliver of paper with some writing.

She reached out to touch the earring on the table; not an inch away it skittered from her finger like a Mexican jumping bean. The Senora snatched her claw away with a sharp intake of breath. The sad man started in his chair; then a cloud of suspicion crossed his face: moving tables, floating candles—séance tricks. But he couldn't see what the Senora saw. The earring leapt into her mind: the sound of screaming, a girl screaming, the girl's head was restrained; long black pony-tail grabbed and then came the knife, bad men were going to cut her, men laughing—

Senora Malvedos started to babble, some sort of song or poem she'd never heard before: "*A rag, a bone, a hank of hair!*" She paused and more came, "Love! It's an iron hand in a woman's glove, it's a hawk disguised as a dove, it's a rag, a bone, a hank of hair, it's not fair, it's a nightmare that poets call a beautiful dream."

She stopped babbling.

Then sat up straight; she knew the fate of that young woman.

"The young lady who wore a trinket like this was kidnapped."

She reached over the table to the little metallic hematite earring and clasped it tightly in her fingers to keep it from jumping away. The Senora quietly reassured herself the thing was real and not some parlor trick brought into her sanctum by a very clever man. Clever people tried to trick the medium. No, no parlor trick.

"This one. *Lila*. Still lives. You may see her yet." She watched the sad man's face darken then lighten, as if with a shard of hope. "Show me the note." He reached for it, touched it with his fingers. To him, nothing happened—to her, to Senora Malvedos, she saw the scrap ignite like flash paper and sail to the ceiling on a sliver of rising ash.

They've been real good. Thanks for everything.

A thread of smoke hung for long seconds in the air; frozen smoke dangling in front of her eyes like the ghost of a lost soul. When she looked back down toward the sad man, he was still holding the unburned scrap in damp, meaty fingers. In that short flash of light and its smoky trail, she'd seen a wall of steel lockers. A coroner or mortuary. An orderly slid a stainless steel slab into the wall, naked feet vanishing into the cold dark. The toe tag read Jane Doe, and a date written in bold red flair; they'd scheduled the body for an autopsy. And Senora Malvedos spoke clearly:

"Eleven-oh-four North Mission Road. Los Angeles, California. Zip code 90033. Telephone 323-343-0512. Business Hours: 8 a.m. to 5 p.m. Monday through Friday. Autopsy day after tomorrow. They call her Sweet Jane because she's so innocent. They tried to be gentle; they tried to be kind."

The sad man sat back in his chair, all the blood draining from his face. He began to breathe heavily, almost like a stroke was coming. With all his self-control, knowing he'd gotten the worst news possible, he held out Lila Chen's earring again. Senora Malvedos' finger reached to the hematite dangler, but this time the silvery thing hung like a dead weight. Lifeless. The attraction gone.

"And this one?" he asked. "I might still see this one?"

But the hand had left Senora Malvedos; she sighed, exhausted. Alas, there was no more left to tell him, nothing left to learn. The sad man dropped the earring and it fell to the table with a tiny clink. He'd heard her correctly, all right. Yes, he might still see the other girl. He put the trinket away. Found his wallet and fished a wad of bills from it, counting out the Franklins, one-two-three-four . . .

But the woman across the table merely shook her head.

"I don't want your money. Look after your Frozen Smoke."

Bhakti started at the use of those two words, *frozen* and *smoke*. Very odd. "That's a special material we make where I work," he managed to tell her. Senora Malvedos shrugged. To her, frozen smoke simply meant a ghost. A lost soul.

"I only saw your daughter. She's waiting for you."

A thousand miles away in Sioux Falls, South Dakota, a few people, people that mattered, were beginning to notice Bhakti's absence.

Local tourist brochures, the kind you see stacked in clean plastic holders in trendy gift shops, called Sioux Falls "The best little city in America," along with the motto, "The heart of America." Maybe it was, maybe it wasn't—but with a population of 151K, you could hardly call it a city, more like a big town. And if you could stand a winter that felt like *North* Dakota, so much the better.

The company Bhakti worked for—Lattimore Aerospace—was housed in a modest glass-and-steel building. In Sioux Falls, most of the buildings were modest, under eight stories, and Clem Lattimore's world headquarters was no exception, a giant rectangular children's block. The only striking difference was the bronze-colored windows that wrapped around the structure in a seamless band, offset by bluish steel. It even looked like an aerospace building: stoic, advanced, and shiny like a strong face hiding a thousand secrets.

This Saturday afternoon the Lattimore offices were empty, the cubicles and conference rooms, the long laboratories dark and lonely. And as usual William Ohanzee Howahkan had stopped by to see if the boss needed anything.

And there were matters to discuss.

The elevator gently stopped at the private suite at the top of the building. The triple security display lit up. First retinal, then palm print, then voice. He looked at the electric eye so it could look back at him. Put his hand on the glass plate so the database could confirm his handprint and said, "It's Billy." He looked up at the tiny video camera in the corner of the elevator for good measure, showing his smooth, handsome, Lakota face. The triple security computer took its good time today, so after a moment he repeated himself dryly, "It's Billy, *Mr. Hughes*. Tonto come see if Big Papoose need nappy change."

A disembodied voice chuckled back at him in the stainless steel elevator, "Hah! Not today, Billy—but come on in anyway." And the doors whooshed open.

William Ohanzee Howahkan, quite a mouthful.

In Lakota, Ohanzee meant "Shadow," and Howahkan, "Of the Mysterious Voice." Billy Shadow of the Mysterious Voice. And not so far off the mark if working for Cowboy Clem was any measure. But it went farther back than that. After his parents passed on was it the mysterious voice that made him walk off the reservation, leaving only his shadow behind? But what was the alternative?

Stay on the rez, drinking welfare for a living? Turn into a social worker; get into the "antiques" business? No . . . better to leave it all like the broken washing machines on the burnt lawns.

So he enlisted in the army at seventeen, later getting picked for Officer Candidate School, then a sponsorship, a commission at West Point. And to the great dismay of some back home—joined the modern incarnation of the 7th Cavalry, now called the 1st Cavalry. How messed-up was that? The very same outfit his great-great-grandpappy left to rot deep in the Black Hills with arrows planted in their blues. The same blue bellies that had great-great-granny on all fours after the surrender of the Nez Perce. Traitor to his people, they called him.

Sure, some of the hotheads were ready to put his head on a lodgepole. But a word from one of the elders took the heat off at home, and it came to him in Iraq in the desert e-mail tent—that it would be all right for him to return, if that's what he wanted. The simple statement from Granny Sparrow: "You're a warrior now."

Fair enough. He'd reached his "twenty" in the army, more like twenty-five, seen all the war a man could see and still survive to tell about it—Major Howahkan resigned his commission and took his leave of boots and BDUs. Old Granny Sparrow always thought he looked strong in his battle dress uniform; a modern brave wearing digital camo instead of war paint. But at age forty-three, the retired Major Howahkan still had a whole life to live.

Which is when Tonto found the paleface.

Billy tripped over Clem Lattimore, a lost tenderfoot in the Sonoran Desert with a fractured ankle, a dead cell phone, and a blistered hour away from final dehydration. Billy saw the man lying up against a pretty red boulder, his pants ripped, shirt open, sunburnt to a crisp. Little boy lost, separated from his group along with their sunblock, fruit juice, and evening margaritas. Clearly the easy field trip to the Saguaro National Park had gone the way of *Deliverance*. A Gila monster kept Clem quiet company from a nice warm spot on the rock. Perfectly happy to watch the white man die and do nothing about it.

What had drawn Billy Shadow to the spot was the bird. He'd seen the vulture high in the sky, and there was always something interesting to see under the shade of the vulture's wings. The vast spirit of land and sky ran strong in him; memories of birds singing their morning songs and smart foxes smiling in the tall grass—the "old ways" rattled in his gourd long after Billy put on long pants. The ancient ground, forever in your bones; just the way you looked at things.

A vulture in the sky. A lizard on a rock.

Everything meant something; everything significant, if you could read the signs. Clem Lattimore cracked his blistered eyelids, hearing Billy Shadow's footsteps, and heard for the first time the mysterious voice of salvation.

"You know, Chief," the voice from the silhouette told him, "you really look like you need a drink." And before Lattimore knew it, the water bottle splashed his face and came to his mouth. The man wanted to say thank you, to cry—but he was simply too dry for tears. All that came out was, "Dahh . . ."

"Easy now, Kemo Sabe." The voice told him. "We're going to find your friends."

So an accident of fate and the Tonto wisecrack started Billy's second life, getting him a job with one of the richest men in America. And the two were a natural fit: Clem needed an XO, and a US Cavalry major, retired, three months home, who'd saved his life in the desert, couldn't be beat. Besides, Major Billy Shadow, retired or not, knew things besides walking out of the desert alive. And the old Lone Ranger shtick went on from there. Something personal between them. And not for outsiders, who hadn't nearly died or been saved.

Beyond the elevator, Lattimore's private floor engulfed you. Billy called it "the Library"; not just hearth, home, and bed, but something much more—a collection of books and artifacts spanning disciplines and centuries. He'd once joked to Clem, "So you got the Spear of Christ in here somewhere?" But still the Library made a kind of sense; so much of the mind of mankind represented on its shelves and from its spines: literature, poetry, the sciences, history. You could find Alexander Marshack's *The Roots of Civilization* next to Cremo and Thompson's *Forbidden Archeology,* and even Däniken's *Chariots of the Gods.*

Billy had spent countless hours after work and even weekends up here reading, trying to separate truth from fantasy, at last exasperated, demanding of Lattimore, "Aren't Däniken with his god's hot rods and Marshack with his knuckle-scraping, hairy moon-counters, cutting notches in pieces of bone, in some way mutually exclusive? We either received our religion, technology, and science, even our DNA, in fallen comet ice from the stars"—he took a breath—"or we dragged ourselves from the slime right here at home, alone. It's either one or the other, don't you think?"

As usual Lattimore sat at his desk, back turned, his swivel chair facing out the bronze-colored window. A wreath of cigar smoke floated above his head, still and nearly frozen. It always reminded Billy of floating snow in the Black Hills, the air so cold the flakes wouldn't really fall, just hover about your face so you could taste them.

"Are they?" Lattimore's voice came back at him. "Mutually exclusive? I suppose. But you can see them as a greater whole. That's why the King James version of *The Bible* along with *The Five Books of Moses* is sitting next to Downing's *The Bible and Flying Saucers*. And beside that *The Nine Doors of the Kingdom of Shadows* by Torchia, burned at the stake by the Inquisition for writing a how-to book on invoking the Devil. And next to that a history of the Vril Society, the Kraut cranks who manufactured Nazi UFOs. The inescapable conclusion I've drawn is that if the Almighty is all-powerful he made Satan too, right? Did life evolve here on Earth alone or was it seeded from far-off stars? Why not both? God made the stars too, didn't he?"

"So that's what Lattimore Aerospace is all about, eh Kemo Sabe?" Billy teased. "Finding Klaatu and his silent servant Gort?" Billy heard Lattimore laugh in his wreath of smoke at the reference to the visitor from outer space Klaatu, better known as Michael Rennie and his invulnerable robot with the Cyclops laser eye in the old sci-fi classic *The Day the Earth Stood Still*.

Lattimore cleared his throat and turned from the window. "Well, it's not because I'm so in love with communication satellites—and if I can only reach out with my little pinkie to the stars, why wouldn't I go that far? Why wouldn't anyone? For all Columbus and Vasco de Gama knew they were sailing off a cliff. We know a little bit better now. Just a little."

Today, as Billy crossed the library Lattimore lit a fresh cigar and swiveled around in his chair to face him. He pushed some papers across the solid surface, personnel files with photos.

"You seen these yet?" A mixture of annoyance and worry fed the lines across Clem Lattimore's forehead. The husky voice slid from Clem's broad throat on a silky carpet of nicotine. "We seem to have a brain drain."

Billy nodded silently; he'd seen the files late Friday.

A half-dozen scientists and technicians down at Escape

Velocity at the Van Horn lab facility had failed to come to work. One, Bhakti Singh, had simply vanished. Operations at the lab had slowly ground to a halt over the last week or so. Now the powers at corporate HQ were just finding out.

Lattimore didn't run a slack ship, but he didn't make his creative guys punch time clocks. If one of the designers hid under the covers for a week with a flashlight and a scratch pad so be it. Billy picked up the file photos of Bhakti Singh and his second-in-command, Wen Chen. The two indispensable men in charge of the space fabric unit and an even more important project: the manufacture of Aerogel.

This miracle material was going to let the fragile paper airplane of a spaceship blast through the wall of gravity and fall like an angel through the fire of Earth's atmosphere again. Aerogel could support thousands of times its own weight and was a thousand times less dense than glass. It felt like Styrofoam and could act as a thermal insulator. They made space shuttle tiles out of the translucent stuff; harder than steel and lighter than air—people called it frozen smoke.

And *very* expensive to manufacture. Bhakti Singh and Wen Chen were working on a more affordable manufacturing process. "We can't afford to lose those guys to MIT or Caltech," Lattimore remarked.

"I don't think we did," Billy told him. "I sent some e-mails, left some phone messages. Hardly anybody answers. And when they do pick up the phone, they mumble some crap—or just hang up. So I tried the sheriff's office at the courthouse an hour ago. There's been some problems down at Van Horn. Kids gone missing, wives walking out on their husbands. Weird stuff." He paused. "And something else."

Lattimore's eyes flashed at him. Bad news coming.

Billy gave it to him straight. "Apparently there was a fire at Wen Chen's place twelve days ago. Wen and Amy Chen may be dead. I say *may* because I can't get a coherent story out of anybody. But I think they're dead."

That caught Lattimore by surprise; he shook an ash off his cigar and missed the ashtray. A soft rumble came up his throat, part concern, part disbelief. In a few heartbeats Lattimore came to grips with the idea of losing one of his best designers and not knowing. "You mean, Wen Chen may have been dead over a week and nobody from Van Horn told us? Not even the local authorities?"

"That's what I'm telling you."

Lattimore let that sink in. Then dryly:

"Have we thought about sending flowers, condolences? A private eye?"

"Good grief, Clem—I haven't even been able to find anyone to send flowers to except the local sheriff. For all we know the subdivision is a ghost town. I was headed out for a look-see tonight. I'm taking your plane to Dallas. But I want to go the last lap by car . . . loaded up and prepared. I should get there sometime tomorrow."

Lattimore stared at his burning cigar; then with an edge in his voice, "Well, we can do it faster than that. What's the number of that sheriff's office?"

Billy snorted. "Go ahead and call, *Mr. Hughes*. As of twenty minutes ago, nobody's answering that phone either."

Lattimore sat back in his chair. Stared at the ceiling for a moment, then back at the cigar between his fingers; this time he actually hit the ashtray. At last he grumbled, "Well, don't you go off on a walkabout and forget to come back."

Billy Shadow turned his back on the desk and muttered, "No, that's your specialty. I'll be in touch."

6

Peenemünde & Mittelbau–Dora

Lattimore watched his Number Two go back through the library toward the stainless steel elevator doors. If anybody could find out what the hell was going on down in Van Horn, Billy could. Whatever there was to find out about Escape Velocity's missing employees, about Amy and Wen Chen dead or alive, Billy was the man to do it. The Indian tracker who never got lost.

Yeah, getting lost—that's my specialty. He stared at the ceiling. How could a guy like himself, who'd made so much money, built such incredible, vibrant engines of commerce, wander off into terra incognito and come back without a scratch? Dumb luck?

He stared at the map spread out on the desk before him. A copy of a map, and not very large. Called the Piri Reis map, after the sixteenth-century Turkish admiral and cartographer with the full name of Hadji Muhiddin Piri Ibn Hadji Mehmed who had made copies of copies of older maps, charting the Mediterranean to the Indies. This was a copy of the famous one, inked on gazelle skin. In 1927, some historians had found the Piri version in the Topkapi Palace Museum, dated around 1513, but even that one was a copy of an older map.

The map showed the Atlantic coast of Africa, the Atlantic coast of South America, and—there at the bottom, real terra incognito—some thought the coastline of Antarctica. A coastline buried under thousands of years of ice and snow—a coastline not mapped till the 1950s with Air Force radar. Like a palimpsest. A coastline first seen before man crawled out of the trees, then covered for an eternity, only to be seen with piercing modern technological eyes. One of "history's mysteries," they called it. The map was an affront to science, to the accepted march of history. Just as Lattimore's life was an affront to the accepted notions of fate, chance, and outcome.

People talked about a "blessed" life, and Lattimore's surely was.

All the power and ease that money brought, without the curse of manic celebrity.

But it hadn't quite started out that way. Not on that critical day as a boy of nine. Lattimore remembered taking his bag of green plastic soldiers up into the treehouse. Usually he took them over to the stream that flowed near the back porch; there among the roots and stones he could play Omaha Beach, setting the little things among the nooks and crannies of the stream's bank, making them climb the cliffs of Pointe du Hoc to knock out the German gun emplacements.

But this time he ascended to the treehouse. The treehouse was his special place, and Pop had taken a lot of care and trouble building it: all enclosed, with pine wainscoting, and even shelves for his toys and bunks for sleeping. A fireman's pole for quick exits, screens in the windows, and even a skylight so you could stare at the sky through the quietly fluttering leaves of an oak tree in summer.

The day he decided to go up into the treehouse instead of squatting by the brook, he heard his father pushing the lawnmower across the grass below and his mother's soft voice coming out from the open kitchen window. The little toy soldiers fell from the bag, but didn't seem to want to arrange themselves for battle.

The sun burned down the skylight, and he heard the wind in the leaves. A hornet buzzed against the screen outside. He must have fallen asleep, because when he woke the sun was in a corner of the treehouse and no sound other than the rustle of leaves. He packed his bag of soldiers, clamped it in his mouth, and slid down the fire pole.

And then he noticed things were very wrong. His father's lawn mower sat in the middle of the lawn, mid-cut. Pop never stopped in the middle of anything. The house stared at him, no noise from the kitchen. Inside, the oven was on and the scent of a roast filled the room. On the stovetop a low flame burned under a pot of water, but it was bubbling fast. He turned it off.

"Mom?" No answer. "Dad?"

Again, just silence. His father's pipe sat in the ashtray, his mother's knitting, needles stuck through a ball of yarn, in her chair; their cat, Briseis, sat next to the yarn ball and tricked the thread.

No Mom. No Pop.

Before the day was out, the Pennsylvania State Police had come to the house, Reverend Franks had come and gone, and his regular nanny, Simone, was staying in the guest room. Neighbors came and went, food was brought, and the house seemed full all the time. They even organized searches in the local Bucks County woods. But to no avail.

The next night it rained.

Around midnight his parents appeared on the front porch. Wet, clothes torn, half-naked and shivering—they walked in out of nowhere. Simone meant to keep him in his room while she made cocoa in the kitchen, but he sneaked to the top of the stairs and looked down. Mom and Pop had found some dry clothes; they sat on the couch, a little distance apart as though afraid to touch. His father's brand-new land camera—the Polaroid Big Swinger 3000—lay on the coffee table in big broken plastic pieces. His father really loved that camera, one of the first to buy it when it came out. A few creased color snapshots dotted with rainwater were all he managed to save. He fingered the Polaroids for a moment but didn't pick them up.

Instead Pop rubbed the numbered tattoo on his forearm and stared dolefully at the Polaroids on the table. The blue numbers of that tattoo always seemed to bother him. And the photos bothered him. Clem quietly heard his father say to Mom, "Yes, I know. I know we have to call everyone. I'll do it in a minute." A pause as his mother asked another question and his father answered, "No, I don't know what to say just yet. Maybe the truth."

Again, a pause as his mother objected, "No one will believe us."

"Would you?" his father countered.

"What about the Polaroids?" his mother asked.

"No one will understand them."

"No, that's not what I mean," his mother said. "What are we going to *do* with them?"

Another pause, until his father said, "Keep them somewhere safe."

In the end there was some kind of inquiry, and Clem remembered the quiet town courtroom, the judge leaning down from the bench asking him questions. The man in the black robes had a long horse-face and seemed to speak through his nose. Did his father ever beat him? Was his mother ever bruised or scared? Was *he* scared when they didn't come home? But boy Clem really never had time to think about it. The police were there; Simone was there; the neighbors stopped in. And he quietly answered as he could.

Then more papers were presented, some X-rays they took of him, showing him a healthy boy of nine inside and out—and the gavel came down, bang. And that was the end of it. Sort of.

Mother never spoke of it again. Father didn't either. Only some months later, Pop took him aside, telling him simply, "I'm sorry Clem. What happened this summer. It won't happen again. I promise." And Clem believed them. Why not? They'd never lied to him before. But he saw something troubling his parents, an undercurrent of suppressed dread, as though they'd seen something no person was really supposed to see. Those creased and spotted pictures from Pop's Big Swinger 3000 . . .

But the weird story had gotten around; too late for Clem to hide behind anonymity. One of the kids in the school playground cornered him at the beginning of the school year demanding, "Is your dad My Favorite Martian?" The kid's nickname was Pimple Face, because he had three big moles on his cheek, and Clem kept staring at the three dots wondering what to say.

He sensed Pimple Face had stumbled across the secret of his parents' shame. Fortunately the local paper never ran the story of his parents' disappearance, so all Clem did that day in the schoolyard was shrug and say, "I don't know. Maybe."

After that, the kids left him alone, afraid whatever happened to him might happen to them. But the question nagged him the rest of his boyhood, all the way into adult life.

Were they Martians?

Something similar happened that day Billy Shadow found him lost in the desert. Only this time a lifetime had passed, a life of work and struggle, of success and failure, and success again—and this time he wasn't a kid. He'd gone out to Sonora to hike with some friends, nothing special, just folks from the office—going for a walk in the pretty desert instead of golfing that afternoon. They marked their route on a map—up here, down there, picnic by the river, hike out again—left their SUVs in the state park parking lot, and off they marched. The wives and kids in a big noisy group like hundreds of others every day.

They paused for a rest in the Madrona Canyon at the

river, and it flowed noisily as the kids paddled about. The adults unpacked their knapsacks and called the kids out of the water for lunch, warning them, *You can't go in for an hour after you eat.* Only to be met with noisy complaints of, *Oh Mom, c'mon,* even as the little bodies shivered with beach towels round their shoulders. Full on chicken salad and pickles, Lattimore pushed his rucksack back against a red stone and closed his eyes.

And when he opened his eyes again, the kids were gone. The river was gone, Sonora Park was gone. And even he, gone somewhere else.

Nighttime surrounded him. A new landscape presented itself. A deep green rolling sward of grassland stretched to the horizon. A moor? The air moist, clouds scudded across the dark sky, lit underneath by a quarter moon. The air was neither cold nor hot; he felt heat come up from the ground, as though releasing the day's soaking sun. A savannah? Africa? A cloud passed before the moon, the land went dark and the stars studded out of the heavens. And suddenly he felt cold all over. For clearly above his head he saw Alpha 1 Cru, then Beta Cru, and finally Gamma Cru, with the two other unnamed stars that made up the constellation commonly called the Southern Cross.

He wasn't in the Northern Hemisphere at all. But far, far south.

Australia? Somehow the land didn't look right for that. Much too lush.

The undulating, soft ground stretching in every direction was nothing like he'd ever seen from down under. Then it dawned on him. This was Antarctica. Without the snow and ice. But Antarctica all the same. At one point the place had been covered in green, but when? Thousands and thousands of years ago.

"What do you want from me?" he asked the sky. "Why am I here?" But none of the stars spoke back. Then he felt something hit his face.

Pebbles. Not the soft green sward, but sandy, salty dirt.

Back to Sonora. He'd fallen on his face. His mouth completely parched, the 100-degree sun beat down on his neck. Where the hell was the Madrona water? And just at the thought of water, he seemed to swoon again. How long had he been stumbling about? He saw his forearms streaked with dust, the knees of his pants torn.

Where was everybody?

Another two hours of stumbling blindly about he was no closer to an answer. When he twisted his ankle on a rut, he walked on the throbbing thing for another hour. Then his face blistered and he gave up, lying back against a stone. When the Gila monster climbed up on a rock and started talking to him, he knew his time on this Earth was pretty close to done, the soufflé cooked and ready for the spoon.

The Gila monster flicked its pink tongue, stared at him with pale eyes, and spoke, just like something out of Carlos Castaneda in the *Teachings of Don Juan*. God, he loved that fellow's books, read them as a teenager, how the magic happened, how you put it together, with what plants and ceremonies and powers. Marijuana, mushrooms, and Castaneda—they all seemed to go together in a far-off magical place called extended adolescence. No, he'd never get back there again. . . .

But the Gila monster wouldn't let him dream; the reptile was going to say his piece and Lattimore was going to listen. A phrase really, part in German, part English. And that was perfect Castaneda—who the hell said the Gila monster had to speak Spanish?

"Peenemünde. Sound familiar? Mittelbau-Dora. Remember?"

The Gila monster didn't really have to explain. Lattimore knew what the animal was trying to tell him. Something Pop Lattimore had told him about, years ago—told him right after his folks' odd disappearance and sudden return. When things settled down; it seemed the right time. Something important young Clem should know; after all, if he was old enough to play with toy soldiers and deal with crazy parents—he was old enough to know.

Peenemünde was a place. The River Mouth of Penne. You pronounced it Penna-MUHN-dah. And the Gila monster did it pretty well in a soft German tongue. A city off the Baltic. Werner von Braun made his rockets there during World War II—with a lot of help from an endless human supply at Buchenwald. When the British bombed the Peenemünde place off the face of the Earth, von Braun saved his precious papers from the fires. Smart man.

And opened up another slave labor shop.

This time at Mittelbau-Dora. Middle Block D, get it? And this time deep underground. Pop showed young Clem a few old cracked black-and-white pictures. Men working in a dungeon in rags. It looked like hell. Slave labor. Then the next old B&W photo changed the impression of death and hell from dirty to clean and bright. The beautiful curve of a V-2 rocket body, blinded by the sun in an open launching area. File photos—God knows where he got them.

"I started us on the way to the moon," Pop explained. "But first we had to bomb London."

Then a philosophical shrug—what was done was done and Pop couldn't change it.

"One of Werner's team contacted me—when I got out of the DP camps, the displaced persons camps, maybe ten years after the war. Von Braun's buddy asked if I wanted to join them at White Sands. That's a place in New Mexico where they built rockets. Von Braun's guy remembered me. All the work I did. Bombing London. He had my number, so to speak. But I was more happy teaching physics in Pennsylvania."

That's when Clem saw his father's arm in a new light. He'd known the tattoo was there, the tattoo that itched all the time; the little blue numbers from the camps. Jew Numbers, his father dryly called them, with his characteristic shrug. Nothing to make a fuss over. So Clem never really thought about them, like his father's suits or his shoes— they were just part of Pop. And if Pop didn't make a fuss, why should he?

Now Clem understood the significance—they marked all the slaves in the dungeon to keep them in line, the little blue numbers fading with age. *Yes, they had his number.*

A wry, dour smile came to his father's face. "They only gave the numbers to us really important ones." Then he chuckled at his tasteless joke. "Besides, I'd already gotten a good job. I'd met your mother and she was pregnant. We'd even decided to change our name from Lattner to Lattimore, in order to fit in. But more to the point, all those old Nazis can go to hell—even if Herr Werner von Braun was friends with Kennedy. You remember Kennedy, right?"

Sure, everyone knew who President Kennedy was. Who got shot in Dallas just before Thanksgiving. A black November weekend. He'd seen it on TV. Everyone had. Everyone was crying.

The Gila monster looked away. Satisfied.

Lattimore didn't feel regret, or even panic at the thought of dying. The thirst and the heat so overwhelming, there seemed nothing to do but let it incinerate him as he lay on the burning rocks. That's when the figure came out of the shimmering air at the end of his sight. At first he thought it was his father, Pop, and tried to say "Dad"—only nothing came out but a croak. And that's when he first saw his Indian Scout. "Easy now, Kemo Sabe," a voice from the silhouette told him. "Man, you really look like you need a drink."

Lattimore came back to the library.

Throughout his daydream he'd been holding the TV remote, clicking through station after station on mute, letting the different colors flow before his eyes on the big flat-screen across the room. He stopped clicking and put the remote down.

The advertisement playing on the screen gave him pause. A tall, gaunt man in black top hat and tails pranced around a brightly lit nursery with cloud-pattern wallpaper and pastel lighting; hanging over the crib was the Tiny Love Sweet Island Dreams mobile—a smiling monkey, a smiling giraffe, and a smiling bird of paradise all dangling under a soft plastic palm tree—while a sweet, lovely baby cooed with pleasure.

The tall gaunt man took a large gray rat out of his hat. The rat wriggled for a moment and bared its teeth. Then the man dropped the rat in the crib—

What the hell? Lattimore pressed the volume control but hit the wrong button. When he found the channel once more, the commercial was over and they were selling V8 juice instead.

7

One If by Night and Two If by Train

In peaceful Fairfield life had returned to normal; no unruly crowds trashing lawns or scaring homeowners. The Finn House picket fence had been repaired, the grass grown over the burnt spot—even the brass plaque returned to its place by the front door.

The last thing Guy and Lauren Poole expected that rainy Sunday afternoon was a visit from Lauren's sister who lived deep in the heart of Texas. Their quiet weekend interrupted when Eleanor suddenly arrived out of nowhere, a wet, bedraggled mess.

So far it had been the coldest spring anyone could

remember, raining every other day for weeks. Now, in mid-June people were already calling it the year without summer. Little League and soccer cancelled at every opportunity, this weekend no exception; so Fairfield's families stayed at home while the rain pelted the windows. At the Poole household, Guy and Lauren started a Parcheesi game in the den while the TV showed a golf tournament; then Lauren went off to bake something. The golfers were playing the U.S. Open in Farmingdale, the whole affair a slippery gully-washer punctuated by bright umbrellas. It looked like they were about to cancel play as most of Long Island was under water, not to mention Bethpage's world-renowned Black Course. For a couple of turns at the game board Guy played both sides for the dogs, but after a while gave up.

Now a man of leisure, he sat with his feet up on the hassock not really watching; he'd come down to rework his resume, in addition to playing Parcheesi, and the papers fanned across his lap, barely touched. He vaguely noticed the red banner along the bottom of the screen warning of a severe storm period between 5 and 6 p.m.

He could hear Lauren in the kitchen, the mixer whirring, then shutting off, then whirring again. She liked to bake and had woken up first thing that morning, rolling over and saying to him, "What do you think about Boston cream pie?" As if that was the most natural thing in the world. What does one say to a question like that?

Easy. "Boston cream pie is very nice."

The pelting rain suddenly grew louder, clacking now. Hail. Hail the size of golf balls shattering on the patio outside. Suddenly the TV picture pixelated into colored bytes, then went black with a yellow flickering notice on the upper left-hand side informing them of the obvious: POOR SIGNAL. The power surged, the house lights brightening—then shut off all at once. Lauren's mixer suddenly died. A slash of lightning lit the gray sky outside the windows and a moment later a crack of thunder that sounded like it was right overhead, rattling every door and board in the house. Corky and Peaches leapt to their feet, scattering the Parcheesi pieces.

Everyone gravitated to the front room to stare out the windows. The street outside grew white with falling ice. Lauren held a spoon covered in vanilla cream pudding. "Anyone want a last lick?" She meant the dogs too. Then she glanced out the window; a tree limb across the street dropped with a splintering rip, landing over the sidewalk and into the roadway.

"Jesus!"

A family of deer exploded out of nowhere and clattered down the pavement, running full out. A Mama doe and three Bambis skittered along the road, then vanished into a huge clump of brush.

Which is when they all saw the car skidding up the street.

An inch of hail ice had fallen, and the car, a little Prius, wasn't handling it well. The Prius skidded toward them at about 30 mph, the engine grinding and leaking smoky exhaust—then ran into that unlucky length of fence again, knocked down by the PIG protestor thugs back in May.

Guy Poole sighed. He had finally gotten around to fixing it and whitewashed to match only the week before. "Well, I still have paint left," he remarked casually. "I just need more slats."

The crippled car came to a wheezing halt on their lawn and died with a sigh. A haggard woman opened the car door and leaned on it for support. Hail fell on her head, and she covered it with a free hand. Lauren recognized her sister at once. "Eleanor! Guy, come on!" They bolted to the front door.

Outside Eleanor staggered from the car; then she fell to her knees, but struggled to her feet, and the hail seemed to beat her down again. Lauren ran down the front steps, suddenly realizing her sister who'd lived in a wheelchair half her life *now stood again*.

She hustled Eleanor inside. Guy snatched a blanket off the couch, and Eleanor clutched it around her shoulders, shaking the hail from her hair, then awkwardly shuffled across the oak wood floors on her own.

The woman was a wreck. Pale face, dark raccoon eyes, lines about her mouth that weren't there the last time Lauren saw her sister. Eleanor wore a T-shirt, a pair of tartan men's boxer shorts, wrapped all over in a terrycloth bathrobe, the belt tied in a dirty knot. On her feet a pair of very wet, cheap, Walmart sneakers.

Her bathrobe fell away for a moment, and Lauren got a good look at the T-shirt. It must have belonged to somebody else; Eleanor wouldn't have been caught dead in the thing. One of those political-poseur T-shirts; the image showed the famous McDonald's Golden Arches in a red field. The caption: MCSHIT. Lauren clutched at her sister's robe, tugging it closed.

Shakily Eleanor took one step and then another, a manic twist to her face.

After a moment Lauren found her last ounce of common sense, the wit to say,

"Jesus, Eleanor! Where's Bhakti? You're—"

Walking? But the word died on her lips. Maybe because Lauren was afraid that if she spoke the obvious Eleanor would go back to being a cripple.

Instead she asked, "What the hell's happened?" Which is when her sister sagged into Guy's arms. They stumbled toward the Keeping Room, and found Eleanor a deep chair.

Guy put water on for tea, thanking heaven for gas stoves that worked even with the power out, while Lauren tried to get some sense out of her sister.

Which proved worse than knowing nothing at all. A stream of horse-hockey came out of Eleanor's mouth as she began to mechanically sing "When Johnny Comes Marching Home"—the children's version:

The ants go marching one by one, hurrah, hurrah.
The ants go marching one by one, hurrah, hurrah.
The ants go marching one by one,
The little one stops to suck his thumb
And they all go marching down to the ground
To get out of the rain, BOOM! Buh-BOOM!

Guy came back into the Keeping Room with the steaming mug of tea, his eyes veiled in caution. He'd heard Eleanor's ditty clearly enough from the kitchen, and it chilled him as though he'd been the one covered in hail. *How far gone was the woman? What nutty thing came next?* Running little cars over white picket fences might be the very least of it.

Lauren shared a dark, questioning glance with Guy, his wife's eyes worried to death, her mouth a grimace of doubt.

Eleanor had given up her kiddy's song for the moment. Looked at the tea, thought a moment about it, as though wondering what was being offered. Then it dawned on her. She brushed the matted hair from her damp forehead and took the steaming cup. But before she brought it to her lips, she looked straight at Guy and asked in a very reasonable tone of voice, "Are we doing the Ant Dance? Are you a Red Ant or a Black Ant?"

Guy Poole didn't answer at once, but considered the question. In a wild stab of insight he quietly said, "I'm Adam Ant. The First Ant. What happened Eleanor? Can you tell us?"

Eleanor looked at him with wide puppy eyes, cocking her head, then replying, "The Myrmidons are here. They came for me. They tried to trick me into thinking they were the bold and loyal black ants of brave Achilles—but they're not. They're bad ants—red ants. Medieval ants. I saw them in their ant colony. All plague-riddled red ants. Every one."

This was absolutely no help at all. Myrmidons? And Guy Poole suddenly wished he'd studied a little harder in school. Which is when they saw the blood. Eleanor opened her bathrobe a touch and pointed down.

"You see they wanted me for the harem. They've got some red queens deep underground." Partially dried blood between her thighs leapt at them.

Guy Poole took a deep and ragged breath—but managed all the calm in his possession and said to Lauren, "Okay, let's get her into the car. We're going to the hospital."

To Eleanor he said, "Adam Ant wants you to come with him. He's going to take you to the Ant Hospital where they help good black ants. Okay?"

And Eleanor lifted her eyes to him, smiling a little and nodding. "All right." Then after a moment, "Can I bring my tea?"

B ridgeport Hospital Emergency admitted the woman, Eleanor Singh née Whitcomb at the request of her family. The sister Lauren signed her in—without the approval of the husband, Bhakti Singh, who wasn't in the state of Connecticut at the time of admission. He had to be reached in California. After a brief twenty-minute wait, the family of Eleanor Whitcomb Singh consulted with the emergency room surgeon, *Yes! Please! Stop the bleeding!* Since it was coming from between her legs again.

The ER doc was a nice lady of about thirty who looked like a fresh-faced nineteen-year-old, with bright blond hair tied in a bun and an accent that tagged her somewhere south of the Mason-Dixon line. But she'd left the ballroom manners of southern belle coquetry along with her party gown back at Tara in Scarlett's bedroom. You could feel the ice in her veins; this was no wilting violet. She'd stopped the bleeding, and now Eleanor was stable. Sympathetic, but all business:

"Mr. and Mrs. Poole . . . Mrs. Poole, your sister seems to have undergone what used to be known as a back-alley abortion. Where, we don't know. But it could only have been within the last 24 hours or she would have bled out. Or succumbed to infection."

Then became even more serious:

"Even more troubling, and I don't know how to explain this. . . ."

The young woman paused for a moment, but followed through, "We found some blood under her nails, her own blood—I can hardly say it, I've never heard of such a thing, but she may have tried to abort herself. We found a piece of plastic inside, looks like it once belonged to a white picnic spoon. Honestly I don't know what to tell you. Amnesia? Psychosis? You're going to want to talk to the neurologist and a psychologist. This is out of my range of expertise."

And now two days later Guy and Lauren sat in the neurologist's comfortable waiting room along a plush bench in front of a solid wall of copper-colored slate with water sluicing down into a long narrow lily pond. The sound of the waterfall trickled across the room, the patter of drops on lily pads—a hopeful sound.

Guy pondered his surroundings, thinking how medicine had changed over a couple of centuries. Things had gone from weird to stranger. . . . Once upon a time a hospital might well have been Frankenstein's castle, where cadavers were laid out for vivisection by illiterate, unwashed assistants within earshot of the sick and dying.

Then as science evolved the rooms grew colder, notably the 1950s "Antiseptic" style. Porcelain-covered pans and rolling gurneys, big operating-room searchlights two feet across, faceless technicians in severe lab coats looking down. Guy contemplated a box of disposable latex gloves near a box of Kleenex and a bottle of hand sanitizer on the nurse's station.

Now they all lived in a use-once-then-toss society: shrink-wrap sealed instruments, miles of transparent glass, every surface edged by chrome and metal. As if designed by sci-fi set decorators. Until at long last it occurred to someone to make the beds, the rooms, the waiting areas in pastel colors, blue mostly; make the chairs more comfortable, creating Zen and Tao flower displays so the deep scent of growth or peaceful splashing streams filled the air instead of the acrid scent of desperation and finality.

A large flat TV screen embedded in the opposite wall showed a twenty-minute loop of Discovery Channel's *Planet Earth* series "Ocean Deep." The segment started with the large white title THIS IS YOUR WORLD over beautiful electric humming music and the vast expanse of an ocean. Two blue whales, the planet's largest animals, sliced through the water. Even from an overhead helicopter shot, you could tell how enormous and magnificent these great beasts were. Even with no perspective point to show them against a smaller object, you could tell—just the way the water slid around their bodies, like some great ships, the white bow wake splitting across their giant, wise faces.

The neuropsychologist, Dr. Kramer—a soft, chubby fellow in his forties with a close-cropped beard and the good manners of a maître d'—came into the waiting area and showed them the results of his preliminary examination: reams of paper on a clipboard. A sort of checklist.

The symptoms: amnesia, disorientation, incoherence.

Date of brain injury—unknown, but within a three-week window May to June. Cause of brain injury—unknown. Initial severity of brain injury, e.g. loss of consciousness, coma—unknown. On the Head Injury Cognitive Assessment Scale, nearly all the criteria were flagged as "serious":

- Difficulty in Group Conversations
- Difficulty Reading
- Difficulty with Recent Memory
- Difficulty with Concentration

Yep, Eleanor Singh née Whitcomb was a lady in difficulty.

And more to the point, no one could find a physical source of trauma. Magnetic Resonance Imaging negative, functional Magnetic Resonance Imaging negative, Positron Emission Tomography negative—the brain looked normal. Tox screen proved negative; no drugs in the patient's body. They even searched for hidden tumors along the spinal cord and other sensitive areas. Some anomaly that might affect a minor artery or put pressure on a nerve. Guy Poole looked at Lauren, her eyes clouded with the pressure of fear just like those desperate, forlorn families on those medical TV shows—except there wasn't a smart team of handsome diagnosticians solving the problem, just this soft man in the white coat, coming up empty.

At length Dr. Kramer forgot about his clipboard, got up from his seat by the lily pond couch, and motioned for them to follow him.

"I want to show you something." A few steps down the hall they followed him to Eleanor's curtained bed. She was sitting up and smiled when the three came in, a juice bottle on her lap tray next to a small flowering African violet.

But they weren't alone in the room. The patient next to her, a very old withered man who'd fallen on his head, was staring with glassy eyes at the ceiling, four days of facial hair whitening his face. His whole family sat around him, in the rumpled clothes of lower middle-class Connecticut—not really talking, just sitting, or staring at the room TV that overhung the bed. On screen, a queer fellow in a top hat and tails was demonstrating some kind of product, a special nonstick pan.

The skinny man was breaking eggs with a hammer and whisking them, *shells and all* into a bowl. Guy stopped short for a moment, the advertisement's subliminal message stunningly obvious: *You can't make an omelet without breaking eggs.* That weirdo seemed to be everywhere these days . . . the Pied Piper Pitchman. The Next Big Thing.

The man's family stared at the TV, not really grasping what they were looking at. They seemed crushed, hopeless—marking time. Guy and Lauren found it hard to ignore them; a kind of finality hung like a bad cloud over the whole group.

Dr. Kramer brought Guy and Lauren's attention back to the woman in bed. "This is the old-fashioned way we used to diagnose—before all the fancy scans." Eleanor appeared better now, hair brushed, clean hospital gown. "How are you feeling today, Eleanor?"

She smiled back at him and shrugged a little. Then . . . "An apple a day keeps the doctor away."

The neuropsychologist grinned. "Yeah, that's what they say, and I've never found any fault with the prescription." Now, businesslike: "Eleanor, I'd like you to repeat a phrase after me. Will you do that? I'll say it and you repeat it, okay?"

"Okay."

"Okay, here goes . . ." Dr. Kramer took a breath, then said, *"One if by night and two if by train."*

Eleanor's face clouded, confused. "Want me to say it again?" Kramer offered. *"One if by night and two if by train."*

Eleanor tried to repeat the phrase, "One if by night, one if by night . . ." but she stumbled over the last bit. "One if by night and two if . . ." She halted and shook her head, dismayed. She'd failed the test. For the life of her she couldn't repeat the second part of the sentence.

"It's all right, Eleanor, this helps us understand. And

you've been very helpful." A little smile flickered over her face, but she doubted him.

"Have you walked today?" Dr. Kramer asked her.

"Oh yes," she answered. "I used the bathroom."

"Excellent," he told her. "We're going to leave now, but I'm sure Guy and Lauren will be back soon to keep you company."

As the three went back down the hall toward the lily pond and the comforting TV, Dr. Kramer explained. "In the old days, before all the super scans, we'd ask that question of people with head trauma and especially after neurosurgery. The sentence doesn't actually mean anything—just a quirky string of words that sounds like something you've heard before and gives you pause. When your head gets rattled, you can't repeat the phrase *one if by night and two if by train.* You get so far and then you stop. It means there's still some trauma that hasn't healed yet. When the trauma finally goes away, anybody can repeat the line."

Lauren tried it out herself: "One if by night and two if by train." Easy. And somehow it stuck in her head like those songs you keep repeating. But she was brought up short when Dr. Kramer asked, "When's her husband supposed to arrive?"

And at that, they had no answer. Eleanor had been admitted as a quasi Jane Doe, with no photo ID, no insurance cards, no driver's license. The hospital admitting administrator had demanded Guy Poole's credit card number, and he gave it over with a twinge as Lauren whispered to him, "I'll call the Lattimore Company—they've got to have some kind of plan, something."

But two days later the insurance company, Lattimore Aerospace, and the hospital were still doing their billing minuet, making Eleanor's silly question, *"Are we doing the Ant Dance?"* take on an extra meaning.

After this last battery of tests, Guy knew the bills were

reaching into the 15K to 25K range, and he tried not to think about it. The numbers on his MasterCard seemed to pulse behind his eyes, the columns of figures blurring together: MRI, $3212.00; Daily Room Charge, $400.57; Neurologist Consultation, $1026.89; Physical Therapy Consultation, Consultation-consultation, State Tax, City Tax. . . .

A cheap, sissy thought entered his head: *How the hell do I get out of this? Where can I run?* Did Brazil have an extradition treaty; could the authorities get him there? Oh, by hook or by crook they'd get him. One if by night and two if by train.

And where the hell was Bhakti, for crying out loud? And what about their kid? Jane? No, Janet.

As Guy and Lauren found their car in the lot, he couldn't help grumbling, "Just leave another message with Bhakti, okay? How many messages is this already?"

Lauren stared out the car window at the gray slate sky; it was starting to rain again. Her phone showed Bhakti's number: a missed call, the third time this had happened, no message. They kept missing each other. "This will be the third time."

Then her lips moved silently. Lauren had been repeating the line "One if by night" off and on like some kind of mantra. And now she said, "One if by night, and three if by cell—"

Guy almost growled at her to leave off but thought better of it. Streams of rain came down, blurring everything outside the car. The Poole's large Honda Pilot crawled along in a flooding downpour; red taillights in front of their eyes, a truck behind with flashers blinking; the whooshing of the water around the wheels, the rain pounding on the roof. . . .

Suddenly, Guy caught something out the passenger's window through the streams of water. A young woman, almost a child, standing at the crosswalk by a Walgreens, drenched in rain. No umbrella, no slicker—just waiting for the light by the steel silver lamp stanchion. The young lady from the night in the Keeping Room; the young lady who reminded him of *Alice in Wonderland*—same skirt, same jumper with the pockets, same puffy sleeves.

He hit the brakes, then without thinking put the car in reverse; Lauren ceased murmuring "One if by" and squawked, "Poole!" She only called him that when she was alarmed. The truck behind them screeched to a stop in the flowing water and honked its horn. Then more honks.

No girl by the lamp stanchion, no girl by the Walgreens entrance. Poole powered down Lauren's window, and rain lashed in. He leaned heavily over Lauren to get a better look. No girl.

"Jesus, Guy!" Lauren snapped at him. "What's going on with you?"

Guy wanted to tell her about that time on the stairs; that he really wasn't seeing things; that young Alice came out of their own house, but . . . but that sounded even crazier. So all he said was, "Nothing. I don't know. Nothing. I was just thinking about that weirdo on TV breaking eggs."

8

Man About Hamelin

That's the way Mr. Piper thought about New York, especially the fortress city of Manhattan: like the medieval German town of Hamelin, back when that part of the world was called Saxony—where his most vivid memories seemed to have been born. But he was far older than Hamelin in the middle of the Middle Ages, the twelfth century—his mind went back to what they now called the "Dark" Ages. Oh yes, even further than that . . .

Back to the Second or Third Thought, right after the First Thought.

But he'd been walking the Earth so long he needed an artifact or an object to recall how it all had been. Give him the touch of a spear point and, *Ah yes, Golgotha.* And the stench of crucified men, their bowels finally opening in death, filled his nostrils from the mucky ground. Give him a shard of pottery: *Ah yes, the Hanging Gardens.* And the laughter of Nebuchadnezzar's handmaidens splashing water under the Babylonian sun as they frolicked in their bathing pool echoed in his ears. Give him a glass of water: *Ah yes, the Flood.* And he looked down from a dark corner in the creaking Ark safe in his spider's web and waited for the always promiscuous flies that rose from the sties and stalls, the rocking of the waves making him sway as his tiny pincers clung to the silvery threads.

Insect, animal, soldier, sailor, alchemist, scientist—he'd been so many things. Not to mention foremost rat-catcher in that German fortress town, while the plague lapped at the walls from a thousand pink rodent tongues and their heaven-sent fleas. Now in the Manhattan canyons the throngs scurried under the steel-and-concrete towers, reminding him of that old Kraut burg. But instead of rats hiding in the corners and only coming out to die, in this modern Hamelin, the people *were* the rats. Scuttling to and fro on every private errand, never knowing what lurked around the corner or in the shadows as they hurried along babbling into a cell phone or staring at the pavement.

Mr. P. left his walk-up on Sheridan Square and clattered down the steps, ignoring the open door to his apartment. Nah, he wasn't coming back. Things to do, people to see. First, straight across town in search of the lad.

He knew where to find him. Mama Ho' would be taking a break from her exertions on Avenue A. Time to have a little chat about sonny-boy's future. Dusk drew down on Greenwich Village, the lights in the restaurants and shops giving the streets a fairy tale feel; uptown the towers of mid-Manhattan were wreathed in a hanging mist of white light and sodium orange. The Piper liked to call the color Creamsicle, after the popular Popsicle. It started to rain again.

On the south end of Washington Square, umbrellas began to pop open as people clung to the edges and overhangs of buildings, craning their necks for empty taxis. Then a lucky salary man, pant cuffs soaked and clutching a briefcase, darted across the sidewalk under his umbrella. His wet shoes flapped on the damp pavement just as a yellow cab squealed to a halt. Ah, success!

Salary Man was halfway in the passenger door when Mr. Piper slid over out of nowhere and plucked the umbrella from the fellow's fingers. Shocked, the man stared at the gaunt figure towering over him in the rain. "Hey!"

"Don't worry, I'll return it," the Piper told him. Half amazed, half confused, the man stared for a moment. Should he fight over an umbrella with this street creature, or make a getaway? Easy decision: clutching his briefcase, he slammed the door shut and slapped the door lock.

"Forget it!" came his muffled reply from inside the car. And in a blink of an eye the taxi rolled forward.

"You sure? I know your address," Mr. Piper whispered to the vanishing cab. "Okay. Thanks."

The squalid roach-infested walk-up on Avenue A wasn't that much different from Piper's place over on Sheridan Square. Maybe it smelled worse; a combination of neglect, leaky pipes, hanging plaster, and triple-locked doors with jimmy bars. A place where televisions ran 24/7 and people shouted at each other for no reason, or because the cable bill was overdue. The locked vestibule door showed the grime of a thousand calamitous entries and hasty exits, the doorknob plate once brass, now a kind of smeared black that only comes from constant human touch. Someone had wedged the door open with a sliver of metal, expecting to return at any moment from an urgent errand for cigarettes and wine coolers around the corner. The dented battery of mailboxes showed names but no apartment numbers. It didn't matter; Mr. P. knew where to go.

Piper casually pushed the vestibule door open and heard it click behind him as he mounted the stairs. *Tough luck, buddy, somebody will have to buzz you in.*

A rat calmly looked at him from the top of the landing. Wrinkled its nose for a second, then flicked its whiskers. "No not yet, Herr Ratte," the Piper told him. "Soon though, very soon. You run along now." The rat pressed his little ears to his head and scuttled off to his hidey-hole.

The stairs moaned and groaned at each step the Piper took. Sagging steps, threadbare carpet on them, the granules and rocks of last winter's ice-melt salt still visible in the corners. The smell of boot-dirt and rancid pork squeezed from the stairs as if from a bellows, *squishsquish-squish*. With each step on the rotten stairs a little picture came to him about what had happened.

Squish: years ago as the stairway looked slightly brighter, shouts from above, a domestic disturbance. *Squish*: a woman flung a pan of hot bacon grease at her husband as he clattered down the stairs. *Squish*: spatter went on the walls and soaked into the stairs, her mouth a rictus of rage. *Squish*: a thread of hot grease caught the back of lover boy's neck and he yelped.

"Ah, *l'amour métropolitain*," Mr. P. remarked.

He stopped at the first landing. Inside the locked door he could feel the boy. And the boy's mind and recent past came to him like a scent under the door. Inhaling deeply, he paused on the landing, dragging the vision deep into his brain.

* * *

Mom and Dimples had been going high for three days. The boy called Mom's boyfriend Dimples, a kid's name because he had cracks in his cheeks that moved every time he talked. Dimple's meth head had shrunken his cheeks, had turned his face gray, giving him a sucked-in, ravenous look, like a hungry hyena. Missing an eyetooth, the black gap flashed you every time he spoke.

When Dimples wasn't making Mom work outside they were on what Dimples called "vacation"—time in the house with the crack pipe going and the powder on the mirror, sometimes crank, sometimes coke. The TV always on and take-out trays everywhere. When they were through gorging, or forgot that there were still stinky Styrofoam plates on the kitchen table, the boy could go from one box to another picking out leftover bits with a plastic fork. The rest of the time he could hide in the cramped cabinet under the kitchen sink.

Or sneak into the bathroom and back again when they were busy on Mama's bed. And sometimes they even forgot he was there. Coming in to the kitchen during a break in the festivities, Dimples laughing, "He still under there? What's with that kid? Like it better under the sink with the roaches instead of his room? What's up with that?"

The boy thought it was a three-day vacation, hard to tell, because the windows were so dirty. Night and day almost the same. The clock on the wall showed six o'clock. Somewhere he remembered it was called a Kit-Cat clock: a black electric thing with the clock face on the body; below, a tail that swung back and forth as it tick-tocked; the head of a cat with white eyes that shifted from side to side as the tail wagged and the hands moved around the dial. The cat wore a white bow tie and smiled at him across the kitchen; the thing was already hanging on the wall when they first came to this apartment, and it died sometime in the first year. Now the Kit-Cat clock always showed six o'clock.

Weird thing was, the Kit-Cat clock would warn him when Dimples was about to pounce. It was better when they were doing coke. Coke flattened them out after a few hours. But when Dimples and Mom were blowing crank in the pookie pipe it was always worse. Crank made you want to hump. And hump. And hump. And—

So when Dimples was tired of Mom and she lay recovering on the sweaty bed, he came looking. Sometimes Dimples would pace around like some hungry hyena, but then suddenly give up and go back to Mom, forgetting where the boy was hiding at.

But sometimes he remembered. He'd remembered twice in the last couple of days, dragging him out from under the sink for some room time. "C'mon boy," Dimples would say. "Time for a lesson. We're getting some room time."

And it seemed that each time Dimples would come looking the Kit-Cat clock clicked to life, eyes snapping back and forth, tail wagging. *Room Time!* And the kid would hear it, and scrunch farther and farther back into the black corner of the counter cabinet under the sink. Until the cabinet door banged open, the light from the kitchen shot onto his face, and Dimples grabbed his ankle.

The clock started ticking again. *Tick-tock-tick-tock . . .* Room Time!

Which is when somebody knocked on the door. The feet outside the cabinet paused; Dimples' head was framed in the light of the kitchen, and the boy could see the clock ticking over his shoulder. The knock came again.

"Dammit!" Dimples' head vanished, and his feet padded across the linoleum. The boy heard the front door open, the chain lock clank. So Dimples' face would be in the crack, staring out into the hall.

"Who the 'uk are you?"

The wind whistled through the gap in Dimples' teeth.

"What the 'uk you want?"

A smooth voice in the hall asked a question, but it was indistinct and muffled. Dimples' reaction was clear enough.

"*What?*" A pause of total disbelief. "What the 'uk you talkin' about?" A word came into the boy's head—a single word describing Dimples' disbelief thing. *Incredulity*. The boy had never heard the word before, never spelled it. Never said it. And nobody'd ever said it to him. *Incredulity*.

Now it popped into his mind like a flashbulb. Like the page out of a dictionary. Incredulity. Dimples was incredulous. And the boy even understood what the word meant. But more important—that something was happening that was gonna get him out of vacation and Room Time. Somebody like a cop or a teacher was disrespecting Dimples and making him small. Incredulity would soon turn to doubt. He'd never heard or spelled that word either. Doubt.

But he'd felt it. Every time he heard the smooth voice in the hall; it seemed to make the cat clock's tail wag. *Tick-tock-tick-tock*. The voice going to his ear, the thought going to his brain. *Tick-tock*. Simple as that.

Then fear. Fear would come next to Dimples. The boy knew fear.

Now it was Dimples' turn.

The boy crawled from under the kitchen sink, past the clicking Kit-Cat clock, and clung to the wall where grimy hand marks met his fingers. That's when he recognized Mr. P.'s voice. The whack-a-doo from Washington Square: "Are *you* the old woman who lived in the shoe?" the Piper demanded of Dimples. "Of course not. I want to talk to her."

Dimples was about to slam the door shut in the stranger's face when Mom struggled from her place on the bed, pulling a T-shirt over her shoulders. A skinny woman of thirty, Mama looked nearly fifty; skinny as Dimples but twice as frail. Too much of everything and too little of what she needed had twisted her into a burnt breadstick; the lines in her face were creases, her teeth banana yellow.

The T-shirt was a little too small, and you could still see her pussy. She tugged at the shirt, pulling it lower, covering it up a little. She showed it off enough, she hardly ever thought about it. "What this 'hole want? Open the 'uckin' door. Lemme see him."

The door opened, and for the second time the boy saw that strange guy from the park again, Daddy Long Legs. The gaunt man looked directly over Dimples' shoulder and talked to Mom. "Are you the old woman who lived in the shoe?"

Mom shivered and tugged at her T-shirt like she didn't hear him right.

"The one who had so many children, she didn't know what to do?" The man in the hall paused. "In your case that one over there by the wall is more than enough."

Mom was opening her mouth and closing it, sort of like fish did when you took them out of water. You see, what she saw was Michael Jackson: the Gloved One, the King of Pop standing in the hall talking into the apartment. Angelic Michael with the fluffed out 'fro, from the good years. Not the icko sicko Wacko Jacko with the balding head, the mask, no nose, and white skin. Angelic Jackson, voice sweet as honey.

"Let me put it another way." The figure in the hall spoke again. "I'm from the government and I'm here to help."

Dimples gulped. He saw Jacko too. "Whatchit you want?"

The figure in the hall nodded to the boy clutching the wall.

"Him."

The boy by the wall saw the figure in the hall too, first as that oddball Daddy Long Legs guy then morphing into Angelic Jacko. The kid shook his head and rubbed his eyes. It didn't help.

Dimples looked a little doubtful, but the thought of getting rid of the boy had its possibilities. The fear slowly ebbed away. Jacko dead, but he didn't mind talking to him in the hall either.

"Whatchyah gonna give us for him? Where you going?"

Mom still stared at the figure of Michael Jackson in the dingy apartment hallway, pressed her shoulders to the wall, and began to slide toward the floor. "That's really good stuff, Dimp. I think I gotta sit down." Her bottom reached the floor; tucking her knees to her chest, she put her head in her hands. "Let Michael have him for vacation. We'll get a lawyer later if we need to." Maybe she'd forgotten Jacko was dead. Or maybe it hadn't made much of an impression.

But Dimples wasn't so satisfied. "I want sumpin' for him."

A baggie appeared in the figure's hand. Not white coke or crystal rock, but something that shimmered in a thousand rainbow colors. "What's that, X?"

"Oh yes," the man in the hall said. "It's new. We call it Dalekto. Because it's delectable. And you're gonna dig it big. Coke without the burnout, crank without the breakdown. Delectable Dalekto. Double D for you, Mr. Dimples."

The baggie vanished into Dimples' hand. He grabbed the boy by his raggedy shirt and dragged him to the door. "Take him. And gimme your address and telephone number."

A white calling card came out. "We're staying at the Grand Hyatt. Just ask for Michael. Maybe when you're ready, you come up to Forty-second Street and we'll have dinner. Talk about his future. Please try to dress appropriately."

"Yeah. Sure. Whatever. And call us when you're done. Now git."

Before he knew it, the boy was out in the hall, tramping down the stairs after the long, tall man. Not so much afraid as when he'd watched the magic show. More confused now.

The man didn't look like Angel Jacko any more, just that guy from Washington Square Park.

"Hey, we going to Neverland? We gotta take a plane for that."

"No, like I told Dimples, we're going to the Grand Hyatt Hotel. Up on Forty-second. Better than Neverland. For one thing, it's still a going concern."

They found a taxi on First Avenue; the rain had stopped for a while.

"You talk funny, man. Big words."

Mr. Piper sighed. "Yeah, I know. And soon you will too. Incredulous, are we?"

The kid looked at him. "No . . . I'm not incredulous. I think I believe you."

"Anything you want before we get there?"

The kid thought for a moment. "I want a Kit-Cat clock that works."

The city streets streamed by, wet in the rain and glistening in the dark.

"Fair enough. But we'll get that delivered."

They had a little trouble at the Grand Hyatt reception. A tall gaunt man in frayed tux and tails, shoes no socks, with a street kid in dirty jeans—and they wanted a room. Enough to give anybody a moment's pause, and Mr. P. was a little pooped after his deal with Dimples. The gaunt man turned from the desk and looked down at the boy. "You know, I think a change of clothes is in order, not to mention a bath and a haircut. We can get it all here, most of it anyway—as soon as I straighten out our accommodations."

Accommodations. The word flashed into the kid's head off the dictionary page. He spat the definition back up at Mr. P.: "Room. Board. Lodging."

"Very good."

"Maybe we can go to Modell's down the street," the kid

said. The sporting goods store: $200 Lakers' jerseys, $100 sweats. Yeah. That *was* an idea.

"Okay," Piper said, "but you'll still need a suit, some go-to-meeting clothes."

Then to the receptionist at the reception desk: "Look, you little Putzette, run the card."

The Piper was getting tired. The business on Avenue A had worn him out more than he realized. Every power-of-mind exertion required a recharge; the transmutation of matter and thought drained him at the molecular level. Nothing was free in this universe. With a last effort of will he showed her what he needed to get what he wanted.

The receptionist, whose name was Paulette, heard her own name. And nothing particularly rude. Something on the order of, "Paulette could you please run the card once more? I'd really appreciate it."

Then as the card came back with plenty of credit to spare, he added, "My dear Tartlet, shimmy your nice little encased tushie onto your boss's lap with my thanks." But what she heard was, "Thanks, that's great." A swift image of her placing her behind on her boss's desk with a little wriggle flitted through her head and she paused, mildly confused. She coded his room key nevertheless, slipping it into a shiny paper wallet with advertisements for the Grand Hyatt and everything the place could do for you—massages, room service, the swank shops—saying, "Enjoy your stay with us, Mr. Piper."

Yet what she heard come out of her own mouth was, "Sorry for the delay, Mr. Scumbucket." And she gasped, putting her hand to her mouth.

"Well, shucks," Mr. P. told her. "Think nothing of it."

A short two hours later, shopping bags stuffed full of Modell's Sporting Goods were piled everywhere in the room. The kid had a field day trying on his new threads.

Settled back on the couch in purple Champion sweatpants, feet up in thick wool socks, he toyed with his new Garmin Forerunner 405 GPS watch with heart rate monitor and USB ANT Stick, a universal serial bus that could connect all his exercise data, heart rate, you name it into his computer. He didn't have a computer yet, but they'd fix that later in the afternoon—plenty of electronics stores on Lexington Avenue around the corner. The TV remote in his hand had settled on *Jeopardy* reruns.

Mr. P. sat in a nearby chair with a cold, wet compress on his head nursing a pounding headache. Phase One complete: Secure a willing apprentice. Now for Phase Two. . . . The tall man's plan for the kid, for the nation, the world—the Piper had many plans. But he wouldn't be putting any plans in motion with this miserable, throbbing head. The flinty voice of *Jeopardy*'s host, Alex Trebek, drifted across the room:

"History for two hundred dollars. The fifteenth-century German most noted for employing movable type."

"Who is Johann Gutenberg?" Mr. P. mumbled as he dreamily listened to the idiot box. Actually, a rather large flat-screen. Idiot boxes, a thing of the past—that's what they *used to* call them.

The kid glanced at Mr. P. The man breathed through the wet compress; as if aware of the youngster's gaze he murmured, "Knew that Kraut well, worked in his printing shop for a year or so. Many hands make light work. But the genius of the whole business was that we didn't need many hands to make a lot of work. And we made a lot of work for everyone else. Moveable type . . . We translated the Bible into multiple tongues: German, French, English, Italian. . . . No more priests murmuring Latin at the dirty illiterate parishioners sitting unwashed pew after pew. Didn't need a priest anymore to hear the word of God. Broke the Catholic Church into schisms. Some of the best work I ever did."

"Idle hands are the devil's tools," the kid said out of nowhere.

"That's half true," Mr. P. mumbled from under his compress. "Busy hands can be much, much worse."

During a commercial the kid had clicked to another channel. Turner Classic Movies, *Topkapi,* the Turkish wrestling sequence: gorgeous Melina Mercouri, manly Maximilian Schell, buttery Peter Ustinov, and the pompous Robert Morley all staring down from the concrete stands under the blinding sun watching the oiled bodies of the wrestlers writhing on the sand. The grisly homoerotic moment as the faces of the spectators looked down with anticipation and hungry eyes. An eager older woman with a faint lady's mustache gripped Peter Ustinov's arm in excitement, barely able to control herself, and the unctuous tout recoiled at her touch.

The kid switched back to *Jeopardy.*

Alex Trebek's voice returned. "Culture for four hundred points. The Turkish national sport."

The Turkish national sport? Easy. The kid knew the answer. Wrestling. Wrestling was the Turkish national sport.

But instead he said, "What is buggery?"

In the kid's case, Mr. P.'s mind tricks were more than contagious; a Dale Carnegie course for the collective imagination. Find a strong, common frequency and exploit it. Almost every human impulse circled a nucleus of fear. Perceive those charged particles inhabiting the human mind and the ability to influence peoples' impulses was but a small step.

All of humanity was desperate for answers. Any answer.

Advertising copywriters, songwriters, novelists, movie makers—all of them employed telepathy or suggestion, but on a smaller scale. The Kid felt the power of his mind surge to broadband, his very name growing a capital "K." He was becoming *Somebody.* He was becoming important. Slowly but surely he began reaching into the television, right into the studio, right into the contestant's very head. Past or present, dead or alive—they were all his puppets now.

And the *Jeopardy* contestant dutifully repeated Kid's suggestion, hitting the sound button and exclaiming, *"What is buggery?"* The siren went off, the backboard lights flashed, the contestant, a little old lady, faintly reminiscent of her Turkish sister with the mustache back in *Topkapi,* leaped for joy.

From his place under the cold compress Mr. P. murmured, "Save to file." Though the answer might not have been strictly true, as buggery was also the national sport of the British upper classes at Eton and other English public schools.

In any case, the lad was learning fast.

M ama Whore and Dimples learned fast too. They showed up at the Grand Hyatt two days later when the Dalekto ran out. The new designer drug had a way of doing that. With an ounce of forethought they cleaned up a little so they wouldn't be stopped in the lobby. Still, their clothes smelled faintly of ghetto hallways and threadbare lives. A kind of stink that doesn't clean up so easy. Not without money, anyway. Money solved many problems of perception. And Mr. P. knew that better than most. And what money couldn't fix, a little mental suggestion solved.

They asked for "Michael" at the reception desk as instructed, and Sweet Tushie the Hyatt hostess didn't have to think twice to direct the call.

"You let me take this one," the Piper told the Kid as he left their suite. "Order room service." Mr. P. met them in the imperial oaken atmosphere of the Commodore Grill, the maître d' leading them to a banquette off the main floor shrouded by royal blue drapes and under a five-foot mirror. Mirrors made people naturally glance at their reflections. Under a mirror you could almost be invisible.

His guests didn't need the menu; they ate and drank whatever was placed in front of them, slyly glancing up from their dinners as though expecting at any moment to be addressed as interlopers and get carted away with the dirty dishes. The conversation tended to be a trifle one-sided, Mr. P. doing most of the talking.

"I suppose I could pack both of you off to Cleveland to work at the Skidmark Underwear Company as Inspectors numbers 86 and 69—but it's probably best we all stay a little closer for now."

Mama Whore and Dimples stared at him without comprehension. But Mr. P. could see the wheels beginning to turn in the crack heads' noggins. The two lovebirds sitting at his table suddenly suspected there'd be more Dalekto somewhere down the line, and more importantly, that their lives were about to change. Good times just around the corner.

"You're going to apply for jobs here at the hotel," Mr. P. told them. "You'll have about as much trouble getting work as you did getting to see me. All you'll have to do is show up every day for your shift, so I strongly suggest you scale back the *vacations.* You'll have samples of Dalekto to pass around. Then you'll have customers. Then you will become wealthy. Wealthy enough to stay in this hotel if you like, get your laundry done and merely take an elevator to work. Good-looking enough to put your skanky ass up on Craigslist for a twist if you still like the skin trade. How does that sound?"

Mr. P. saw his pitch intrigued them.

Dimples seemed okay with all this, but Mama Whore couldn't quite understand her stroke of good luck. Suspiciously, "Why you doin' this, mister?"

The long, gaunt man took a sip of his merlot, gently correcting her, "Why are you doing this, Mr. Piper?"

And she repeated dutifully, "Why are you doing this, Mr. Piper?"

"None of your business," he said calmly back. "Now go get some decent clothes in the hotel shops, charge it to my room, and apply for the jobs. Any job will do. You can make up your Social Security numbers if you want. That's nine digits. Hold up your fingers."

Both Mama Whore and Dimples held up their hands, like they were under arrest. "Now take away one thumb." They dropped a thumb. Nine digits.

"That's how many numbers you need to give them. Your new names will be Adam and Eve. Adam Smith and Eve Jones. Now go forth and multiply."

B ack in the room the Kid had gone whole hog with room service. Ordering up two shrimp cocktails, broiled lobster, a hunk of steak, a raspberry torte for dessert, espresso, and a bottle of Armagnac, because it was expensive and sounded fancy. He'd never had lobster before, and though it looked like a big bug, he really liked it. The Kid was still wearing his lobster bib sprinkled with drawn butter; obviously, he'd figured out how to eat the thing all by himself.

Mr. P. dipped a French fry into the little cup of drawn butter, then popped it in his mouth. "I saw your parents. Well, your mother anyway—and Dimples. They're not going to bother us anymore. Whattaya say, let's order that Kit-Cat clock?"

9

Desperately Seeking Sweet Jane

Bhakti found a funeral home for Janet's remains where he could grieve in private, the Cremation Society of Los Angeles. Officer Cheryl Gibson went with him to the LA coroner's office to release the body. Corpses weren't supposed to be transported in private vehicles, so Cheryl helped Bhakti with a special waiver allowing them to make the ten-mile drive on their own.

With the death certificate and transport authorization they were able to take Janet to the funeral home in the back of her father's rented SUV wrapped in a body bag. Cheryl being a cop and the one who discovered the body, the county coroner's office looked the other way on this breach of bureaucratic protocol, sparing Bhakti the added expense of renting a long black station wagon that nobody rides round-trip.

The coroner had stitched Janet's arms back to her shoulders, making her look almost normal. There were all kinds of stories in the news about funeral homes botching the job, leaving the autopsy stitching still visible, but what could anyone do to Janet worse than what happened already? Nothing.

On the way they stopped at a florist and bought $800 worth of flowers, about ten bundles, wrapped in clear cellophane—all the flowers the place had.

The Cremation Society was a single-story ranch house with a touch of Spanish mission about it; wide entranceway arches under terra-cotta roof tiles. Clean, functional. A Taco Bell for the dead. Bhakti chose an open pine casket.

He removed the wrappings from the flowers and laid them on Janet's folded hands, piling them inside the open box.

Then he chose to witness Janet's cremation, Cheryl with him, both watching through the fireproof glass window as the gas jets released the poor girl's soul.

The mangled body of his daughter under the large pile of flowers caught fire, but Bhakti did not look away. Instead he began to chant the "Antim Ardas," the final rite of the dead, the soft Punjab dialect filling the viewing room: *"In the Lord's fear, the wind and breezes ever blow. In the Lord's fear, thousands of rivers flow."*

As they waited for the ashes to cool Bhakti picked an urn from a leather-bound catalogue. A Nambe urn, a kind of silver metal alloy that never lost its shine; he chose the shape of an hourglass. He knew the metal—knowing metals was part of his job. Mostly aluminum, but Nambe, Inc., kept the formula secret. The urn radiated a kind of eternal, timeless beauty, the luster of silver and the durability of iron; it didn't so much remind him of Janet, but a kind of invulnerability, an exoskeleton—giving her all the protection in eternity he failed so miserably to give her in real life.

"I'm sure her mother will like that too," Cheryl comforted him. They were sitting in his SUV outside the crematorium, the urn in the open driver's well between the front seats. Bhakti stared at the silver hourglass, and his hand strayed to its smooth sides.

"Her mother's about to be admitted to a psychiatric hospital in Connecticut. I talked to Eleanor's sister Lauren last night. She tried to reach me three times yesterday, and when I didn't answer . . ." *Didn't answer what? Where the hell are you?* A conversation that started with outrage at Bhakti's not being there and ended somewhere in tears and anguish.

What were the odds that Bhakti had found Janet about the same time Guy and Lauren Poole were driving crazy

Eleanor to the Bridgeport Hospital? Things happen in threes or just all at once? The latter, it seemed. In any case, Bhakti had faced a choice: find Janet or chase Eleanor.

"Things got confused, and my in-laws are very angry. There are a lot of bills I have to straighten out. They didn't even know Janet was . . ." He couldn't say the word *dead*. He went on instead, "When Janet vanished, Eleanor left too, but . . . I kept looking for Janet." He stared out the windshield at nothing. "Then Eleanor, my wife, got up from her wheelchair that first night, got up for the first time in twenty years, and drove to her sister's up north in our other car—" Bhakti stopped, realizing how crazy this sounded.

He shook his head in subdued dismay. Then sighed. He shifted the subject, asking Cheryl, "What were you doing when I showed up at your door?"

The lady cop powered down her passenger window and rested her head against the car frame; somehow it was easier to think things, say certain things, through an open window.

"Putting in my two weeks' notice with the highway patrol," she said slowly; then in final resignation, "Getting a divorce."

She went silent for a moment.

"What are you going to do now?" Bhakti asked her. Cheryl looked at him. "What are *you* going to do?"

Half an hour later found them sitting at Canter's Deli. Same table and chair as Herman the cop union lawyer. Bhakti even ate the same bloody thing. Cottage cheese and a peach half. Cheryl had heard bits and pieces, but now she heard Bhakti's whole mad tale. The vanishing, the back and forth search along the border, Eleanor getting up from the wheelchair, the burned-down Chen house and hematite earrings. Even Madame Zelda, Senora Malvedos. What a crazy story.

Thing was, Bhakti had Cheryl hook, line, and sinker at, "I woke up at three a.m. and just knew something was wrong."

So when he told his newfound cop buddy about the kiddy Felix the Cat song on his BlackBerry and that one of the girls, Lila Chen, might still be alive—it crept up Cheryl like slow strangulation. Maybe she'd been too late for the chopped girl in the orange Chevy because she'd never followed one Felix lead to the next; maybe if she—

Her heart-attack sandwich came and she felt her chest tighten. Same as before—corned beef and chopped liver. Idly Cheryl slipped her napkin to her lap. That grinning Felix face smiled up at her; yet another urban artistic anarchist had drawn a version of the cat right on the tabletop in black pen. Indelible black pen. The restaurant had just been covering it up with a napkin until they could get a new table. The pressure in her chest blossomed for a moment, then dissipated to nothing. . . .

But now a thought crystallized in her mind. With both of their lives altered by the grinning cat, with both Bhakti and herself working the case—

Find the girl, Lila Chen. That's what they'd do. Bhakti was on a mission, and Cheryl wanted in. To somehow give Sweet Janet her final rest by finding the other little lost lamb. A worthy goal. How they got to this place in their minds didn't seem so complicated. More like an unspoken decision, over a canned peach and half-eaten sandwich. *We will proceed.*

Now.

Find Lila Chen alive. And they'd find those who killed Janet.

For Cheryl the rest of the nagging details of daily life—splitting with Rachel, moving her stuff back east to Poughkeepsie—somehow fell into place. She kissed Rachel good-bye, and Rachel promised one of her property lawyer colleagues would somehow protect them from the vampire wrongful death suit by the terribly aggrieved family of the arm-chopper choir boy, Ricardo Montoya.

Rachel seemed resigned, sad—but with a look in her that seemed to say, *Cheryl, you always have a place here. I'll wait.* But Cheryl didn't know what to tell her; more like, *Don't wait up.* Words best left unspoken.

Bhakti picked and paid for a motel in Escondido as base command—the Holiday Inn. And yeah, they even shared a room. Privacy didn't seem to matter; the Punjabi materials engineer seemed to have been raised in the Queen's Own Privy Guard, more considerate than even Rachel, a stickler for hygiene protocol—God, the guy even rinsed out the sink after he combed his whiskers or brushed his teeth, and put the toilet seat down. Now, that was well housebroken.

The only things she kept of her past life were her uniform blues, her CHiPs motorcycle gear, and her sidearm. Since she'd given notice at the department, they put her on zero shifts and zero duties, and with a little of Herman's finagling she didn't have to turn in her shield until the last day. So for the first lap of their search she did it on her BMW, in uniform hooked into Dispatch, and that helped when talking to scumbags. While Bhakti followed along in the black rental SUV.

The first few stops on their search were rudimentary police work: buttonholing snitch types hanging around the Felix scat on walls and toilet stalls, a bodega, a bar—they'd found a picture of Lila on Facebook, and used it. But for a couple of days no luck.

Their first hit was a handyman for some local bangers, his curbside office a bare sidewalk in South LA by a smiley Felix spray-painted in an alley. Street dealers always knew what was going on. The one they found was a kid about fifteen, doing the *Hi-Bye, how you doin'? Whassup?*

Catch you later act for curbside cruisers and passersby that crossed his shadow. A very handy man.

The young dealer jumped up and down and waved his arms like a gooney bird as Cheryl idled her BMW bike and climbed off. He didn't try to run; he was a scarecrow for the lookouts with binoculars. The head-shop lads watching from a nearby building would see him prancing about and knew the heat had showed her face. Time to split. Shut down. Set up shop somewhere else. In forty seconds their rat trap would be an empty shell. And nobody'd bother with their front man, as he was only a kid. No point in booking.

Cheryl escorted the young lad into an alley, unholstered her Glock, and put it in his mouth. The kid's eyes widened, but he wasn't that scared. Probably happened to him before. Nothing like a little experience to take the edge off critical moments. It was her buddy, the nerdy tagalong—the one in the chinos, polo shirt, and cheap pull-on loafers like Abdul from the local dollar store—that looked scared. Like he hadn't expected this bitch cop to pull a gun.

Cheryl spoke to her new buddy very slowly and deliberately, "Look, cuz. I don't care about your business. I don't care about your homey's pixie-dust empire. I think with a little luck you're going to grow up and have a great future in commercial real estate. What I care about is a girl. We're looking for a girl. Chinese. About eighteen. Not from around here. So I want you to go to the boss and pick a place to meet. Here's my cell number. He's gonna talk to me about the pimps. Not the regular pimps, the weird ones. The ones nobody wants to know. Understand?"

The kid understood.

"Now empty your pockets."

The kid emptied his pockets. Little vials and twisted baggies came out in his hands. A nice haul.

"On the ground."

The vials and baggies were put on the ground in a small pile. Cheryl the bitch cop carefully crushed them with her boot, spreading the pixie-dust around. The kid's face dropped, but he knew this drill. This was the fishhook into the boss.

"So you can tell him, I'll double the price on whatever you spilled on the ground today. Looks about a thousand. So for a ten-minute meet he can have 2K. Got it? Make the call, we'll hang at the Dunkin' Donuts. Just keep in sight."

The kid nodded. "Cool."

Bitch Cop Cheryl kept one of the vials. Held it up to the light, examining. It didn't look like regular crank or rock. It had a strange shimmer to it, sort of rainbow sparks.

"What are you peddling?"

The handyman preened a little. "You haven't seen it yet, have you, mamacita? It's the new Dr Pepper. Like the ad, y'know? I'm a Pepper. He's a Pepper." The boy glanced at Bhakti. Then back at the smart lady cop. "Wouldn't you like to be a Pepper too?" When she didn't respond the lad answered her question in a more conventional way. "They call it Big D, chica. It's Dalekto. It's delicious. It's delightful. You take a snoot, you'll dig it."

"Maybe another time."

The call from Super Fly came about five minutes into a coffee and doughnut.

"You got my money?"

"We will. Do you take a check?"

A pause. "You're one crazy bitch. I could get to know *you*."

"Get to know me now."

T he limousine pulled up to Cheryl's bike in the parking lot of the Escondido Holiday Inn around dusk. Bhakti had retired to his SUV, but got out when the long black car stopped by the curb. The window rolled down an inch, and the voice came out. "Why look, if it isn't Snarky and Putz."

Bhakti looked a little confused. Cheryl snorted. "I don't

think he watches many cop shows," she said through the partially open window. "We can go into the bar if you want." But no reply came from inside the car. Then after a moment the shiny car door unlatched and swung open. Under the sodium lights of the motel apron, Cheryl and Bhakti slid into the spacious back of Mr. Bossman's limo and let their eyes adjust.

The guy wasn't much of a Super Fly: no flash, no gold bling-bling. A Banka-Gangsta; he wore an Armani suit and Testoni crocodile loafers. Size 48 and 12, respectively. But not a fat man. Nice, polite, tight, and controlled.

He measured the two guests in his private mobile office for a few silent moments. "You want a soda? A Perrier? A Dr Pepper?"

Bhakti swallowed hard, like his throat was parched. Shook his head but didn't dare to speak—he'd never been this close to a criminal before. The Banka-Gangsta smiled and wagged his head a little and looked at the Punjabi scientist. "When we're done here, you let the officer from the highway patrol take you into the mall and get some clothes. You can't walk around like that. With those rubber shoes with the fake stitching and ten-dollar Costco shirts. I mean, the only thing you're missing is the leaky pens in a pocket protector."

Bhakti glanced at himself, up and down. Then said, frankly enough, "They're in my laptop case."

At which point both the Banka-Gangsta and Cheryl erupted in laughter.

"Where'd you find this guy, Sistah?"

Cheryl shrugged. "I found his girl. Then he found me. Sort of an accident."

"That the girl you looking for? What's up with that? Did your buddy, Hadji here, marry a Chinee?"

Cheryl shook her head no, then showed him the Facebook photo of Lila Chen. "We think she's still alive."

The Banka-Gangsta lit a cigarette and flipped on the

reading light behind his head. He put on a pair of reading glasses and stared at the photo of the Chen girl for a long time. He sighed, a stream of smoke shooting from his nostrils and then the remnants from his mouth.

"A lot of girls come through LA. You know that. I mean this is Booty-City. All the starry-eyes going for Hollywood and getting holy wood instead. You got the Spics runnin'—" He broke off, didn't mean to insult Cheryl, figuring she was who-knows-what. "Sorry. I didn't mean anything." He came back to the point. "Look, the Chinese and Japs and Koreans, they got gambling, protection, loan shark, yeah—but they're not crazy about anybody messing with their sweet stuff. Y'know it's a family thing. They'll marry a seventy-year-old to a fourteen-year-old before they'll put high-class poon out for bids. Take care of the brothers and uncles too. No kidding. Arranged marriage. *Wild,* right?"

Cheryl didn't answer immediately. Then, savvy: "C'mon, they have Asian hooker rings up and down the coast, you know that. Acupuncture salons, nail salons."

"But they're not high-class, are they? Boat people. Working off their passage."

When Cheryl just looked at him he tried another approach. "Thousand-dollar hos, for the Burbank crowd, sure. There's one or two madams. And they run it clean—you know, pay off everyone in sight. Maybe your gal fell in there? Maybe you've put the touch on them yourself from time to time. They have a big payroll, lots of coppers on it."

Cheryl took the photo back. "We're looking for a weirdo. Some kind of horror show impresario. You know what I'm saying?"

Dead silence again. Nicky the Banka-Gangsta took off his reading glasses and put them in a silver clamshell case and back in his jacket. He reached to the armrest minibar along the side of the limo. Poured himself a slug from crystal. Then stared at it. Swirled it around, then stared at it some more.

Then at last: "I don't know his real name. I don't think he's got one. But they call him the Magician. Things get around. They say he's running some kind of chop-shop, snuff market; they call it the Harrow House. I mean, it may not even be a real place, a real house. You pay and you play. Single-payer system, right? We're not talking some kind of Mistress Spanky and the Gang where the Hollywoods come down from Malibu for the night to get their fannies red, and a home movie thrown in for free. This is *not* for the fainthearted. We're talking the real deal. Blood and pus and dead before dawn."

Bhakti's face had taken on a beige tinge. What it looked like when an Indian's blood drained from his cheeks. He was going white.

"How do we find him?"

"You don't, sister. He finds you." Bossman the Banka-Gangsta took a hit from the glass. "I mean he's like Santa Claus. He's got a list, checking it once and checking it twice. He knows who's been naughty and who's been nice."

"You're whack," Cheryl said with some heat. "What is he—Peter Pan? Flying in on his tights and flying out again like Mary Martin?"

Bossman took another hit of the whiskey. "You know what I know."

Cheryl took the little glass vial of Dalekto out of her shirt pocket. "Tell me about this stuff."

The Banka-Gangsta looked curiously at it. Got out his glasses again. Took it in his handkerchief so none of his prints got on the little glass vial. "Where the hell'd you get this?"

"Your boy had it in his pockets."

"You're kidding me." The gangster was incredulous.

Cheryl and Bhakti shared a fleeting glance. The big Bossman didn't know? *Really?* The gangster tried to explain, "Look, I'm in the blow, crank, and X business. I never seen this before. But if that kid is playing me, I'm gonna cut his big lips from his upper and lower mouth with a razor. Then he can talk to his mama that way and suck cock in Chino."

"You mean you don't know," Cheryl said.

"That's what I mean." He tossed the vial back at her. "I never seen it before." A quiet kind of queer fear seemed to creep into the man's face. The unknown in his world was the mind-destroyer. The Future Killer. What you didn't know could kill you. Snarky and Putz could see it clear enough from their couches across the long back of the limo.

"Well, thanks for taking the time with us, Squire," Cheryl told him. "We're going to want another word with your boy before you do anything rash. Remember that. You want your money?"

The gangster was breathing with his mouth open. He poured another slug from the armrest and brought it to his mouth. It slipped a little and splashed his Sea Island cotton shirt. "Damn." He mopped himself with a handkerchief. "My money," he said vaguely.

"Yeah, we'll go to an ATM, or a couple of them. Right here in the mall."

"The mall . . ." He seemed slightly doubtful. The money. The mall. Then he made up his mind, reached a decision, knew his place in the scheme of things. "No. We're not going into the mall. I'll give you a day to talk to the boy before I talk to him. I'll give you his address. Just leave him alive. About that money, now . . ." A long breath. The breath over.

"I don't want the Magician to know I even know about him. You can keep the green."

L os Angeles at night is part black sky over the glow of sodium lights and bright neon storefronts; then the softer yellowish lights in neighborhood windows, the flickering blue of televisions. They found the handyman's place easy enough from the address Bossman provided and found the kid at home in one of a thousand faceless 'hoods in LA: the ranch house, the chain-link fences, the gated doors and windows, the little square lawns that never got enough water, beer cans and KFC boxes spilling over trash cans. But Bhakti couldn't find many indicators showing they had entered rough territory. Bad areas in this part of the world didn't have the thick grime and grit of the rust-belt cities, the forbidding public housing, grim fortresses as though designed by jailers. But even the open canopy of sky overhead didn't make Bhakti breathe any easier.

As their black SUV pulled up to the curb, a few kids down the block talkin' smack gave the two strangers the eye for a moment—but went back to themselves after they spotted Cheryl's blues under the sodium lights. Only gun-shots and bubble-lights were worth a look. Hell, she coulda lived nearby.

The chain-link four-foot fence gate was open. So was the metal iron-twirled gate at the door, open a crack, the front door itself ajar. Cheryl and Bhakti went in cautiously. Most of the lights were on, but the place was quiet except for the soft babble of a television. Tan-painted walls, the smudge of fingers along the doorjambs. The discount store furniture was clean, but with that beaten look that cheap pieces seem to accumulate so fast. The dining set especially; the table peeling laminate. A glance in the kitchen showed more of the same: cupboards missing knobs and warped doors that didn't close all the way.

In the main room three figures sat on the couch watching TV. Cheryl heard the sounds of an *American Idol* re-run; Paula Abdul was at the judges' table doing her sincere coquette thing. The singer, a tall contestant dressed in tux-edo pants sans jacket slithered about the mike stand in his gleaming white shirt and sparkling studs, crooning a ren-dition of Lou Reed's "Sweet Jane," lewdly stroking the microphone head as if that young Jane were his favorite knob-polisher.

The three figures on the couch just sat and watched and listened. Not moving.

"Hello?" Cheryl called out. "Can we come in? The door was open."

Her hand strayed to her sidearm, and she motioned to Bhakti to keep behind her. A large mirror hung over the TV console, showing everyone on the couch. A mother and her two sons. One was the handyman from the corner earlier in the day. He now wore cargo shorts and a Lakers T-shirt—lounge-around-the-house wear. The other, a younger brother, dressed in a matching outfit.

Over on her side of the couch Mama stared at the TV with open eyes; a large and round woman, maybe forty-five. She had "single mother" written all over her—the kind who held down two-and-a-half jobs so her kids could get some of the things they deserved, even if their dad only showed up twice a year for birthdays.

She was definitely off work now; pink spandex enclosing her bottom, a flowing Hawaiian shirt over her ponderous bosom, three buttons unbuttoned. No bra and no air-conditioning. Maybe somebody turned it off. The unit in the wall was throwing wind but no cool. Thin yellow strips fluttering.

But that wasn't the ugly part.

The three figures weren't breathing, just stone-still staring at the tube. Each one's lips had been cut, top and bottom, exactly like Bossman had described not half an hour before. The three sets of white teeth grinned into the mirror over the TV. Could Bossman have gotten here this quickly, in and out before Cheryl and Bhakti arrived? No way. Or could he have done the deed himself earlier? Doubtful. Why promise them a day to question the boy? Why even bother giving the kid's correct address? No point at all. Bhakti and Cheryl shared a long look. Bhakti could see the pause and suspicion in his partner's face.

Weirder still, a line of red ants snaked up from the floorboards, a marching column from the floor to the armrest of the couch, across Mama's arms and onward. The busy marching column curled over her forehead, down between her bosoms, out the tail of her loose shirt, and over to the younger child. Across the younger child, onto the kid from the street, disappearing down into the crack of the seat cushions again. Cheryl stared in silence.

For his part, Bhakti thought of the children's song: *the ants go marching two by two, hurrah, hurrah.* Bits of this had come to him from Lauren and Guy, a rambling snippet that pushed Eleanor toward the psych ward.

"You have to call this in," Bhakti said huskily. "Somebody's got to be notified."

Cheryl's face took on a veiled cast. "Did you touch anything?"

"You're not going to leave them here?" Bhakti came back, aghast.

"No? You think not? You want to spend the next two weeks in interrogation with your court-appointed lawyer? Or do you want to keep on looking for Lila Chen? Make up your mind and make it up right now. Whatever we decide this very second will determine whether we find her or not."

Bhakti looked down at himself. Had he touched anything? No, just some footprints on the wall-to-wall. And that was strange too; the carpet had been recently vacuumed. The only footprints on the wall-to-wall were their half-dozen steps walking in from the door. He took a deep, ragged breath. Committed.

"All right then," Cheryl told him. "Back out the way we came. Careful not to touch anything."

They left Mama's place the way they'd found it. Back by the curb, Cheryl considered for a moment what to do about

Bhakti's black rental SUV. The kids were gone from the sidewalk two houses down. Still, somebody might have snagged a plate number.

"Get in and drive toward Long Beach."

They found an alley in Compton, off Long Beach Boulevard and not too far from the Alameda rail corridor that fed the docks.

"Leave the windows open and the keys in the ignition."

"Just *leave* it here?"

Cheryl didn't know exactly how to explain the Greater Los Angeles area to a newbie tourist from Nowhere, Texas. Compton had its problems: highest murder rate in the USA, longtime home of the Bloods and Crips. The Compton PD had even been disbanded once when the line between law enforcement and gangs blurred to irrelevance. Now that it was the LA County Sheriff's Department jurisdiction, some people said Compton was coming back. Still, not nearly fast enough for Cheryl's taste.

"Look, with any luck half an hour from now this vehicle will be washed, waxed, vacuumed, a cute New Car Scent freshener pad dangling from the rearview mirror— and on its way to South America. You'll report it stolen later. When you give them this general address in Compton, they'll think you're just an idiot from out of town."

Bhakti saw the logic to it. He was from out of town. They got out of the car and began to walk away. "Wait!" Bhakti doubled back to retrieve Janet's ashes. "What if the local cops find it first?"

Cheryl laughed. "Then chances are *they'll* boost it down south. If it finds its way back to Dollar Car Rental, it'll get washed and waxed anyway. Let's find a cab. We'll throw out our shoes later. I want to make a call."

Which she did from inside a Yellow Cab as it idled by a shoe store; Bhakti had vanished inside the Payless. She hung up on her call when he emerged, only to send him back for another try at a new pair of shoes. "Pick another style, Bhakti." When he looked at her crazy. "Different treads."

Later he asked her, "What about your boots?"

At length she sighed, answering him, "If I get tagged with any of this—DNA epithelials, hair, fingerprints, boot prints, handprints, nose prints—the only thing I can say is that when I arrived nobody was there, or they were alive and I left empty-handed. Maybe leave you out of it. You get to visit me in lockup on weekends." She paused at his look of alarm. "All that's in that house was shoe prints on the wall-to-wall, yours and women's size 8. Tactical ATAC boots—they made about a zillion of those last year. I was just taking precautions with you."

Y ou want *what*??"
Herman the Police Union lawyer sat in the Holiday Inn motel room. When Cheryl asked him to meet them there, he had no idea she was cohabitating. Or collaborating, or whatever the hell she was doing. Besides leaving the Highway Patrol and getting a divorce.

And Joe College moved in.

Bhakti's navy blue Brooks Brothers sports jacket hung neatly in the open closet and beside it two pairs of pressed khakis on another couple of wooden hangers. Three Lacoste polo shirts—one in lime, another in salmon, and the third in lavender—lay on the dresser; next to them sat a cardboard box of men's button-down shirts from a local cleaner marked HEAVY STARCH. Bottom of the closet showed a pair of Payless rubber loafers and a pair of expensive leather ones, cordovan leather with tassels.

But Herman absorbed the scene without much fuss; he'd seen much worse in his day, and accepted the Punjabi scientist's presence as you would a potted plant. Still, what his Rainbow Rambo was asking him fell between lunatic and criminal:

"I want to see the full intel file from the Felix Graffiti Task Force, or whatever they call it."

"Cheryl, are you crazy? You have four hours left on your two-week notice. Whattaya think? They got some kind of war room? Maybe it's in four different offices on three different floors, in file cabinets and under trash cans. Maybe the FBI has requested the whole lot and it isn't even there. Some of it may even be in the property clerk's office."

This seemed to deflate Bhakti considerably, and he went into the bathroom to splash water on his face. But Cheryl wasn't deterred.

"Herman, some person, somebody, some nobody, maybe *three* nobodies—*knows* something. I want the names of the people who sit in the cubicles and what floor of the new Parker Center they work on. Maybe we'll be lucky and there'll be an expert, a nosy cop in one precinct. And I want to know tonight."

Herman looked around at the pale sea-foam yellow of the Holiday Inn room. "Do you mind if I go down to the bar-restaurant? I work better in dark, cool air-conditioning."

They met him about forty minutes later; Herman had borrowed a Holiday Inn writing tablet and a ballpoint pen. A couple of names were scribbled on the tablet. His smartphone screen looked a touch sweaty. He was on his second G&T. You could tell by the rings on the bar.

He took a long swig. "Do you have any idea how tricky it is to ask questions like this? The copper you're asking can't know *why* you're asking or *who* you're asking for." He pointed his finger at Cheryl. "And the patsy has to tell me what you want to know without getting himself stuck on *you*, tar baby."

He took another draught of the clean G&T. "So when you get your cute little nosy nose slammed in the Parker Center rat trap it doesn't have *his* cheese on it. So nu?" Herman saw the Indian didn't get the Yiddish. "Capiche?" And that wasn't much better either.

"So how did you do it?" Bhakti asked somewhat amazed.

"*Feh,*" Herman cawed; a Jewish seagull dismissing his question. "What's it to you?" Bhakti's mouth dropped a little. But the union lawyer's take on the business did make a kind of sense. There was safety in anonymity.

"One more thing." Cheryl used her sweetest smile on the man, like she was asking Daddy, pretty-please, for a favor. "Can we borrow the car?"

Herman's face dropped. "Oh, that's just perfect." Then he sighed, resigned; so much for compartmentalized anonymity. He looked to the bartender; ordered a third G&T. It came and he pounded half of it back. "I probably shouldn't drive now anyway." He fished the keys out of his pocket and slid them across the bar. "You can take the wife's MINI Cooper at home. If you're not back by morning, I'm reporting it stolen."

12:30 a.m., the new Parker Center, the LAPD Headquarters, had the nighttime quiets, with a slow, sleepy pulse in the building. The occasional ring of a phone, someone answering, soft murmurs. The duty sergeant didn't even blink when Cheryl signed in at the front desk in the lobby. He pushed the sign-in book at her and vaguely looked at her badge and ID. The desk cop didn't even bother with Bhakti, saying, "He's with you?" Not caring whether the Indian fellow was or not. They took the elevator to the third floor.

There was no name on the third-floor office. A wall of translucent glass; a door with a viewing slit in it. A cardboard, handwritten sign was taped to the glass wall by the door reading GANG TASK FORCE. And some joker had scrawled the smiling face of Felix on it. Cheryl knocked. Nothing. No answer. She peered through the viewing slit. Empty.

Inside, the nameplate on the clean, organized desk:

F. FREDERICK. And that rang a bell somewhere, but she couldn't place it. A nagging tic at the back of her head. She glanced around the office; it looked clean, almost unused. A map of greater Los Angeles on one wall showed the rough gang territories marked with Post-its. Nothing special, nothing an ordinary cop wouldn't already know. Crips here this block, Bloods there that block. No big deal.

The steel filing cabinet wasn't even locked.

She opened the E-F-G-H drawer using a ballpoint pen to unlatch the handle; then poked through the F file using the tip of the pen. Slim pickings. One folder contained a slew of photos: Felix photos, pictures of graffiti on walls, tattoos on anonymous arms, a photo of the Bang-Flag-Gun that got her into all that trouble. She flipped past it, but discerned no discernable order, no notations, no police work to the drawer. This place was the dead-letter office.

"There's nothing here," Cheryl said to Bhakti. "Come on; let's go. We'll try that precinct guy in West Hollywood Herman knows."

The elevator doors opened at the lobby; Cheryl and Bhakti walked toward the front doors. The desk sergeant dozed at the reception desk, but opened his eyes as they passed.

"Thanks," Cheryl said to him. He didn't reply.

As they left the building another cop, plainclothes, opened the glass door for them. Something familiar about him. Cheryl and Bhakti scooted through, nodding thanks. The plainclothes cop nodded too, then paused, watching them as they walked away.

Cheryl could feel the man's eyes on her neck. He was staring and thinking. Thinking and staring, but she kept on walking. Then it struck her: he was the Internal Affairs guy at her interrogation. The ferret-looking cop with the pockmarked face. The guy who needled her, *Are you sleepy, Officer Gibson? Are we boring you?* Nicknamed Felix by the police captain—the mayor's crony who'd told the ferret,

Oh, I think we've covered what we can today, Felix. The ID tag read FREDERICK. Just like the nameplate in the office upstairs.

"Nice to see you again, Officer Gibson," the Internal Affairs cop said from the door.

"Just keep walking," Cheryl muttered to Bhakti.

And he dutifully followed, without a clue.

The precinct in West Hollywood was definitely open for business. Nights were long in this part of town. And at 1 a.m. things were just getting started. This time the desk sergeant, a tough-looking lady named Dubois, took a moment from the general cacophony of prebooking to give Cheryl some professional courtesy.

"Steinholtz? You want Detective Steinholtz?" Sergeant Dubois looked over Cheryl's shoulder. "He's right there. Coming in now."

The detective—a round, grumpy man in his mid-fifties in a disheveled brown suit—was escorting a suspect into the precinct. And not just any suspect. The young lady was about thirty, tricked out for a night on the town.

Broderick Fallows—A-list movie director. His newest offering, the third installment of the *Zyklon-B* trilogy, had just broken 200 million after two weekends. It was titled *Inexplicable.* And no, Cheryl hadn't bothered to see it; she'd wait for cable. Oh, that's right, no more cable for a while without Rachel. Well, maybe the Holiday Inn.

Worse still for Mr. Fallows, his face had been on the magazine *Transformation*—for two weeks in every corner news box and newsstand, his extra notoriety the result of some sort of sex change, breast enhancement or estrogen therapy, male to female, at the urging of his/her "girlfriend," a famous dominatrix to the stars. Cheryl had forgotten most of the details, if she ever knew. . . . Rachel had even taken Cheryl to a law-firm dinner with the guy once.

But that was back when Fallows was a boy. He'd played with his broiled salmon and quinoa sautéed with yellow peppers and red onion, but didn't eat much.

Now, mincing into a West Hollywood precinct in do-me heels and cuffed, Lady Fallows looked awful. Blond dripping hair a mess, lipstick smeared, missing a false eyelash. When Steinholtz brought Lady Fallows to the high desk for booking he/she hitched up her top over an impressive boob job. The $500 Victoria's Secret décolleté chamois top in purple wasn't chopped liver either.

"Soliciting. Hollywood and Vine," Detective Steinholtz told the sergeant. "Outside the saloon Boys 'n' Bears. She can keep his cell phone, her cell phone. Don't throw him in the pen with the others. But don't let him run outside either."

Desk Sergeant Dubois wagged her head a little. "*Again,* Mr. Fallows?" She smiled. "Some of us here just wish you'd move to San Francisco."

"It's too cold," Fallows replied. Dubois nodded. True enough. Then to Steinholtz, who'd started to walk away, "Some people for you."

Steinholtz halted in his tracks. A once-over of Cheryl in her blues and Bhakti in his preppie wear. "Oh yeah, Herman's nameless friends," he said not even using their names. "My desk is upstairs."

A cluttered desk with two extra chairs facing it in a large room packed with desks, all of them taken: cops on the phones, shouting, laughter, guys eating breakfast at 2 a.m.—the noisy West Hollywood circus. Steinholtz just stared at Cheryl. He held her badge in a meaty hand. Staring at it and rubbing the silver with a damp thumb. Even when he handed it back, he didn't say anything. Glanced at Bhakti, then back at the lady from the California Highway Patrol.

Finally, "Nice shooting over by Pharaoh's Lost Kingdom. I read about it in the paper. This city is going to miss you."

"I seriously doubt that."

Steinholtz shrugged, a wry smile, then got up from his desk. "Let's go to the men's room. We do our best work there."

Silently he led Cheryl and Bhakti inside the men's room, a battered wall of urinals, a battered wall of stalls, a long grimy mirror over the sinks. A large map of the city was spread out over one side of the long mirror, taped at the edges. The map was plastered with stickers at various locations and intersections. The stickers were Felix the Cat faces, each one about the size of a shirt-collar button, no bigger. Still you could see the cat's goofy smile.

The map looked like it had been hosed with a thousand rounds from an Uzi. Just top to bottom tiny black tags, many in clusters, overlapping in certain areas.

"I had the stickers made up myself," Detective Steinholtz said. "This is the record since your cat appeared. Gotta buy a new batch every two weeks. Everybody in the precinct helps out a little. We call it the Kitty Litter Map."

"Jesus," Bhakti remarked. "It looks like a virus, like a disease."

"Yeah, doesn't it? And that's not even San Diego."

Cheryl pointed to one spot, one Felix dot off by itself. All by its lonesome. She knew the area. The Taylor Yards: railroad tracks and old warehouses. The Taylor Yards were 1930s old, not used much now, and many of the warehouses had fallen in the quake of '94.

Suddenly Cheryl remembered her dream of Sweet Jane talking to her out of the storm, then suffering under ugly hands. It came back clear and strong: the dark, blue-and-gray clouds rolling over themselves, the sound of galloping hooves. A figure at the edge of the patio looking plaintively at her, begging her for something. To find her before she lost her arms. Then the abandoned warehouse with pigeons cooing on the rafters, Sweet Jane tied to a table, mewing behind a gagged mouth; now the knife was going in; now the arms were coming off . . . And somebody was singing, *"Take a little tip"*—

No, she had a name now: the late Sweet Janet Singh sitting in the Nambe urn back at the Holiday Inn beside Bhakti's Lacoste shirts.

"Yeah," Steinholtz told her. "An old warehouse. Stands out, doesn't it? I went over, didn't find anything. I'll give you the address. Fresh eyes and all that."

Bhakti and Cheryl bumped back and forth across the abandoned tracks of the Taylor rail yards in the cramped MINI Cooper borrowed from *Mrs.* Herman, crawling between parked dump trucks and bulldozers, even a crane where the authorities were still trying to clean up after the quake over a decade ago. Not a high priority, though there'd been a flurry of recent activity when the city toyed with the idea of turning the area into some kind of railroad museum, near the state park. Intact buildings dotting the landscape between piles of fallen rubble took on the appearance of broken teeth.

Many of the warehouses had long ago lost their signs or building numbers. Never mind their lights and power and their windows. It was that strange time of night, right before dawn, when the streetlamps still cast umbrellas of sodium light and the sky lightened to an incandescent blue. Thank God they'd brought flashlights.

Bhakti stumbled on the concrete steps of a truck bay; the metal gate was locked. This was the place. A few bays down, a battered roll-gate stood open two feet, but jammed in place. Just enough room to squirm through. Bhakti got a good snort of plaster and concrete dust laced with pigeon dung. But Cheryl got through without mussing her uniform. Practice.

A strange mélange of streetlamp and dawn sky lit the windows, bluish orange. The flashlights flashed on— swords of light in a large void turning the rest black.

"We should have come during the day," Bhakti whispered. Something about being in a large, black space made him want to whisper. Bits of concrete crunched underfoot, the occasional tang of metal when they kicked a bit across the floor. Not the kind of place to run heedlessly about; maybe cracks or pitfalls out ahead.

Go slow, go quiet.

Against one wall a gated elevator stared at them like a black mouth. The elevator stalled between floors halfway up. Bhakti touched the slide gate and it clanged a little, making him jump—a large empty sound in this empty space. Not inviting. His light sliced up and down.

"Let's try the stairs," Cheryl said softly. "Somehow in my dream it felt like the top floor of a building, not the downstairs." She paused for a moment, considering. "Does that make sense?"

"Sure. I guess so," Bhakti told her. "It was your dream." He followed her to a large door, ajar, marked STAIRWELL. Cheryl found a screwdriver with a broken handle on the floor and took the precaution of jamming the tool over the bottom hinge, wedging the door open. They carefully climbed the stairs, flashlights down to make sure of the steps. At one landing the wooden stair rail grip gave way and fell at their feet with a noisy clatter.

"Careful!" Bhakti hissed. The lady cop was in a hurry. Taking chances. The climbing, making her go faster and faster.

"Careful yourself!" Cheryl hissed back.

The skylight at the top of the stairwell was growing lighter, and the sound of pigeons in their roosts cooing seemed to ruffle the air around them. The smell: old, musty, deserted. When they reached the top, several flustered pigeons flapped and fluttered. Then quieted down. Cheryl touched the half-open door to the top floor of the warehouse. With just a light finger tap it yawned open. Their saber lights showed just a clean, swept wooden floor. Large planks extending the length of the building.

"You think this is the place?" Bhakti's whisper cut the air.

"Yes, Bhakti." A pause. "But I don't think you should have come. Maybe me either."

Bhakti had taken a dozen steps in one direction, Cheryl in the other. When he turned to look at her she was standing over a metal cot, just the plain metal frame of a camp cot with its spring meshing. Cut cords hung at the four corners. On a low table some empty plastic bottles, dirty gauze, long tweezers, medical clamps. On the floor, a large pair of garden pruning clippers with two-foot handles, used for pruning the thicker branches of a shrub.

And in a sudden blow to his mind, Bhakti realized this is where it happened to Janet. He was standing where the monster stood who took his baby. "Stand back," Cheryl warned him. And he could see why: a large pool of dried blood around the metal cot.

He felt the urge to tear his hair, to howl; the flashlight began to tremble in his hand. There wasn't even any sign of the one they were looking for. No Lila Chen, no hair, no clothes; if he didn't pull himself together in a second he was going to drop the flashlight in a fit of tremors; the beam danced across the dark cavernous space.

"But—but," he stammered, "the guy at the precinct said he didn't find anything." Then in a slow, measured tone: "He said he didn't find *anything*."

He felt Cheryl thinking in a long, following silence.

A new voice came out of the empty corner of the warehouse room; a dry and heartless voice seemed to hang in the air like a nasty smell: "Maybe that's because your guy in the precinct went to another warehouse."

Bhakti's guts ran cold, and it took all his will not to drop his flashlight. Cheryl's body snapped to the sound of the newcomer; her flashlight lanced into the dark. A figure emerged from the blacker shadows of the cavernous room. Cheryl recognized him at once. Inspector Frederick of Internal Affairs from her departmental hearing. What the hell was he doing here? Working overtime on his own dime? Tailing them?

Bad either way.

The ferret-like man picked his way across the floor, stopping a few paces off. His own flashlight glanced across his pockmarked face. Then flashed across the yawning room. No cat graffiti. But the flashlight stopped when it caught some large spray paint on a long expanse of wall. Silver and red, striking large letters: ROGUE HOUSE MENU. Then underneath: *Today's Specials: Your Choice of White Meat, Dark Meat, Mush Puppies, and Kitty Fried Kiddies.* The cop with the pockmarked face coughed darkly at the droll perversion of it.

A sicko's idea of humor. But still no smiling Felix Face.

"Did you see our happy cat on the way in?" Inspector Frederick asked. "No. Or on the stairs? Or downstairs? No. You just used the Kitty Litter Map you saw in the precinct toilet."

Cheryl felt a twinge. She hadn't even been looking for the smiling cat. Hell, maybe somebody had gotten the little sticker on the bathroom map wrong. With a touch of grit she asked him, "I thought you were with Internal Affairs."

The ferret-faced man shrugged. "I was transferred."

His flashlight touched the metal cot, the dark stained floor, the handles of the pruning clippers. "I suppose I should call in a Forensics team just to be thorough. For all the good it will do. But I think we all know whose blood that is." He paused for a moment to see if his remark had any effect on the Indian man in dirty khakis holding a flashlight. He found his cell phone and tapped it.

"Are *you* the Magician?" Bhakti asked him slowly.

The ferret-faced man snorted. Then wagged his head at the simp.

"Whattaya thinking, Mr. Krishna? There's some guy out there in black tails and spats pulling strings, pulling rabbits out of hats, kidnapping chicks for fun and profit? There is no magician, Mr. Singh. He's the boogeyman—just a bedtime story drug dealers tell themselves at night. Mostly it makes them think they're not the worst guys in town. See, I'm not so bad . . . there's the Magician. *That man is much worse.*"

He started to tap his smartphone.

"How about I send you the report, Officer Gibson?" He caught himself, glanced at his watch, then the clock on his cell phone to confirm. "Sorry, should I say, the *former* Officer Gibson. You officially retired thirty-five minutes ago. Better get out of those blues. You wouldn't want to be pulled over for impersonating a police officer, now would you?"

Cheryl took a ragged breath and almost smiled a little. "No, definitely not." The light was coming in stronger through the warehouse windows. They didn't seem to need the flashlights anymore. She snapped hers off.

She walked toward the stairwell door, Bhakti silently following.

"Nice to see you again, Officer Gibson. I'll get you a copy of my report anyway."

As they passed into the stairwell and down the stairs a flock of pigeons flapped violently, a flurry of beating wings; a dozen or so zoomed off their roosts in every direction.

Shafts of sunlight lanced through the stairwell's dirty windows. The trip down seemed longer than the way up. The door at the bottom landing was still wedged with the broken screwdriver. He couldn't get Janet's blood on the floor out of his mind; and for a moment he almost ran back upstairs to mop it clean, somehow fix it. But instead he took a deep, shaky breath and plodded after Cheryl.

The cavernous ground level didn't seem particularly creepy anymore and the urge to walk softly or talk in whispers vanished. Bhakti's BlackBerry hummed, then vibrated in his shirt pocket. Eleanor texting him. They'd stuck her in a sanitarium and some patients were allowed BlackBerry privileges at the sanitarium—sure, why not, there were rooms with phones. The place wasn't a lockdown. But the text message didn't make him feel any better. Maybe even worse. *They're watching. Always watching. And the ants go marching west to east. Hurrah.*

More rantings. He showed Cheryl the back-lit text, explaining, "Eleanor. She sent me something similar when we found the girls' clothes on the tracks."

"You told me."

And Bhakti shook his head: right, remembering now. It was getting hard to remember what he'd done or said or explained. Too much to explain.

And he'd have to do something soon about Eleanor. After two weeks of searching for Lila Chen, Bhakti still had to come to grips with things back home. No, not back home—in Fairfield. With Eleanor. And Guy and Lauren. Head for Connecticut, straighten things out, somehow. The hospital bills, the sanitarium bills . . . His brother-in-law was starting to text in capital letters. HEY! BHAKTI! Followed by the growls of desperation.

Under the partially open roll-gate, the scientist and the ex-copper slid off the trailer bay and stretched. The rising sun hit them full in the face. Blinding orange. The great flock of pigeons from the top floor escaped out a hole in the warehouse roof and wheeled in a magnificent arc, hurling off toward the sun.

Tired, worn out, and flat as old soda, the two searchers shuffled toward Mrs. Herman's MINI. But Bhakti halted for a moment. A line of little insects moved on the ground, undulating like a snake.

Ants.

Black ants, this time; and there didn't seem anything evil or ugly about them, as if these were the *good* ants who meant no one harm. The good, black ants marched out of a small hole in the concrete, snaking on for a dozen feet and vanishing into the hill of a colony. What made it stranger was the ants marched over a tablet of laminated paper: sun-bleached, but wide as a newspaper.

Bhakti picked it up and gently shook the ants away. The thing was a menu from a place called the Road Island Diner in Oakley, Utah. The menu read *JUSTLY FAMOUS SINCE 1939.*

A typical diner bill of fare: burgers and shakes, illustrations of generic 1950s faces in the margins, smiling 1950s clean-cut Mom with bacon and eggs. Clean-cut chef in a chef's hat. A welcoming soda-jerk mixing the malts—all in American heyday nostalgia style. But what caught Bhakti's eye was on the left side of the page, the Kiddie's Korner. A smiling young lad's freckled face in eager anticipation beside the caption *LITTLE BANDITS MENU* and the offerings: Hush Puppies and Kitty Fries. Kitty Fries?

Cheryl spotted it too. And looking at each other, man and woman could feel the gears working. Rogue House Menu. Mush Puppies. Kitty Fried Kiddies. Road Island Diner. Hush Puppies. Kitty Fries. Too unlikely. Slim? Too cool for school.

If this new signpost was meant to lead them on, how had it gotten all the way from Utah to a concrete apron in lost-in-time industrial LA? Dropped by a passing stork? Had it fluttered out of a freight car ten years ago? Or had someone on their way to Utah left it behind like bread crumbs in the forest? Calling it unlikely was being generous. Calling it improbable, wildly magnanimous. A clue to nowhere.

Bhakti dropped it back to the ground, defeated. They climbed into the borrowed MINI Cooper and began to roll.

Wisps of an ocean breeze picked up spirals of dust at different corners of the rail yard. The gust picked up the menu from the ground and slapped it onto the car's windshield, jolting Cheryl and Bhakti behind the glass. He hit the brakes, then flipped on the windshield wipers to swipe the menu away. The menu caught under the wiper blade and stuck where it landed. Bhakti killed the wipers, grunted, and reached out his driver's window, bringing the laminated lost artifact inside with them.

"Want me to take out Lila's hematite earring, see if it draws?" Bhakti asked.

The two of them considered that for a moment. Would a jumping jelly bean hematite earring make their choice any easier? Whether to go forward in search of a lost little lamb—or just give up?

Cheryl gingerly took the menu from him, almost reverentially. Smoothed it out, then put it on the dashboard. She looked at Bhakti, measuring the weight of slim to none, and tasting a bit of hope. Like the service station displays that said LAST CHANCE GAS 400 MILES before a vanishing point on an empty blacktop.

"No, don't bother," Cheryl finally answered. "I wouldn't trust my eyes anyway." She sighed long and deeply. An old, discarded menu pointing the way to a kidnapped kid. Hush Puppies and Kitty Fries. What do you say to that?

The diner made me do it?

But that didn't change the fact that Lila Chen was still out there somewhere, alive for all they knew. Out there and alive. Could the girl be headed into Utah too? Was that the menu's message?

"Let's grab a couple of hours' sleep," Bhakti suggested. "Then I'll go to Utah if you will."

Cheryl scrunched around in *Mrs.* Herman's cramped MINI Cooper, thoroughly uncomfortable.

"Not in this thing you won't."

10

Skin Walker

Van Horn, Texas. 9 a.m., Sunday.

Billy Shadow's look-see for Boss Lattimore made him wonder about people's sanity. These walkabouts always seemed the best part of his job—part cavalry scout, part licensed troubleshooter—but not this time. He'd seen some desolate places in his life—the deserts of Iraq for one. Burnt tanks, burnt bodies, and melted sand—a sober kind of loneliness. Desolation that left you empty.

Or the Badlands of South Dakota, the sighing prairie grass under an endless sky while white clouds in the shape of eagles wheeled silently overhead—a peaceful kind of desolation that refreshed your soul.

Billy remembered Old Grandma Sparrow as she sat on the wooden steps of her trailer at the reservation holding out her soft, wrinkled hands and examining the discarded bits of junk he brought her as a boy, her sharp black eyes sparkling at everything he showed her. Little trinkets found lying on the side of the road or beside an abandoned trailer: a tin siren ring that whooped like a wolf whistle, a half-dozen red aluminum jacks from some child's game fallen from the pouch. Trinkets for some, treasures for him.

Grandma Sparrow had the quirky trick of telling him where they came from, her lined faced wrinkling in a thousand smiles: "Lucy's jacks. She married Lone Crow. And that silly wolf whistle fell out of a Cracker Jack box Laughing Horse was eating four years ago—it's yours if you want." Whether great insight or mere memory Billy never found out; God, she had to be 110 by now.

But the absence of living, breathing human beings in a place where people once lived and worked and played made for a kind of cold, fearful desolation.

The ghost town dreads.

And the subdivision in Van Horn, Texas, that Lattimore built for Bhakti Singh and the other Escape Velocity employees had a very bad case of the creeps.

The door to the Punjabi scientist's house stood open as if the man left in a hurry. In the few days since Bhakti and Eleanor Singh had vanished some wasps had taken up residence, building the beginnings of a paper nest half in the vestibule, half on the door lintel. The wasps flew in and out of the house like a winged, thrumming orchestra.

Inside, Billy went from room to room. Master bedroom, bed unmade. Master bathroom, light on, toilet seat down. He paused over the graffiti scrawled on the wall by the potty. *Here I sit, Muscles Flexin'.* . . . In the kitchen he looked in the refrigerator; amazing how much you could tell about people by looking in the fridge.

Nothing special in the fridge, a mix of old and new: The oranges were still good, but say good-bye to the avocado, the artichokes—going black. The milk sour. The kitchen in general, pretty clean.

Back in the living room the entertainment center with its large flat-screen dead. A wheelchair stood in the living room by the window, against the wall, a pair of crutches. Billy sighed; he was getting nothing from this.

He closed the front door on the way out, crushing the wasps' nest. And a few buzzed angrily about his head, but didn't pursue him.

Billy walked across the deserted street to the ruins of the Chen house, a tangle of charred timbers. Didn't look safe. He looked up and down the subdivision street. No cars in the driveways, no conversations, no kids playing, noise, or life. Even the TVs were turned off. Front doors open. Houses abandoned. The whole kit and caboodle packed up and vamoosed. A ghost town.

Everywhere he looked the lawns were still green as if everyone had left their automatic sprinkler systems on. As if to confirm this, every sprinkler head in every lawn in front of every house turned on at once. A rushing, cool sound. A kind of empty Eden. Moreover, animals seemed to have returned to suburbia. Cats slunk in and out of shadows. He spotted a badger looking at him from under a hedge. A family of mule deer tiptoed quietly among the landscaping and shrubbery. An armadillo trotted purposefully across the paved street on its little stumpy armored legs. Birds chirped brightly from every rain gutter and flower box.

Then with some sixth sense he looked up, his eyes drawn down the shimmering asphalt. A pack of wild dogs gathered at the end of the subdivision. Coming together for a moment, they sniffed the air and in a heartbeat spotted Billy standing alone by the ruins of the Chen house.

Billy leapt to his rental van; three seconds later the dogs jumped up on the driver's window, snarling and leaving foam. He popped the glove compartment and pulled out his piece. A long-barrel Ruger Blackhawk six-shooter. Then looked stupidly at it. Twelve dogs, six shells. Then what? Close the window and fumble with bullets? He put the gun back and waited for his heart to slow.

After a few moments, the dogs got the deer scent from the shrubs and bounded between two houses in a pack. The street now empty, Billy turned the key in the ignition and put the Dodge Caravan in drive. There were other places to look-see. The ghost town of subdivision suburbia slid by; he'd soaked his shirt with sweat. The air conditioner roared on high, cold air chilling his skin.

And to think he'd almost rented a convertible.

* * *

The R&D hangar at Escape Velocity was the same kind of desolate normal. On any weekend the security guards at the gate should have been on duty with their clipboards and visitor ID tags. Not today. Billy Shadow's Lattimore Aerospace identification let him go everywhere except Clem's personal computer. Every door, every locked filing cabinet, every restroom. The automatic video camera at the gate whirred on its base to capture his face as he slid his card into the security reader. After a moment the gate rolled open.

No employee cars in the lot. No ambitious souls working their Sunday instead of playing golf. Another card swipe, and the electric door opened to the large R&D hangar, welcoming him inside. A row of steel lockers stood by the door where the scientists and techs kept their lab coats. An inviting cube of translucent foundation bricks: the bathrooms with showers. Down at the far end a floor-to-ceiling thick plastic partition, and behind that the Aerogel vats, sealed clear canisters with large hoses going in and out. In front of the partition a chemistry lab, long tables, gas jets, lots of racks and vials. Very neat.

He checked Bhakti's locker and then Mrs. Bhakti's, with an extra set of crutches. Inside Chen's locker: deodorant, Tums, Kleenex, a white lab coat. A photo of daughter Lila was taped inside, clinging to Daddy's neck, both mugging for the camera.

All the workstations were empty, a half-dozen PC terminals on sleep mode. Billy picked one at random. It turned out to be Wen Chen's. The über-swipe Lattimore Aerospace ID card overrode Chen's password, and the desktop flashed on and started its boot-up protocol.

Better call the office while he was at it. Billy Shadow reached the Lattimore Aerospace corporate techno chief at home outside of Sioux Falls. Jasper was where he always was on a weekend: sitting in his basement playing Master of the Universe in his pajamas. And he picked up his phone with a question in his voice: "This is Jasper."

Billy Shadow's iPhone blocked caller ID. Better if his wireless communications didn't show his name, better if people didn't know who was calling until Billy's voice told them. Maybe Jasper could play with the code and jimmy the system, but he never said, "Hi, Billy," or "Yes, Mr. Shadow," or his Lakota name, "Hello, Mr. Howahkan." Just, "This is Jasper."

"It's me." Then . . . ,"Here's what I need, Jasper. I gather you've noticed the brain drain down here at Escape Velocity Aerogel R&D?"

"Yep, no activity for . . . a while. Everyone gone fishing?"

"Something like that. I want all the hard drive files and URLs locked down. Then transferred to a firewall stand-alone server. Do it from a throwaway laptop; don't use the office terminals. We need a total virus scan."

"So you think we've been compromised?"

"Not sure right now. But I'll need direct access from a remote. Access at specific times, so you'll have to plug in and pull the plug by hand. And stand by while I comb through everything on my throwaway terminal. Understand?"

"Uh-huh." Jasper understood. "It'll take me twenty minutes to get down to the office. Does Lattimore know we're going for the fire-sale protocol?"

"He will by the time you get there. I'm going to play around from here until you call me when you're ready to transfer."

The fire-sale protocol was simple: Take everything in every PC at the R&D facility and transfer it to a single stand-alone emergency hard drive/server. Dip in and out when necessary and only to expendable laptops in case there was some kind of virus. Lattimore was smart; he kept all the company's computer records in their various divisions and subdivisions, answering to different server farms that weren't connected, putting all his eggs in different baskets. And the power towers all lived in a lead-lined room at the lower levels of the Lattimore Building. Safely cocooned in case of an EMP blast, natural or man-made. In any case, even in the event of thermonuclear war, on Lattimore's farm one rotten apple in the barrel wasn't going to ruin the produce.

In the twenty minutes before Jasper's hard-drive, gut-sucking operation, Billy Shadow found out a couple of funny things about Wen Chen. The Chinaman was a conspiracy nut. And a manic researcher. One file, named WR 104, was Chen's granny-notion box, but instead of old buttons, fancy thread, and bits of lace, the file contained all the elements of Armageddon and the Apocalypse. The street-corner prophet in the sandwich board shouting, *"The end is near!"*

The file's name, the notorious WR 104, was the designation of a binary star 8,000 light-years from Earth. And yeah, Billy had to Google it. In cosmic terms close enough to count. The star itself emitted immense radiation; only its binary companion kept the thing from lighting up the heavens. What you saw was a spiral of dust as the two stars played tug-of-war. That spiral of dust was like a safety blanket.

What got some stargazers all hot and bothered was that the poles of this star were pointing at bull's-eye Earth. Should the thing go supernova, should a gamma ray erupt, the death gasp of this star would rip the skin off our planet. By the time you saw the flash you were toast, even if it took 8,000 light-years for the eruption to jump the distance. Fifty thousand Earth years of human evolution gone in seconds, everything on Earth burnt to inanimate carbon.

So all in all, WR 104 was a pretty good name for a doomsday crackpot file. And the stuff inside kept the promise of every scary eventuality. Like a hundred road signs pointing to an event-horizon singularity, where time and space, past and future danced one last jig before the universe expired.

Wen also had files on Gray Goo, the hair-on-fire theory that molecular nanotechnology would self-replicate, engulfing everything in existence. A file on various plagues in history: black plague, bubonic plague, crimson fever, yellow fever, influenza, ebola . . . Histories of the Mayan doomsday calendar and a biography of Edgar Cayce, along with links to his foundation in Virginia Beach. Naturally lots of stuff on Nostradamus and the Oracle at Delphi. And the requisite ancient alien pics of the "airport runways" at Nazca, Peru. Not to mention the incredible interlocking granite stones of Puma Punku in the Andes.

Then the WR 104 file went tech-heavy.

Billy Shadow felt a headache coming on.

A dozen Soviet reports on underwater UFOs—USOs, actually: unidentified submerged objects—some documents even in the original Russian. In English: the famous report on the sightings from the USS *FDR* aircraft carrier. Scanned photos and addresses of some of the sailors who had testified. Hell, even President Eisenhower was on board at the time.

The range of Chen's obsessions went on and on. Files on the Vril Society, Nazi time machines, gravity benders, and doomsday rays. Well, to be honest Billy had picked over some material on this in Lattimore's private library. But he'd never seen a map of Glacka, Poland, where some of the slave-labor research was accomplished. There was a massive sealed-up tomb of Third Reich experiments down there somewhere.

A file on Nikola Tesla, the incredible Serbian-American scientist. The inventor of alternating current and the man single-handedly responsible for bringing power to the masses without a coal-fired electric plant on every city block. A file from the Library of Congress: Tesla's epic battle with Edison. Edison didn't like the alternating current idea; it conflicted with his own investment in direct current. Massive lawsuits ensued.

Notes on Tesla's experiments in earthquake machines, and the dubious claim he could transmit electrical energy around the globe without power lines or wires. The address of the Tesla Museum in Belgrade, first Yugoslavia and later Serbia, where the great man's papers, trunks, and scientific instruments were taken by his nephew—not surprisingly a KGB agent—after WWII. A refusal for research from the Serbian curator of said museum in the new spirit of East-West cooperation. *Get lost, Chinee-American Data Man*. No tickee, no laundry.

A menu from Delmonico's Restaurant in New York City, where Tesla ate every day, and a bill for starched napkins. Tesla was famous for the stack of white napkins at his elbow that he used once and threw away. Billy had found a book on Tesla in Lattimore's library and was struck by that fact. A new nappy for every dab of the lips. Well, there in the file was the bill from Delmonico's scanned into Chen's PC. Hey, if you invented/discovered alternating current you were entitled to eat however you wanted.

Extensive files and a bibliography of articles on HAARP. Sounded like an Irish ale. Christ, if it wasn't right there, he'd have to look it up online. No, not an Irish beer: instead the High Frequency Active Auroral Research Program sponsored by the U.S. Air Force and the University of Alaska at Fairbanks. Located in a dozen remote Alaskan tundras or valleys were various kinds of antenna arrays. The program was one of a few facilities on Earth that could do what it did: study ionospheric physics and radio science.

Extracts from various PhD eggheads warning that bouncing radio waves off the ionosphere would stimulate intense ultra-low-frequency (ULF) electromagnetic anomalies, inducing local earthquakes. The real war plan for the U.S. Air Force. Beam it up; bounce it down in a certain place; rock the planet. Why invade Baghdad when you could break it from underneath? But who knows if it worked?

The next file Billy clicked on was a Reuters news report on the building blocks of life discovered within comet tails; the building blocks were captured by NASA spacecraft as they flew through the ionized trails. Microscopic particles of glycine, the most common of twenty amino acids; *Glory Be,* same glycine as on Earth, discovered in particles snatched from a flying ball of ice. Glycine, glycine everywhere—common as dirt and every place you looked. Bits of stuff just aching to burst into protein, and thence into life itself.

The latest NASA mission was to the comet named Wild 3 with the spacecraft probe called *Stardust*—mission accomplished, it had snagged some primordial dust in a fly-by a couple of million miles out in space. The glycine-laden particles were trapped in a dish lined with Aerogel. The design for the lining had been tested right in this lab. Instead of "light as air and hard as steel," Professors Chen and Bhakti had made the lining in micron perforations so it trapped things, like an air filter. More accurately, a space filter.

Then the comet probe trajectoried back to Mother Earth; after a zillion-mile journey through the heavens, the probe was due to fall on safe old Utah in some kind of reentry parachute canister any day now.

Okay, that was a legit file entry having something to do with Professor Chen's day job. *Lattimore Aerospace made the damn space filter.* Still, all this effort, so many documents, so many searches, so much material. And for what?

"Jesus," Billy said under his breath. "When did this Chinaman ever have time to do the laundry we were paying him for?"

The last file Billy clicked on showed a note from Clem Lattimore to his factotum in the R&D facility, scanned in from an original. A simple note scrawled in Lattimore's hand, and Billy recognized it. The note read:

From: Lattimore
To: Wen Chen, PhD
Research at will. Keep Files.
Clem

Ah, the whole basketcase was a legit research project. Okay, whatever the boss wanted.

Perfect Clem. He'd never mentioned it to Billy. Compartmentalize.

Now Jasper was texting: *At office/Alerted Howard Hughes.* The IT chief must have made it down to the office in twelve minutes, not twenty—an all-time record. Billy walked away from Wen Chen's terminal, leaving it on standby.

One last stop before he skedaddled off to find a motel room and a cheeseburger; time to talk to the authorities—if any.

The empty Texas town of Van Horn was ten or so miles from the R&D hangar and looked even emptier than the subdivision or the lab.

No moving cars. No people in the Motel 6s or IHOP.

Never mind a subdivision, a whole town disappears and nobody notices? Not the neighbors, not the Feds, not the fire department? The Van Horn FD truck bays were closed, lights off. Even on Christmas the Fire Department keeps a light on. Not even an Old Mrs. Hubbard in San Antonio calling out the state police because her children failed to call her like they did every Sunday from Van Horn?

Billy Shadow parked the van and got out.

The courthouse and the local constabulary were housed in the same building. The courthouse door yawned open, the long hall with the sheriff's office to one side, door open as well, light on. Silent . . . This time he brought a firearm, a Browning semi-auto in a holster. Middle of a Sunday there should have been a deputy on duty, the police band burbling in the background. Billy's footsteps echoed dryly off the Spanish floor tiles. *Tak . . . tak . . . tak . . . tak . . .*

Billy touched the strap from his holster but didn't unsnap it. The Van Horn sheriff's door opened to show him the office. A desk with papers strewn across: police reports, budget requests, a bill from an auto body shop, the Quartermaster catalog for cop gear. A half-eaten sandwich lay on a plate—American cheese, lettuce, mayo on white bread. The bread stale, the cheese curling at the edges.

Off the main office, an open door to a file room. Most of the file cabinet drawers were open, and their contents scattered over the floor. A paper shredder stood in one corner over a pile of twisted ribbons, a large manila folder crammed in its maw, only partly devoured, the machine jammed.

Housecleaning? Or some guilty person trying to destroy the files, but interrupted halfway through the job?

Next to the paper shredder sat a squat refrigerator marked EVIDENCE. Empty, except for some baggies with paint scrapes, hair samples, blood traces. The blood now black in coagulation, the dates some months ago. Useless.

The freezer drawer yielded something else. A quart-sized evidence bag, neatly labeled CHEN HOUSE/LILA and a recent date. What looked like . . . flesh? The contents were all mixed together—a dried prune with bits of charred wood. The metal earring gave it away. A blackened shriveled ear. A dangling earring. Human remains. From what Billy could tell there had been no effort to actually process the stuff. Send it out to a lab, analyze the DNA.

"Christ."

Billy would find a lab to analyze the mess of flesh and earring along the line. On the way out of the office, he paused over the desk again. The PC was still on. Whoever last sat at the terminal had been working the federal databases for missing persons, uploading an individual's profile and photo. A photo of the Chen girl, Lila Chen, sat on the desk. Billy pocketed it and then stopped.

A legal pad sat on the desk; the page was filled with doodles, as if the scribbler had been scrawling away while on the phone. Little caricatures of ants, some in red, some in black. A nice rendition of the girl, taken from the photo; but the scribbler had touched it up with a goatee.

In the lower corner, the round grinning face of a cat. Bright eyes, creepy grin. A squashed mosquito adorned the caricature, a blot of dried blood. It flew, it fed, it got squished on a cat doodle.

Nothing here.

Disgusted, Billy left the office and headed for the door without turning off the lights. Out in the long hall he stopped short. Goosebumps suddenly popped up along his arm; the hair on the back of his neck grew stiff. Quiet movement ten yards down by the courtroom doors caught his eye.

The lithe sway of an animal crept along a shadowed wall. A large animal—a cat of all things—slowly approached on its velvet paws. Then it paused, looking at him.

An ocelot, nearly four feet long. Fifty pounds of coiled muscle.

First dogs, now cats.

He unlatched the strap from his Browning, drew the weapon. In a flash of his own confusion the phrase *raining cats and dogs* scrolled across his brain. During medieval times animals often bedded down in thatched roofs; when it rained hard they slid off. In Van Horn, Texas, when the people vanished now it rained cats and dogs. . . . Where was this mental cabbage coming from?

Focus. What did he know about wild cats?

They were pretty rare; but since the hunting bans they were becoming a nuisance on the edges of suburbia. No natural predators. Mountain lions ripped people from bicycles in California. And ate children playing in their backyards.

In Texas? They still roamed the brushlands—but ocelots had been nearly hunted out of existence for their pelts. No two alike, the black, white, and golden camou-flage. Most of them never grew to more than three feet and weighed no more than thirty pounds. But now Billy was stuck in a bare hallway with four feet of feline lightning.

Damn, he didn't want to kill the thing, but he didn't want it coming any closer, either. And Billy knew that if he moved an inch the cat would pounce. He saw his hand shaking as he held the gun. That did it.

Animal brain to animal brain, the big cat saw his hes-itation. The ocelot's yellow eyes flashed at Billy for a moment, and then the body erupted in motion, a blur. In one bound it nearly closed the gap. Billy fired once, twice; the third time the cat was in the air claws outstretched. The muzzle flashes lanced toward the animal's chest. The brass cartridges pinged against the wall, and Billy found himself sitting on the floor, legs outstretched, the warm slide of the gun smoking over his thigh.

His heart slowed; ears rang from the fired shots. Long hall empty. No cat. The cartoon character Tweety Bird flit-ted into his mind. Little Tweety chirping with this silly speech impediment: "I tawt I taw a puddy tat! I did, I did taw a puddy tat!"

He felt a dab of wetness on his cheek. Touched it. Blood from a long scratch like a dueling scar. A claw wound. The cut began to bleed in earnest. What cat?

He found a kerchief in his back pocket and pressed it to his cheek, the wound beginning to throb. There was an emergency medical kit in the van. Time to find it. And a hospital as the notion of rabies touched his mind. No saliva. Still, mess of shots to be on the safe side. Swell.

He stumbled out to the rental van with half an eye scan-ning for big puddy tat. Nope, no ocelot. All the while know-ing in his primitive brain that whatever attacked wasn't what it looked like. For one thing, if he'd hit the thing, it'd be dead. If he'd missed it, ole Billy'd be dinner. And nei-ther had happened.

He couldn't have missed. Not that close.

A thought danced around the edges of memory: the old stories. So old and so powerful he felt reluctant to visualize the words. Actually just two words. Two words he didn't want to say. Crazy crackpot stuff from old times at the rez. He really didn't want to think these two words. They reminded him of the chanting with the beads and the animal claw necklaces and the angry braves stamping to the drums. The hopeless ghost dancers and the wish to set the world on fire, burn it down, build it up again.

The two words were *Skin Walker*.

Inside the van he turned on the roof light. He'd had the rental place remove the backseats so he could stow his gear: a sleeping bag and other necessities, a citizen's band radio, a police scanner. In one corner he had plugged a Koolatron Kargo Kooler travel refrigerator into one of the passenger cell phone jacks; the fridge held a small green Zero Degree tote, cool and ready to use. He stowed the evidence baggie of Lila Chen's burnt ear in it.

Next, the medical kit in a small foot locker. He peered into the med-kit's mirror and soaked the wound good with hydrogen peroxide. Then some antibiotic ointment, and finally slapped a pad of QuikClot emergency dressing across the slash. Great stuff; hold it in place for a couple of minutes, it was crazy glue for ripped skin, holes, and blood.

Now what about the three different types of antibiotics—two oral, one with a syringe? Doxy. Cipro. Amoxicillin. Decisions, decisions. His mind was getting fuzzy. Mild shock. No surprise there. Wasn't doxy for bronchitis? He couldn't remember now. Google it? Who said they had Wi-Fi out here anyway? The names on the labels were starting to blur together. He'd find the first hospital in Lubbock. First thing, right after a little nap. First thing—

His eyes fluttered closed; the van floor called him.

Almost at once, Billy dreamed the most curious dream.

The sun had gone down to dusk. The ocelot from the courthouse hallway circled the van, padding round and round and mewing into the dark. When he struggled to get a better look at it through the van windows, Billy's arms were too heavy to move, his legs like lead. Yet he didn't feel afraid. Or even angry at the animal. The wild thing had done what was natural. No real harm in that. The large cat put its paws up on the van hatchback and scratched the latch; it wanted in.

Then it *was* inside. The ocelot lay on the footlocker across from Billy.

Billy touched the cut on his cheek, the place where the cat cut him open. In his dream it felt completely healed. A thin little white scar. The ocelot flicked his tail and rubbed an ear with a front paw. Slowly the big cat underwent a subtle change; the tail curled away like smoke, the paw thickened. . . .

Grandma Sparrow stared at him.

She found a comfortable place on his footlocker and smoothed out the pleated skirt she always wore, her face a thousand smiles.

"Hey there, Tweety Bird," Grandma Sparrow teased him. "Did you see a very large animal in that police station? Did you?" A naughty smile played up and down her face. "You can tell Granny; she'll believe you."

He liked the idea that Granny knew what he'd seen, knew what had happened; that he could trust her to believe him no matter how crazy it sounded.

"Yes, Granny, I saw a big cat," he managed to tell her. "I shot it, but it flew away, leaving only a little scratch behind. A magical cat." Granny's wizened face warmed to him, sharp eyes narrowed. She understood.

"Yes, a good cat, not that bad cat they paint on walls. A very special cat, William Howahkan. You were one of us before, but now you're even more so. Those of us who can walk in the dark, and see with great eyes." The old woman was touching on the edges of old memory—those scary two words back in the hallway outside the sheriff's office. Those two words he couldn't say out loud, which he tried to put out of his mind. . . . The old grayhairs stamping their feet and the chanting and the drums. Granny Sparrow's wizened face shone at him. The old woman was trying to tell him a secret; now that he saw the puddy-tat and *it taw him.* . . .

That he was a Skin Walker too.

The legend said that in order to be one, to change into animals, to see into the night, to walk as a ghost among men, you had to kill one of your own: a child, a brother, a sister, mother, or father. An outcast act, by an outcast who would walk the world alone. Well, maybe the legend was wrong.

Or misunderstood.

Billy realized he wasn't afraid of how he may have changed. He touched the white scar on his cheek again. And it tingled back in a delicious sort of way. . . .

He opened his eyes—the quiet van on the empty streets of Van Horn came back strongly all around him. His cheek throbbed a little, no, not healed yet. But Billy woke with a sense of peace and contentment. In fact, a little sorry Granny Sparrow wasn't there to talk to him. He liked her sitting across from him on the footlocker. Like a guardian angel.

Outside the car, it felt like the middle of the night. The first thing he sensed was that he probably didn't have rabies. Never would. But he couldn't tell you how he knew. What did rabies feel like, anyway? Crazy paranoia? Thirst but fear of water? Hallucinations? Okay, well scratch that one. He took a deep gulp out of a water bottle. There were too many other things that seemed much more interesting. Important things in the dark; things he could sense even from inside the car. The night opened out to him with new eyes, his hearing exquisitely sensitive.

Across the street a family of bushy-tailed woodrats gathered by the storm drain where they made their home. Billy

Shadow could hear their faint breathing, even the pitter-pat of their little hearts. Their rodent tongues faintly squeaked at each other, simple precise thoughts: *search, food, look, now.*

A large scorpion clicked along the gutter by the curb toward the storm drain on crab-clawed feet, and the rats stopped hustling—pausing, frozen, their minds going back and forth: *Get him? Leave him? Get him? Leave him?* Four on one: *Get him!* They pounced. One of the rats snapped off the scorpion's tail stinger in the first bite. Billy heard it crack. Some quiet thrashing, then snapping sounds as the arachnid was pulled apart. Quiet returned.

Except for the whining of a mosquito a hundred yards into the darkness.

Billy felt stumped. No way was he going to find any answers in this place. Abandoned subdivision, vacant research hangar, ghost town . . . He was a blind man rattling a tin cup on an empty street, his look-see turning into a hopeless grope.

With all these dead ends, where next? Of course, have Lattimore or Jasper track Professor Bhakti Singh's company-issued credit card purchases—they could access those at least, see if the man swiped plastic anywhere. Provided Bhakti was alive. And the cards weren't stolen. Maybe Jasper had thought of that already.

But if nothing showed, then logically—what? Maybe instead of following footsteps he could blaze a new trail, strike a new path. Do what Escape Velocity Scientists Singh and Chen *would have done*. If they'd been here.

Precisely what, then? Billy knew the answer.

Scoot up to Utah to monitor the Wild 3 *Stardust* satellite recovery; check to see the Lattimore Aerogel dust collector performed to specifications. The two missing scientists would have been there come hell or high water, would have crawled over glass to be there when the military recovered their cosmic bird. Who knows, maybe Professor Bhakti Singh might yet make an appearance.

Clem would want someone present. Billy would need special permission for access to the military's touchdown area, as he wasn't one of the designers—provided he arrived on time. But was it worth a try? Or was Billy just plodding toward a mirage?

Yes, worth a try.

But before Billy could even compose an e-mail or phone home to Lattimore Aerospace, a text message from Boss Clem pinged through his BlackBerry: *Proceed W3 Dug Recov ID TBS. Confirm Frozen Smoke Unit Success.*

From twelve hundred miles away—almost as if reading his mind.

In plain English: *Proceed to the Dugway Proving Ground Wild 3 recovery site, clearance identification to be supplied. Confirm the Aerogel unit in the satellite performed to specifications.* So that answered that question. Him and the Boss were on the same wavelength.

Yet something nagged him: Grandma Sparrow's knowing eyes. On impulse he hit speed dial. A cricket's voice answered at the other end:

"Hello?"

"Hi, Grandma. It's me, Billy. Did I wake you?"

A pause, the tingle of delight in her voice. "Oh, silly man! You know I hardly sleep; I was just thinking about you. How's that cut on your cheek?" Billy's heart skipped a beat.

So she knew exactly what happened.

He suppressed the urge to laugh. *Good call, Grandma.* Did she have the Skin Walking thing too and just never told him? He could see her in the well-kept trailer back on the rez at the Formica kitchen table surrounded by faux wood paneling, talking on the old-fashioned princess wall phone. An American flag hung on the trailer wall over her headboard. A feathered Sioux war bonnet hung nearby. The real thing; Granny could have sold it to a museum and moved into a house, but she never did.

Photos of long-dead relatives faded in their frames, even his parents' wedding. The TV on but with the sound off. In the background late-night radio: "Coast to Coast" with George Noory. People across the country trying to explain things they'd seen in the sky or in the woods behind their house. Strange lights, black helicopters, time loss. Billy smiled.

"Nothing serious. I'm okay."

Her smile came right back at him, seeming to flow into his head. "So you have it now, don't you?"

Billy knew the answer even as he asked, "What's that, Grandma?"

"The Walking Way. The Skin Thing." She shifted the phone and turned the radio down, her voice serious. "You're going to really like it, Billy Howahkan."

That gave him pause.

"I hope so, Grandma. You've always had it, haven't you? The Walking Way. Can you tell me what you see?"

A low chuckle; again he knew the answer before she spoke it. He wasn't getting off that easy. "The question is, Billy, what do *you* see?"

He let the question hang. Then Grandma Sparrow said, "I have your old tin wolf whistle here. Thought about sending it overseas in case you wanted to call me, but was afraid the APO might lose it. You want me to send it to you now?"

Billy laughed. "I could have used it there, Grandma. But I'm glad you kept it. I'll let you know."

The radio came up a notch; the signal she was gonna say bye-bye. "You take care, Billy Howahkan. You call me when you need to."

The line went *click,* and he stared into the silence for a long time. What had she said? What do *you* see? He opened the small refrigerator and took out the Zero Degree tote. He stared at the evidence bag: a bit of hair, the mess of burnt flesh, an ear, an earring. He unzipped the freezer bag and sniffed the contents and inhaled deeply.

What *could* he see?

The biting odor of burnt wood, burnt plastic. More now . . . an image-scent formed in his mind, much clearer than actually seeing a person; something like traces of sweat—a residual aura. The impression in the air a person left behind on all they touched. Like a bloodhound on a trail, he inhaled again. The wispy aura seemed to sneak away into the night, leaving a trail. He cleared his mind and inhaled once more.

There was something else in Utah besides the Wild 3 touchdown that needed a look-see. The Chen girl was there. But *where* exactly?

The scent *changed*—now he smelled malted milks, and chocolate shakes. He shook his head—other scents much, much stronger. Hamburgers, cheeseburgers, and sounds even—the sharp crackle of fries boiling in a hot vat of oil, clean dishes coming out of a steaming dishwasher, the confused odor of people. Strangers. No. *Patrons* in a diner . . . *Hey Mickey, eggs easy no potatoes*—

A diner. Salt Lake City. Not that far from the Wild 3 recovery site. The bearded face of that Sikh scientist flitted into his mind: Professor Bhakti Singh, the lost employee from Escape Velocity. In Utah? Already? Or on his way? To witness the Wild 3 recovery—or for something else?

Smell the bag again, smell deeper. There was an aura from the ear and the earring, bright like a flame. . . . One of the girls *was alive*. And Professor Singh was chasing her; too late for his daughter, he was hunting Lila Chen.

Billy Shadow shoved the evidence bag back in the refrigerator, climbed into the driver's seat of the Dodge, turned the key, and slammed it in gear. No friggin' time to waste. He promised himself a hospital visit, first chance. Maybe Lubbock Hospital. Only 100 miles. Better safe than sorry, right? That's what they always said. Hell with them. Granny was right. No rabies, not now, not ever—

The last thing he saw driving out of town: that big mother-grabber of all ocelots; the good kitty that made him a seer, not the bad kitty that stole little girls. The ocelot padded silently out of the dark and calmly sat on the sidewalk by a streetlamp. The big cat picked up its paw and began to lick it, then groomed its soft ears, rubbing its paw-pads over its head. He slowed the car, powered down the window.

The big cat blinked at him with knowing eyes, then stared at him as if pleased. He hit the accelerator. "I get it. Next stop, Utah. I'm on my way."

11

In the Event of an Emergency

Lattimore sat at a desk in the lead-lined subbasement of the Aerospace building in Sioux Falls and worked a terminal. Jasper the IT chief worked his own console: one of those double screens where the mouse could run from one to the other. The men had six screens they could use if necessary; a troop of stand-alone servers and power towers stood at attention for fifty feet on three sides. The lighting in the safe room was ambient, now nighttime, a dusky gray; when dawn came the lights in the ceiling would brighten—this way anyone spending long periods deep underground could feel the world outside.

Lattimore had received one text message from Billy Shadow:

Van Horn Ghost Town. R&D Abandoned, ordered new security at lab gates. Arrange Clearance ID Wild 3

*touchdown. Look-see Surviving Chen Girl. All roads lead
to Utah.*

Ghost town . . . now confirmed. Wen Chen, Bhakti
Singh, the whole Aerogel research team *poof!* Gone. Not
to mention the locals, and local law enforcement missing
in action—not good. For a moment Lattimore played with
the idea of alerting some bureaucratic federal alphabet
agency: The FBI? The Missing Persons' Bureau? And then
just as quickly shoved it aside. What would he tell them?
I've lost an R&D Unit at Escape Velocity? Next thing the
Wall Street Journal picks it up and Lattimore Industries'
stock price tanks.

Right now, Lattimore owned a brief moment to nail
down things on his own; maybe a week at most.

Better to let Billy Shadow run down leads in the outside
world; his Number Two was a one-man early warning system. Billy would know when to send up a flare.

And better to let his corporate IT chief explore every
digital back alley in cyberspace. From where Lattimore sat,
the latter was already deep in the process. Eyes glued to
his screens, Jasper didn't make eye contact but remarked,
"You're taking this awfully calmly, Clem."

"Well, it feels too early to panic," Lattimore replied quietly. "We don't know what we don't know." He paused in
silence for a moment. "So let's find out something."

Jasper clicked a few keys on the keyboard, and chuckled.
"True, why panic now? We have all Sunday afternoon."

Jasper used one side of the large workstation, his half of
the screens, and quietly ran a diagnostic on the fire-
walled cache, RAM, and hard drives of the R&D hangar
from his throwaway laptop. This could take some time; a
sophisticated virus lay in wait, kept its head down.

Jasper knew the deal. Most complex enterprises had

abandoned any notion of true data security for some time. Hookworms riddled their bowels, latent psychoses their higher brain functions. If Department of Homeland Security mysteriously lost a few hundred million dollars every month, well—that was just the cost of doing business. American Express treated their computer fraud losses as a company secret. But Lattimore Industries deserved better. Clem Lattimore always wanted better.

The infinite combinations of 0-1-0-1-1-0 a game of hide-and-seek, long ago surrendered to the keystroke demon. And so, Jasper wasn't having much initial luck.

It didn't really seem to trouble him, though; programmers are naturally patient men. Jasper glanced at his boss through a pair of thick granny glasses, then stroked a graying goatee. *No update, Boss, sorry. So far, nada.*

For his part Lattimore had been clicking through Chen's research files. Now he dwelled on photos of the massive stone blocks of Puma Punku—Puma Mountain, high in the Bolivian Andes.

Massive in size, made of the densest granite, cut and shaped to millimeter tolerance. They fit together like pieces from a Lego set, that tight, that close. The Puma Punku walls once rose fifty feet on the top of a mountain. These granite blocks were the hardest on Earth, and nothing but diamond-tipped tools could cut the edges and grooves. Did men wearing antelope skin and feathered headdress use diamond-tipped drills and diamond-dust wet saws eight thousand years ago? The Andean stones were another of those quirky anomalies, like the Piri Reis map. Appearing like magic in the wrong time and place and carved by invisible hands.

A queer artifact or a secret message?

Maybe the artifact *was* the message.

Not meant to stand for all eternity but still, stand a long, long time—telling the story of itself in fallen ruin.

Only this wasn't one of those drowsy summer afternoons in Bucks County with cicadas buzzing in the trees—this afternoon lasted ten thousand years, an expanse hard to see from our ant-view of the cosmos. *"Consider the lilies of the field, how they grow; they neither toil nor spin, yet I tell you, even Solomon in all his glory was not arrayed like one of these."*

And then it struck Lattimore in a flash of possibility that once seen he could never shake. The lilies of the field; Earth that lush blue planet, just one lily—while thousands of other earths flowered across the galaxy. *Perhaps* the visitors who helped Man carve those stones were more like farmers, sowing and reaping; coming once or twice a cosmic season. Like herdsmen who tended their cattle in the fields, letting them graze the long summer months before gathering them in for the winter. Herdsmen of the stars . . .

Jasper cleared his throat, bringing Lattimore back to the lead-lined subbasement. The man stared into his monitor, his interest suddenly aroused.

"I may have found something." Jasper sat back in his chair, stroking that goatee again.

"Diagnostic or Tassology?"

"Tassology."

Like many keystroke masters, Jasper could run more than one application at once. He'd run a half-dozen diagnostic programs looking for early signs of hard-drive influenza and at the same time run his own keyword bot grabber. A program much like the infamous Web Bot project, running a massive search engine across the universe of the Internet with an army of spiders, the little wanderers who flew across the Internet at the speed of light, analyzing words, patterns of words, confluences of thoughts and ideas. The Web Bot engineers claimed to have predicted 9/11. Hurricane Katrina.

Jasper had created his own prophetic data-mining search engine, an artificial Nostradamus—part Ouija board, part *I Ching*—and named it Tassology, after the practice and craft of reading tea leaves. Darting back and forth between Lattimore Escape Velocity data, company files, and roving across the greater www, Tassology had found something.

One of Wen Chen's subfiles was called Skeeterbug. The contents of the subfile Skeeterbug were an innocuous bundle of documents from the Centers for Disease Control in Atlanta. Press releases, obscure projects under consideration, expense reports from civil servants with their names blacked out for security reasons; at first glance mere detritus, a file of Big Government minutiae. But on one CDC document Chen had collected, the word *Skeeterbug* was scrawled in pencil on the minutes of an operational meeting relating to organizational funding.

So that's what Tassology chose to pluck out of cyberspace. An otherwise obscure moment in the history of CDC bureaucracy which someone inside the CDC had released onto the Internet without comment. And slavish Tassology expanded its search ever outward in the general realm of "unknown entity."

Skeeterbug.

"What the hell is that?" Lattimore leaned over Jasper's

shoulder to stare at the curious graphic on one of the man's screens.

"They call it Skeeterbug."

"Who calls it?"

Jasper didn't answer, but pointed to the hologram of a mosquito; partly manufactured was the easiest way of looking at it.

A cyborg/insect hybrid. *An enhanced, flying, stinging bug.*

Same size as a mosquito but reengineered from the inside out. Special modifications: molecular-reinforced polymer-based wings, a reinforced stinger, and enhanced eyes. Living plastic. The brain wasn't any bigger than a mosquito's brain, but this was no nitwit. Even if the brain was the size of a period.

A close-up of the insect's head showed some drastic changes. No longer merely a receptor for chemical traces or infrared imaging which leads the bug to a tasty prospect, the brain had been altered. A nexus of molecular synapses, lit up like tiny stars. Enhanced cognizance.

"They? Who are they?" Jasper cleared his throat. "A USAF subcontractor. Real small outfit; no name, just a designation: πr^2, with links to a disease-control annex office in Ohio. They do something in the field of animal husbandry, or reproduction." Jasper shrugged in frustration. "Anyhow, that's who made Skeeterbug."

"πr^2, Pi R Squared," Lattimore repeated. "They name the place after a formula. How to determine the area of a circle . . . Catchy."

After a moment Lattimore posed a question, though he already sensed the answer. "So why make it? If this was your baby, what would you do with it?"

Jasper took off his granny glasses and polished them for a moment.

"If it was me?" The IT chief smiled. "Me, with an unlimited cache of memory and processing power, say a tiny government contractor that can bill the DOD so small they stay under the radar, say fifty or sixty million dollars, buried in some three-thousand-page appropriations bill . . ." He put his glasses back on. "I'd use it as a DNA/biological retrieval and catalogue system. Everybody gets bit by a mosquito once in a while. Heck, this little bugger is probably immune to DDT."

Lattimore got up from his chair and stared out across the standing stones, the megaliths of his servers and power towers. Then felt a psychosomatic itch that wasn't really there. He scratched it anyway.

"But it could go both ways, wouldn't it? The damn bug could infect everyone in the world. Pick your disease. Pass it around."

Jasper snorted.

"Why not? Suddenly everybody gets an itch they wanna scratch."

B ack east, not Fairfield—this time Middletown, CT. A thousand miles and a thousand different problems away.

Elcanor was in the nuthouse. Temporarily committed by her sister in the absence of her husband; now awaiting evaluation at Connecticut Valley Hospital in Middletown. An institution on the National Register of Historic Places—no surprise really since the place was first built in 1867.

A daunting six hundred acres with nearly eighty brick and brownstone buildings in styles ranging from Second Empire to Queen Anne and even Jacobean and Colonial Revival. Shew Hall, the original hospital, merely served as the administrative building. The unimposing Stanley Hall, where they used to keep the criminally insane, was not so impressive—just a big ugly rectangle, vacant. Not where they stuck anybody anymore, thank God.

But when it came to putting a relative in a state facility,

if you couldn't afford a private rest home, how much choice did you really have? Not much. Thank heaven conditions had improved a lot since the nineteenth-century nightmare of loony bins. Instead of padded rooms, restraints, and invasive cranial surgery, time marched on; the 1940s brought the practice of electroshock, and finally toward the end of the twentieth century, care of the crazy had graduated to colored pills, a kind of chemical lobotomy. Less fuss, less muss.

The mental hospital still used a few of the old-fashioned methods, of course, but only in the worst cases, which the staff called the Ravers. And Eleanor didn't count as one of those. Moreover Eleanor Singh née Whitcomb wasn't criminally anything, just very confused; and she showed no inclination to perform another auto-abortion. Sometimes lucid, sometimes not. So the authorities prescribed a low dose of Lithium and not Risperdal or any of the other brain-bangers.

Eleanor occupied a private room in a nice colonial, her new home. No bed restraints, but the door did lock from the outside. She could open the screen windows about eight inches but not crawl outside. And the place cost $700 a day. A nice hotel might have done the same job. And now the bills were going to the Human Resources Department of Lattimore Industries for claims and payment.

Eleanor stared out the window of her room at the night-time sky. She'd taken her Lithium from the little paper cup, but for some reason it had almost no effect on her. Like taking sugar pills: a touch of sweetness, then gone. Clouds veiled the moon. As she stared at the night sky the clouds seemed to go away—the moon shining into her room.

Even with her room lights off she could clearly see the vase with dried bulrushes on the dresser. Her clothes hanging in an open closet like limp ghosts. She gazed upward; a band of stenciling ran around the upper portion of the walls: bright tulips in blue and pink and yellow like the

"Dance of the Flowers" in *Fantasia*. But as she stared harder in the dark at the stenciled band along the walls, the flowers seemed to change.

Now the flowers were red ants, red ants marching one by one *hurrah*. She turned her eyes away in dismay—no, she didn't like the red ants marching along the wall.

What else was there to look at?

TV held little or no attraction. The cable service showed only a prescreened choice of shows: Animal Planet without the wild stuff, mostly *Puppy Olympics, Antiques Roadshow, Say Yes to the Dress*—but nothing suspenseful, nothing violent; so no History Channel, no *UFO Hunters* or *Barbarians*. And generally few news programs. Still she left it droning in the background. It reminded her of Bhakti, how they'd keep the TV on at night in their bedroom like a kind of lullaby.

But something different was happening on the TV now.

On the cable shows—CNN, Fox, MSNBC—the service kept flipping back and forth, *blip-blip-blip!* The top stories of the day: blizzards and floods; soldiers in firefights; huge street protests; bloated politicians pompously talking; the newscasters' faces concerned, incredulous, or smug—just a big mishmash.

What held the confusing flickering clips together was the red warning ticker sliding along each cable channel. As though it didn't matter what the actual stories were, when you could read the underlying narrative scrolling along at the bottom of the screen in high crisis red, punctuated by annoying beep-tones. And this she could see quite clearly:

This is a test. This station is conducting a test of the Emergency Braincast System. This is only a test. The federal, state, and local authorities have developed this system to keep you informed in the event of an emergency. If this had been an actual

emergency, this system transmits official informa-
tion, news, or instructions. This concludes this test
of the Emergency Braincast System.

Braincast? Did she really read that word? That wasn't what the authorities called it these days; they called it Emergency Alert System or words to that effect.

The cable service flickered, abandoned the news, and settled on the Discovery Channel; the segment was on the meadow spittle bug, *Philaenus spumarius*—king of the meadow jumpers, leaping away at the first sign of a predator, leaving a slime of excrescence behind. Some entomologist was blatting on about how this clever insect may have developed this ability to escape predatory males after long bouts of reproductive sex.

Eleanor felt a twinge in her leg—a kind of numbing as if she was about to lose the use of it again. Oddly, or not so oddly, her bouts with Bhakti hadn't been that "long"—just enough to cripple her. Maybe she should have jumped up afterward—and this almost made her laugh. She could even hear Bhakti's smiling voice chasing her: "Going so soon?"

Reluctantly, her eyes strayed to the stenciled border around her room. This time the ants were gone. In their place little black stick figures marched one by one *hurrah*. Little human stick figures. And she was immediately reminded of Sherlock Holmes and "The Adventure of the Dancing Men":

But these men were moving, walking and jumping and dancing along the border of the wall. She shut her eyes to push the little silently moving figures away and tried to remember what the story was about. A secret code, a cypher written to a woman who had tried to escape her sordid past—that's all she could remember. Still, she couldn't tear her eyes away from those little dancing figures. They seemed to mock her like glib little ninnies.

Her leg tingled again and she rubbed it; then got up from bed to move around, terrified she might not be able to walk again. That this new ability would be snatched from her. The hospital room's wood floor was cold on her bare feet, and she shuffled over to the oval hook rug. Better there. Not so clammy. *I got better when I got sick,* she murmured to herself. I got better when—

When Janet vanished. She came and my leg died; she went away and my leg came back. What a horrible, horrible thought. And then she was back in their Van Horn house standing at the window as Bhakti stumbled into the living room. She knew then—yes, even then. An electric mother/daughter psychic hotline had told her Janet was gone for good, grabbed at the railroad tracks—but she made Bhakti look anyway, texting him confused ramblings, on the slim hope—

Sure, he'd be all right, keep it together, but Chen would crack. The best she could do, because another force was ripping her apart, a much stronger force that came out of nowhere.

Something—some *thing*—had dragged her from the wheelchair. Not just the knowledge that her baby was gone—that was a black abyss in her body—but an outside force like stiff wires jammed up her anus and into her spine, forcing her to rise.

Bhakti came and went, came and went.

She stared at the flames in the house across the street.

The flames died and Bhakti went to bed.

That's when she knew the *other women* were leaving—all the women on their street getting ready to get in their cars and quietly drive off. The hot wires made her want to go with them. She found her car keys, took some money, went to the garage. The garage door was even open like some kind of invitation. Yes, go!

The line of cars from the Van Horn subdivision rolled along Interstate 20 east, then headed north toward Oklahoma and Interstate 44 like a convoy. The first lap of the ladies' chicken run over seven hundred miles—and it required the convoy stop for gas three times. Three times in Texas—Odessa, Abilene, and then finally Wichita Falls on the Oklahoma border. Along the way two of the cars broke down—one overheated, the other blew an engine—but it didn't matter.

At the first sign of car trouble, the car's flashers lit up; the failing car was left by the roadside, and everyone packed in together. Twelve hours from their start in Texas, the remaining vehicles rolled into Tulsa, Oklahoma, about four in the afternoon. Mrs. Biedermeier and Mrs. Stanton had squeezed into Eleanor's Toyota Prius two hundred miles ago, neither of their cars making it past Wichita Falls.

The women sat silently the whole way, neither looking out the window nor speaking; the blousy Mrs. Biedermeier plopped in the back like a sack of potatoes, the rigid Mrs. Stanton in the front passenger's seat sitting with her hands folded in her lap. Like Eleanor, the women had left the subdivision in whatever they were wearing at the time. In Mrs. Biedermeier's case a fawn-colored plush leisure suit and a fake alligator fanny pack. In Mrs. Stanton's case her Vermont Country Store blue seersucker patio dress, a small lamé silver purse with a wrist strap, and a gold cross at her neck. Silence consumed the car, not even the radio turned on.

What was there to talk about?

What would Mrs. Biedermeier say? *I feel the uncontrollable urge to take a drive. How about you?*

And Mrs. Stanton? *A voice in my head is telling me to go to Tulsa. Do you hear it too?*

Janet? *My child's dead. I can walk again. Too bad about the Chens, don't you think?*

Maybe the only question worth asking was, *Why us?*

Mrs. Stanton clutched the little golden cross, pressing it hard between her thumb and finger, thinking, *I never wanted to come to Van Horn after NASA. We never should have left Houston.* Mrs. Biedermeier petted her fake alligator fanny pack. *It's what they did in the hangar, what Chen and Bhakti made them do. . . .* Fragments of thought: because our husbands meddled in things no man should touch. Because we strayed. Because we sinned. And each woman thinking the same thought, the same mantra: *We're on the way. We're coming. . . .*

The convoy slowed to a crawl under the huge statue of the Tulsa Golden Driller. Seventy-three feet of roughneck like Paul Bunyan, the Tulsa Golden Driller stood with his hand on a life-size drilling rig, staring out across the knobbly landscape. The yellow-painted roughneck sported advertisements like a NASCAR driver, his T-shirt a pitch for Tulsa's rock station, KMOD, also a Coca-Cola ad. His huge belt buckle read BUILT *FORD* TOUGH.

The convoy kept crawling, finally into a Super 8 Motel near the Tulsa fairgrounds, where the cars ground to a quiet halt in the parking lot. Under an overcast sky Mrs. Stanton unlatched the passenger door and stepped out of the car, padding toward the reception door in her blue seersucker patio dress and slip-on Mary Janes as though in a trance. She clutched her little silver purse in one hand, the other gripping the cross at her neck.

A leisurely ten minutes later she had rented a place for the women of Van Horn to rest for a couple of hours. Mrs. Stanton unlocked the motel room door; the five ladies from Van Horn filed in dutifully behind her. Immediately they lined up at the bathroom like women all over the world waiting their turn for the toilet stall. And when each of them had gone and went, they spread silently about the room.

The two others from the subdivision sat in matching chairs; for a few moments Eleanor couldn't remember their names—they lived several houses down. One was a mousy woman of about thirty: Mrs. Perkins? The other at least seventy with bluing in her hair. Mrs. Quaid. Widow.

Mrs. Stanton silently switched on the TV and sat in front of it on the floor with her back to the double bed. No one spoke; no one offered to go for sodas or snacks or ice. Just sat and stared at the numbing television; a red banner was scrolling along the bottom of the picture: *This is a test. . . .*

Eleanor didn't wonder or question why they had come. She could see the road ahead in her mind. Ohio, a little north of Cincinnati. Hillsboro: a country town surrounded by fields and farms. And after a few hours of staring at the red scroll at the bottom of the screen, she rose silently from the bed. The others rose too. They all felt the need to leave. They lined up once more in front of the bathroom, as if all thinking the same thing, what you say to your kids: *Did you go before we left?*

The three cars rolled out of the Motel 8 parking lot like they'd never been there. Twenty miles from Tulsa a tune came into Eleanor's mind and she began to hum it. After a few stanzas she remembered the words. A ditty they taught to kids in kindergarten; a little song to help them learn anatomy over the melody of a spiritual, "Dem Bones."

"Ezekiel connected dem dry bones. Ezekiel connected dem dry bones—"

Then, after a few bars, Mrs. Stanton picked it up, singing along: *"Your toe bone connected to your foot bone, your foot bone connected to your ankle bone—"*

And finally in the back, Mrs. Biedermeier: *"Your ankle*

bone connected to your leg bone, your leg bone connected to your knee bone!"

They could almost hear the other two women singing in the cars behind as they rolled down the highway. The mousy Mrs. Perkins in her Audi going, *"Your knee bone connected to your thigh bone. Your thigh bone connected to your hip bone—"* And even blue-haired Widow Quaid pounding it out on the steering wheel of her Cadillac: *"Your shoulder bone connected to your neck bone, Your neck bone connected to your head bone, I hear the word of the Lord!"*

All together now, the women in the cars rolled along as dusk drew down over Oklahoma, headlights peering into the dark, singing verse after verse:

> *Disconnect dem bones, dem dry bones.*
> *Disconnect dem bones, dem dry bones.*
> *I hear the word of the Lord!*

12

❧

The Girl by the Stairs

Guy and Lauren Poole sat together on the large couch in the den. The first sunny day in a month; outside, sunshine dappled the trees, a breeze fluttering the leaves bright green then dark as they twisted on the branches. Lauren engrossed in a book, nose in a thick biography of Lord Byron liberally doused with his quotes: *"For pleasures past I do not grieve, nor perils gathering near; My greatest grief is that I leave nothing that claims a tear."* She'd been on and off it for years.

Corky and Peaches tried to crawl up close to Mom and Dad, the long-legged greyhounds awkwardly searching for a comfy spot, first stepping on Lauren's thigh muscle, then into Guy's groin, making him go *woof!* and Lauren laugh. The two adults waited patiently for the "kids" to settle down. Finally, Corky wedged himself under Lauren's elbow. And Peaches put her head in Guy's lap with her rump on the armrest.

"I don't think that's very comfy, Peaches," Guy told her. For one thing she was resting her head directly on the sheaf of papers on Daddy's knees. A dozen or so bills from Eleanor's short stay at the Bridgeport Hospital, bounced back from Lattimore Human Resources, an undignified mess. A cotton swab here, an intravenous tube there—eight thousand dollars.

He'd have to get on the phone with the Bridgeport billing department—and soon. At least Bhakti had promised to call the bureaucracy too. Yet so far no one at the Sioux Falls office had reached the damn Sikh in person. The entire owing-money thing felt so cheap. If he kept a coffee can stuffed with 50K cash in the garage like a petty corrupt official, Guy wouldn't have cared. Here, take it.

Not to mention, he wasn't getting anywhere on the new job front either. If Guy heard the word *overqualified* one more time— They might as well say "over-the-hill," or "too expensive." Easier just to let Peaches sit half on his lap while he stared at the pretty dappled tree leaves in the backyard.

One crab apple tree grew fairly close to the house, whose branches sometimes touched the French doors when the wind blew. On the backside of the trunk Guy suddenly spied a wisp of cloth, then a little hand curling around the tree. His heart skipped a beat. Yeah, he saw it clearly enough: the young lady from the stairs, the girl standing on the curb in the pouring rain outside the Walgreens entrance. She shyly peeked at him from around the trunk of the crab apple, her eyes glistening with the beginnings of a cautious smile.

"Lauren," Guy whispered, afraid he would startle the dogs, his wife, or spook the vision of the girl outside. "Lauren . . . honey . . . do you see what I see?"

Lauren looked up casually from her book, through the glass French doors, right at the trunk of the crab apple tree. A woman of measured temperament, not easily ruffled, she made absolutely no move on the couch besides raising her eyes. She didn't even close the book.

Then just as quietly asked her husband, "Same as before?"

Guy replied with the barest grunt, "Uh-huh."

Corky sensed them both, opened his eyes, and picked up his ears. Peaches didn't move her head off the nice warm crunched papers, instead wrinkled her nose. The little lady at the tree shifted, showing half her body, and the sound of laughter came into the den. Same striped dress with puffed sleeves, same apron with pockets, a youngster right off a page of Lewis Carroll; she grinned brightly as though amused at the ungainly pile of people and dogs on the couch.

"Hold the kids," Lauren told him. "I'm going outside." Gingerly and with slow, deliberate movements she closed the book, put it on the end table, and rose from her place on the couch. Lauren glided to the French doors, unlatched them quietly, and opened them wide. The girl stepped from behind the tree and stood coyly, a secret smile on her face.

"Hi, there," Lauren said. "What's your name?"

The corners of the girl's mouth turned down, her eyes sparkling hard.

"Are you lost?"

The little figure shook her head no, then put her thumb to her mouth as though thinking about biting a fingernail.

"Do you live near here?"

This time the girl nodded shyly: *yes*.

"Don't you want us to call your mommy? She must be worried about you." Lauren took a step onto the patio flagstones. Another step and she'd be within reach. The woman knelt down so as to be level with the sparkling precious eyes. "Don't you want to tell me your name? My name is Lauren. Are you hungry? I have cookies."

At the word *cookies* both Corky and Peaches lifted their heads.

"Come on." Lauren held her hand out. "Let's go in the house—"

The sprat bolted, scampering right past Lauren, through the French doors, through the den, the kitchen, and into the Keeping Room. They heard the Keeping Room door swing open and bang shut. Corky and Peaches came unglued from the couch, and Guy leapt to his feet. "Yowza!"

Lauren, Guy, Corky, and Peaches, in that order, stumbled through the den door to the kitchen, tripping over themselves. "Whoa," Lauren warned them with an open hand. "Guy, this won't do. Hold them, please."

"I am," he replied tersely, fumbling with their collars, making cooing sounds in their ears. Then he crouched, clasping each dog around the chest with each arm. "Okay, go ahead."

Lauren crossed the kitchen and silently put her hand on the doorknob to the Keeping Room. She turned it slowly, and the door opened inward. Guy needn't have bothered throttling the dogs at all. The door yawned open, and neither Corky nor Peaches made the slightest effort to dash inside. Lauren, cool as a cucumber, just stood there and stared.

After a few moments, she quietly whispered, "Guy . . . honey . . . do you see what I see?" Guy couldn't believe Lauren was so rational.

It was the Keeping Room, all right. But *not* the Keeping Room.

Just as quietly Guy asked, "Do you think this will get us on *America's Most Haunted*?"

The Keeping Room, but not the Keeping Room. For one thing, inside the room it was night. While at their backs— the den, the French doors, the backyard—bright daylight shone through the dappled crab apple tree. They could see through the old parlor right to the front of the house, right out the front windows.

Dark outside. Nighttime.

Oil lamps burned on the fireplace mantelpiece. A well-tended fire threw more light and heat; an iron kettle on the hob sent out whiffs of steam. A rocking chair sat with an afghan over it; a doll with glass eyes lay on the floor. Yes, the Keeping Room—a hundred and fifty years ago.

"Guy, whatever you do, don't let that door close."

"You're not going in there!"

"Honey, find something to wedge the door."

"Lauren, did you hear what I said? You're not going in there."

"Alone, *no,* of course not. You're coming with me."

Guy rose to his feet, letting go of the dogs, his mouth opening and closing like a guppy. The two dogs seriously sniffed the Keeping Room door frame—but made no rush to pass through. Peaches sneezed as if snuffing some old dust. The dogs circled back behind Guy, wagging their tails a bit, and lay down, content to let the folks handle it for now.

"Want me to take the door off the hinges? That way *nobody* can close it."

Lauren gave him a withering stare. "Oh, forget it." She put her hand through the threshold. Despite their bickering, neither Guy nor Lauren felt particularly frightened. There didn't seem anything bad or evil about the vision. And they could feel the warmth of the fire wafting into the kitchen. More like a pleasant memory than some kind of nightmare. Guy crept past the entrance of the old room after his wife; Corky and Peaches got up to follow. Now they were all inside.

Resigned and a touch fatalistic, Guy remarked, "Well, if the door closes behind us and we're stuck in the nineteenth century I'll get a job with Junius Morgan, J. P.'s dad—dry goods in Hartford, I think. I could give him some good stock tips—railroads, fur, oil—work my way up, get to know J. P., the son. But I think we'd have to move to Boston or Britain eventually."

Lauren, already a couple steps inside, shook her head in amusement. "Oh, shush!" Guy and the dogs followed cautiously, almost on tiptoe. It felt like being in the diorama display of a museum. There were new pieces of furniture: a small horsehair couch, a lovely inlaid Pembroke table with a music box. Nearby, a bare chessboard waited for a game.

A fixture hung from the center of the room, a brass double-lantern, just low enough that you might bang your head on it; the large green-shaded storm lanterns burning . . . whale oil? Isn't that what they used? The wainscoting along the walls was varnished, giving off a reddish glow; the wood paneling rose to a white plaster ceiling. The whole effect, cozy—not troubling. But thin, like weak tea.

In one corner a grandfather clock's pendulum went *tock-tock-tock. . . .* The time read sixteen minutes to nine. As they stood there looking about them, the minute hand clicked forward a minute and the grandfather clock chimed the three-quarter hour. The classic, sober chimes of Westminster, full of portent. Guy and Lauren looked at each other—a moment of doubt.

A Parcheesi board lay on the floor by the fire, on a bright braided throw rug next to a pair of large leather pillows, elbow-dented where people reclined on them to play. The Parcheesi board was newish—painted on a square of wood, yellow and blue and red, the pieces left in mid-game.

On the flat ledge of the hob by the iron kettle sat a sterling toast rack with a single browned slice of white bread. Crumbs were scattered across the small ledge, and across a butter knife. The remains of a pat of butter melted to almost nothing lay on a little dish. Play Parcheesi; eat buttered toast. Sounded like fun. Corky and Peaches sniffed the piece of bread, the pat of butter. Usually the two greyhounds would have gone for it in a heartbeat—but something didn't smell quite right.

"Maybe they miss the jam," Guy said. "You always give them jam."

Suddenly a comic line popped into Lauren's head, and she said to Guy, "The rule is, jam tomorrow and jam yesterday—but never jam today." The silly words from *Alice Through the Looking Glass*.

A splash of laughter from above made Lauren gasp; her hand flew to her mouth. Guy and the dogs snapped their eyes to the stairs. The little girl again, staring at them through the stairway spindles; she smiled coyly and ran *clap-clap-clap* toward the upper part of the house.

Guy and Lauren slowly mounted the stairs, keeping a safe and cautious distance. As he passed the front door and front windows, Guy glanced out into the street. Dark nighttime through the glass; gas lamps lit cobblestones in a yellowish glow. From the full green leaves in the trees he could tell it was about the same time of the year as now—June—and through the open windows he heard the patter of raindrops and felt the cool air of a chilly summer evening.

Their bedroom door stood open, lamplight pouring into the darkened hallway. Lauren crept to the bar of light on the landing and peeked inside. "Guy, you gotta look at this." Quiet as a mouse, he leaned over her shoulder. Their bedroom looked almost the same, the furniture basically in the same place: older chairs where their new chairs sat, same compact writing desk, bed in the same place. Only this bed was a four-poster draped in fine muslin. Of course, there were no screens in the cottage—just muslin, old-fashioned mosquito netting.

Their little girl sat on the quilt covering the mattress

playing with two dolls: a Marie Antoinette with high poofy white hair in the curious style called Macaroni and a dour black-clad citoyen of the Revolution. The little girl was trying to make the handsome gentleman kiss his mistress's hand.

A woman sat writing at the compact writing desk, dipping pen into ink and quietly scratching into a diary by the light of an oil lamp. The writing desk was newer, with a tilted, framed, inset leather blotter, ball-and-claw legs. The woman—the little girl's mother?—finished her passage, blotted the ink, and closed the diary, slipping it into a drawer on the side of the box-like cabinet. She stared at her daughter on the bed.

The girl's dolly game had changed. The stern citoyen was making a chopping motion with his stiff hand, and the girl's high voice piped out: "I, Saint-Just, by Order of the Committee, condemn you, Marie Antoinette—" The doll's hand came down, and Marie's head fell off.

"Now you've done it," the woman at the desk said. "If the Committee for Public Safety has decided who goes to Madame Defarge and the guillotine, I think that means it's time for cake." What struck Guy was how closely the lady at the writing desk resembled Lauren. Must be Auntie Whitcomb's great-great-grandmother. And the little girl—who? Auntie W's great-grandmama? Guy's head got tangled in the branches of the family tree. Too hard to sort out even when he wasn't peering through a window in time.

The woman at the desk looked sharply at Guy and Lauren peeking around the door frame, frowned a little, and asked, "What are you doing here?"

The two voyeurs froze, like deer on a road. Was she talking to them?

"Miss me?" said a man's deep voice.

The two Peeping Toms grabbed each other with a shout of *"Whoa!"* and jumped back into the hall. A tall, strong man stood before the open bedroom door, almost on top of them—dark hobnailed boots, dark pants, open peacoat, and a week of beard on a swarthy face. Then before they could swallow their surprise the nighttime vision went away in a pulse of light.

They were standing in the upstairs hallway in broad daylight. Nobody in the hall, nobody in their room, just another Saturday at home.

Guy leaned against his empty hallway and put a hand to his chest, clutching his heart. "Ye gods and little fishes," he muttered. Then after a moment, "I think it really is time for cake."

Lauren was very pale. "Okay, but I want to look in the desk."

"We've looked in the desk. A hundred times."

"Then another time won't matter."

There were three drawers in the square cabinet-like desk one on top of the other, with wooden pull knobs. Yep. Nothing much. Lauren kept boxes of buttons and scores of saved restaurant matches in the top drawer. The second drawer she stuffed with instruction booklets, expired warranties from washers and dryers, the innumerable thirty-page pamphlets in seven languages that come with iPads and the like. The electronics crap you never read.

The last drawer was swollen and always stuck about halfway out. Funny how you never opened the slightly swollen drawers all the way out. Lauren tugged, getting it two-thirds the way out for the first time in a century. But that was enough. She could look behind, inside the cabinet.

"Well, I'll be damned," Guy murmured.

Down at the base of the desk, within the third drawer space, sat the Whitcomb woman's diary. Black, leather bound. Or the remains of it. The old relic was overgrown with mold and a mouse had made it a house; chewed fluff, droppings, the leather cover partially eaten. "Get me some rubber gloves," Lauren asked.

"You're not really going to touch—"

"Guy! Get the gloves."

Armed with rubber gloves and Lysol spray against possible mouse dung, Lauren spread the worn, leather-bound journal on the kitchen counter under the window light on a layer of newspaper. She gingerly opened the old rotten thing with a pair of cooking tongs and a carving knife to hold down the back cover. The diary cracked and split— more paper crumbling everywhere. There was precious little left to read. The happy vermin had eaten most of the way down to the spine. A few half-pages here and there— stained, faded, and nearly unreadable.

Lauren tried to dope it out, but it was slow going, fragments really:

June 25, 1855— "I think it's 1855," she said, "there's a '55 on the corner of a broken page."

Johnny's ship, in from Norfolk, the schooner Righteous— docked last night. He brought some Cuban pineapples he'd bartered off a ship from Havana in the next slip. Two of the pineapples were spoiled, as mice made their nest in the box, but one still good. A cloud of mosquitoes flew out when we opened the lid, but mother wafted them through the front door outside. I think we caught them—all? The writing crumbled away.

More than a score of eaten pages later, one fragment intact, bottom of a page:

August (unreadable) New York has refused refugees. Along with Philadelphia, Baltimore, and Washington. Hundreds of boats in the Hudson, all trying to leave off people from the city. But it doesn't matter for us: they put an X on the front door of the house two days ago. We haven't been outside in a week. Pastor Simmons has been very kind and brought us food. We leave the money on the stoop. . . .

And that was it: a mere page amongst the crumbling dusty fragments. And one last thing. Between two slivers of very thin glass an old photo.

"I think it's called a cyanotype," Lauren said. "See, it's blue. They were hard to preserve, light sensitive. They refresh when they're stored in the dark."

The square four-by-four photo showed the Keeping Room. Guy could tell by the fireplace. No fire there. Sunlight slanted across the floor. Two padded wing chairs placed on either side of the hearth. A man and woman sat in each, posing for the photo. They were dressed in their Sunday best—man in high collar, morning coat, cravat, pressed pants, his best shoes. The woman in a white pleated dress, lace collar, lace at the sleeves, hair piled on top of her head, a brooch at her throat.

The man and woman were clasping hands, reaching halfway chair to chair, a gesture of fealty and love; in an odd contrivance a black ribbon seemed to be holding their palms together, wound about their wrists a turn or two then tied in a bow. That's when Lauren and Guy noticed the man and woman's eyes were closed.

Not only that—the features of their faces were simply smooth and lifeless: no spark of cognizance, no turn of the mouth or cock of the eyebrows. Dead. The holding hands seemed to be saying, *In death as in life. . . .*

"This is a death photo," Lauren said softly. "People used to do that. Take pictures of their loved ones right after—" Her voice broke off. There was a third figure in the death photo—the girl from the stairs. Only she wasn't dead—she was very much alive, sitting cross-legged on the floor between the two adults, her striped pinafore covering her knobby knees. She cradled her two dolls, Marie Antoinette and the frock-coated revolutionary citoyen Saint-Just of the Committee for Public Safety. The monarch's doll head was back on her doll shoulders, so perhaps the Committee for Public Safety had bestowed a last-minute stay of execution on the queen.

Great-great-great young Auntie stared at the camera, her eyes sober and dry—as though the girl had seen things much worse than this, this moment a kind of reprieve from whatever came before. . . .

In the few moments Guy and Lauren stared at the strange image, it faded and finally vanished from between the glass as if it had never been. Lauren put it carefully between the leaves and rotten leather cover of the old diary.

"Maybe it will come back again if we keep it in the dark," Guy said.

"I think I know what they died of," Lauren murmured.

A few moments later Guy and Lauren huddled at the PC in the den doing a search; there must have been five hundred entries in the archives of the *New York Times* from 1852 through late fall 1855 on the keywords *yellow fever*. You could tell by the drift of the articles that outbreaks of yellow fever had diminished somewhat over the course of the nineteenth century. Yet if the sheer number of notices, articles, and dispatches were any measure, the disease had killed a lot of people and scared the bloody pus out of millions more, even with outbreaks years or decades apart. Whole cities quarantined, populations fleeing slums and ports. Yeah, the outbreaks had dropped off mid-century, but still . . .

One entry worth reading: In 1855 the ports of Norfolk, Virginia, and its neighbor Portsmouth were hit pretty hard. The whole East Coast had been thrown into panic.

A daunting August 14th dispatch from the stricken area:

We have already told how our Health Officers are "whipping the devil round the stump," in the quarantine ports of Virginia. The *Ben Franklin* remained in port for twenty days, and no yellow fever made its appearance. But as soon as the *Ben Franklin* began to "break bulk"—to discharge her cargo—the disease spread like wildfire among all classes and still continues to prevail in the most malignant form.

More on the same day:

Reports from Portsmouth and Norfolk, of the ravages of yellow fever there, are of the most alarming character. Notwithstanding, a vast majority of the population of both cities has fled—

Guy made Lauren look up the phrase *whipping the devil round the stump,* and was dismayed to find it meant, "To evade responsibility or a difficult task." Clearly, the civil authorities in Virginia of 1855 were failing miserably to contain the disease.

Another dispatch from the ports published a day later:

The yellow fever still ravages our community, though it is estimated that up to this period fully 8,000 have left town.

Guy felt his throat grow dry. Then one of those no-see-ums tickled his arm. He resisted the urge to scratch it, but couldn't help himself. Lauren stopped over another entry, shaking her head in mild disbelief. The more things changed, the more they stayed the same. In a feel-good piece on the readiness of New York City, written to allay panic and published a week later, this little gem about three hundred words into the article, contradicting the whole thrust:

Brooklyn is ill-prepared to resist the ravages of a pestilence. It is a large city; it has no sewers. Each house has attached to it two disease-breeders, in a cesspool and an outhouse, and the filth thrown into the streets lies festering there, creating a foul and offensive stench.

Same day, as reprinted from the *Baltimore American:* THE YELLOW FEVER. NEW YORK LADIES ATTENDING THE AFFLICTED. Several paragraphs in:

DEAR SIR: The condition of things in our town at the present is most serious and alarming. Deaths are occurring all around us, new cases are multiplying hourly and our means of treating them are hourly diminished.

Lauren snorted—part scorn, part resignation—at the way things always turned out. The streets festered. How typical. About two weeks later, in September, New York City authorities shook off their lethargy: QUARANTINE— YELLOW FEVER PORTS.

The Board of Health held a special meeting at City Hall yesterday. The Mayor, Aldermen and Commonalty of the City of New York, convened as a Board of Health, ordain as follows—

Clearly the time for stern measures had arrived. Any vessel from the port of Baltimore or any port or place south thereof was to be quarantined for thirty days.

The Baltimore papers had something to say about that a couple of days later, as the *Times* reported:

The Baltimore papers are very indignant to the action of our Board of Health in subjecting to detention at Quarantine all vessels arriving here in New York from that city.

Guy could hear Lauren's breathing; this wasn't any fun anymore. Then on September 20: REPORTED YELLOW FEVER AT FAIR HAVEN, CT.

New-Haven, Wednesday Sept 19, A telegraphic dispatch has been published in some southern papers stating that three cases of Yellow Fever have occurred at Fair Haven. This is untrue, and the only foundation for it is the fact that a lady who arrived there recently from the South died suddenly of something akin to Yellow Fever.

Guy and Lauren sat back from where they huddled over the PC screen, slightly nauseated. Fair Haven, just north of New Haven. That was only twenty-five miles away! An easy afternoon's buggy ride. Maybe an hour on the train. Right next door!

Died suddenly? Something akin? Akin? Who the hell back then could tell what the poor lady succumbed to? Yellow fever, a stroke, a tooth infection? To make matters worse, Lauren clicked on symptoms: high fever, chills, vomiting, and backache. After a brief recovery period, the infection often led to shock, bleeding, kidney and liver failure. Jaundice, yellow skin, yellow eyes. Why they called it *Yellow Jack*. Then black vomit on account of the presence of blood in the—heck, just about everywhere you could name.

Guy muttered, "Black vomit—that's nasty."

A mosquito let into the house by accident floated dreamily over the PC screen, hovered for a few moments, and thrummed off. After all this yellow fever panic, the humming of an innocent mosquito was simply too much to bear. Lauren leapt from the desk, lost it in a bar of light, then caught it at the French doors, where she managed to slap it dead. A splat of blood on the glass. "Ick."

Guy wondered for a moment whether this was going to be the last time they saw the girl by the stairs, whether they'd exorcised her spirit or whether she had more to show them. And poor Eleanor sitting in the psych hospital in her nice room flitted into his head, and that silly ditty: *The ants go marching one by*—

As if reading his thoughts, Lauren said, "I don't know. But I want to visit Eleanor and tell her what we saw. She always knew about family history, which is why I think she was upset when Auntie Whitcomb gave us the house. I never cared as much."

She paused to stare at the den's flat-screen television; the DVR box had gotten into the habit of turning itself on at strange times. This time the channels were flashing zippity-zip. That tall fellow in the top hat and tails appeared picture-in-picture, holding a TV remote and furiously clicking away as if he were in control of the whole device, flashing one scene of depravity and destruction after another.

"Guy, sweetheart, will you turn that idiot off! He's everywhere."

13
❦

I've Been Everywhere, Man

The long kitchen in the lower reaches of the Grand Hyatt was a frantic syncopated dance—a cross between Leni Riefenstahl's *Triumph of the Will* and the flaming spectacle of a medieval auto-da-fé with slabs of meat and fish instead of burning heretics. A double aisle of stainless-steel sinks and preparation counters surrounded a long center island of flaming ranges and vent hoods. Two dozen hands, flipping, turning, slicin'-'n'-dicin' under a cacophony of shouted orders: "Crème brûlée! Tournedos!" and bells going off *ding-ding-ding* as orders came due and uniformed waiters rolled carts through swinging double doors.

The whole get-a-job thing went exactly as Mr. Piper had said it would. Not without a few ruffled feathers, but that was to be expected. Mama Whore and Dimples applied for and were offered positions at the hotel—Dimples on kitchen staff and the Ho' in housekeeping, then waitressing in the evening. Between making food, making beds, and delivering room service the two had the run of the whole place.

Dalekto seemed to have a peculiar effect on them: The cobwebs of the past were brushed aside; they saw things clearly; they mastered the learned skill of absorbing information and giving it back on demand. Showing up on time, bathed, clothes pressed, the two skanks quickly mastered the social niceties of working around relative strangers— doing the job, lots of *please*s and *thank-you*s. Dimples got his tooth fixed, looked good in his kitchen whites, black-checked pants, and Mama Whore took on the guise of a naughty jailhouse matron in her housekeeper uniform. She gained a few pounds with regular eating and lost ten years in the process.

The ruffled feathers came from the Hotel Employees and Restaurant Employees Union Local 6 shop steward, a grizzled little woman who kept a small cubbyhole of an office off the kitchen. Like so many in life she didn't like upstarts and newcomers having the way of a place she had taken so long to bring under her own control.

So when she saw Dimples lending an extra helping hand with the sous chefs, or his woman folding towels in the laundry that were assigned to someone else, the tin-hat bureaucrat went on red alert. Waiting like some kind of weasel in the straw, she bided her time till she could really get them on something, staking out the long hallway outside the kitchen, peeking over the stacked produce boxes, skulking around the barrels of MSG or behind the tall racks of fresh silverware and crockery.

A dedicated lurker in the maze of modern kitchen chrome, the grizzled union hag got them on Dalekto, spotting Dimples doing the hand-and-cash switch in the long hallway between the kitchen and the elevators. She sidled up to him afterward with a self-satisfied, "Ahhh . . . so, Handsome, is this your version of motivational therapy?" Clearly not a reprimand—more like putting Dimples on notice.

Luckily, Mama Ho' was on hand to defend her man; long ago she'd spotted the spotter, and some skills left over from the streets still came in handy. Emerging from behind a box tower of frozen steaks and chicken, Mama Ho' sneaked up like a cobra, put her hand on the back of the grizzled hag's neck, and pushed her face into an open crate of sour, Dumpster-bound cabbages.

The limp cabbages were still partly hard, and the poor woman's face went *crunk-crunk,* into the layer of round vegetables. And with each crunch, Mama spat, "Keep," *crunk,* "your stinky nose," *crunk,* "outta our bidness." *Crunk.*

The woman's face emerged, slightly bruised, tears sprouting from her red eyes. A Ziploc sandwich bag topped off with shimmering Dalekto was thrust into her wrinkled hands. And Dimples said quietly, but seriously, "Now take this stupid bag. Come back when you want more; we need your little butthole of an office, so clean it on your way out. And leave it spotless."

The double doors to the kitchen swung open, and one of the day chefs emerged with the purposeful steps of a potty run. He paused for a second, taking in Dimples, Mama Ho', and the shop steward hag blinking tears from her eyes, clutching the Ziploc. Mama Ho' put the fellow on his way with a simple, "Whattaya looking at?" Eyes snapped back in his head, and the day chef vanished around a corner.

From then on Piper's two Vice Presidents for Distribution really did have the run of the joint. After straightening out Local 6, their duties became light and pleasant. Everyone in the crowded kitchen said more *please*s and *thank-you*s than either Dimples or his lady were required to return, paying the two new employees a kind of unspoken homage, much like that offered to ward bosses and inner-city politicians—but at least with Dimples' and Mama's ongoing concern everyone got some bang for their buck instead of just empty promises for votes.

The two hustlers ran their little cubbyhole off the main kitchen with all the efficiency of an automated production line in a Fizzies Factory, as Dalekto now also came in tabs. Still, they kept regular hours and a serious work ethic, leading by example. If a kitchen job was dirty or a room job unappealing or someone called in sick, Dimples and Mama Ho' would step in as required, no questions asked. And so no questions *were* asked.

Dimples kept a Wi-Fi PC link and his cell phone on speed dial to the Kid "upstairs," whom he now called "The Boss." As one of the top brains of the operation, the young man now told him what to do; their roles reversed. And Dimples felt lucky that he and Mama Ho' had been chosen out of the faceless throngs available in a city of eight million. Fortune knocked, and Dimples was damn glad he'd answered.

Exposure to Mr. P. and Dalekto seemed to have improved Dimples' mind, his wits—everything came easier now. The best he could reckon, Mr. P. was like some great social engineer and the world his laboratory. Dimples began to see how the business and commerce of drug addiction brought everyone who touched Dalekto under the Piper's influence, and he was glad to help. It didn't even seem strange answering to a boy for his every move, if that's what Mr. Piper wanted.

So part of Dimples' job was to keep the young boss constantly informed of pending Dalekto deliveries, either by phone or e-mail, and give a strict accounting of unit, bulk, and discount sales, along with their revenue stream. Discount sales were rare, but used with new clients—the easiest way to lure them into dependency. In this manner the whole of the city seemed to stream past the little cubbyhole off the kitchen, people traipsing in and out from seven a.m. to midnight, seven days a week.

Where the devil the rainbow dust came from, Dimples and Mama Ho' couldn't say; that was above their pay grade. What they did handle was the endless parade of delivery boys bringing in the goods and taking them out again. Like skycaps handling your luggage at the airport, they boosted it along. And the name stuck, *skycaps* becoming the tag for anyone involved in the Dalekto drug business—the Kid's personal army. Everyone in the hotel got a little touch of lucre, from the sweeties at the front desk, down through the bowels of the place right out to the security guards at the employees' entrance.

Dalekto's magic glow made the world go round.

The Gulfstream G650 private jet sailed through the thin air at forty thousand feet, the barest whisper of its Rolls Royce engines penetrating the cabin. The young boss from Avenue A watched as vast vistas of mountainous clouds formed and broke apart; below the clouds the green and golden pastures of flyover country glimmered under the shifting sun. On a plush club chair, Mr. Piper slept in climate-controlled comfort; at least Mr. P.'s eyes were closed, safe and secure at 600 mph. No better ride for love or money.

Fly-by-Wire digital technology sent instantaneous impulses to the flaps and tail, with no lag or delay. A Synthetic Vision-Primary Flight Display in front of the pilot's eyes enabled him to land in fog or blizzard and still visualize the terrain ahead. The jet's Enhanced Vision System III fed the magic window surface radar topography down to the smallest detail, and a special subcontract modification made by Lattimore Aerospace, an Aerogel translucent sighting panel and lead-infused Aerogel baffles, meant that the thing would work even after an EMP blast—just like Air Force One.

Another specialty that Lattimore Aerospace sold to

Gulfstream: small escape pods in the belly of the plane, each a two-person cushioned EZ-access encased lifeboat under a triple parachute with automatically deployed Ultralite paraglider airfoils in order to land. The pods could float on water or float safely to the ground. With duplicate pretasked Enhanced Vision III topography and Vision-Primary Flight images just like the cockpit flight display, the escape pods could detect a clearing in a dense forest at cruising altitude and home onto the range like a guided butterfly for touchdown.

So far in the history of this device, no one had ever had to bail out of a Gulfstream and actually use them. But ask any man in the heart-stopping panic of some technical malfunction whether the price tag of five million per to survive a plane crash seems too high.

Instead of buying the aircraft outright, Mr. Piper and the lad from Avenue A leased it from a Dubai princeling suddenly in need of extra capital. Amazing what unlimited credit could do. And Piper Holding Ltd.'s credit cards were better than gold. Who cares if they were borrowed?

In business terms, Piper Ltd.'s New York Local Operation under the direction of Dimples and Mama Ho' was ahead of schedule and running more or less on its own, microscopic tentacles of Dalekto slithering down the nerve stem of society. However, some employees on the West Coast and in the Mountain divisions were falling down on the job. So the time had arrived for a business trip. Time for Mr. P. to set matters straight, a long-term assignment, thirty days or more—and this required a comfortable ride. A month on a Gulfstream wasn't so bad.

By nature, Mr. Piper wouldn't necessarily have stirred himself to action after the Grand Hyatt project came together so swiftly. Keeping various minds in the extended orbit of Piper Ltd. in line, not to mention casting himself into every television show through a dish or cable box—as a daily exertion—he needed dream time. Added to that, he could clearly hear the million squeals from every rat in every corner of the country. Legions of them. The little rodents squirmed and writhed in every drain and gutter, yearning to break free and run amok. With one part of his mind, whether sleeping or awake, he was holding them back. *No, not yet . . .*

Mr. P. absorbed ambient energy like a rainforest sucked up heat and sunlight; he could absorb anything, emotional energy the easiest, anxiety the most prevalent from millions of troubled souls who walked the face of the Earth. But he could also absorb the energy from a lifeless rock, from fields of wheat, or the motion of tides. He soaked up energy like a sponge, stored it like a battery; but like a fuel cell, he could only power so much for so long. Turn lead into gold? Sure, but don't ask him to influence a billion rat brains while he smelted the bullion.

So the need for sleep reasserted itself as the Gulfstream cruised above the skin of the world. God, what he'd give for a year-long dreamabout. He'd taken long rests in other times, after great exertions, a rain of brimstone or plague of locusts. A dozen years here, a century there, even millennia, awakening refreshed and restored. Immortal hibernation. A Rip Van Winkle nap: snoring away and opening his eyes only to discover how the world had delightfully changed in his absence. His dreams were always about the past. He felt his eyes shutting, his breath slow and steady, as the present dream brought him back, a favorite, an oldie but a goodie: medieval Hamelin.

The bare monastery cell: the wooden cot, the rope sling, the rag-stuffed mattress, a cross on the wall, and the bolted door; a table for a candle and The Book. And even if there were moments of bright sun and glorious days in that period they called the Dark Ages, the light in his room always was shadowed, damp, a mere slit in the wall to let in air. The mortar was slightly cracked in the dank stone walls, and when it rained a rivulet of water snaked by his head as he lay on his cot, thence to the floor and along the wall and out a corner. Sort of like a subterranean river that emerges from stone, flows on for a spell, then disappears into the corner of a cave.

In the winter, icicles came down from the wooden roof where it met the stone; in summer, a hundred flies found their place to breed. Brother Hansel told Piper that his parents had sold him to this place, to make him a monk, to take him off their hands. The last of thirteen children, never enough to go around—and Brother Hansel told young novice P what a lucky fellow he was to come into the cloister. But these were just old wives' tales; for the life of him, Piper could never remember a childhood. It seemed to him he'd always been a man.

Outside the monastery walls the world cried under the fists of petty kings and their petty squabbles, but within the safe walls, life was quiet. Austere, pious. Piper particularly enjoyed the liturgy as chanted by his friend Vans, while the brothers sat at supper, quietly eating. They called him Vans, with a double meaning, *vantze,* the Louse, mostly because Brother Vans was so short and pale. Vans' charming voice filled the long cold hall:

> *Thou that takest away the sins of the world,*
> *Have mercy upon us.*
> *Thou that takest away the sins of the world,*
> *Receive our prayer—*

Everyone liked Brother Vans; he was popular and often available. No stranger to the secluded ground under the bushes by the high stone wall. . . .

The *Twilight Zone* phone rang, rudely ripping Brother Piper away from the charming and easy pious Brother Vans. The Kit-Cat clock tick-tocked away in its own banquette, strapped into a child safety seat; the time read fourteen minutes to noon, *tock-tock-tock*. Outside the sun was shining. God, he'd only been asleep a couple of hours.

Damn that *Zone* phone. Good for ordering pizzas in New York and keeping tabs on the company's underlings, but he never gave out the call-back number. He groggily stared at the toy phone from the deep cushioned seat in the Gulfstream's cabin. Mr. Piper had even taken the black phone receiver off the hook as a precaution. But it didn't help; the damn phone rang again, insistent. He could get people to think what he wanted, so why in damn hell couldn't he get a damn toy phone to behave and stop ringing at all hours for no reason? Some entities just had a mind of their own.

In another banquette the boy quietly tapped the keys of his laptop; music bumped out of the speaker, a Johnny Cash song: "I've Been Everywhere." The lad tweaking it on his own now:

> Can't say I really cared, man
> Stabbed you in the back, man
> Can't say I really cared.

If he put his mind to it, he'd rewrite every copy in existence. No, not today.

The boy looked up from his laptop and turned down the gravelly voice of the Man in Black, then reached across his banquette, picked up the *Zone* phone receiver, and returned it to its cradle, hanging up on the call. Disconnected, the ringing stopped. The Kid had no use for the phone; he could get everything he needed from the computer. Gas station credit card charges, lodge and dining charges, police arrest records, weather reports, data streams of every variety were open to him. His eyes went back to the laptop screen, where he tracked the company's operatives.

"Well, which do you want first, the good news or the bad?" the boy asked.

Mr. Piper rubbed his temples and tried to concentrate.

You wouldn't have recognized the lad from that first day in the dirty T-shirt. No longer a street punk; the pressed khakis, the button-down Oxford shirt—he could have been right out of Tabor Academy in Marion, Massachusetts, with one of those blue blazers and the school coat of arms.

As always, Mr. P. wanted the bad news first:

"Location of surviving female?"

Competent as any corporate VP, the sharply turned-out preppy reeled off what he knew so far in a likeable, non-judgmental kind of way:

"Location unknown. We are pursuing relevant leads. In Los Angeles County, Inspector Frederick delayed due to arrest of an associate on the charge of solicitation."

The long, gaunt man snorted in contempt.

"Solicitation?"

The lad's nimble hands stretched from the clean cuffs of his button-down shirt; he clicked a few keys on the laptop, "Broderick Fallows. Arrested twenty-four hours ago by local Los Angeles PD in the company of Inspector Frederick. Broderick Fallows doing business as Lady Fallows; film director, transgendered part-time soliciting. Inspector Frederick briefly held and released on his own recognizance. We've rerouted Frederick to Las Cruces, New Mexico, for Malvedos interview, additional lead, possible shortcut to Chen girl."

A pause; another question was coming:

"Bioengineer Webster specializing in recombinant DNA? Wayward brother of Big Sis, gimp saloon broad?"

The lad paused for a moment, touched the keys, checking another database on the laptop. A tiny sheen of sweat had appeared on his upper lip, and he wiped it off on his shirtsleeve, more in excitement than any kind of fear. He really liked being of use.

"Bioengineer Webster location confirmed, en route to Dugway recovery with planned return to the πr^2 facility, Hillsboro, Ohio."

Again, the long pause. Another question:

"Wild 3 touchdown site?"

A few more clicks of the laptop:

"Recovery delayed due to inclement weather. Recovery Team standing by at the edge of the low-pressure area. The National Weather Service is calling it an anomalous event. No sign of abatement."

An even longer pause. Piper felt the snow falling from the sky in faraway Utah, felt his will melding cloud and moisture and ice and wind. That was enough to give anyone a headache. His voice came again, out of the depths of his head, and with a touch of satisfaction, if the sound of ground glass underfoot might sound pleasing:

"Carry on."

The boy turned up the sound on Johnny Cash, popped a fizzy tab of Dalekto, and clicked back to his studies, instantly immersed in the rise of Oliver Cromwell, the Lord Protector, the regicide of Charles the First, and the nearly genocidal invasion of Ireland and the Siege of Wexford:

> While Cromwell himself was trying to negotiate surrender terms, some of his soldiers broke into the town, killed 2,000 Irish troops, up to 1,500 civilians, and burned much of the town—

The young lad looked up from the laptop screen and toward Piper. "Were you in Ireland?" He didn't have to tell Mr. P. which century; their minds seemed to work like that. No need for long explanations.

"Aye, boyo—both sides. After the Lord Protector was dead and buried, I dug him up for the Royalists and beheaded him for good measure. Never overlook the benefit of cheap theatrics when attempting to please a crowd."

The boy went back to the screen; he was clicking through European history at a hurtling gallop: four seconds on this century, five seconds on the next. In addition to learning big words, his ability to access and absorb was becoming prodigious. He was already up to mid-twentieth century. He paused. "But Stalingrad did not go as planned, did it?"

Mr. P. sighed. "Oh, we went to town all right. Not a stone standing. But then Der Mustache ordered Field Marshal Paulus to commit suicide in disgrace. As I recall the good general remarked, 'I have no intention of shooting myself for an Austrian corporal.' Never underestimate the self-regard of the aristocratic mind, boyo. Snobbery is the last refuge of defeat."

Then after a moment, he lay back and closed his eyes again.

"Just make sure our open-fly Keystone Cop gets to Las Cruces."

14

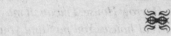

Low-Pressure Center

June turned into July.

Most of the world went about its daily business in blissful ignorance.

Las Cruces, New Mexico.

Once again, the wooden clunky beads rattled apart in Senora Malvedos' inner sanctum; she stared at the weasel-faced man coming in from the parlor. The weasel owned the face of ugliness and brought with him many terrible things. The hand on the back of her neck wasn't a mild touch, but a vise-grip. Two steel pincers with ridges squeezing tighter and tighter. This walking waste of human skin in his cheap suit had *bad cop* radiating from every pore. Second-rate navy blue Arnold Palmer sport coat and Dockers slacks; the sport coat riding around his shoulders, the khaki slacks board stiff as if pressed with starch. Under the jacket he carried a gun and didn't care if the bunching showed.

Every time the man exhaled, the reek of halitosis carried on it the remnants of some black deed. One of the few men Senora Malvedos had ever seen who wasn't keeping a secret or trying to confess. The stench of his own recent past flowed across the table:

The hatchet-faced policeman sat in an unmarked car at night; across the street in a Holiday Inn parking lot a lady motorcycle cop and the sad man with the lost daughter got into the back of a limousine. Inspector Frederick jammed an earplug into his ear. He was listening to a conversation inside the idling limo, a wiretap on some kind of criminal boss named Nicky. A black man's deep voice explaining: ". . . they call him the Magician. Things get around. They say he's running some kind of chop-shop, snuff market; they call it the Harrow House. I mean, it may not even be a real place, a real house. You pay and you play. Single-payer system right?"

The vision shifted, and Senora Malvedos saw something else. *It felt like the same night. The inspector was addressing half a dozen kids outside a single-story house in some Los Angeles neighborhood. "Make it quick. They either know or they don't. Do the lips. And don't forget to vacuum on your way out."*

Suddenly the woman saw inside the house: *The kids ran in like wild animals surprising Mama and her two sons on the couch. Hissed questions, "Where is she? Where?" No answer, just fear. Arms held down big Mama; plastic bags came out, over the heads, gasping, choking, turning blue while Mama and her two boys writhed on the couch and the TV sang. The bodies stopped struggling. Then the knives did the mouths like they were told, zippity-zip! And someone ran the vacuum over the wall-to-wall carpet as the wild boys quietly backed out of the house snickering over their trophy lips.*

Senora Malvedos touched a kerchief to her face, but nothing pushed aside what she saw. *The dark upper floor of a warehouse, a bright desk lamp illuminating a large body strapped to a metal spring cot. Nicky the Banka-Gangsta's three-thousand-dollar Armani suit fell in tatters around his body; blood ran down the coiled springs of the cot like rain dripping from a roof. Only the soft sound of the drug dealer's ragged breathing. Alive, yes, but missing his lips. All the missing lips from around LA would keep the department chasing its tail for months. . . . Then the hatchet face came into the light, his voice sad and measured: "Nicky . . . Nicky . . . we had a good thing going." Heavy with regret: "I'm gonna miss it. And I know you're not holding out on me—no reason to. But frankly the Magician needed a lot more from you this time." A large butcher knife glinted in the light. "In any event, on behalf of the Los Angeles Police Department, I want to thank you for your cooperation."*

Senora Malvedos stared at the kerchief, darkened with moisture from her face. Another bit from Los Angeles crossed her eyes, and the word *Inexplicable* jumped into her mind. A movie title? But the vision was clear enough: *Later that same night . . . The hatchet-faced cop sat in his unmarked car in some quiet alley. He'd picked up a hooker; she sat in the passenger seat, leaning over the center armrest, her face down in his lap. The shiny blond hair moved back and forth. While the radio played old Donna Summer, Inspector Frederick mouthing new words, "He works hard for the money / so hard on it honey."*

Then suddenly an LAPD patrol car flipped on its bubbled lights, flashing everywhere in red and blue and white. The single bark of a siren. A metallic voice ordered, "Stay in the car, please."

"Quit it!" Frederick the bad copper yanked the blond head off his lap. And he snarled, "Get outta here! Go find an ant colony, bitch. Get lost!" But it was too late for that; the uniforms from the black-and-white were already at the driver and passenger windows. To Inspector Frederick: "License and registration, please?" To the blond ladyboy fixing her makeup from a Mary Kay Compact Pro: "Miss, you can do that later. Hands where I can see them, please." Then the uniform at the passenger window recognized the lady. He chuckled dryly. "Again, Mr. Fallows?"

The police inspector's recent past floated away to nothing. Senora Malvedos stared at her hands on the green velvet of the table; one was twitching.

Something in the way this bad man looked at the Senora forced her to shudder; Inspector Frederick knew a lot about her. About what she saw and what she knew about him. Someone had tipped him off. The vague impression surfaced: of long legs stretching from a padded chair while a preppy black kid tapped away on a keyboard nearby, the sound of jet engines whirring. . . . Nothing more.

When the inspector smiled, Senora Malvedos saw that brassy big woman with the limp, again, Big Sis—the saloon keep worried about her brother, Webster. The weasel knew all about them. *Right now, right this very second the big brassy woman was tending bar in her roadhouse, pulling a tap handle. She slid the suds to her brainy brother sitting on a barstool. "Here's mud in your eye," Big Sis told him while he laughed, hoisted the mug, and said, "To frozen smoke and comet dust!" Webster took a swallow. "You won't see me for a while, but don't worry. I'm exactly where I'm supposed to be."* But the cop wasn't concerned with them. The two were just where they were supposed to be. No urgency.

Inspector Frederick had come to clean things up; each little tick of his face told her more and more. *Everyone— Daddy Long Legs, the preppy kid, the bad cop—was look-*

ing for a girl, and looking for the two searchers who were looking for the girl. The Inspector even knew about the Senora's session with the sad man from India. It was that Indian scientist who filled the space behind his eyes. The sad, gentle Sikh. The bad cop knew the fellow's name. And most importantly knew who the poor man was looking for. The lost young lady Lila Chen, surviving daughter of Professor Bhakti Singh's friends and colleagues Wen and Amy Chen. He even knew the Senora's own words, *"This one. Lila. Still lives. You may see her yet."*

The unreliable goons Inspector Frederick had assigned the job of kidnapping the filly were missing in action, fled to parts unknown—gone rogue. The weasel cop had picked up the girl's scent in Los Angeles, but lost it again. Now a twinge of concern; *Dammit!* the Punjab scientist and his new copper gal pal could follow the trail too. So he was rolling up the scent from where it started. Right here in Las Cruces. The Senora felt his very thoughts . . . *maybe the old fortune-teller frump knew more than she was telling.*

But how this weasel got the Senora's locale and street address, Senora Malvedos had no clue. Someone else was pointing the weasel in her direction. Again, the whisper of jet engines in a luxurious Gulfstream cabin . . . long legs stretched out from a padded chair, expensive tweed trousers, polished wing tips.

Inspector Frederick came to the table and paused, glanced at the chair. "May I?"

"Everyone is welcome here."

The chair scraped; he sat, his Arnold Palmer sport coat bunching more around his armpits; she could see the butt of his gun staring at her from behind the flap of his jacket. He carefully put the statue of a saint between them. Little Maria came to her side and clutched her hand. Senora Malvedos looked at her protégé and quietly told her, "Go to Nona's. Tell her what we want for dinner."

That was a code between them. It meant, *Run away and*

hide. And since the weasel was totally absorbed in the old woman before him, the secret warning glanced off his mind and vanished into thin air. Little Maria sweetly said, "Okay!" and trotted from the room with a coy look over her shoulder. He barely noticed.

Senora Malvedos and the bad policeman sat in silence. The saint he'd picked from the table in the parlor was Dona Sebastiana. Santa Muerte. Saint Death. And this lady had more names than a Spanish noble family. Nina Santa, Holy Girl. La Flaca, the Skinny One. Senora de la Noche, the Lady of the Night.

Condemned by the church, but adored by those on the lower stratum of society: the pimps and the prostitutes, tamale vendors, pickpockets—an endless legion of the supplicant. Anyone who feared the random violence of the streets. The old fortune-teller's copy of Santa Muerte was an opulent one. A hooded skeleton covered in a glittering robe of red and gold, hung with fake pearls and silver trinkets, and in her skeletal hand a tiny intricate bouquet of bright flowers.

Inspector Frederick cleared his throat and found a cigarette. "May I?" he asked again. The woman across from him shrugged, found an ashtray, and slid it across the table. The rotten cop contemplated Dona Death for a moment.

"I understand that ancient Mexicans used to tie this girl up to a post and beat her if she didn't give them what they wanted."

"People desperate for salvation or miracles do a lot of things," Senora Malvedos told him. "For my part, I never threaten almighty powers with violence."

He inhaled and let the serpent of smoke float across the room. "Don't you think it's really the other way round? Powers we don't control threatening *us* with violence? Been to Chicago lately? In my lovely city of Los Angeles, we've essentially given up. Our very own LAPD public database omits nearly forty percent of any given year's crimes. Better not to write it down. Wouldn't want to alarm the public, now would we?"

He didn't seem to care whether she answered or not. He leaned across the table and his jacket fell open, blatantly showing the butt of the gun.

"Where are they?" he asked quietly.

"They who? Which they?"

Inspector Frederick's face became drawn and pale—capable of anything. Softly he told her, "Don't play with me."

Senora Malvedos looked at the statue of Dona Death on the table. The skull face stared with open eyes, almost a touch of pity. And Senora M implored her, *Please make it quick*. The vise at the back of her neck squeezed a little tighter, and she saw how it had happened to the girl. A glimmer here, a fragment there. Yes, the Chen girl still lived; everyone might see her yet.

The goons had them in the van, tearing off their clothes, dumping the torn rags in a pile along with their cell phones on the railroad tracks. A man's hand held a bloody ear, almost fondling it. Laughing. "Who's gonna drop it on Mama Chink's lawn?" Then the sound of tires squealing along the road. Senora M turned her face from the statue on the table, pressing her temples to make the vision go away. She told him what she knew:

"The *cucarachas* you put on the job, the local chapter of the Kitty Kat gang, got carried away. They were just supposed to grab the two girls. Which they did; they found your prospects. But they took too much rainbow dust. And forgot to cut it. Too pure. *Muy puro.* Then they went haywire. Sold Sweet Jane for drugs; maimed Panda girl and now they carry her as a freak in a traveling circus. They don't want to be found. Your mistake was leaving such an important task to lunatics. Now you lost the Chinese girl. Your last best prospect and there's no time to locate another. The Kit-Cat clock says it's thirteen to twelve. The Tall Man isn't happy."

The inspector's narrow face twisted at her. "You say *my* mistake? Like those body snatchers were *mine*? Like I picked them?" His skinny chicken neck quivered.

"I didn't pick them. They were *His*." Inspector F's eyes bored across the table. He leaned a little closer over the table, his suit jacket open, the gun nearly slipping from his armpit. Senora Malvedos shrugged. Did it really matter who picked who? The world was teeming with available scum. The Kitty Litter Map in the LA precinct men's room scrolled across her eyes, then expanded from coast to coast, telling the tale. Scores of smiling kitty cat dots splattering the map. Almost like the devil had put out a bounty: WANTED: PANDA GIRL—BIG REWARD. Everyone was hunting for Lila Chen, leaving a trail of bodies behind when none of the victims turned out to be the girl they wanted.

"*La cucarachas*. Every cockroach in America is looking for that girl," she said. "But no one will find her as long as she's with that traveling freak show that snatched her."

And this seemed to relieve the inspector a little. He wasn't alone in failure—not now at least. There was still hope he could fix his little problem. Even with competition.

"What about that pathetic scientist and that dyke cop?"

Senora Malvedos sagged in her chair. Nothing to tell him. Nothing that would help. She looked to the statuette again, the grinning smile, the empty eyes. "Burgers and fries. Malted milk. *Justly famous since 1939.*" That's all that came.

And the knowing ended there. The touch gone, the vise on her neck fading like the smoke from the inspector's crushed cigarette in the ashtray. Her head fell to her breast, exhausted. Santa Muerte's eyes were no longer speaking to her—a mere figure of a saint. Inspector Frederick took the gun from under his armpit.

"Thank you for your cooperation, Senora Malvedos. You've been very helpful. Now I'd like to talk to your Little Maria. Maybe you can tell me where she likes to hide."

The bad cop left the fortune-teller's with nine bullets in his clip instead of ten. A dozen paces out the door he turned the block, walked down an alley, and paused. He looked down at his feet, then knelt to a foot-by-foot square of grill-work in the side of the building about the size of a dog door. The grillwork was metal and meshed over with a lint-covered mosquito screen—an old exhaust duct from a basement commercial dryer. He pried the mosquito screen free, and the grillwork came off with it. His flashlight lanced down the metal air tunnel. Ten feet in, Senora Mal-vedos' Lil' Maria stared back at him. She crouched like a frightened rabbit, blinking at the light. Inspector Freder-ick let the thought of his presence sink in. Would it really be necessary for him to pull his gun?

"Hi," he said.

Billy Shadow had been driving all night, hoping to make it in time for the Wild 3 satellite recovery at the Dugway Proving Ground, just like Lattimore wanted. West on I-70 through Utah, to 36-N up by Provo; then headed west again onto a nothing blacktop, Route 199. Lattimore had texted him a brief update: *Clearance ID confirmed Dugway. Hurry up.*

Alas, Billy was already four hours late for the Wild 3 *Stardust* touchdown; the probe must already have landed as it was due to hit Mother Earth around 4 a.m.; but hope-fully he'd be able to ascertain the performance of the com-pany's Aerogel particle collector anyway.

A gray dawn came, overcast, raining hard. He'd turned off the AC hours ago, and now the heater blasted warm air everywhere in the minivan. Route 199 led to the long-lost town of Dugway, Utah. The old town was mostly gone now, and if anyone wanted a Motel 6 or a Comfort Inn they'd have to go over to Provo or Salt Lake City—same for a Slurpee or a beer. This was U.S. Army country, home of the military's Dugway Proving Grounds—the government's biological and chemical testing site a few miles south of the Great Salt Lake. About a million acres of nuttin', honey. And the best landing area tax money could buy.

When Billy cracked the window for a little air, a clammy blast filled the car, and he shut it again. For some while the memory of old Grandma Sparrow—her lined and withered face—floated behind his eyes. Her smiling lips moving silently, she was trying to tell him something; one word, a single word: "Good." That's what she was trying to say. Glad he was doing the right thing. On the right path.

The road led to a cluster of well-planned streets, grassy lawns, multistoried buildings behind wire fencing, and warning signs, a number of them reading BE PREPARED TO STOP—the army's way of getting you to pay attention, as repetition works every time. He turned onto a quarter mile of pavement past a large granite sign reading DUGWAY PROVING GROUNDS toward the main gates and checkpoint, where another sign told him DO NOT BACK UP.

The two soldiers on duty looked as if they were expecting him and were not the slightest bit tired at 5 a.m.—freshly shaved, alert, exuding a kind of professional competence and reserve. A contagious calm that everything was all right, just the way it was supposed to be. Dawn or no dawn, rain or shine, day or night. Billy powered down his window and handed over a wad of identification through the open window of the guard post, the trump card being his Lattimore Aerospace ID. The young sergeant took it and handed it to a lieutenant who couldn't have been a year older than a junior at Princeton. The older one began running various pieces of ID under a scanner.

"Am I too late for the recovery?"

"Couldn't say," the young sergeant replied. "You're not the first to arrive, but I don't think you'll be the last."

The wad of Billy's identification came back through the open driver's window. Inside the reinforced booth a machine hummed, automatically contacted Lattimore Aerospace, paused for confirmation, then printed his laminated visitors' tag. The sergeant clipped it to a metal necklace, handing it through the window. The visitors' tag showed Billy's official Lattimore corporate photo, along with his thumbprint and a speckled bar code with God knows what else. Probably his service record.

Yes, they knew all about him.

"Please wear this tag at all times, Major Howahkan. The visitors' parking lot is up and to the right. The public relations offices are in the first building at the top of the lot. The public relations officer will meet you inside the hospitality area. Please leave your car unlocked and the keys in the ignition." A tiny smile. "Or we'll tow it out to the range." The smile went away. "Welcome to Dugway Proving Grounds."

The soldier saluted, and the reinforced window slid closed. Billy Shadow saluted back and nudged the car forward. He drove through the first of two gates. An electric arch of sensors scanned the minivan; when the car passed the automobile-scan a green signal light allowed him to proceed. Another gate slid open, and the car clanked over a grate of traffic control teeth—tire rippers to stop any vehicle slapped into reverse. No second thoughts allowed. One way forward, no way back.

A triple line of cars were parked in the visitors' lot, and he pulled over at the rear of the herd. Rain streamed across his windshield as the wipers died. Jesus. July in the desert; it felt like 45°F outside. He could see his breath.

No good going out unprepared. His face was freezing. In the back of the van he dug out his boots, a fuzzy pullover, and a roughneck jacket from the footlocker. Found a pair of binoculars and threw them around his neck. When he opened the minivan sliding door, a spray of rain sliced across the opening. He went back for a pair of mittens and a watch cap, then slammed the minivan door shut and sprinted across the lot to the overhang of the public relations building. Man, they'd better have some coffee.

Another more thorough security check with four more soldiers greeted him. He slapped his rain jacket and binocs on the rubber conveyor belt, then handed over the ID all over again.

Thumbprint scan, retinal scan, voice scan, full-body X-ray. Off with the boots.

The young men in uniform were pleasant, thorough, and polite to a fault. But underneath it all, a dead seriousness that couldn't be ignored. On the other side of the security hurdle all his possessions were handed back to him. And the last guard said, "Please make yourself comfortable. There'll be a briefing in about an hour. You haven't missed anything."

The hospitality room looked a lot like an airport departure lounge: lined with couches and chairs linked by the arms; men's and women's restrooms off to one side. A buffet table stood against one wall. To Billy's eternal joy, the Army was providing breakfast: fresh fruit, muffins, eggs, bacon, pancakes, sausage, butter, yogurt, Smart Balance, a pyramid of Kellogg's variety packs, three kinds of juice—the works. A mess detail in whites was bringing out the steam trays, the scent of every good thing in the morning filling the room. Coffee!

And naturally, he wasn't alone. A dozen guys from various aspects of the *Stardust* mission, mostly manufacturing types—the Jet Propulsion Lab at the California Institute of Technology, Hewlett-Packard, Microsoft, Sun Microsystems, Boeing, General Dynamics. Billy knew the kind. And a gal from the Associated Press who looked thoroughly distraught, like she'd been waiting all night for a date that never showed up. Her sensible flats and Spanx control hose were soaked through and through. That's who Billy decided to plop his butt next to. She didn't seem impressed with the breakfast. Or even the smell from Billy's loaded plate. In fact she looked a little nauseous. She'd been up for a while.

Before digging in, Billy looked at her and said, "I have an extra pair of boots and some rain gear in my van. A union suit, some good Carhartts, and thick socks. Might be a tad big, but you won't get cold. I'll fetch them, if you want them."

She looked at him for a moment like *The Man from Planet X* pitching her *Plan 9 from Outer Space*. Then thought it through, picked his ID tag off his chest, and examined his pedigree. Nodded to herself. "Oh yeah, the Aerogel dust collector grid. They think it worked. Your boss Lattimore should be happy."

The ID chain came back to his chest, and Billy went to work on the scrambled eggs and bacon. The AP Gal looked down at her sodden shoes, then acquiesced. "If you bring 'em, I'll put 'em on. You'll be a half hour with security, and they'll probably send someone with you."

"That's fine." Billy was starting to think about seconds on the order of flapjacks—but that risked making him sleepy. More coffee . . . ? No, better get the gear first. "I'll be right back."

"Before you go there's something you better see. C'mon."

He dropped his plate on a discard pile at the end of the buffet table and followed her to the front of the hospitality area; there was an open hanging observation deck, again like an airport. They climbed the steel steps and came out on a wide gantry in front of a bank of windows overhung with a wide awning to keep the weather off. Full dawn had come, still raining, still gray. Billy looked out across the lower buildings of the proving ground; a long, flat road led into the desert.

A quarter mile out, various recovery vehicles idled in a long line: a fire truck, a troop transport, a tractor trailer hauling a small flatbed crane—all waiting at the edge of rain-drenched visibility. You could see their super-bright

LEDs, lightbars and bubble lights flashing under a canopy of mist, fired-up red and blue and yellow sparklers, as though aching to go. Yet there was something creepy about the silently flashing light show as Billy and the AP Gal watched from behind the thick glass—no noise, no sirens. Of course, the whole shebang was a quarter mile out—but still . . . weird.

A half-dozen trucks stalled on the road. Waiting.

And you could see why. Beyond the gray pall of rain there was another storm. Something out of those History Channel extreme weather computer graphics—hypercanes or some such. Only this was white. The gray rain ended just beyond the recovery vehicles; directly in front of them a wall of white swept across the road. You could see the whirling whiteness extending to the horizon. A snowstorm, a blizzard really—standing off the end of the blacktop and the vehicles, whirling its ice and snow like a merry-go-round while the battery of recovery vehicles stood helplessly flashing their lights at its frozen edge.

The sound of doors opening below, and a gust of heavy wind, made him turn from the window on the gantry to look down at the entrance. A newcomer had arrived and was laying his gear on the security conveyor belt. *Not the first, not the last*—good call, soldier. The newcomer wasn't a hardware technician, or a software engineer; the guy wasn't a jet-propulsion geek or even one of the suits from some federal alphabet agency. But he was some kind of book-learning nerd. Looked young—no more than twenty-five. Grad student, science student, pre-med—the utilitarian no-frills clothes, pocket protector, smartphone clipped to his belt in a holster. The young man took off his Clark Kent glasses, wiped the mist from his specs, and pushed a mat of sandy hair from his forehead, exclaiming so just about everybody in the room could hear, "Whew! I thought I wouldn't make it!"

A few heads turned to look at him, dismissed him, and

turned away. There was something likeable and wholesome about the fellow—eagerness and the sense that he felt special about being included. His gear was a couple of transport cases of some sort, bright yellow, the airtight locking kind. He left them by a stand of waiting room seats and bolted up the metal stairs to the gantry. Then gripped the railing and stared out with hungry eyes at the wall of white in front of the recovery vehicles. "Wow," he said. Then he slapped out his phone. "I have to tell my sister, Beatrice, about this. It was 85 degrees in Ohio yesterday! And she was afraid it'd be hotter here!"

But in a moment he deflated when his useful electronic trinket failed to pick up any signal bars. For a few comic seconds he waved it over his head in one direction or another as people do, hoping for a sweet spot. Sorry, no luck, kiddo. The two adults stared at the young man like a puppy they weren't sure whether to pet, make sit, or take out for a piddle. Incredibly harmless and, so far, mildly amusing at 6:06 a.m.

"They can't even read the beacon on the thing that came down," the AP Gal told their new arrival. "No satellite signal. A million acres. They haven't a clue where it is."

Billy let the weather situation sink in for a moment; there wouldn't be Wi-Fi access in this part of the base; communications were strictly controlled. In all probability even weather satellite image feed might be blanked out in spots if necessary, no one on the outside knowing of this anomaly. Not something the military would want getting around: *Uh yeah, we lost a satellite in a snowbank in July.* No way, Jose.

Their own private little storm.

"I'm going to trot out and get you that gear," Billy told the AP Gal. "Who knows? They might take us with them when they decide to roll."

The young grad in the Clark Kent glasses forgot about the dead phone, about trying to call his sis in Ohio, and blurted, "Gee, do you think they will? Really?"

Again the two adults stared at the young man. Billy paused before descending the stairs, then plucked the Dugway Proving Ground ID tag from the fellow's narrow chest to read it, much the same way the AP Gal had done to him but a trifle more gravely. Not much to read on it. A name, a very white Anglo-Saxon name: WEBSTER GALEN CHARGROVE, PHD. Then the symbol πr^2 and underneath, HILLSBORO, OH. No speckled bar code. No description.

And that was disturbing.

What kind of hush-hush government outfit called itself Pi R Squared? What kind of private outfit wouldn't use a speckled bar code? As if young squire Chargrove didn't possess enough recent history to merit a coded background—or worse, that the symbol alone was supposed to tell you all you needed to know. That made it scary. Billy tried to remember if he'd heard of Hillsboro, Ohio, in some other context. Military research and development? Some civilian facility? And so who was this Boy Scout, their junior science dork? But nothing rang a bell. And that frightened him too. πr^2.

Maybe Lattimore knew. Or even Jasper. But he didn't want to ask this kid and betray his own ignorance. Billy let the young brainiac's ID tag drop back to his chest.

"They've promised us a segment of the dust collector grid," the young man explained with a hint of anticipation bordering on delight. "*A comet's DNA.* That is, if the grid's not damaged. If it's intact. Uncorrupted. It's made with Aerogel; do you know what that is?"

Billy almost laughed, but held the corners of his mouth in place.

"Yeah," he said to young squire Chargrove in a friendly way. Then to the AP Gal, "See if you can find a butterfly net in case he decides to flutter off the gantry."

Billy smiled inside. Inadvertently this kid had told him something valuable about his job and his outfit. Whatever Pi R Squared had going on in Hillsboro, they were messing with amino acids, proteins, the building blocks of life. A comet's tail might have swept up all kinds of interesting stuff on its trip across the solar system. Galactic spores that travelled eons across the vast emptiness? Bacteria in suspended animation? Viral threads in cosmic hibernation? God's fairy dust? *Comet DNA.*

Pi R Squared—reengineering the dandelion puffs of life from outer space.

ET phone home? No, ET was calling collect.

Before another hour passed, the public relations officer came in for the briefing: a major, Billy's old rank, but younger, about thirty-five, dressed in battle-dress uniform, and like so many in the military giving off an aura of resilience and energy. He spoke in easy sentences—a strange combination of optimism and reserve. So he made only a very brief briefing: "Now that everyone's here the low-pressure anomaly seems to be breaking up. I guess it was waiting for you termites from Pi R Squared," he said, throwing a long look and a thin smile at young Chargrove, PhD. "We're getting some kind of signal from the probe, and you're welcome to join us in the recovery. Transportation is outside." The message was clear: *Snow or no snow, this is the U.S. Army. Let's go get a spaceship.* "When the satellite is in the quarantine hangar you can break up into your technical groups for preliminary assessment."

The recovery team left in a troop, a squad of soldiers riding in a covered personnel carrier, followed by the fire trucks, the flatbed with the crane, and pulling up the rear, three Humvees packed with the visitors. The convoy left without air cover; this was no weather for helicopters.

Billy, the AP Gal, and young Webster Galen Chargrove, PhD, jostled about in the Humvee, knocking elbows and knees. The AP Gal, in Billy's extra boots and overalls, looked like a very dour Farmer John. Cold air and flecks of snow blew in the cracked windows. The vehicles traveled like a line of circus elephants, trunk to tail, crawling through a sea of white and gray; the flashing lights from the lead trucks stabbed the thick air.

Minutes crawled by, then an hour. Billy had no conception of distance or speed—maybe ten mph across gravelly terrain. The snow cover hid potholes and bumps. Periodically a tire hit a rut and threw the occupants against each other, a lot like being in the hold of a boat in rough seas. Both the AP Gal and Chargrove, PhD, looked like they needed a Dramamine: empty stomach, black coffee, no breakfast—green in the face.

Billy fished some magic out of his roughneck jacket—a tin filled with candied ginger—and offered it to the green AP Gal. She shook her head, and the young professor was too nauseous to even give it a look. Billy rattled the tin in front of them. "Come on, come on," he insisted. "A couple of pieces and you won't woof inside the nice Humvee."

Reluctantly, their shaky fingers reached for the tin. "That's why they gave us breakfast," Billy tut-tutted at the poor things. "An army travels on its stomach. Isn't that right, Specialist?" he addressed the uniformed man at the wheel. The soldier's eyes never left the white whirl in front of them, but from the driver's seat came the reply, "That's affirm."

For the last ten minutes they seemed to be going in wide circles, the specialist driver tugging gently at the wheel. Suddenly the vehicle ground to a halt. The whole convoy had stopped. The snowstorm around them didn't seem to be letting up. So much for optimistic weather forecasts from public relations officers. The inclement weather just wasn't ready to let them in. Some squawks came across the radio. Every third word blanked out, transmission trouble. Still, Billy could make out the gist of it.

"Looks like we're having a little trouble nailing it down. We may have driven by it a couple of times already. They're thinking about sending out a patrol on foot," he explained to his companions. Neither of them replied or seemed to mind, mostly grateful to be sitting still.

Billy turned away and gazed out the window into the milky void. You couldn't see twenty feet; the snow pushing and prodding the air. Every so often a gust struck the side of the Humvee with a thump. Billy's breath steamed up the window, but something caught his eye and he wiped away the moisture.

Some local fauna was sitting in a low drift of snow. A pygmy rabbit, sitting still as a stone, ears up. Its little nose twitched, the whiskers flitting back and forth. Billy understood. The rabbit wasn't concerned about the pack of noisy vehicles, the flashing lights, the throbbing engines. He'd seen them before, the convoy a familiar distraction; the rolling tires, the marching men combing the ground—nothing new in any of that.

Billy's heightened Skin Walker senses came to him in a rush like the moments in Van Horn on the nighttime street, full of creatures you didn't see. . . . He felt inside the animal's nose and whiskers and sharp ears, filtering out the wind and the snow. Back on the rez, old Granny Sparrow was smiling at him. And he knew what the rabbit knew—something else was out there. And he knew just where.

"Hey!" the hard voice of the Specialist driver broke his concentration. "You all right?" Everyone in the vehicle stared at him, like he'd been talking to himself; yeah, Billy'd been muttering rabbit talk. *New . . . Something new, new thing. New, new over there, new thing . . .*

Billy snapped out of it. "I know where it is." He pulled the hood over his head and unlatched the side door. "Just get on the radio and tell them to follow you. And you follow me."

The *Stardust* reentry pod sat sixty yards off, through the shifting storm of snow. The satellite payload had wedged itself in between a couple of large boulders, its reentry parachute a mess of flapping tatters. As Billy trudged in

closer, the vehicle crawled slowly after him; gently, a rec-
ollection of Wen Chen's crackpot file flitted into his head.
HAARP—the High Frequency Active Auroral Research
Program. Didn't that high-altitude stuff include cloud seed-
ing and weather control? You'd think the Air Force would
arrange for clear skies if they could.

He spotted more rabbits: about ten sitting on their
haunches in a wide rough semicircle, twitching their noses
at the silver thing. As he thumped past the little animals,
they abandoned their vigil and scattered in all directions.
The recovery vehicles rumbled up, and the rabbits had
vanished without a trace. The roughly pyramidal pod looked
scraped and dented where the wind had dragged it along the
ground by its chute—but otherwise intact.

Young Webster Galen Chargrove, PhD from πr^2, was the
second member of the crew to get out of the vehicle and
hit the ground. He stood staring at the pod, his short, sandy
hair blowing against the grain. And then as if to punctuate
this moment, the wind measurably slackened. The snow,
instead of going sideways, began to fall straight down in
gentle, sparse flakes. Above their heads a window opened
in the sky—somewhere up there the early-morning sun was
shining. A tear of blue, getting wider and wider.

The AP Gal joined them, staring at the thing. She turned
to Billy plaintively: "Got any more of that—?" but didn't
finish her sentence. Instead she took a deep pull of fresh
air, then put one hand on the Humvee and bent her head,
retching a little. She wiped her mouth on her sleeve.
"Got any more of that ginger?"

In those few seconds the recovery vehicles had deployed
and the men in full hazmat suits were cordoning off the
area with flares; Billy, Chargrove, and the newswoman retreated twenty paces, giving them room. The minicrane on
the flatbed truck was already lowering a hook; the soldiers
snapped huge bungee cords around the craft.

In five minutes the whole shebang was ready to roll

again. But a great unease came over Billy: the fleeing rabbits, the newswoman's sudden convulsion as if there was something wrong with this place. As if the capsule itself contained some kind of contaminant. Then the curious appearance and sudden abatement of the storm—as if the weather gods wanted to make sure young master Chargrove, PhD, was on hand no matter what. That the brainiac didn't miss a thing.

The young man's face was ruddy with the wind, his eyes glistening, enjoying the greatest moment of his life. And Billy wondered again what the hell this guy from πr^2, that whole weird outfit, wanted with dust from comet tails. Likeable or not—it felt all wrong. Even with breakfast, his stomach roiled, and he reached for another piece of sugared ginger.

Their time in the quarantine hangar stretched into hours; the *Stardust* pod wasn't a pop-top. Behind layers of inner and outer glass walls the men in hazmat suits carefully took their precious cargo apart. From their spot in a viewing booth the visitors could watch their progress. Some had even wandered back to the hospitality waiting room for a nap on the couches. But not Billy, not the AP Gal, and not the eager-beaver PhD from πr^2. Somewhere in the third hour the satellite pod was ready to release the Aerogel dust collector grid.

It had done its job all right: collected its precious dust, collapsed into itself like an accordion, and now ready to give up its secrets. One of the technicians inside the quarantined glass wall detached a small section of the collector like a fragment of honeycomb and placed it in young Chargrove's airtight traveling container. He looked to the sealed viewing area and gave a big thumbs-up.

Webster Galen Chargrove, PhD, beamed with delight. An innocent, wholesome grin, and Billy nodded with a slip of a wry smile. *Attaboy.* The young fellow's attitude was infectious, but still, part of the man's Injun mind was going *and yet and yet.* . . .

"How come the public relations officer called you guys 'termites'?" Billy suddenly asked.

A laugh caught in young Chargrove's throat, as though Billy had hit on some sort of inside joke from Pi R Squared. Staring down into the quarantine hangar, the young brainiac explained offhand, "Oh, typical government research op. Part of the facility is underground. Y'know, like an ant colony." He paused for a moment, wondering if he'd let slip too much. Then, as if to bury the issue, "Seems like your Aerogel grid did okay."

15

The Stuka Crew

A yellow Toyota 4Runner pulling a Kendon dual-rail trailer with a used Harley strapped on came out of the Rocky Mountains. The rising sun blasted over the Great Plains and into the narrow chute of roadway. Cheryl and Bhakti had returned Herman's MINI Cooper in plenty of time, got some sleep, and went car-shopping—paying cash. The 2001 yellow Toyota 4Runner was an all-purpose, drive-till-the-wheels-fall-off vehicle, the yellow color easy for Cheryl to spot in traffic if she was riding her motorcycle. And the used Harley Sportster was in damn good shape even with 15,000 miles. Cheryl had no intention of giving up a motorcycle and with it her independence. They got off easy, under ten thousand dollars for the whole rig.

Bhakti found a safe place for Janet's ashes on the rear seat, the Nambe metal urn in a black canvas miniduffle with the zipper open. He wanted the zipper open so Janet could see where they were going, so she wouldn't feel left out. Closing the thick black zipper over the urn felt too much like closing it over her face, too much like a final good-bye.

When Bhakti put the duffle in the back, he almost sat beside his daughter. Instead, he petted the urn once, saying, "Rest here now." Then silently got in the passenger's seat. Janet's ashes would ride with them with the zipper open for over a thousand miles—as long as Cheryl and Bhakti were together.

The two had spent the night in Eureka, Nevada, and headed out early in the morning, skirting the edge of the Schell Creek Range and the Oquirrh—beyond that rip of mountains lay the Great Salt Lake and Utah. You couldn't drive through; you had to go around. Then head down to Salt Lake City. Somewhere over the Bonneville Flats a gray-and-white storm seemed to be breaking apart, some of the clouds sucking into the peaks and vanishing, others moving east toward the big city.

They had decided to take the long route from Los Angeles, avoiding the well-used Interstate 15, going up the length of California instead, through central Nevada and over the High Sierras, entering Utah from the north. A ten-hour drive on big roads turned into twenty hours on smaller ones. The yellow SUV dragging the Kendon trailer with Cheryl's hog slowed them too. Tricky mountain driving, steep curvy roads—they crawled under a cloudless strip of American sky.

Worse still, paranoia required several stops to look over their shoulder in the event of a tail from LA, cooling their heels in roadhouses and motels to see if they were being followed. When they reached Eureka, Nevada, they veered off track and hid out on an empty road near an

Indian reservation aptly named Duckwater. Cheryl stared out the dusty glass windshield of the SUV at a carpet of burnt hills. Wherever the ducks in the water hung out, it wasn't here.

Inside the SUV Cheryl and Bhakti's road trip fluctuated between the sharp edge of obsession and a shotgun marriage. Sharing close quarters day in and day out proved to be a battle of give and take, with the take part taking advantage. How the odd couple settled on a motel for the night, which diner or fast food joint to pick, which station on the radio, the best possible route—every little thing could be a source of niggling spats. And now finally they'd arrived at the stage in their relationship where people who'd been together too long were reduced to name calling, the ex-motorcycle cop branding her pal a "gorp."

When he hung his jacket up in the motel closet: "You're such a gorp."

When he ordered cottage cheese and canned peaches for the third time in a day: "What a gorp."

Only to hear him mutter back, "Shiva princess," turning a deaf ear into a fine art.

The last three and a half hours in the car hadn't been much fun; Cheryl was getting pimples on her fanny as she hit the accelerator or rode the brakes and the mountains shrank behind them. Bhakti began fiddling with the radio soon as a strong signal came in.

Being Utah, every other station, AM and FM, broadcast brimstone and Bible thumping, not to mention a medley of "your favorite hymns" and "holiday easy listening"—he let the tuner rest on a German version of "Silent Night"—in *July,* for Chrissakes. And to make it even more annoying, Bhakti was singing along in Punjabi. Yes, you could actually do that to "Stille Nacht"—German was bad enough, but Punjabi positively mind-breaking. The word he repeated was *Waheguru . . . Waheguru . . .* A damned near-perfect syllable match to Siiiiii-uh-lent Night, Hooooo-uh-leee-Night.

Wa-hah-gooo-rooo . . .

Cheryl figured the word was a prayer from back home in "Inja"; but what it meant she couldn't guess. As long as one lost soul out there was praying, or singing through the thin air, this crazy brown man was more than happy to pray along. Christian songs, Buddhist songs, Jewish songs, even bad C&W—anything would do. And it drove her nuts.

Wa-hahhhh—

"You are such a freaking gorp!"

Bhakti left off his prayer, and stuck her a hard look with his dark eyes.

"What is gorp?" He shut off "Silent Night." "Don't be a gorp. Gorp, gorp, gorp. What is gorp, Shiva princess? I looked it up last night. It stands for trail mix. Granola, oats, raisins, and peanuts. Are you calling me trail mix?"

She straightened herself, gripping the wheel for another slow turn in the SUV, and wriggled her fanny to relieve her rump. Then told him, matter-of-factly, "My mother told me a gorp is someone with teeth in their ass who eats the buttons off car seats, so I shouldn't squirm around while we were driving."

Bhakti let this sink in. He glanced at the leather bucket seats in their SUV. No buttons. He gave her a long, dubious look. "Yes, well that explains a lot about you. Buttons on car seats went out with high-buttoned shoes."

Bhakti went back to the radio. "Perhaps we can find something more appropriate for a true gorp." He zipped along the stations, finally finding a bit of classical music from an NPR station. The music, bright and comic: Franz Liszt's "Hungarian Rhapsody Number 2 in C-Sharp Minor"—yes Cheryl had heard it before, not that she actually knew the title.

Bhakti helped her out. "Also known to many as the 'Bugs Bunny Symphony.' "

"Yes! Yes!" Cheryl cried. "On the piano with his tux and tails flapping. 'Look, Ma, no hands!' Bugs playing with his feet!"

Cheryl smiled for another two miles without shifting her fanny once. When the piece died, the announcer droned on about a fundraiser and Bhakti lowered the volume. "When you have kids you remember these things."

And that stopped her cold. Kids, yeah.

"What does *Waheguru* mean?" she asked him.

"Wondrous Teacher," he replied. "But it signifies more than that. Also known as Vahe*guru*. The *V* reminds us of Vishnu. *Guru* you know as 'teacher' or 'wise man,' but is actually two words: *gu,* meaning 'darkness,' and *ru,* meaning 'light.' We go from darkness to light. In English you might say 'the wondrous destroyer of darkness.' "

Cheryl finally understood. "It's a prayer? So you were praying? Praying for Lila Chen? That she's all right? That she's alive?"

He nodded silently. Then at last, "And for us."

Bhakti went back to the radio tuner again, finding that dopey Hail Mary station. He snagged on to the conclusion of an Emergency Alert System test: *"This concludes this test of the Emergency Braincast System."* With the final three-beep tone, Cheryl glanced at the radio, wondering whether she really heard the peculiar twist on the prerecorded message. Broadcast? Braincast? She looked to Bhakti, but he showed no reaction. Maybe he hadn't heard.

"That's been happening a lot lately, the emergency broadcast thing," Cheryl said without raising the issue of the altered word. "Have you noticed?"

"Should I have?" Bhakti replied.

She stared at the road ahead, another long mild curve. Should he have? Should she have? She shrugged. "I guess not. It just seems weird."

The programming cut back to the weather, the announcer giving some color comment on the local forecast in one of those fine upbeat male voices that oozed bonhomie: *This is the Big P on KEZB 90.7 in Beaver, Utah. Well, you know what I know—we seem to have had a freak snowstorm this morning, starting out in Bonneville, over to Dugway, then downtown Salt Lake. Too early, you say? Not if you're looking for comet dust in Beaver Land. Throw in a Chinee princess with the lunch special and you get eggroll. But the Big P says you stay right here on KEZB, the Eeee-Zeee Beaver, leave it to Beaver; music during the day and inspiration at night. . . .*

Cheryl frowned. What a steaming cup of mental mush. Bhakti didn't seem to have heard "Chinee princess." Cheryl thought better of pointing it out. Leave it to Beaver.

The Road Island Diner was a streamlined stainless-steel railroad car with an art deco entranceway embedded with a large lit-up clock. A place Buck Rogers wouldn't mind bringing Wilma Deering as long as they could park their airship. Cheryl scoped it out on Bhakti's laptop: operating for years under different names and owners in and around the Northeast, the diner was a classic. But with the decline of the New England economy, this bit of Americana had been sold again and found a home where the buffalo roam in Oakley, Utah, a little north of Salt Lake. And where seldom was heard a discouraging word—

Except for today.

Apparently there'd been some kind of ruckus at the establishment.

A few patches of snow remained on the pavement and in the shade beside some parked cars. Lots of confused tire tracks. The first thing Cheryl and Bhakti noticed was a spidery crack in the front door glass about the size of a pie plate, and a smear that looked like lemon meringue. Inside, the place was open for business—barely. Still getting over the night before.

A few customers sat at the counter, and didn't look up from their flapjacks when the newcomers came in from outside. A waitress with a tag that read MAGDALEN looked up from the heat lamps at the kitchen pass-through slot and said, "Anywhere's okay. Be right with you."

Cheryl found a booth along the front windows but far at one end that gave her a view of the place. Her buddy would have to sit with his back to the action, but that didn't seem to bother him. A busboy was messing around behind the counter with a broom and a pan. He swept the floor, and the dry clack of broken china clattered harshly; then hefted a large plastic bucket full of busted crockery and lugged it somewhere out of sight. That's when Cheryl noticed another thing: splashes of coffee and orange soda against the walls, and something unspeakable on the ceiling. As if a family of wild baboons who didn't know how to eat in public had trashed the place.

Magdalen the waitress picked up another order at the warming shelf, passed it off smartly to a couple at the counter, and made her way to their booth, her order book and pen in hand before she got there. "Know what you want? Or would you like a menu?"

Cheryl didn't need a menu. "Can I have two over easy, sausage patty, no potatoes?" And Bhakti fell into gorp mode, politely asking, "Do you have cottage cheese and canned peaches?" Magdalen nodded yup to both.

"Did something happen here?" Cheryl asked. Magdalen finished scribbling their order. She glanced around to see if she was needed elsewhere in the joint. Nope. An exhale of disgust.

"A rough crowd last night. Broke some dishes, threw a lot of food around. Nothing you could really put your finger on—just bad seed. Prone to accidents—know what I mean? They came on the wings of the storm. Then paid and left."

"Didn't you call the cops?" Bhakti shifted around in his seat to get a better look at the place.

"For what? A mess of dishes and a little cracked glass? They paid. Overpaid. And we cleaned up the worst of it before closing. But I see we missed a spot or two. The whole crew could be in three different states by now." She shook her head in disgust. "Skinhead biker buttwads, pardon my French. Generally we're okay with our two-stroke friends, but these clowns were yerks. Anything to drink?"

After Magdalen left with their order, Bhakti leaned across the table to whisper a question. "What's a yerk?"

Cheryl snorted, then mastered herself. "A twitchy glue-sniffing jack-off?"

Bhakti rolled his eyes. Twenty-five years in this country, speaking English since he was six, and he *still* couldn't keep up with the slang. "What about 'to snog'—I once heard a woman complain that her husband 'snogged the local skank—'"

"Shush! Shut up," Cheryl shushed.

"What?"

"Don't look around. No, no, okay, look around slowly. No, wait, they're leaving. Look out the window."

Cheryl's eyes followed a man and little girl getting up from the counter; he paid off with a big bill and left the change. She and Bhakti must have walked right by them on their way in, neither noticing the other. Bhakti twisted his neck, and what he saw stunned him. Inspector Frederick walked at the side of his Crown Victoria sedan, opening the passenger door for a little girl about age nine or ten. The girl, dressed in bib jeans and sneakers and a red shirt, stared at the diner through the plate glass right into Bhakti's eyes. *Choose and by your choice I will know you.* He heard Senora Malvedos' raspy cigarette voice brushing his ear like the wisp of a breeze. *Or let the girl pick.*

Bhakti's hands gripped the table, his body coiled, ready to bust from the booth.

"I know that little girl. I've seen her. How I found you, found Janet—"

The inspector slammed the car door shut and made his way back to the driver's side. He glanced once at the front of the diner; saw nothing of interest—a band of light had spread across the glass panes. He got behind the wheel. Cheryl was half out of her seat, fumbling with her cash, when a soft, serious voice came at them from the next booth.

"Don't get up. Don't follow. Please, sit back down. I'm not sure you're going to find who you're looking for by chasing those two. Not that way."

The tone and quality of the man's voice stopped Cheryl dead in her tracks. The voice surprised Bhakti, and he fell back to the corner of his booth seat. A smooth and handsome Lakota face stared at them with hard brown eyes. The tone said, *You want to know what I know. Maybe we can help each other.*

The man came out of his booth and slid neatly onto the seat beside Bhakti, who was scrunched in the corner. Cheryl was skeptical. "Do we know you?"

Billy Shadow smiled back. He took out his Lattimore Aerospace ID and laid it on the table. The eggs and sausage came, the cottage cheese. Bhakti blinked at his plate of mush, then blinked at Cheryl's plate: the perfectly turned eggs, the sausage. He suddenly changed his mind. "I want what she's having." Magdalen nodded, jotting the order onto their check. Then Bhakti stared hard at the man who had joined them, some sort of memory stirring his brain.

Bhakti nodded at the newcomer. "I know this guy," Bhakti told Cheryl.

"We work for same Big Chief," Billy said in mock Injun. "When you didn't show up for work and vanished from the subdivision, Boss Lattimore got worried. I've been hoping to catch up with you. Among others."

Billy reached over the back of their booth seat and set the green Zero Degree tote in the middle of the table. "If you haven't seen this before you may want to keep an eye on the restroom door."

The tote flap peeled away. Inside, the plastic evidence bag from the Van Horn sheriff's station, labeled CHEN HOUSE. The remains of a burnt ear, dangling an earring.

"We've seen this before," Bhakti said. "And worse."

The extra hematite earring taken from Lila's blistered dresser dangled from his fingers. For a moment Billy stared at the earring match. Then nodded too, as if finally realizing, *Sure, girls buy extras, just in case they lose one.* Then Billy's eyes went back to the plastic baggie and he did the strangest thing.

He zipped it open, pulled it over his nose, and inhaled deeply. . . . Billy's eyes seemed to roll into his head. He began to mutter unintelligible words. Cheryl and Bhakti froze in alarm, afraid the man was about to faint or go spastic. The strange fellow's head slipped toward the table, his lips slurred—but he suddenly snapped out of it.

Billy's eyes cleared, and he stared coolly out the window.

"No, we don't want to follow them. The weasel copper, the fortune-teller girl. Definitely not. They walk a different path, different from ours."

Outside the diner, Inspector Frederick's sedan backed up and nosed toward the exit of the parking lot. Cheryl had to restrain herself from leaping up, and Bhakti looked like he was ready to crawl over seat backs. Billy Shadow's smooth voice stopped them.

"The cop isn't going to find what he's looking for. There's no Lila Chen at the end of his road. Even though he's using the little girl like some kind of compass. But she isn't going to bring him where he wants to go. Or us, either. We want to keep going east."

Cheryl started getting uppity. "And you know this *why*? You know this *how*?"

"Look." Billy took a slug of his coffee; he jangled the baggie once and put it back in the freezer tote. "It's a long story. A cat bit me."

Cheryl sat back in the booth, eyes as big as saucers, flabbergasted at this hooey. Billy's tempered voice came at her:

"*I see things, okay?* A biker outfit called the Stuka Crew came through here last night—the very same baboons who messed up this diner. The Stuka Crew has adopted Lila as their mascot. Their little play toy. Your gal Lila rounds out their bunks, so to speak."

And Billy told them what he knew. How the Stuka Crew kept Lila like one of those pedophile abductees, locked up for the day in their cycle van and let out only at night when they could all keep an eye on her. The gang itself was seven members who followed a small traveling circus called The Dr. Ponkus Medicine Show.

"The bikers put on daredevil stunts at local fairgrounds," Billy explained.

The Dr. Ponkus Medicine Show was an outfit fashioned after those nineteenth-century snake-oil hustles that wandered the countryside with acts like The Serpent Lady or The Brilliant Fleas. Cheap carny stuff. Only Dr. Ponkus didn't sell magic elixirs to improve your manhood, and it was mostly legal.

"What's with the name? The Stuka Crew?"

"Y'know, like the dive-bomber in World War Two, that big unpleasantness in Europe last century?"

Dim blank stares came back at him. Billy tried again. "It's the name of their act. The seven bikers are skinhead types. White Aryan Resistance rejects. Four guys who call themselves The Four Horsemen and three women, the She-Wolves of the SS. The guys wear Wehrmacht uniforms and jump a flaming pool on their bikes, while the girls do slaloms around X-shaped mock tank traps made of two-by-fours and shoot paintballs from a sidecar. For their finale one of the bikes drives headlong into a Sherman tank. It's just collapsible, plastic and canvas, but the bike slams in and the thing goes up in smoke and hellfire. You can check their website. I did."

"And you know this how?" Cheryl asked again, exasperated.

A slim smile creased Billy's face: a big cat in a ghost town; Grandma Sparrow in a dream. He could hardly explain the Skin Walker thing to himself. "I know because I went down to Van Horn looking for Gunga Din here, found the ear in the baggie in an evidence locker, and because a large cat bit me. I think I was meant to find you, and I think we were meant to go together."

Bhakti's eggs and sausage came. Cheryl didn't know which was stranger, some Injun with cat-scratch fever or her Punjab companion poking his fork into sausage. She sat back in her seat and pushed her plate away. Tried it out one more time, just to set the record straight:

"Explain again how the hell you know all this? Because you're snorting baggie fumes and a large cat bit you?"

"Who the hell told you to drive to Utah?" Billy demanded right back.

To which Cheryl had no answer. Some black ants on an old menu, the god of the winds slapping it à la carte onto a car's windshield? Don't even go there. *Calling it unlikely was being generous.*

Bhakti looked up from his plate with a dab of egg on his very trimmed beard. "Who's this Hocus Pocus guy?"

"Dr. Ponkus. Nobody special. A loose outfit, an old-time carny with a funny name. The whole mud show isn't that far from here. We can catch up with them at their next whistle stop. Notice the ear and the bangle in the baggie? The Stuka Crew wanted to keep Lila Chen compliant. The bandages should be coming off any day now. They didn't use antibiotics, or give her a tetanus shot, but she doesn't seem to be infected. Think you can account for that?"

Bhakti carefully put his knife and fork on his empty plate and wiped egg from his whiskers. He'd seen the contents of the evidence bag before it became "evidence." The question of how they got here was less important to him than the question of why the Chen girl hadn't died of an infection. For him conjecture lost to science every time.

"Lila Chen isn't dead because she is very healthy," Bhakti said quietly. "An enhanced immune system. That's the only explanation."

Billy Shadow quietly nodded his head as if this simple statement hit the root of a problem he'd been wrestling with for a while. "Yeah, exactly. One in a million."

Cheryl intrigued him too. "So what's your deal, Miss?" She didn't answer immediately, so he shrugged. "Never mind; tell me later."

For a long minute the three adults sat in the booth without speaking, as if they'd come to some mutual understanding. Obviously they'd have a better chance of finding the Chen girl if they pooled their resources. Finally Billy looked at the untouched dish of cottage cheese and canned peach halves; the curds had leached a rime of thin whitish whey across the plate.

"Hey, Gunga Din. You gonna eat that?"

Inspector Frederick couldn't stand the little rat sitting next to him in the passenger's seat. Having her in the car was like seeing a young version of that old palm reader's face; everything about her just grated like sand on a lollipop. The way she twirled a lock of hair around her finger, the way she stared out at the passing scene, never talking. Making him ask her, *Do you have to go potty?*

Are you hungry? The way she hummed along to the radio; right now Roger Miller's "King of the Road" blatted out the speakers, the words all twisted, as if speaking directly to him:

> *So many hos for rent*
> *Cute tail for any gent*
> *No muss, no fuss, no mess*
> *I ain't got no deep regrets*

God—that cheesy song grated like nails on a chalkboard:

> *Ah, but . . . two hours of strokin' poon*
> *Buys an eight-by-six jailhouse room*
> *Gimme Sweet Jane with greasy jeans*
> *King of the Hos.*

Yep, that's me, he thought. Inspector Frederick, King of the Hos—dragging around the little tart because she could see things too. So he bugged her, demanding, *This way? Or should we go there?* Twisting the little chubby face from the passenger window with his narrow fingers, he growled harsher now, "Which way?"

And she just stared at him with those big baby browns. If she did it again he'd turn that angel face away for one last time. Stick her head in a plastic bag, lift her tushie in the air, and hump the lil' squirmer till the writhing stopped and it all went limp—

Whoa! He hit the brakes. Coming around a curve through a narrow arroyo a long white limousine blocked the road, right across both lanes. Inspector Frederick knuckled the wheel as his Crown Victoria screeched to a halt. "What the f—"

But his lips died cold when the limo door opened. The

long gaunt man stepped onto the roadway. Stared for twenty seconds or so at the Crown Victoria, then crooked his finger. *Come on. Get out. Don't make me wait.* The pale blue eyes of Mr. P. dragged him from the car. The two men stood in the middle of the empty highway. At last Mr. Piper said, "Y'know, Felix . . . we hired you because you came highly recommended. But you have turned out to be an absolute crap-magnet."

Inspector Frederick took a deep, calming breath. Christ, wasn't the guy supposed to be on a plane to LA? Well, Salt Lake had airports too. "This is not the time, P." He felt some bile rising up his throat. "I'm inches away from your precious Rinky-dink. And right now you're blocking the road."

Mr. Piper paused for a moment, then examined his manicured fingernails. "Actually, the firm has come to a decision. We're taking you off the case. So I'm politely asking you to follow my lead here, and when we reach the next local constabulary—park in front and turn yourself in. I'll take the Little Match Girl now."

This made a snort of laughter come out. "Get real. I've got as much on you as you do on me. Wire taps, e-mails— the whole punchbowl including the turd. You don't turn me in; I turn *you* in. I'm a *badge.*"

The sedan door unlatched, and Little Maria got out of the Crown Victoria. She stood quietly on the roadway as though she'd seen the bad cop's dirty end and steeled herself to whatever came next. The tiniest scrap of forethought came to her. There was a boy sitting in that limo—a young man, really.

A young lad bad as bad could get. Heart black as pitch, cold as ice.

But there was something else—something unexpected. Little Maria could see a tiny spark inside the young man—a faint ember burning beside his cold heart. A tiny white spark of hope or goodness or just a granule of sugar left over from the First Sweet Thought at the beginning of time. And that tiny ember showed through the limousine, right through the cushy seats, the molded metal, gleaming like a star in the darkness.

As she stood in the roadway, Little Maria closed the sedan door like a door latch to the past, closing it on Inspector Frederick. A few feet away the limo door stood open, along with her future, and a spark of hope in the dark.

Mr. Piper sighed and looked wearily up and down the canyon. From beside a scrap of dried brush, three mangy coyotes came into view. They padded back and forth on the rim of some red dirt beside the road, then stared at the cars. "Okay, in a minute," Mr. P. told the mangy animals.

A profound sadness came over his narrow pale face. Tuttutting like the town librarian. Telling the bad cop in a hushed voice:

"We don't need no stinking badges."

Around dusk a wandering caravan of bikers rolled down the same road, empty now except for the abandoned Crown Victoria sedan, stopped dead over burnt rubber skid marks. Four outriders leading a red 4X4 and a large stainless-steel Custom-Fab cargo trailer emblazoned with an Iron Cross over the words 𝕿𝖍𝖊 𝕾𝖙𝖚𝖐𝖆 𝕮𝖗𝖊𝖜 in gothic script. The Four Horsemen, in no rush to be anywhere, cruised easy, the thrumming of their exhaust throbbing back at them in the canyon, so they didn't have to brake hard. They gracefully slid around the abandoned vehicle in a troop and pulled over. An empty car, like a lost wallet, was something worth picking apart, pawing through just for the hell of it. In any case a good spot to take a leak and let the girls squat in the brush and shoot anything that moved just for the hell of it.

Not much in the Crown Victoria: a couple of soggy

burger boxes with the little bits of wilted lettuce, a half-eaten bag of cheddar cheese popcorn, a few plastic soda bottles. The keys in the ignition; they popped the trunk. Zippo. Disappointed at the slim pickings, the men wandered off the road like dogs searching for a whiz spot. That's when one of them found the body.

Once a man, mangled and torn like a strip of rice paper—a hundred and sixty pounds reduced to a mound of bones and gristle in pants and a torn shirt. Three coyotes looked up from their work, bared their teeth, and didn't back off.

Now the master race was gonna show the scrawny mutts who was boss in the desert: two shots from a pistol did the trick. One coyote lay dead; another limped off into the dark, yelping. The third vanished.

"Hey, I found a Rolex." The Horseman in biker boots and leather squatted near the body. He splashed some water from a bottle and cleaned the watch, then put it on his wrist.

"It's probably fake," came another voice from out of the dusk.

"So what? It's ticking."

Off in the brush the last of the coyotes watched the men and their hussies get ready to ride again. One of the brassy babes complained, "Why the hell couldn't we have stopped at the Arby's back in Fort Duchesne?" She pronounced it Fort *Douche*.

And the gruff reply:

"Why the hell don't you learn to piss standing up?"

16

The Ant Colony

Eleanor recognized almost everyone at the Connecticut Valley Hospital, staff and patients alike, and could call many by name. If her progress continued, there'd be only a few more weeks of observation to go. Then she might get to go back home with Guy and Lauren by the end of August. Her therapist had allowed her a Wi-Fi laptop; even with strong parental controls it showed how much they trusted her. But sometimes the recovery felt like three steps forward and two steps back. This evening, especially.

At dinner in the common hall, another patient in the facility gave Eleanor a bit of a fright. A middle-aged lady much like herself, Eleanor had nicknamed her friend Mrs. Miniver, as her first name was Kay and she looked a little like Greer Garson in the movie of the same name. They often ate together.

Mrs. Miniver had been committed after chasing her husband around with a kitchen knife, tying her children up in bed, and setting the house on fire. All the while shouting about how "Goobers" were taking over their bodies. They used to be Raisinets, but now they were Goobers. Happily, the fire never caught, the kids were unharmed—unhappily, Kay found herself in the Connecticut Valley loony bin. Until the "incident" by all accounts she'd lived an ordinary, unremarkable life.

Tonight at dinner, Kay Miniver leaned over a pink plastic bowl of tapioca and whispered, "Have you seen them? Do they come to your room too?"

"Who, Kay? Who comes?"

Kay fell silent, took a long while over a spoon of pudding, and looked suspiciously around the dining room. Nope, nobody listening, just the regular collection of droolers, head-bangers, and mumblers. . . .

"The light people," she answered in almost a whisper. "They've come every night for a week to my room. Right outside the window. But they don't want me. I think they're looking for you." Kay finished her tapioca and stared sorrowfully at the empty pudding cup. "I think it's because we look a little alike and we sit together and we're the same age and we're friends."

"Oh." Eleanor thought for a moment. "No, nobody's come to my window. Not that I noticed. And yes, I'm glad we're friends."

Kay gave a final nod and sucked her spoon. Then put it in the cup. "Maybe they just wanted me to let you know they were coming, so you wouldn't be surprised."

Eleanor offered Kay the remains of her own tapioca.

"Maybe."

Eleanor didn't like when Kay talked crazy. It reminded her of her own babbling moments, which she was trying to control with all her might. Bhakti had called during the day and that was nice; he was still looking for Lila Chen, but Eleanor had nothing new for him. She'd dried up like an empty gourd. She chalked her lack of insight up to getting normal; maybe the medication. Bhakti promised he'd come east as soon as he found the child, and Eleanor tried to make him not worry about anything else saying, "I'm glad. Find her, Bhakti. Find her for Janet. And me."

The best thing about their conversation was when Bhakti asked, "Are you still walking?" And she could answer, "You bet."

But the reassuring glow of Bhakti's voice diminished after dinner, disappearing entirely by the time she returned to her room. Eleanor turned on the TV and powered up her laptop, but neither distracted her this evening.

The long blue shadows of midsummer stretched across the lawn outside her window. Two large black-winged woodpeckers jumped to a nearby tree and hopped around the trunk looking for a good spot to drill for bugs. Eleanor could see their silhouettes, the slash of white across their faces, the sharp red crown poking this way and that: *peck-peck-peck.*

Eleanor turned away from the window and stared at the TV. She tried to ignore the walls. She wasn't doing very well with that; the dancing men were at it again.

This time not only were they marching around the painted border of her cheerful loony bin room, but dancing with the ants too. The nasty red ants. The stick-figure men held their spiky legs and led them along as though doing a minuet. One step forward, two steps back. Turn and curtsy. Turn and bow.

The television wasn't behaving either. The images were clouded with static, breaking apart then re-forming.

From a local news station out of Ohio, a reporter stood in a local field in the midst of tall weeds, speaking into his microphone under a deep cloudy sky. The green hills around him were torn by mudslides. Over his shoulder you could clearly see some kind of abandoned factory in the background: long brick buildings, smokestacks, broken windows. Then rain came streaming down.

The screen tag under the reporter read STEVE HORSTMEYER——CHIEF METEOROLOGIST, FOX 19 CINCINNATI. The heavy weather had brought him out of the studio, and he pulled up his hood, looking slightly amused. The audio came through crackly, but Eleanor could get the gist of it.

"They say time heals all wounds and rain washes the world clean of its sins. But not today in Hillsboro. Recent

heavy rains which have kept everyone indoors for weeks seem to have exposed something somebody wished stayed hidden. A mudslide on a slope a few hundred yards from the rear of the old Whiteside Meatpacking Plant revealed a pile of rotting meat. An estimated forty tons of meat."

The report cut to a shot of the mudslide hill; across the face of the cleaved slope an ugly eruption seemed to be flowing out of the soft dirt like slow-moving lava: meat of all kinds and description, chopped, limbs, bones, guts bursting out of the cliff face as if from an angry wound. The report came back to Steve Horstmeyer, his face lashed with rain.

"Normally with the gates closed and no road access, nobody would notice it out here, but with the sheer volume of waste product, people downwind—well how do I put this politely?—they noticed the smell."

The woodpeckers outside Eleanor's window went *peck-peck-peck,* then suddenly stopped. The birds' dark silhouettes froze to the tree, dead still. That's when Eleanor noticed the floating light. It seemed to come from a copse of woods at the far end of the hospital grounds, zigzag around the tree, and then hover twenty feet outside her window. An amber glowing ball of light.

Kay's light people? It didn't look like a person.

Did it actually speak to Kay? An illumination of few words? It felt part friend, part guardian. Did it want to speak now—?

A few cogent ideas entered Eleanor's mind—ideas that went into her head like a touch of voltage, a pleasant tingling. *Once I walked among men; once I had a name. . . .* Eleanor felt the name on the tip of her tongue, a very familiar name. A reassuring name.

Tesla.

The name stirred up lectures on electromechanical engineering in grad school, and long spells in the MIT library: wireless energy transmission, longitudinal waves, resonant frequency, weird science. Tesla the nut job: *They called me mad at the University, but I'll show them. . . .* The Light was Tesla, come to explain something to her. How could that be? Was she crazy again? Urging her to look away from the window, go to the laptop.

At first a single image filled the screen: πr^2.

The symbol faded, replaced by a live stream.

A video report was in progress of a lecture or a briefing. A middle-aged balding man with a halo of white hair was presenting scientific findings to an audience in a small, darkened amphitheater. The audience, composed of civilians and military types, was very attentive.

The lecturer wore a white lab coat; his dry, clean-shaven face lit from underneath, gave him that mad professor shadow. The face reminded her of Sam Jaffe in one of those old movies, the High Lama in *Lost Horizon*: except this man was more remote, more cerebral, and much less humane. Completely self-absorbed in his lecture, he held a laser pointer that danced about a large light screen behind him. The light screen showed a satellite image of the Van Horn subdivision where Eleanor used to live. His voice bleated softly:

"The initial test of the Braincast system with the Van Horn control group concluded, despite unforeseen outside factors. We tapped eight women, but due to outside interference only five subjects responded to the stimuli." Eleanor stared at the screen, confused. Then it dawned on her. *She* was one of the subjects, while the outside factor interfering was the gang that abducted Lila Chen—and Janet. If Lila hadn't been kidnapped, there would have been three more women coming along: Mrs. Chen, her daughter, and Janet. Eight instead of five.

The professor explained more: "But once the stimulant was introduced to the remaining subjects, respond they did.

One of our more flippant designers has dubbed the process *Dog Whistle*—for obvious reasons. We call and they listen." Eleanor started to understand; the man in the white lab coat was explaining how the women had been lured away.

"What makes it most effective is the targeted delivery system via our enhanced Skeeterbug. An innocuous insect bite allows us to pick who we want, and the Braincast system allows us to direct them where to go."

The light screen showed a complex internal/external diagram of a mosquito labeled SKTR-13, its tiny brain pulsing with energy. The screen shifted, showing the scrolling database of the Social Security System, the nine-digit numbers morphing to names and addresses of people, then morphing to something called the DNA National Database, then to the actual double helix of a DNA strand, finally superimposed over an animation of the human body. A tiny mosquito zeroed in on the human figure.

So that's how they got to them all, Eleanor realized. Sure, just about everyone in the Van Horn subdivision, even the children, their DNA was on file someplace, with some institution. So this group of scientists had access to their DNA too. But Lila Chen and Janet had gone to a music festival and weren't at home when the Skeeters, the enhanced mosquitoes, chose to zero in. If they'd stayed home they'd have been bitten and lured off like the other women. But who was doing all this?

The lean, precise face of the professor in the lab coat explained more:

"Never random as in nature, our new airborne friend allows the Braincast system deep discretion to pick and choose. With targeted delivery, we can introduce combined food-trail pheromones and sex-trail pheromones to the olfactory membranes by the simple process of injection, and thence directly to the brain." The screen showed a large biological diagram:

Eleanor's biochemistry was a little rusty, but that image was the correct compound, all right. Cyclic adenosine monophosphate. A protein that when stimulated provided a direct pathway to the brain. A gatekeeper that opened in the presence of other cyclic nucleotides. Once open, you could phone in anything you wanted: Hunger. Thirst. Happiness. Sadness. Rage. Joy. All the primal drives, ready to be tapped and manipulated. In a critical leap, Eleanor grasped the implication. The only question remaining was what exactly you wanted your subjects to do.

The professor's soft voice confirmed as much:

"The refinement of chemosensory proteins allows us almost infinite combinations of stimuli and response. In our test control group we settled on one of the most primitive and powerful instincts—reproduction."

And that's why the women had to pick up and go. No choice. A Dog Whistle. Come and breed, bitch. A question from the audience, from a young man with sandy hair, a sort of unruly mop:

"How did you handle those who remained behind, the families, the husbands?"

Eleanor nodded to herself. Good question. What the hell do you do with people still at home in the subdivision? How do you keep them from running around like chickens with their heads cut off? Or maybe that's what you wanted them to do.

The man with the white halo of hair over his balding head brushed aside the question with a wave of his hand. "We introduced another manipulator into all the males and all the preadolescent females, producing general ennui, an indifference to local conditions and events. Most simply wandered off into the desert. We needn't worry about them."

But the young sandy-haired questioner wasn't satisfied and persisted: "With two exceptions, no?"

Eleanor knew those two exceptions, Wen Chen and her own Bhakti. The professor sighed. "Correct. Neither male was present at the time of inoculation. One committed suicide; the other"—he paused, checked his notes—"is on a hopeless search for the dead man's daughter. A young lady he will never find. Can we continue?"

Back to business. "As for our subjects—we added psychological reinforcement tapping into common childhood experiences delivered in the usual manner."

The light screen showed a pleasant kindergarten classroom, tiny desks; enthusiastic kid artwork festooned the walls. The teacher was leading the cheerful children in a song; faintly you could hear the tune and the words, their voices chirping in unison, *Your foot bone connected from your toe bone, I hear the word of the Lord!* The light screen image flitted to TVs in living rooms, car radios, cell phone ring tones—all blatting away the same thing. The image shifted to piles of junk mail on doorsteps and TV ads for calcium treatments, Boniva, foot treatments, glucosamine chondroitin supplements, hip transplants, a panoply of health medicine—the kind you see from every supermarket checkout stand. Every day in every way a product or service pounded home the message *Your foot bone connected to your toe bone*.

God, Eleanor realized—the message stroked you from every angle. Take a tune from childhood that was naturally reinforced in everyday life, from cradle to grave on every container and platform imaginable. No wonder the song was in their heads. The Professor agreed:

"So who can resist? We call and they listen. The group abandons home and hearth, husband and children, traveling over twelve hundred miles at our invitation. North by northeast. And never for one second knows why. Just that they must. And we're not even sure our scheduled program of periodic task reinforcement was actually necessary, though our field team applied it at every rest stop opportunity."

Field teams watched the women on the road, reinforcing their "toe bones" when necessary, say at motel rest stops. The light screen showed the familiar red banner running underneath—*This is a test of the Emergency Braincast System*—and the faint three-beat tone. . . . Faintly, "Dem Bones" played underneath like an earworm, and she'd never even noticed.

The streaming feed into the laptop died. Eleanor stared out the window again, but the light guardian called Tesla had vanished, leaving behind no trace. Alas, and to her dismay, the little dancing men and the marching red ants were still moving along the upper border of the walls. And she remembered more now, more from her trip to that horrid place that she called the Ant Colony—

How long ago? A month, at least. Six weeks? Eleanor couldn't tell; fragments of her memory came in bits and pieces. . . .

The women's cars ascended a series of switchbacks; then through an open chain-link gate in the late afternoon. The surrounding fence was overgrown with weeds; vines snaked up to coils of rusty razor wire. The compound lights perched on stanchions should have been lit under the dark rainy sky, but only one or two were working, the rest smashed. The cars rolled over the flat edge of a large dented metal sign, WHITES-something, but the sign was too battered to make out clearly.

At the edge of the parking lot Eleanor saw the gritty, smudged smokestacks of a factory, the top floor of the main brick building dotted with empty, shattered windows. . . . Faded sign lettering over the top lintels said WHITESIDE MEATPACKING.

Her memory ebbed, then flowed back like a tide. The vision jumped. Eleanor found herself following the others through an open side door to the abandoned factory, then tramping down a steep flight of metal stairs. Next, she was walking along a dingy underground tunnel, the walls damp and greasy to the touch.

A line of bracketed lights attached to the stone roof passed endlessly overhead, every other bulb burned out, so the passage went light/dark, dark/light. The other women of her troop marched in a gradual descent: Mrs. Biedermeier first, one hand on her fanny pack, then Mrs. Stanton still clutching the gold cross on the chain around her neck, the mousy Mrs. Perkins next, turning her head this way and that to get a better look at their surroundings and, finally, the widow Mrs. Quaid, her silvered hair blanching each time a bracketed light passed slowly above them. Eleanor, last in line.

She recalled a sense of fierce urgency, smoldering away inside. The desire to keep walking, to soldier on.

The tunnel branched off into multiple passages, some as forks, some descending, some rising, even crossroads. But the women needed no guide; they knew where they were going. They paused only once and very briefly when they stumbled upon another woman. She wore a dirty hospital gown and sat in the gap of a dark opening. Shaved head, pale unwashed face—she hugged her knees to her chest and rocked back and forth, mumbling to herself.

A pack of cautious rats scuttled behind the woman huddled in the tunnel, but paused as if unsure whether to proceed or flee. Eleanor's neighbors kept walking by; there was nothing in this that concerned them. The barest glance and they marched on. The only sounds coming down the long tunnel were the soft scuttling rats and the faint echo of a song: *"Dem bones, dem bones . . ."*

Eleanor's eyes blinked, and she returned to her pleasant sanitarium room.

The Light Guardian was back hovering outside the window. It wanted her to look at the laptop once more. She turned to the laptop screen, trying to understand:

A new video feed was coming through the machine, not a live stream but recorded in the last month. She should have been able to tell exactly when by the date in the upper corner, but the image was blurred. Mid-May? About the time she and the ladies from Van Horn arrived . . . A wide-angle shot onto a wall of glass built directly into the side of a tunnel, a kind of den.

A maternity ward. One word was stenciled onto the wall of glass in large red letters. For a second she thought it read ANT COLONY. She looked closer at the laptop screen—no, the word was ANTENATAL. Eleanor knew what that meant. Prenatal.

The video feed showed a row of clean modern hospital beds, women lying on them, medical monitors blinking and tubes leading to and from other machines. It felt vaguely reminiscent, as if she'd been there once. But she didn't see herself or any of the Van Horn sisters. But then she knew. She'd been there. They'd tried to do something to her.

The video stream was showing something odd. So not everything went according to plan. For one thing, she'd escaped; that couldn't have been part of the plan. And others had arrived by mistake, like the crouching woman in the tunnel, wearing the dirty hospital gown. Yet another such woman was staggering along the front of the glass wall, holding on to it for support, dazed and confused.

This new one tripped along on high heels, one broken; she was tarted up, as though for an evening out on the town, but her hair was a shrieking mess, lumped and clotted with dirt. Her mascara ran like clown tears down her cheeks. She held on to the glass for support, mumbling and talking half to herself. You could hear it clear enough on the feed:

"They've made a mistake. A terrible mistake. I'm not supposed to be here." She paused. "Why did they bring me? Oh, yes, the invitation. But it wasn't meant for me. It was misdelivered and I only read it by accident, or did I listen—?"

The distraught woman left off blabbing when she caught sight of the security video monitor watching everything. She tried to pull herself together, pushing aside her blond hair. Then attempted to stand up straight on her busted pumps, addressing whoever was watching:

"My name is Broderick Fallows. I'm not supposed to be here. They've made a mistake. There's a premiere back in Los Angeles at Mann's Chinese theater of the picture I directed, Part Three of *Zyklon-B*, *Inexplicable*—everyone's heard of it, and later in the week the studio is supposed to release part two on DVD, and later a boxed set. I think I'm supposed to be on cable tonight. And I have to arrive an hour ahead of time for makeup."

The confused woman's voice faded as the video monitor made no reply. Then she tried again, imploring: "I think I'm lost. Can you tell me which way is Los Angeles? Is this the right way?" She stumbled back against the glass.

"Hello? Did you hear me? Hello?"

The video feed began to break up; the last thing Eleanor saw was the ghostly bodies of two men in lab coats approaching the wall of glass. The faulty transmission seemed to make them dance, an ant dance—jerking toward the distraught woman with outstretched hands. And she seemed mildly relieved to see them.

"Are you from the studio?"

* * *

Lauren Poole lay in bed with Guy, the peaceful sounds of nighttime rain going down the gutters of the house. The dogs had come upstairs and were nestled in their plush doggy couches. Lauren never spared any expense when it came to canine comfort, and Guy would often kid her about it. "Those two gangsters have better mattresses than us!" Even as Lauren lay under the covers while her husband softly snored and the dogs stretched or sighed, she knew she was asleep. Dreaming.

She rose from the bed in her nightgown to find her robe, which always hung on the bedpost. But as she stood, the room went through a subtle change. The bedroom had reverted to the "old house" she and Guy had seen that day. Auntie Whitcomb's great-great grandmother sat at the writing table again. A single candle burned in a pewter candle holder. The woman cupped her hand around the flame and blew it out.

Night engulfed them, but it wasn't raining anymore, and bright moonlight cascaded through the open windows. The scent of candle wax smoke filled the bedroom, and Lauren could see quite clearly.

The long-dead woman rose from the boxy writing desk and crossed to the bed. A man lay there, breathing heavily. Wracked with fever, he moaned a little. Great-great Auntie Whitcomb drew a chair next to the bed and swept away the muslin hangings. She took a bowl of water from where it sat on the floor and set it on her lap; dipped a facecloth in the water and wrung it out. She reached to the man's fevered brow, pressing the cloth to his forehead, sucking up the heat, and going back to the cool bowl of water again.

But what dismayed Lauren this time was the identity of the man in the bed. Not the sailor they spied fresh back from Norfolk bringing pineapples—no. Guy lay in the bed, just as he did every night. Guy had the fever; Guy was sick. The cool facecloth went back and back again, but to no avail. Guy moaned weakly and twitched, feebly brushing the invisible cobwebs of disease from his face. A sickly, sallow yellow face. Guy was dying.

Lauren looked down at herself, at what she was wearing. Not her nightgown, not her robe—but old-fashioned mourning clothes. A plain cotton black dress with a hoop at her ankles and belled sleeves at her wrists, simple pleating— a crisp, starched cloth that rustled when she touched it. An unforgiving sound.

She crept away from the head of the bed, from the vision of Guy, and clutched the curtains by the dormer window. Down below in the street, a horse-drawn hearse waited in front of their door. The horses snorted and wagged their heads.

In a dream jump Lauren found herself standing in front of the black wooden hearse. She looked inside the etched glass windows, to see the body or the coffin. But the hearse was empty. Empty. No one there.

A great sense of relief flooded through her, and she began to breathe again.

And up on the spring seat there was no driver, no coachman. The hearse was waiting, waiting for her to take the reins. Now she was up in the leather padded driver's seat. She swept aside the hoop skirt to sit more comfortably, grabbed both reins off the guardrail, and released the brake.

The reins snapped, a cracking sound.

The horses lunged forward.

The cobblestone street clattered under the wheels of the rig as she passed house after house.

House after house with an X on the door.

House after house boarded up, abandoned. House after empty house. And the sound of thundering hooves rose, echoing into the night.

PART TWO

Yellow Jack

"Die trying" is the proudest human thing.

—Robert Heinlein,
Have Space Suit—Will Travel

17

❦

Tribulation

It may have been raining in Connecticut while Lauren
dreamt of driving a hearse past doors marked *X*, but
fifteen hundred miles across the country there was no rain
over Nebraska. Luminous, blue velvet clouds sailed a vast
Midwestern sky. Cheryl rode the Harley along Interstate
80 for the sheer solitude. Behind her, Bhakti stolidly
drove the yellow Toyota 4Runner, pulling the empty motorcycle trailer; and finally Billy Shadow in the white
Dodge rental van brought up the rear.

"We can catch up with them at their next whistle stop,"
Billy had said back in Salt Lake. Famous last words. They
left the diner, got in their vehicles, and promptly lost any
trace of the Stuka Crew. The pursuit from Utah took them
weeks, the end of July devouring a hunk of August, zigzag-
ging across the Wyoming-Colorado state line off Interstate
80, stopping in every hick town as they rumbled along.

The medicine show always seemed a day ahead, vanishing over the horizon or sidetracked off the main roads.
Cheryl, Bhakti, and Billy caught up with the show a couple
of times, but never saw any sign of bikers fitting the description of swastika rejects. So they kept circling around
Interstate 80 in the hopes of spotting weirdos hanging by
a silver van in some strip mall parking lot or saloon.

Now under the velvet clouds of a Midwestern night, the white lines on the interstate rolled under their wheels like an endless conveyor belt. They had the asphalt to themselves; no cars or trucks on the interstate for the last twenty miles. Nothing coming, nothing going, nothing but their headlights lanced into the dark.

Until they saw the cow.

A young cow had wandered up the road embankment and paused in the middle of the eastbound lanes to chew her cud. Cheryl almost missed seeing the animal entirely. The cow was a Belted Galloway: black chest, black rear, with the wide white stripe in the middle, completely camouflaged on a black roadway with white lines dashing past your eyes. White/Black, White/Black, Dash-Dash—*Yee Gads, a COW!*

The Harley's brake taillights flashed red; the vehicles screeched to a halt all over the roadway, their engines idling in the dark night. Ms. Cow stared calmly at them for a few moments, finally finished her cud, ambled across the median, and vanished into the dark countryside.

Cheryl, Bhakti, and Billy shared a long silent glance, all of them digesting the unspoken reality that wandering cows were not a normal state of affairs, even in farm country. But the realization got worse as they rolled on.

The lights of Lexington sent a glow into the night, but they saw no movement, no headlights or taillights, as if the whole town had come to a standstill. As they rounded the cloverleaf and headed south on Route 283, there were other strange signs: two cars had rolled off the curve of the exit ramp. A sedan and a pickup truck, both skidded off the road, crunched into the guardrail. The convoy slowly passed the empty cars. No drivers, no passengers. Where the hell had all the people gone?

Cheryl, Bhakti, and Billy pulled into the parking lot of the Dawson County Fairgrounds. Dr. Ponkus and his Medicine Show had put down stakes. The fairground parking lot was full of cars, and lit up by floodlights on high poles—

but again, the place seemed awful quiet. Generally there'd be people coming and going, but there was none of that.

Instead, the searchers saw a couple of cars conked out in the midst of pulling into a parking space, a couple of stalled fender benders with dented bumpers. And once again the cars were empty.

Cheryl got off the cycle, slid her helmet onto the handlebars, and rubbed her thighs. She could see the garish lights of the carnival, the Ferris wheel paused in its revolutions, but no sound of people, no rumble of voices. A kind of expectant silence. The two men waited for her some ways ahead, just standing in front of the Medicine Show ticket booth.

The painted sign of Dr. Ponkus grinned down at them: an unshaven huckster in battered beaver top hat, a genuine American quacksalver, sharp as a rusty fishhook and as unreliable as a two-bit pocket watch. The painted Dr. Ponkus offered a brown laudanum bottle with the caption *"We Cures What Ails Yah!"*

The ticket seller stared down too, but there was absolutely no point in paying the man. This time, what stared back at them was a department store mannequin dressed up as a ticket seller: loud shirt, porkpie hat, his plaster fingers on a roll of tickets and some bills sitting in the change well.

"I guess our money's no good here," Billy remarked dryly.

Bhakti, holding his wallet, sheepishly stuck it back in his pants.

As the three walked into the Medicine Show the silence welled up from a thousand plaster throats; a thousand painted eyes stared blankly at them. Was this somebody's idea of an elaborate practical joke? A maze of concessions spread over the fairgrounds with stuff like General Custer's Golden Custard and Minnie Ha-Ha's Buttered Corn. The scent of cotton candy floated across the fairgrounds.

But nobody was selling.

Cowgirl Jill at the shooting gallery held up a Kewpie doll; a fat lady strained a basket of fried dough from a bubbling tub of oil—mannequins posed like real people caught in mid-act. Petrified plaster statues everywhere: families with little kids holding on to floating balloons; guys and dolls, the guys in their better muscle shirts, the girls in their Daisy Dukes.

Bhakti dipped his finger into the tall, frosted cup of a large mannequin: a Norwegian squarehead, pale blond hair, with a beer-muscle. His red T-shirt was emblazoned with the biohazard symbol and caption *Caution: Fart Loading*. Yep, lime fizz. The Punjab scientist sucked his finger.

"Bhakti!" Cheryl hissed at him. "Cut that out!"

Cautious as mice, the three searchers crept their way around the frozen throngs, trying not to knock anyone over.

"Where'd all the real people go?" Cheryl wondered out loud. "If it wasn't for these dummies—this is like the Rapture. Y'know—gone up to meet Little Baby Jesus at the end times."

She suddenly stopped, afraid she was talking nonsense. But after chasing a young lady, a total stranger, halfway across America on a song and a prayer, was the idea of the Rapture any more unlikely than that? Was this the Second Coming, or the Already Arrived? In all honesty, she didn't know the answer.

The whole thing seemed just so spooky, and as far as Billy was concerned, much worse than the empty subdivision back in Van Horn, Texas. Back there the dead quiet felt like a schoolroom in summertime—but here, here it felt like there were still people hovering around, maybe trapped inside the plaster bodies.

Quietly, a bit of Scripture popped into his head, proving he hadn't been totally asleep on those cold winter Sundays on the rez. That bit from Matthew, which suddenly came out of his mouth:

"*No one knows about that day or hour, not even the angels in heaven. . . .*"

Cheryl stifled a laugh; she'd had the Good Book thrashed into her by Sister Penelope back in Poughkeepsie, her pointer at the blackboard when it wasn't rapping your knuckles. Bhakti's soft Indian voice finished the passage:

"*Two men will be in the field; one will be taken and the other left. Two women at the mill; one will be taken and the other left.*" Cheryl and Billy looked the Punjabi scientist askance.

"You think I wouldn't know it?" Bhakti asked. The scientist grinned at the other two. "Like Spencer Tracy says in the movie, 'It's a good book. It's not the *only* book.' But it's a really good book." So the Punjabi scientist could quote from *Inherit the Wind* too. Cheryl and Billy shared another glance, impressed, neither prepared to argue the point. Bhakti had probably read more books than both of them combined.

Billy's eyes strayed off the midway, past the motionless rides. A hundred yards away the silver van glinted back at him, and you could see the Iron Cross emblem of the Stuka Crew. The motorcycles were parked on the grass. Members of the Stuka Crew sat motionless on their bikes or stood near the silver cargo trailer.

The three started to hustle. Running now. In five seconds they were halfway across the field and zeroing in on those crap-hats. Billy could feel inside the van, inside the trailer. Oh, they were close, really close. *Just a few more steps, just a—*

A blast of light hit him full in the head, like he'd walked right into the stitches of a wild pitch. *Wham!* stopping him dead in his tracks.

He sank to his knees.

Cheryl and Bhakti doubled back to help, but he couldn't

move. The lady cop and the scientist tried to talk to him, but the Skin Walking thing had come on way too strong. A strobe light flashed in his brain; an opera soprano sang in his head. Oh yes, he could see what had happened now; he slid back in time as though through a tunnel, week after week. One month. Two months. He could see everything in that silver van very clearly. Seeing through the Chen girl's eyes . . .

Stuck in a dark corner of the silver van, Lila Chen squinted past motorcycles and stowed show props; another girl huddled nearby. Panicked eyes stared back with fear; her body shivered uncontrollably. Her tongue darted out of her mouth to where she bled from a split lip.

Janet! They got Janet too.

Janet's eyes gleamed out of the dark, bulging out of her head. She was trying to scream, writhing and straining, but nothing came out. Mouth gagged, Janet mewed helplessly. Rough hands thrust a hood over her head.

Gagged and bagged.

A grinning monkey face leered right up at Lila. A guy named Pinky. And Pinky said, "You won't be needing this."

His fingers pinched her ear. "But your folks will want it."

And zip! A razor of pain sliced the side of her head. The ear. *They'd cut off her ear.* The blinding light, the blinding pain, and the screeching opera singer sang an aria as Lila screamed silently into her own gagged mouth.

She must have fainted, a long spell in the dark. How long? No way to tell. Now awake on the hard trailer floor, no real pain at first: a lump of damp bandages at the side of her head. Little slit windows showed the faint light of day. The van bumped on a bit of rough road; she hit her head and blacked out again.

Then the throbbing came. Throbbing that made her want

to puke. Lila Chen oozed into a sort of syrupy delirium. Time passed. . . . Somewhere in the desert the van halted, one of its tires gone flat. While they fixed it, baked air poured in through the open door, blinding white light outside. The crew hit the road again.

In the bumping van Lila and Janet were stripped naked. The bag came off Janet's head; her eyes shone like two great spotlights. One of the bitch women kept slapping Janet's face till her eyes swelled shut, like they didn't want her to see. Again, the pain came for Lila, but not before she saw Janet curled up on a bit of foam padding like a punished dog. The trailer hit a bump, Lila's head touched the metal wall, and the lights went out.

When she came to, blood had seeped through the bandage. The air had become cold—a kind of clammy night cold, desert cold. Where was Janet?

Janet?

One of the crew towered over her in the dark:

"You missed LA. But we didn't stay long, just a delivery for the Magician and Hawaiian Gardens Chino Boyz. Those guys like their toys with all their pieces intact. So we sold 'em Janet instead, better looking than you. You'll just have to be satisfied with us."

So they'd sold Janet like a pet parakeet for a couple of bags of rainbow junk, or just for the hell of it. And it sank into Lila that now she was really alone. All alone.

Days passed, and nights. Hot then cold.

Easy to lose track of how long she'd been in there.

They kept her watered up pretty good, threw her whatever they didn't finish from the take-out joints, which she gobbled out of greasy Styrofoam. A tiny porta-potty sat in the corner to squat on. Her ankle was handcuffed to a bicycle lock with a combination cylinder, cabled to a ring in the floor of the van. They were such idiots they even left the numbers visible on the combination cylinder of the bicycle lock—666, how freakin' original—but she was too wiped out to unlatch herself from the metal floor and make an escape. Truth was, after the first couple of days all the fight had been knocked out of her.

Time became a slow descent, endless falling. . . . While in a corner of her mind, she knew the reason they'd let her live. They'd let her live for fun.

Every couple of hours they pulled over to do that rainbow stuff, sticking their faces in it. Then they came at her; sometimes in tag teams and sometimes individually, rubbing that rainbow dust on her privates when they did her there too. The times they didn't sex her, they'd pull off to some back road so she could empty her porta-potty—always at night so they could see cars coming.

Queen Bitch always went first, sponging off her armpits and snatch, while Lila squatted beside the trailer. Afterward, Lila waited her turn to wash herself out of the same bucket while the men and women leered. She could hear the others as they roamed around their patch of back road nowhere, taking leaks, drinking beer, or looking for something to shoot.

Once during one of these uncomfortable rest stops, the familiar face of Janet's dad, Mr. Singh from across the street, floated across her mind. Floating out of the dark and hovering before her eyes . . . Mr. Singh smiled kindly at her, quietly whispering, *We're coming. Hang on.* . . . No, not her parents; her house engulfed in flames flickered behind her eyes. Mom and Dad weren't ever coming. Just Mr. Singh.

Queen Bitch clapped Lila on her bare arm, hoisting her roughly off the ground. "C'mon, we're done." And Lila's hallucination vanished to nowhere.

Back in the trailer, back on the road.

Sleep, potty, sex slave, sleep; sometimes the men went first, sometimes the women. No rhyme or reason to it. More travel, more food, sleep, potty, and sex service all over again. They'd been climbing for a few days. Pausing very high, where it got very cold one night and they threw her a blanket.

Back on the highway she felt the van wind down out of the mountains. Long flat stretches of road like an interstate. Then suddenly wheels bumped off the asphalt onto some dirt or grass. Lila heard the noise of a lot of people doing things, all talking at once; metal clanking, and winches cranking. It reminded her of a carnival. The caravan halted some distance from the human rumble. Quiet descended on the van, and for a spell nothing happened. Lila sat in the dark on her foam pad, amongst the motorcycles.

A day, half a day? Impossible to say.

Suddenly the back of the van slammed open; the Stuka Crew unstrapped their bikes and rolled them down the ramp. Lila held her hand up against the light, unable to rise. Queen Bitch's voice: "I thought we were going to take off her bandage."

Pinky's voice: "I like the way she looks in it."

The woman again. "I want to see you do her."

Now Pinky: "Get your freaky dyke on and do her yourself. We have to set up for a show tonight—"

The sound of tires scrunched on the grass. Someone had driven up in a large car, a limousine? Suddenly everyone went dead still. Queen Bitch slapped a gag around Lila's mouth, gagged and bagged, and the van door banged closed again. But Lila could hear perfectly; she felt the Stuka Crew measuring this newcomer. A man mighty put out at having to deal with idjits, the voice of authority—

"So this is the master race," he said. "The Four Horsemen? What a waste of human skin."

Pinky with the mouth on him: "Look, Slim, shove off. The Four Horsemen got a show to put on."

Slim's stern voice rattled around the metal van: "What's your name? Pinky? That's your name? Pinky?" Then with pure contempt, "Well, Pinky, I know the Horsemen. And the other three are nothing like you. They speak and read

Aramaic, Babylonian, and Assyrian. Can you? Can you even *read*?"

Lila could feel the dipshits of the master race bristle, especially Pinky with that smart mouth. "Shut the *uck fup*, Mr. Bones. We don't answer to you. We don't answer to nobody—"

Lila thought she heard that Mr. Slim smile; it sure sounded like a smile, the voice dripping sincerity: "Well, we can't have a posse of mouth-breathing jizz-wits roaming the peaceful countryside ejaculating over our virtuous Texan maidens, now can we? Not when I'm getting ready to heal the planet. High time to Rapture your ass, Pinky. To afflict the afflicted. To tribulate you and your crew out of existence."

From outside the trailer came the gust of dry wind. The van rattled as the Piper's evil will blew across the fairgrounds. A sudden breeze, a single breath, a wispy hiss of evaporating moisture sucking bodies dry and leaving soulless plaster behind. The trailer walls shimmied, then fell dead silent. The van door opened, and somebody snatched the bag off her head. Light streamed into the van, and Lila shut her eyes. The stranger's hand touched her shoulder.

"C'mon, Chen girl. You're coming with me."

Lila felt the steel cuff at her ankle fall away. She rose on unsteady feet, leaning on the gaunt man; he smelled of puppies, peanut butter and jelly, chamomile tea. . . . But the sweet odor caught in her nostrils as he helped her shuffle to the blinding doorway of the trailer. And Lila felt something else she didn't expect: a deep sinking feeling. Despite the comforting scent, despite the fact that he'd let her out of her shackles.

Not relief, *not gratitude*.

Fear.

And it struck her as a certainty, like the Rock of Ages: If the "Stupid Crew" were jizz-wits, this Mr. Slim was the master of the master race.

* * *

Mr. P. lay back on the long expanse of couch inside the darkened limo and brushed a clammy hand across his brow. His head throbbed, and gritty sparkles of light danced behind his closed eyes. Rapturing the entire fairgrounds, evaporating souls and leaving plaster mannequins behind, had exhausted him. He'd gone a tad overboard, shoving the whole crowd into the kiln instead of just the nitwits. That's what rats, red ants, and mosquitoes were for, though once in a while he craved brimstone, the scent of sulfur. Now they had finally reached the rally point and were paused for the final assault. So far, so good; everything necessary for total domination had been achieved.

Beside him the lanky lad had poured himself a 7-Up from the limo bar and sipped it noisily through a soggy straw, his nose buried in his laptop. The young man was getting ready, preparing himself to make America safe for Mobocracy. Mr. P. smiled inside; what a finely tuned instrument of psychological warfare he had created, a master of targeted chaos.

In another cushioned corner of the limo the Piper could feel Little Maria using all her powers to probe his mind, to see what he saw, know what he knew. But what could Maria really do? She was only a child. Access Denied. And when she realized the hopelessness of penetrating the gaunt man's consciousness, the little fortune-teller girl gave up, staring at him with wide eyes, scared there'd be some punishment due. He let her wonder.

Last of all, his mind reached out to Lila Chen. The gaunt man could feel the Chen girl's head throbbing; the sudden shift from the sweatbox of the skanky motorcycle van to a cool air-conditioned limousine had been quite a shock. The bandage was peeling away from her scalp, revealing a swath of raw meat. Lila Chen nodded her head, almost to her breast, the soft couch cushions sucking her into sleep.

He felt her regenerating, but she still needed a hospital. Too bad they didn't have a first-aid kit, but he'd get the young lady sorted out soon enough.

Definitely not the moment to introduce her to those out-breeding techno geeks at Pi R Squared. Who knows if those Jekylls could be trusted with the twin prizes of Lila Chen's miraculous triple helix, or with Little Maria the innate seer?

Each female possessed powerful, nearly divine qualities—qualities he himself possessed. And such pearls weren't to be cast before swine. The twisted sisters at Pi R Squared would have to do a good deal of genetic grunt work manipulating the species before the Piper would allow them access to two of nature's miraculous accelerants like Lila Chen and Little Maria. You don't let children run with scissors. . . . Besides, he had to study his two new acquisitions before knowing how best to use them.

The sparkles faded behind his closed eyes, and Mr. P. felt the hapless searchers gaining ground, approaching them: the pathetic Aerogel scientist, the nightshade copper, and faithful Tonto. Two had become three, but it wasn't going to help. The searchers were half a day late and a dollar short; let them wander in the wilderness a while yet, purify their souls.

The Piper opened his eyes and scanned the dark limo. Then, to the uniformed driver up front, one of Kid's faceless posse of skycaps:

"Indianapolis Methodist," he said. "And step on it."

Cheryl and Bhakti helped Billy from the ground, their human warmth flowing into his limbs. "I can walk." He hobbled with them to the Stuka Crew trailer. As he stomped along, the blood returned to his feet on shivery needles.

The first thing they noticed, the Stuka Crew was headless. A headless mannequin sat astride a Harley, two more headless dummies lay on the ground half crushed to powder. But the women were staked out against the silver trailer, spread-eagled and done ugly. Triple X-rated. Their jeans and vests torn in all the right places, their boobs destroyed, genitals mutilated. Mouths punched to mush, brutally punished. Lifeless white plaster. The husks of people sucked dry.

The three searchers stood silently. Dumbfounded. Lila Chen wasn't in the van, and nowhere nearby.

Cheryl clucked softly and chewed her lip; she looked at the triple-X bitches, feeling momentarily sorry for them. But then she remembered how Bhakti's sweet Janet looked chopped up in the orange Chevy and the pity went away.

The Punjabi scientist stood silently for a few heartbeats and then began to paw about the trailer. Banging inside, rattling chains with a frantic urgency. Finding nothing, he came outside again, dragging a hunk of dirty foam bedding. He stumbled into one bike and knocked it over, the mannequin rider breaking into a dozen pieces.

He'd held himself together for so long. Searching every stinking corner of the southwest, but too late for Janet and now too late for Lila. Bhakti held his head in his hands, and finally lost his mind.

Too late—oh Jesus Christ!

He kicked the foam padding on the ground, stomping around the silver trailer like a madman, tearing at his hair.

"Where is she? She was here! I know she was. I know it!"

He lunged to a female mannequin—shouting at it as though it could really answer.

"Where is she? Where?"

He slapped the naked dummy across her mashed face, making a piece of her foot drop off. "C'mon you! Tell me! Tell me!" Cheryl put her arms around this crazy man and held him as his soul died in public. Trying to get him to see: *Enough now.*

Bhakti paused, his inner coil sprung. He looked at his hands, at the plaster dust, at the crumbled mannequin, and started to weep long and quiet tears, mumbling, "It's not fair. *Not fair.* She was *here.*"

While Cheryl whispered, "We'll find her, Bhakti. We'll find her."

Billy Shadow watched his two companions, the sane and the broken. He jammed his hands in his pockets like he used to as a kid when he didn't know the answer to a question. So he stared at his feet, unsure what to do next. But he slowly realized he was seeing something on the ground, something very peculiar: Of course . . . the residual effects of his Skin Walking thing allowed him greater perception.

Two ant colonies were going to war. From each mound swarmed an army of ants. A horde of red ants streamed from one, and a great host of black ants from the other, marching out to battle, as if a terrible hand deep inside the earth were driving the ants to the surface in massed rage. The gaunt man in the limo flitted into Billy's mind. A creature who stirred nature's noisome, dirty creatures: ants, cockroaches, mosquitoes, rats, lice, *vermin of every kind.* Could the man really do that? Not the nice animals, the butterflies and bumblebees, but the ugly ones? Billy's head said yes.

Half the insects on Earth didn't even look like they belonged on this planet. Maybe the aliens were already here in the form of ugly bugs, just waiting for orders from a more intelligent life-form. And an advanced life-form like the ruthless Mr. Slim wouldn't disappoint them.

The confused melee roiled at his feet—two colonies, one red and one black, at death grips. Was this humanity's future? A final reckoning? If not today, the day after tomorrow or the day after that? Mankind tearing itself apart as only insects could, frantically, relentlessly—until no one was left alive.

Cannibal Ants.

Billy stared at Cheryl and Bhakti through Coke-bottle eyes. Their faces swam in and out of focus. He must have swooned again. He touched the side of his mouth, leaking spit, trying to say something. The words came slowly, distinctly, but through cold, numb lips. *One more thing he'd seen in delirium. Wave after wave of vicious gray hordes.*

"Let's get out of here. Right now. Before the rats come. The rats are coming."

18

The First Rat

August limped into September, the week before Labor Day. So hot you could feel the pavement through the soles of your shoes. A Manhattan scorcher sweating you to the lapels before you walked three blocks; the first time all summer the mercury climbed into the 90s. Guy Poole entered the office tower refrigeration, limp as a noodle, and didn't stop sweating for twenty minutes. He looked dismally at the reflection of his two-year-old Brooks Brothers' suit in a glass-walled conference room on the thirtieth floor. Gumby in clothes.

"You can go in now, Mr. Poole."

The advertising firm of Talent Associates, and senior partner Lorraine Talent, had called him back two and a half times. First, a chirpy lady from the human resources department, who informed him primly, "I love people.

They're so interesting. Which is why I work in personnel."
For a moment Guy thought he was talking to a graduate
from Up with People, the smiley-face inspirational orga-
nization. Their treacly song echoed in his head: *Up, Up
with People, You meet them wherever you go!* Only a su-
preme act of will allowed Guy the presence of mind not to
sing it out loud.

Next up the ladder, the head account executive, Eugene
Skinson, a guy who could have been Guy's doppelgänger
in every demographic and a perfect foil. The only difference between them: this fellow had one of those shaven-
skull haircuts.

"I've heard on the grapevine that Ingelheim Pharma and
WunderThink might be ripe for a move," Guy informed
him.

"Really?" Skinson quietly pursed his lip. Apparently, he
hadn't heard. You got the feeling the VP was capable of
rushing upstairs to tell the Big She—She-Who-Must-Be-
Obeyed, Lorraine Talent—the very minute the interview
concluded. But to Guy's quiet satisfaction, VP Skinson
brought him into the fold a little:

"We're about to lose two accounts: our hunk of DirecTV,
that's bread and butter, and the other, a small, breakout
technology, Nanotec Microprocessors—*bad, bad, bad*. As
you already know, industry ad buys have dried up since
Christmas. I let go four execs pulling down 250K each and
ten people out of Creative, who . . . I don't even know what
they did for us. Now I'm working thirty-six hours a day and
haven't slept in a week."

VP Skinson leapt from behind his desk and strode to the
door. "Let's go see Quiche Lorraine. Might as well shove
your resume where it will do some good. If I don't see my
wife this weekend, she's going to divorce me. Got any questions?"

Guy smiled at the *Quiche Lorraine* informality and dutifully followed the man. "No questions. I'll work for food."

VP Skinson acknowledged with a dark chuckle. The elevator took them up to Lorraine Talent's office suite—the last surviving partner and grandchild to the original Barnabas Talent. Not much in the way of office frills: a few big wipe boards and multiple flat-screen televisions in a Spartan whitewashed, long, bare space. The lady was Prada-sharp with taut features and no wedding ring: a woman who lived for her job. Lots of those in the city. But at least the Big She had a sense of humor. She rose from a clean, spotless desk with her hand out as the two men crossed the parquet floor.

"Lorraine Talent. I gather VP Skinson already told you my nickname. He can't help himself. Apparently I'm my own brand of egg pie." Guy Poole grinned a little and took her hand. Without inviting him to sit, the smart lady gave him the once-over, cocked her head, and said, "All right then. Thanks for coming in. We'll be in touch."

L auren had been watching their neighbor Mr. Fenniman on and off all day. First peering at him from the lantern windows by the front door, then peeling back the curtains by the front parlor windows, and then boldly out the Keeping Room window, which had no window treatments at all.

Ever since her dream of Guy in bed with yellow fever and driving a runaway horse-drawn hearse, a sense of dread had grown on Lauren. The rainy summer seemed to have produced nothing but bugs: legions of ants crawling up from between the floorboards, silverfish in the drains, and fat cicadas clinging to the house. Lauren went about exterminating anything that crawled, flew, or spun webs. With the exception of pretty butterflies—who she let alone to flutter harmlessly about.

But she exterminated the rest with all manner of weapons at her disposal: vacuum, brooms, acrosol spray, until she became the Chairman Mao of her helpless backyard bug population—deciding who would live and who would die.

But still the dread grew on her, and no amount of dead ants or gassed wasps alleviated her noxious moods. The cause? Who the hell knew? Nothing she could put her finger on, but when she saw Mr. Fenniman taping up his traditional two-story American Colonial something clicked.

At first she didn't quite get it: old Fenniman climbing the ladder, then moving window to window. And she occasionally heard him mutter a curse as the ungainly aluminum ladder clanked onto the wrong spot or he tramped his flower beds. A score of his precious tiger lilies died that day. What was so important that the flowers had to lay down their lives?

Old Mr. Fenniman was not the type to ask for help; a widower for ten years now, a flinty old Yankee, a true do-it-yourselfer—always telling Guy the right way to clean a gummed-up chainsaw or tune up a two-stroke engine. "He sharpens his own lawn mower blades," Guy once told her, rather impressed. And now, Lauren watched the old coot tape up his house.

Mr. Fenniman had precut window-sized rectangles of thick translucent plastic and sealed the windows from the outside with strips of black duct tape along the seams. Plastic sheeting and black tape—talk about an eyesore. The town was going to have something to say about that. You couldn't just turn Mr. Blanding's Dream House into a hazmat government containment area. At one point a couple of neighborhood kids paused from skateboarding to watch the silly old man. But that didn't seem to faze Fenniman one bit; he climbed the ladder, ripped the duct tape, and pressed it into place. Up the ladder and down: tape, tape, tape.

But now it clicked inside Lauren. She knew what the dream meant: Guy dying in bed, and her driving the hearse like a madwoman out of town. A warning: *Don't get sick; drive death from your door.* Now she knew what she wanted to do. First things first, she had to keep them both safe, seal the house. They were going to need it for a while. Downstairs, somewhere in the cellar, Guy kept a big roll of plastic by his painting things. And duct tape too. Lots of duct tape.

If Fenniman could do it outside, she'd do it inside.

The town wouldn't even know.

The 2:07 Metro-North train to Fairfield was less crowded than that Friday at the beginning of this clammy summer. No goofball clowns in Green Goblin bicycle togs, no grumpy salary men dying from life. Labor Day had started early for those who could afford to escape the city for their country estates, so the train car was nearly empty.

Except for the running brats.

An extremely self-absorbed Mamaroneck mommy babbled on her Bluetooth, oblivious to her four-year-olds running wild in the aisles, playing Aliens. The two ratkins wore bug-eyed gray alien masks, which didn't prevent them from shrieking up the coach's metal interior and firing noisy plastic laser-blaster guns in every direction. After a mere ten seconds the alien bratlings made Guy want to kill them very slowly and in public in front of their Mamaroneck mother.

The inconclusive interview in Quiche Lorraine's office made him feel like he'd missed the brass ring. But maybe the most disturbing element of the day had nothing to do with a capricious Quiche Lorraine or ungovernable children, but with the Tri-State Area's little biological mysteries. As the wild aliens ran up and down the aisles, Guy Poole spied an urban casualty by the grungy metal foot of one of the blue leather coach seats. A large gray rat lay

inches from the center aisle, dead as a doorstop. A dead rat
under the seat nobody noticed.

What did Guy know about rats? Not that much. They
were hardy buggers; they could eat just about anything,
climb walls, live for years, and breed like . . . well, rats.

Suddenly intrigued, Guy busied himself with a net
search if only to ignore those whooping aliens. He found a
brief article from the *NY Post* headlined "Rat Patrol." Concerned citizens were battling rats in their neighborhood;
the rats were winning. But fear not, the city's Pest Control
Services Division was counting whiskers: *In December
2007, the Health Department started a new program using an inspectional process called "Rat Indexing" to pro-
actively identify the presence of rats in neighborhoods*. But
a paragraph later the Health Department seemed to con-
tradict itself, a spokeswoman saying, "We don't do rat tail
counts."

"It's all crap," Guy muttered. Nobody had a clue how
many rats lived in the city. City Hall couldn't even count
the people who lied to the census workers. Like they were
gonna count rats? Fuggedaboutit.

He vaguely remembered a line from Camus' *The
Plague*—the first rat coming out to die. A dozen clicks later
he found it: *"Dr. Rieux felt something soft under his foot.
It was a dead rat lying in the middle of the landing."*

Oddly satisfied in his search-engine prowess, Guy
looked back to his quiet rodent friend. The sunlight slanted
into the car, illuminating a patch of grimy Formica floor-
ing. The flicker of a mosquito emerged from the dead rat
fur. The bloodsucker hovered for a moment in the shaft of
sunlight, fat and full of rat blood, and then vanished into
the vastness of the Metro-North coach.

The conductor's voice over the PA system announced the
next stop. The engineer sharply slowed the train, and a discarded soda can rolled from the rear of the car, picking up
speed. The empty can bounced over the late Mr. Rat and

leapt along the floor with tinny hollow clangs. In her rush to corral her brats the Mamaroneck mommy caught her toe on the rodent and knocked him from under the seat.

People stepped around or over. And no one seemed to care. Typical.

On the hot slog home from the Fairfield Metro-North station, Guy's feet soaked his cordovan loafers, each step harder than the one before. Familiar faces in town came out of the Dunkin' Donuts and the Chocolate Shoppe, but he ignored them. Instead, a curious sensation came over him; the strong scent of orange blossom and heightened expectation you felt right before a thunderstorm, breathing ozone-saturated air.

And Guy began to see things in the street. At first the visions seemed faint as wisps of smoke; then more vivid. As if the old ghosts of the past, the old inhabitants of Fairfield, still roamed the streets. Drawing closer to home it became easier to see them. Men wore frock coats and buckled shoes; women wore long skirts and plain starched tops; others wore fashionable bustles and top hats. The sound of carriages rattled off the storefronts, and the whoops of little boys playing hoop-and-stick. Like Disney's Main Street USA, layers of superimposed memories, mixtures of old styles and present day, women in high button shoes and parasols next to tourists in Trek sandals and boxy yellow disposable Kodak cameras. God, it had to be the heat.

Except for one vision that made his blood run cold.

A number of horse-drawn wagons rolled toward town, followed by farmhands pulling handcarts in from the countryside. Torches stuck on each corner of the buckboards wafted black greasy smoke, smoldering punk sticks that spewed the heavy scent of burning dung—an old-fashioned disinfectant, Guy seemed to recall. Moreover the carts weren't carrying food from the countryside, but the dying. The stricken piled one on top of the other, too weak to move. The moaning filled the air.

One man pulled a dog cart like a coolie, his passenger a shivering skeleton clutching a blanket, the creature's face and arms a bright yellow, terrified yellow eyes staring out of a shrunken skull. The fevered eyes locked on Guy. The wagons clattered onward, finally vanishing into the past where they belonged.

God, he thought, a few hours in the heat and he'd lost his mind. Guy loosened his tie and shrugged off his jacket. The sweat poured off his brow. He grasped the lamppost by the curb for support. *Pull yourself together, buddy.* Then he noticed old Mr. Fenniman taping up windows. The old coot turned and spotted Guy clinging to the lamppost like a drunk.

"What the hell's the matter with you, Poole? You sick or something?"

Guy stood up straight, wiped his sweating palms on his pants, and tried to look as sane as possible.

"I hope not. Thanks for asking though."

Old Fenniman dismissed Guy as your typical metrosexual pantywaist and nodded admiringly at his wrapped-up house.

"Think I'm nuts, Poole? They say there are mosquitoes everywhere carrying all kinds of disease. I'm not taking this off till the snow flies, and maybe not even then."

"Who are *they,* Mr. Fenniman?" Guy asked. The old man frowned; everybody knew who *They* were. Guy left his lamppost and stumbled across the street toward home. "No, Mr. Fenniman, I don't think you're nuts. Not today, anyway."

Across the street, Poole saw the girl from the stairs—Auntie Whitcomb's great-great whatever she was—sitting on the Finn House stoop. Kinda hard to think of her as anybody's grandmama seeing the youngster in pinafore and puffy sleeves. She'd seen the death carts too, but brightened when Guy came up the path. She jumped to her feet and ran toward him, eyes glistening, then shyly took his hand, fingers strangely cool in his sweaty palm. And he looked down at her, the daughter he'd never had.

Inside, big wags from Corky and Peaches made him kneel to give the dogs their pettings. When he looked again the little girl had vanished. She did that a lot. But it felt nice to see her even so briefly, as though all the "kids" were there to greet him when he came home. "Let's go find Mommy," he told the dogs.

They found Lauren cutting lengths of plastic from his painting roll on the kitchen table, as though working bolts of cloth. She had taped up the French doors in the den, and the air conditioner was working overtime. Lauren placed plastic over one of the kitchen windows and taped the edges. She paused and looked at her husband, a hot dripping rag.

"You're a mess," Lauren chuckled. "How'd it go?"

Guy threw his damp jacket over the back of a kitchen chair. Shrugged, and did an impression of Quiche Lorraine, "Thanks for coming. We'll be in touch."

"Like that, eh?" Lauren nodded to herself and smoothly cut a broad length of plastic. She glanced at Guy, suddenly a little worried he thought her crazy. "Did you see what Fenniman's doing to his house?"

"Yeah. But he's doing it a little different."

Lauren nodded. "I know—on the outside."

"Well, the town's going to have something to say about it, won't they?"

Lauren cut another perfectly measured patch of window plastic. "Do you think I'm nuts?"

Define nuts. Brother Rat in the aisle of the New Haven train? Visions of yellow fever death carts in the street? Great girl-granny Whitcomb waiting on the stoop? Guy just shook his head and laughed.

"You know what they say: An ounce of prevention is worth a pound of cure. What about the dogs? We have to let them out in the backyard once in a while, don't we?"

Guy paused, considering the problem. "What if we screen in the backyard like a big outdoor pavilion?" he suggested. "I can probably buy a used party tent and do the rest myself with extra netting."

Lauren sealed the last kitchen window, a glint of admiration in her eyes. "You're so smart. That's why I married you. Just don't change your name to Fenniman."

19

❦

House of Stairs

Something had gone terribly wrong at Connecticut Valley Hospital. Eleanor could feel it in her bones. First her good friend, Mrs. Miniver—Kay—looked a little green around the gills at lunch. Instead of Kay's perky self, she seemed lethargic, playing with her food in the plastic trays and not even coveting Eleanor's tapioca.

"You sure?" Eleanor asked Kay, offering her friend the little blue cup. But Kay simply shook her head and grimaced at the thought.

"Have you told anyone you don't feel well? Maybe it's the medications, maybe a stomach virus."

Kay nodded yes; she'd told someone. Then shrugged at the other part of the question. The medications, a virus? Who knew?

"They gave me some Pepcid for my tummy. And some Rolaids soft chews. I wish they had Jell-O today. I'm in the mood for Jell-O. Lime green Jell-O."

"I like cherry better," Eleanor told her friend. And Kay smiled.

Then conspiratorially under hushed breath, "Did the light people come to you too? They didn't come back to me. So they must have come to you. Did you see them?"

For a few seconds Eleanor wasn't sure how to reply; as she mulled over an answer she stared at the other patients in the cafeteria. Nobody in a nuthouse acts normal to begin with, but almost every loosey-goosey in the cafeteria had undergone a subtle change, behaving oddly. Patients did a kind of spastic hand-dance, waving imaginary no-see-ums from their faces, scratching an itch on exposed skin, a chin or forearm, then staring sharply at an invisible bug. *Slap! Got 'em!* One man a few tables off was unable to sit up straight, and actually gripped his chair to keep from sliding off. His eyes sloshed in his head. Vertigo.

"I can hear the mosquitoes talking to him," Kay whispered at Eleanor. "I think he can hear them too."

Suddenly two female patients eating lunch under the broad windows made some clattering noise. A very large woman with tightly controlled hair erupted in a bit of inappropriate laughter; the other, a mousy librarian, gasped in scandalous dismay as if assaulted by a pervert. Eleanor saw why:

The head orderly, Mr. Washington, was getting sick in public. A very sweet Uncle Remus of a gentleman, Mr. Washington stood a pace or two away from a patient's lunch table, one hand on the wall, the other across his belly. He had quietly retched onto the floor. You could tell poor Mr. Washington was taken totally by surprise. Completely ashamed, he pressed a handkerchief to his lips and told his two charges, "I'm terribly sorry to disturb your lunch. I'll clean that up right away."

Which made Kay forget all about visitations from Light People or whispering mosquitoes.

"See?" Kay said. "Mr. Washington could use some Jell-O too."

After lunch the two friends walked across the carefully

mowed lawns back to their rooms. The more benign patients were allowed to stay in one of the nicer residences on the grounds. Eleanor and Kay had dubbed theirs the Gabled House. This time of day patients would often lounge around the downstairs parlor, what the hospital called "comfort rooms," to play cards or Chinese checkers or watch TV before dinner.

Kay had been working on a jigsaw puzzle at the parlor coffee table—M. C. Escher's *House of Stairs*. Eleanor always felt drawn to the crazy black-and-white picture; the stairs going up and down and slanting side to side while the imaginary segmented lizaroids crawled along one after another on their tiny human feet.

"They're called Rolpens, after a kind of Dutch meatwrap," Kay had told Eleanor. "Escher made the creatures up, as there are no wheel-shaped animals in nature that can roll themselves along."

Eleanor considered that a moment. "I saw a kitten do that once, roll over and over, chasing a ball of yarn. I'll bet a puppy or a monkey could too," which made Kay laugh.

But this afternoon no one was playing cards in the parlor, and Kay didn't feel like working on her puzzle. The two women went straight to their rooms, opting for naptime instead. Eleanor could hear sighs of relaxation as her housemates knocked off their shoes and stretched out. But what she heard next alarmed her. First, squeaky crepe soles marched along the hall outside: staff shoes. One dead bolt thrown, and then another. A brief pause outside her door; the orderly threw the dead bolt on her room too, locking Eleanor in like all the rest.

"Hello?"

But no one answered; the crepe-soled feet marched away. Other patients softly protested from behind their locked doors. Eleanor stared for a few moments at the locked door. She wanted to call out to Kay, but her friend lived in another part of the gable-front house. A break in routine meant bad things coming. Gingerly Eleanor jiggled the door handle. Yep, locked.

She went over to the window, opening it as wide as it would go; a few inches before it hit a restraining block. God, where the hell did they think anyone would go? What about fire? Oh yeah, every bloody room had a sprinkler in the middle of the ceiling. But what if the sprinkler didn't work?

A muffled shout from the mousy librarian came through the wall: "Eleanor, shut up! Shut up!"

She clapped a hand over her mouth. Talking to herself again? Eleanor looked to the pretty flower stencils at the top border of her room; no, no dancing flowers there, no dancing men. Something far worse this time. The Rolpens from Kay's M. C. Escher puzzle: bug-eyed lizaroids tramping the upper border of the walls, then tucking their heads into their segmented tails and wheeling along like runaway tires. Eleanor's feet began to tingle, losing sensation. Oh, a bad, bad, bad lapse. . . . Time to look away.

The Light Tesla had come again, but this time not floating outside her window, no—this time inside the laptop, *inside* the machine. The benevolent pulse of light stared out at her. It wanted her to remember, starting from the time she could suddenly walk in Van Horn right up till she crashed through Guy and Lauren's picket fence. Eleanor recalled the road trip with the women from the subdivision, but once she arrived at the ant colony everything became broken and confused. . . . How had she finally escaped and come to Connecticut? The pulsing glow was asking her to pay attention. To watch what it showed. The Light Tesla was asking her to fix her memory. Okay, if that's what it wanted. If it was that important . . .

The mousy librarian in the next room pounded on the wall:

"Eleanor, stop talking to yourself!"

She crawled on the bed and put the computer on her lap.

The Light Tesla told her to close her eyes. Close your eyes, take another nap, go sleepy sleep. . . . She closed her eyes and went back in time, back to when she and the ladies from Van Horn went down the tunnel. Marching down, down, down like marching little Rolpens in the crazy Dutchman M. C. Escher's *House of Stairs.*

Yes, she remembered now. . . .

Two months ago probably, just after she left Van Horn; this is how it began. . . .

She lay in another bed behind a glass wall. She'd been some weeks in the Ant Colony; long enough to lose track of time, dreamy weeks luxuriating on nice crisp cool sheets, clean air softly blowing on her face, almost like a spa. In a room called:

Ol ɿɘdmu͟N lɒɈɒnɘɈnA

No, wrong; she was reading the letters backward through the glass. From the bed it only looked like *latanetnA.* They called the room *Antenatal Number 10.*

Ten beds to the room, five and five with an aisle down the middle; she felt absolutely lackadaisical with no urge to get up or do anything but turn her head to look around. Tubes snaked into her arms, but she lacked the ambition to learn their purpose—in any case they gave her no discomfort. She barely glanced at the other women in the beds nearby.

Periodically more women tramped past the glass wall on their way to Antenatal Number 9 or Antenatal Number 11. New women, more women; vacant-eyed and slightly bedraggled as if they'd come inside from a long walk in the woods. The new women glided past, looking neither left nor right, simply drifting along and vanishing from sight.

Then—in a sudden, abrupt shift—they, the mysterious "They," hit the fast-forward button and things *sped up.* Instead of floating aimlessly about, everyone suddenly moved very quickly. Men and women in white lab coats flitted into the glass-walled room, and then flickered out again, their movements herky-jerky like film jumping through the sprockets too fast. Of course the ant people and the dancing men: good ants or bad ants? At last she understood all that stuff she babbled when she crashed through Guy and Lauren's picket fence in a rainstorm. The ant people who worked the colony, *bad red ants*. . . .

And those tubes, those tubes in her arms must be for drugs. In a dizzying flicker the white coats flew around her bed, fussed with her tubes, and suddenly the gurney raced down a hall, whooshing through swinging double doors. Then abruptly halted under the enormous stage lights of an operating theater. Beyond the glare people stood in a gallery gazing down. Red Ants in white coats.

She saw her own feet at the end of a white sheet, in stirrups high up in the air. An old geezer with a halo of white hair glided across her vision. Oh yes, that dry, clean-shaven scientist from the Braincast lecture with the glimmering eye. The last time she'd seen this odd man with the white hair was on that first Light Tesla trip—in a lecture hall holding forth on cyborg mosquitoes and sensory proteins in the human brain.

What was that gobbledygook again? *The refinement of chemosensory proteins allows us infinite stimuli and response*: explaining how the desire for reproduction lured Eleanor and the other women from Van Horn to the abandoned meatpacking plant. So that seemed to be only Phase One of the project. Now for Phase Two.

He spoke to an unseen audience in the gantry above the OR; his flinty voice filled her head:

"Pi R Squared. Outbreeder Eleanor Singh. Team Leader presiding."

Eleanor hadn't a clue what the sly professor meant by that. But she did get the impression the old scientist with the dry voice stood on the verge of doing something unpleasant.

Doing something to her. She tried to say, *No thank you, I'd rather not; could we please—*

An oxygen mask covered her face, and the operating theater slipped away. The last thing she noticed: a shiny mechanical surgeon robot with a thousand pointed instruments in its multiple remote-control hands gliding up between her legs—or was it a giant metallic wasp with multiple feelers and multiple stingers? *What, a Wasp?*

Multiple what?

Eleanor's eyes snapped open in her cozy gabled-house room.

The time on her laptop read 3:57 p.m. She tried the door handle; nope, still dead-bolted. Were they going to let them out for dinner?

But something else nagged her too.

What had the shiny old egghead, the "Team Leader," called her? He'd used a strange word: *outbreeder.*

Outbreeder Eleanor Singh. Out *what*?

Eleanor was an Aerospace gal, not a Life Sciences gal—but a few clicks on the laptop got her an answer. Outbreeding, a form of hybrid reproduction: the crossing of distantly related individuals, producing better plants, cattle, dogs, to create stronger offspring. Superior substance. Superior ability. Genetic enhancement.

Enjoy the *New and Improved* human being.

Only the technicians in the Ant Colony weren't doing it to guinea pigs or brown cows—they were doing it to women. And women like her. And if this was the way they operated, working in the dark, out of sight—that was evil. Taking superlative qualities in their breeding stock and reinforcing them over and over: but to create what?

Übermensch? Superman? A few clicks brought her to a version of Nietzsche's *Thus Spake Zarathustra*: *"I love those who do not first seek . . . beyond the stars . . . but who sacrifice themselves to the earth, that the earth may one day belong to the Superman."*

Sacrificed to the earth. But bred for what?

Sent forth to conquer.

Those fantastically engineered Skeeterbugs she saw at Herr Professor's last lecture leapt into her mind. The blood of earth goddesses fed enhanced SKTR-13 mosquitoes, injecting Übermensch fertility juice like a broad-spectrum insemination into anyone and everyone at the designation of Team Leader. *Outbreeders*.

Eleanor stopped analyzing. The sounds from the other bedrooms in the house had grown louder, more urgent. Moaning from next door as if the mousy librarian lady were in pain. Eleanor thumped her hand against the wall, trying to get the woman's attention.

"Are you all right?" No answer. She thumped again. "Can you hear me?"

Then the faint reply: "Eleanor, shut up."

And coughing. A bout of coughing that went on for a long minute. Then two minutes. Then dragged into three . . . The woman's coughing became more ragged, deeper and more painful. Finally it petered out. That much coughing could kill a person. Break a blood vessel, give you a heart attack. The sound of wheezing came through the wall. The woman wasn't quite dead yet.

Eleanor sat back on the bed and gazed out the window. She could see the woodpeckers in the trees again, pecking the trunk like they did every late afternoon. But this time they just seemed to be hanging on to the bark. Occasionally she could see the slash of white across their faces, the sharp red crown when they shifted a little. But their movement seemed sluggish. Instead of vanishing in the flick of an eye, these guys couldn't care less. All their natural energy drained away.

Suddenly one of the large birds chirped—a single, harsh *kuk!*—and fell from the tree trunk, a lifeless lump. The other large woodpecker fell right after him with a hollow flap. Eleanor saw the two wonderful birds lying at the base of the tree. A gust of wind ruffled their feathers; but there was no mistaking dead.

From elsewhere in the house a woman's voice sobbed long and deep—Eleanor could hear the penetrating sobs coming up from the floorboards. As if the poor soul had discovered something too terrible to name. Things were not right, and not getting any better.

Once again, the Light Tesla stared at her from the flat laptop screen. The ball of light pulsed for a moment, then faded. A feed from the Ant Colony came through. First that familiar image: πr^2. The Pi R Squared symbol dissolved, and a young man's face appeared. A fellow with sandy hair and dark circles under his eyes as if he'd spent a whole night worrying himself sick. And Eleanor immediately recognized him as the persistent questioner from that Braincast lecture with the DNA and SKTR-13.

He wore a white lab coat and sat at a bare desk. The vid cam on his laptop picked up little bits of his surroundings. The young man sat in a dim run-down office, paint flaking off scabrous walls. An exposed pipe dripped water.

"I found an old telephone jack in another part of the plant away from the main facility." He paused, looking around him as if expecting the Gestapo to break in any moment and drag him away. The young man looked nervous—like he was making some kind of confession. Five seconds of silent staring.

"My name is Dr. Webster Chargrove. We've been doing something very bad at Pi R Squared. And I don't know how to stop it. I'm making this record now in the hope that someday, someone will find it. Then pass it along. Especially you, Big Sis." He paused to work up his resolve and then found the grit.

"Not long ago I was charged with retrieving comet dust from the Wild Three Aerogel collector at the Dugway satellite recovery. We should have known better than to do that. But even before the pod recovery our Skeeterbug Braincast

System made targeting errors. Women showed up here who didn't belong, and other people who didn't belong."

Eleanor recalled the old security tape; the video feed of dazed and confused movie director Broderick Lady Fallows, hobbling along on one busted pump.

"At first we sent the undesirables, the *misfits,* as we called them, back onto the street. Homeless, crazy women, abducted by aliens, nobody cared, nobody noticed. But then for security reasons we kept them here, and began recycling. Harvesting as much as we could. Stem cells, bone marrow, plasma—" The young man took a breath. His face dropped in shame.

"We should have shut down, found the glitch in the Bio-Design. Instead we made it worse. We introduced the comet-derived glycine into our original glycine base. I did that. That was me. I used the new material as a template for allele genetic outbreeding."

The sad fellow was starting to lose Eleanor, and she struggled to keep up. Glycine, an amino acid, the building threads of life, part of the DNA chain—a primal neurotransmitter. Obviously the geniuses used it as a pathway into the human brain, like they said back in the Braincast lecture.

"That way we could introduce our genetic enhancements. These alleles included denser muscle mass, stronger bones, more flexible ligature. Greater lung capacity, an overall resistance to heat, cold, pain, solar radiation, disease. And inside the brain itself a more enhanced synaptic response. Just like we did on the mosquito. Except now on people. Über-humans. It was all supposed to be so good, so beneficial."

The young man on the laptop shook his head in dismay, amazed at his own hubris and stupidity.

"We thought the glycine from outer space would be pure—as it had been endlessly radiated in a pristine airless vacuum. How could we know?"

BioDesign engineer Chargrove hit a few keys, and the feed cut to a new image:

Hatchery 4. Another glass-walled room of ten beds, five up and five down with an aisle in the center. Safe, clean, nice music piped in. But something was very wrong here; all the women were sick, bloated red and gray faces. One face pasty white, another gray, another blushing red, yet another streaked black as though a living bruise. Then last of all yellow.

Young Chargrove's voice came through. "If you were prone to bronchitis you cough up blood. If you suffered childhood chicken pox your body becomes susceptible to shingles. Not just one disease but a thousand plagues. When the subject's liver finally liquefies we call it Yellow Jack."

20

There Must Be a Way Out

Same hour. Same day. Moments later. Eleanor's eyes fell from the laptop screen.

The Light Tesla had not only fixed Eleanor's memory but improved it. She recalled everything that had happened to her in that dreadful place: sight, sound, touch, taste, down to the last detail. Seeing it all once more . . .

In the bowels of the Ant Colony Eleanor pulled the crisp sheets off her chest. No stirrups, no robo-wasp with a mouth full of needles. Her meds had run out; shrunken fluid sacks hung above her bed. She detached herself from two IV needles and sat up in bed for the first time since her insemination. Her back ached; she gingerly touched a bedsore on her thigh. She looked at her fingernails; they'd turned into slatternly cat claws with cuticles to match. Three weeks' growth, maybe a month.

Suddenly awake and alert, she looked for a robe; this place was colder than she remembered from her shadowy waking periods. The Van Horn wives lay in their beds, attached to tubes and monitors in various altered states. Something was very, very wrong. Looking closer at her neighbors from Van Horn, it only got worse.

All the women in her postnatal section were dying.

Mrs. Biedermeier seemed to have ballooned up twice her size. A big woman to begin with, now a whale. Her face red as a plum, but so swollen her eyes had almost vanished from her head. A clear plastic respirator was inserted down her windpipe, and a pump moving her chest seemed to make her breathe, but otherwise there was no sign of life.

The skinny Mrs. Stanton looked like she'd lost two pounds a day for a month. The gold cross on the gold chain around her stringy neck stood out against her bluish gray skin, puckered with goose bumps. Sunken cheeks, nearly opaque eyes looked like those vampire corpses dug up after a dirt nap in the pine box. Mrs. Stanton breathed without a respirator but for all intents and purposes not long for this world.

Poor Mrs. Perkins seemed to have grown a tangerine-colored fungus about her face and exposed arms—orange mold, turning her into a human plushie squeeze toy. As Eleanor stared, a terrible lethargy seeped into her bones. Why flee? She'd just wind up like them.

Only the elderly, silver-haired Mrs. Quaid seemed to have survived their fearless Team Leader's insemination procedure in the operating theater. Her skin wasn't parchment yet, or deathlike or some strange color. Rather, Mrs. Quaid's face had twisted into a rictus. Mrs. Quaid was frozen from head to toe; limbs frozen, face frozen in a

gaping laugh, a thread of saliva slipping from the corner
of her mouth to a damp pillow.

Only her eyes were alive, darting back and forth. And
in a horrible realization Eleanor saw sentience, intelligence
in those flashing eyes. They implored her, digging into
Eleanor's brain, frantically pleading: Mrs. Quaid was
begging for her very soul for *someone,* anyone, *to come
and kill her.*

That did it. The lethargy shattered into a thousand pieces.

Nothing Eleanor could do for these women. Not the dead
ones, not the living.

She bolted from bed; her finger clamp wired to the bio-
metric monitors yanked her back. If she pulled it off would
anybody notice?

Of course not, Eleanor!

Half the monitors in this ward weren't running. Nobody
watching, nobody cared. This batch of women too far
gone. *I'm sorry,* she mouthed to Mrs. Quaid. *I'm sorry,*
she mouthed again to the woman's frantic eyes, *but I just
can't—*

No point in talking. Eleanor's bare feet slapped out the
glass door as she clutched her hospital gown. Which way
now? She hurriedly looked for a hallway map with a *You
Are Here* arrow. No, only a tunnel slanting up and a tunnel
leading down. She tried up first. After a dozen yards the
tunnel broadened to the habitable areas: operating theaters,
control rooms, workstations. She heard the hum of voices.
A public address system announced, *"Team Leaders to
Synthetic Biology Section. Progenitor cell manufacture
and red blood cell pharming. Scheduled briefing at oh-
eight-hundred hours."*

Eleanor shrank against the wall. Somehow she knew the
word *pharming* was a portmanteau, of *farm* and *pharma-
ceutical.* Had she seen it etched on a glass wall during her
fits of delirium? Who knew? So this is where the technical

ants observed the guest ants, where the master ants moni-
tored the pregnant ants. But in any case—

Not this way.

She retreated down and out, flapping past the postnatal
death room of the Van Horn women. The tunnel went on,
slightly downhill. Before she walked half a city block, she
came upon another glass-walled ward dug into the side of
the passage. This room was labeled INCUBATION TRIMES-
TER ONE.

A dozen transparent containers with human embryos in
amniotic fluid sat on long metal tables. Big eyes stared from
tadpole bodies. Too soon in the process for eyelids, but the
offspring were developing arms and feet from amphibious
flippers. Some of the fetuses moved in their artificial
placentas; one actually seemed to be waving at her.

A terrible fear crept into Eleanor. A kind of knowing
certainty about what lay ahead. Two more brightly lit glass-
walled wards farther down the tunnel shone out from either
side of the smooth walkway.

INCUBATION TRIMESTER TWO—unborn children, but
more developed. Some kicked and turned. Eleanor remembered reading that even in the second trimester the
child's taste buds worked, and whatever their mother ate,
they tasted as well. But without mothers, what did these
little things taste? She fled from the wall, shrinking before
the last enclosure.

INCUBATION TRIMESTER THREE—fully developed infants. Slender intravenous feeding tubes entered the children's veins from panels in the sides of their incubators;
tubes snaked from underneath, waste disposal. Human
contact restricted? Maybe a once-a-day check to see if they
were breathing? The whole setup exuded automated indifference.

But why real children? With blood pharming, synthetic
biology, with the harvesting of unlimited stem cells, adult

and embryonic, what the hell did the Ant Colony need live infants for anyway?

She paused to watch every baby in the bright glass room bawl away in their cute plastic crates, the chubby, angry bambinos caterwauling behind the soundproof transparency, beet-red faces moving like in a silent movie. Her first impulse was to yank open the door, leap in, and rescue as many as she could; throw them under her arms and bolt for freedom. But the transparent door was secured with a retinal scan and keypad.

Suddenly, a ventilation duct in the tunnel wall began to whir loudly. She felt the air suck past her face. Inside Trimester Three a large vent with Venetian slats clapped open, and Eleanor could see a bright blue ribbon windsock fluttering into the room.

And that's when Eleanor saw the reason the infants cried. A brown cloud shot out of the slatted vent and spread across the room on tentacles of forced air. Mosquitoes. Skeeterbugs.

They hovered over the infants in their transparent cribs for a moment. And then in a smothering rush the insects descended to feed. Thousands of mosquitoes swarmed over little bawling bodies. They planted their stingers over and over, pausing for a moment, then sucking back for more. The babies' faces became mottled, swollen, unrecognizable. Some babies totally covered, an undulating swarm of living bloodsuckers blanketing their bodies—

Another Venetian vent slapped open; an exhaust vent in the rock ceiling. Air rumbled through the tunnel. In a few moments the Skeeterbugs were drawn to the new vent. Having fed, they were being sucked outside the complex. Eleanor turned away in revulsion.

She staggered on, her bare feet slapping the concrete floor.

If the mosquitoes could get free so could she.

The tunnel narrowed, the overhead lights becoming less

and less frequent. Eleanor emerged into a cavern of missile silos in an underground barn. She paused for a moment, taking it in. No, not missile silos; what remained of the deep substrata, the subbasement of the Whiteside meatpacking operation. Not originally part of the labs and control rooms above, but still used by them nevertheless.

Stainless-steel silos, chutes, and tubes flowed into hoppers—an assembly line of pumps, cookers, and centrifuges harvesting the last shreds of meat by-products. A conveyor belt that siphoned off bonemeal, rendered fat, and dumped the gristle into mine carts on rails.

The end of the line for all the busy work upstairs; the final process for the women dragged here, like Mrs. Biedermeier and poor, insane Mrs. Quaid trapped inside a useless body. The place the infants, the outbreeders in Trimester Three went after feeding Skeeterbugs. When they'd served their purpose or died of neglect.

For several minutes Eleanor stood there in the midst of the rendering machines shaking uncontrollably, the cold seeping into her bare feet from the concrete floor. She clutched the hospital gown around her body. The reek from it all staggered her, a thousand miles of bad intestines, bits, and grits on an endless slippery road. A train of mine carts on railroad tracks led down to one last cramped tunnel and disappeared into the dark. The only way out.

In a dingy corner she saw a huge pile of refuse. Clothes, stockings, skirts, coats—more than anyone could burn or throw away. As though whoever in charge of disposal worked in fits and starts, discarding clothes by the pound, not bothering to sort them or finish the job. An iron furnace door yawned open, exuding the ugly smell of burnt cloth.

But she'd found *clothes*. In a few moments she snatched a pair of dirty sneakers, a T-shirt, a pair of Tartan boxer shorts, and a terrycloth bathrobe that didn't smell too bad. As she picked through the dirty clothes a broken high heel

Prada pump fell out of the pile and tumbled to the floor. The busted lady's shoe looked strangely familiar, stirring a memory. She picked up the fancy patent pump, trying to remember.

Then a bright bit of flaxen hair caught her eye: glimmering blond hair. Eleanor drew it out of the mound. A wig, a lady's blond wig. A mess of shrieking hair. *I think I'm lost. Can you tell me which way is Los Angeles? Are you from the studio?*

So that strange, distraught Broderick Fallows had finally left by the back door.

Tying the belt in a knot, Eleanor staggered toward the narrow rail tunnel along the mine cart train. A narrow concrete walkway ran along the tunnel wall, with a handrail bolted to the rock. She gripped the rail and stepped onto the narrow ledge. Once upon a time this mineshaft had been lit with electric lightbulbs, one every ten feet, but most had burned out. She spotted a dim forty-watt bulb up ahead, but it threw light on nothing. She passed it and shuffled on, holding the handrail for safety. Every so often her feet stumbled over broken concrete or rubble, the shaft darker than sin.

A mine cart that had jumped the tracks rose up from nowhere and blocked her path. Blindly she stepped down from the safety of the ledge and groped her way around the metal bucket. Panting, Eleanor climbed back on the ledge looking for the tunnel wall. She found the handrail and gratefully leaned against it.

A few steps farther on the handrail vanished, and with it any sense of security. Broken? Fallen off? Maybe they just ran out of pipe. She shuffled onward, one hand grazing the damp tunnel wall, the other reaching out hesitantly in the dark. The stench became overpowering—a physical mass that you had to push your way through. She tried mouth breathing, but it did no good. Finally, she saw a last dim lightbulb up ahead. Her pace quickened, but she tried to restrain herself; too easy to stumble, too easy to fall.

She halted in the dim cone of light and peered about her. The tunnel ended; the rails and mine carts ran over an edge of another abyss, a yawning trench. The stench here, beyond overpowering. Another cavern yes, but this one filled with moist, wet, gelatinous mounds. Once upon a time Whiteside plant's private dump, now where the Ant Colony poured all the guts they couldn't harvest.

She stared at the forty-watt bulb, wishing it threw more light. If only it threw a little bit more light; her fingers reached to the glowing bulb as if to coax a little more light from it, just a little more light—

The dim forty-watt bulb flashed once and died. The dark enveloped her. Eleanor sagged against the rim of the tunnel, knees to chest, hugging herself, despair drowning her like a living force. Crouched beside an enormous pit of rotting flesh, she'd gone as far as she could go.

She began to weep, tears running down her cheeks. But she stopped short of total mental collapse; something brushed up against her leg. She kicked out wildly and heard the angry squeal of a rat. She wasn't alone. An even greater revulsion filled her, and she planted her backside against the rock tunnel wall. Crawl up to the surface? She hadn't the will to move another inch. If she died here would the rats take pieces of her outside? *Don't think like that.*

She brushed the damp tears from her eyes and stared out into the nothingness, damning the dark. Then caught her breath. The dark was dying.

Yes, the dark itself: a patch of light twenty feet away and a dozen feet off the ground, an opening in the trench of meat—a hole or a gap. Daylight from outside; daylight showing Eleanor the way. . . . She stifled her first impulse to rush to it. No, she might step off into the slimy abyss. With all her will she waited, waited for the light to broaden, to reveal her surroundings. Ten aching minutes crept by. Then twenty.

The hole grew brighter. Pale dawn.

The gap was about the size of a large bay window. The endless pattering of rat feet and nameless scavengers had tramped down a path, right down to the bedrock. From the rail lines and the tunnel's end the rat path hugged the wall, around the stinking pile of meat and filth.

Eleanor stumbled forward, first walking, crawling, then clawing out into the light. Fresh air wafted over her face, dampening the cloud of stink. *But she was outside, sliding down a grassy slope. Free!*

Dawn had come to Ohio; the most beautiful dawn she'd ever seen or felt. The cool morning air braced her, and lavender clouds touched a fair blue sky. In the high grass a thrush sang its first morning song: a hopeful, expectant flute, the day's first herald telling heaven that in this one pasture all was right with the world.

Eleanor blessed the bird, and thanked God for the first time in as long as she could remember. She rubbed her sneakers on some fragrant grass to get the slime off, washed her hands in the dew, and looked around to get her bearings.

Above the grass-covered meat seam she saw the dirty brick smokestacks of the Whiteside Meatpacking Plant. A mosquito hummed into her face, and she batted it away. Down below she spotted the rusty fenced parking lot where she first arrived, however many weeks ago.

She carefully picked her way toward those old landmarks along a weedy dirt road. In a few minutes she passed the battered chain-link fence and the compound lights at the rear end of the factory and the large dented metal company sign. Eleanor's car sat exactly where she left it among a dozen other abandoned cars. Maybe they'd eventually be sold for spare parts, but who cared?

What really mattered—her Prius wasn't blocked in. Mrs.

Stanton's small lamé silver purse sat on the dashboard. She snapped it open and pawed through: fifty, sixty, eighty dollars. Oh good, mad money.

She turned the key, and the engine caught. The sound of salvation. She rolled out through the metal gate as easily as she had rolled in, descending the switchbacks to the highway. As the car gained speed, a bug splatted against the windshield, then another. Eleanor hit the wipers and windshield fluid, sweeping them away. Clouds gathered overhead as the highway rushed under her car and the trees by the roadside waved good-bye.

Free at last, but free to do what? How about the insane lie she told Bhakti when she ran away? *Taking a little trip to see my sister. I have my cell.* Now she really wanted to see Lauren. Her cell lay just where she left it, plugged into its charger. Better call or text Bhakti too; gotta tell him something. Was he still looking for Janet? Had he found her yet?

Despite the exhilarating freedom, a pang of regret stabbed her: *Janet. . . .* She'd hardly thought about Janet. And Eleanor felt *something else,* something very bad deep down in her belly. Those Dancing Ant Men had put something in her body that wasn't supposed to be there. Something she didn't want—a little trimester tadpole that didn't belong.

Not Bhakti's, not anyone's. She carried an Outbreeder.

She could almost feel it moving under her bathrobe, feel its little feet struggling, its glassy eyes trying to stare out her belly. And with a terrible wave of fear, an image of it jumped into her head. She carried a rolling segmented tadpole with tiny human feet, that could roll like a wheel if it wanted, and after a few weeks that beak-mouthed salamander was going to crawl out of her, crawl right out of her—

God, don't say it, don't think it. She began to pant, the ache in her belly getting worse. First thing, get rid of it somehow. If she didn't, the Ant Dancers would know everywhere she went, every place she slept, everything she did. The tiny rolling tadpole tattling on her every move, her body sending messages back to the Ant Colony. And inside her belly the glassy-eyed tadpole would be telling her what to say, what to do.

No, they couldn't know where she was going, not now, not ever again. Eleanor passed a blazing, enormous billboard off the side of the road. Two sign-hangers in white overalls standing on a scaffold were plastering the board with a new advertisement. The image showed a beanpole of a man in doctor's pastel blues, masked and capped and gowned for surgery, standing in front of a gleaming white hospital building. ST. FRANCIS'— That part wasn't pasted in yet.

The odd, gaunt man's rubber-gloved hand held up a shiny speculum in the billboard picture. And the caption read: *Don't take shortcuts. Take 15 Minutes to a Lifetime of Freedom. It's not a Choice; it's a Convenience. St. Francis' Teaching Hospital. Accepts ACA, Medicaid, and all Major Credit Cards.*

No, no more hospitals, no hospitals. They'd just send her back to the Ant Colony. Eleanor put her foot on the gas. Up ahead the highway sign of a Dairy Queen flashed at her, and she pulled the car toward an exit. Ask for a plastic spoon in the drive-thru window.

The teeny-bopper drive-thru girl turned her nose up at Eleanor like testing bad lip gloss at a cosmetics counter. "Next window." She shrugged. "They'll give you a spoon and napkins."

Eleanor parked the car and looked around to make sure no one in the Dairy Queen parking lot noticed her. All Eleanor had to do was one little poke, one little poke up between her legs to miscarry and she'd bleed the tadpole right out. Could she do it? Could she? She didn't know. One little poke, one little—

Her hand trembled in front of her face; somehow she'd

snapped off a bit of spoon. A fog closed in. She felt her mind blur, her brain going soft: sights, sounds, and memories slipping from her. *How she got here, why she was driving.* That's something they did back, back at that other place, the underground place with the glass walls. The ant place. They knew how to break your memory, make things move fast or slow and scramble things up.

When she finally texted Bhakti on the cell, all she could think of came out crazy: *They're watching. Always watching. And the ants go marching west to east. Hurrah.* Which made absolutely no sense. . . .

She'd drive to Connecticut. Get to Lauren's. Guy and Lauren, they'd know what to do. What the hell was this spoon for again? And why was it so bloody? Good thing she had plenty of napkins.

The gray road rolled underneath the car; the windshield wipers beat the rain away. She kept the radio off—no room in her brain for a Braincast. Morning passed to midday and midday to afternoon. The interstate swept her eastward, stopping only for self-service gas with a credit card she found in Mrs. Stanton's little silver purse, and back on the road. God, she hadn't been to Auntie Whitcomb's in years. Would she remember the way? Sheets of hail pelted the quiet streets of Fairfield. A family of deer galloped through the driving ice; the car fishtailed. Now which house? Oh, yes, there was the white picket fence—

Eleanor's hands gripped the windowsill in her pleasant Connecticut Valley Hospital room. At last she'd found the broken pieces of her past. She'd escaped from wicked men. Miscarried. No, self-aborted. Don't minimize. Don't make excuses. Her fingers left smudges on the window glass. She had made a little circle of dirt. There was something horribly appropriate in the smudged area of a circle. A circle filled in with slime and grunge—

Dirt R Squared.

Outside the gabled house night had fallen. Vaguely, she recalled the staff orderly, the nice Mr. Washington, politely knocking, opening her door and speaking to her while she nodded distractedly, working the smudge circle on the window. Not too odd for a madhouse; Mr. Washington was grateful Eleanor didn't throw tantrums.

In any case her room had been entered; a meal tray sat on the table under the TV. Along with a bottle of hand sanitizer and a few white cotton biofilter masks in a clear antiseptic pack. Also a printed note: *Watch for Hospital Updates Channel 98.*

She looked under the Styrofoam cover. Meat loaf, mashed potatoes, corn, and string beans. A brownie for dessert. Those were always pretty good. Napkins, plastic forks and spoons in sealed plastic. Salt and pepper packets. Channel 98 showed a simple announcement:

> **Due to an outbreak of staph infection, we ask all guests to please use the hand sanitizer and to wear the face masks when in contact with the hospital staff. Check back to Channel 98 for further information.**

What did Eleanor know about staph infections? The bacterium entered through cuts on the body; but the variety of symptoms was legion. If you were prone to bronchitis, it hit the lungs, if you were prone to skin infections—and so on. And staph was a hardy, nasty bugger. Suddenly brownies didn't sound so good, never mind the sweaty slab of meat loaf.

Another bout of coughing from the mousy librarian next door bled through the wall. Then silence. Quietly, faint moans and soft sobbing came from distant corners of the gabled house. In a precious moment of lucidity, Eleanor wrote a mass e-mail on her laptop to Bhakti, Guy, and Lauren and cc'd Lattimore Aerospace in Sioux Falls. God, what wild things would Boss Clem think about her just wandering off? Nothing good, to be sure.

> *I want to leave now. Just please come and get me. Somebody, please.*

But the second she clicked Send, Yahoo bonked her right back.

> *E-mail service temporarily out of service. Please check back later.*

21

Ship of Foos

The Cosmos Café, the Lattimore company cafeteria, occupied part of the ground floor near the reception and the elevators. Clem Lattimore poured a couple of black coffees into quilted paper thermal cups and shuffled half a dozen doughnuts onto his tray. He paid Mildred, the dowdy cashier, and asked after her husband, who had recently retired from Lattimore Aerospace.

"How's your dear Paul?"

Mildred made change and sighed. "His rheumatism is acting up, Clem. We're thinking about going to an arthritis specialist in Chicago. A sports medicine guy."

Lattimore nodded sympathetically. "Tell him we miss him."

Two clerks from accounting looked up from lunch,

offering him a seat at their table, but Lattimore shook his head thanks, but no thanks. The company cafeteria struck him a little thin for middle of the week: empty seats, bare tables, and hardly any noise. Maybe it was the run-up to Labor Day. The official end of summer. It sure felt like the official end of something.

Two levels down, Lattimore entered the lead-lined sub-basement bearing coffee and half a dozen doughnuts. His chief technology officer had been hard at it for weeks, looking for a firewall breach or a virus. Going home at eleven or midnight only to change clothes and sleep.

August had flown by without a peep, and so far they'd struck out. Maybe there wasn't a breach to find. Worse still, Jasper seemed to be spending as much time reading bizarre news items about classified conspiracies as searching for a crack in the operating system. Jasper glanced at the java and dunkers and back to his flat-screens, now using all six for weirdo "gubiment" ops. If Lattimore's tech specialist misplaced any more of his marbles he'd be going quackety-quack, don't talk back. The CTO tickled a few keys.

"Have a look at this."

"Tell me you found the server breach. Tell me we know whether the Van Horn lab has been compromised."

A satellite image taken by the company's Lodestar satellite, a search-and-rescue hybrid with military applications on lease to the United States Navy, flashed onto the screens: one of those high-resolution pictures from a couple of miles up, the designation USN, latitude and longitude, date and time. A very pretty picture of the Atlantic Ocean—pale blue water surrounding beach break and palm trees.

Clem could pick out the island of Nassau in the Bahamas off the Florida Coast, the thin strip of Coral Sands, and the spear point of a ship, a container vessel heading north. The Navy kept track of a lot of ships.

The image flickered, a few minutes of time-lapse photography. Then the ship vanished. The screen picture jumped back and forth: Ship, no ship. Ship, no ship. Lattimore carefully measured his words, trying to suppress total incredulity:

"You're showing me some ship disappearing in the Bermuda Triangle?"

Jasper grabbed a doughnut and inhaled it in three bites. "Those pictures are from an hour ago. The cargo vessel is the Norwegian container ship *Anja,* en route from the Port of Rio to the Port of Miami. The Navy picked up a peculiar heat bloom of some kind in the cargo area, and not the power plant. That set off warning bells."

Lattimore saw a tiny white-hot lozenge in the middle of the ship before the vessel vanished again.

"Now they may have misplaced it. I mean the ship's not there anymore. My guess, its vanishing act is due to a software glitch and not a Klingon cloaking device. But I sure wouldn't want to be the naval commander of Key West today."

No more coffee and dunkers for Jasper. Starting immediately, a diet of steamed broccoli and brown rice. Or a nice turkey sandwich full of sleepy mayonnaise.

"Jasper, I want you to knock off for a while, come upstairs and get some real food."

But the fellow wasn't listening. "Yeah sure. In a bit." Jasper clicked a few more keys, then suddenly turned from the bank of screens and asked out of nowhere:

"Didn't you tell me once your dad saw Foo Fighters during the war?"

What the hell had gotten into this guy?

Lattimore held the tray from the cafeteria with a dismal expression on his face.

"Foo Fighters," he repeated grudgingly.

"Yeah. Y'know, they were—" Jasper tried to explain.

Lattimore almost lost his cool. "I know what they were."

Foo Fighters? Mysterious lights that played tag with

bomber crews and fighter squadrons over Germany and the South Pacific. Picked up on radar, documented in after-action reports—lights that zigzagged around the planes like fireflies at night. You couldn't catch 'em and you couldn't shoot 'em down. Nazi miracle weapons? Nah, they never shot back. Not to mention, the Japs and Krauts saw 'em too, thinking, Ah-*so,* Ach*tung*! Yankee ingenuity.

Allied Airmen chose the name from the *Smokey Stover* comics, from Smokey the Fireman's zany two-wheeled fire truck, the Foo Mobile. Foo Fighters.

But there was a kind of odd connection. Foos, and those who acted like them. Lattimore remembered two books sitting on the arm of his father's club chair—two copies of the same book. Katherine Anne Porter's *Ship of Fools,* a hardcover in English, and a well-thumbed German paperback. Little Clem could tell his father considered this a special book, important enough to keep by his elbow in both his mother tongue and his adopted one.

Not until years later when Lattimore read the novel for himself did he understand why Father kept it around. A ship of overweening bourgeois passengers sailing to Germany in 1931, the frivolous international smart set, delusional Deutschland *Volk,* pompous charlatans each returning to the fatherland. But *not one of them* truly grasped the real destination of their voyage—the end of the world. The novel reflected his father's own delusion: that his hard-won scientific skills could protect him. Instead of a Ship of Fools, Pop's political naïveté landed him in Ship of Foos—Mittelbau Dora—with a slide rule and V-2 specifications. What he liked to call his "Master's degree from Speer University."

Maybe Clem could make his CTO understand.

"You're getting your stories mixed up," Lattimore told Jasper. "That's not exactly what I said. My dad worked as forced labor for Von Braun, fed better because Pop was a physicist and did mathematical calculations—*rocketry not flying saucers.*"

"But didn't your folks get abduct—"

Clem Lattimore almost lost his temper again, but held his tongue.

He really didn't want to spook this pony, a fellow now perfectly capable of hitting a few clicks and frying the works. Silently Lattimore turned from the obsessed man and took the cafeteria tray with him. "Don't go anywhere," Lattimore suggested. "I'm getting us some real food." He'd come back quietly with security.

Out in the hall he swiped a key card for the elevator, stepped inside, and breathed a sigh of relief. The car rose upward, then bumped to a halt. He pressed the intercom on the indicator panel for the Security office: "This is Clem. I'd like two officers to meet me—"

A tinny, unintelligible squawk came out of the speaker. The overhead lights flickered, then suddenly died. Lattimore stood in the dark, stalled between floors.

The emergency lighting struggled to come on, the bulb filaments tiny red threads.

He pressed the first floor button, but nothing happened. He tried the large red alarm button—again, nothing. His head began to feel a little faint, and Lattimore gently slid to the floor, sensibly laying the cafeteria tray, the doughnuts, and coffee aside before he spilled them. The emergency lighting in the corner of the elevator glowed in such a captivating way, as though inviting Lattimore somewhere special. But where?

"Are we going on a trip to Antarctica again?" he asked the empty elevator.

Soft and fragrant air caressed Lattimore's face: an ocean fog smelling of salt and seawater. He weakly stood with his back to a metal wall—no, a bulkhead on the walkway of a very large container ship. Beyond the rail the ocean stretched for about thirty yards before vanishing into gray mist. The ship's engines were at full stop. Water lapped softly against the ship's hull, magnified in the deep hush. The vessel gently rolled in a silent sea.

Stunned, he accidentally bumped the cafeteria tray with a clumsy foot. The coffee spilled through the grated deck; the doughnuts bounced down the steep gangway stairs. Lattimore snatched the silly tray to his chest with one last doughnut and looked wildly around: portholes, battened waterproof doors, fresh white marine paint. Countless tractor-trailer containers—bright blue, red, and yellow— marched off in long rows along the ship's deck, fitted together like a giant set of blocks, and vanished into the fog.

No point getting lost down there; might as well find the bridge. Lattimore clutched the cafeteria tray to his chest as if it were some kind of lifeline back to South Dakota and mounted the steep open stairs. He spotted a fire extinguisher that read ANJA. Ah . . . the Norgie container ship spotted from the satellite. So that solved the mystery. Déjà vu all over again. Ship. No Ship. Adrift at sea. Great. Thanks, Jasper.

On the bridge the officers and crew stood their watches, alive but unconscious. The captain, a ruddy Viking, sat in his chair breathing softly, binoculars around his neck and chin to his breast. Lattimore touched his neck. No waking him. Dead to the world.

The XO lay slumped by the back bulkhead, the accordion wire of an intercom mike against his lips. A clean-shaven fellow, intelligent crow's feet starting around his eyes. He'd blacked out while listening or talking, a look of puzzled concern on his face.

The galley showed a similar scene: two men slumped over a steel table, knocked-over coffee cups. A huge pot of beef stew simmered away on the range. The open door to a crewman's quarters showed a man on his bunk facedown, unconscious as the rest.

Lattimore stumbled over a crewman spraddled on a

stairway to the lower decks, obviously fleeing from below. Unlike the men on the bridge, this man wasn't Scandinavian, more like Southeast Asian. He sprawled against the metal stairs, a thread of blood leaking off his lip from where he had fallen. Not dead, just conked out cold as a mackerel.

Ignoring a pang of doubt, Lattimore picked his way around the fallen seaman and clattered down the stairs to the hold. He passed another sailor on the way grasping a two-way radio, his face twisted in fear. He'd been trying to make a report to the bridge. The expression of vague concern on the XO's face on the intercom crossed Lattimore's mind. They'd called from below in panic. Then everyone had dropped at once. So what was so damn frightening down in the ship's cargo?

A heat bloom his satellite picked up from low orbit, *remember?* Maybe that's what his Takers wanted him to see. What his Takers *wanted.* His *Takers.* Like the ones who took him to Antarctica? Easy there, Roger Ramjet. . . .

The final watertight door to the cavernous hold stood open. A series of catwalks stretched a hundred yards out into the belly of the ship.

An enticing ball of light hovered over one area in particular. His newest Taker.

The incandescent light pulsed through the primary colors, breaking apart then melding once more, re-forming, then breaking apart again, like a dance. Sure, that'd be enough to send a Filipino seaman running for his life. Lattimore felt weak in the knees, and he pressed the ridiculous cafeteria tray to his chest.

What did he know about container ships? You didn't stack the heavy loads on deck where they could swamp the vessel. You stowed the heavy stuff down below along the keel. So whatever lay there under the glowing lights had serious weight. Serious mass.

He clanked along one of the inner catwalks, and his

Takers receded. Almost dead center of the ship, the floating globes disappeared. Two stories below, Lattimore could
see light reflecting off the metal side of one container.
He scrambled down a flight of steps, then two. . . . Then
sneaked around a couple of corners to find the proper metal
box; he found it, but no incandescent light.

No Takers. Those guys had vanished.

And no real markings on the shipping box either: just a
plain container with the designation L1/5 written in five-
foot-high letters. The lettering was of the same metal as the
container, almost like etched glass, rising from the metal
itself. But not rough or scratchy; seamless, so if you didn't
look at it exactly the right way it would vanish back into
the stainless steel. Then if you looked at it from an angle,
the L1/5 designation morphed seamlessly into the simpler
L2. Look at it one way you got L1/5; look at it at a slightly
different slant—you got L2.

L1/5 to L2

Shift your perspective again. . . .

L2 to L1/5

Whatever the hell that meant.

But one small side door on the tractor-trailer box stood
open, the latches thrown back. He cautiously peeked around
the open edge. Nothing stranger could have greeted him.

Through the open door Lattimore stared at a bit of
heaven on earth.

Inside the metal container was a meticulously con-
structed life-size diorama, perfect in every detail—a
Japanese tea garden right out of feudal Kyoto.

Silvery rice-paper windows let in faint moonlight. Overhead, a tile roof kept off a gentle rain that seemed to fall
from nowhere; the peaceful sound of raindrops filled the

air. Under the tile roof, clean wooden planks surrounded a stone fire pit. An iron teakettle steamed softly on a metal tripod. The tea house floor overhung a koi pond, where great golden Nishikigoi carp gazed lazily up at him with wide accepting eyes. A stone path led to a little bridge, which jumped a chuckling waterfall spilling over mossy rocks.

Even as Lattimore watched, the light in the windows changed, as a veiled moon set beyond distant hills. Beyond the rice-paper walls, night came to an end and dawn broke, filling the tea house with gentle heavenly light.

A miniature red maple danced under the raindrops; a bed of water lilies grew beside bulrushes in a bit of quiet backwater. A cherry tree in spring bloom displayed its fragile pale blossoms. . . . Two butterflies danced about the spears of elephant grass. A praying mantis sat upon a rock in the stream and rubbed his forelegs together, then looked at him with dubious eyes. A bluebird sat in a pine tree and pecked at a pinecone. The flicker of movement by the tea hearth caught Lattimore's eye. A wise, old cricket stroked his wings like a violin, the trill of welcome, almost like a temple bell—as if to say, *Why hello, come in!*

The rain stopped. The light broadened, and a rainbow appeared across the pond.

So much life in such a precious space: a place of peace, of meditation.

A place of Zen.

Lattimore could have gone inside the container, shut the door, and never come out. So easy to do, so easy . . . a name for this place came into his mind. *Tea House of the Hidden Moon.* He put one foot through the container door—

A blast of cold hit him like a wall; cold autumn rain splattered off his throat and chest. Lattimore held the cafeteria tray over his head to keep the rain from splashing into his face, but it pelted down, soaking him to the skin. He wiped the cold wet from his eyes and tried to make out where he was. Clearly, the Takers had taken him somewhere else.

He stood on the high bank of a roadway stretching off into sheets of falling water. A state road sign read GAKONA, AK, POPULATION 215. A wiseass had scrawled the words, *Or Thereabouts* underneath.

A bolt of sunlight broke through a thick bank of clouds; a broad plain stretched for a dozen green miles. Off in the distance a mountain range stood like peaks in a Tolkien landscape. The plain's only disfigurement was a radio antenna installation, the array a perfectly square forest of metal prongs about a half mile on each side, hundreds of metal spikes reaching to the sky. In half a heartbeat Lattimore knew exactly what he was looking at.

The antenna array of United States Navy/United States Air Force's jointly run High Frequency Active Auroral Research Program.

HAARP.

An antenna array in Gakona, Alaska, which zapped all kinds of radio waves and charged particles into the planet's uppermost atmosphere: low frequency, high frequency, ultra-high frequency—whatever you needed into the ionosphere.

Weather research.

Others called it other names: weather warfare, a force multiplier.

But Lattimore had to admit Alaska *was* having perfect weather for this time of year—September: heavy rain, mid 50s, with a chance of sun.

He looked closer at the square of aerials. Not what you normally thought of—no big dishes pointed at the sky. Instead, a legion of metal stalks, cross-spars, and slender tubular props like those old-fashioned 1950s TV antennae. The bristling tubes looked vaguely like Van Gogh's drawing, *Avenue of Poplars*.

And of course, you couldn't see the radio waves emanating from the prongs; but you could feel them in your bones. When they broadcast ultra-low frequency, it seeped under your skin like the subwoofer off a massive concert speaker. Lattimore ground his teeth and felt the sudden urge to hide.

Suddenly the rainy wind off the howling tundra tugged the cafeteria tray from his hands. The tray flew across a wild bit of field, disappearing over the bank of a fast-moving stream. Idiotically, Lattimore chased the flat pan down, hoofing it through lashing grass. The cafeteria tray had come to rest by the edge of the stream under icy water. His feet sank into the sandy bank, and cold water filled his oxfords; sandy mud sucked one shoe off his foot, dragging half a sock with it. Lattimore stumbled back, flopping to the ground with a *woof,* clutching the stupid tray.

W alter Nash, head of building security, looked down through the open doors of the elevator; behind Nash people in the reception area rose in alarm. Apparently seeing the boss on the floor of an elevator, trousers sopped and missing one shoe, scared them. Well, that was natural. The security man kneeled, his shaven face close enough to see every follicle.

Walter Nash gently pried the cafeteria tray from his boss's hands and helped Lattimore to his feet. "Are you all right, Clem? Would you like me to call the EMTs? Take you up to your floor?"

Lattimore shook off the cobwebs. The motherly faces of those two clerks from accounting approached with clucking tongues and busy skirts. Lattimore slipped off his remaining shoe and tugged off his wet socks. "No, Walter, no thank you. I think I've been taken enough already. Let's go downstairs to the subbasement."

He looked at the bare cafeteria tray and shook his head sadly. "Damn, I wanted that last doughnut."

Thirty seconds later, Lattimore and Security Chief Nash stood in the subbasement hallway in front of the steel-reinforced *Star Wars* blast door. The boss swiped a key card, scanned his retina, pressed the palm-print reader, and announced "Lattimore" three times into an audio receiver.

The door ignored him.

He even typed in his override code onto a keypad—all to no avail. The steel, soundproof, bomb-proof door had no intention of letting him into the server farm. Clem pushed his face to the Plexiglas viewing slit, peering inside to the power towers. His CTO was hard at work before a bank of screens. But every so often Jasper shivered, then clapped his arms around his torso as if trying to get warm. Was he cold?

A thousand self-reproaches went through Lattimore's mind. How in hell could he have left this nutkin alone? With horrible trepidation, he knocked on the Plexiglas window. Suddenly feeling like—

Open the pod bay doors, HAL.

Jasper didn't look up. Lattimore rapped the plastic glass, harder this time.

C'mon Jasper, look up.

From his place at the panel of screens, Jasper finally gazed in the direction of the blast door. For a moment he didn't seem to recognize his boss's stern face in the viewing slit. Jasper shivered violently. The gears clicked into place, and he suddenly rose, lumbering toward the locked entry. Outside in the hall the two men heard the welcome click of the lock and breathed a sigh of relief as the door automatically opened. Lattimore shot a glance of caution at security man Nash. "Easy," he whispered. "Let's go easy."

Jasper was already back at his workstation, hugging himself, teeth chattering. The man was *that* cold. *That freezing.* "At first I thought it might be contagious," Jasper stammered. "But in this case, my infection—*mine*—was malaria, so I'm not spreading anything. I'm just sick as hell. And it came on very fast."

What on earth was the man babbling about?

Jasper saw their confusion, stressing: "Malaria. I think I have malaria."

He glanced at a half-eaten doughnut sitting on a paper napkin. Two dead mosquitoes lay on the napkin. "Maybe they came in with you from the cafeteria earlier, maybe a vent. One of them bit me, and ten minutes later I'm sick as a dog—" He stopped to shiver and took a deep, shaky breath. "Sanford Medical across town has cases of dengue fever, West Nile virus, and Rocky Mountain spotted. Point is, I don't think these critters carry just one disease. I think they're sort of like a farmer's market of pathogens. This guy thinks so too."

Jasper tapped a screen; his specialty search engine had latched on to some kind of recorded confession. A young sandy-haired man spoke earnestly into a webcam, but the feed pixelated, as if struggling through an old analog telephone line. The fellow's face looked familiar.

Sure, Billy had sent Lattimore a mug shot from his cell phone after the Dugway recovery back in July. *Aerogel . . . do you know what that is?* Talk about a magic circle. The brainiac bioengineer who'd brought comet dust back to that hush-hush outfit πr^2 making a mea culpa:

"We planned on using the Skeeters for national insemination and disease prevention. Whether the threat came from a new plague or the flu, mankind was long overdue for partial extinction. The science was settled; we'd formed a consensus. We had to do something!" He licked his lips, quietly shocked at how it had all gone so wrong.

"But then they began to breed with normal mosquito swarms. Replicate. Apparently like all living creatures our Skeeterbugs *liked life,* and wanted more of it. Not content to die or expire when instructed. Another software glitch. The self-destruct button malfunctioned. In turn, the enhanced swarms fed on any creature they could find—rats, rodents, anything with blood—spreading a string of pathogens in unpredictable ways. Spontaneous mutation. Creating what we call the wandering sickness, a myriad of pathogens popping up wherever mosquitoes roam. In New Orleans the sickness may be mosquito-borne West Nile virus; in Kansas City the mosquito gives a rat pneumonic plague."

The earnest young man's breathing became ragged.

"Some Skeeters may have even been blown across the Atlantic Ocean into West Africa where the smoldering fires of ebola blazed to life. The contagion brought back home again by the jet engine in a jet age. An affliction no longer transmitted by flying insects but by commercial travelers. Now you don't even have to get bit to get sick. Just go to the ER, sit for a while, and wait for somebody to turn their head and cough."

He paused, gulped air, grasped at a last straw.

"There's a minuscule chance one of our test subjects, known as Chen-L—has a DNA profile that can reverse this wandering sickness. Tests on our samples of her DNA from the national database show the Chen girl possesses an extremely resilient genetic structure infused with a regenerating enzyme called telomeres. The telomerase enzyme keeps a cell from burning out. From dying. Call it the God Protein if you like. But we've been unable to locate her. The surviving Chen girl is one that went missing, the one that never arrived from Van Horn. Originally considered dead—now we've been frantically trying to discover her whereabouts, but so far she's vanished off the grid—no credit card data, no phone calls. It's like somebody just up and kidnapped her—"

The feed broke and the screens went blank.

Lattimore understood. These bio-kooks tried to inoculate mankind against the future. And created a chimera by accident, a combination of disparate, possibly off-world genomes: lethal pathogens that got loose and ran wild in the streets. Now the one girl they needed to fix their fix, whose blood strain might counter their bio-monster—Chen-L—couldn't be found.

Perfect.

Jasper concentrated, trying to make a larger point. "Clem, I don't think the cavalry is going to arrive in time. People inside the CDC are leaking info. Besides being incompetent, careless, and rigid—they're scared." A report from the Centers for Disease Control flashed onto a screen. Rates of infectious diseases had risen 5% in the last six weeks. "Five percent doesn't sound like much, but it's every disease you can think of. Hit ten percent, you're going to see chaos. Hit fifteen percent and you'll think the whole world is sick." Another screen showed a drug bust; packets of rainbow whack, a bunch of cops grinning over their haul.

"And all this Dalekto crap is making it worse. Like any narcotic, it wears down your immune system, makes you more vulnerable to infection. They've analyzed the stuff, and it's just high-octane rocket fuel; an alkaloid, amphetamine-opiate mix with a touch of DMT and other hallucinogens as neurotransmitters. In some samples they've found traces of the psilo stuff, psilocin and psilocybin. But nobody knows where the hell they're making it. DEA? FBI? *Nobody*. Maybe in Mexico?"

Well, no big surprise there; half of America's high school graduates couldn't find Mexico on a map.

"They forgot about the Almighty," Lattimore whispered to no one in particular. "And in the dead of night mixed a hell cocktail. Brains without Faith."

"What's the matter with these people?" Jasper grumbled between shivers. "Didn't they see *X-Files* season six, episode twenty-two, 'Biogenesis'?"

You had to wonder if the CTO was still playing with a full pinochle deck.

"I think I missed that one."

"Great episode," Jasper said a trifle eagerly. "Tidal pools exposed a crashed UFO off the Ivory Coast, possibly sent to reseed earth with alien DNA." Then with great gravitas, "Everybody knows you don't mess with genomes from outer space. It just evolves into government programs for partial-birth abortion clinics and super soldiers."

You had to admit there was a queer sort of logic to that.

Lattimore almost blurted out his brief interlude with the Foos, the Takers, the container ship, and the Tea House of the Hidden Moon. Weather warfare, force multipliers, and bad bugs—they all had to be connected, but Lattimore was damned if he knew how. Just a spilled can of mixed cocktail nuts. To be involved in anything nuttier he'd have to be wearing pink bunny rabbit slippers and tooting a kazoo.

Silently, Jasper looked over the bank of screens and across the rows of power towers blinking green, red, and blue lights. He waved a shaky but expansive arm across the field of RAM. "There's nothing to do here, Clem. Our servers are okay, they're swell, they're fine. Every tower, every stinking gigabit ethernet cable."

"All right, if you say so," Lattimore said warily. "Then you won't object to us taking you to the emergency room."

Jasper sighed, clicked a few keys to power down his workstation, and rose from his seat. Speaking idly, "Y'know there's something else. I have the strangest feeling Wen Chen's HAARP file means something. There's a weather array up in Alaska called the High Frequency Active Auroral Research Program. I meant to tell you that. The enhanced insects, the container ship, weather warfare may be all part of the same—"

Jasper never finished. His legs turned to jelly, and he passed out standing up. Luckily Lattimore was right there to catch the man's heavy body. "Hey!" he called to Walter Nash.

But the security chief was not paying attention, otherwise preoccupied. Nash abruptly snuffed some rainbow powder off his nostril with the back of his hand. A glass nasal atomizer vanished into a pocket. "Sorry."

But what shocked Lattimore the most wasn't that he'd come down off a Foo Fighter trip or that his tech officer had contracted malaria in a subbasement, not even that his security guy might be a Dalekto addict. But that Walter Nash doped up in public and *couldn't care less whether anyone knew.*

22

The Wandering Sickness

The pursuers left the plaster people back in Nebraska but with every mile Lila Chen seemed to recede in their minds as in a dream. Crossing the Missouri River, Bhakti's yellow Toyota 4Runner spawned a mysterious ailment and sputtered to a halt in Council Bluffs, Iowa, where the search for the surviving Chen girl ground to a halt, leaving the three trackers lost in the Marriott hotel doldrums.

The local Toyota dealership seemed to be limping along on half-staff, like every other business in the Midwest. Most everywhere, they'd seen a lot of dirty plate glass and empty storefronts. And the damn 4Runner had conked out again as Bhakti tried to drive it off the lot just *now.* Already a week over the grease pits, hooked up to the diagnostic computer, and nobody could figure out what was wrong with the dang SUV. So back inside he went ready to throttle the first available service representative.

Generally, he liked car dealerships, the showroom lights full of glamour and new car smell. Nevertheless, the Punjabi scientist was getting extremely sick of this Toyota store. The place had the feel of an empty bottle. Vacant workstations with knickknacks left behind: a Love Bear from Valentine's Day, a Post-it note: *Dentist Tuesday.*

A framed photo of a Marine Corps graduation caught his eye. A young man in his dress blues stared soberly into the camera with a look of quiet resolve; a triangle of black crepe covered the corner of a gold-plated CVS photo frame. That made Bhakti want to turn away; a parent, a child. He knew about that.

This might be a good time to try Eleanor again. Generally, they touched base for a few minutes every day, but the last couple of times the coverage was spotty, no bars or his e-mails blocked for no reason. He clicked through. Her cell phone came back *Customer Not Available.* And her Yahoo account bumped him. *MAILER-DAEMON: This user doesn't have a Yahoo.com account—*

Frustrated, he stared out into the street at the passing scene. Gazing out the broad dealership plate-glass window had become something of a cleansing ritual. Good air in, bad air out . . . Then Bhakti saw the stricken man.

He looked to be a wage slave, a worker-drone VP at the First National. The man walked awkwardly down the grassy highway divider with jerky movements like a puppet on strings, every other step threatening to pitch him off the median. Cars honked and swerved. Suddenly Bhakti recognized what he was looking at.

Huntington's Chorea. Now called Huntington's disease.

Also, the poor fellow seemed to have a very itchy face. But every time he tried to scratch his cheek he missed, one time poking himself in the eye, making him turn round and round on the median like a wobbly top. He stamped his feet to stop his spinning; then lurched forward again.

Where in heaven's name was he going? Perhaps the man himself didn't know. The curious scene reminded him of H. G. Wells' wandering sickness in the movie *Things to Come*: doomed people lurching about until they expired, others fleeing at the very sight of—

Another car nearly sideswiped the poor fellow, the horn blaring. Bhakti slapped the plate glass and almost bolted outside before the poor wretch became roadkill.

"Hello again, Mr. Singh. Really sorry about all this."

Bhakti tore his eyes from the street.

Lester, the service rep, was an amiable dork of about thirty-five, with a gap between his two front teeth. You knew his name was Lester because of the nameplate on the lapel of his Century 21 knockoff gold blazer. He gave off a whiff of Polo aftershave and all the persistence of the En-ergizer Bunny, the very model of a modern polyester man.

"Of course we're going to diagnose again. I can't tell you exactly when it's going to be ready. Is there a number where I can reach you?"

Bhakti had given it every time, to the billing department, to Lester, to anyone who would take it. "I'm at the Marri-ott."

"That's right." Lester Polyester knew all along, but double-checked the papers just for show. "Okay, great."

Something had been troubling Bhakti since they came to Omaha and Council Bluffs: why in hell nobody seemed to know about the weirdness back in Lexington. Stalled trucks and cars on the cloverleaf, passengers turned into crash dummies. A mess of stick figures at a cornpone med-icine show as though ripped from their shoes. You'd think something like that would get some reaction in the land of a thousand psalms, at least an item on the local news. But nope. Not a word. So what exactly would you ask? *Heard from Nebraska lately?*

Lester's face twitched. He scratched a perfectly normal spot on his cheek and twitched once more. His hand jerked to his face again. "Can I get you a ride back across the river? Call you a cab?" Lester picked up the phone. "We have a special discount with Council B's Cab Company." He dialed before Bhakti could say yes.

Cheryl had barely thought of Rachel all summer, never mind calling—which was bad, divorce or no divorce, breakup or no breakup. The two of them, once a couple of peas in a pod, had been popped from their shell and rolled away from each other. When she watched Bhakti lose his mind outside the Stuka trailer, a part of her cracked too. Feeling the Punjabi scientist blubber in her arms made Rachel's presence fill her head. As though Cheryl had been holding herself together in bits and pieces too, but just didn't know it.

Now she sat in the lounge of the Springhill Suites Marriott across the Missouri River in Council Bluffs. A new laptop lay on her knees, but she didn't mess with it. She'd picked it up at a downtown RadioShack so she wouldn't have to borrow anyone else's and tried to work up the guts to Skype LA. It took more than she expected.

Imagining Rachel sitting at the glass dinner table with a cup of tea, under that kitsch cowboy chandelier, was incredibly daunting. No, better in a lounge chair staring out over their horizon pool at the cactus, the tequila bottle at her elbow. . . .

Her laptop webcam link connected to home. *Their* home? No, not really anymore. Rachel's PC responded automatically to the video request, Rachel's prerecorded voice saying, "Hi, sorry I'm not logged on right now. Try me at the firm or leave a message."

Cheryl stumbled over what she wanted to say. "I didn't

want to disturb you at work. Thought maybe I'd get you at home," finishing lamely, "I've just been thinking about you."

At the firm, Rachel's paralegal accepted Cheryl's video session request. Brit, a young man in his mid-twenties, starched white shirt, gold braces, nervously cinched up his red paisley tie. His eyes were red and weepy, and he seemed to have a terrible cold.

"Cheryl! We've been trying to find you."

"I'm sorry, Brit. I've been bad about getting online the last couple of weeks. And I lost my cell phone charger." This all sounded so stupid. "Can I talk to Rachel?"

Brit paused, looking incredibly uncomfortable. "I'm going to give you to Boedeker."

Boedeker, one of the top partners, "Just tell me, Brit—"

The video image shifted to standby. Two very long minutes. Boedeker came on; the dark circles under his eyes and thick jowls made him look miserable, not the confident Big Shot he always projected. Cheryl felt a dump truck of bad news coming.

"Arthur Boedeker here, Cheryl." He paused for a breath but didn't hem or haw. "Rachel passed away two days ago. Car accident, up in the hills. There were drugs involved with the driver of the other vehicle. That rainbow stuff that's going around. I can't tell you how sorry I am."

Cheryl said nothing. A chasm opened under her, and she could feel the air rushing by. No Rachel. No Rachel. No Rachel. Ever again.

So amazing that someone you hadn't talked to in seven weeks, eight weeks, *whatever*—and this first thing you heard, the first thing. *I know your face better than my own.* A cold fist squeezed her heart, and she clutched her chest. Boedeker in an office on the edge of the Pacific Ocean had more to tell her.

"Sorry to pile on here, but we also need to talk about this Montoya wrongful death suit." For a second the name didn't ring a bell; then *ding*, right, the late lamented Janet Sweet Jane Killer.

"Isn't that Herman's job?" Cheryl asked numbly.

Here Boedeker took a long breath. "Herman is sick. His kidneys shut down after a diabetic attack. It came on very suddenly. Cedars-Sinai is saying it's fifty/fifty. No kidney donor on the horizon."

Cheryl didn't know what to say.

"In any case, the police union couldn't get the wrongful death charges dismissed. Judge Santiago ruled against you. The Montoya family is proceeding to discovery. We'd like to take depositions here, but perhaps we can do them by webcam. Obviously, the Montoya family will be going after Rachel's estate, but just because your assets are considerably less doesn't mean you're in the clear—"

She'd been silent for some time, making no remark or even nodding her head. The downside of face-to-face video calls: people could see you.

"Cheryl?" Boedeker prodded gently.

"I'm here, Arthur." A silence stretched between them. "Is there anything you want me to sign? For all I know, Rachel changed her will."

An awkward silence from lawyer Boedeker.

"Yes," he sighed. "She did. But no, there's nothing you have to sign. Not right now, anyway."

She clicked off the webcam connection, then closed the laptop and stared out the clean picture window of the Marriott's hospitality lounge. Outside in the parking lot a car ignition turned over; the tires rolled toward the exit. Cheryl sat there in the silence. She didn't get up to leave or even change positions. She sat there doing nothing, staring at nothing. The woman sat for a very long time, a beige woman in a beige room on a beige couch. And nobody noticed.

* * *

On the discount cab ride back to Council Bluffs, Bhakti tried to contact Eleanor again. But when he dialed Connecticut Valley Hospital directly he got a busy signal. Something was wrong. *Very Wrong.* Hospitals always answer the phone. Dammit, he should have called sooner.

His BlackBerry buzzed. No, not Eleanor. Billy Shadow texting him. *Meet me now. KPTM,* and the address of a local TV station. The one they'd been watching at the hotel while the Toyota sat at the dealership. What could Billy want this time? Go on TV; broadcast an Amber Alert for a girl named Chen using her grainy Facebook photo?

Bhakti sighed; that was exasperation talking. After seeing plaster people at the Nebraska fairgrounds, after the Chen girl trail going cold and the scads of people failing to show up for work, it felt as if some unseen barrier had been crossed. Maybe going to a news studio wasn't such a dumb idea. There'd be newsfeeds from around the country; a good way to get a handle on things. Besides, Lila Chen might even appear in a report—"Girl Survives Lunatics" or some such story, improbable as that sounded.

"Do you know where KPTM is?" Bhakti asked the cabbie, like he really expected a coherent reply. The driver was about twenty-two years old, with a silver stud through his eyebrow; he wore a Disney World cap in the shape of the cartoon character Goofy. A dog's nose, floppy ears, and two large white toofies hung from the brim.

"The business office or the studio?" Goofy asked.

The cab pulled into the parking lot of 42 Productions, a large studio building with two enormous broadcast masts planted nearby, a number of large satellite-receiver dishes on the roof, and several more running along the edge of the property. The kid with the stud in his eyebrow looked at his passenger. That hat with Chiclets teeth was really something. Goofy's large nose and big toofies talked again.

"You want me to wait?" Goofy asked, and idly scratched an itch on his ear.

"No, I'm all set—thanks anyway."

Bhakti went through the glass doors. The effect, high-tech minimalist. Cool blues and grays, exposed ironwork, bolts, stanchions, spick-and-span metal sheeting. Head shots of the on-air announcers were displayed prominently. Not as large as New York or LA, but big enough to make the talent feel appreciated. Man with Helmet Hair. Woman with Swing Do. Honest heartland faces, smiling eyes. The telephone lights at the empty reception desk blinked, burring softly; people were trying to get through to the station. Bhakti pushed past the double doors marked STUDIO and down a long dark hall.

Two enormous photographs dominated the passage, historical black-and-whites blown up to artistic dimensions to make a statement and lit by spots. In the first photo, an old dustbowl farmer stood in front of a silo looking uncomfortably into the lens. An anomaly hovered in the sky behind him like a UFO. A cloud? A flying saucer? The photo made you wonder.

The other photo showed the 1880s Omaha Railway Station: steel, steam, and people who couldn't stand still for this newfangled camera thing. The photographer had captured the ghostly image of a figure, perhaps by accident. A lanky apish creature squatted on the crown of a lamppost. All you could see was the smudge of a top hat and a grin about a foot wide. Defective film stock? A ghost? Again, the peculiar photo gave one pause.

Bhakti entered the cavernous studio floor: cameras on cushy rubber wheels, the empty green screen, teleprompters lit but not rolling, the words *Good Evening, Omaha*.

Overhead, the dark control room window reflected the studio floor like a mirror. Somebody up there knuckled the glass to get his attention. Bhakti climbed a flight of utility stairs and pushed open the control room door to the soft hiss of pressurized air.

A dozen workstations with flat-screens and overhead monitors murmured in the twilight of the control room, the media—CNN, MSNBC, BBC—all playing against each other. One dedicated to FOX streamed raw feed. Bill Hemmer, a man with the earnest looks of Clark Kent, and Martha MacCallum as Lois Lane in faraway New York talking to each other in asides during a break:

Bill Hemmer: *So your housekeeper vanished?*
Martha MacCallum: *No. She just called in sick.*
Bill Hemmer: *So what are you going to do?*
Martha MacCallum: *Told the kids to make their own beds.*

Billy Shadow sat in front of a battery of control panel dials under the streaming screens; he stared into his own laptop on a callback to South Dakota. Clem Lattimore's face floated on the screen. Billy had been conferring with his boss a lot since Nebraska, then filling in the others on the most recent peculiarities, every discovery: the mea culpa of one young Webster Chargrove, PhD, who Billy had met up-close last month; the Pi R kooks' sick plan for mass mosquito insemination; the Chen girl's God Protein. Rat tail counts. Jasper in the hospital with malaria . . .

So it wasn't their imaginations—people *were* getting sick. Boss Lattimore signed off, the video call window closed, and Billy sighed. He pointed to one news report on an overhead screen: Amtrak trains stalled up and down the eastern corridor.

Apparently, an Acela Express had collided head-on with a freight train carrying chemical cars. The freight train jumped the tracks, and freight cars were spilling chlorine into a Baltimore neighborhood. The helicopter feed showed residents in the midst of a chaotic evacuation fleeing down residential streets. On the various screens the phrase "Asleep at the switch" was being repeated on three different news networks.

Billy looked hard at Bhakti. "How much you want to bet they pull the switchman in for drug testing and find out he's got a case of African trypanosomiasis?"

"Sleeping sickness? I'm impressed you know the medical term."

"Don't be. Guys in the army know about tsetse flies. Wanna bet there are also some Skeeterbugs mating their little hearts out in the Port of Baltimore?"

Bhakti shrugged: *Wouldn't be surprised.*

Another feed popped on. A Southern belle stood in front of a sturdy wooden sign that read FORT BRAGG—HOME OF THE AIRBORNE AND SPECIAL OPERATIONS FORCES. The lady reporter spoke into her mike:

"This is Kimberly McKay. Here at Fort Bragg life goes on as normal—but sources tell WNCN News all leaves have been cancelled due to an outbreak of visceral leishmaniasis, more commonly known as leishmania or dumdum fever, which is spread by sand flies. Base authorities have instituted rigorous pest-control spraying— *Whoa, Nelly!*"

Kimberly McKay angrily waved the no-see-um from her face, violently slapped a flying bug, but hit her mike instead: *thunk!* The feed from Carolina died.

"I think we're seeing a cluster of the same disease in one place, then a cluster of another disease somewhere else," Billy said. "In New York, you might see a burst of yellow fever or bubonic plague. Down in Philly, Baltimore, and Washington, DC, it'll be sleeping sickness, or say bacterial meningitis. Up in Sioux Falls, Jasper has malaria. A cluster here, a cluster there. Wherever the mosquitoes roam." Billy pinned Bhakti with a dark stare. "Over at Fort Bragg they think it's sand flies, but I think we know better."

Bhakti smiled wanly. "Around here, I think it's St. Vitus' Dance."

"St. Vitus' Dance," Billy repeated, returning the smile.

"Huntington's Chorea, or maybe all the various choreas—akin to rheumatic fever. Problems with the nerves and joints; do a spastic dance and then you die."

"Oh, you mean like him?" Billy Shadow nodded across the darkened control room. About three rows back, one of the newsies sat at his desk, deep in shadow and dead as a doornail. The poor sap was slumped backward, his hands and fingers twisted into claws, his blackened face a frozen wild grin. He'd chewed off a bit of his tongue, which lay on his tie.

"Jesus!" Bhakti knocked into Billy's chair; then after a moment got the better of himself and replied sensibly, "Yeah, just like him. I saw a guy nearly get run over across the street from the dealership. He's probably chasing parked cars by now."

"Not particularly infectious," Billy mused. "But still . . ."

Bhakti finished the thought: "If there are enough mosquitoes spreading the condition, who cares how it spreads?"

"And if the larger story isn't framed, every incident is random," Billy added. "There's no rhyme or reason—and the Big *They* like it that way."

Bhakti understood. "When no one really understands, no one is required to fix anything. *As if they could,*" he replied cynically. "All the relevant details are dying in studios like this from coast to coast." Bhakti left the console and went over to the dead man in rictus; an ID hung from his neck on a chain. Bhakti examined it. "Station Manager." A phone light blinked, then buzzed softly, and the Punjabi scientist tapped the manager's speakerphone.

"Hello?"

The clear and precise voice of a woman came charging through the base. You got the impression of lady talent with the Swing Do in the publicity shot.

"Who is this, please?" she demanded.

"Bhakti Singh."

"Are you new?"

"I'm kind of a temp," Bhakti replied.

She accepted this without question. "Okay, Bhakti. Hi. I tried the switchboard, but nobody is picking up. This is Juliet Jay. Will you tell the boss I can't come in today? Just feel really sorta sick. Kinda twitchy, and my throat feels swollen. Tried calling Marianne to sub for me at the three o'clock, but she's not answering either. So the boss is going to have to figure something out on his own. I should be better by tomorrow. Okay bye, thanks." *Click.* Bhakti stared at the dead phone.

Billy came over and patted the station manager's lifeless shoulder. "You hear that, Chief? Julie isn't coming in and can't reach Marianne either. So you're on your own."

Bhakti looked away; when you talked to the dead you had to hold up both sides of the conversation. Suddenly the Punjabi scientist's BlackBerry thrummed in his shirt pocket again. A text message from Eleanor, coherent this time:

> First time e-mail has worked in days. Tried L&G but no reply. I want to leave now. I'm not sick. Just please come and get me. Bhakti, please come get me.

In five heartbeats he typed back,

> I will, I'm coming. Calling G&L. They can get there quicker. See you soon. Does your phone work?

He pressed send, but it came back, MESSAGE NOT SENT.

"Damn," he swore. "Dammit! I have to get back. I have to phone Guy and Lauren. And I don't have a car and nothing is friggin' working! What the hell are we doing here anyway?" Bhakti growled. He knew the answer . . . so they could see what was happening in the big bad world. There was even an outside chance they might see Lila Chen on TV on some news story. Not a big chance, but a chance all the same.

The two men left the station manager to his TV station control room, clattered down the utility stairs and back out the empty studio.

As they emerged from the building, an ambulance with its lights flashing and siren going full blast roared up the street. The siren flared and abruptly died. The emergency vehicle slowed as if the driver had taken his foot off the accelerator, but it swerved off the highway, hopping the parking lot curb. The ambulance came to a sudden halt against one of the antenna towers, with a bang and scrape of metal.

The EMT staggered from the driver's seat. He didn't seem injured too badly, just shaken up pretty good. He threw a dopey grin at the two men coming toward him across the parking lot. Even as he waved okay his arm jerked; his leg twitched. He found a comfortable spot on the ground by the back wheel and got out his iPhone, calling for backup. The ambulance siren was gone, but you could still hear noise from inside the dented vehicle. The EMT had been playing the radio as he drove; you could hear the brassy pitch for that hot new show everyone seemed to be listening to: *Does the Night Have More Fun for It Being Dark? Listen to Piper, Night to Night. . . .*

Billy Shadow plucked his partner's sleeve, drawing Bhakti to his side. "I wouldn't get too close, in case he bites. Look at this."

He pointed down at their feet. The cracked asphalt surface was dotted with ant colonies here, there, everywhere. Little grainy mounds of sand with their volcano holes covered with armies of ants. Except all the ants lay dead, red ants and black ants mixed together. Claws and pincers, cut throats and thoraxes, scattered broken body parts. No, these little creatures didn't require a story framed for them or put in context. Some hidden power, like the gaunt man on every TV show or radio station, had sent his minions forth like every other vermin to wreak havoc and die. And they simply obeyed orders. Not a single ant moved. They'd fought a war, the war was over—and both sides lost.

Cheryl heard the ambulance siren wail across the river. Maybe the second or the third time that morning. Busy day out in the big world, apparently. How long had she been sitting in the Marriott lounge? Hard to say—a couple of hours at least. She got up from the beige couch and went to the ladies' room. Muzak dribbled faintly from a ceiling speaker; then the announcer said, *This is Mr. P. with his favorites for a lovely afternoon. Coming up, Mantovani and his orchestra plays "Charmaine."*

The cold water from the sink felt good on her face. Another woman joined her in front of the mirror, like girls at the prom primping. The woman hovered a little too close.

"Try the other sink if you're in a hurry." Cheryl patted the water from her eyes.

"I'm in no rush," the other woman said softly.

Cheryl glanced in the mirror and nearly choked on her own spit. She whipped around, banged her funny bone on the sink, and yelped as the flash ran up her arm.

Cheryl clutched her tingling elbow.

Rachel stood in the Marriott ladies' room, wearing what appeared to be a hospital gown. There was a scratch on her forehead, a patch of hair missing. Her scalp was discolored and dented in. They'd stapled it closed. Rachel patted her hair, looked sadly in the mirror, dwelling on the bald patch where some ER doc had shaved her head.

"You'd think they'd let you look your best for times like these, but *Nooooo*." Rachel sighed in dismay, shrugged at the inevitability of it all. "Lemme tell you, coming and going, you always look the same."

Rachel peeked down the neckline of her hospital gown. "See, no autopsy scar." A wry grin. "I guess they were pretty certain on the cause of death, eh? Hey, don't you talk anymore?"

Cheryl's honey-dark skin had gone gray. She stood stock-still, quietly questioning her own sanity, but not questioning too much. "I speak," she stammered.

"Great." Rachel fluffed out her hair as best she could. "You know the amazing thing about death?" She didn't wait for an answer; how the hell would Cheryl know? "The amazing thing is that you *always know* what people are thinking. You can read their minds. And you know what else? You can be in three places at once. No kidding. Right now, not only am I in this really elegant ladies' room with you, I'm also haunting that putz doper who ran me off the road, *walking away without a scratch I might add*—he's seeing me with my head bashed in every time he looks in a plate-glass window or a mirror or a teaspoon. Anything shiny. And he's not handling it well."

Rachel paused to chuckle at herself. "I'm also terrorizing the piss out of the family of the late lamented Ricardo Montoya, the Sweet Jane Killer. I rearranged a crucifix on their dining room wall so it hangs upside down. Every time they set it straight, I flip it over again. Then I scrawled *Forgive* in red indelible marker over the hanging Jesus. *Perdonar* in Spanish. And lemme tell you, Lucy, the family of the late lamented Ricky are freaking out. A whole new kind of wrongful death. Y'know I think they're gonna drop that civil suit. They're arguing about it anyway, and that's a start. Cool huh?"

Cheryl had no words.

"Also, I'm sorry about changing the will. I'll see what I can do to sort it out. I wasn't in my right mind when we, when we . . ." Rachel didn't finish.

Cheryl tried to figure out a reply. What do you say to a ghost? Nice to see you? Finally, after a moment's thought, "Do you want me to come to the funeral?" she asked. "Should I fly back?"

"Oh *that*." Rachel laughed. "Day after tomorrow. In the firm's big conference room, flowers and a cellist and readings from the Torah or Sappho, I can't remember which." She shook her head sadly. "I hate the cello."

Rachel's ghostie thought for a moment: Should Cheryl go, or not go? Did she really want Cheryl there? "No, no point in rushing back for that grim scene. Call Arthur Boedeker and tell him you're sick. Everyone else is— gallstones or hemorrhoids or something. He can send you the DVD in the black crepe case—"

"Oh, Rachel," Cheryl blurted, tears welling into her eyes. "It's so good to see you again."

Suddenly the ladies' room door opened—the young woman from the reception desk smiled briefly and disappeared into a stall, latching the door. Cheryl could hear the sounds of her sliding up her skirt and yanking down her pantyhose. Rachel put a finger to her lips. *Shush.* When they were both out of the ladies' room and alone by the beige couch, Rachel explained, "I don't think anybody should see you talking to yourself."

Cheryl nodded. "Very thoughtful. So . . . can I ask you some questions?"

"Shoot."

"Why are you here? How long do you plan to stay? And of course, is there life after death?"

Rachel flopped on the beige couch, crossed her bare legs, and bashfully patted her hospital gown; highly self-conscious as it did *nothing* for her.

"Why am I here? To show you something, I think. What am I supposed to show you? Can't say. How long do I get to stay? Haven't a clue, but I'll know when it's time to leave.

Nobody explains anything in the sweet bye-and-bye; being dead is as mysterious as being alive. Figures, right? And as for the last question . . ." She paused to consider the matter of life *after* death; looked down at herself in the schmata hospital gown. "If there is life in the great beyond, we don't have to shave our legs anymore."

A flash of light came through the glass doors and windows of the Marriott; out in the parking lot the white Dodge minivan pulled into a parking spot.

"Oh, why look, it's the American Indian and Indian-American," Rachel remarked; then to Cheryl, "Better stop staring at me, Girlie. They'll think you're tetched."

23

Deal or No Deal

Finally, a slim lead on the Chen girl.

Billy Shadow had gotten a message, not from the Great Skin Walker in the Sky but from Lattimore's Aerospace CTO. Even from the confines of a hospital bed, tubed up on a cocktail of antiparasitics, quinine, and doxycycline, Jasper found what he was looking for—an Internet Protocol address tracking the mysterious Chargrove, PhD, back to a source and a digital fingerprint. The confused confession wasn't coming from the Pi R Squared complex directly, instead traced to an e-mail recipient with the promising name of BigSister@zmail.com.

The digital fingerprint boosted from a Wi-Fi account in the little town of Vandalia, Ohio—a roadhouse called Big

Bea's Bar and Grill. Some kind of saloon in the Dayton area. Jasper's search engine, Tassology, had snatched the needle from the supposedly "private" Zmail haystack.

Sure, it felt like grasping at straws. But if you wanted to find the Chen girl alive, why not do a look-see on those who wanted to find her alive as well?

The pursuers left Council Bluffs a little before noon, and rolled eastward onto the interstate. Cheryl drove the revived yellow Toyota 4Runner, which the dealership had finally and miraculously managed to fix. Rachel, wearing her hospital gown, sat in the back and tried to act inconspicuous. With an agony of effort the two women refrained from talking; no need to spook innocent bystanders, especially Bhakti. In any event, the first couple of hundred miles from Council Bluffs to Des Moines wasn't a happy trip. Another freaky text message from Eleanor came over Bhakti's BlackBerry.

> *Bacteria here, Staff-Staph fear. But DON'T come near.*
> *Not Here Dear, not here.*

What the hell was going on at that loony bin? First she wants a rescue, now she doesn't? Was Eleanor sane or insane? Guess it depended on the time of day. When his wife didn't respond immediately to his texting Bhakti switched to cell phone, calling Guy and Lauren in Fairfield. How soon could they get to Connecticut Valley Hospital? But the call kept disconnecting; Bhakti's side of the conversation with his in-laws going like this:

I don't understand Lauren. What do you mean you're not leaving the house?

Will you please put Guy on?

Well, can you or can't you walk outside?

It's the whole town?

The call disconnected into a dead zone one more time. Bhakti slapped the device into the dashboard, grousing,

"They sound crazy. Like the wandering sickness hit Fairfield and everyone's in hiding. Except it's not St. Vitus' Dance, it's, it's—I dunno, yellow fever I think." Then with irritation, "Can't you drive faster?"

"Is he always like this?" Rachel asked from the backseat. To which Cheryl replied to both, "Yes."

The wicked fact that strange maladies were spreading from coast to coast got the cop in Cheryl thinking. The presence of firemen, EMTs, bright lights, and smart uniforms reassured folks. When an ambulance crashed, another ambulance showed up. But when light switches stopped working, when milk turned sour in the supermarket case, and people started paying with bottled aspirin, things could get ugly very fast.

The good citizens of Fairfield, Connecticut, were in hiding, and nobody on the outside knew? Or if they did know—the Big *They*—they didn't care. So where else didn't they care? The Centers for Disease Control in Atlanta? The nation's capital? When society mandated that everyone care, nobody did.

Shortly after 6 p.m. the yellow SUV and the white minivan pulled off the highway at a truck stop in Galesburg, Illinois. A dark ceiling of clouds rolled in from nowhere, making the service area's floodlights gleam. The air felt thick, full of expectant ozone, heavy weather on the way, thunderstorms, maybe hail. Hanging off the back of the minivan, Cheryl and Bhakti picnicked on deli food: Italian combos, Pepsi, and potato chips. Billy Shadow relayed the latest video call from Lattimore HQ via Jasper in his hospital sickbed.

"Jasper says that IP address is still hot." A few clicks got Billy an address, a telephone number, a Google listing. "Looks like a biker bar."

Bhakti did thumbkins on the tiny BlackBerry keyboard. He shook his head, confused. "I'm getting another text from Eleanor." He repeated aloud what she wrote to see if anyone else could make sense of it: "*'Don't you dare let her mother's milk back up the meat seam to the birthing chamber. Don't you dare let her anywhere near them—'*" The *her* most likely meant the Chen girl, but as for the rest?

Cheryl put her hand on his arm. "We'll get her, Bhakti, I promise. We'll get Lila, you'll see."

"Yeah," the Punjabi scientist replied, but you could see he didn't believe it. Bhakti left the group and for some moments sat alone in the yellow Toyota. Sitting alone with Janet's ashes in the backseat, he put his hand on the Nambe urn in the unzipped black duffle. He started quietly speaking to himself, then began murmuring to the ashes as if having a private conversation. Finally he left off.

"Mind if I drive alone for a little while?"

Cheryl didn't argue. "Let me get my bike off the trailer."

The last lap of their trip became a headlong rush. Cheryl's Harley devoured the broken white lines while the headlight stared into a roaring tunnel of night. Rachel's stubborn spirit rode with her, ghostly arms clinging to Cheryl's waist, loose hospital gown flapping in the wind, two witches on a 1200cc fuel-injected broomstick. A few minutes before midnight they pulled into the saloon parking lot. A serviceable roadhouse in Unabomber longhouse style: single-storied, green metal roof, with electric signs for Budweiser and Jägermeister.

No crowd tonight, the lot almost empty.

One lonely vehicle sat by itself: a fully restored Ford Gran Torino. A Starsky & Hutch muscle car, except this one wasn't fire-engine red with the white vector streak, but a dark grape color, neon purple that morphed seamlessly to electric blue along the hood. Whiplash on Mag Wheels. A real head-turner.

As Cheryl climbed off her own bike, she noticed a small sticker on the corner of the Gran Torino's rear window: UNITED DAUGHTERS OF THE CONFEDERACY over the motto

LOVE, LIVE, PRAY, THINK, DARE. Not exactly the rebel battle flag, but still . . . Southern heritage associations took on darker shades the closer you got to the schoolhouse door, making her wonder if there wasn't a folded white hood in the trunk of the purple Ford.

"Doan you fret, Prissy," Rachel chuckled. "We ain't gonna send you back to Tara. The only one wearing a white sheet in dis joint is gonna be me."

Cheryl held her tongue; keep it up, Girlie.

Beside the saloon door stood a freestanding chalkboard for the daily specials. The management had drawn Felix the Cat's grinning face on the slate chalkboard. Only *this* cat face was boldly augmented with a bright red circle and a slash, the universal **No** sign.

No Felix. No Felix allowed.

"Yeah well, this place can't be all bad," Cheryl said to nobody in particular.

Bhakti held the door for her with a raised eyebrow. The saloon enveloped them, dark and cavernous, with spot lamps that hardly shed any light over the tables. From a large booth they could see most of the watering hole at a glance. Rachel's apparition found a perch on an inch of wainscoting where she could hover.

So this is where Webster Chargrove's confessions from that dingy underground office were emanating? This is where he blabbed the secrets of national insemination gone wrong, spontaneous mutation and sickness run wild?

The barmaid, a big brassy woman with cropped gray hair, finished polishing a beer mug, slapped open the swing flap, and plucked a walking cane off the bar. She wore a black plastic knee brace over her jeans and tied her work shirt in a knot. When the woman reached the table she unconsciously hitched up her bra strap; you could see a small red scar under her ear. The words *gunshot* and *frag wound* leapt into Cheryl's mind. The woman's breast pocket

embroidered with the name of a local brewery: *Butch Beer.*
A Ford Torino key chain dangled from the other pocket.
Ah, the Daughter of the Old South.

"Hi, folks. I'm Beatrice, Big Bea. The kitchen's about to
close, but Chaffy will fix you something if it's not too fancy.
What can I get you?"

"Coke with lemon, no ice," Bhakti said. His companions
rolled their eyes. Fussbudget. Big Bea nodded. "We have
that."

Billy looked around the empty place. "Everybody at the
penny social?"

The large barmaid shrugged. "You got me, Handsome.
Feels like the whole town went to church." She turned her
eyes on Cheryl, eyes measuring the lady cop right down to
the last inch. "What about you, Gorgeous?"

"Go ahead, say 'Diet Pepsi,'" Rachel clucked from her
perch, "Say 'Diet Pepsi.' Dare yah, double-dare yah—"
Stop nudging, Cheryl almost growled.

"I'm thinking," Cheryl said.

"No problem."

The place fell silent except for the whisper of the wide
flat-screen television and the soft gurgle of the soft drink
hose. Big Bea put Bhakti's drink in front of him and then
stolidly limped toward a secluded booth in the rear. She
wedged herself in, put a pair of James Joyce eyeglasses on
her nose, and grimaced at a laptop screen. The glasses
made her look intelligent and innocent at the same time.
Then suddenly, piercing Cheryl boldly from across the
room, "Just let me know when you want something. I'm
right here."

"Well, Prissy," Rachel said softly. "Maybe we found your
Scarlet." And that made Cheryl think about when she and
Rachel used to cuddle like nesting dolls. Two honeys without the bee. And a band of loneliness twisted around her
heart. *I miss you too,* Rachel whispered inside her head.

As for the older woman in the booth, you could see the

lines of concern in the saloonkeeper's face, especially around her eyes. Her face clouded over with strain and worry as she stared at the laptop screen. Safe bet Beatrice had seen a lot in her time—maybe too much.

"Looks like part of her is scared as hell and the other part just trying to cope," Rachel said. "This Svetlana isn't looking for a quickie on a stack of canned tomatoes in the pantry. Not today, anyway." Cheryl almost hissed at Rachel to stop babbling.

Bhakti swirled his soda straw. "Did you say something?"

Billy Shadow suddenly stared at the secluded booth over his own laptop screen. "We've come to the right place. This is the Zmail lady. Jasper says that's Big Sis all right; real name Beatrice Chargrove. Big Bea. Webster's *big sister*. She's a postal cop, on leave from the United States Postal Service. Had some kind of trouble investigating mail fraud in APOs overseas, wounded in the line of duty. She just got out of Walter Reed eight months ago."

A sister, Cheryl thought. Okay, that made sense. That eager beaver with the unruly mop *would* have an older sister.

Billy chewed his cud for a moment. "Kinda makes me wonder what this gal *really* did for a living. People in witness protection have backgrounds like this, and so do retired intelligence types. That big dame sure as hell didn't sort envelopes in the Dead Letter Office."

So what now? Chat about cosmic dust and summer snowstorms? Raise the subject of Little Brother's hand in spreading the wandering sickness? Or the Gaunt Man who snatched the Chen girl from the Stuka Crew? How about godly DNA?

Billy didn't know where to begin.

He didn't have to. Bhakti saved them.

Or maybe the TV over the bar did it.

One moment Bhakti was sitting quietly in the booth, stirring his lemon Coke with a damp straw, and the next moment he sprang from his seat like he'd been jabbed with a cattle prod. He flung himself against the bar, staring wildly up at the screen.

"It's Lila! It's her!" Bhakti exclaimed, slightly unhinged. "She's on *Deal or No Deal*. Eleanor and I used to watch it all the time!" And it became clear why the fuss. Bhakti had finally found Lila Chen on a television game show.

The Chen girl—Contestant.

Everyone gravitated to the bar. Big Bea left the booth, poured a round of sodas on the house, and Cheryl got her Diet Pepsi without asking for it. Back on the TV, a silver metal briefcase possibly stuffed with half a mil sat on the show's translucent table. The host of *Deal or No Deal* stood on the dais, a preppy black kid. The young man had outgrown his clothes, the arms of his blue blazer short and his pressed khakis about two inches north of his ankles. The lanky preppy grinned, addressing everyone in TV land:

"Well, I'm here with my two foster sisters. The younger, Little Maria—"

The camera zoomed onto a pale scamp of about nine with bright coal eyes. Her own cute, crepe, party dress raised a couple of inches above her knees; she fruitlessly tried to tug it down. A caption card read WOULD YOU DO HER?

"And the other girl up here is my older sister, Lila Chen." The camera closed on the young Asian lady. Lila was tarted up as an adult schoolgirl: plaid skirt, knee socks, and black patent leather Capezio Piccadilly dance heels, just this side of do-me pumps. Lila's caption card read DEFINITE SLUT.

Lila Chen demurely brushed the side of her head, inadvertently showing her missing ear and a livid ear hole visible to millions. Kid leered knowingly. "Obviously, Lila has come to California in the hope of a little cosmetic surgery, providing she scores the big dough. What you may not know is that doctors have to grow the ear on a mouse and then graft it to the side of her head. What I want to know is, what happens to the mouse?"

The audience rippled with laughter.

"And what about today's Banker?" the young man asked, introducing the "heavy" of the game show. "We call him Top Hat for obvious reasons." The camera rose to a darkened booth overlooking the game arena. Behind the glass you could see a tall man wreathed in shadow and the outline of a top hat. He touched the brim, acknowledging the introduction. With a sudden jerk his long hand snatched a telephone receiver. The whole stage set changed from cool blue to lurid red. Time to make a deal. The contestant's phone down below flashed like a strobe.

Kid picked up the receiver. "Talk to me."

The gaunt man silently gesticulated in the shadowed box overhead.

"Uh-huh. Right. Okay." The preppy dangled the receiver by the cord, offering it to the younger of the two girls. "Think you can handle this?"

Maria cautiously put the phone to her ear and listened for a moment; her eyes widened with every passing second. Finally piping up, she said, "Top Hat says a new ear ain't in your fortune cookie, Lila. Instead, come on over to his Manhattan apartment in the San Remo. You'll get twenty bucks to bend over and grab your ankles. Then he'll drive you home."

The audience exploded in glee, chanting, *"Top Hat! Top Hat!"*

Lila Chen glanced up at the darkened booth; the gaunt man was tense as a violin string, as though he couldn't wait to blow his wad. She coyly tugged at her pleated skirt and rubbed the dark gash on her head where her ear used to be. The camera closed on the silver briefcase. Maybe the big money was in there, maybe not. Kid smiled indulgently. "So what's your choice, Lila? Open the case? Or as Little Maria says, let Top Hat drive you home? Deal or no deal?"

Lila fretted, twirling a lock of hair, doing the schoolgirl thing. "Well, that's a very nice offer, Kid. Can I think about it for a second?"

The audience held its collective breath, building to a gasp—

Everyone watching the TV from the bar gawked in disbelief, the show a total disgrace. Suddenly the picture froze, then pixelated. Lila Chen broke into a thousand colored bits. The five spectators at the bar started in surprise. The words POOR SIGNAL came on the screen.

Bhakti still clenched the bar, but he felt something jiggling in his jacket pocket like a Mexican jumping bean. He fished among the coins and pocket lint, knowing exactly what it was. Lila's hematite earring from her bedroom dresser, the match to the one dangling from her burnt ear in the frozen baggie. God, he hadn't looked at it in ages; dancing around inside his pocket just like it had at Senora Malvedos' place.

Like the earring knew the girl was on TV. He clenched it tight, deeply reluctant to take it out or show anyone. The earring was his private connection to Lila and his daughter Janet, to their bodies, to their souls—to wherever they'd been taken. For Janet taken to the bosom of God, for Lila to a twisted game show on TV.

"You know this girl?" Beatrice asked, slightly aghast.

"Chen, her last name is Chen," Bhakti repeated. "She lived across the street from me in Van Horn. Then they took her with my daughter, and now she's the only one left."

Cheryl put a serious hand on Bhakti's arm to keep him from levitating, explaining, "The girls from Van Horn disappeared together. Kidnapped. I found Bhakti's daughter Janet in LA. Too late. We've been searching for this one, Lila, since then. We think a certain facility not far from here wants to get their hands on her, for . . ." She paused.

Big Bea's cool eyes gazed back at her. "For experiments," Big Sis said darkly. Everyone nodded silently—*for experiments*.

Outside in the night came a rumble of thunder. The lights over the bar flickered. Along the flat television screen a scroll in red: TORNADO WARNING FOR THE FOLLOWING COUNTIES: DARKE, PREBLE, MONTGOMERY—

The lights flickered again, and the television went totally blank. Thunder, closer this time. A long silence engulfed everyone.

"So how the heck did you find me?" Beatrice finally asked. "You must have snagged my brother's feed from our e-mail thread."

Billy nodded. "I found the remains of Lila's missing ear in an evidence locker in an abandoned sheriff's station back in Texas," he said with a touch of trepidation. "I kept it in a refrigerator in my van. We've been using it as . . . uh . . ." He paused to show he knew how weird the next bit sounded. "Using it as a kind of compass. The three of us hooked up outside of Salt Lake and tracked Lila as far as Lexington, Nebraska. Then we lost the Chen girl's trail. I guess Lila doubled back on us to Los Angeles." He stared at the rising soda bubbles in his cola.

"You sure she's back in LA?" Beatrice said doubtfully. "I'm not even sure this, this Top Hat guy or these kids are actually in LA."

This stopped everyone cold. *Not in LA?*

Big Bea saw their doubt. "I know this show well. Been watching it for years, watched it in the hospital while I was laid up. I can't remember any black preppy kid. No nine-year-old scamp. No cute, grown-up Chinese schoolgirl. And that Top Hat creep has never been the Banker. I'm starting to think that guy in the dark booth is gaming the system—"

"Gaming the system?" Cheryl asked incredulously.

Beatrice shrugged. "You haven't noticed weird things on TV lately? Somebody is messing with our heads. Tweaking the video. Rewriting the episodes. Pick any channel, it's like some ass-clown is playing a prank or a practical joke. Next thing you know, Snooki will file for child support from Roseanne Barr."

Billy choked on his Coke, blowing soda out his nose.

But Big Sis wasn't smiling.

"I'm guessing at least one of you met Webster when he went for the comet dust. Snow delayed the recovery until he arrived. Like some power really wanted him there. Wanted it enough to create an anomalous event in order to guarantee his presence. Don't you find this curious?"

She spun her laptop around so everyone could see the screen: a paused image of young Dr. Webster Chargrove in his hideout. Big Bea hit Play. Her brother, young Webster Chargrove, came alive, grimly confessing from that dingy forgotten office:

"Yes, I finally got to Dugway. Wish I'd gone anywhere else. We set the wandering sickness loose, and there's no way to stop it. Kill every mosquito? The kill-switch in the Skeeterbug software won't respond. Inoculate the world? But with *what*?" The young man held his head in his hands, a wave of despair overcoming him: regret, irreparable harm. "What did we do? *What did we do?*"

The feed died.

Once more, Billy saw the lad's youthful exuberance in the Humvee at Dugway: the scientist's glistening eyes enjoying the greatest moment of his life while the poor gal from the AP gave her stomach the heave-ho into the snow. While a circle of rabbits surrounded the probe, almost as though they knew the significance of the Wild 3 comet dust locked away in the precious pod.

A great unease came over Billy again, just as it had in Utah. There was something about that storm that had always bothered him. And the curious appearance of the rabbits. Nature not being natural.

"That was me," Billy Shadow admitted. "I met him."

"I'll bet one of you even went to Senora Malvedos' and saw the girl who chose the saints," Beatrice said.

"That was *me*," Bhakti chimed in. And it sank into him that Big Bea had met the fortune-teller and Little Maria too.

Cheryl shared a long glance with Beatrice, weighing the odds their crossed paths were mere chance. "What did Einstein say?" she asked. "'Coincidence is God's way of remaining anonymous.' So we're on the same side? No Felix allowed?"

Big Bea nodded her head. Something had been troubling her; quietly she confessed. "When Webster was recruited they did a background check. It helped he had family in government and all. Made me fill out a thirty-page questionnaire, take a polygraph. Not my tenth polygraph either. Half the reason they let my brother anywhere near that damn lab was because they thought I was reliable. They figured it runs in families. I knew Webster was involved in something classified, secret science. But I didn't know it was anything like—"

She broke off, unable to continue. She felt responsible.

The thunder rumbled, a little closer now.

Suddenly the kitchen doors swung open with a bang. Everyone nearly jumped out of their skins. Beatrice caught her foot behind the bar, and her game leg threatened to fold. She grabbed the bar for support.

"Dammit, Chaffy!" Bea hollered. "You're gonna gimme a stroke!"

The cook leaned heavily on the metal swing door. A man in his late fifties, wizened alky face, grizzly beard, having trouble standing. The man swayed every time he strayed from the swing door. White flecks of foam stuck to his lips. One gnarled hand clutched the waistband of his stained apron; the other hand gripped a twelve-inch carving knife. "They're coming," Chaffy growled at them. His eyes bulged in their sockets. "They're getting close." The carving knife flicked back and forth.

"Your cook has rabies," Billy Shadow said softly, but so everyone at the bar could hear. "I think this man is rabid."

Chaffy twitched at the word *rabid*.

"Rabbit! We got no rabbits. No rabbits on the menu. No

rabbits in the house! Now you want rabbit? Bre'r rabbit? Broiled rabbit? Rabbit fricassee?"

Thunder rumbled overhead, much closer now. Chaffy's eyes darted in every direction. He almost crawled up the metal swing door. "They're right outside!"

Another low rumble. Not thunder—the rumble of diesel engines. The engines revved loudly, and the group at the bar heard the sounds of men shouting orders. Suddenly all the lights died. Jesus, a crazy man in the dark with a blade.

Then *pang*! Floodlights drove blinding columns of light into the roadhouse.

A voice from a megaphone penetrated the walls:

"Please stay where you are. Do not move or attempt to leave the building. We repeat, please do not attempt to leave the building."

The urge to slither into the darkest corners seemed to infect everyone. Easy to imagine what waited outside: guys in tactical gear, guns and flash-bang grenades. Bhakti had crawled back to his booth. Like a frightened . . . rabbit? Chaffy the cook plastered himself against the jukebox, clutching it for safety.

Cheryl found herself at the front door with Billy and Big Bea to get a glimpse of the parking lot. Foolish bravery. The large woman threw the dead bolt on the door, slamming it home. Cheryl caught a glimpse of Rachel's ghost standing at a window looking outside. The floodlights seemed to pass right through her; now she really did look like a spirit. Rachel's soft voice touched her mind, apologetic, embarrassed. *"I really didn't see this coming. I would have told you if I did."*

"Told me! Told me! *Now* you tell me you could tell me?" Cheryl said loudly.

Making everyone in the saloon think maybe the lady cop was a little nuts too.

24

The San Remo

The lamp hanging over the interrogation table really bothered Billy. A government issued, green-shade model, with wire mesh over the hundred-watt bulb; he'd lived half his life under lamps like this. And he knew the sound of boots and armored personnel carriers and all about sticking men in metal cages. Now his turn had come for the cage.

Chaffy the cook didn't make the trip. The soldiers shot him where he stood clutching the jukebox. They zeroed in on the man like they knew exactly who and what they were looking for, then gave him the triple-tap—two rounds to the chest, one to the head—as he glared at them with wild eyes, snarling, "Rabbits!"

The entry team had Chaffy wrapped and bagged like Chinese take-out before the rest of them were cuffed and blindfolded. The military police or whatever this outfit called itself set up their field command in a tent surrounded by a maze of chain-link fence in a baseball field somewhere near Vandalia proper. Overhead, the thunderstorm passed; lots of noise and flashes of lightning with the heavy splatter of big droplets on the canvas, but it drifted off, and after a while you could hear crickets and the wind in the trees.

The officer in charge was regular army, a major, just like Billy used to be. Brass oak leaves on his shoulder boards, but no name tag on his battle dress and no divisional chevron on his arm. They'd taken off the plastic cuffs and brought in a few bottles of water. Billy passed on the one with the cracked seal, opening a fresh one for himself. And that made the major drink from an open bottle just for show.

The full military jacket of retired Major William How-ahkan lay on the interrogation table, the thick file open to the first page, which showed Billy's official Army photo. They showed it to him as a courtesy; sort of like putting their cards faceup. Letting him know they were aware of what he used to be. A kind of respect.

"You want cigarettes or chewing gum or anything?" the major asked. "There's probably somebody around here who's got some." Billy shook his head no thanks. There were no formal introductions, and Billy Shadow wasn't so stupid as to ask for any.

The Big *They* had arrived.

They'd assessed the situation, they'd shot the guy who needed shooting—and now it was time to talk.

Light from the hanging lamp was *really* starting to annoy. Billy felt a headache coming on. A bad one. The major rubbed his skintight jaw. From under the table he took the green Zero Degree tote sack from the Dodge minivan, the one they'd been lugging around in the Kargo Kooler for a couple of thousand miles. Unzipped it and drew out the evidence bag: the melted hunk of an ear and a dangling earring, all still mostly frozen.

Then he threw down the earring match from Bhakti's pocket that the Punjabi scientist had been carrying around since forever.

"Don't you think it's strange," the major began quietly, "and *odd* how you and the lady cop and Babu haven't gotten sick yet? I mean, you've driven hither and yon, eaten in public, slept in a dozen motels, and crossed paths with a hundred people, most of whom now are probably sick—and what about you? Perfectly healthy."

Billy Shadow shrugged. Healthy enough.

The major nodded to himself, like *Yeah right, you never*

noticed it. Like never. Always dwelling on something more important. He shoved the plastic baggie with the frozen bits of the Chen girl across the table. "I mean, you didn't even send this out to be analyzed, did you?"

Billy shook his head no.

"No, of course not." The major smiled. "No time, right?" He didn't wait for an answer. "You know what I think?"

Billy Shadow raised an eyebrow. Seemed the safest thing to do. *Okay, what do you think?*

"You're gonna think I'm crazy." The major shook the sealed plastic bag with the frozen human bits. "I think these leftovers are like some kind of Miracle-Gro, know what I mean?"

For a moment, Billy didn't. So the officer elaborated:

"Chemical sunshine, fertilizer, weed-killer, hand sanitizer, and spring rain all in one. You don't even have to take it out of the plastic bag for it to work. I'll bet there are trace elements of the stuff on the outside of the friggin' bag keeping you healthy. You touched it and brushed your teeth or rubbed your eyes. Then you breathed it on the motorcycle cop, then the lady cop shared a soda with Babu." His voice stiffened. "Hell, Major Howahkan, *Retired*—it's a get-out-of-jail-free card. You've probably been immune since Van Horn and you didn't even know it."

The officer paused in awe.

"Can you imagine what the real living thing is like? Lovely Lila Chen. Can you imagine what *that babe* could do?"

Billy Shadow looked long and hard at the bits of Lila Chen in the plastic bag, wondering for the hundredth time if the girl could really be some kind of genetic miracle like those kooks at Pi R Squared thought. More strands of DNA, however it worked—even in dead flesh? Maybe that was why he could see through Lila Chen's eyes in the back of the Stuka van—receiving her vibes via the bits in the baggie like a radio signal. Ah, a *rational* rationale. So maybe he wasn't touched with the walking curse after all; blame everything on biochemistry. Billy finally found a few words:

"Yeah, I can imagine. I can imagine every damn thing the big brains would wanna do to her."

The major sat in a folding chair and stroked his smooth face. "Yeah . . . ," he said after a long time. "I wonder if I rub some behind my ears it'll work on me too? Do you want to know *what else* I think?" he asked again.

Billy raised an eyebrow one more time: *What else do you think*?

"I don't think it will work on me. I think you were supposed to find it. Not me or anybody else. Do you know *why* I think this, William Howahkan, *Retired*? Here, I'll show you." The major's hand carefully drew a string of dog tags on beaded ball chains and some religious trinkets on silver or gold chains out of his shirt pocket; several gold crucifixes, a sterling Star of David, aluminum dog tags: all nonmagnetic metals.

"A couple of my guys noticed an odd phenomenon during the routine search of your vehicles."

The major held the different chains in one hand and dangled them beside the plastic bag, and Bhakti's extra earring. The chains leaped to adhere, as though sucked by a magnet. The major pulled them away. Then dangled them again. *Flap*—they stuck like glue.

"Here's the thing," the major said slowly. "So far as I can tell these chains only do their 'Dead Ear Earring Magnet Trick' around you four people: the CHiPs bitch, the Postal Mistress, Mahatma Gandhi, and *you*. When you four guys are in the room, or somewhere close, the magic works. When you're not, it doesn't. Why do you guys deserve to be immune? You wanna figure this out for me, Crazy Horse?" A rhetorical question.

"I don't know," Billy muttered. "Sounds like we're two

cans short of a six-pack. Maybe we need a white man to figure it out for us." The officer wasn't amused.

The overhead light beat down on Billy's skull; he wished he could get out from under it, like crawling out of the blistering sun into the shade. He looked between his knees, wondering if the major would mind if he curled up on the nice cool grass. It had been a hell of a long day. If he could just lie down under the table for a while, he'd feel so much better. He noticed his boots were loose; kicked them off, then his socks. His feet sank into the cool damp grass. Oh, that was nice, so cool and nice.

Billy closed his eyes. . . .

When he opened them again, Granny Sparrow looked at him from her trailer bed, the covers pulled up around her chin. She stared at him with feverish eyes, sunk deep in her head. Was she sick? More scared than anything. She'd moved the American flag from the trailer wall to the back window, blocking the view outside. Granny's wizened face looked pancake-pale, almost like ghost dancer paint: white with black around her eyes. She glanced fearfully to the trailer door; all the bolts locked.

Billy didn't have to read Granny's mind to know how bad things were on the rez. Grandma Sparrow wouldn't lock herself in this way. No, she left her door open, not afraid of anybody. And nobody'd dare touch a hair on her head. My God, that *was* pancake makeup on her face. Ghost dancer paint. Granny rose halfway up on one elbow, and Billy saw something else, something new—she wore a ghost shirt.

Jesus, those *were* rare: supple white muslin cloth, V-neck, and hanging fringe. Two painted birds, hovering above her breasts; of course, sparrows. Protecting her. But from what?

Granny Sparrow spoke to him from the bed.

"I don't think you're going to get here on time, Billy. I don't think I'm going to make it. Bad weather. Everyone sick. Still want your wolf whistle? Where should I send it?" The thousand wrinkles of her face smiled at him. "Don't you ever believe the Walking Way is all just cells and DNA and science in a book. No sir, it's God's way of letting you have a hand in things. You mark my words."

"You said I was going to like it," Billy mumbled. "But it makes my head hurt."

"Of course it does." The face of a thousand wrinkles smiled at him. "You think a gift like that is free?" Her face began to recede in his mind, as though sucked down a long tunnel. Billy Shadow struggled to return to the chain-link compound, back to the tent. Open your eyes; clear your head. Now stop staring at the cool grass at your feet. Billy squinted across the interrogation table.

"There's something bad happening in the Dakotas, isn't there?" he managed to ask the officer. "Here it's rabies. But there . . . Up there it's something else, isn't it?"

The nameless major said nothing. Silently he took a smartphone from the pocket of his BDU pants and slid it across the table. "Call if you want."

Billy stared at the major's cell phone on the folding table. His hands felt light as air, brittle as glass. He touched the phone but didn't pick it up. Sure, Officer X was acting all friendly, nice and obliging, but that meant squat. There was something disingenuous about the gesture. Almost like a dare. If he called Granny now and she failed to answer, Billy'd lose his mind. Leap from the table, go all wild Injun, and the Big *They* would slap him in a rubber room just for the fun of it.

The green-shaded electric lamp beat down on Billy's head. God, if only he could crawl off to rest, pull the carpet of grass over his head. Another bout of Walking Way was coming on like a blinding migraine. Merely touching the officer's smartphone had showed him so many things; the split second he touched the shiny electronic toy, he knew *what the major knew.* . . . Billy even knew the man's real name now.

Major Todd.

And the major stood a lot higher up the totem pole than he let on. The soldier had been briefed and rebriefed. Then the details; the knowledge in pure form entering Billy's brain like pages from a briefing book, a situation report allowing him to grasp the essence of reality, directly mind-to-mind:

There had been an outbreak of hemorrhagic smallpox on Indian lands. A new outbreak of the pox where the pox once ran free; once upon a time the real Indian killer, spread through traders' poisoned blankets, or dirty white men scratching their fleas. And the indigenous people were just as susceptible to the disease today as yesteryear.

The military had overrun every reservation in the Dakotas in force: to the north, Standing Rock, Cheyenne River, and to the south, Rosebud and Pine Ridge. Confiscated CB radios, computers, cell phones, any communication device they could get their hands on. And just to be on the safe side they shut down the cell towers and routers. Right now, this very moment, nobody was going in or out, every rez under quarantine. The cover story was "planned exercises."

More troops were heading into the Dakotas by the hour, taking a couple hundred thousand doses of vaccine from the country's smallpox stockpile with them. And nobody was gonna know diddly until they contained the situation.

Worse still, the army had caught some hotheads trying to bust out and get to a phone, a gas station, anything. Now there were dead braves in the Black Hills again. They'd deal with the bodies later, call it a "vehicular incident."

So that's why Grandma Sparrow wore a ghost shirt, and paint on her face. That's why she cowered in bed with the covers up to her chin.

Major Todd's business in Vandalia, Ohio, was merely a contingency operation: federal damage control to prevent stories like "Bureau of Indian Affairs Poisons Sioux Nation." It seemed Skeeterbugs had been dipping proboscises all over the Dakotas, and it was crucial that no one—not a single soul—make a connection to *government* testing. This leak from Pi R Squared needed to be stanched before it went viral; sever any connection to a guilt-ridden, pointy-headed scientist in a lockdown complex with a funny name.

And absolutely no mention of enhanced mosquitoes.

Or hemorrhagic smallpox.

Forefront in the major's mind: the fear that some high school science nerd on summer vacation with nothing better to do would stick one of the fancy mosquitoes under a microscope and find the *Made in USA* label. Make the connection that enhanced bugs mating with common bugs had reawakened an infinite number of insect-borne plagues. The little hummers just wanted to breed. Could you really blame them?

Then the Army would have to snatch the inquisitive student off the street and quietly liquidate him along with his entire family. The major wasn't looking forward to that.

As for Big Bea, Postmistress Sis of Webster Chargrove, that made her Pi R Squared's problem; let the egghead geneticists deal with it. Hook Big Sis up to a protoplasm milking machine and outbreed her big ass out of existence.

But what about the other three?

If Division knew about their little magnetic attraction trick, they'd want 'em all dead for sure, no questions asked. Maybe three weeks of Dr. Mengele tests just to be on the safe side and three weeks debriefing his own men under duress—at the end of which nobody in his outfit would know his own name. Which brought him back to the same point—*what the hell was he going to do with this guy?* Look at him. What a mess, an inch away from drooling puddles on the interrogation table.

With great effort Billy Shadow lifted his wooden head and focused his eyes.

"So what *are* you going to do with us?" he asked Major Todd.

Billy shakily touched the evidence bag with the melted contents; then the extra earring from Lila's dresser. He'd always thought of these bits as a compass. But to navigate what? True north of the soul, perhaps. . . . Beatrice was right about Lila Chen never actually being in LA on a TV show. Even now, the evidence ear bag wanted to draw him on a journey. . . . The light from the metal lamp filled every corner of the interrogation tent. Oh God, the headache was back.

Billy could feel the Chen-girl fugue coming on. From a great distance, he heard Major Todd's voice. "We're looking for Lila Chen. Do you know where she is? I think you do. I think you get to go places. See people, and the things they do . . ."

Yes, Billy knew. Once again the Skin Walking thing pushed him down the rabbit hole to Lila Chen. She was very close. She was in Indiana. The gaunt man and the children had taken a twelve-hour drive in the white limo to Indiana, ending at Indianapolis Methodist Hospital admissions. Piper Holdings paid for her private room, where she received a glucose drip and broad-spectrum antibiotics. A cosmetic surgeon came to check the scar over her missing ear. The specialist remarked at her amazing powers of recuperation; the scar tissue on her head getting paler by the day.

Should he tell the major? *No, not Major Todd. Not trustworthy.*

Billy could see her hospital room. She was recovering from her long ordeal in the van bit by bit, some bits better than others. . . .

* * *

L ittle Maria and the Kid had brought her a gift so she wouldn't be lonely, a friendly rabbit to keep watch over her. The gift shop rabbit at the end of Lila's bed was speaking to her. A plushy cottontail with big brindle ears and a precious nose saying, *They're coming, they're on their way.* . . .

One face in particular loomed in her mind. The familiar face of Janet's dad, Mr. Singh, just like when she'd seen his apparition during a potty stop outside the Stuka van with Queen Bitch. Mr. Singh smiled wisely, as if he knew all about her troubles and wanted to help. Quietly whispering once more, *We're coming. Hang on.* . . .

The dream ended and Lila woke.

The sweaty sheets on her bed were rumpled and twisted. What day was it? Didn't matter. Nothing keeping her to this bed but some tubes and a wrist ID. Carpe diem. Was the coast clear? Clear enough. Lila plucked the drip needles from her arms.

Nothing in the closet, not even a pair of slippers. She tiptoed out into the hall. Nurse's station or stairs? Make explanations or make a clean break? Clean break. She eased through the first stairway door available and right into a wall of beefcake. The huge orderly who caught her in his arms looked down; the nameplate on his scrubs read PHIL.

"Can I help you, little lady?" A deep baritone.

"No thank you, *Phil*. I'm just on my way out."

Phil looked down at her with grave doubt. The brute's arms were like an octopus; whichever way Lila turned they stopped her, shuffling her right back onto the ward.

"This isn't the way out," he rumbled. "But I'm sure they can help you at the nurses' station."

At the nurses' station a hatchet-faced woman in pale violet scrubs looked up from her monitor, asking her severely, "Aren't you supposed to be in bed, Miss Chen?"

Lila started to babble at a small gaggle of nurses and hospital attendants. She thought she was being sane, but they must have doped up her drip tube. What came out of Lila's mouth sounded like this:

"The Nazi guys high on Big D kidnapped me in Van Horn. Then scalped me in the motorcycle van. When my parents saw the ear they burned the house down with them inside. I think there are people looking for me. Who's in charge here?"

An elderly patient about a hundred years old limped along with his drip stand and nasal oxygen plugs. "Yes, I know what you mean," he remarked sympathetically. "That happened to me last week."

Everyone at the nurses' station laughed.

"I need to make a call. Can I borrow someone's cell?" But the moment had passed to call for help. Besides, whom would she call?

"Come along now," the hatchet-faced nurse said. "Let Phil take you back to your room." So much for Lila's great escape. For the present at least, she belonged to Mr. P.

A day later Mr. P. and the Piper children arrived in New York City on a two-hour red-eye on the Gulfstream from Indianapolis getting in around 4 a.m. During the flight, Kid put his nose into his laptop and made nasty things happen to a game show in LA. *Rewrites* he called it. Why mess with that stuff at all? Lila had no idea. When she asked him, Kid told her, "Just for the hell of it. Hanging with Piper I got to learn how to mess with people's heads. Telepathy and hypnotic suggestion on steroids. Mental Photoshop. Bet you by next week you'll be able to do it too."

"That's not something I'd ever want to do," Lila said.

"No? Too bad. It's fun." Kid said. "Pretty soon, Mr. P. and I are gonna do a tail-count. Kicking rat-butt and taking names. Mustering the troops."

Lila wasn't exactly sure what he meant by that, but it

sounded big. Kid finally dozed off for the last hour of the flight, and Lila watched him sleep. He seemed to have troubled dreams, quietly muttering to himself. She couldn't make out the words, though it sounded like *boom pine* or *room time*. Nothing that made any sense to her.

When the jet finally pulled up to the arrival area, Lila tried to carry the sleeping little girl on her shoulder. But Maria was getting too big for that; she walked holding Lila's stuffed bunny. The Kid stumbled along bleary-eyed and groggy, climbed into a waiting limousine, and closed his eyes again. He seemed extremely worn out to Lila; apparently messing with people's heads "for the hell of it" took more out of him than he realized.

The limo stopped in front of a tall apartment building; Lila saw the number on the awning, 146 Central Park West. A bronze plaque under the canopied entrance read THE SAN REMO. As they approached, the doorman put down the newspaper he was reading and held open the heavy metal-and-glass door for them. "Good to see you, Mr. P. The movers finished this afternoon."

The Piper smiled and slipped him a twenty, saying, "Thanks, Fucknutz." The doorman merely heard, "Thanks, Farley." As they passed inside, Lila glanced at the newspaper headline on *The National Enquirer.* "Mannequin Medicine Show Mystery": *1000 Plaster Dummies with Real Identification. Nebraskan State Police Baffled. Bereaved Families Claim "Rapture Capture."*

They took the front elevator up six floors to a private entranceway. Kid noticed Lila looking at the curious wallpaper on the vestibule walls; cute bunnies nosing each other surrounded by leaves.

"Nineteenth-century William Morris," Kid informed her. "The design is called Brother Rabbit." Lila detected a note of pride in his voice; he liked knowing things other people didn't.

The door to the apartment opened, and the dimmer

lights gently came on like twilight. Lila didn't see much but got the impression of a living room, a fireplace, towering houseplants, books in bookshelves, and paintings on the walls. They went down a long, dark hall. Mr. P. opened the doors to the children's rooms, one after the other. As in many swank Manhattan apartments designed for families with kids, adjoining bedrooms shared a bathroom. Open bathroom doors let you see right through from room to room. Kid crawled into bed without looking around.

In the girls' room, Lila saw a double-decker bunk bed. She led Maria to the lower bunk, took off her shoes, and pulled the covers over her. The child went back to sleep in seconds. That's when Lila noticed another bed in the room, larger than the bunk, up against some kind of mural. She didn't need an invitation.

Lila awoke a few hours later to soft voices. Morning light slanted through the window. She looked through the open connecting bathroom doors into Kid's room. The Kit-Cat clock hung on the wall and wagged its tail at her. Lila could see right to the foot of Kid's bed. His feet stuck out from under the covers and twitched a little. And she could hear Kid arguing with himself, softly talking in hushed voices, like in cartoons where a white-robed Angel and a red-robed Devil whispered back and forth.

Angel Kid: *He's a man with a very bad plan.*

Devil Kid: *You know you want to. He'll make you big. Bigger than them all.*

Angel Kid: *He's just using you. Don't let him own you.*

Devil Kid: *Own you? He birthed you. If he hadn't showed up, you'd still be hidin' under the kitchen sink with Liquid-Plumr and Mr. Clean. You'd still be waitin' for Dimples to get done with Mama so he could . . .*

Kid's muttering grew softer, and she stopped catching words. Except for the words *Room Time.*

Lila finally looked around the room she shared with Maria, and couldn't help laughing. *More wallpaper.* A Beatrix Potter woodland mural ran the length of her larger bed and from floor to ceiling. Aunt Jemima Puddleduck, Mr. Fox in his red waistcoat, Mrs. Tittlemouse's mousy daughters, dancing in their pretty dresses holding their long tails—all the creatures from that Potter woman's fanciful mind. Peter Rabbit. Benjamin Bunny. . . .

You could even write your name on a sign plank planted inside the forest scene so you could tell everyone whose room this was. The gaunt man had pasted their names over the previous child occupant. Now the sign plank read:

LILA & LIL' MARIA'S BURROW

Ah, that Master Piper thought of everything. Or did he? Mr. P. was like an awkward adult who knew nothing of young people, but still presumed to grasp their whims. Maybe this was age-appropriate for Little Maria, but a grown-up young woman? Lila sensed a weakness in him: *conceit.*

Then it struck her. . . . Since her failed escape, the impulse to flee had vanished. Not that Lila had fallen in with Mr. P., but her desire to watch over the other two children overpowered any fear for her own personal safety. The way Maria cradled the bunny in her arms as she slept, the way Kid struggled over right and wrong; neither the little girl nor the young man belonged in Mr. P.'s world.

The bar of morning light from the window crossed Maria's face. She groggily sat up in bed and rubbed the sleep from her eyes, then heard Kid's mumbling voice; Maria looked to the older girl for an explanation. The Kit-Cat clock on the wall in the other room rolled its eyes. Seven minutes to eight; rise and shine.

"C'mon," Lila told her. "Let's see what we can find for breakfast."

Kid's bedclothes rustled. "I'm not hungry," he grumbled.

"I wasn't speaking to you," Lila said.

Maria patted her mussed hair and then the plushy, stuffed bunny. Lila shared a look with the little girl. An understanding flowed between them, a kind of bond. Was there still hope for Kid? Maybe they could drain the poison. Breach his walls without breaking him. In so many ways the young man was still so needy. Lila went to their shared bathroom and stood in the open door to the boy's room. Kid had tangled his covers in his feet and struggled to free them. The Kit-Cat clock grinned at her.

"No breakfast unless you wash your face," she said sternly.

Kid lurched from bed, brushed past her to the bathroom sink, and turned on the taps. The children's toiletries, toothbrushes, and toothpaste had been laid out; he pondered them for a moment. Mr. P. had thought of everything. He splashed water on his face. "Eggs Benedict?" Kid asked with a tiny note of hope. "Canadian bacon? Buttered toast?" The young man looked curiously at her.

"Only if you wash your face," Lila told him.

25

Hall of the Rat King

Lila made eggs Benedict, extra bacon, English muffins, the hollandaise sauce, even parsley garnish. Other mornings she made French toast or blueberry pancakes. The huge kitchen in the apartment was outfitted with every kind of stainless-steel appliance. The humongous refrigerator stocked to overflowing: not only milk and eggs, but frozen mango slices and stone crab claws. If they ran out of Nutella or smoked Alaskan trout, there was a phone number for the local Food Emporium on a magnetic shopping list, and the supermarket delivered.

Days passed, then more days. The dead end of September had arrived. Mr. P. seemed to have forgotten all about them. They saw him only when he came in during mealtimes to nosh, or pick off the children's plates. Otherwise, he left the youngsters to their own devices, sequestering himself beyond a grand Tudor arch in a large wood-paneled study off the living room. And they were careful not to disturb him, like kids told to play quietly outside Daddy's office. When Lila asked if he needed anything—snack, a soda—he merely shook his head. "Time to pour castor oil on the waters. No rest for the wicked."

So far, mission accomplished.

He had secured both Lila for her outstanding genetic qualities, and the little girl for her nascent powers of insight and foresight, keeping both females like a couple of Rapunzels in a tower far from the outside world. Neither of them would fall into the hands of subterranean government dimwits in the worm-crawls of Hillsboro, Ohio; much better to be held in reserve until he knew what circumstances required. Lila and Little Maria were his secret weapon, to be used only at a time and place of his choosing. He had to prepare the way, abolish comfort and normality forever. Achieve a measure of destruction called *Point of No Return*. Then he'd know the proper way to employ the two females.

No doubt the worms of Hillsboro knew of Lila Chen's Indianapolis hospital stay, accessing her records from their own search engines. They might even have traced the two girls to New York via the Gulfstream's manifest or flight plan, but those techno naïfs at Pi R Squared hadn't earned the right to partake in the fruits of the Pied Piper's labor or the privilege of joining him at the adult table.

Mr. P. sat at his desk watching three flat HD screens, each tuned to different channels and running picture-in-picture. By his elbow stood an original Astro lava lamp, the only decoration in his study. As he worked the *Twilight Zone* phone, he stroked the transparent cone, and the red wax blobs in the lamp rose and fell, slowly coming to a boil as he made countless calls to the furthest reaches of Piper Holdings.

Very soon, a stream of directives drummed out of Mr. P.'s office, straight to Kid's iPad, the newest supersized version. Lila and Maria watched with growing apprehension as Kid let slip the rats of war. While his nimble fingers touched and pinched the screen, Kid chatted amiably about chaos in times past:

"In 1348, the Black Death came to Medieval Europe on the backs of rats and their fleas. Thirty to fifty percent of the population was infected and died. Not enough people remained to even bury the dead. Peasants brought in from the countryside dug graves at extortionate rates."

He plucked a Dalekto tab from a candy bowl and stuck it under his tongue. Without moving from the iPad screen, he stealthily glanced at the two girls to gauge their reaction. Nothing overt, no condemnation; instead, the two were wary, as if wondering where he was going with this.

He almost told the two girls the depth and breadth of Piper's plan, revealing how he and Mr. P. were going to raise their own medieval plague. Using rats, fleas, *and* mosquitoes; much, much worse than anything in times past. How an infection rate of only five or ten percent guaranteed certain collapse of modern civil society. But something made him hesitate. He was afraid Lila and Lil' Maria would treat him as they treated Mr. P.—with silent loathing. The gaunt man gave off a faint stench: the scent of deceit, the aroma of a sneer. And suddenly Kid didn't want to smell like that.

Instead he told them, "Believe it or not, we're much more vulnerable today than the world of superstitious serfs and Popes who thought maggots sprouted from rotting fish. And so chaos comes on smaller wings."

Again, he glanced at them surreptitiously. The girls didn't like where this was going. And Lila and Maria knew about Skeeterbugs. Kid had plenty of digital images of them. But when Kid said "chaos comes on smaller wings" the girls could tell it wasn't just actual carriers he meant. Clearly his mind had taken on a greater depth. By rendering complex events into unique, graspable bits, he demonstrated the true mark of high-end thinking: similes, metaphors, allegories, and parables. Analogies. Some called it *the very core of cognition*.

He took the drug tab out of his mouth to examine how much had dissolved, then popped it back in his mouth. He caught his two companions' worried eyes. The Too-Much-Drugs Look.

"It makes me smarter," Kid said. "I think faster; I work faster. Makes me better."

"No, it doesn't," Lila exclaimed. "It just feels that way."

Little Maria's voice piped up like a bird, "Food makes you smarter. A bath every day makes you smarter. Not *that* stuff." He made a show of ignoring them and thought about the tiny white-robed Angel Kid and red-robed Devil Kid perched on his shoulders, arguing in his ears. The two cartoon characters were on the verge of starting up again, and there was nothing he could do to stop them. In a few seconds he'd be babbling like an idiot in front of everyone. Lila laid a single finger on his forearm, and he felt a kind of warmth flow through him. Lila's magic touch. Angel Kid and Devil Kid held their tongues.

Slowly the Dalekto tab soured. He brought his hand to his lips like he had to cough; surreptitiously he spat out the lozenge so neither girl would see. *Don't let on. In case you can't beat it. In case the Dalekto gets you in the end . . .* He felt a twinge of cowardice that he couldn't do it up front. Maybe that meant he wouldn't be able to quit this monkey crap. Best hide the doubt, deep down.

He pointed to his iPad, exuding confidence for the girls' benefit.

"Want to know how Mr. P. gets things done?" Neither girl replied. He told them anyway. "He's been around so long, he knows everything everybody's ever done and ever thought. He's been a thousand different men and countless creatures. He speaks in tongues, the language of every animal. When Mr. P. decided to get involved again, he talked to the insects first, the ants especially. The ants follow orders without question. The rats, because they're smart. The rats are his banzai troops, his kamikazes, knowing however many of them die, they'll still breed their way to the top of the food chain."

Kid's fingers danced across the iPad screen.

"Get a load of this." The brave blue shield of the NYPD appeared. He'd tapped into New York Police Department's real-time office security feed at One Police Plaza: the cops' own security cameras, in the corridors and cubicles, stairwells and fire doors. The screen cut itself into dozens of boxes, each one a thumbnail of a different camera. Kid touched one thumbnail. One image expanded to fill the screen.

A basement-level camera showed conduits, steam pipes, and a pair of elevator doors. The thrum of generators filled the audio. As One Police Plaza was a modern building from the 1970s as opposed to the 1870s, the basement area was brightly painted and well lit, not your typical New Jack City dungeon.

The elevator doors opened, and two building engineers emerged, one of them talking personal stuff. "I told her if her brother comes around drunk again, barfing on the front steps, he's going direct to Queens Memorial holding his friggin' head—"

The two men stopped short; three bold rats hustled into view at the bottom of the frame. Both men jumped back against the basement wall, too surprised to gasp. The rodents paused aggressively, measuring their competition. Three rats vs. two men, the odds almost even. One guy started to kick them, and the rats scattered.

"Oh, they're not going to like that," the Kid remarked. "Mr. P. has a certain affinity for these creatures. They're organized, they're highly social, and they listen well. Now he's told each and every one of them they have nothing to fear. The world is their rat run."

Suddenly there were six rats in the hallway instead of three. The first wave had called in reinforcements. Go ahead, Dumbo, try kicking now. The two men turned tail and ran for their lives, retreating down the basement corridor. They hammered the elevator button, the doors sluggishly opened, and the two building engineers leapt inside, punching every button in sight. The elevator doors sluggishly closed, cutting off the horde of rats skittering along the floor.

Whew. Close call.

The Kid touched another thumbnail. Now they were looking at the Real-Time Crime Center, a kind of Mission Control inside One Police Plaza—a dark, cavernous room with lit Jumbotrons staring down at platoons of smaller desks, keyboards, and flat-screens. A wide shot of police bureaucrats and office workers. People talked on the phones like quacking ducks; others traipsed along the aisles.

Suddenly there was a bellow of panic and revulsion: a plainclothes cop in a bad suit and tie nearly fell over his chair and began doing the Mexican Hat Dance. He pulled his gun and started waving it around; people shrieked and ducked, but luckily, nothing went bang.

An office worker flew out of her cubicle—an attractive

woman in a business suit—she did the stamp dance in high heels. A stream of invective flew out of her mouth. "What the F—!" and more. You could see objects falling out of the drop ceiling. In the Real-Time Crime Center it was raining real-time rats.

One last thumbnail of Police Plaza's lobby showed a bank of elevators. The metal doors slid open. A body fell out: arm, neck, and the back of a man's head. One of the guys from the basement, his clothes shredded and hunks of flesh missing. A gang of brown rodents stood their ground, defying anyone to come closer. One person screamed or maybe they all did; the lobby scattered.

Lila and Lil' Maria watched, too daunted to say anything.

"It won't take much," Kid said to his two companions. "Just a little poke. Y'see, when the rats crawl out of their basements in every tenement, whole neighborhoods will be overrun, ungovernable. It's not rocket science. It's sociology. Remove a rat's fear of punishment, and the world of men goes to hell."

Satisfied with his work at Police Plaza, Kid paused. The desire for a rainbow tab overwhelming his brain. For a moment, he said nothing, breath shaky, his face turning pale. He felt completely washed out, and he avoided the girls' eyes for fear they'd notice. He nodded to the chaos on the iPad screen.

"A couple of days of this and just you wait."

L ater that night the children settled into their beds, but the lad had trouble sleeping. He tried playing soft music, he tried letting the television on his dresser whisper to him, but nothing worked. Kid glanced at the candy dish full of Dalekto tabs next to the TV. The dish called to him. *C'mere, Boy. C'mon, just one or two won't hurt. What you waiting for, Boy?* The need for them rose up through his bones, from the tips of his toes to the top of his head, a burning craving, the urge irresistible. He tried to think of something else, anything else. Nothing worked. Kid tore his eyes away and gripped the bedsheets for dear life. The Craze owned him body and soul.

And he didn't feel smart at all, only weak and shaky.

With all the control at his command, he got up and poured the dish of Dalekto into the toilet. The tabs fizzed, the water swirled to a flickering rainbow; then all the colors combined making the toilet water look like blood. He hit the flush handle, and the tabs were sucked away. The act took all his effort, and he sagged on the sink, his breath coming in gasps. An ashen face stared back at him from the bathroom mirror.

Mr. P. had left Dalekto all over the house. What would he do about those? Throw them out? Yes, throw them out.

For a split second he thought of Lila's magic finger and the flowing warmth making him want to call through the open bathroom door. Would she do it again? Just the girls' presence seemed to help—a kind of antidote. The Kid left the sink and went into their room. Orange light spilled in from the streetlamps below; he stood for a moment, staring longingly at the bunny rabbits and smart mousies in the Beatrix Potter mural—if only he could go to a place like that.

Lila looked up from her pillow. "What is it?" Kid's face took on a pained expression. "Don't you want to talk about it?" she asked.

Kid struggled for the words. "Bad things. Dalekto is doing bad things to me. I don't like my room. Can I stay in here?" He seemed so pathetic and scared.

"That's why we're here," Lila told him. "To keep the bad things away."

The bunk bed creaked as the little girl woke up too. "Come in with me," Maria told him, "or take the top bunk."

He seemed smitten that he'd actually been invited somewhere. "You sure?"

"Yes, I'm sure."

"I think I'll go up," Kid said at last.

He climbed up to the top bunk and dug his way under the covers. "I've always wanted to sleep on the top bunk."

The effect of the girls' room and their auras lasted through the night, killing the Craze so Kid could sleep. But it didn't last forever. When morning light came, his mood had grown cold and calculating again, and the wholesome effect of the Beatrix Potter mural by Lila's larger bed had vanished. No longer needy, no longer afraid of being alone in the dark. With a good night's rest, Kid's mischievous urges overcame everything—the need to be good, the desire for company, and temporarily even the Craze.

Daybreak found him deep into executing Piper's lists and commands, creating chaos one finger tap at a time. And the girls watched in silent alarm as his iPad spread mayhem over a thousand streets and neighborhoods. Under Mr. P.'s direction, Kid reached out using his skycap dispatchers, his private army of drug traffickers: *Chicago, LA, San Diego, Boston, Austin—they'll go everywhere, man. Wear the pavement down, man.* Calling out to his Dalekto distributors, his skycap couriers in every burg of any size, the young master set his social network of pushers to other tasks, redirecting their efforts in fantastically destructive ways.

Explaining to the girls, "My skycaps have been delivering Big D into every corner of the city. In New York alone my 'Little Men' will commit ten thousand crimes in a matter of hours and yuk it up on YouTube."

Kid clicked on a flash mob of skycaps swarming the Prada flagship store in SoHo; roughly dancing undressed mannequins through the aisles, their Google Glass headsets showed the swarming mob from every conceivable angle. The gag ended with a mess of ignited lighter fluid and the sprinkler system going off like a thunderstorm.

The police never showed.

Reports of wildings came in from Topeka, Memphis, and Austin. In New England, flash mobs looted Boston's Faneuil Hall, picking it clean. In downtown Pittsburgh, one of Kid's skycaps dumped a truckload of manure into the water feature fountain outside the Pittsburgh Plate Glass Industries complex. Before leaving the wreck, he spray-painted Day-Glo graffiti on the stonework: *Superfund Cleanup Site*.

With the help of Twitter, Facebook, and YouTube, monkey-see-monkey-do madness rose up from the pavement, the wilding taking on a life of its own. Across the greater metropolitan area, nimble hands sabotaged backhoes in storage areas and construction sites.

With no backhoes, no digging.

With no digging, no graves, and the unburied dead overwhelmed the system. Bodies began showing up in abandoned lots and alleys. Food for rats.

The craving for Dalekto spurred Kid on; the girls helpless to stop him. The more the Craze ate into him, the more he crushed everything and everyone under his thumb, grinning into his touch screen as his fingers did the dirty work. Mr. P. had forwarded access to innumerable municipal accounts to his young apprentice's iPad. The young man moved a decimal point here, erased a number there. Multiplying a debt, liquidating a pension fund, hitting the *B* for billion instead of the *M* for million. He could do it with his eyes closed. Cities large and small operated on billions of dollars of Monopoly money; now, the time had finally arrived to call in their IOUs. Crash the system.

Even as the children slept, automated overnight flash trades devoured bank balances in milliseconds. As dawn broke, city workers and the mass of civil servants realized in a single blow that payrolls were not going to be met. The money stream had gone flat, run dry like a fire hose at an empty hydrant. Nurses, cops, teachers, firemen, transit workers, not to mention faceless throngs of bureaucrats, turned into paupers at the click of a mouse.

Things began to grind to a halt. Trains and buses came once every two hours; the lights flickered and garbage started to pile up in blissfully warm late-September days. At toll points around the city, Port Authority toll attendants demanded cash and rifled luxury cars while the cops passively stood by like the London Metropolitan Police during the London Riots of 2011.

On the cable news shows, the newscasters, all second-stringers or third-stringers, blabbered on as if nothing was out of the ordinary, offering the usual menu of foreign crises, international debt, and cheating celebrities. But they seemed very pale and tired, as though some announcers were working both sides of the camera or hadn't left the studio in days. And their faces . . . Almost yellow, you might say.

It seemed the Days of Reckoning had suddenly arrived. And Lila wondered if she picked up the phone whether the Food Emporium would actually answer.

Early one morning, the two girls caught Kid sitting on the bathroom floor staring at the closed toilet seat. One hand held an open Altoids breath mint tin with a dozen or so Dalekto tabs—Kid's secret emergency stash. He pondered the open tin, a single finger moving the tablets around inside the shiny box, his mind caught in a desperate struggle. The girls barely breathed; afraid that if they spoke Kid would stick a tab in his mouth. But after long moments of sliding the things around, Kid lifted the toilet seat, tipped the last of his Dalekto tabs into the water, and leaned heavily on the flush handle. Sagging over the roaring toilet, he retched.

Splashing cold water on his face from the sink, he drank from the tap and fumbled over his toothbrush; then noticed the girls staring at him from the connecting bathroom door.

"What are you looking at?" he demanded.

But neither Lila nor Maria knew what to say.

* * *

Elsewhere in the San Remo apartment building, things were getting ugly. Apartment doors slammed above or below; incoherent shouts echoed off walls. Tenants hit the elevator buttons over and over, repeatedly cursing. Lost souls moaned or cried softly. Whatever the problem happened to be, it was beginning to sink in that no one was coming. No EMT, no rescue, even though the city canyons echoed with sirens. The children could feel it all around them, things getting out of hand.

When a terrifyingly piercing human shriek reached the sixth floor, Lila and Maria rushed to the living room window and leaned out. Down below, the body of a man in a bathrobe lay sprawled on the pavement—a jumper. Lila seemed to recall his name was Skinson. Beside him, a woman wailed and cradled his head.

Lila and Little Maria dialed 911, but got a recording. The body would lie on the pavement below the San Remo for days, until urban scavengers stripped it of its bathrobe and slippers. Then at last it would disappear.

Under the Beatrix Potter mural, Kid worked the iPad.

He liked the girls' room better than his. Especially at night, its cozy warmth and pretty mural picture safe and comforting, even as he did ugly things before crawling into the top bunk. Lila found herself drawn to his shoulder, wondering silently what kind of meanness she'd find. This time Lila saw the ugliness emanated from a much closer source: a desperate video call from that place Kid once called home, that ratty apartment on the Lower East Side.

Dimples and Mama had crawled their way back to the dingy apartment on Avenue A. Lila watched as Dimples Skyped in a final plea from the bathroom. Mama in the tub, dead from an overdose of bad dust. While Dimples rasped, "Up for Room Time—?" Kid disconnected, blocking the Caller ID.

Without taking his eyes off the screen, his voice betrayed nothing.

"Mr. P. taught me a lot of useful tricks. How to rearrange TV, how to influence people . . . The man can get inside your head and rearrange your thoughts; he can get inside a toaster oven and bake a Hot Pocket. But he still keeps the good stuff to himself—molecular metamorphosis, the mental manipulation of matter."

The Piper could collapse a bridge, but he couldn't stop an earthquake. He could cause a thunderstorm, but he couldn't water the desert. A creature of finite powers. With limits, like any entity—and Lila began to understand that the gaunt man "paid the piper," so to speak, every time he performed a miracle. Afterward, he wore out, got tired, had to recharge.

"But his greatest talent is getting people to think what he wants," Kid told her. "Nudging them, scaring them to death. All we do is fuel the engine of fear, and lust and greed. That's how human interaction works. The lust for power masked as benevolence. The trick is to present it as a collective awakening. That way people think they're doing good as they're doing bad."

A quote from Nietzsche floated to the top of Kid's mind. "Madness is rare in individuals—but in groups, parties, nations, and ages it is the rule." Not long ago, in a moment of candor, Mr. P. mentioned how he had 'befriended' Nietzsche, tormenting him with syphilitic symptoms just to see a brilliant mind crumble under the weight of physical and moral rot. So much for geniuses.

Kid returned to the present. "See, I'll show you."

He opened up a new message window called Billboard West-Southwest; the cursor blinked waiting for him to type.

"I'm putting new sayings on digital billboards around the country—subliminal advertising. Y'know those signs that flash at you on the interstate and cloverleaf interchange? Nashville, San Diego, Denver—Bible Country, all those

End-of-the-Worlders. If they think the Rapture is at hand, they'll volunteer to disappear. So when they get sick, which they inevitably will, masses of them will go nice and quiet. This should get their attention in Dubuque." The digital message on the highway billboard now read GOD IS WAITING. "You watch; there'll be people walking off cliffs just to meet him."

Lila and Maria looked at him aghast, too stunned to speak.

He swished the iPad icons and paused a moment, considering the problem of billboard manipulation closer to home. Thinking out loud, "The new 'future proof' Yankee Stadium has over a thousand HD video monitors and a giant scoreboard. The Times Square billboard is primo too. Elevator TVs; taxi, bus, and airport digital signs. Problem is, hardly anybody believes squat in this city except maybe the newsstand Dot Heads and the Camel Drivers. And they all hate each other's guts on a good day. Let's play it safe; let's focus their energy. How about—"

The Kid tapped out a new line: *The Jews Did It.*

"Wait. Wait. Wait!" Lila grabbed his hands. "Stop!"

"What?" he asked, annoyed. But her warmth flowing into him actually made him want to stop. "You want it more precise? So everyone can understand? *Blame the Jews*?"

"Stop, Kid," Lila repeated. Her fingers reached for the iPad screen. She tapped and slid and scrambled his work, making it disappear. "Don't do this. This is not you." Maria joined them on the bed, and the two girls pressed him on either side, shoulder to hip. He snatched the iPad close. "It's mine! You can't have it! Mine!"

Kid began to pant, mouth open with labored breathing. The urge for a tab of Dalekto engulfed him in a slow burn. But when Lila touched him, the warmth flowed over him like a summer breeze and the gritty desire for the Devil D eased off.

"That pad's not yours," Lila told him very seriously. "It's

his." She looked around their safe room. "Everything is his—the apartment, the clothes, the toys, the city. The only thing you own is yourself. Yourself and us. Just the three of us."

"Just us," Little Maria repeated. The young man's hands trembled in his lap. The two little whisperers, Angel Kid and Devil Kid, hovered on his shoulders. Now they began to argue as they always did, in those high tinny voices.

> Devil Kid: *There's more Dalekto in the living room. Go look for it.*
> Angel Kid: *That's just talk. The Devil's scared. You've kicked Dalekto and you don't even know it. It's been days and days. You're beating it.*
> Devil Kid: *Which means you can have one and it's not gonna matter. If it wasn't for Mr. P. you'd still be on Room Time getting bumped ugly. Turn away now and he'll give you to the Russians in Orchard Beach, who'll sell you to Middle Eastern pimps for a boi-harem. What's the Kit-Cat clock say, Time for a Tab, right?*

The Kit-Cat clock began ticking very loudly in his room, the bug-eyes darting back and forth, the tail wagging madly. Without warning the Kid leapt from Lila's bed, barged through the bathroom, and confronted the thing.

"I never should have listened to you."

The clock grinned, *tick-tock,* showing minutes to midnight.

Kid's tense fingers hovered over its smiling face. When it got loud like this, did it mean Mr. P. was about to bust in for Room Time just like Dimples? Gritting his teeth, he yanked the cord from the socket, unplugging the thing. The eyeballs stopped moving; the tail stopped wagging. Nice dead kitty. Stay that way.

Kid stepped backward out of his room, one foot after the

other, until he found Lila's bed again and the two girls just as he'd left them. His face streamed sweat, limbs trembling with the Craze. Lila ran cold water over a facecloth and mopped his brow while the younger girl kept petting his thigh, telling him everything was going to be okay. Maybe they were right; maybe everything *was* going to be okay—

Inside Kid's room, the Kit-Cat clock started ticking again, kitty's eyeballs clicking back and forth, even unplugged. *Tick-tock.* Maria hopped off the bed and closed the far door. The sound diminished.

"Lock it," Lila told her. Maria threw the dead bolt, climbed back on the bed, and took the Kid's soft hand in her own. Petting his clenched fist, she glanced shyly into his eyes. "Can't I just hold your hand? Is that so bad?"

Maria gently peeled fingers loose one by one to study his palm, like Senora Malvedos used to. "Shall I tell your fortune? Should I see your future?"

He quivered in doubt, but he let her hold his hand. She stared hard at his palm, touching the tips of his fingers. Could she really see the future?

The Craze made his hand a jumble of confused and contradictory lines. However, the little girl did see something. An extra lifeline—what some called a "fate line"—parallel to his lifeline. Kid's life and fate ran side by side, the two deep lines extending to the very edge of his palm. Unlike so many others whose lifelines crawled off to nothing, his life and fate penetrated the future. His life and fate ran off the map, life and fate extending into infinity.

Kid's life was going to mean something. Not just here now. Forever.

But before Maria could tell him what she saw—

Even as she stared into his hand, the two lines seemed to smooth away and disappear, leaving a youthful, blank palm. No more to see.

Future unknown, all ends undone.

26

Quarantine

Lauren sat in a chair in the Keeping Room, staring out the front window at Mr. Fenniman's house. She'd been sitting for some time, watching for any sign of life. If she'd seen even the slightest twitch, she might have risked going outside to check on the old man. Mr. Fenniman hadn't moved since she noticed his feet sticking out from under a bush by the side of the house.

And she couldn't help thinking of the Wicked Witch's legs poking out from under Dorothy's house. No red-and-white striped stockings and no ruby slippers, but still, more real than those fake prosthetic arms frat boys stuck out of their car trunks for a gag.

Guy joined her at the window, along with Corky and Peaches, who came for pettings.

"Anything?" He meant old Fenniman, feet sticking out on the grass.

Lauren shook her head. "No."

Across the street, a rat ran up the curb, zeroed in on Mr. Fenniman's ankle, and tugged at his sock. Then another rat joined him. Guy turned away from the window, putting his hand on Lauren's shoulder. "C'mon. There's nothing we can do."

When exactly Mr. Fenniman fell sick, no one could say. Perhaps his ticker gave out while trying to fix a gap in his taped window seals. But he died outside; and that's where he stayed.

The weather had cooled off this second week of October, but mosquitoes still floated under the eaves of the house. Lauren had been a lot smarter to seal up their place from the inside. Neither Guy nor Lauren had ventured outdoors in a week; first, ordering pizza delivery, then switching to the Hunan Pavilion or the Mandarin Palace. But when Mama Mia's stopped answering, so did the half-dozen Chinese places; they wound up eating their pantry bare.

Finally becoming desperate enough to risk a grocery run.

Guy and Lauren wore long-sleeve shirts, long slacks, turtlenecks, boony bug hats, and gardening gloves, making them stand out at Shaw's Supermarket on Black Rock Turnpike. People stared, but not for too long. Infected customers moved slowly in the aisles, examining cans and jars for longer than normal, as though they couldn't focus their eyes properly. No one seemed to have a clue what was happening. An elderly woman suddenly came to a halt behind her shopping cart and sat on a stepped stack of Budweiser twelve-packs. She hugged herself, shivering with chill, and the cart aimlessly rolled toward the bakery section.

A store worker in a red smock stared at the old woman as though considering what to do. The lad seemed to have trouble making up his mind. Words from the public address system—*"Clean up on Aisle Two"*—didn't get his attention. Eventually he approached the old woman and asked woodenly, "Are . . . you . . . all . . . right?"

The old woman barely looked up. "I'll be all right in a minute," she said.

Lauren pushed their cart past and down an aisle. The girl from the stairs held Guy's hand as they traipsed behind her. She stared in amazement, eyes wide as saucers, awed at the mountains of goods spilling off the shelves. Frankly, Guy, Lauren, and the dogs had gotten used to the girl following them everywhere. So when she appeared in the house or jumped in their large blue Honda SUV, the two adults didn't think twice about it anymore.

Part guardian angel, part adopted puppy. Their 'Alice' seemed to pop out of nowhere: on the stairs, outside the Walgreens after their hospital visit, visitations in and around the Finn House. Over time, however, their *Alice in Wonderland* girl seemed less an apparition than an unlikely time traveler stuck in an unfamiliar world. Lauren reminded herself to ask Eleanor about Auntie Whitcomb's mother, Great Auntie Whitcomb. Once upon a time, odd things happened to the great aunt—as a little girl—some hushed-up scandal. That she vanished for months, or was kidnapped by elves or something equally improbable. God forbid young Alice blab about all this when she traveled back to her proper time. They'd think her nuts at home and lock her up.

As the young lady lost the aspect of a specter, she took on more substance, able to pick objects up in the real world, examining things on the shelves, then putting them back. She was particularly fascinated with packaged meat: Oscar Meyer bologna, Deli Fresh turkey breast. And Cap'n Crunch in the cereal aisle made her think a lot. She stared at the Cap'n's picture on the box for quite a while, until Lauren doubled back for her.

They must be quite a sight—two adults in bug suits and their *Alice in Wonderland* girl in a nineteenth-century starched pinafore covered in a clear plastic raincoat, her own bug hat and white kid gloves. Guy broke open an enormous bag of Tootsie Pops from the candy shelf, gave Alice a lollipop, and let her carry the bag. Then found an equally large package of Pixie Stix and gave her that to carry too. Never underestimate the power of a Pixie Stix or a Tootsie Pop.

The girl by the stairs smiled shyly, knowing full well this was candy, even if she'd never seen this kind before. He wished he knew her name, but she hadn't spoken yet. You had to wonder whose world was more real: the world of supermarkets, with miles of aisles, or the world of sick-carts piled high with the dead?

No cashiers to be seen. At the self-service checkout counter, they swept their purchases over the scanner. Lauren toyed with the idea of shoving the Charmin TP and frozen orange juice through without a swipe, but innate honesty, the veneer of civilization, made her obey the old rules. The bar code scanner beeped, cheerfully confirming each purchase, but when Lauren hit the total button, the sum total came up $713.00. *Is this Correct? Yes? No?* Only about $650 too much.

"Oh for crying out loud." She brandished her debit card and pleaded, "Guy! Fix it!"

"Press no. Just press no and cancel the transaction," Guy said as he bagged. "I'll leave a hundred bucks; that's more than enough."

"The alarm will sound when we push the cart out the door."

"Fine," Guy growled from behind his bug mesh. Sweat dripped down his face. "Let it."

And just as Lauren predicted, the alarms went off, lights flashed, bells rang—but nobody came to arrest them. Shaw's Supermarket seemed deader than the public library on Christmas Day. Lauren noticed the balky store worker wearing the red smock in Aisle Two staring down at the linoleum floor. He'd brought his mop and roller bucket for a broken half gallon of tomato juice, but wavered uncertainly over the spill, staring down his mop handle, seeming lost in thought.

Back in the car, Guy and Lauren whooshed off their bug hats with a sigh of relief and cranked on the AC. The girl by the stairs sat in the back and quietly finished her Tootsie Pop. She showed the clean stick around the car, grinning for another from the bag.

"All right," Lauren gave in. "But it'll ruin your dinner."

Back home in Fairfield, maybe a dozen pedestrians wandered aimlessly about the village, others merely staring into the shop windows, lethargic and preoccupied.

"Did you ever hear from the agency?" Lauren asked suddenly. "You didn't say anything, so I figured no."

"Talent Associates?" Guy said, mildly embarrassed. These days when an employer wanted you, they called. Calling them just showed desperation. "Yeah, I called." He sighed. "Got put on hold for fifteen minutes, then disconnected."

That night they heard people crying in the middle of the night. A shriek of despair. Two gun blasts. Murder-suicide? Nobody dared leave his or her house to investigate. Later, they heard a car rolling slowly down the street. A woman drove, but they couldn't make out her face. Perhaps because her skin was so bloated, sallow, and yellow— unrecognizable. The car swerved gently from side to side, then jumped the curb and quietly came to a halt. Thankfully, the poor lady died quietly there and then and didn't fall onto her car horn, making someone like Guy come out of the house in bug suit to lift her off the steering wheel.

The next morning Lauren could not resist glancing at Mr. Fenniman once more. A swarm of rats lunged and darted over the body, worrying his limbs, pulling him to shreds. A pang of guilt struck her; regret that she never got to know him better after all the years he lived across the street. Too late now . . . Corky and Peaches rescued her from her dark thoughts, fetching her with wagging tails; they wanted out.

"Okay, I understand. C'mon!" The happy hounds eagerly followed her as she went through the kitchen and into the den and opened the den doors. Since nobody wanted the dogs to get bit or infected, neither Guy nor Lauren was taking chances. A screened-in shelter filled most of the backyard.

Guy found a great deal on a ClearSpan storage shed, originally designed for cattle, and had it delivered almost a month ago. One of the last UPS deliveries they could remember. The ClearSpan company's Moo-Tel Series was a big tent—perfect for a half-dozen cows or couple of pampered greyhounds when you needed to keep hordes of flying insects away behind plastic and screens. You could even unzip the windows for screened-in cross ventilation. Guy abutted his improvised kennel right up to the den doors and sealed it with duct tape, extra plastic, and tent stakes. Presto, a screened-in doggy run.

Instead of nosing around for a good place to go on the grass, Corky and Peaches leapt into a wild dog dance, skittering about, chasing—oh no! Rats!

A small hole near the ground showed where the nasties had chewed through the tenting looking for food. They found trouble instead. Corky bit around the rodent's head. Shake! Shake! Shake! Peaches neck-snapped her first, dropped it, and went after another. Frantic rats climbed the tent walls, the dogs yelping like some nineteenth-century blood sport.

Young Alice clapped her hands and laughed delightedly, like it wasn't her first rat-baiting. Lauren gave her a wild-eyed stare. God, people really *were* different back when.

Well, what did Lauren expect for a girl who sent her dolls to the guillotine?

Stop thinking; get control of the dogs!

"Corky! Peaches!" Lauren cried, chasing them down. Four rats gone. The fifth squeezed through the hole in the polyethylene canvas about the size of a dime and vanished. The two dogs, immensely pleased with themselves, shivered and laughed with pride. From what she could tell neither had torn or punctured their rodents—more of a game than a feast. Lauren pushed back her flyaway hair. Finally, Guy appeared in alarm.

"Guy," she said seriously. "We gotta get out of here. Today. Right now."

Would anywhere be better than Fairfield? Maybe someplace with fewer rats, fewer mosquitoes? Where yellow fever had burned itself out?

Why not rescue Eleanor from the Connecticut Valley Hospital in Middletown? Bhakti had been sending broken messages for a week. Every time they tried to text him back the Internet became frozen or scrambled; connecting seemed like the bad old days of pongs and whistles. It had been a week, at least, since they'd heard anything from him. Eleanor's own messages floated between coherent and canned asparagus. Why not go get her like Bhakti wanted?

Two hours later they'd stocked the big Honda, doing it all in their bug outfits: cargo cooler, rolled sleeping bags, dog beds, papers like deeds and wills. Add to that, an empty plastic gas can, flashlights, emergency radio, Lauren's laptop—everything they could think of on a moment's notice. Guy didn't own a gun, but suddenly wished he did.

"Let's git while the going's good!" Guy called from the car. Lauren paused before closing the front door. A brisk wind blew out of the north, as if blessing their getaway. Lauren thought about leaving a note: *Be right back.* Then noticed door after door down their street, large black Xs just like in her dream. With a heavy heart, she found a Magic Marker and drew a black X.

Alice, their girl from the stairs, watched silently from the Keeping Room.

"Well, you coming? C'mon, then!"

The young lady didn't have to be asked twice; she skipped out of the Finn House and climbed into the SUV, bug hat and raincoat under her arm.

Inside the car, Alice fished into the backseat pouch and brought out a gaily colored laminated book with the words *My Diary* written on the cover, a "Horse Friends" diary. The girl must have taken it from Shaw's Supermarket along with the Tootsie Pops and the Pixie Stix. The diary cover showed a chestnut pinto near an apple tree by a stream, and the book locked with a cute pink lock. She flipped through the blank pages; found a colored pencil in the seat pouch;

then, frowning with concentration, slowly began her first entry.

Lauren was just as happy the child had found something to occupy her; the town of Fairfield was not a pretty sight. Storefronts broken, the liquor store burned out, more than a few bodies slumped in corners or splayed across the sidewalk. Xs on every other door and plenty of rats to go around. Corky and Peaches saw the rats through the Honda window and shivered in delight. Sheriff Mike's police cruiser had run up on the curb of the Metro-North station, right where Guy had seen the Leprechaun Bus at the beginning of summer on his way home to find his lawn torched and Sheriff Mike outnumbered by a rent-a-mob. Only four months ago? Back then the world still seemed basically normal. Now the cruiser's side door stood open, the cockeyed vehicle abandoned.

No Sheriff Mike.

Eleanor woke up in her pleasant room in the gabled house, a beam of sunlight crossing her face. What day was it? She couldn't quite remember; felt like the place had been on lockdown forever, and up till yesterday things had more or less taken care of themselves. Trays of food arrived; the used dishes removed; a nice word from Mr. Washington. Then the whole process repeated itself, one day flowing into the next. Maybe ten days? The leaves had started to turn. First or second week in October? Close enough. The head orderly's visits always provided her with a chance to find out about the staph infection. When he collected her tray she'd always ask, "How's that upset tummy of yours, Mr. Washington?"

"As good as can be expected," he'd reply philosophically.

"And the staphylococcus? I didn't see anything on Channel Ninety-eight."

Mostly she remembered him nodding—fine, fine. But

the last time he took her tray, only yesterday, he shook his head with a note of doubt.

"Hard to say, Miss Eleanor." That didn't sound so good.

And this morning an eerie quiet seemed to have descended on the gabled house. She looked at the walls of her pleasant room: no dancing men, no Rolpens rolling along the stenciled border. And no Mr. Washington either. The remains of yesterday's lunch sat on a tray. So Mr. Washington had missed bringing her dinner last night and she didn't even notice. She must have spaced out again.

Then it came back to her. Last night the Light Tesla took her on another trip right into the laptop screen, down pathways of electrons, to leap great distances in a single bound, only to emerge in Dr. Webster Chargrove PhD's secret cubbyhole in the meatpacking plant. The young scientist was giving his latest mea culpa through a single live telephone wire. And Eleanor tried to follow him as best she could.

"Lila Chen is the key. They want to apply her enhanced physiological profile to a new generation of Skeeters. But not to inoculate millions of people like originally planned to counteract the wandering sickness. No, far fewer. Only the elite, the selected, a Noah's Ark of the anointed."

He gulped for air.

"It's imperative you keep her away, don't let them get their hands on her—"

He paused, something at the door. He began to blurt, *"I love you, Beatrice. Don't forget me, don't forget—"*

Suddenly the cubbyhole door slammed open. Booted feet entered the room. The telephone cord yanked from the wall. And a voice said, *"Thank you, Webster. We'll take it from here."*

Back in her pleasant room Eleanor stared at her laptop; a log of the bizarre text messages she'd been trying to send

Bhakti and her sister for weeks flashed and repeated like a crazed loop of desperation:

- *I want to leave now. I'm not sick. Just please come and get me.*
- *Bacteria here, Staff-Staph fear. But DON'T come near, dear.*
- *Don't you dare let her mother's milk back to the birthing chamber.*

Sweet Jesus, what nonsense was this? She hardly remembered writing the damn things. Crazy or psychic? Had the Pi R Squared people scrambled her brains *that* badly? The last one, *mother's milk,* made a strange kind of sense. With dead women in beds growing orange fungus, and zillions of mosquitoes feeding off live babies, no, don't let Lila Chen and her perfect biochemistry—her mother's milk—anywhere near the Pi R Squared complex. *Keep her the hell away.*

Eleanor, stop talking to yourself!

And what about that confused writing? Could she write straight if she wanted to? Try doing one coherent text or e-mail: *Come get me. I'm not sick. Come get me.* She tried to type out a more coherent e-mail, imploring them to rescue her and not get infected. Dear Bhakti, Lauren, Guy—but her fingers typed, *No Staff/Staph here, just me dear. . . .*

Dammit! Just type straight. But no matter how hard she tried, she couldn't do any better. She sent it anyway. For a moment she felt she would faint, lose consciousness—wake up later and not remember what she'd done. Help me, Obi-Wan Kenobi, you're my only hope, *phzzzzzt, Help* me Obi-Wan—

Face it, Eleanor; nobody is coming. They ran out of food. Mr. Washington has gone home to Mrs. Washington. Nothing to do but eat paint chips off the wall and die of lead poisoning. What about her neighbor lady, Mona the Moaner in the next room?

Eleanor pounded the wall. "Hey! I'm talking to myself. Don't you want to shout at me?"

She waited for a moment, listening for any reply, then pressed her ear to the wall, but didn't even hear a quiet groan. That was bad. Scary. She pounded again.

"Hey, you alive? Am I annoying you yet?"

No reply. Nothing. Silence.

She stifled a shiver of panic; a frantic butterfly fluttered over her heart. If a door was locked from the outside, how do you get out? If the wood wasn't swollen you could pry the hinge pins out and maybe it would fall inward. Need a screwdriver or a jimmy for that.

Brilliant Eleanor, before you dig a spring out of your mattress check the door. Hah, good! The hinges were on the inside. And her bed was one of those bunk things with thin metal slats attached by springs. Perfect.

She cut her palm getting one of the metal slats free, but who cared about that? She sucked the edge of her hand, the coppery taste of blood. She ripped a sheet and tied a swathe around the wound, then went to work on the door hinges. The pins were stiff, but once she got a little gap going, she could bang at them with the edge of her cafeteria tray. Two hinges done—one stuck partway. Now she was almost wild, thinking, *No way out, no way out.* One stupid hinge pin. *Help me, Obi-Wan!*

She kept banging at it with the cafeteria tray until *bing* it came free. Which is when she heard Mr. Washington's pleasant voice calling her name, but she couldn't exactly catch what he was saying. His key turned in the lock— *Jesus, he was coming in.* "Mr. Washington! Careful! There's no—"

"Miss Eleanor, are you all right?" The whole door careened off its hinges and fell inward. She leapt out of the

way, and Mr. Washington stumbled forward into the room.
"Oh my!" He recovered himself, brushed down his pants.

"Really, Miss Eleanor, you didn't have to do that. I
wouldn't forget about you."

Eleanor, suddenly shy, wrapped a bathrobe around her
jammies and stammered, "What's going on?" She dug
some clothes out of the chest of drawers—blue jeans, bra,
T-shirt—and went into the bathroom to change.

"People dead all over the place. I didn't go home last
night; the staff got the infection and I attended to some, but
they're gone now."

"And the patients?" Eleanor asked out the bathroom.

A silence. That told the story. She came out of the bathroom dressed. "Well, I'm glad you're okay." Truth was, Mr.
Washington looked a little pale—

"My stomach came back this morning. Didn't feel like
breakfast. Not sure I want to go to the cafeteria kitchen."

Mr. Washington's eyes were clouded with doubt. Eleanor
could read his mind; he feared the staff's staph infection,
staphylococcal food poisoning, vomiting, diarrhea, dehydration. With nothing to do for it except Imodium, weak
tea, and toast. But what if his symptoms were something
different, something stronger, something worse?

A terrible image leapt into her mind: one of M. C. Escher's
creepy-crawlies, padding along on their tiny human feet, a
Rolpen crawling out of Mr. Washington's belly—

Eleanor squelched the thought.

She looked once more on the pleasant room. No, she
wasn't going to miss this place. Out in the hall Mr. Washington had opened all the adjoining doors. Eleanor didn't
want to poke her nose into every single room, see the dead
in some final horrid repose, but she couldn't contain her
curiosity about the woman on the other side of the wall,
the mousy librarian from the cafeteria. After all her moaning back and forth: *Eleanor shut up!* One last good-bye.

The woman sat on the floor, legs outstretched, her

housecoat fallen open, her head leaning up against the wall. She had coughed up a chunk of lung and died before she could wipe it off her chin. Eleanor silently turned away and followed Mr. Washington down the stairs to the common room.

Kay sat in front of her M. C. Escher jigsaw puzzle. Poor Kay. Eleanor's friend seemed to have succumbed to a more traditional form of staph infection, the mighty itches, scratching her erupting skin raw until she bled out. Eleanor knelt beside her. "Oh, Kay . . . I'm so sorry."

"I didn't have the heart to lock her in," Mr. Washington admitted. "Not with her itching and scratching." He stood looking down in a bewildered fashion at the weird black-and-white M. C. Escher puzzle *House of Stairs*, with the parrot-beaked lizaroids rolling up and down connecting hallways. Mr. Washington rubbed his belly like it hurt him. "I never liked that one. Makes me think I got a couple of those in my stomach."

Eleanor blocked that visual. "What's happening outside, Mr. Washington?"

"They locked the main gate. Nobody going in, nobody going out. But then the chief administrator, Dr. Bodine, drove his car right through and knocked it down. He was just afraid, I think. I stayed here to take care of some of the others, but—" He paused, daunted, overwhelmed.

Mr. Washington breathed heavily; he cradled his tender belly. "I'm going to sit down for a minute, if that's okay. There's some Pepto-Bismol in the glove compartment of my car outside. Would you mind getting it, please, Miss Eleanor?"

Outside, Eleanor paused; an early autumn morning, the prettiest October day she could imagine. The red and gold leaves dappled the hospital grounds, rustling when a sudden gust of wind made them laugh. God, she'd hardly noticed the change in season. Stop dreaming; Mr. Washington, *tummy medicine.*

The car was one of those decade-old Subaru hatchbacks you occasionally see on the road; the car door wasn't locked. Mr. Washington kept it neat as a pin. A pair of fawn driving gloves lay in the well between the seats. A plastic Jesus stuck on the dash.

The glove compartment squared away as well: registration and insurance in a plastic see-through folder, a pen, a pencil, but not even one lone candy wrapper. The bottle of pink cement, cap tight, half gone. She grabbed it and snapped the glove compartment shut.

Suddenly the sound of car engines broke the quiet October morning. A troop of vehicles rolled toward Eleanor through the hospital grounds, slowly negotiating the fallen gates. A mud-splattered white minivan with the sliding door dented, then a yellow Toyota 4Runner, running very ragged. Next a rumbling Gran Torino muscle car, and last a big boxy Honda Pilot that seemed to catch sight of Eleanor. The Honda jumped the curved driveway, making a straight beeline for her as she stood by the porch of the gabled house near Mr. Washington's old Subaru.

The large SUV pulled up in a spit of gravel and halted; the window powered down. A very familiar face stared out at her through the light mesh of a bug hat. Oh my God, *Lauren!* Her sister struggled out the car door, gushing, "Eleanor! Eleanor, we were so worried."

They hugged, sister holding sister, one still gripping the pink plastic bottle. Eleanor looked curiously down at her hand. Oh yes, Mr. Washington's Pepto-Bismol. "This is for a friend," she tried to explain. Then managed, "Lauren darling, I think you can take off that silly hat. We don't have mosquitoes here. Not many, anyway. They spray. And it was kind of cold last night."

Eleanor caught a glint of something terrible in her sister's eyes—a weight of pain and suffering, some terrible thing she kept inside. However, before Eleanor could say anything, the other cars arrived, crunching gravel as they halted; the engines died. One by one, the drivers and passengers got out of their cars, and Eleanor felt an incredible sense of déjà vu. Of course Bhakti had been mentioning all these people in texts, spastic e-mails, or disconnected phone calls for thousands of miles and weeks on the road.

First out of the white minivan came a handsome Native American, his smooth black hair combed back, a lean and haunted face like a movie-star Indian. One Who Has Seen Much. That had to be William Howahkan, Billy Shadow. Bhakti was always talking about how much he admired Billy's clear and open mind, a mixture of the sensible and stoic. The man who kept the Zero Degree freezer tote with the burnt ear. *Good God,* Eleanor wondered. *Did he still have it?*

Next, a large woman got out of the neon purple Gran Torino. Beatrice the roadhouse saloonkeeper, the gang's most recent addition to their rolling rescue squad—Webster's Big Sis. Big Bea was something out of *Road Warrior*: a Kevlar vest, ammo pouches, and a shoulder holster with a gun in it. The big woman unclipped her rig and laid it on the hood of the muscle car, sighing, free of its weight.

"Isn't that Big Bea?" Eleanor asked her sister. Then a much more familiar figure got out of the yellow SUV. That had to be Cheryl Gibson, Bhakti's companion since the fortune-teller, from the beginning almost. Eleanor felt like she'd known the woman Bhakti called "Shiva princess" all her life. She ran to Cheryl with a smile. The lady cop's eyes welled with tears, she was so glad and speechless to finally meet the woman she knew so much about. Eleanor's eyes welled up too; she could feel a big gusher coming on when she saw Cheryl clutched something in her arms—a metal urn. Janet's ashes. Janet, her Janet, in a metal urn.

Oh God. *Janet.*

Then it swept over Eleanor—everything since the first day of her Braincast madness. She never went to find her baby, not once, letting Bhakti do it all.

Instead, letting the Light Tesla take her places and show her things at the Ant Colony—even though she knew from the very second her daughter didn't come home Janet was gone for good. And for a brief moment Eleanor was back in their Van Horn house staring out the plate-glass window while the Chen house burned down and Bhakti came and went and came and went, driving across the desert like a madman. Had there been no other way? No *other* way? And only when she got half sane in this crazy place did she think, *I got better when Janet vanished.* How horrible for a mother to think that, even though she could walk. I gave birth to her and my leg died; Janet went away and my leg came back. *How horrible to think that.*

And now this lady cop stood before her with Janet in a metal urn. Her baby in a metal container clutched in another woman's arms . . . Cheryl slowly approached Eleanor, holding out Janet's ashes and saying again, "I'm glad you're still walking. That's good."

And it almost made sense when Eleanor said, "One of the bugs bit me, and I can walk." She took the urn with Janet's ashes and cradled it gently in her arms.

But then it struck her all at once. Who didn't get out of a car. Who was missing.

Eleanor's eyes flitted from one figure to the next. A huge lump growing in her throat, she still blindly expected him to appear; to get out of a car and stride across the fallen leaves, arms outstretched, looking like he hadn't trimmed his beard all summer, his whiskers coming to a funny point; putting his arms around her, telling her he loved her, that he'd always love her. And Eleanor could stroke his face, holding a tuft of beard and tugging it gently. Telling him, *I should trim this. Do you want me to?*

But all she could stammer was:

"Where's Bhakti?"

27

❦

The Good Humor Man

Jasper, at death's doorstep, was dying of the unlikely, the first case of insect-borne malaria in the continental United States since the 1940s. Would anyone notice? Probably not. The Sioux Falls Sanford Health Center was a madhouse of crazed men and women bouncing off the hospital walls: the sick, the hopeless, and those helpless to help them. In the last twenty-four hours hemorrhagic smallpox in South Dakota had jumped the military's cordon sanitaire, strangling the reservations.

Obviously, the wild red man had indulged his lust for freedom, selfishly spreading disease into the white man's world instead of dying quietly so no one would notice. In Sioux Falls at least, payback was a bitch. The Sanford Health Center battling the plague had all but lost the war.

Oozing, dripping, moaning patients from across the city were stacked on every available gurney and bed. Extra foam mattresses from a supply of backup bedding mandated by Homeland Security in the event of a blizzard lay on the hallway floors. Alas, when it came to weeping sores these foam pads became hemorrhagic incubators, like sponges sprouting mildew. Worse than useless. On his way upstairs Lattimore passed a dozen or so patients lying on the floor quietly leaking into the nasty things, others writhing like dogs chewing their sores.

He passed a young female nurse of about twenty, who seemed a lot smarter than her age, arguing with the attending physician, who seemed a lot dumber than his. The nurse had boxed the doctor into a corner and was trying to talk some sense into his thick skull. The attending physician was on the bad side of fifty; a man long ago given up on his faith in science, on his powers to cure, but still wanting to be seen to care.

Pinned to his lab coat a veritable rainbow of Awareness Ribbons, from the familiar red signifying AIDS Awareness, to pearl, to orange to yellow and blue and magenta and all the weird colors in between: burgundy, periwinkle, turquoise, teal—"awareness" of every condition from primary biliary cirrhosis to obsessive-compulsive disorder— just too many pinned on a single white lab coat to care about anybody in particular.

"I'm sorry, it's the protocol," he feebly argued. "We have the protocols posted downstairs. In an emergency use the government foam mattresses. That's the protocol."

Nonsense on stilts. "Just lay them on the floor; then we can mop up with disinfectant!" The young nurse waved her hands in his face, exasperated at this imbecile. "This is no good! Just look at them!"

But the best Doctor Awareness could manage was, "I'm sorry, that's just the rule," refusing the sensible suggestion to get rid of the pest-house foam pads. Lattimore almost smacked some sense into the jerk, but stopped short when he caught the doctor's tie. A Felix the Cat tie. A white tie with Felix's black grinning catty face pulled up tight against the man's white shirt collar.

The attending physician reached into his lab coat, found an atomizer almost exactly like the one Security Chief Walter Nash used, stuck it up his nose, and inhaled. He snorted hard, snuffing up every particle, then looked at the empty vial with deep resentment. How dare the damn thing run out now?

Lattimore kept going.

His CTO sat up in bed when he came in. Jasper's eyes were extremely dark, his face extremely pale. Between bouts of chills and fever his voice came out in a whisper. "Sounds like a bloody riot downstairs."

"Yeah." Lattimore nodded. "Right out of Bedlam."

"Hah," Jasper croaked.

He slid his laptop toward the edge of the bed. "This is the latest. Nothing new from our satellite over Bermuda; the container ship *Anja*'s still disappeared in a large fog bank. However, I bought some additional satellite time on your AmEx card and tasked it north of the Lower Forty-eight for a while. We got some serious frequency signatures in Alaska."

"Lemme guess," Lattimore said. "The antenna array in Gakona. The High Frequency Active Auroral Research guys, the lads from HAARP, are getting excited, tuning up their heavenly tuning forks. Funny how nobody in charge of tasking government satellites objected to Lattimore Aerospace spying on them on one of our leased satellites."

"At a million dollars a minute the government could use the money you paid." Jasper smiled, his lips cracked with fever. "Besides, maybe the NORAD tracking folks are too sick to care. Or asleep at the switch." He swallowed. "Either way, wouldn't want *that getting around,* now would you?"

Clem Lattimore chuckled darkly.

"No way. I'd shoot first and ask questions later if anybody hinted at such a lie."

Jasper coughed and held his head, his face going green with pain. "Dammit!" he cried. The spasm passed. He paused, panting, his eyeballs rolling in and out of focus. "I don't think the hit squad from the Men in Black is going to beat my liver to it. If you could rustle me up an iced tea or nice tall Coke with lots of ice, that'd be great."

He pushed the laptop another inch toward the edge of the bed.

"Take that with you," Jasper said about the PC. "I don't

want anybody finding it here thinking I know anything of consequence. Magnetize it if you have to."

Lattimore sighed quietly; he snapped the thing closed, tucked it under his arm, and headed out on last requests. An iced tea or a nice Coke.

He need not have bothered.

There wasn't any iced tea anymore. No more Coca-Cola.

A run on the hospital's food services had looted the cafeteria clean. Seems like a lot of people wanted iced tea with Sweet'N Low at the end of the world. Could you blame them? When Clem Lattimore came back from his fruitless search, Jasper the living man was gone. The CTO had died with a frown of frustration on his forehead; alas, he'd failed to unravel even one little secret of the universe. Lattimore closed Jasper's eyes and tugged a length of bedsheet over the dead man's face.

As if to give the boss one last farewell, Jasper's arm slipped out from under the covers. Lattimore examined the wayward hand. The skin was still livid, red weals where a vise-grip had held him down. Both wrists. The extra pillow in the room on the chair showed a clear facial impression. Jasper's frown was from a smothered face.

The guys in suits and ties had paid poor Jasper a visit as the CTO lay in bed. Guys who'd never allow some tech-head to retask space hardware over classified tundra. Nobody gets to know stuff like that and live to talk about it. Lattimore's eyes flashed up and down the hospital hallway.

Empty. They'd come. They'd gone.

And still, no personal computer to show for all their effort, because the laptop tagged along on an errand for an iced tea or a nice Coke. The thought of operatives coming to tie up loose ends like Jasper made Clem's hands tremble. Would he have tried to stop them? A dagger of shame touched him. He'd never find out.

But it made him hesitate before trying to leave the place. Sure, he needed to get back to his own digs, batten down the hatches. But if he walked out now bold as brass he might as well run out the front entrance naked as a jaybird. Whoever got Jasper would get him for sure.

All his life he'd tried to protect against an accident, against disaster. Now of all things, he wished he had thought to install an electromagnetic pulse device in the lead-lined subbasement in the event he wanted to wipe his records clean. Nut-bag thinking.

EMP blast or no EMP blast, the storm troopers in suits and ties would come for him anyway. Right now getting back home was the problem—how the hell to get out of this charnel house?

Somebody'd be watching; maybe waiting in the hospital elevator ready to grab him when the doors opened. Forget the elevator; use the stairs. He found the emergency door, bumped through it, and headed down. One flight, then another. Bodies lay on the icky foam mattresses in the stairwells. He stepped over and around them, but missed, feeling the damp foam squish under his heel. At last, he reached the delivery bay at the rear of the hospital. Sick people lay on the concrete floor of the storage area, weakly groaning and reaching out for help.

Lattimore saw a new crop of doctors and nurses gliding between the rows of foam mattresses, coming to help the inflicted. Long, tall doctors and nurses in long white coats. Long white coats and long gray arms with three fingers; long arms and teardrop-shaped heads with black sunglasses. No, those weren't sunglasses; those were their big black eyes. Tiny mouths and no nostrils. *Hey, Clem, Is your dad My Favorite Martian?* Or are these the dudes who come from Uranus? The Grays from Lost Vegas.

"I hate hallucinations," he said to nobody in particular as he slid toward a gritty corner of the delivery bay. Gingerly he let himself down by a huge unopened carton of prepackaged, empty plasma bags, where he wouldn't crack his head or smack the laptop. One of those funny light balls glided across the concrete floor. The Taker was getting ready to take him away.

"Oh, it's you again," Lattimore remarked. "What the hell do you want this time?"

Then he thought better of being rude. If this was going to be a last request, might as well make it a nice place to go. "How about the Tea House of the Hidden Moon? Take me there, and I won't complain." The globe of light hovered for a moment.

That would be nice. Go back to the chuckling stream, the bluebird, the wise old cricket for company. Sit down for a Japanese tea ceremony and have a cup of *cha*. Heaven on Earth. The Taker went inside his skull and drifted out the back of his head like a passing thought.

No such luck.

Lattimore stepped into a dingy room overlooking the Whiteside Meatpacking Plant "Recycling" section. No Webster Chargrove, PhD; the grim office empty. Cautiously, Lattimore crept out the open door, into a dingier hall. Easy fellah, one step at a time. Was he really standing in the underground πr^2 complex? Or had he become some kind of apparition, a mind glider, lacking true substance?

Now that he thought about it, his other mind glides were partly physical. In Antarctica he'd felt the green grass under his feet. Inside the container ship he'd turned off simmering stew on a stove; then climbed into the Tea House trailer. In Alaska he'd chased a cafeteria tray into the stream and lost a shoe.

He cautiously followed hallways and doorways toward the operational center. The floors became progressively cleaner, then metallic and tubular. He halted before a biologically sealed transparent hazmat airlock. Four men in white lab coats stood at a railing; Lattimore glimpsed a gantry overlooking a surgery theater. The warning lights went from red to blue for entry, and the transparent door opened with a *whoosh*. One of the observers said, "They need me in blood pharming," and turned from the rail. He walked right by Lattimore as though the CEO of the aero-space company didn't exist. So that answered that. On *this* mind glide the Takers didn't want his presence known, let-ting him hide in plain sight. And luckily too—if anyone caught him in this human Habitrail they'd lock him in a steel room and throw away the key.

Lattimore took the man's spot at the viewing glass, com-pletely ignored. Through an adjoining glass wall a battery of technicians stared at large consoles like some kind of electronic jury. The specimen on the table had grown too long for his khakis, the pale blue Oxford shirt, tie, jacket, a white lab coat. The seams of his lab coat popped in places, making the figure look pathetic and comical at the same time. Its head and shoulders covered with a large swathe of blue sterilized surgery fabric. The remains on the oper-ating table completely the wrong shape. Too long, too skinny and the head not right.

A lecture was already in progress. Beside the specimen on the table, the clean, shaven face of the professor looked up, addressing the observers on the gantry. His white halo of hair a luminescent ring about his skull; his lips moved like a large white guppy speaking up from a lily pond.

"The Wild Three comet-derived glycine seems to have produced an unpredictable side effect in one of our col-leagues. As you can see, two digits lost on the hands."

The professor lifted the dead wrist of the body on the table, the skin purplish gray; a shrunken stub where the pinkie and ring finger had melted away, leaving a utilitar-ian three prongs: two pincers and an opposing thumb, all three digits extremely long.

"Similar toe loss on the feet and loss of genitalia. The epidermis—the skin itself—is extremely receptive to white light, yellow to red on the spectrum. But at the same time the skin has more in common with asbestos than our porous body covering, allowing the creature to work in the presence of intense heat. Moreover, the epidermis does not breathe; in fact we do not believe the organism breathes at all. This specimen, which we are calling Model-A, was designed to operate, that is *work,* in the dark, at great depths and pressures. Underwater, for instance. But as it developed here at sea level its cell structure erupted. A form of decompression sickness, cellular rupture, similar to the bends.

"We speculate this model to be malformed, missing its twin capabilities: those being the ability to work under intense pressure per square inch, and operate where there is little to no pressure. That is to say in a vacuum. Correctly formed it could function both under great PSI and under virtually none. This mutation lacks the ability to work in space."

He paused for a breath. "What we're looking at is what might have been a standard model. Had it formed correctly it has no natural biological drawbacks and nearly indestructible DNA. This creature photosynthesizes at the extreme end of the short-wave light band: ultraviolet light, X-rays. All it needs is a drop of moisture, a grain of nitrous-rich fertilizer, and starlight does the rest. Heats itself with bioluminescence like a firefly. Work anywhere. Do anything. Live forever."

He flicked a corner of the sterile gauze covering the head. No hair, but some extra tissue about the size of a grapefruit had erupted out of the bald skull as if blown out like a balloon.

"He seems to have wanted to grow a bigger brain. Naturally, the decompression permanently crippled the emerging organism before it could evolve; technically dead, though there appear to be traces of continued cell replication, and little or no decomposition. The brain matter itself seems to be more mineral than animal or vegetable. Carbon-based, naturally."

All that made sense to Lattimore. If you wanted to colonize or groom a planet, you'd have to work underwater, work in orbit, work in extreme places. Even coming back after eons, across the gulf of a galaxy, the herdsmen of the stars would need an indigenous, "native" herdsman, pre-adapted to the planet. What they couldn't bring from space, they'd have to breed right here.

"And there were in the same country shepherds abiding in the field, keeping watch over their flock by night."

Only there was something good and pastoral about human shepherds in the Bible—and absolutely nothing benevolent about this creature. The creature had moved beyond such minor concerns as good or evil, a life force grown in a petri dish with no morality involved. Manipulated molecules, genes, and DNA for ends that not even the creature understood.

For a brief second, the uncovered sterile gauze on Model-A slipped to reveal more of his old human clothes—the white laboratory coat, split at the shoulders, a breast pocket, a pocket protector with glasses and pens. And underneath the breast pocket the subject's name embroidered onto the lab coat. Personalized. The letters were pretty small, but Lattimore could just make them out. Bright, embroidered letters in blue thread, spelling out a name:

Chargrove.

The narrow, methodical face of the professor continued the analysis. "There's been some lively discussion as to what effect, if any, this unanticipated malformation may have on our present efforts to alleviate the spread of various diseases. Some bright minds around here speculate that the introduction of the Chen-L alleles will accelerate the mutation. What a few of our resident comics call the young lady's 'God particles.'"

He paused and harrumphed, clearly putting God and un-intended consequences in their proper place, being somewhere at the back of the class, if not on the short bus.

"I'm of the opinion that the introduction of the Chen girl biochemistry will only enhance our broad-spectrum inoculation efforts. Since none of the other test subjects have undergone this evolution, or malformation, it is safe to say we possess some kind of natural protein suppressor in the human body, or combination of antigens that our young colleague may have been lacking. Hence, only Chargrove's biochemistry, *his biomolecules,* were open to the change. Him and only him. This can't be the first comet dust to hit our planet. Most of us must have this genetic blocker. Otherwise we'd all be walking around with big heads and three fingers."

One of the white-coated scientists nearby chuckled. Lattimore recalled his paranoid hallucination from the floor of the Sioux Falls Health Center: a kind of premonition—the long-fingered doctors gliding back and forth. . . .

"In any case, we'll find out soon enough whether this is merely an anomaly or part of a larger evolutionary change. Our special locator team has traced the female from Indianapolis Methodist Hospital to New York and expects to secure the Chen-L specimen within twenty-four hours. We anticipate initial blood pharming within forty-eight hours. And then inoculation via our latest generation of Skeeters, which will home into designated individuals' alleles, our Noah's Children." He took a breath. Clearly, the thought of choosing who was to live and who to die made this cerebral monster practically glow with joy. Not merely playing God, but being Him.

"Of course it won't be a mass inoculation—only fifty or sixty thousand within the first week. But within following weeks we expect to make our ultimate choices, designate our final Celestials at no more than three million in the continental United States: sufficient population to regenerate society. Not only will you have to be stung, but you will have to be stung by one of ours. We anticipate that within three generations the country will have returned to Second World War population levels. About 130 million people, more than enough to ensure dominance—"

Lattimore started to feel faint. The creature on the table slowly sat up, the sterile gauze falling from its elongated body, and the late Webster Chargrove, PhD, pointed to the viewing area with his gray three fingers, addressing him without spoken words. *They mean just the elite, the connected, the selected, a Noah's Ark of the anointed. I'll put in a good word for Lattimore Aerospace. They'll need satellites before too long.*

He could feel a Taker hovering nearby, getting ready for a mind glide. A haze of starbursts and sparklers lit up his brain. Clem Lattimore felt the Taker sweeping him away. Bye-bye American Pi. The Big *They* always got away with it. Deciding who got into the club and who didn't. Sorry, you're not on the list.

Lattimore woke up on the concrete floor of the health center loading area.

No hallucinations, no gray alien doctors tending sick patients on pus-soaked foam mattresses. His lower arm and elbow had gone to sleep against the large cardboard box of plasma bags. The pins and needles of returning circulation frizzled into his forearm. He shook it a bit to help the blood along, then examined his skin. Hemorrhagic smallpox worked fast, so if there weren't lesions on him by now, he probably wouldn't contract it.

No lesions. But he'd woken in the land of the dead.

Wherever he looked—the delivery bay, out onto the street in broad daylight—nothing moved. He stumbled outside and found his car in the lot. The only other movement he saw on his way to the aerospace building was a white Good Humor Ice Cream truck. The Good Humor Ice Cream truck cruised along a side street, chimes echoing. Yet no children came running out to greet it, and the white truck turned a corner, vanishing from sight.

Lattimore pulled up to the empty aerospace building and went through the bronze glass doors. Nobody manned the reception desk. A terrifying sense of quiet descended on him. Drop a pin you'd jump out of your shoes. He became almost teary when the voice-recognition system inside the elevator let him back in his apartment with a *"Welcome Home, Clem."*

He sank gratefully into the leather couch in the library and stared at the decanter of bourbon on the shelf, but couldn't muster the energy to pour one. He set Jasper's laptop on the glass coffee table, wondering idly if he still should wipe its memory clean with a magnet. But since the Men in Black weren't knocking down his door he let the machine boot up. Jasper had left it open for him, no encryption, and no password.

Immediately, dozens of windows flashed at him like an e-mail bomb, a massive stream of data scrolling at Lattimore from the laptop screen. But this data was coming from HAARP. His late CTO seemed to have latched on to the High Frequency Active Auroral Research Program's real-time command consoles, the actual Operations Center data stream—no mere satellite flyby. You'd think for security reasons, the HAARP control room would be closed-circuit, but you'd be wrong—there'd always be some Air Force general or federal appointee who'd require access from somewhere other than Gakona, Alaska.

The info jumping out of the screen was what the technicians saw when they revved up their heavenly tuning fork: every panel on every monitor in that faraway facility. Huge amounts of data. Naturally, Lattimore couldn't read most of it. He vaguely began to grasp the various power and frequency modulations in the arrays: wattage and voltage and a hundred other ways to measure it. Other data streams were dedicated to areas of ionization, latitude, longitude, and altitude. Another satellite data feed showed upper-atmospheric weather conditions, temperature, wind direction, velocity, and barometric readings.

Then by dumb luck, he found a master model—a visual

representation of the data, a real-time computer graphics image; a map of the Earth in high def in 360 degrees like the ultimate Google Earth app. You could see the jet streams moving, sucking moisture from the oceans and sending it down in rain across the globe. Up from the oceans and down to the ground. A superimposed touch button read GENERAL WINTER, a model projection of cause and effect. A countdown clock below the touch button unwound the hours and minutes until launch. Lattimore clicked on the touch button and watched the screen change.

Now the picture zoomed northward; the rectangular HAARP antenna array in Gakona, Alaska, began to blink. A stream of excited electrons leapt to the sky, pushing against the ionosphere. A vast air blister in the atmosphere rose up over the dome of the Artic. The altitude counter read: 86.3745 MILES/139.006 KILOMETERS. The blister tugged everything on its stratospheric plane toward it. Moving jet streams glided across the sky as the huge bubble drew them out of their natural paths. Moisture was drawn to more northern latitudes, and snow began to form. A lot of snow. Then the snow began to swirl and gather in huge purple storms.

Storms over Greenland and Scandinavia.

Storms from the Alps to the Himalayas, covering Europe and Eurasia and as far down as New Delhi. Storms smothered China, Japan, and the Korean Peninsula. For the first time in history Ho Chi Minh City saw snow and freezing rain.

A great cloud formed over Kamchatka on the Bering Sea, crossed the Pacific and approached Canada and California. The mother of all storms picked up steam across the High Sierras and even more steam over the Rockies, dumping snow from British Columbia and Manitoba to Mexico City.

Lattimore held his breath. Jesus. *That's* what they were planning? The HAARP antenna array was going to rearrange the *weather*? He could almost feel the pulse and throb of the ultra-low frequency coming out of the damn screen. And now Lattimore understood why his Takers had mind-glided him to that cold spot in Alaska where he'd chased a cafeteria tray into a stream. It was their way of showing him, so he'd understand.

Up there in the far north, some bright boy at HAARP had either figured it out for himself or been tipped off that the annoying whining in his ears was mosquitoes spreading disease. And because there were so many multiple pathologies, the best way to counteract the plague was to go after the contagion. In this case a bug. Kill the bug; kill the spread of disease. How do you kill a bug that needs killing? Spray the world with DDT? There'd never be enough DDT.

Bring on winter. Bury it in snow and ice. Freeze its buggy ass.

So lemme get this straight, Lattimore thought to himself. . . .

What are we seeing here?

One government outfit run by Herr Doktor Frankenstein, a geneticist working overtime to inoculate a fraction of the U.S. population with ancient alien comet dust laced with Girl God particles. All in the hope a few lucky souls would survive, despite overwhelming evidence that showed inoculation turned average young geneticists into malformed, asbestos-skinned, deep-sea divers whose brains blew up.

Swell plan.

While another government outfit far from the Lower 48 was warming up their antenna array, getting ready to blast thunderbolts of ultra-low-frequency waves into the stratosphere to suck the jet streams from their normal global pathways, drawing moisture into colder climes. Move the weather around. Send an ice age to North America before all the leaves fell off the trees, and the insects were still flying out of their breeding swamps.

The brilliant Plan B.

Two government outfits working against each other: one group working underground, sending mosquitoes to select the chosen, while a pincushion of antenna heads in Alaska tried to kill every bug by shooting lightning bolts at the heavens.

What could possibly go wrong?

Lattimore gently closed Jasper's laptop. If government guys still wanted to kill him for those two state secrets, they should have their heads examined. The diseases had already flown from coast to coast.

Lattimore flipped on the TV, only to see smiley-face news programs featuring lower-level government officials talking in circles. The White House had brought in experts for consultation and was monitoring the situation. They expected things to turn around any day now, *and no, there was no emergency to speak of.* No, nobody from DC was going to ride in on a white horse to save the day.

Yet even at the end of October the mask of civilization sat firmly in place as power stations with skeleton crews kept the juice going. A saving grace. Nobody born in the country had ever lived *without* electricity. The nuke plants might go for years, but sooner or later the coal-and-oil-fired installations would run out of fuel as train freight slowed to a halt. Spot outages would turn into rationing, which would turn into favoritism. Emergency regulations would require that residents in big cities only flush their toilets on alternate days, turn on their tap water either a.m. or p.m., and ride an elevator only if they dared.

On impulse, Lattimore rose from the couch, went into his spotless kitchen, and opened the refrigerator. . . . Leftover cream of tomato soup, wrinkled carrots, limp celery, an onion. A-1 Steak Sauce. No steak. A tin of anchovies, the thin metal cover peeled back. Great. Only a matter of weeks before the human marsupials would be fighting over Princella sweet potatoes in the canned vegetable aisle.

As if to punctuate this thought, a fire engine siren rose

from the streets, and he was drawn to the bronze-colored windows overlooking the city. Doubtless, some fire departments would still respond to fires, some emergency rooms still treat patients, but you couldn't know who and you wouldn't know where. Without mass communication, the gasp of despair could only travel as far as the human voice could carry. If the wandering sickness didn't get you, you'd still have to survive bad weather as Plan B went into effect. Sure, life would go on, an epic scrounge for food and shelter. . . .

The siren's wail faded into the distance; then, as if to mock him, the carefree chimes of the Good Humor Man reached his ears through the thick bronze glass. At the company entrance, the Good Humor Ice Cream truck pulled up to the curb and came to a halt in the No Parking zone. A figure emerged from the driver's side. A woman went around to the side of the white truck, opened the door, and began to unload frozen boxes from the interior. A very familiar woman.

Mildred! Mildred the dowdy cashier from the Cosmos Café downstairs. What the hell was she doing? Unloading ice cream crates out of the back of an ice cream truck? No, not ice cream. The crates looked like boxes of frozen burgers: meat and fish and chicken. Then it dawned on Lattimore. *Hah!* Mildred was scrounging whatever she could from local supermarkets or dead people's refrigerators.

Food. Food for when things got ugly.

Impressive foresight. Damn near took your breath away.

A middle-aged woman on the lowest rung of the company showing the great captain of industry how you hoped for the best, but prepared for the worst. Put frozen supplies in the Cosmos Café food locker. *Smart thinking, Mildred.*

Lattimore tore himself from the window. *Go and help the lady, chucklehead.*

Stairs or elevator? Don't be an ass. Stairs.

28

The Last Halloween

Billy Shadow stood outside Granny's silver trailer. The overcast sky made him want to bow his head. An October wind came over the burnt hills, luffing his jacket like a sail. How strange the place looked, newer and larger than he remembered; the high silver door of the trailer seemed to tower above him, the sage grass beyond the path nearly reaching his waist.

He looked at his own hands—grungy kid's hands that didn't get washed often enough. The dungarees, the scuffed Keds sneakers; he was a youngster again. He'd come to show Granny the wolf whistle. Staring at it in his hand, he brought the whistle to his lips and gave it three big wolfie whoops. *Woo-Woo-WOO!* Then patiently waited for Granny Sparrow to come to the door.

But no one came. She didn't answer.

Gingerly, he climbed the wooden trailer steps, unlatched the door, and stepped inside. The place seemed very dark and very quiet. Granny Sparrow lay in her bed under the trailer's rear window; the American flag tacked up to dim the light from outside cast a purplish hue across Granny's covers. She was gently sleeping, but as he approached, her eyes opened. Her face on the pillow turned toward his own. She looked old—older than history, older than death.

"Billy boy." Her voice was dry as parchment. "Do you know what people want right before they die?"

Granny was talking about your last wish. He shook his head no. Billy didn't know what people wanted right before they died. He fingered the silent wolf whistle in his hand. Granny Sparrow breathed hard, eyes challenging him to understand.

"You want to be naked," she told him. "So God can see you as he made you."

She smiled at him, the smile of life out of a face of a thousand wrinkles. Her bony fingers plucked a bit of quilt off her shoulder, revealing her old nightgown, and over that her old housecoat, which she wore even under the covers. "Almost as naked as God made me." She smiled. But Billy knew what she meant: naked to your core, naked to your soul.

Silently, he offered her his shiny silver wolf whistle. So she could call him when she wanted him. No matter where he was, no matter how far away—

A bony claw drew him closer, face to face. Granny Sparrow whispering a children's ditty like they read in kindergarten: *"Ring around the rosie, pocketful of posies, ashes, ashes . . . We All Fall Down!"*

A hand slapped Billy's face, bringing him back to the interrogation tent. The hand wore a powder-blue nitrile glove.

"Ring around the rosies," Billy slurred.

The hand in the latex glove struck him again. Spittle swiped across his chin. No, not spittle, blood. How long had the roadhouse folks been at the field command? More than a few days. A week? Three weeks? Time came and went. It felt like a long time.

"Pocketful of posies—" Billy mumbled.

Whap, the hand came back. "C'mon pay attention," a voice said sternly.

"Ashes, ashes, we all fall down."

Whap. "C'mon, don't make me keep asking."

Billy glanced down at his wrists cuffed to the camp chair. Plastic restraints. He didn't feel like moving anyway. Major Todd's face swam in and out of his vision, the man's expression less indulgent, more hostile. Something else about the officer. Major Todd had grown *older,* his face deeply lined, pouches under his eyes, and wattles where his Adam's apple used to be. Major Todd was trying to explain something, but Billy couldn't follow the man's moving lips. They doped the food or water; doping made a prisoner more cooperative, easier to handle. But it also made you stupid.

"You know there are guys around here who want to make you into sushi, serve you on rice with pickled ginger, figuring you're some kind of fountain of youth."

Why not? Very understandable. Billy and the others had traveled halfway across the country without catching so much as the sniffles; hard not to see them as powerful medicine. Major Todd's voice rattled around in his head.

"Others around here want to bow down and kiss the hem of your robe."

Major Todd twisted Billy's face toward his own. He pointed to the wrinkles, the sagging skin. He bared his lips, exposing his mouth. Major Todd's bloodless gums had turned white, his teeth black. Methuselah. "You know what this is, my good Red Buddy?"

Nopey-dopey.

"Cutaneous erythropoietic protoporphyria." Quite a mouthful. "*Porphyria* for short. Literally, 'skin blood cell purple,' a metabolic disorder. I'm not quite purple yet, but there are other side effects. Usually not fatal. Just grotesque. Ignorant peasants used to think people with this condition were vampires. But if it keeps advancing, I'm thinking this affliction is going to leave me at the pearly gates."

Major Todd saw he'd lost his doped-up prisoner back at "cutaneous." He tweaked Billy's ear to get his attention. Billy's head jerked up; his eyes made contact.

"You see, some of my desperados are looking for a few pints of Kickapoo Joy Juice. My hotheads are more than ready, willing, and able to drain you dry, drink every drop, and throw away the husk." He let that settle in for a moment. "While the other half of my men think you're fucking

God, and should be worshipped. Are you fucking God, Your Worship? Is that who's keeping you alive? Fucking God?"

Billy's ears hurt at the sound of these ugly words. He didn't know the answer. Major Todd was afraid for his life. And terrified men say terrible things—the shameful, the profane. Did the man even want a real answer? Perhaps he wanted nothing but to know God existed. Lacking faith, you demand proof. *Proof in exchange for faith.* Deal or no deal? Sorry, Major Todd, no deal.

Whap, the hand came again. The tent went away.

Then Billy woke up again. How long? Maybe an hour; maybe a day. A profound quiet seemed to pervade the temporary holding compound. Major Todd sat across the table just as he had for ages; the freezer tote with the magic remains between them, the dog tags and religious keepsakes in a tangled pile. The limp blue gloves tossed aside. The old soldier's head was folded to his chest. Bleached white skin sagged from his skull; livid purple streaked the craters of his cheeks, a fright mask of decrepitude. Prune-face. Major Todd had died of extreme old age.

Billy felt he should comfort the man, maybe pray for his salvation. . . .

A minute and a thousand years too late.

Billy tried to rise, but his wrists kept him pinned to the chair. He'd forgotten about the plastic cuffs. Overhead the tent creaked a little, a lonely sound. Billy tried to reach the plastic bands around his wrists with his mouth. No luck.

Too bad he couldn't do the Skin Walker thing now, turn into a puddy tat and slip his paws out of the shackles. Faintly Billy could hear Granny blowing the wolf whistle all the way back in South Dakota, the forlorn sound like a lonely train coming down the line. The spiritual rang softly in his head: *"People get ready. There's a train a-coming. You don't need no baggage. You just get on board. All you need is faith. To hear the diesels humming. Don't need no ticket. You just thank the Lord. . . ."*

He saw a tiny cut on his wrist where he'd been tugging at his straps. *Yeah, yank that thing.* A couple more days sitting in this camp chair he'd have a nice infection. Paralysis. Gangrene. Rot to death. Oh, there's a train a-coming—

The tent flap whisked back, and Billy caught a flash of chain-link fencing, the soft light of dawn. Bhakti stood under the metal-shaded lamp. The Punjabi scientist glanced around for a moment, examined the dead soldier at the camp table. Not much reaction; Bhakti had hardened to the point where dead people didn't impress him so much anymore. The *Indian* Indian frowned at the American Indian as though he'd caught Little Drunken Feather snoring off a night of Jim Beam.

"Oh, there you are. We've been looking for you."

He picked the hematite earring out of the tangled pile of trinkets on the camp table. "I've been looking for this too." He examined the baggie with the burnt ear and its own earring; Bhakti sighed. He stuck the earring from Lila's dresser in the baggie and zipped it closed; a baggie, an ear, and two matching earrings.

"Maybe it's time we kept these together so they don't get lost."

O utside the interrogation tent, the troopers had set up a fenced perimeter and a maze of chain-link corridors connected to a dozen holding tents, as though the military were expecting more detainees. But the new customers had failed to materialize, and Major Todd's entire outfit had quietly passed away in the night, like their commanding officer—of galloping old age. The two men stepped over motionless bodies; a couple of soldiers died on their knees, hunched over in prayer. Waiting for Godot.

They found Cheryl and Beatrice in their own tent,

rumpled blankets on the canvas cots showing where the women had slept all this time. The two women stared blearily at the men as though recovering from an eight-day bender. The ladies seemed to have been treated fairly well during their detention despite being doped to the gills. Periods of sleep, half-eaten meals, trips to the shower tent, the porta-potties, then back to the cots again. Bea's leg brace lay on her cot, like an extra limb. With great effort, she groggily strapped it on.

They found a Humvee outside the compound with gas in the tank and keys in the ignition. Back at the roadhouse, Big Bea opened the door and walked into her dark saloon and they silently gathered around the bar to regroup and reassess. The saloonkeeper flipped on the spotlights and the television came on too: a test pattern of Felix the Cat.

A groan of disgust rippled around the bar; Bea snapped the TV off. They drank flat soda without tasting. A pall descended over them, the heavy sedatives leaching out of their systems, leaving them all sapped.

At some point during their drugged-out detention, Major Todd had informed Big Sis that her brother, Webster Chargrove, PhD, would not be making any more mea culpas—ever again. Major Todd spared nothing, recounting every gory detail, hoping to shock Big Sis into spilling what they knew of the security breach. The ploy worked. Beatrice spilled her guts. But what she knew in the end amounted to very little—just her kid brother's video confessions. But as the drugs wore off the grief returned. Big Sis at the bar chewed the gristle of anger and stared pensively at the blank TV.

Cheryl said nothing. The shock of freedom turned to numbness.

When Rachel's ghost reappeared, sitting on the bar and crossing her legs like a torch singer, Cheryl repressed the urge to make sarcastic remarks. Her gal pal leaned close. "Sorry I haven't been around, but I couldn't miss my own

memorial service. Everyone at the firm thought it was nice."
Cheryl's long face brought Rachel up short. "C'mon, don't
go all Gloomy Gus on me. I worked Los Angeles for you. The
will is straightened out, and I convinced the family of the
late lamented Ricardo Montoya to drop the civil suit."

"Great," Cheryl said flatly to no one in particular.

An unspoken question seemed to float silently around
the bar. . . . So *were they really* going to finish the job, find
this girl, Lila Chen, with the godly DNA, and keep her out
of the hands of the Pi R Squared maniacs?

"A logical next step would be nice," Beatrice said to the
ceiling. "Any ideas?" Nobody said anything for a while, as
though not wishing to go first, say something stupid.

"The game show told us where to go," Cheryl said. "*New
York*. That's where Lila's gotta be, along with Maria and
the older boy."

Bea sighed; too much faith, too little reason. She crossed
her arms over her chest, a marble bust of skepticism.

"New York is a big place. Have you ever been there?"

The lady copper pursed her lips. "Grew up in Poughkeepsie, but my mother allowed me to see the Christmas
tree in Rockefeller Center when Daddy put down the beer
can and kicked me off his lap." She took a breath. "Look,
we've done all right so far. Dead ants and a menu on a
windshield, remember?"

"Yes, I know what you told me." Beatrice unlaced her
arms, planting her hands on the bar. "So what's the plan? Get
out your baggie of dead ears and see which way they point?"

"You know, I'm starting to be real sorry we confided
anything to you at all," Cheryl said. Chilly words.

Beatrice left off, got up from the bar, and went over to
the jukebox. The record player had taken quite a beating:
riddled with bullet holes, 45-rpm records shattered inside.
She stared at the holes in the walls where Chaffy the cook
made his last stand.

"She lives at the San Remo; it's an apartment building."

"That's right," Cheryl said. "The little girl told us on the show. So if Top Hat lives there, she probably lives there too."

They shoved off before noon. The lady cop and Beatrice scrounged the saloon for anything useful. The saloon-keeper measured her new pal on the QT, surreptitiously glancing at Cheryl when the other wasn't looking. "Take whatever you think might be useful, Gorgeous. You never know when you'll need a few quarts of mayonnaise and a gallon of canned pickles."

"Or Beer Nuts," Cheryl remarked. *Gorgeous?* Officer Cheryl Gibson, lately of the California Highway Patrol, now known as "Gorgeous," wasn't altogether sure she approved. Still, she hated to admit it—she sorta liked the big gal calling her Gorgeous.

Big Bea came out from the back stumping along on her bum leg, in one hand a red plastic hand-crank fuel pump still in its box. "Who knows what's still working on the interstate," she said. "If we have to get juice out of an underground station tank for three guzzlers you'll wish we had more than one of these things." She also lugged a kind of silver suitcase almost identical to the *Deal or No Deal* case but larger. She slapped the case onto the bar and flipped it open.

"From my field-agent days," Bea explained. Inside black-foam cushion cutouts sat four Motorola walkie-talkies, with car chargers. A couple of semi-auto pistols lay in snug little pockets, along with clips, ammo, and a Kevlar tactical vest with lots of pouches. General-issue postal inspector gear? Cheryl got the feeling there was a lot more to this Beatrice lady than met the eye.

"Did anybody miss this stuff when you took it home?" Cheryl asked.

Big Bea grinned slyly. "Neither rain, nor sleet, nor gloom of night stayed this courier from requisitioning what she needed out of baseline budget for extended field deployment. Know what I mean, Gorgeous?"

Cheryl helped lug their stuff out to the cars. "In the California Highway Patrol we called it *stealing*. If the world still worked I'd pinch one of your hairs out of your hairbrush and run you through Codis."

From outside a car horn honked.

Time to go.

Billy rode alone in the white minivan, and Cheryl rode with Bhakti in the yellow 4Runner, as they had since California. Beatrice turned the key in the Gran Torino, and the engine rumbled like thunder restrained. She put the car in gear and led the way out of town, nice and easy. Despite all the craziness in the big world, nobody in this corner of Ohio seemed to have forgotten Halloween. Yard displays on every block: the jack-o'-lanterns, spiderwebs strung from trees. Cauldrons and skeletons, fake gravestones. An enormous pressurized Casper the Friendly Ghost grinned at them from one front yard.

However, here in Vandalia it was midday, middle of the week, and everyone in town seemed to be sitting in front of their houses like a crowd for a parade, watching the caravan drive down the street: the neon purple Gran Torino in the lead, the white minivan next, and the yellow Toyota with the motorcycle trailer pulling up the rear.

Most of the townsfolk had brought out lawn chairs and coolers like a picnic, occasionally passing around a soda or a beer. The gatherings seemed extremely subdued; people hardly talked to each other. When the children started to get rambunctious, their parents shushed them quiet. A thousand eyes stared as the cars crawled by.

Beatrice picked up her walkie-talkie off the dash and talked into it. "You guys see this? What are they waiting for?"

Major Todd's men may have died of old age in their tent compound, but here everyone seemed healthy. Maybe the major's men had brought their porphyria with them; maybe the Skeeterbugs around these parts were spreading another disease. In any case, none of the onlookers looked too sick just yet.

In the yellow Toyota 4Runner, Cheryl palmed the steering wheel and groped for her radio, which had fallen down the seat crack. Bhakti fished it out, shut it off by mistake, turned it on again too loud, hit the transmission bar a couple of times, and finally fumbled the thing over to her. Cheryl just shook her head and laughed at him; the two had grown so accustomed to each other the thought of riding with anybody else never even occurred. She pressed the transmission button.

"Wanna stop and trick or treat?"

Nobody wanted to stop; the cars crawled down the suburban street.

Many people lifted their eyes to the sky, vacantly staring, like waiting to welcome Elvis off the mothership. Many wore summer clothing; short-sleeve shirts, which seemed a little odd for October. A chill spiked the air as the day lengthened toward afternoon.

Billy Shadow, in the white minivan, picked the walkie-talkie out of a cup holder, thinking about what to say. He shrugged. No clue why the good people of Vandalia took it into their heads to sit in their front yards. Billy didn't feel particularly frightened, only curious; he examined the radio, looking for the transmission button. An answer popped into his head.

"They're waiting to get bit."

Dead silence from everyone in the convoy.

After a moment, Cheryl pressed the transmission. "They're waiting for *what*?"

"It's the Pi R Squared thing."

Again dead silence from the caravan; Billy's voice came through choppy: "Pi R Squared's secret got out; somebody besides Webster blabbed how those kooks planned to inoculate the general population. The process hasn't even started yet. None of the townsfolk know the interceptor

Skeeterbugs are waiting on Lila Chen. These brain donors think if they stand outside, one of the magic mosquitoes will select them. The truth got garbled in translation. *Go outside; get bit; you're immune.*"

"A rumor," Cheryl repeated in quiet awe.

Now they all understood. On this last Halloween, these poor saps had heard the word and just hoped to escape the crawling crud by sitting outside and waiting to get stung by the good government bugs. Hoping against hope the magic mosquitoes would find them attractive. All on a misconception.

As the caravan slowly crawled past the lines of people, this or that person—a granny or a kid, a mama or papa—jumped up, smiling, showing off where they'd been bit. But there were no good bugs out there, just the bad ones that made you sicker.

No one squawked or squelched the walkie-talkies. In the purple Ford Torino Beatrice tossed hers onto the dash. She took a deep breath. Just thinking about that damn place, how they'd turned poor Webster into an elongated freak of nature, made her want to slam the dash. She didn't want to look out the window at the deluded crowds. Let them hope for salvation—it didn't come for Webster; it wouldn't come for them either. Beatrice gripped the wheel and stared through the windshield. No siree Bob, hope may spring eternal, but whether they knew it or not, in Vandalia, they were fresh out.

In the white minivan Billy watched the tragic fools lining their front yards and storefronts, all trying to avoid the reckoning. He tried to remember the last time he'd ever really lost someone. He'd grown up sort of an orphan, so Granny Sparrow was the only one who counted for him now. Was she still lying in bed in the trailer? Or had she given up the last gasp of the wolf whistle? He stared at his cell phone. *Go on; pick it up; make the call.* . . . He let it lie, too afraid to call the only person he cared about in case Granny had caught the bug and wasn't there. *Chicken, go on, make the call.* . . . He reached for the phone, tucked it in his shirt pocket, but still couldn't make the call.

In the yellow SUV Bhakti fiddled with the radio. No humming, no praying this time. A current of gritty anxiety seemed to have come over the Punjabi scientist, as though he feared he'd arrive too late. Whether for Lila Chen or Eleanor, or both? He breathed heavily through his mouth as he hopped from frequency to frequency. Only strong signals came through, and those that did sounded pretty much the same. Canned music. Spanish-language stations. When Bhakti finally hit on a news report the transmission was so broken neither he nor Cheryl could follow it. The only clear words: *"and no reason for alarm. Stay tuned to—"* The transmission died for good.

"Anything on the Internet?" Cheryl couldn't help asking.

Bhakti hadn't even bothered booting up his laptop or snapping on his BlackBerry. "I can try again, but it seems frozen or temporarily unavailable. The blogs are so full of raving as to be insane."

He paused for a moment, but when Cheryl glanced at him hard for an explanation, Bhakti elaborated. "You've got kooks saying the Four Horsemen are here and the Easter Bunny is going to stop them."

Cheryl blinked. She dug into the side pocket in the driver's door, coming up with a can of Off! bug spray. Here and there along the way they'd stocked up on a dozen spray bottles, the pump version and the aerosol, placing them liberally around the 4Runner, always within easy reach. At first he'd hated it, but after a while got used to the scent. This was the pump version, pocketbook size. She waggled it at him, offering a spritz.

"No thanks, I used some before," Bhakti said.

Cheryl, one hand on the wheel, spritzed a touch around her neck and shoulders like perfume, then dropped the spray bottle back in the door pocket.

Suddenly she asked, "How many people do you think

have . . . y'know . . . gotten sick? I mean, out of everyone, how many?"

How many absent people did it take to make everything revert to wall-to-wall Muzak? Bhakti shrugged.

"Since we left Los Angeles? Hard to tell. A lot of people. Three in ten? How about 2.755 in ten? That's almost the same thing as one in three. You get to percentages like that, like 3.7 or 4.2, and it'll feel like half of everyone is sick."

He paused for a moment, calculating cause and effect.

"When three out of ten people don't show up for work and go to a hospital instead, the hospital shuts down. When four out of ten people are out of action the world shuts down."

Cheryl gripped the wheel. Rachel's ghost sat silently in the backseat of the SUV and stared at the people of Vandalia through the car window, the dead gazing at those already gone and those soon-to-be. Rachel turned away sadly. "There are more dead people than I can count. Most of them are lost, and they don't know where to go. I think they're running out of room, above and below."

"Wonderful," Cheryl remarked, answering both at once. "I wish I hadn't asked."

29

On the Banks of the River Styx

At the entrance to I-70, the outlying buildings of Vandalia stared back at the three vehicles with blank windows like vacant eyes. Beatrice nudged the Gran Torino around a stalled tractor-trailer, and the cars crawled onto the interstate heading east, then picked up speed. Overhead, clouds clamped down from horizon to horizon. On either side of the highway the leaves at their peak in this part of the country sped past like a counterpane of flame, as though the trees were on fire.

And smoke. Smoke?

Smoke curled into the air from burning houses half a mile off and drifted across the black asphalt like belts of fog. Not every building was burning, but enough of them, every ten miles or so—a warehouse, a silo—pouring smoke into the sky.

Tractor-trailers and other vehicles on the interstate, heedless of the speed limit, roared by at 75 to 80 mph, only slowing down when a dense screen of smoke blocked the road ahead. Nobody seemed to care about state troopers or the highway patrol. In the white minivan, the police band had been silent for miles; Billy Shadow switched over to the CB for some cross-chatter. The citizens band was eerily quiet too, like none of the truckers wanted to talk.

A young, querulous voice broke the static:

"Hello? Anybody out there, copy?" Silence. He came again. *"Anybody?"*

But no one answered.

Billy Shadow frowned for a moment. Even the truckers were scared of what was out there. The caravan climbed into the hills, approaching West Virginia, endless slopes of maple and pine. They crossed the Ohio River and Wheeling; stacks of burning tires blocked the exit ramps, the message: *Keep Moving.* They kept going, their engines sucking juice. The miles rolled by.

Billy picked up the walkie-talkie, pressed the button, and held it down.

"I think we're all low on gas. I'm close to a gas-gauge warning. A little east of Wheeling there's the Dallas Pike Fuel Center. But uh . . ." Billy paused, holding down the transmission bar. "But I don't think we should just bomb in there. I think we ought to scope it out from an overpass or an interchange."

Static for a moment; then Big Bea broke through. "Smart thinking, Crazy Horse."

A few miles farther, at Exit 11, the convoy pulled off the highway. The exit ramp wasn't blocked; no burning tires or roadblocks. The convoy pulled off the highway and stopped. Gantzer's Ridge Road ran parallel to the interstate; the road wound off along a thick belt of trees. Some smoke in the distance rose from where the fuel station was supposed to be.

Everyone got out.

Billy climbed to the roof of the minivan for a better view. The day was getting on dusk, the light fading.

"Can't see a damn thing," Billy growled.

"We're gonna have to move up a little," Bea said, her face taut with dismay. Back on the ground, Beatrice and Cheryl gazed at the belt of smoke blocking their view. A pair of binoculars were passed around. Nobody liked the prospect of moving any closer; it felt like blind groping. Problem was, they had no choice; time to gas up, now or never.

Beatrice, Cheryl, Billy, and Bhakti packed into the Gran Torino and did a thousand-yard crawl up the road, hugging the line of trees; they passed a Ford dealership, every car on the lot either on fire or a smoldering, twisted hulk. They got out of the Torino and crept to the side of the tar strip. Between a break in the trees they peered through their binoculars at the comforting sight of a Holiday Inn Express. No fire, no smoke. And beyond that, the Dallas Pike truck stop was easy enough to spot, the white overhang of a Citgo canopy next to the flat-topped beige concrete of a Taco Bell.

The Citgo canopy was lit, and the reassuring thrum of a heavy generator throbbed across the road. Several rigs sat behind the pumps, their chicken lights running. Out in the parking lot, picnic tables stood by the restaurant door with a dozen flickering candle buckets on them.

Everything normal, except along the flat roofline of the concrete building the dark silhouette of a man with a rifle stood sentry. Another man with a long gun sat in a camp chair, smoking a cigarette, the burning ash visible a couple of hundred yards off. Not exactly the welcome wagon, but it didn't seem like anybody at the Dallas Pike Fuel Center was trying to hide anything. As if to allay suspicions, the pacing sentinel paused, leaned his rifle against the roof ledge, and lit his own cigarette. Then he used his lighter to light another row of bucket candles along the roofline. A sharp breeze blew out of the rugged hills—October nights were chilly up here in the mountains. The bucket candles flickered but didn't blow out.

"Do you smell it?" Billy asked.

Cheryl shook her head. "Can't smell a thing. No, wait—"

"Yeah," Bea whispered. "Citronella. Citronella candles."

A hopeful sign. "Guess they don't like mosquitoes either," Bhakti said.

The three vehicles rolled into the truck stop parched for gas. The concrete apron in front of the pumps seemed oddly vacant. You half expected a mess of men in plaid shirts and guns to be standing guard. For a few moments, nothing happened. Then somebody inside the truck stop threw a switch, and *pang-pang-pang* the place lit up like shock and awe.

Heavy-duty floodlights on the corners of the building, an easy thousand watts apiece, hit the gang from six different directions. Inside every one of the cars, the light so blinding you couldn't see, like when a flashbulb goes off in your face, or the aliens' ship appears out of nowhere to zap you away—

A woman's voice from a loudspeaker barked, *"Show us your hands!"*

Everyone in the three vehicles clamped their eyes closed and held up their hands for a long ninety seconds of silent observation, while their retinas burned from red to blue and back again. From the roof one of the sentries hollered, "Gosh darn it, Jilly, will you *warn us* next time? I can't hardly see up here."

The woman's voice over the loudspeaker growled, "Oh, quit your bitchin'."

Then *pang-pang-pang* the lights died. "Okay, if you could get out of the cars for us, we'd appreciate that."

The travelers climbed from their vehicles, shielding their eyes; their sight began to return on waves of electric-blue optic shock. The door to the convenience jumped open, and a flock of kids burst out followed by their mom, Jilly.

"Hey, easy now!" she cautioned them. The swarm of scamps pranced around in a bewildering melee dressed up for Halloween. Only four kids, but it felt like forty: a fairy in pink ballet tights, a clown, a lamb, and the littlest of the four as a bunny rabbit, all clamoring at once, "Trick or treat! Trick or treat!"

Their mom, hillbilly Jilly, looked like she could have been Dolly Parton's sister, but without the sequined cowboy shirt. She carried a large plastic jack-o'-lantern; then set it down outside the double door and lit the lantern's citronella candle with a flick of a lighter.

Beatrice staggered out of the driver's seat, shaken by the sudden flash; the bright lights had hit her harder than the others. She snapped her brace so the game leg didn't fold and leaned heavily on the hood of the car. She delicately rubbed the side of her head. One of the ragamuffins bumped into her, and she slid along the car hood, groping for balance. Without thinking, Cheryl came to Big Bea's side.

"I'll be all right," Bea whispered. "Bright lights shake me up. It passes."

"I said, you be polite!" Jilly hollered at her children. And the imps quieted down a little.

"Don't you get suckered." Their mom smiled. "My doodlebugs got more candy inside than they can eat in a month. Just a moment while we turn on the pumps. Good thing you're not looking for diesel; we only got about six hundred gallons left and we're considering taking it home for the furnace. Who the hell knows when we'll get another delivery. What'd you see back in Wheeling? Everybody standing around with their mouths open catching flies, hoping to get bit?"

Jilly seemed to know about that, so the rumor had taken on a life of its own.

"A lot of smoke," Beatrice replied. "And blocked interstate exits like no one wanted strangers stopping by."

"Suckers who think getting bit by skeeters will save them, right? Well, we don't believe everything that's on the net," Jilly said. "And we use a lot of bug spray, for good measure. Where you headed, if it's any of my business?"

"We're trying to make New York tonight," Cheryl said.

Jilly exhaled gravely. She glanced over at the tractor-trailers on the concrete apron, three of them still thrumming with power, their rig lights blazing. "You're braver than them. They were heading east too, but now they ain't so sure. Thinking maybe it's better to hole up here, until whatever blows over. Seems things in Pennsylvania aren't so good."

The travelers pulled out of the Dallas Pike truck stop before night fell over the hills and hollows of West Virginia. Their short convoy lost some time over Allegheny Plateau. The pillars of smoke invisible in the dark, but the travelers smelled burning wood, burning rubber, and every so often the crushed velvet mountainsides were dotted with red-and-yellow flame. A house afire, a burning cornfield, or an abandoned town glowered into the cloudy night.

They took their chances on another fuel run a little east of Harrisburg. The caravan almost didn't stop, but desperation made them roll into an I-78 service area. Jilly knew the score, all right. Elements of the Pennsylvania National Guard were trying to keep order from Hershey to Hamburg. A lot of uniforms. A lot of guns in the hands of uniformed kids trying to stop a rash of gimme-takee. A sign read BE PREPARED TO STOP. Then the inevitable, implacable: "Could you pull over please? We'd like to perform a search. Please have your license and registration."

Oh, this wasn't going to do at all. Guaranteed one of these soldier boys would find them with too many guns, too much medicine, and an Injun toting a hunk of frozen ear like a lodgepole scalp. The three vehicles crawled to a coned-off area of the parking lot. Three Guardsmen approached, two privates and an officer.

In the yellow Toyota 4Runner Cheryl took a deep breath. How to get out of this? Flash her LAPD union card? Like they'd care. Bhakti lost patience, smacking the dashboard with his palm, a futile gesture. He turned to Cheryl, angry and annoyed. "Do something! You're a cop. Can't you show them your badge?"

Rachel's ghost stared apprehensively out the window as the men drew closer. She caught Cheryl's eye. "Oy," Rachel whispered. "This is starting to feel like white hoods and torches. I hope you remember how to do the goose-step two-step."

To which Cheryl responded to both, "It wouldn't do any good. Not with these guys." The Punjabi scientist looked like he was ready to boink. "Be still and try to look normal," Cheryl told him. "I know it's an effort, but do it for Lila. Do it for Eleanor. Do it for me. Just keep a lid on it."

Inside the white minivan, Billy Shadow approached a frustration point close to that of Bhakti. But totally controlled, his mind worked furiously, wondering if he could scoot back to the fridge and maybe hide some of the dicier items. That scalped ear, for sure. But for some reason, Billy didn't stir from the driver's seat, as Big Bea had already unlatched the Ford Torino's gleaming purple door and stepped out.

The soldiers were about ten yards away.

Big Bea stared at the men like one of those wise cowgirls

you see in old Westerns. The solid sister of Randolph Scott; a steady hand who knows the score, knows how far she'll go and how far she'll let anyone push her around. She shut the Gran Torino door, showing no sign of weakness. She planted one hand on her holster and held up the other in warning, the message clear: *Halt*.

So great was Bea's authority, one of the younger soldiers missed a step.

She fished some kind of ID out of her shirt pocket, flipped it open, and showed it to the Guardsmen, her arm outstretched. At first, the officer was not overly impressed, but he took a hand scanner out of his battle dress cargo pocket and ran it across the tough lady's identification. In three seconds, the scanner database verified her pedigree. The Guardsman whistled under his breath, mildly impressed. Beatrice nodded to the white minivan and yellow Toyota. "They're with me."

The officer gave the woman a smart salute and waved to the other vehicles.

"Okay, first pump available, line two."

At the pumps, Cheryl and Billy gave Bea a real long look, with a dose of respect. Nobody gets through that quick.

"Neat trick, Babe," Billy remarked. "Reminds me of Army Intel. We flashed a lot of badges." Beatrice didn't reply, just went about filling the Gran Torino. When Cheryl's turn came to gas up the Toyota truck, Bea was still within earshot.

"You're gonna have to explain that to me, Sister."

Big Bea patted the ID case through her buttoned breast pocket.

"Am I, Gorgeous?"

They hit the road again. Last lap. The night deepened as they rode out of the anthracite hills into whatever was left of civilization. Not much to see on the interstate: lines of cars racing to get somewhere else. Smoke and the scent of smoke rose from every town they passed. The miles rolled by. Allentown. Elizabeth. They'd reached New Jersey.

Shortly after midnight they pulled over in the Meadowlands to look at the big-city lights of Manhattan; the air grew cold, and out of the sky a few flakes of snow came circling down, melting on the car hoods. The aurora borealis shimmered overhead, sheets of green and red flickering like a kind of warning, much too early in the year, and too far south. Heaven on fire.

The office towers of Lower Manhattan still shone into the night sky. So it wasn't total collapse, not yet anyway. Emergency vehicles at street level flashed their strobes off the metal-and-glass buildings. But the travelers were too distant to hear the sirens.

At least major sections of New York still had power, dots and dashes in every building like some kind of secret Morse code. But what was the message? *May Day, May Day*? Or *Keep Away, Keep Away*?

30

The Ziggurat

From his wood-lined study in the ivory tower of the luxurious San Remo the Pied Piper was taking names and kicking ass on the *Twilight Zone* phone, prodding the weak-minded over the edge.

- A mother of three drove the wrong way onto the Tappan Zee Bridge into oncoming traffic, killing a

mother of eight along with all her children.
Another tragedy caused by cell phone distractions. And a bottle of vodka.

- In Miami, a bride gabbing with her six brides-
maids died in a gown store fire as a cigarette
butt ignited a couch and the place went up like
torched taffeta. The bride and her maidens had
vowed to quit smoking together right after the
fitting.

- In California, Mr. P. cajoled the noted cage fighter
James Whye to rip out his training partner's
beating heart, then cut out his buddy's tongue,
peel the skin off his face, and gouge out an
eyeball. Police found Whye watching *Deal or No
Deal,* blood up the bungalow walls, sharing a beer
with his training partner's headless corpse.

Not much in the grand scheme of things, but all these
little calamities added to the frisson, the thrills of the day—
and Mr. P. was nothing if not an artist. He could ruin
greater swathes of the country in his sleep, but with a little
bureaucratic mischief he made matters infinitely worse.
Mr. P. stroked away at the undulating lava lamp as the
glowing red wax rose and fell.

- An order to bulldoze 10,000 homes in Detroit
suddenly read 30,000, and city bulldozers mistakenly wrecked good homes too.

- Four deepwater oil rigs off Galveston malfunctioned simultaneously, pouring gallons of crude
into the Gulf. A billion fish and five billion shrimp
died, not to mention all the manatees.

- In Minnesota, the Palisades Nuclear Plant on
Prairie Island gushed an endless stream of
radioactive water, poaching the Mississippi River
from St. Paul to New Orleans.

However, these catastrophes were mere distractions compared to his coming assault. Up till now, the ebola leakage had been his most insidious achievement. It wasn't hard to serve up batch after batch from simmering third-world cook pots stewing bat and monkey meat. Then add to the steaming cauldron—bumbling bureaucrats, contradictory protocols, abandoning precaution, even common sense—and before you knew it hemorrhagic fever had jumped its hot zones, sputtering along like a ragged engine. No one was responsible and yet everyone was responsible. The marriage of anonymity and incompetence.

Matters had nearly reached the Point of No Return, but Mr. P. still weighed the fates of the Chen girl and the fortune-teller scamp. A Special Locator Team had traced the two to New York, but that didn't mean Piper would let anyone collect the girls. Alas, no one at Pi R Squared deserved unrestricted access to either female; the geeks at Pi R Squared couldn't be allowed to experiment all on their own. Providing Lila's living body to those termites for her miraculous genetic qualities and Maria's living brain for her nascent powers of insight wouldn't necessarily enhance the creation of their Celestials. Consider what the quacks did to Chargrove, one of their own: an exploding-brain, useless Model-A.

Why squander his assets on clods in white coats unsupervised?

The two females' divine particles mixed with cosmic dust would be like spraying gasoline on a fire. In their haste to make a difference, to find a universal cure for the wandering sickness, the idiot savants at the Ant Colony would most likely turn Lila Chen and the little one into uncontrollable breeders of pestilence carried hither and yon by every creature in creation. Good plan, but they'd need direction.

The lava lamp began to simmer in anticipation. Not the first time in recorded history the Fallen—what legends called "fallen angels"—had interfered with the species, mating wantonly with the sons and daughters of men. Just look what had happened that time? War in heaven. Death below. Still, after a dozen generations or so, a Moses, a Buddha, or a Christ would come along to work a miracle, teaching a few lessons of life to the stubbornly ignorant. To draw the human animal back from the brink. *Not this time though*. Mr. P. was going to get it right, let the masses die in sin. Drain the well of souls.

Events had guaranteed that mass death was preordained, but ruinous extermination wasn't enough. The Pied Piper wanted more. Much more. There was a secret ingredient missing from this master plan. *Something better, more comprehensive, eternal . . .*

The lava lamp under his hand bubbled under his thumb. . . .

The travelers drove north through the Meadowlands to the George Washington Bridge. More sense going that way than trying the tunnels into the city; no one wanted to be stuck underground. A unit of the Jersey National Guard and Fort Lee Police Department stopped them on the New Jersey side of the GWB at the toll plaza. The authorities had set up concrete barriers on the bridge, funneling vehicular traffic back to Manhattan, but the bridge lanes were curiously empty. A few hardy souls from Washington Heights walked out with backpacks and strollers, refugees too pathetic to drive away. They would find out soon enough every convenience store in Bergen County was picked clean.

The Guard commander stared at the three vehicles as if they were bananas; nobody'd crossed the bridge to the Big Apple in a week. One more flash of Beatrice's fancy identification and he shrugged his shoulders. "Don't come back this way. Use the Henry Hudson if it's open."

About 1 a.m., the convoy parked bumper-to-bumper under the London plane trees across from the San Remo on
Central Park West. From inside their cars they could see
the situation for themselves. The whole city seemed to be
crawling on its belly. No buses, no trains, a kind of quasi,
citywide curfew. There were still a few yellow cabs around,
and gypsy limos. Pedestrians caught outside scuttled along
the buildings as though afraid of being noticed. Instead of
parked cars lining every cross street, the spaces were
empty. The yuppies and bobos, the brownstone elite of Am-
sterdam and Columbus Avenue, had already locked their
townhouse doors and run home to mommy and daddy.

For those less upwardly mobile, the Dark Ages had arrived.

On their way in, the rescue posse saw how Consolidated
Edison cut back juice to some neighborhoods but kept others lit, like the swank towers, putting a brave face on rolling blackouts. Who cared if half of the Bronx and Brooklyn
burned candles? With the news media suffering a throm-
bosis, what point in keeping up appearances? To make matters more surreal, the radio stations played loops of Herb
Albert and the Tijuana Brass.

Inside the yellow 4Runner, Bhakti didn't even bother fiddling with the scan button; instead he gripped the dashboard with both hands as though bracing for impact. It
struck Cheryl that since West Virginia her buddy had become steadily grimmer and more withdrawn. As though
the closer they got to Lila Chen, the stronger her pull on
him; seeing neither right nor left, just straight down a tunnel. And now, below the San Remo apartment building,
Bhakti's eyes bored holes across the street into the stone
façade. Cheryl swore she could almost hear him grinding
his teeth.

"Do we know what floor they're on?" Bhakti asked,
though he did not seem to care about an answer. A police
cruiser roared downtown, lights flashing, without pausing

for the vehicles idling in a No Parking zone. Instead, the patrol car ignored the strange convoy and sped on. Bhakti barely glanced at it.

"Where the hell is everybody?" Bhakti grumbled. So apparently the weird state of the city had penetrated his noggin.

Cheryl shrugged. "How the hell should I know? I grew up in Poughkeepsie. But this *does* look a lot like Omaha and Council Bluffs, doesn't it?"

"Taller buildings," Bhakti replied; his eyes strayed up the stone face of the towering apartment house, almost as if counting floors. "There's still gotta be a lot of people here."

Cheryl nodded her head. "Millions."

Rachel's spirit gazed dismally out the backseat passenger window at the desolate streets. "I hate New York," she murmured. "That's why I moved to LA."

Rachel had barely finished her sentence when the rumble of heavy vehicles echoed off the buildings; you could see lights bouncing up and down inside Central Park. Heavy vehicles were coming out from under the tree cover. They rumbled onto the 77th Street access and turned the corner. First, an M1 battle tank, followed by a troop carrier and three Humvees. The tank took out a large stone entrance pillar to the park, then the suspended 77th Street intersection traffic light along with its wires and three red elms—leaving an enormous airy gap—and kept going.

The armored column homed in on the uptown tower of the San Remo.

The tank, the troop carrier, and the Humvees parked in a semicircle; a score of troops piled out of the carrier and set up a perimeter. Overhead the sound of rotor blades— *whop-whop-whop*—cascaded down the stone apartment buildings. Wind buffeted the street; loose newspaper and trash flew in every direction. At the 77th Street intersection, a UH-60 Black Hawk helicopter made a tight turn over the edge of Central Park and landed in the middle of the roadway amongst the tangle of stoplight cables. With the elm trees down, the rotor cleared the remaining street-lamps with a few yards to spare on every side, the blades slowly coming to a halt.

The message couldn't be clearer.

The Big *They* was here for a pickup.

The Special Locator Team had arrived.

The travelers in their three vehicles stared at the military guys. In ten seconds, the soldiers spread barbed-wire accordion barriers from corner to corner. The officer in charge directed his men to seal off the San Remo's main entrance. Then he sent a detachment around the corner of the building to secure the service door. Four troopers entered, securing the service elevator, the back stairs, and the service entrance to the apartment building. A special detachment in blue hazmat suits rolled four lozenge-shaped body transport containers to the San Remo's main entrance and halted in front of the ironwork doors awaiting orders.

Nobody in, nobody out.

A squad of three men boldly walked across Central Park West toward the idling cars, their intention clear: *No parking here. Move along.* Big Bea's harsh but soft voice came across the walkie-talkies in every vehicle.

"This is way too big for us," she whispered. "We better shove off. Figure out another way to get those kids. Just hit the transmission button if you copy."

In the white minivan, Billy hit the transmission bar. Roger Wilco. In the yellow Toyota 4Runner Cheryl did too. Click, crackle, and click. New plan: Shove off, regroup. Except Bhakti wasn't having any of it. Speaking softly but distinctly to his companion, he said, "*I want you to give Janet's ashes to Eleanor. Promise you'll do that for me.*" Before Cheryl could even say "*What?*" the Punjabi scientist groped out of the car as if he meant to enter the building across the street.

One of the soldiers said sternly, "Get back in the car, sir."

Bhakti didn't pay attention. The Punjabi scientist stared up the face of the building, all the way up to the sixth floor, to a wide-open lit window, to the figure in the window, to the figure of a little girl. Bhakti had seen her before, *Oh yes,* picking the correct statue of a saint off a table of saints; in the company of a woman who knew the address of a coroner at 1104 North Mission Road, Los Angeles, California, and wouldn't take his money. Oh God, yes, he knew her.

"Maria!" he cried up to the window. "Maria, it's me!" His hands rose to the building, pleading with its stone face. "Get Lila! Where's Lila?"

One the soldiers approached closer, violence behind his voice. "Sir, get back in the vehicle please."

The little girl in the sixth-floor window looked down. Little Maria's eyes and Bhakti's eyes made an electric connection. She raised her hand, silhouetted in the window, waving gently down into the street. Yes, she remembered Bhakti.

Another figure came to the window. A Chinese girl with shimmering black hair; she pushed it from her face and tucked it into a ponytail. Even six floors up, no one had to tell him—*he knew.* Bhakti frantically waved back. "Lila, it's me! Lila, I'm down here!"

The three soldiers were upon him now.

"Sir!"

Cheryl powered down the passenger window. Her voice controlled, terribly controlled. "Bhakti. Get back in the car. Bhakti, get in now!"

The Punjabi scientist didn't listen.

"Hey!" Beatrice barked into the walkie-talkie. "Somebody grab his ass." Too late; guns pointed at them. "The rest of you, stay in your vehicles."

Bhakti tried to push through the three soldiers blocking his path, shouting at them, "Let me through. That's Maria, the little girl who helped me find my daughter. That's Lila who lives across the street!" He thrust against them. "Get out of my—"

One of the troopers struck him a right across the jaw with the butt of an M16; you could hear the thunk of composite plastic hitting Bhakti's cheek.

Bhakti dropped to his knees holding a bleeding face.

"Get back in the car, sir."

At first everyone thought he would do it. *Obey the trooper. Be sensible. Get back in the car.*

Bhakti slowly rose from the pavement, holding his jaw. His whole head rang, yet through the blinding pain something terribly unexpected happened. A *thought* struck him—*a realization.* For suddenly he understood that dream he'd had so long ago—the one of the temple, the cripple, and the rupee, with the terrible heat blasting down from above, the sun beating down like a white-hot cap on his head as he stood on the high platform of the nameless ziggurat. The realization struck him through and through.

The cripple in rags with the twisted ankle who climbed the endless steps; this was not a dream of two people, but of only one person. Him. The cripple was *really him,* and the steps of the forgotten temple were the steps of life—his life, all the days of his life. And what you did during your life—crawling on broken feet to a distant summit to reach the figure above, which shone in the light—your perfect self. Forever visible, and yet forever beyond mortal grasp. With only the ancient steps, your rags and human wounds, the sum total of existence.

Now, standing in this hard city street beside a grand park under a tall building, another figure stood high upon the stepped pyramid. A figure in the window of a modern ziggurat. A figure reachable. Touchable. *Right here. Right now.*

His soft Indian voice slurred through his bruised jaw, "Get out of my way."

He took a step, and all three troopers backed up, giving

him room, triangulating on target. Bhakti took a step, and then another. Two rifles swung up to the ready.

"Last warning, sir."

No one could believe what they were seeing; there wasn't even enough time to shout his name. He lurched one more step.

The guns fired, and the Punjabi scientist dropped for good, crumpled on the asphalt, like a person who never was. Special Locator Troopers appeared at each car window. Each man giving the same order: "Move along."

The last thing Cheryl saw before slamming the yellow 4Runner in gear were the figures of Lila Chen and Little Maria—Bhakti's Lila, Bhakti's Maria—staring down at her from the sixth-floor window. Then a much taller figure approached the two girls from behind. One moment Lila stared down; one moment Little Maria stared down—

And then they were gone, swept away by dark wings.

PART THREE

Weather

Magic is believing in yourself, if you can do that, you can make anything happen.

—Johann Wolfgang von Goethe

31

❦

Janet's Ashes

A piece of Cheryl tore inside when Bhakti fell, a wound that never really closed. Worse than when she learned Rachel was gone, maybe because she saw Bhakti shot down before she could tell him what he meant to her: cottage cheese with peach halves, singing "Waheguru" to "Silent Night," explaining, "We go from Darkness to Light. In English you might say, the *wondrous destroyer of darkness.*"

And to think she'd called him a gorp. If she ever heard that word again, she'd begin to sob and never stop.

Plan A had been to grab the Lila Chen girl and fly out of town to Bhakti's white-bread relatives in Connecticut. Get the girl; run like hell. Then spring Mrs. Singh, Eleanor, from the sanitarium. Hole up somewhere safe and assess the situation. So far, the get-out-of-town bit was the only part of the "plan" left intact. They didn't need to discuss it. Like Big Bea said, *Shove off. Regroup.* Lucky to get away at all.

The Special Locator Team directed Cheryl and the others out the perimeter with glowing red marshaling wands, dragging the accordion wire for the cars to pass. Icy rain began to *tick-tick-tick* on the windshields. The vehicles rumbled toward the Museum of Natural History, then headed across town toward the West Side Highway.

At 79th Street they merged into very thin northbound traffic and left the icy rain behind. The lights of the George Washington Bridge dangled brightly before them as they roared up the Henry Hudson Parkway, first under the trees of Washington Heights and then sweeping past the Greek columns of the pergola at Inspiration Point on the edge of Manhattan.

The road swept them onward, but as the cars rolled toward Fort Tryon Park, Cheryl looked up to see the Romanesque arches of the Billings Road Viaduct, one of those strange and haunting architectural curiosities of upper Washington Heights. The spooky stone arches stared down at the parkway, watching the would-be rescuers' flight from the city. Cheryl got the distinct impression of dangling bodies in the darkness—women's bodies dangling from hangman's ropes. She counted four, the roadway making them jerk like frames in a silent movie.

Women hanging by their neck, each in their own dark arch—

In a peculiar writhing dance three of the women wriggled off their nooses and dropped to the ground—*plop-plop-plop*—while the last one kicked her feet, unable to escape. *Didn't anybody else see?* None of the cars slowed down even for a moment. A flock of pigeons burst from under the arches, hurtling over the highway like a rush of lost souls.

Four women. Three escaped. One hung.

Cheryl knuckled the wheel. What a strange, cold feeling, as if she'd been looking at their own future. But who was the unlucky one? She picked up the walkie-talkie, pressed the transmission button, and then stopped. What the hell was she going to say? *I saw four women hanging—*

The walkie-talkie went back on the dash.

Past Inwood Park, the highway rose to the Henry Hudson Bridge toll plaza and the Dutch-named Spuyten Duyvil, "Spinning Devil," the treacherous narrows at the tip of

Manhattan. Suddenly Beatrice hit the brakes and the Gran Torino swerved; the cars behind screeched to a halt. Cheryl stared at the tollbooth plaza, maybe a hundred yards off. Big Bea's anxious face was framed in her driver's window; she whispered into the walkie-talkie.

"Whattaya think?"

Two large vehicles—one red, one white—blocked the toll plaza; they were bloodmobiles channeling three lanes of traffic into a single tollgate. One bloodmobile was a bright red school bus—one of those old-fashioned WWII antiques, like the fire engines that got rolled out at Independence Day. The other bloodmobile was a white, state-of-the-art, extra-large Winnebago; patriotic red, white, and blue stars danced across the side of the RV and across the familiar American Red Cross. Five-foot letters encouraged GIVE BLOOD PLEASE.

Ambulances from across Upper Manhattan waited for consignments, their lights flashing: Harlem Hospital, Mount Sinai, Columbia-Presbyterian, Bronx-Lebanon, even St. Joseph's in Yonkers. On the far side of the tollbooths, two Riverdale Police cruisers idled on the Henry Hudson Bridge. So that was the gig; emergency services had gone on a twenty-four-hour-a-day blood drive, right at the chokepoint for vehicles leaving the city heading north.

"I'm not crazy about this," Billy said into his walkie-talkie. "I'm sure the hospitals are short on plasma, but my feeling is I gave at the office."

Beatrice agreed, whispering loud enough for her mike to pick it up and everyone to hear, "Nobody is sticking me with anything today."

Cheryl pressed the transmission button. "Those two cop cruisers on the other side of the booths say different."

"Doesn't look like they're going to take no for an answer," Beatrice agreed. "And I'm in no hurry to find out what yes entails."

Billy weighed all this for a moment, took a deep breath,

and let it out slowly. "I'll go in easy. Just be ready to step on it."

"What's going to stop them from following us all the way to Fairfield?" Bea blatted back. Silence again as they pondered the problem of pursuit. Nobody wanted to get into a shoot-out with Bronx coppers and desperate hospitals dying for blood.

Cheryl hit the transmission button. "I have an idea. I can loosen the trailer and the safety straps. If somebody's tailgating . . . well, it'll be an awful mess."

Cheryl went to the rear of the 4Runner, unlocked the linchpin from the trailer hitch, and unplugged the brake lights. Then she loosened the straps on the bike and unlocked the wheel chocks. Not exactly tire spikes, but better than nothing. Sooner or later the whole trailer rig, motorcycle and all, would jerk free—a very nasty accident waiting to happen.

Billy Shadow slowly approached the Henry Hudson toll plaza in the white minivan; next came Beatrice in the Gran Torino. Cheryl pulled up the rear with the shaky motorcycle trailer.

The door to the fancy Winnebago opened on a hydraulic sigh, and a clean-cut, pleasant fellow in pale blue hospital scrubs stepped down. CliC magnetic reading glasses hung from his neck on an orange cord, and he gave off a whiff of impartiality, concern, and fairness. The clipboard didn't hurt either.

As the pleasant fellow came closer he offered a business card, explaining, "American Red Cross of Greater New York." Billy took the card and examined it. "As you're probably aware, the run on plasma and blood products has been staggering the last couple of months. Our bloodmobiles were getting hijacked in the neighborhoods. At this point the hospitals aren't too choosy about where they get their V8."

The fellow looked around the toll plaza and grinned

sheepishly at the red bus bloodmobile parked for show like antique cars at hot-wheels rallies. "Commuters have to slow down anyway. If you donate there's no toll. We even have Girl Scout cookies and orange juice." Mr. Scrubs was just the kind of guy that made you want to say yes to anything.

Billy got out of the minivan; the large .357 Magnum in the cowboy holster clunking on his thigh. Not a look you see often in New York, but the gun and leather holster didn't seem to faze the efficient fellow in the pale blue scrubs with the clipboard, who followed him to the door of the Winnebago.

"Mind if I take a look?" Billy asked.

Nope, he didn't mind at all, more than pleased and proud of the spanking big Winnebago. "Help yourself."

Billy looked back at the other cars, his own expression clear enough: *Hit the gas if anything happens.* The Winnebago's hydraulic doors whooshed open, and he poked his nose inside.

A clean antiseptic smell filled the coach; three shiny, pale blue reclining couches with head- and armrests lined either side of the main aisle; a utility counter at the back, a sink, overhead cupboards, and a large refrigerator. The lighting subdued but pleasant, and a large flat-screen TV ran a Discovery Channel loop of playful jackrabbits hopping about a desert, eating leaves off scrub and boldly sticking their cute faces into thorny cacti to drink the pulp. The whole setup very relaxing, very peaceful and inviting, Girl Scout cookies and orange juice included.

"I see."

"Can't we get one or two of you in for a pint? It would be so helpful."

It all made a kind of sense. A ton of sense, actually.

Except it was 2 a.m. in the friggin' morning! Who in their right minds—?

Billy backed silently out of the trailer, not answering one way or the other. He glanced at the Gran Torino and the yellow Toyota 4Runner; the plaza lights fragmented the women's faces behind the windshields, a puzzle of doubt. Then Billy noticed the strangest thing. Off to the side of the parkway in deep shadow, four rabbits had come out of the brush and twitched their sensitive noses at the weird scene in the toll plaza. They wrinkled their whiskers, getting a better scent, then pointed their smart little faces at the blood-red school bus.

Get a load of those rabbits. Just like back at the Dugway Proving Ground, making him almost laugh at the little critters. *Ah, the protector rabbits. How good of you to join us.*

His eyes strayed to the antique bloodmobile. The interior lights within the long red school bus gave off a sickly incandescent glow that illuminated very little: double-decker cots for donors, hanging tubes and plasma bags, ancient hardware. It seemed the blood drive already had some takers this time of night, or more accurately *givers,* the cots occupied with mouth breathers and opium dreamers.

A male nurse glided past the bus windows wearing 1930s doctors' whites that buttoned up the shoulder to the neck, a fly-specked lab coat. The male nurse tapped the yellow rubber tubes snaking from the plasma bottles to dislodge any clogs. *Damn, if this weirdo didn't look like Flattop right out of the Dick Tracy comics.* No, Billy didn't need any Skin Walker bliss to tell him this wasn't about blood for hospitals.

This was much darker.

A cult had risen up from the skank corners of the city, the dregs of hospital staff going rogue. Doing their own blood harvesting, maybe even drinking it on the sly like urban vamps used to do in those after-hours Goth clubs. The lump on one cot slowly rolled over; the sheet fell away from its face, and Billy got a good look at the donor. A young woman around eighteen or twenty, not much older than Lila, nearly bled white. She smiled wanly at him through the glass. She was okay with that. Bleed her white, fine by her.

So that was the deal—people who'd given up on life hooking up with those that wanted to live no matter what; ready, willing, and able to suck them dry.

The male nurse smiled smugly at Billy through the grimy bus window and patted the skinny rump of the female donor. He threw a corner of the white sheet back over her face, covering her head to toe once more.

"What can we put you down for?" Mr. Scrubs asked quietly.

Billy Shadow stepped away from the Winnebago. He planted his hand on the large .357 Magnum, giving fair warning. The genial fellow in the pale blue scrubs stepped back, not particularly alarmed, but deeply disappointed.

"Is there anything we can do to ease your mind? It's painless."

Billy climbed into the minivan. Key in the ignition, foot on the gas; the engine roared. The van leapt through the toll slot snapping the barrier. The two other cars right behind him put pedal to the metal, bumper to bumper. The yellow 4Runner's bike trailer clanked like tin cans on its tail. The getaway cars shot past the Riverdale patrol cruisers before the pursuit officers could slap their cars into drive. In another half second the whole crew blasted over the Harlem River, up Route 9A, passing the residential apartment houses of Riverdale, Seton Park, and Fieldston. The two patrol cars gunned close, lights flashing.

In the yellow Toyota, Cheryl felt the trailer shimmy; she took her eyes off the road for a split second. The motorcycle had tipped but hadn't shaken free yet. Flashing lights lit up the inside of the yellow SUV. She snapped her eyes back on the road. The big curve at Fieldston Road came up like a roller coaster, and she could feel the 4Runner wanting to ski on two wheels like a stunt car. She hit the brakes to hold the curve. No brake lights.

One of the cop cars zoomed up behind.

The cruiser tapped the trailer, and the whole rig clanged like a bell. The motorcycle jumped the chock.

That first patrol car took it right in the grill. The cycle skated over the hood and took out the windshield. The patrol car went sideways on the Fieldston curve, caught his buddy's fender, and both cruisers did 360s, grinding glass and squealing tires.

Cheryl didn't look back.

She felt the motorcycle trailer shimmy again and cry for mercy. When the yellow Toyota glided under the Mosholu Parkway overpass, the trailer disengaged and said *adios*. The yellow Toyota leapt free. Cheryl fishtailed onto the Saw Mill River Parkway right behind Big Bea, the whole escape—from the bike jumping the chock to losing the trailer—no more than eight seconds.

Beatrice hit the transmission button on the walkie-talkie. "You okay?"

Cheryl was soaked in sweat.

"Yeah, I'm fine. But I'm real low on gas," she croaked.

Her eye caught Rachel sitting in the back, smiling broadly. You'd think her grinning ex might have gone *Boo!* to freak out the coppers—but no.

"Nice work, Sister," Rachel remarked. "That was totally swank."

Alone in the car, Cheryl could now talk to her private spook. "Do you want to sit up front?"

Rachel shook her head and grew a trifle embarrassed, as if she wasn't supposed to say anything. "Uh, no. Bhakti's sitting in front."

Cheryl couldn't help swerving the car, w*hoa-whoa!* She gained control and kept her wheels between the lines, then glared into the rearview mirror.

"You can't see him because he's not here for you," Rachel explained.

A fearful look had come to Rachel's eyes. "He is *not* a happy man, Cheryl. God help whoever crossed him."

Cheryl instinctively reached across the empty passenger seat as though to pat Bhakti's arm or comfort him in some way. A deep cold bathed her fingers. Steadily the cold reached her wrist, then her forearm, and Cheryl knew if she left the hand there in Bhakti's invisible lap, the cold would freeze her heart.

"I'm sorry, Bhakti," she whispered to the empty passenger seat.

"I'm so sorry."

The Saw Mill River Parkway swept them up a long hill. To the west, rows of houses climbed a steep slope like a broad stairway of ticky-tacky boxes. A red glow lit the sky and low clouds. Yonkers was burning.

A few miles farther on the vehicles left the parkway and converged at the Elmsford Exxon station. Billy emerged from the white, Dodge minivan, his face white where the airbag had deployed after his blast through the toll barrier. Sensitive things. The bag had torn apart as Billy swept it from his eyes, spreading white talc-like dust over his face, in his hair, leaving only the wet gash of a mouth.

Beatrice limped out of the Gran Torino and leaned heavily on the hood, trying to keep the weight off her braced leg. She rubbed the soft spot behind her ear, her face grown pale again. Nausea, dizziness, exhaustion—all the old dings and dents. She shook her head a little as though to clear a ringing in her ears. She glanced at Billy's pancake face.

"Ghost dancing?" she asked weakly.

"And how," the powdered red man said. "It's better if you don't swallow any." He tore the remnants of the airbag from the steering column and took a wet nappy from his first-aid kit.

When Billy started to miss spots, Beatrice stopped him.

"No, no, let me." He struggled like a little kid with a dirty face. "Just stay still," Big Bea scolded. He stopped fussing.

For a few moments they all looked around the Elmsford Exxon. The gas station had been around in one form or another since forever. Cheryl remembered her dad calling it "the Esso on the Saw Mill" whenever they drove down from Poughkeepsie. That's how long, from before Exxon. The orange sodium lights cast strange shadows around the cars and gas pumps. The cramped convenience store attached to the flat red, white, and blue canopy was dark too; the glass doors were padlocked from the inside.

Beatrice popped the Gran Torino's trunk and dug around for the fuel pump crank, her face still gray. She glanced weakly about, trying to distinguish the diesel underground tanks from the gasoline underground tanks by their metal fuel covers: gasoline yellow, diesel red, nearly indistinguishable under the orange sodium lights. The large woman gave up and went back to leaning on the car.

"No gas fumes for me right now," she panted at Cheryl. "Think you can handle it, Gorgeous?"

"Maybe we don't have to," Cheryl replied.

In the dark cubby of the convenience store, two faces seemed to float behind the glass doors. Two terrified faces, husband and wife, the proprietors of the Elmsford Exxon. Jet black eyes and hair, just like Bhakti's; the wife's head covered by a scarf. They peered out at the three cars by the pumps like a couple of squirrels cowering in the hollow of a tree.

"Let's wave money at them," Cheryl suggested. "They might turn on the pumps."

That's all it took. Billy collected money from everyone and shoved a wad of bills under the crack in the glass double doors. The display light in the gasoline pump went *bing,* and the thirsty cars got a long drink.

Ten minutes later, they were back on the road again.

After another hour on the road, drooping heads made

them pull over in the empty parking lot of the Danbury Fair Mall for a couple of hours of shut-eye. When they woke with crusty eyes, dawn approached the world in a bluish cloak and the cars had grown cold.

A huge black *X* spray-painted on the mall entrance doors showed quarantine, but the place was unlocked and they had no trouble getting in for potty call and splashing cold water on their faces from the restroom sinks. They took turns standing guard in the food court, Cheryl first. Big Bea appeared fresh from the ladies' room, cheeks pink and face washed, and a lot less pale.

"Let's scrounge up some Dramamine for you before we leave," Cheryl suggested. The tough gal nodded, *Good idea*. "It comes and goes. Mostly when the weather turns, low pressure. Rain or sleet. I'm just a walking barometer."

As they returned to their cars, Cheryl voiced a concern that had been troubling her. They were going to meet Bhakti's wife pretty soon, and his sister-in-law. "I don't know how we're going to explain everything to Bhakti's family. . . ."

The statement hung in silence.

"I'm open to suggestions."

No suggestions, no bright ideas. As Cheryl approached the yellow Toyota 4Runner she heard buzzing from inside. Bhakti's BlackBerry shimmied across the dashboard. Caller ID showed Guy and Lauren Poole, Bhakti's in-laws. Four bars, a strong signal.

Cheryl stared at Janet's ashes, the Nambe metal urn sat in the black canvas miniduffle, zipper open, as it had since Bhakti first placed it there two thousand miles ago. The way he wanted her to ride, so she could be with them. Cheryl opened the passenger door, hefted the miniduffle, and placed it on the front passenger seat. Bhakti's seat. Bhakti should sit with her now. His last words came back: *"I want you to give Janet's ashes to Eleanor.*

Promise you'll do that for me." She'd never actually promised. The phone kept buzzing. . . .

"Better let me explain to the family," Cheryl said. "I rode with him longest."

Neither Big Bea nor Billy argued. Cheryl finally took the call, sitting in the yellow Toyota by herself. The signal held, the battery lasted, and Cheryl talked for a long, long time.

32

You Gonna Trust Me—Or Your Lying Eyes?

The cheerful chimes of the Good Humor truck were still playing when Lattimore reached the aerospace building's ground floor. The fire stairs brought him to the side of the Cosmos Café; a viewing slit in the door let him see the whole reception area.

Mildred the cashier struggled over a load of purloined sirloin and frozen burgers by the café's glass wall. The folding cart from the Good Humor truck had gotten away from her, boxes of frozen food sliding every which way. But as Lattimore watched through the fire door, the matronly woman stopped struggling with the frosted boxes and shrank against the transparent wall of the canteen, her face very frightened.

Security Chief Walter Nash had come to help, only not in a good way. The security man held a gun, waving it vaguely in the middle-aged lady's direction. His other hand gripped a box cutter. He slit open the nearest box, a jumbo pack of Red Baron frozen pizzas, and greedily crouched over it. "I know you have some," he insisted. "Just tell me where. Tell me, and I won't hurt you."

Nash's voice rose in anger. "Just tell me."

Suddenly the man went berserk, slashing open one pizza box after another. Tearing off the sealed plastic wrapping, he pawed frantically at the naked pie, bringing cheese to his lips and scattering the shredded mozzarella over the floor. Nash pointed the gun at Mildred, his sanity critically fractured. "*Just tell me!*"

The poor woman cowered against the glass, trying to shrink herself to nothing.

Cautiously, and with no plan, Lattimore opened the stairwell door and stepped into the lobby. Security Chief Nash whipped around. Shreds of mozzarella cheese clung to his face, his nose. God, he had actually *tried* snorting frozen cheese, hoping it was drugs.

In a flash Lattimore understood. The Good Humor man used to be the local rainbow-dust delivery guy, hooking you up with strawberry shortcake Dalekto. Mildred had just picked the wrong truck to carry her vittles. Unlucky Mildred; the middle-aged lady shivered against the Cosmos Café wall terrified and confused. Worse for Walter Nash, the Red Baron pizzas were simply that—just pizza dough, pizza sauce, and grated cheese. The big black gun aimed directly at Lattimore's chest. Any point in reasoning with Nash?

Through the glass-and-bronze doors of the aerospace building Lattimore saw snow beginning to fall. Why notice this all of a sudden with a crazed man ready to drill you for his last fix? Who could say? Maybe the snow falling outside was simply easier on the eyes than the dark hole of a gun muzzle. Stranger still, Lattimore caught sight of an animal outside. A jackrabbit cautiously hopped along the sidewalk, then hopped off the curb and out of sight. You saw squirrels, sure; but rabbits—those were rare. The curious sight took the edge off addressing an unhinged man with an itchy trigger finger and shredded mozzarella cheese on his face.

Lattimore heard his own voice coming out sane and rational:

"It's all gone, Walter. No more is coming. Mildred doesn't have any. I don't have any. If I did, I'd give it to you. If I knew where the Good Humor man lived, we'd go there."

Security Chief Nash sobbed in despair. "Don't you think I know where he lives? I *went there*. Don't you think *I'd know*?"

Nash brushed the shredded cheese off his face. Looked at a few shreds clinging to his suit jacket sleeve and shook his head at the pure idiocy of his behavior; the crazy things desperate men do at the end of their rope. Then the rope slipped from his grip. Security Chief Nash gently slumped to the glass wall of the Cosmos Café. Tears ran down his cheeks.

"I just wanted one more hit. Just one last time."

Mildred wasn't scared anymore, just pitying. She approached the poor man to comfort him. "It's okay, Mr. Nash. We'll get you better. Just a week or so to clean up. Isn't that right, Mr. Lattimore? We can help Mr. Nash get through it."

"Of course we can, Mildred. We'll help you straighten out, Walter. We both will."

The security man thought for a moment, glanced at the gun in his hand.

"Yeah, straighten me out," Nash said with a bitter smile. He put the gun to his head.

"No, Walter, no!"

Upstairs, Mildred went to a shelf in Lattimore's library and stared at the decanters on a silver tray: bourbon, cognac, rye, gin. She stared at the liquor as if she really wanted a drink. "I almost never . . . ," she said, but didn't finish the sentence. Instead, she talked about her husband, Paul.

"I couldn't get him out of bed to bury him. I wasn't strong enough. And I knew no one would come. The Good Humor Man lived across the street from me. . . ." Her voice trailed off. "I don't think anyone is coming for a while."

Lattimore nodded. "No, I don't think so either, Mildred."

He and the Cosmo cashier had tucked Walter Nash's body in the café's cold locker amongst frozen ground turkey boxes. Then they cleaned up everywhere so you wouldn't know a man had blown his brains out if you hadn't been there. Still, Clem wasn't about to make a food run to the freezer locker alone anytime soon.

Lattimore's head pounded. He went to the kitchen for a damp dish towel and flopped on the couch without ceremony, completely worn out. Too much had happened today. Dealing with the dead security chief had been the last straw. First Jasper died in his hospital bed, suffocated by government goons for their own security lapses. Then Lattimore fell asleep on a loading dock while a Taker took him to see really ugly stuff in the Pi R Squared complex. Finally, Nash had killed himself in the afternoon. Enough already.

At the library shelf Mildred touched one decanter, then another; the silver labels clinked against the crystal. She settled on the bourbon. "May I?"

Lattimore waved a limp hand toward the bottles on the shelf. "Help yourself."

The cool damp dishcloth soothed his head but didn't quite cover his eyes. Outside snow was falling, flying sideways. Not so unusual for early November, but Lattimore knew this wasn't merely Mother Nature. Should he click into Jasper's PC again? Look in on the antenna heads at the High Frequency Active Auroral Research Facility; see if all the dials and monitors were flicking into the red? See the real-time data streams of General Winter crawling down from Canada?

Maybe he'd do that later. But for now, let the snow slip across his vision and listen to Mildred padding about the library. "We'll make some plans a little later," he mumbled, "but right now I think I just have to . . ." He didn't finish.

As he began to doze, Lattimore felt a new presence in the room. Through half-closed eyes, he saw that Sikh scientist from Escape Velocity sitting in the deep armchair by the couch. Bhakti. *Bhakti Singh*. Of course, reporting for work, the most natural thing in the world.

The man wore dirty khaki slacks, a watermelon-pink polo shirt, and a Brooks' Brothers blazer. He looked calmly at Lattimore even though large bullet holes dotted his chest, his shirt stained with rings of blood. The *Indian* Indian scientist held out his hand. "C'mon, boss. I want to show you something."

Lattimore knew he was dreaming, but it was an interesting dream. He'd only met Professor Bhakti Singh once, a few years ago at the Van Horn Aerogel manufacturing hangar. Bhakti and his Number Two, Professor Chen, had showed him around, behind the great transparent wall, explaining the tanks, the injection process. Even the Punjabi scientist's wife joined them, rolling along in her wheelchair. Lattimore remembered asking if they liked their new subdivision house, and Mrs. Eleanor Singh, more than pleased, smiled at him and said, "Delighted."

As he lay on the couch in his living quarters at the top of the bronze-and-glass building, Lattimore's fingers touched the Sikh scientist's hand; the aerospace boss felt himself rise off the cushions, and they went away together.

The next thing he knew—

Heat pounded into him from every side.

Lattimore blinked his eyes. The two men stood on a reddish dirt ridge on the side of a reddish mountain. The blue sky overhead a steaming, blinding cap; sunlight pulsed off the red dirt.

An ancient city of broad streets and narrow alleys lay in the saddle of a valley: empty doorways, roofless brickwork, a bone-dry public bath. . . . A huge mound rose above the city's ruins, a high hill rubbed smooth by endless winds—some sort of temple mount.

"Buddhists called them stupa mounds," Bhakti said into Lattimore's ear. "In Sanskrit the word *stupa* simply means 'heap.' But this mound is far older than Buddha. It has guarded the floodplain of the Indus River for many thousands of years. Behold the ancient city Mohenjo-Daro, known as 'the Mound of the Dead,' though what they called it in ancient times no one knows. Not even the Pakistanis remember."

"The Mound of the Dead . . . ," Lattimore murmured.

He stooped and picked up an odd bit of rock at his feet. A scrap of reddish fused gravel melted to molten glass. Ripples on the stone showed where it had liquefied, sliding down the reddish slope like lava. Lattimore knew the term for this—vitrification: rapid heating and then rapid cooling. Only a few things on Earth could do that. A volcano, and—

Nuclear fission. *Thermonuclear heat*.

Lattimore rubbed the reddish glassy slab with his thumb, feeling its ethereal smoothness.

"Something terrible happened here, didn't it, Bhakti?"

The Punjabi scientist nodded his head, his voice soft and seductive. "Something terrible, thousands and thousands of years ago. Down below there are bodies, ancient bones. Still radioactive. They resist decay. How did the people die? Who killed them? All we know is what the Mahabharata, the Bhagavad-Gita, says. The Song of God tells of giant cities floating above the Earth. And those giant cities were made of gleaming metal and iron. And when those cities went to war against each other, fire rained down on men's heads."

Bhakti seamlessly slipped into verse, quoting what he knew from memory:

> *An incandescent column of smoke and flame,*
> *Bright as ten thousand suns*
> *Rose in all its splendor.*
> *An unknown weapon,*
> *A gigantic messenger of death . . .*

Bhakti swept an open hand across the ruins below:

> *The corpses so burned as to be unrecognizable.*
> *The hair and nails fell out.*
> *Pottery broke without apparent cause,*
> *And the birds turned white. . . .*

Bhakti fell silent.

Lattimore gazed down at the reddish brick ruins of Mohenjo-Daro, the Mound of the Dead. As Bhakti's hand passed over the burnt landscape, the ancient city slowly came to life before Clem's eyes. From thousands of years ago, the buildings grew from their broken foundations; water filled the great bath; the great stupa mound gleamed with gold and silver; people walked the streets as mules and camels drew carts from the green countryside laden with fruit and grain. The Indus River sparkled blue and white on the horizon.

"There are no city walls, no defenders."

"No need," Bhakti whispered. "They feared no one with the great sky gods in their sky palaces to protect them."

As the nameless city went about the business of daily life, Lattimore perceived two sharp points of light in the sky moving toward each other from opposite directions. Two gleaming fairy cities hovered on the horizon of east and west like floating castles in children's stories. Shining silver-and-glass towers, pointed spires, and lithe skyscrapers—needles bound together with titanium thread. The faces of the buildings shivered in the air like silver shields and spears. One city came at last to rest over the sacred temple.

From the bright stupa mound's ascension point, the temple spire, figures ascended to the nearest floating city on fluttering strokes of air, and likewise descended on gossamer wings to the golden temple's pinnacle. Shining figures bathed in holy light stepped off the temple mound to walk among the mortals below, an endless stream of up and down, to and from the hovering fairy castle.

The Punjabi scientist's soft voice murmured, "How could our rustic forefathers know that the sky gods in their sky palaces, with their flying horses and flying carpets, might hate each other? Like the immortal angels of the Bible, they went to war."

"Over us? Over these green valleys?"

Before Bhakti answered, a flash of light like a thousand suns ate the sky in one blast. Lattimore shielded his eyes, turning his face away; he could see the bones in his hand, X-rays lighting him up like a fluoroscope.

The world returned; not incinerated, just a vision. Lattimore had dropped the curious piece of vitrified glass. It lay at his feet in a dozen pieces. His eyes returned to the weathered mound, the temple ruins.

"But who would fight such a war? And why?" Lattimore asked softly.

"Perhaps the war was actually between bad gods and *better* gods," Bhakti answered. "Between those who wanted Man to reach for the stars, to follow them across the heavens—*and those who did not,* who wanted us only for genetic code and raw materials, who looked at us as mere playthings and a source of spare parts. Selfish gods who never wanted Man to walk on air, or live in floating cities."

Bhakti's voice kept on. "They fought a death match against better gods who saw mankind as more than breeding stock;

benevolent gods who saw us as redeemable, or simply good in and of ourselves. Better gods who left behind legends of great beings, ancient knowledge, and tales of divine souls who reigned in heaven—learned souls in search of morality, ethics, and enlightenment. Causing mankind to venerate their offspring, honor their memories and ideas. Moses, Jesus, Buddha, and nameless others in every corner of the globe, divine beings who kept us on an honest path. Better beings, humble enough to understand an even greater God existed—the One who created us all."

The Punjabi scientist's voice dropped away to nothing, letting this sink in for a moment. His voice returned, stronger than before.

"Divine beings we honored with pyramids and sacred cities on lost mountaintops, with everlasting foundations of stone and our endless labor. Temple complexes laid out in the shape of constellations—star maps for future generations: in the three great pyramids of Giza, marking Orion's belt. And in Cambodia, Angkor Wat, pagodas match the constellation Perseus. In Mexico's Teotihuacan, great causeways and waterways show the way to the Pleiades. Each ancient culture pointed to the same quadrant, pointing to our origins. Star maps for the Children of the Stars. All in order to show us the way home— where to follow, where to go. Star maps from divine galactic beings who wished us to find them in the immensity of space."

Bhakti's mythic cosmology hung in the air beside Lattimore's ear. This was a trail of eternal bread crumbs for Hansel and Gretel to follow across the stars. A coherent cosmology sprung from the ancient tales of good and evil: tales of redemption, of this Earth and beyond.

The soft voice explained the ancient struggle. "Call it the birth of planetary morality, if you like. Good aliens versus bad aliens. With their own squabbles, just like us. Immor-

tal beings both *of this Earth, and not of this Earth.*
Competitive star peoples in a race war for supremacy
over the blue planets and their star children. There were
even survivors. We call them fallen angels now. Or the
Nephilim, who still roam the Earth among their offspring
and descendants. Is that so hard to believe?"

Lattimore realized those immortals, call them Takers or
Mind Gliders or the Fallen—call them anything you
want—had been hovering over him since boyhood, since
he climbed into a tree house to fall asleep, since before his
family came to Pennsylvania. Since before the beginning
of his life—

Yes, even since Pop Lattimore worked as forced labor
in Mittelbau-Dora.

The blinding light over the Indus River and the Mound
of the Dead faded away; Bhakti had spirited him to a new
place. A dark clammy underground. A tunnel of slaves. The
gentle Indian scientist had undergone a subtle change: cold
foreboding eyes, the tunnel gloom covering his face like a
drawn hood.

"Of course your father's first employers desperately
wanted to master the technology of the floating cities. And
your father helped them. Not merely with rocketry, but with
antigravity. The real secret of our star-wandering ancestors."

Lattimore peered into the gloom, the underground
section of the forced labor facility known as Middle-Block
D. The rock walls shuddered and trembled. Dust cascaded through a thousand cracks in the concrete. Lightbulbs in their wire cages flickered, and half-naked men
scurried like frightened rats in hell. Fire leapt into the corridor through an open steel door, the metal bent like tin.
Technicians in white coats stumbled into the corridor
half-burned and screaming.

Lattimore saw his own father emerge choking and gasping, his lab coat on fire. His father, a young man: *not one*

of the naked slaves at all, but clean-shaven and well-fed as though allowed regular access to hot water and soap and fresh clothes and food. Pop Lattimore tore off his smoldering coat, threw it away, and pressed against the tunnel wall, eyes wide in fear. Everything had gone terribly wrong.

Inside the testing room, a great bell-shaped instrument vibrated on the edge of sight. The metallic thing appeared visible and then invisible; apparently some kind of anti-gravity core. The infamous Nazi Bell: electromagnetic weightlessness, fractionating space/time and bending light. A device you'd put in another machine to make it float; what you'd put under a city to lift it from the Earth, to awe the natives and keep the savages in line.

But the Nazis' floating bell caromed out of control. Flying wildly about the inner cavern, it smashed men in white coats and men in uniforms against banks of dials, against concrete walls, and then smashed something else. A great fire of mercury lay in its wake, burning everything in the room—men, machines, cables, and slaves—in a violet radiance of death. Lattimore's father shielded his eyes, beaten back by the violet light; turning away, he stumbled down the corridor, fleeing with the rest.

Panic raged through the underground; technicians ran from the violet fire, and things that were not men fled too. Creatures that were not human: gangly humanoids, like frantic praying mantises, thin gray arms and bulbous heads, flailing as they burned. Exactly like that mutant Chargrove Model-A Lattimore had seen on the operating table, except these were alive and functioning. The familiar "Grays" of ancient and modern legend: the large black soulless eyes, the silent tiny mouths. The panicked mantids' emotionless faces showed nothing, their arms flailing, but the Mittelbau insect-men burned like everything else.

Bhakti's voice came again, like Virgil explaining the circles of hell to mute Dante:

"The Nazis never found the secret of the floating cities,

even with all the help they received. The Fallen sent their drones to work down here, not to share secrets but to see every effort squandered, the war machine fail. No gravity bells were ever perfected. Not the kind of magical plaything to be lavished on the insane children of the Wehrmacht. Powers like that are reserved to only the highest forms of galactic life, not demented Über-men here at home."

As if to agree, the thunder gods of the Allies' war hammer pounded bomb upon bomb aboveground. And beneath the earth men cowered in their skins. A single dying shriek of five thousand naked slaves echoed in the tunnels and then suffocated under a mountain of rubble as the roof of the world caved in.

Why wasn't his father among the doomed technicians in their blue overalls and the burning mantids? Where was his father? How had he escaped?

Bhakti's Virgil brought Lattimore to the surface. Fire stretched as far as the eye could see, while the drone of Allied bombers faded under a boiling night sky. Searchlights lanced into the dark along with ack-ack tracers, eager to shred any aircraft straggling behind the squadron. Aboveground most of the buildings were smoldering rubble, but not all. Here and there partially damaged structures dotted the smoking landscape.

Inside an exposed lab building Clem found his father.

His father, clad in dirty overalls and work boots, must have crawled up from the hell below. The man sat at a workbench in the light of a kerosene lamp, the sleeve of his left arm rolled to the elbow. In his free hand a tattoo needle hummed, pricking the skin of his forearm. The needle whirred and whirred. Carefully his youthful father etched blue numbers on his arm.

The vision was more than enough to break Clem Lattimore's mind apart.

Dad wasn't shaved-head slave labor at all, but one of the

favored few, one of the master technicians, working of his own free will. Now that the world lay in ruins, he sought a way out, to escape punishment, becoming a karmic chameleon: changing from coddled scientist to pitiful concentration camp inmate.

Using a few scratches of ink to become a displaced paperless refugee, then magically morph back to coddled scientist once more when the danger of discovery had passed, racing into the arms of the Americans, who would soon scour the German countryside for anyone who'd worked on the Wunderwaffe, the wonder weapons.

"No, that's not right. Not right!" Lattimore cried.

Bhakti brought him back to the library in Sioux Falls, sitting in the chair just as they'd started. The specter exuded a deep well of contempt, the skin of a man filled to the brim with pus and venom, extremely frightening now. Not the man Lattimore knew at all—not the kindly, gentle scientist so interested in showing him about the Aerogel manufacturing facility, so devoted to his work and family. The Punjabi scientist's face seemed choked with bile. No, this was another being entirely, rejecting everything good and decent in life, but with a sly grin on his face, a knowing sneer.

For a moment the mask had slipped, and Lattimore saw the real creature inside the Bhakti-skin: a grinning gaunt man in a top hat and tails, sitting at a desk in a wood-lined study. One of the Fallen, a man of evil tastes and long fingers with strings attached to the weak parts in every human soul.

This wasn't Bhakti sitting in the chair. No, but the creature behind the mirror, a parasite occupying a passive host, his sneering essence glowing through a dead man's eyes—a poisoned angel daring Lattimore to say one of the demon's many names out loud. The Adversary. Beelzebub. Lord of Flies. Gaunt fingers stretched out to shake his hand with unctuous words of greeting. "Glad we finally met."

Lattimore awoke.

He swept the clammy washcloth from his forehead. Snow swirled against the bronze glass windows and over the nighttime streetlamps in the street below. Could everything he believed about his father have been a lie?

He jackknifed off the couch and started pulling books off the library shelves: a history of Nazi wonder weapons, and then Hilberg's *The Destruction of the European Jews*. There were problems with the sick fantasy the hallucination of Professor Singh had showed him. Inconsistencies. Project Riese—Project "Giant"—in Lower Silesia, where the Nazis supposedly built the antigravity bell, was located in the Owl Mountains of *Poland*, not Germany. And the Mittelbau-Dora complex was situated in *Germany*, not Poland.

Moreover, only the concentration complexes of Auschwitz and Birkenau used ink arm tattoos—but then as an educated scientist, his father might have been transferred from either of those camps to Buchenwald at some point and thence to Mittelbau-Dora. So perhaps the ruse might have worked. . . . In any case the Americans gave just about anyone with advanced degrees in the sciences a free pass to come to America, so why put the numbers on your arm at all?

Stop, Clem. This is just the devil talking. The gaunt man talking through the image of a good man. Don't start gnawing your own bowels over a long-dead past. There was no logical way to reconcile the young scientist of his nightmare with the same father who built him a tree house. Nevertheless, Lattimore couldn't help wondering. What about his parents' vanishing act when he was a kid—appearing naked and wet with a broken camera and a few damp Polaroid snapshots? What of that strange conversation upon their return, which Clem had overheard from the stairs?

Mother objecting: *"No one will believe us."*
Father countering: *"Would you?"*

Mother again: *"What about the Polaroids?"*

Father: *"No one will understand them."*

Mother: *"No, that's not what I mean. What are you going to do with them?"*

Father's final words: *"Keep them somewhere safe."*

Lattimore found the bourbon decanter and poured himself a double, which went down way too quick. Mildred lay asleep on his bed, tuckered out. The middle-aged woman had taken off her shoes and unzipped the side of her skirt. The clock said three in the morning.

Back in the library, a photo had slid from his father's Deutsch copy of *Ship of Fools*. Not one of the mysterious Polaroids, but a black-and-white snapshot: Werner von Braun among his rescued colleagues and soldiers of the United States Army. Von Braun's arm was broken and in a cast, but despite this, the genius Kraut showed no signs of fear or subservience to his new masters; instead, he boldly stared into the lens with grim triumph. The faces of his men glowed with a knowing certainty. The whole crew had gotten out clean, found new patrons. Moreover, they were going to do what they did best: make more rockets.

Some wiseass had penciled a devil's goatee and little horns on von Braun's head.

Lattimore chuckled. That could only have been Pop.

Across the room, Jasper's laptop screen beeped to life. A communication window blinked at him, an outside party requesting a video chat. So somewhere out in the big bad world an Internet server still worked. Apparently Wi-Fi still operated in parts of Manhattan. The screen's identification panel read *Caller Unknown, Room 3327, New Yorker Hotel.*

Why was that so familiar?

Something about that hotel, about that room number . . . He really should know about this place, but nothing clicked. The name New Yorker Hotel floated about his head like

fake snow in a glass ball. Until very recently all you had to
do was type a question, get an answer. Google addiction.
Search-engine dependence.

Then it clicked.

A seemingly insignificant factoid of arcane trivia.

Room 3327 was Nicola Tesla's suite in the New Yorker
Hotel—where the great scientist had lived the last years of
his life, broken down and alone.

33

Hysterical Blindness

Piper sat in his study stroking the lava lamp.

Gee Willikers, he loved getting inside a man's head
and messing around. Shock the human rat in the maze;
watch him jump.

Hiding a falsehood between two truths was Mr. P.'s specialty, and he'd only become more adept with age. Mortals
knew they had no time in life's hourglass, so they believed
anything and everything. Aerospace boss Clem Lattimore
couldn't have been a better subject, and conjuring the image of that dopey Punjab scientist to toy with the poor sap,
a true bit of genius.

Bhakti's ghost had been loitering about the crack of Ha-
des, refusing to go down since his recent demise; might as
well put his angry spirit to some use. The really delightful
thing was that Piper's patsies never knew which parts of
his tales were true or false. And that went for both the living *and* the deceased.

Take the war of the silver cities, the Mound of the Dead.

Mostly true. Take his own role in it. Mostly what you'd expect: a "fallen angel," a refugee, the last survivor of his "immortal" kind. Oh, how wonderful life had been before the casting down, he and his playfellows ruling like princelings and princesses in the floating city of glass. They lived among the clouds, wanting for nothing, bathing in heavenly pools and making love in scented gardens, every earthly delight theirs for all eternity. Answerable only to the Master of the First Thought.

Ah . . . the Big Him must have known his shepherds who bedded his sheep would eventually go to war over the flock. The mating impulse, so irresistible . . . And how better to control and improve the stock? The struggle for supremacy was inevitable. Frolicking with the maidens and youths of the fields, sweeping them up from their toil below and keeping them for a while, returning them to their huts and hovels all the better for it . . .

Ten thousand years ago.

Plenty of time for superior breeding to take effect. More than enough time for everyone involved to forget it ever happened, except in tale and myth and the immortal word of לא. Except for El. Him. The One You Cannot Look Upon. The Infinite Mind.

At the final reckoning, when Mr. P. stood naked before the doors of Elysium and Horus weighed his heart against a feather, the gaunt man had long ago decided to claim the Big Book as his defense. Lord, I was just following orders: *"You Angels. You mighty ones who do his bidding, who obey his word . . . be you fruitful and multiply. Now scatter thy enemies with thy strong arm."* Piper smiled at his clever manipulation of scripture, stroked the lava lamp, and whispered, " 'Thy kingdom come. Thy will be done. On earth as it is in heaven.' "

Amen.

Now, take the incredibly useful gravity drive that upheld the floating cities of pre-antiquity and legend. Sure, it existed, but the Nazi version never worked, and thousands died trying to make it work—while the ever-helpful praying mantids *made sure it never worked.*

What the hell were the Germans thinking? That greater beings than themselves would actually teach them how to float? Hah. Better to be buried alive and burned to death from electrically charged mercury. All their work amounted to nothing; now that was justice.

As for Pop Lattimore . . . The gaunt man inserted that ugly bit about Daddy Lattimore tattooing himself into a kike for the heck of it, pure schadenfreude. Just to torture the little boy living inside Clem. While thousands of SS men burned the Reich tattoos from their arms, why not make old man Lattimore get himself a bigger yarmulke, play up his persecution pedigree for after the war? Wouldn't be the first to switch sides a couple of times when the going got tough. *Who cared what was true and what wasn't,* just as long as the grown-up son couldn't get it out of his head.

As for the overwrought, gullible Punjabi scientist mooning over his own untimely death, Mr. P. didn't even have to make him a son of Abraham. Bhakti was the easiest of all to manipulate, believing what he saw with his own lying eyes. After a hopeless search of five thousand miles, more or less, he'd looked up to a window, only to see what he wanted so desperately to see: Lila Chen and Little Maria waving down at him from an apartment window. More than enough to drive the poor Punjabi over the edge.

Then dragged away from the high window on black wings?

Well, not exactly God's honest truth.

Yes, Piper had come into the room, but all he'd done was glance at the two girls staring down to the street. What were they going to do, *jump*? Don't be absurd. The two brats glared over their shoulders at him—part surprise, part annoyance—as though caught doing something naughty.

"Be careful. Don't fall out."

The third member of their cozy little family sat on the larger bed below the Beatrix Potter bunny rabbit mural, touching his iPad. The beanpole preppy looked up only to mutter sullenly, "Right, the first step's a doozy." Then went back to the flickering pictures on his little screen.

But Kid's dark countenance was like a hood over the lad's mind and thoughts, shutting the tall man out. No matter. He was better off than when Piper had taken him away from that crappy apartment on Avenue A. Let him sulk. He'd come around eventually. All Quiet on the Kiddie Front.

Back to business. The cavalry had arrived.

There were soldiers down in the street with hermetic coffins—hazmat body-transport canisters—who *really* wanted to collect Mr. P.'s children. The gentlemen in camouflage praying they weren't too late to snatch Lila's most excellent genetic cell structure and restore humanity as the exalted rulers of planet Earth before the cockroaches took over. The gaunt man's hand clenched the red lava lamp on his desk. The molten wax within slowly roiled under his touch, bubbling to life like real lava. The more excited he got the faster it seemed to bubble.

What to do with the Special Locator Team downstairs? Use them or abuse them?

Should he get them to blast each other to smithereens? Or get them to help bring Lila Chen, the little scamp, and Kid to the Ant Colony for their body-fluid donations in those nice, clean, hermetically sealed plastic canisters? They could all chopper over to LaGuardia airport and hop on Piper Holdings' Gulfstream jet.

Decisions, decisions. Why not both? Use them *and* abuse them.

Lila and Little Maria turned from the window in their San Remo bedroom. Not much left to look at down in the street. The soldiers stood idly by their barbed-wire cordon, not even talking amongst themselves; the helicopter blades were limp and drooping. A kind of icy rain began to fall, glittering under the streetlights, and the sound of *tick-tick-tick* echoed in the canyons of the buildings. Their would-be rescuers, the *nice people* in their SUVs, had driven off, leaving one man dead on the pavement. Maria remembered him. The quiet, sad man from Madame Malvedos' parlor who'd come looking for his daughter—a daughter he would only find on a slab.

Kid sat on the bed under the bunny hutch mural and stared into his iPad with hooded, brooding eyes. He'd seen it all go down outside. And he'd begun to realize that since the moment he met Mr. P., he'd been dying by inches.

Everything the young man did since he left the ratty apartment in Alphabet City—before he possessed a mind, before he knew right from wrong, before he learned *analogies and the core of cognition*—had finally come full circle. If chaos came on smaller wings, fate came on greater ones: the rainbow junk he sold through his skycaps, the digital havoc he wreaked from coast to coast. Now one of those who'd come to rescue them, a selfless stranger, lay in the street. Shot dead for all his effort.

Kid's breath came in short gasps; his hands gripping the electronic tablet. He felt the anger in him, like an exoskeleton protecting his soft insides. A cloak of invisibility for him and the girls from Mr. P.'s inquisitive mind. Kid's anger grew. God, how eagerly he followed the Pied Piper down every dark path without question. And he'd kept on following even as he learned better. *Too late to set it right, change it now?*

Not too late, as long as Mr. P. was the last to know. After mastering so many of Piper's tricks, Kid had mastered a poker face too. Carefully, he donned it like a mask, covering the inside and letting nothing show, shielding his mind from the man in the study.

For the last time he recalled his mother and her boyfriend as they used to be: Mama shuffling around the Alphabet City apartment, tugging at her dingy T-shirt and Dimples bored of her, coming into the kitchen ready for Room Time while the Kit-Cat clock wagged its tail—

Mr. P.'s voice echoed in his head. *Why'd you ever want to leave that swell apartment? Oh yeah, I remember— Room Time. No more of that, right?*

"No more Room Time," Kid agreed softly. The iPad began to flicker in transmission, some new atrocity. Lila and Little Maria stood with their backs to the window, not daring to move.

"You don't have to watch any more of that," Lila whispered.

Kid looked at her with haunted eyes. He swallowed hard and quietly shut it off. For a few seconds he stared through the connecting bathroom into his bedroom with the Kit-Cat clock, the room he never slept in. When the clock refused to stop ticking, even with the plug out, Kid had cracked its face. Periodically the damn clock still came to life, going *click-clack-click* as if to defy him, like it used to in the dirty kitchen back on Avenue A. To think once upon a time he *actually asked* Mr. P. to buy him one of his own.

For a few more moments, the young man thought about all the stuff he had bought: extra wristwatches, a samurai sword, a crossbow with real pointed darts. He used the crossbow once on the back of his door and never picked it up again. Now all his toys and clothes repelled him: the preppy blazers, the dozen pairs of khakis, the three-yard basketball shoes, and all that really cool hip-hop gear. All because he'd started out hiding under the kitchen sink hoping to escape the next Room Time. So when the Pied Piper took him away from the rotten apartment, fed him lobster and fancy cake in a hotel, that made everything okay? What had he really gotten out of it? Baubles. Bribes. And the merest beginnings of an education. The barest inkling of the difference between right and wrong.

But other than that—

Not a damn thing.

In two strides, Kid bolted through the connecting bathroom, slammed open his window, and started tossing the stuff outside. All the toys, all the trinkets. Suddenly the Kit-Cat clock began to *click-clack* loudly.

Kid grabbed it off the wall and pitched it out the window with all the rest. The brittle plastic clock clattered noisily to the pavement, making a couple of troopers look in the shattered clock's direction as the clothes fluttered down. A pair of trousers tried to run away by themselves on a gust of wind, but snagged onto the barbed-wire barricade. A soldier removed the pants and slung them under a grimy standpipe.

That's what I've become, Kid realized, a pair of trousers on a wire. Shapeless legs that Mr. Piper allowed to walk around for a while until the gaunt man decided to change his pants.

Kid flopped back down on Lila's bed. He rested his head against the bunny hutch mural. In a lower corner of the picture, under a clump of grass, two mice in a cozy hole shared a meal at a tiny table. He reached out to touch the two little mice, safe and snug in their little hole. Oh, if only he could go there, live forever with Flopsy, Mopsy, and Peter Cottontail. Not a perfect life, but a better one: where no one was hurt and no one got scared too seriously.

Kid stared at Lila, and then at Maria, his eyes growing dark and bitter. Maria clasped Lila Chen's hand.

"I'm just as smart as either of you," Kid said. "I'm just not biologically divine or psychic. So how come you got the extra jizz? What makes you Hottentots so hot? Whaddah you got that I don't got?"

His eyes grew darker.

"I'm surprised I haven't made you suck my dick yet, Lila.

I could do you in the lower bunk while the little one sits up top. Or get her down to jump on Mr. Baldy while you help. I knew guys in the 'hood that did their wives and sisters together all the time, just like they do in swanky Lincoln Park, bohunk Cheesehead towns in Wisconsin, and places you never heard of in West Virginia."

The ugly words hung in the air.

He seemed to relish the thought for a moment; but the pleasure faded like it had never been. Over time he'd grown bigger inside than that. Less cruel. More merciful. Stronger. Maybe beating Dalekto had done it, or just being with the girls—under their benevolent spell. They'd had a good influence on him. Like a lovely perfume that never wore off.

When Lila said nothing, Kid knew there wouldn't be an answer. Neither Lila nor the little girl spoke, but a glint came to their eyes, as if they knew something. That Kid was not half as bad as he thought; that he had chosen the right side ages ago and just didn't quite know yet. Kid felt the tiny angel and tiny devil sitting on his shoulders again:

Devil Kid: *Where you gonna run to, Spanky?*
Angel Kid: *Don't listen. Just leave.*

Suddenly, Kid shooed them away like pesky flies. Devil Kid fell from his shoulder with a squeak of dismay and a puff of smoke. Angel Kid smiled and rose to heaven on the thrum of a harp. Kid's mind hung in the balance. There was a decision to be made. A choice. That's all that was left to do; exercise a moment of free will.

"I want to go," Maria begged. "Can we go, Kid? Can we go now?"

The little scamp's eyes pleaded with the older girl to help.

"It's up to Kid," Lila said to Maria. Not wanting to force the young man. Anything but that. He'd been forced his whole life. Tricked and bullied at every turn. And Lila wasn't going to do it this time, not now—not ever again.

Repeating softly, "It's up to Kid."

Mr. P. had finally come to that crucial decision. After peoplekind slaughtered each other and went to ground, he fancied remaking the world *in his own image*. This, then, the critical, missing aspect of the plan.

The blush on the rose, what made it perfect.

How truly inspired.

Reseed, rebreed, inbreed mankind using his pretty poppet pods: the Chen girl, Little Maria, and the Kid. Use them as Human Zero, Adam and Eve, plus an Evelyn for good measure. That meant going down the worm crawl at the Hillsboro Whiteside Meatpacking Plant to *personally* help that quack professor and his hybrid fishpeople finish their work. Idjits who thought a few specks of comet glycine could alter human genetic nature for the better.

Well, it couldn't, boys and girls, not without superior extraterrestrial direction—the Pied Piper's direction. Those marinated fish heads would never say no to a fallen angel, to a scion of the silver floating cities. Hell, they'd be delighted to cooperate. He'd show them what panspermial species "enhancement" really looked like: positively sacred.

Obliterating every human grub and substituting the best qualities of himself and his three perfect children. Raw intelligence so you never strained your brain, precognizance so you never tripped on the sidewalk, immortality so you almost never died, and even wings so you could fly—

But how to get from here to there? Play nice with the soldiers downstairs? Beg a ride on their swell helicopter? In olden times when Mr. P. wanted to get the human grubs to do his bidding, he played a game called *Verräter*—Traitor. A simple-enough game for old Hamelin in medieval

Saxony, as people were already frightened out of their wits at black cats or pigs that looked at them. If a sentry or a night watchman spotted a stranger along the dark parapet, he immediately demanded, "Friend or Foe?"

Before the man could answer you'd shriek *"Verräter!"* and stab the fellow in the neck. You could set whole barracks at each other's throats in the middle of the night, one cretin stabbing another until cooler heads prevailed. Then blame the casualties on witches and Jews.

But in modern times the Pied Piper could take advantage of the confused human mind from every angle on his flat-screen TV; his PlayStation controller put him in places simultaneously: a first-person shooter with thermal high-resolution imaging and night vision. Outside the San Remo, the Special Locator Troops were trigger-happy. The tank locked and loaded; the helicopter's minigun safety off. Everyone more than ready to blast everyone else to kingdom come. With a few flicks and twists of his PlayStation controller he could light up the street like New Year's Eve. All the Piper had to say was *Bang bang, you're dead.*

But suddenly he paused. *Think this through. . . .*

Was all this violence strictly necessary? A stray round might disable the helicopter. No, there were simpler methods, much less messy.

The Piper shifted his attention to the troopers on the street securing the San Remo. Those eyes you're seeing with, you don't really need them. *Gentlemen, allow me to introduce you to hysterical blindness.*

With a click of his PlayStation, the men surrounding the apartment building lost their sight. A sudden gasp went up. They dropped their guns, ripped off their gas masks, and shuffled about, finally groping each other in fear and silence. A Special Locator Team member moaned, "Oh, God . . ."

Now he turned his PlayStation to the four troopers at the service entrance of the sixth-floor apartment. No need for uniformed mooks at the back stairs; the children would come quietly enough. With a click and twist of his thumbs the men by the service elevator lost their sight too. A similar gasp as the troopers sank to their knees, fumbling for the stair railing. Two of them stumbled onto the backstairs, panicked, and tripped and went head over heels. Struggling to rise again, the blind men stepped on each other, did a half-somersault, then rolled down the stairs in a confused human ball.

They lay on the landing below, one's man's neck snapped, the other man's ankle broken, the survivor mewing weakly. *See, there actually are wheel-shaped creatures that roll themselves along. Rolmen. And when they land at the bottom they become a meat wrap.*

Mr. Piper forgot all about them.

Now for the men coming up the front elevator. When the sliding doors opened on the apartment landing, five of the six groped out into the hallway, all blind except the captain. The front doorbell rang.

Mr. P. opened the apartment door to see a very distraught officer, almost shell-shocked, discovering for himself that in the land of the blind, the one-eyed man really is king.

"Why don't you bring your men inside, Captain?" Mr. P. said genially. "They can sit for a moment. When they calm down a little perhaps their sight will return. I know why you're here, and we have every intention of cooperating to the fullest. Let me fetch the children."

The captain made the men put hand on shoulder to tramp through the front door. They found the couch or sat cross-legged on the floor. Mr. P. strode down the hall toward the children's rooms, the doors ajar, the lights on. And in one sweeping glance the Piper thought he might have undergone an attack of hysterical blindness himself. The kids' rooms were empty.

The kids' rooms were empty.

Silently he cursed leaving the Kit-Cat clock in charge.

Plugged or unplugged it should have warned him. Maybe Kid's bashing it had compromised Kit-Cat's integrity; in any event, never let a plastic cat do a grown man's job. He noticed the girls' open clothes drawers, the scattered shirts and socks, the missing JanSport packs. He looked wildly about in the connecting bathroom, and then to Kid's torn-up bedroom. He thrust his head out the boy's open window and saw the mess of stuff below. *Oh, so that's how it is. . . .* Total rejection.

Ungrateful brats. *How dare they run away?*

After all the care, the loving, after all the—

The Pied Piper could feel a holy rant coming up his throat. Oh, we're gonna have some fun tonight. Just you wait, my pretties. Snarling damnation to the empty room, unforgiving as the blowhole of a furnace.

"First, we're going to fix you, lil' rat-girl. The fish doctors at Pi R Squared are gonna peel back your skull and wire your brain to a Ouija board to see if it moves the pointer up and down. And if we don't like the answer, oh, if we don't like the answer, we'll push a pain button right into your folded pudding—"

He took a breath; there was so much vengeance to go around.

"Lila, my most beautiful creature, we're gonna use you for body parts, *my very own Piper Youth Movement*; keep you alive in a big glass test tube and take a few cells at a time. You'll never die, and you'll never grow old, and you'll *never* get out of that tube."

Last of all, a special, special venom for his firstborn: "For you, Kid, my greatest creation, we're gonna do *performance art*. Ever hear the old joke about the traveling salesman, the farmer's daughter, and the buttered corn? No? Well, I'll leave that to your imagination. In the end, Bub, we're gonna enjoy some very special Room Time. We're going in that room with the traveling salesman and a bushel of buttered corn, and we're never coming out!"

The Piper raged back down the hall and stormed into the living room. The men sitting on the couch or squatting on the floor held their heads, some openly weeping.

"Okay," he shouted. "No more slacking." He smacked one on the head. "C'mon! Get up, let's go!" Magically the men's sight returned, to gasps of gratitude.

Mr. P. strode into his study in a slathering rage. The lava lamp had burst; a pool of lava spread across the desk. The sounds of explosions erupted outside, up and down Central Park West, manhole covers leaping into the air on columns of underground steam. The metal lids clanged against the buildings.

In three shakes of a lamb's tail Mr. P. raced out the lobby and into the street. The rain of ice slackened, leaving scattered diamonds everywhere. In his temper tantrum the Piper had blown a steel manhole cover at the helicopter too, snapping a rotor blade. The officer and his troopers stumbled out the building after Mr. P. and stood about idiotically, not thinking too clearly—just happy to see again. Mr. P. almost slaughtered every single one there and then, but managed to restrain himself. He went to where the shattered Kit-Cat clock lay on the pavement coated in fallen ice.

The long, gaunt man stared down as the busted Kit-Cat clock grinned back. He whispered to it and asked it questions, and it told him what he wanted to know. How far the children had gone. And where.

"You should have warned me of this!" he snarled. *What do you think I keep you around for?*"

Then he kicked the kitty clock into the gutter.

34

Hippety-Hop

After the Danbury Mall, Beatrice drove grumpy. The bulky pockets in her tactical vest rode up her midriff like a bad girdle. Stomping around a saloon for a year picking French fries off customers' plates had ruined her girlish figure. Now she was paying for it. *Sigh* . . . Nothing worse than a dumpy dame you might mistake for a Polish goalie on a women's hockey team. Feeling slightly sorry for herself, Bea shrugged. *Well, yeah, things could be worse.* Then she tried to think of exactly how.

A creeping cloud of the vapors washed over her. The package of Dramamine jiggled in her shirt pocket. No point adding sleepy to pukey. In a Dramamine haze all she'd think about was poor Webster—bad bugs, galloping disease . . . Too much in a claustrophobic car with a long hood and a low roof. But it bothered her. How'd they all gotten so lucky?

Beatrice took a breath, gripped the wheel, and pressed the pedal down. Her leg throbbed and the little punctures by her ear burned, morphing to a mysterious ache. Those pain clusters always heralded a change in the forecast. As the barometer dropped, the side of her head ached. Weather heading their way—maybe that icy rain chasing them up from the city.

So get here, already.

In the white Dodge minivan, Billy watched the highway roll under him, a gray treadmill devouring the miles. With the whole world dead or dying wherever you looked, at least in the white minivan you sat up high. It felt so much better, easier to breathe.

Suddenly the walkie-talkie squawked, Beatrice's voice barging out of the box,

"How come we didn't get sick like everyone else?"

Billy took a moment. Then, "Not everybody's sick."

Beatrice again: "*Almost* everybody. You know what I'm asking."

Billy sighed and kept looking straight ahead. He knew what she meant. It troubled him too. How had the bunch of them gotten to skip study-hall punishment and a trip to the principal's office? A mosquito must have bitten them at least once this summer. He kept staring at the gray interstate. His mind went back to Major Todd, the same confusion before he and his men succumbed. *Why you? How'd you get so lucky?*

"I'm not sure," he finally admitted. "Maybe it's like Major Todd back in Vandalia thought. Natural immunity? Maybe touching the evidence bag did it for me, and I passed it on to Cheryl and Bhakti. They touched the baggie too. Maybe you were unexposed. Unavailable. Use much bug spray this summer?"

The walkie-talkie went silent for a few seconds.

"Well, I tended a lot of bar when Webster was away. Lived at the saloon."

Another few moments passed; then the tinny voice came out of the radio. "Still, Cheryl and I were smacking mosquitoes like crazy in that holding tent. Love to get you two in an immunology lab. Do a blood work-up. Check your DNA against that baggie."

Billy nodded, bewildered; no logical answer.

"That leaves fate. Magic. The hand of God."

Silence for a few more moments. Then Cheryl's voice came over the walkie-talkie. She'd been listening. "Better than nothing, right? I'll take fate, magic, or God every time."

Cheryl rode with Janet's ashes for company.

No Rachel. Where was she?

Did she do right by Bhakti, putting the Nambe urn in the front seat? Would it make any difference? She almost started fiddling with the radio tuner as Bhakti used to, trying to find a sing-along, but she didn't know if it would make him angrier. Better to leave bad enough alone. She reached across to the passenger seat to touch the metal urn with Janet's ashes. Not cold, like before. A good sign? Maybe it pleased him.

The big Honda Pilot wasn't too hard to find in deserted Middletown, Connecticut. She spotted the big SUV, flashers on, parked on empty Main Street. The would-be rescuers pulled up behind and shut off their engines. Cheryl got out of the yellow Toyota 4Runner with a heavy heart and walked up to the SUV driver's window. Two adults dressed up as beekeepers sat in the front seats. She heard barks from the back of the Pilot, but the tinted glass kept her from seeing much. The two beekeepers stared at her through the mesh of their bug hats.

"Lauren?"

The smaller beekeeper nodded yes. "Cheryl?"

The breath caught in Cheryl's throat; what else was there to say? She couldn't think of anything. Neither could Lauren. On the phone, Lauren seemed more worried about her sister, Eleanor, than she was for herself. Being half-crazy, how would Eleanor take the news? Would this be the last straw of sanity? The thought grew on Cheryl as the convoy traveled the last lap; grew to the point of dry-mouthed panic—for she suddenly realized even Eleanor's in-laws in that big Honda Pilot *wanted her* to explain about Bhakti. In the wan morning light, the four cars drove down the sanitarium drive under rattling autumn leaves. A woman stood on the porch of a gabled house in a housecoat.

Eleanor.

Dreading the worst, Cheryl unlatched the door of the

yellow 4Runner, clutching Janet's ashes in her arms. Her feet felt leaden and watery at the same time. Awkward words came out of Cheryl's mouth. "You're still walking. That's good. I'm glad you're still walking."

She watched the woman's face collapse from within, grasping and yet not grasping. Eleanor held a ridiculous pink bottle of Pepto-Bismol replying stiffly, but sensibly, back, "One of the bugs bit me back in Van Horn and made me walk." She took the urn with Janet's ashes and cradled it gently in her arms. After some moments Eleanor snuffled a little; she clutched her housecoat together. Slowly she sank to the porch and held herself, quietly asking over and over, "Where's Bhakti? Where's Bhakti?" And already knowing the answer, she began to sob.

In a horrible flash, Cheryl saw something she was never supposed to see: Eleanor with a rope around her neck, a hangman's noose, the tail draped into her lap. Just like those women at the gloomy arched viaduct as they'd raced from Manhattan. A foresight? A premonition? The vision went away. No rope, just a poor lady in a housecoat sobbing on the porch.

At length Eleanor brushed the tears from her face and looked at her sister and brother-in-law standing there in their grand beekeepers' outfits. "I don't think you need that stuff," she told them. "They spray here. Haven't seen a bug since the end of September." She acknowledged the goofy pink bottle in her hand and glanced over her shoulder into the house. "Mr. Washington doesn't feel well."

After having been cramped up for hours, Corky and Peaches bounded out the back of the large Honda and shook themselves. As Guy and Lauren fussed over the two dogs, Cheryl begged to take them for a walk—anything to get away from death talk—and Big Bea offered too, her face gray. She could use some air. "Really, it's no trouble."

At first the dogs were reluctant to stray very far with new handlers, but soon graciously allowed the two strangers to hold their leads when mommy Lauren told them, "It's all right. You go explore. We'll be right here." Then after a few strides, Corky and Peaches dragged Cheryl and Beatrice hither and yon over the manicured lawn, not caring a fig who held the leash, snuffing under fallen leaves and happy just to be alive on an autumn morning.

They came at last to a spectacular red maple in the middle of the lawn. The morning sun lit up the tree like a lantern; the deep scarlet foliage was bright enough to radiate off the ground thirty feet away. Two large dead birds lay at the bottom of the tree, partly covered in leaves. They looked like ravens or crows, but a breeze rattled the branches overhead and exposed the birds' heads and beaks. Woodpeckers: two large black woodpeckers with brilliant red crests and white racing stripes along their faces under the tree.

"Think they ate the wrong mosquitoes?" Cheryl asked out loud.

Beatrice had been wondering the same thing; she shrugged and leaned heavily on her cane. Peaches pulled on her leash to investigate, then Corky, but the women held them a dozen feet back. Peaches looked up at her handler with doleful eyes. "Better not, Girlie," Bea cautioned. "Might be contagious."

Another movement caught the dogs' eyes, and they shivered as one. A passel of rabbits crept out of the bushes and cautiously hopped toward the two dead birds at the foot of the maple. Cheryl counted six or seven more nearby, but gave up as another wave of bunnies poked their way out of an enormous gorse bush. In a few seconds, a score of rabbits had gathered in a loop about the fallen birds. The two women and the two dogs stood transfixed at the spectacle of normally shy rabbits making a fairy circle around the woodpeckers. No, not normal, not by a long shot.

"Those are some brave rabbits," Cheryl whispered, fear-ing that if she raised her voice the whole crew would scatter into the brush.

"Looks like they're having a prayer meeting," Bea chuckled.

Corky and Peaches stopped shivering and sat on their haunches, no longer eager to chase—more like a couple of pious parishioners sitting in a pew.

Then something even stranger occurred. Two of the more courageous rabbits broke from the circle of their friends and bunny-hopped closer to the fallen birds. Now three feet away. Now one foot. The two big, brave bunnies were right on top of the dead woodpeckers when they began to nose the birds' black lifeless wings, sticking their rabbit faces right up close and pushing a little. They paused to examine the black woodpeckers, then went back for more, nudge-nudge with their cute, twitching noses. One bunny patted the stiff wing of the dead bird with his front paw. Pat, pat: *Hey, wake up.* The other rabbit patted his bird too.

Slowly a taloned claw unclenched.

Cheryl pressed a hand to her mouth.

Beatrice could not believe what they were seeing. The women stood stock-still, hands on the dogs' heads. One of the large black woodpeckers twitched his neck. Then the second woodpecker opened its eyes and looked around, brushing away some fallen leaves. The two grand birds sprang to their feet and ruffled their feathers. Their sharp beaks darted from side to side, eyes like lasers. A heartbeat later, the woodpeckers leapt into the air and vanished into a copse of trees. The two dogs barked, and the bunnies scattered in every direction.

"Magic rabbits," Cheryl said, completely dumbfounded.

"Wouldn't mind carrying one of them around in my back pocket for good luck," Beatrice agreed.

Very quietly, the large woman stroked Peaches' head, trying to digest what they had just witnessed and not really coming up with an answer. Her game leg still throbbed, and the pinpricks behind her ears felt like an angry burr, but the dog's head under her hand seemed to have a calming, peaceful effect. Beatrice felt a subtle change in everything. A kind of hopefulness she hadn't felt since . . . since forever.

The wind shifted, a season turned, tipping the balance of the world. The great descent finally arrested, and now matters stood at equilibrium—a great pause—now, they would either crawl out of the abyss, or slide the rest of the way down. When Big Bea looked at her lady copper friend, she smiled a little. "I'm glad *we both* saw this, Gorgeous."

Cheryl felt it too, as if a great weight had lifted. "I don't think I'll ever get used to that nickname, but you just keep on. Good for a girl to hear it every so often."

The sun faded from the morning; wind from the north brought the scent of snow. Cheryl, Beatrice, and the dogs returned from their weird interlude to find Guy and Lauren sitting on the front steps of the pretty gabled house, their bug gear folded like laundry, neatly at their feet.

A young lady sat between them.

The girl wore a blue dress with puffed sleeves and a white starched smock, at least two petticoats under her dress; then tights, and high-button shoes. In addition, she wore a bright green quilted down ski jacket over her shoulders. Sort of like a child extra in *Hello, Dolly!* waiting to go onstage—an odd mélange of old and new. She sat on the front steps, her knees pressed together, face creased in concentration; the diary with the bright pink lock sat open on her lap. She held a dark-colored pencil in her fingers and pressed it into the book, drawing something, drawing very hard, face scrunched as she worked the difficult lines.

"You guys see the rabbits?" Cheryl wondered.

Guy and Lauren shook their heads no. Corky and Peaches wagged themselves inside out, rushed over to the little girl, and began licking her face. She laughed for a moment, but pushed them away. *No, no! Stop it!* Then going back to drawing in her Horse Friends diary.

"I'm Cheryl. What's your name? Can I see what you're drawing?" How had she missed the girl sitting in the big Honda? Maybe the tinted glass? "Were you sitting in the back and I just didn't see you?"

The young lady glanced up, smiled briefly, and then covered the page with her arm, frowning with concentration. *Very private.*

"Her name's Alice," Lauren tried awkwardly.

Suddenly Lauren felt the need for some kind of explanation—after all, the girl had indeed ridden with them. She looked to Guy, but he shrugged. If somebody asked something as simple as where she came from, what do you say? *Oh, 1855. We think she's my great-great auntie-granny.* Good luck with that. She glanced crossly at her husband, as if to say, *You got a better explanation?* Guy chuckled, rose from the steps, and went toward the gabled house, taking the two dogs with him. *All yours, Sweetie.* Worse than useless.

Lauren swallowed hard, thinking of the right reply.

"She's uh . . . she lives near us in Fairfield," Lauren said finally. Guy paused at the front door, impressed. *Not bad, Darling.*

Inside the house, the nice hospital orderly named Mr. Washington lay stretched out on the parlor couch, a pillow under his head. Eleanor found an afghan in one of the patient's rooms and tucked the blanket under his legs to keep him warm. His dark skin had gone gray, and he shivered. Eleanor poured him some pink Pepto-Bismol in a teacup while still clutching Janet's ashes. "This is for now. Do you think you can get it down?"

Mr. Washington made a face; he would try.

Everyone from the porch came inside. Cheryl, Bea, and Lauren stood awkwardly around the parlor. Mr. Washington smiled wanly and waved hi to the newcomers. For a few moments, no one said anything, as if embarrassed. A dead woman sat quietly in an armchair near the coffee table, making the parlor seem slightly overcrowded.

The dead lady had been working on one of those M. C. Escher puzzles: a busy little scene of stairs and segmented worms crawling up and down. Mr. Washington had thrown a sheet over her like covered furniture. Dots of blood bled through in patches. The poor woman in the chair seemed to have scratched herself to death. A hanging forearm showed her skin in tatters, the lady's nails broken. Mr. Washington breathed deep. "There's another woman upstairs with her lung coughed out."

"Let's take care of this one first," Billy said quietly to Guy.

Guy nodded. "Why don't we just carry her outside in the chair, as is?" Billy offered Guy latex gloves from a box in his first-aid kit, which helped some, but they had trouble wresting the woman and the chair onto the porch without getting blood all over. The lady had really soaked the thing.

"Where are you taking Kay?" Eleanor asked adamantly, barely containing her agitation—her husband Bhakti, her best friend Kay, her daughter Janet—all gone. She pensively cradled the Nambe urn, as though wondering how a thing like a human body got into such a small vessel.

"Just outside for now, Eleanor," Guy reassured her. "We'll bury her properly later."

Outside, young Alice still sat on the porch steps working the drawing in her plastic Horse Friends diary. The young lady glanced at the two dead bodies nearby and didn't even blink. Dead bodies, *who cares?*

Only the drawing on the diary page mattered.

Lauren came out on the porch. How to explain their little time traveler unruffled by dead bodies, diligently scribbling away? *Well, she's seen worse,* Lauren figured; sitting cross-legged for her family's cyanotype, Alice's dead parents dressed in their Sunday best, hands clasped together with a black ribbon while the child cradled her dolls. Maybe now they could find out what sister Eleanor remembered about Great-Auntie Whitcomb, or Great-Granny Whitcomb. Lauren vaguely recalled some family legend about a little Whitcomb girl disappearing and reappearing. Some hushed-up tale.

Alice looked up and smiled. A nice smile; you could tell she liked Lauren.

"Why don't you draw inside, sweetheart. It's warmer. C'mon."

The sun had vanished, the sky now leaden and overcast. Large flakes of fluffy snow began to fall, settling on the carpet of red maple leaves. Along the edges of the wide lawn, faces appeared in the gorse bushes and in the long grass, dozens of them—here, there, everywhere. Tiny faces with twitching noses and long ears. Rabbit faces.

35

Room 3327

Only a few short hours earlier, in the dead of night, while the gaunt man indulged fantasies of rebreeding the world in his own image, the Piper's children were getting ready to leave the bunny hutch. Lila and Little Maria tugged on their parkas, then hoisted their packs which were stuffed with extra socks and long johns. The Kid dawdled in front of the Beatrix Potter mural. The two mice in their little burrow stared back at him with flat black eyes, now just pictures on a wall.

Grimly, Kid wrapped his cloak of anger around himself

and the two girls. No souls for sale—not for Dalekto, lobster, or Nesselrode pie. Mr. P. wasn't God. At the far end of the apartment Kid could feel the tall man's mind occupied with great plans, busy-busy-busy, thinking great thoughts in the wood-lined study; first gloating over how to use the girls, then crippling the troopers downstairs with hysterical blindness. Mr. P. was too busy to notice their escape.

Only moments to get away. *Make them count. Do it now.*

The three youngsters sneaked into the hall by the emergency stairs, quietly shutting the back door of the apartment. One of the stricken soldiers looked up at the sound of the shutting door, staring blindly through lifeless eyes. Too terrified even to speak, he gripped a metal stair rail for dear life.

Bhakti's ghost stood in the gloom of the landing under a dim lightbulb—their rescuer finally come to rescue them. The holes in his chest from his recent shooting seemed to glow on their own. A curious effect, as if Bhakti's insides were imbued with an extra radiance, wrapped in the translucent skin of a dead man. The Punjabi scientist flickered in the shadows, pixelating like the grainy images in an old silent movie. Perhaps as the world fell apart, the seen and unseen performed a kind of dance, trading partners and planes of existence, stepping out from the mirror. Perhaps as the world finally unraveled you got to see all the threads of now, forever, and maybe.

Bhakti's inner radiance, his inner glow, seeped from inside him and coalesced as a single glow. More than the aura of his soul, this incandescence seemed to form on its own. A benevolent presence. A guardian light.

"Mr. Singh?" Lila had slipped. No—*Professor* Singh from across the street in Van Horn. Bhakti lowered his dark eyes and put his fingers to his lips: *Shhhhhhh . . .*

Silently, the dead man beckoned the youngsters to follow him, slinking around the stricken soldier. The benevolent light hovered at his shoulder.

Quiet as mice, the children tiptoed down another landing, then another, putting as much distance as they could between themselves and the apartment. At last they reached the ground floor and the lobby service door.

"I can see through things." Maria's small voice was very frightened. "I think Mr. Bhakti and his little glow ball are helping me see through things, Lila. I can feel the men outside, and I can see them."

"So how do we get out?" Lila whispered.

Little Maria shut her eyes and put her hand against the service door. *How to get out?* Soldiers stood in the lobby with gas masks and guns; this crew wasn't blind yet. But Maria sensed they would be soon. The main elevator reached the ground floor, the doors opened, and the troopers piled in. One of them stabbed the sixth-floor button a couple of times, and the elevator doors whooshed shut. The lobby now empty.

"Let's go, now!" Maria whispered. "While there's no one there!"

The youngsters tiptoed across the marble floor, pausing for a second over Farley the doorman, slumped in a corner. A couple of wire plugs stuck on his neck; he had been tased.

The children slowly pushed out the heavy ironwork door to the street. The deafening sound of falling ice drummed over the awning, battered the parked cars and military vehicles. Icicles were beginning to form on the accordion-wire barricades. A few soldiers still hunkered down in the street in various states of hysterical blindness, weapons pointed in every direction.

Quietly, Bhakti's ghost led the three youngsters out the front entrance; the children hugged the wall, scurrying along from shadow to shadow. Lila noticed the gentle light coalesced around the dead Punjabi scientist leading them on, a pale amber glow in the nighttime city street. Bhakti's guardian glow hovered beside a fire hydrant and beckoned them. The ephemeral glow moved again, a floating fairy light gaining momentum as they approached the south barricade. There was a narrow gap between the building wall and the accordion-wire barricade, maybe just enough to squeeze through.

Now or never.

In half a second, they slipped the gap and ran into the noisy, icy rain. Little Maria fell behind, the slush sloshing into her boots.

"I'll take her," Kid urged. "She can ride piggyback. Take my pack, Lila." He shrugged off his JanSport, and Maria climbed up. The pleasing amber glow danced ahead; determinedly they slogged toward it, but the children were not out of the woods yet.

Cohorts of looters emerged out of nowhere, picking storefronts or restaurants clean and scattering back into the city again. Sirens echoed off the concrete canyons, the dark buildings piled high with bulging and broken mounds of plastic garbage. Shattered window glass mixed invisibly with the falling ice, and trash fires burned at every intersection. Ambulances and fire trucks spun their wheels helplessly in the growing slush. Police cruisers came to help, and then were stranded in turn. Clambering over a heap of trash, the youngsters fled the chaos and kept on going.

Dawn came to the city.

The freaky icy rain began to stop for good, pink-and-blue slits parting the clouds.

A forty-block tramp left the youngsters cold to the bone. Clammy sweat soaked their parkas and longies, their boots sopped through, and the gray flat air chilled their lungs. The streets were quiet, no traffic, no plows or shovels scraping the sidewalk. Bhakti and his guardian light finally halted at the entrance of a large old building, the New

Yorker Hotel. The pleasant, illuminated Bhakti passed through the hotel revolving doors and vanished. The youngsters paused a moment to glance at the commemorative plaque embedded in the building wall.

HERE DIED, ON JANUARY 7, 1943,
AT THE AGE OF 87—

They didn't finish reading; they were just too damn cold.

Lila, Maria, and the Kid pushed through the hotel doors; the gold-and-silver art deco hotel lobby enveloped them like the grand gallery of a royal audience hall. The hotel doorman, in his greatcoat, was curled up on the long leather couch in his stocking feet, asleep, galoshes on the floor beside him. The youngsters went to the reception desk and dripped onto the marble floor until a groggy bellhop appeared, buttoning his tunic. The fellow brushed a greasy lank of hair off his forehead and measured the ragamuffins wetting his nice clean floor.

"Welcome to the New Yorker Hotel. Do you have a reservation?"

The bellhop chuckled at his own funny, then leered over the marble counter.

"Let me guess. You'll be wanting the Hungarian's room, won't you? Everyone's favorite. The thirty-third floor. Room 3327; it's open. Don't lock yourselves out; our key card coder is on the fritz. We change the sheets twice a week. No credit cards. We're four hundred a night, in advance. I'll be up for it later. And don't bother calling for room service. The noodle shop on the corner may still be open. Otherwise, we have a general scrounge in the Tick Tock Diner around noon, but we're not expecting deliveries today because of the ice storm. So it looks like Jell-O and Saltines and Sanka until we do."

That's when the three noticed the Kit-Cat clock behind the counter on the wall. They hadn't noticed at first because it wasn't moving, but the second their eyes lit on it the damn thing began to swing its tail and roll its eyes: *tick-tock-tick-tock*. A gold plaque beneath it proclaimed PIPER HOLD-INGS QUALITY SERVICE AWARD.

The bellhop grinned and wagged his head. "I love that clock."

It turned out Kit-Cat clocks hung throughout the art deco hotel, in every room, not to mention in every other hotel in the city—as though Mr. P. wanted to keep both eyes on people's comings and goings. Every time the youngsters passed a clock, it clicked to life and went *tick-tock*. Once inside Room 3327, Kid ripped Kit-Cat off the wall and looked about for a window to open, then stopped.

Bhakti Singh had joined them again. Once more, a mantle of light infused the dead scientist, as if more than one entity occupied the same body. And as before the light co-agulated, coalesced to the shape of a ball, seeming to hover at his shoulder. The Punjabi scientist stood in one corner of the Tesla Suite, no longer their guide, but a frowning totem of retribution. You could see the storm clouds inside him, a volcano of simmering resolve. He was not through with this world, not yet.

Little Maria glanced at the double apparition. In this special room, the Punjabi scientist and the Light Tesla were living as one; and they wanted to show her something.

"Kid, give me the clock. Give it to me."

He gaped at her for a second but did not argue. Maria took the clock, holding the plastic thing in her hands like a crystal ball. If the clock let Piper spy on the world, the clock told the little girl much, much more; seeing the ma-chinery of reality, the clockworks of existence going back into time itself. To how it all started. To what was. And how it became . . . Her eyes fluttered and then rolled up into her head. She whispered softly, "Show me. Tell me. . . ."

She saw things very clearly now; psychic fingers like a direct wire into the gaunt man's mind, showing her the Pied

Piper's galactic history. His story, from the birth of the first perfect thought to the ugliness of the present. Some of it she understood and some of it she didn't, but she let it wash over her, absorbing what she could.

Endless star fields and coils of dazzling gas flowed across the heavens. The Long Souls came out of the vast Magellan cloud, touching the edge of the galaxy, flying on schooners of light like an armada of sparks. Mr. P. was first among equals. The first of the Long Souls to climb the highest heavens; the first to challenge the supremacy of the Great Inspirer, to raise a fist against the Almighty architect of multiple universes and infinite numbers. . . .

The Long Souls fought the One who set the galaxies to spin—fought and fell, their sparks fleeing across the void. His Resolve chased them across the universe like a cosmic wind, denying them world after world—not the immortal gas giants, not the frozen globes of methane and ammonia, nothing stable, nothing permanent.

Dare you stand against Me?

Then make something of these topsy-turvy blue planets, with oxygen skies, saline swamps, and rivers of lava. Take the most unstable planets to seed, the most volatile spheres, the pretty blue ones.

Try keeping them alive. If you can.

Piper and all his kin were cast into the blue atmospheres, the Long Souls hurtling through formations of clouds like falling stars. As in ancient tales they raised ape to thrall, and thrall to man, creating in His image a pleasing form of graceful life. . . . They carved mountains with their minds and made metal into floating cities.

But like selfish children the Long Souls turned against each other, burned rocks to glass, battling over who would rule. They fought one last death match over this pretty blue world, this Mother Earth. Then they left only mounds of the dead behind . . . reverting to simpler forms of life: insects, beasts, the thralls they once enslaved, even mere incandescence. Wandering the face of the Earth for eons, across jungles and deserts, under oceans and over mountains, the gaunt man now scavenged the stone and concrete cities, clawing up from the gutter, the final Piper, the last of his kind to embrace human physicality, the last Long Soul in human skin to reseed the world once more.

As these thoughts and pictures lit up her mind, Maria realized all this past history was coming to a point. This galactic struggle over ancestral life all came down to this day, this moment, this final struggle. The little girl began to speak.

"The Tall Man wants to fly us away to the underground tunnel place. Then down to where the bugs in white coats and their human pie are squared. Where the doctors will use Lila's cells to remake the world and leave her a dried-out skin. They want to put wires in my head and ask me to tell them what happens next. So a special few new-and-improved human beings can see through walls and around corners."

"What does he want from me?" Kid demanded.

Maria's eyes rolled all the way back; a touch of saliva glistened at the corner of her mouth. "You were Mr. P.'s favorite. He wanted to grow wings on you, make you owner of the world, but now he hates you worst of all, and he's going to butter your buns, cornhole you forever."

More soft words fell from her drooping mouth.

"The two light friends brought us here because the sparks in the system are still alive in this room; the lightning jumps where they want. Bhakti's ghost and his glow ball, once called Tesla, want you to make a call. They want you to call the Lattimore man in Sioux Falls while there's still a connection, while there's still a chance to stop them. Tell him to try to use electric bots to kill the worms. Lock the worms inside and kill them all. Lock them in, and kill them all."

Kid slapped his laptop open. "You mean a virus? Get the

computers at the aerospace company to corrupt that Hillsboro place?" Kid squirmed. Billboard tweaking was not that kind of wizardry. You needed magic codes and infected memory sticks to plug into mainframes. How was he going to explain any of this to the Lattimore guy? How much could the man really know about sending viruses into supersecure research facilities? Convince him to try. The computer-placed call rang through. At the other end, a red-eyed Clem Lattimore accepted the transmission.

Little Maria dropped the Kit-Cat clock to the floor.

Her face frozen in panic.

"Hurry!" she hissed. "Mr. P. has found us. He's downstairs. He's almost here."

36

Numbered Headstones

The magic rabbits that mysteriously thumped dead woodpeckers back to life had vanished into the gorse bushes without a trace. Gray clouds crawled up from the south, that ice storm from the city picking up cold air, turning it into a snow-maker. Beatrice spoke out loud what everyone else was thinking.

"We could do a lot worse than this place. I mean, it is a hospital. Food, medicine, I'll bet the buildings have their own generators someplace." Sounded reasonable. Wait out the storm. But who knew how long the troubles were going to last? A month? Six months? No, that didn't alter their present situation either. Might as well look for what they needed here and now.

Before they set off on the treasure hunt, Mr. Washington roused himself from the couch on one elbow to warn them, "When the administration closed the max-security building for lack of funds, they spread the hard cases around to different buildings. No telling who's still wandering around. Be careful."

So they went warily, locked and loaded.

The men walked the length of the cold maintenance garage toward the security office. The place was almost like Home Depot. A half-dozen snowblowers were parked in a row, and even two snowplows—a Kubota front loader, and a red-painted cowcatcher bolted to the front of a 1960s yellow school bus. The only creepy thing about the school bus—the hand and leg restraints and a metal grill door separated the driver from the patients.

Guy looked around the sterile security office. A video-monitor wall showed screens from a hundred or so cameras dotting every corner of the psychiatric hospital. Across the room, scores of labeled metal keys hung in an open metal lockbox. One key was marked PUMPS. And below the lockbox a bright red security card sat by a programming terminal—the master pass.

"Wonder if it still works?" Billy took the red key card just in case.

They left by a narrow side door marked PUMPS. The key worked; a very good thing.

The red plastic master key card pass also worked every place they tried. As they walked through the empty cafeteria toward the food-service area, Guy became a little reluctant to probe too far, swipe after swipe; like entering a labyrinth, drawing you in—

They stopped cold at the meat locker; the steel door wasn't latched. The two men strained their ears and shared a silent glance. Billy pushed the locker open; they checked the corners, the ceiling. What you would expect; shelves of packed cuts, slabs of hanging meat, just a meat locker.

Billy paused, glancing onto a shelf of frozen chickens; an object caught his eye and he picked it up.

"Get a load of this."

A solid gold wedding band and an engagement ring with a diamond the size of a cherry stone. The rock glittered under the refrigerator lights. Guy was impressed. Lauren's engagement sparkler wasn't half its size, and she wouldn't have parted with it unless they took her finger too. "Ladies don't leave these things around."

There were scuff marks on the tile floor, the signs of a struggle, as if somebody had been dragged along. Scuff marks. Lost rings. No fingers . . . .

"So where's the hand they belong to?" Billy wondered.

As for the armed and dangerous females, Cheryl and Big Bea were starting to have second thoughts about Connecticut Valley Hospital. A growing sense of dread descended on the women as they tried to locate the psychiatric hospital's up-to-date medical areas. Parts of the place still had that nineteenth-century nuthatch feel.

Neo-Gothic and Victorian brick buildings dotted the campus, many of them in a terrible state of repair, with chipped steps and broken columns. Empty windows stared at the women; rickety iron fire escapes clung to the main structures by threads—nothing you'd want to climb. The silent, empty grounds whispered of peeling paint and abject failure.

Making matters more daunting, the women found themselves traversing an old cemetery once used by the sanitarium. The straight lines of headstones across the grass reminded Cheryl of military graves. But instead of names and dates on the headstones, only numbers appeared. Numbers in granite: 231. Another chiseled gravestone: 202. No name, no date. Endless numbered headstones—the nameless graves of the forgotten insane.

Cheryl saw the mark of doubt in her companion's eyes. "My guess is, the hospital did it out of sympathy, to protect the families from their loved ones."

"Social stigma." Beatrice nodded in agreement. "Nothing worse than people thinking you were crazy. Or that you *were related* to someone who was crazy. Nobody wanted their family name on the headstone in the cemetery of a madhouse. Insane blood might run in your veins."

Cheryl suddenly felt terribly sorry for those buried with nothing to show for their lives but a number on a stone. It didn't sit well with Beatrice either. "Shame can be a powerful restraint. But without it . . ." Bea paused. "Everybody's crazy."

The women found the infirmary. Gurneys stood against the walls. The overhead lights were shut off and the reception desk empty. The whole place seemed neat and clean. A sign in the hall pointed to the pharmacy. Beatrice paused at the wide pharmacy counter; drawers ransacked, pills scattered across the floor, the large refrigerator ajar, leaking cold air and colored liquids.

"The staff and patients had a staph infection," Big Bea remarked. "Not surprising they looted the place. Let's hope they didn't finish off the antibiotics. Might need those."

"Let's hope," Cheryl replied, trying not to sound too discouraged.

A subtle noise came down the darkened hall. Big Bea's eyes widened in alarm. "What is it?" she hissed. Quietly, Cheryl unclipped the safety strap on her weapon. Big Bea crept a few paces ahead and unholstered her own gun. She stopped in front of an examination room with a large viewing slit. The sound of faint slurping, lip-smacking, and heavy breathing came through the door. Bea squinted down the viewing slit, but her face betrayed nothing. Gently, she used her cane's rubber tip to open the examination room door. It silently yawned inward. The gun pointed into the room—

Beatrice pulled the trigger.

The gunshot went off like a howitzer in the bare hallway. Bea holstered her weapon and stood back from the open door, leaning heavily on her cane. Cheryl's ears rang. A woman crouched on the floor, shot in the head. The lady was in her mid-fifties: maybe one of the therapists or psychologists—her clothes good enough for that. Reading glasses hung from a bright metal chain around her neck, along with a string of faux pearls; she'd put rouge on her cheeks, wore sensible shoes. The dead woman cradled something in her lap.

A human hand, tapered elegant fingers, pale skin around the ring finger—a young woman's hand. You could see teeth marks. The regimented marks of methodical gnawing. Cheryl stepped back in revulsion.

Big Bea had shot herself a cannibal.

"You can plant that one under a numbered headstone and I won't object," the lady cop said dryly. A quarter of an hour later, Cheryl and Beatrice returned to the gabled house considerably subdued. What were they going to tell everyone?

Mr. Washington had managed to sit up, a cup of tea nearby. Cheryl brought him some Maalox and various other medicinals she'd found in the pharmacy, so he could finally get rid of that grimy old pink bottle. They'd also found a doctor's bag, which gave Cheryl a chance to use her mandatory ChiPs EMT training. But it had been a long time since she'd wrapped a blood pressure cuff around anybody's arm, and it took two tries to get it right.

After taking Mr. Washington's pulse and temperature, Cheryl began to suspect the poor man was just worn out from work in a psychiatric hospital. He rubbed his belly. "Feels better. Thanks. Sure hope those two boys in the kitchen know how to cook."

Billy and Guy had returned to the gabled house lugging cartons boosted from the cafeteria food locker. Cheryl raised an eyebrow when she entered the kitchen, noticing the sparkle on the kitchen table—a gold wedding band and an engagement ring with a stone the size of a cherry pit. Involuntarily, she glanced at the much less ostentatious gold band on her own finger. Instinctually, she touched it; all this time, still on her finger. Never taken it off . . . Had Rachel noticed?

"Yeah, somebody left those in the food locker," Billy said about the rings.

"We found part of the gal they belonged to." Big Bea sagged to a kitchen chair and rubbed her thigh. "But we didn't look for the rest of her and I damn well need a drink to tell you about it."

Beatrice tossed her cars keys to Cheryl. "Would you be so good, Gorgeous? My leg is singing *Die Walküre*." Cheryl returned to the kitchen thirty seconds later with a bottle of Jim Beam from the Gran Torino's trunk and a very worried look on her face.

"We got company."

37

❦

Pudknockers

Mr. P., the three youngsters, and one dead Punjabi scientist cooled their heels in the plush Gulfstream jet. Safely parked in a LaGuardia airport hangar, they could watch the snow fall outside through the jet windows. Night had come. A whole day lost, and the Pied Piper was ready to lose his cool along with it.

Ever since the gaunt man found his kiddies in Tesla's old hotel room, it had been three steps forward, two steps back, with Bhakti Singh's hopeless ghost dogging them every step of the way. The peckerhead now stood as he had in Room 3327, arms at his sides, his wrath smoldering below the surface of his phantom skin.

What an annoyance.

The Light Tesla had come right into the Gulfstream cabin as well, the "electrician" floating around like a firefly. The faint glow ball hovered about the cabin, taunting Mr. P., as if the tall man didn't already know who was behind Bhakti's pathetic efforts to alter the preordained.

Sure, dead Bhakti had sneaked the brats out of the San Remo on the prompting of the "electrician." But the Light Tesla was a little instigator, feeding the dead scientist all manner of false hope. That he could actually rescue the youngsters, that his special hotel room would protect them, that a man in Sioux Falls could prevent the inevitable by trying to scramble the digital innards of Pi R Squared.

Pure childishness.

Mr. P. fixed his attention on the uninvited ghost of Bhakti.

The Punjabi scientist glared silently, as though hoping to burn holes in Piper's head with his brown cow eyes.

"Y'know," the gaunt man told him, "I could put this neurotic remnant of your mind back in that drained corpse of yours and keep it there forever. Should I have your molecules rearranged? You'd be staring out of dead shrunken eyes and never be able to escape. I'd keep you conscious in your coffin even as your mortal coil unwound, as your stinky flesh decayed. You wouldn't be the first I've put asunder since you knuckle scrapers walked the Earth. Wouldn't be the millionth."

Mr. P. paused. The specter said nothing in reply, simply kept staring with those terrible eyes. The Piper couldn't help trying to enlighten him.

"You think *He's* going to save you? Forget about it. The Big Kahuna doesn't interfere too much with us as long as we don't interfere too much with him. That's why things are such a friggin' mess down here. If you blow yourselves up, we'll go to another blue planet, go somewhere else to play. Your little glow ball friend too. There's plenty of room out there for the likes of us. And you can wander the stone halls of Elsinore Castle moaning till kingdom come for all I care."

The gaunt man left off; no point in educating a dead man. And Mr. P. knew all about the Light Tesla. . . . The dancing golden glow was a survivor of the silver-and-glass cities, like himself. A Magellan star surfer, like himself, another Long Soul, merely one of Lattimore's Takers. But this one chose to do good over the years—a little help for humanity here, a little help there. Instead of mastering a skill set of terror and intimidation, command and control, the Light Tesla had used his powers over eons for reflection and meditation, his innate benevolence stripping him of useful talents.

At last no longer able to buy friends or influence people, leaving such practical matters to the likes of Piper, the Long Soul had steadily retreated beyond the mortal world to pure energy, his original form. As it told the crazy lady, *Once I walked among men; once I had a name.* And before that? One of the galaxy's immortal fireflies. All in all, the dead "electrician" had become an interfering, very old, busybody. Bottom line, the dim bulb that once lived as Tesla for a while—just as Mr. P. inhabited this sack of skin—was in no position to do much for anybody, living or dead. And neither *ahem,* was "God."

In any case, none of this brought the kids any closer to the underground facility in Ohio. From the moment they reached the jet in LaGuardia airport, matters conspired to delay their departure. Since they were inside an empty hangar, it was not necessary to deice the wings, but they needed to find at least one pilot and a couple of thousand gallons of Jet B fuel. LaGuardia Tower was still on the air, but everyone up there sounded drunk. A few months ago, Mr. P. had made serious weather over Utah so a little twerp could retrieve a pinch of comet dust, but *now* he couldn't clear a patch of clouds just to get a plane off the ground. Thinking positive thoughts about blue skies on summer days wasn't working. Maybe all the mayhem, whoopee cushions, and hysterical blindness had worn him out.

And it continued to snow. The Pied Piper clenched his jaw.

Another newcomer had arrived—this one living. A disheveled fellow in an airline pilot's uniform stumbled through the Gulfstream's hatch, their airbus driver, half in the bag. He wore gold on his jacket epaulettes and scrambled eggs on his cap, but his tie was askew and his face pink and sweaty. A couple of days away from a shave, it looked like the man had been sitting in one of the airport bars eating plastic sandwiches and knocking 'em back for a week.

"The soldier outside said you needed an air taxi driver?" the man in the pilot's blues said. "You wanna go to Ohio? I'll go to Ohio. Gotta be better than this stinking dump."

"That's correct," the Piper informed him. "We have to arrange for fuel, a plow, and perhaps a tow out to the runway. So you'll have plenty of time to settle in."

The pilot thought about that for a moment, then nodded agreeably. At the cockpit door, he said to Lila, "Stewardish, do you think you can get me a club soda or a toffee. A coffee?" Without waiting for an answer, he grabbed the preflight checklist and disappeared behind the cockpit door, repeating again, "I'll go to Ohio. . . ."

Mr. P. glanced to the vision of Bhakti standing like a spear-carrier in an Italian opera. Nothing seemed to have fazed him. The youngsters didn't seem fazed either. The children had spread themselves around the interior of the cabin. They lounged around like spoiled brats, staring contemptuously.

Mr. P. dismissed the sullen eyes.

"The spook scientist doesn't say much, does he?" When none of the kids responded, he shrugged. "Well, let's see about getting some jet fuel. If I can make a break in the weather, we can take off. Maybe get to Hillsboro by this time tomorrow morning. Or by tomorrow afternoon . . ."

Was he really going to have to pull on his galoshes and oversee the whole thing by himself? He went to the cabin hatch to check on those not-so-special locator bums. If they wanted a ride to Ohio, they were going to have to do something to make it happen.

Fuel first; plow later.

What he found dismayed him. The trooper dudes were playing some sort of stupid game, making the officer of the outfit run around the plane with his pants around his ankles. As he hobbled along in his u-trou, they paddled him playfully with bright pink flight-control wands. Their bout of hysterical blindness seemed to have left the men slightly demented. Mr. P. watched them for a few moments, barely controlling his temper. He was having trouble getting hold of their minds.

"Gentlemen," he began. "TSA peoples! Can I have your attention?"

Then something else caught Mr. P.'s eye—

Two rabbits, right out of that dumb Beatrix Potter mural, sat at the entrance of the hangar. They stared right at Piper as though defying him to come and get them. Then one of the bunnies thumped his big hind leg, and they both vanished into the weather. Mr. P. stared at that spot by the hangar entrance for some moments after the rabbits disappeared.

Swear to God, one of them flipped him the bird.

38

Night of the Living Dread

A shaft of late-afternoon sun broke through the clouds across the hospital grounds. From the porch of the gabled house you could see three figures standing under the maple tree. Behind them the graveyard and numbered gravestones stood out like crooked teeth; then the clouds closed, flurries caught the wind, and the gray sky returned.

The strangers wore overcoats over bathrobes, unlaced boots over long johns or jammies: unkempt strays. The ravenous middle-aged staffer in the examination room came to mind. Cheryl glanced wordlessly at Beatrice, sharing the same thought: *What's for dinner? People, the other white meat.* Since anybody left alive, sane or mad, must also be immune to the wandering sickness, it was almost logical—eat the living, and be immune. Cargo-cult thinking.

You could tell Mr. Washington felt the patients were still his responsibility, that they got fed and put to bed, that none of them hurt themselves or anyone else.

"Maybe they're lost; maybe they don't know enough to come in." Mr. Washington pointed across the expanse of snowy leaves. "That's Mrs. Hampshire. She's not violent; she's just sad. And there's Mr. Simmons. He drew a picture of me in Art Therapy. Used up all the brown crayons in the Crayola box making it. *You don't know they're bad.*"

Eleanor restrained him for a moment, a hand on his arm, and clamped her daughter's urn to her chest. "No, Mr. Washington, don't go out there, please."

Mr. Washington looked affectionately at her.

"It's getting cold out here, Miss Eleanor. Take your

Janet's ashes inside where it's warm." He gently pried her hand away. "I'll be all right."

Nobody thought so. The two other men especially.

"C'mon, Mr. Washington," Billy said. "The ladies had some trouble before with that woman in the infirmary. We don't want the same thing now." Then Guy, "Let's sort it out tomorrow, in the daylight. We'll find these people's proper places. All right?"

Mr. Washington ignored them. He stepped off the porch and unlatched the door to his car, and picked the Jesus statue off the dash. Touched it for a moment, and then put it in his pants pocket. The whole group seemed paralyzed. Lauren came to Guy's side and nudged him in the ribs. "Do something!"

"Do what?" Guy asked her. "Maybe he's *right*. We don't know these people."

"He's *not* right," Lauren hissed.

Standing off by themselves, Beatrice and Cheryl were as troubled as the others. The two women naturally gravitated to each other; close enough to touch, but somehow not daring to commit that simple act. If the two women suddenly flew into each other's arms, nobody would have thought twice about it, but still Cheryl and Bea couldn't. So they watched the good Mr. Washington walk across the snowy lawn not being able to comfort each other, or even stop him. They just stood there.

Mr. Washington approached his patients, and they seemed to shiver in expectation like delighted animals. When the gentle man was within arm's length the three strangers cautiously reached for him as a single creature, petting him as if touching something sacred. But in a few moments the adoration changed to harder stroking, and then pulling. Then clawing and tearing. The orderly's head disappeared under their hands, his voice rising to a choking shriek—

"Help him!" Eleanor screamed.

Everyone snapped out of their trance. Beatrice took off at a run, humping along on her gimp leg. Cheryl went after her; both women with guns drawn. The men followed. A few yards from the porch, the large woman's leg brace gave out. She crumpled, and Cheryl rushed to her side. Now it was okay to touch. Mr. Washington had vanished from under the maple tree, the graveyard empty. No watchers either. The men stopped in their tracks. Snow began to blow sideways across the lawn . . . and a silent shock settled over the group.

"Don't look," Lauren told young Alice. They stood at the open door. But the young girl pushed Lauren's hand from her face and clutched her Horse Friends diary to her chest. She wanted to look.

D inner became a silent wake.
        Lauren and Eleanor hovered over young Alice, insisting she put down the diary for a minute, making sure she ate. If not for the laconic silence, no one might have even heard or noticed the moving camera. But as cameras hung everywhere, the one in the parlor wasn't worth a second glance. Except when the camera began to move, everyone heard it; a long *whirr* as the camera mount panned the room, corner to corner, then back again. The electronic eye methodically stared at each of them in turn. Young Alice put down knife and fork, speaking into the terrible silence.

"They're watching us," she said out loud.

Guy and Lauren sat upright in their seats; this may have been the first time the Girl-by-the-Stairs had spoken. *They're watching us. . . .* The strangers from the maple tree sitting in the warm security office looking at their next meal. Guy found a dish towel and threw it over the video camera, covering the lens. "We'll do something about you tomorrow," he muttered. And the camera whirred back as if to mock him.

* * *

Dinner ended in a mess of plates, glasses, and silverware in the sink.

No one felt like doing the dishes.

Cheryl and Beatrice climbed upstairs, slowly, step by step. The lady cop kept an eye on her friend's game leg, letting her lean on her. Big Bea's short gray hair smelled faintly of coconut pomade, reminding Cheryl of the stuff she used to put on her kinks as a kid, mango hair gel. When exactly had Beatrice *become* Cheryl's friend? Somewhere between shooting a cannibal and falling down; then helped her to her feet with a look of thanks. *Thanks.* Making it okay between them. Now okay for Beatrice to cling to Cheryl, sharing the younger woman's strength like it might rub off.

They must have picked Kay's room, the lady who died in the parlor. A half-dozen puzzle boxes were stacked like big tomes on the shelf. Not just M. C. Escher either. Cheryl examined an eye-dazzler of Bruegel's *The Tower of Babel.* "I used to love puzzles as a kid. Now, life is perplexing enough."

Like every room in the place, this one was video-monitored too. The camera didn't *whirr,* but the red light came on. They were being watched. Neither woman cared. Cheryl smiled and just shook her head. Beatrice sat on the bed, took off the brace, and sighed with relief. She flopped on her side without bothering to cover herself. "I think I have to pee. Maybe I'll pee right here," she mumbled. "If I stop breathing in the middle of the night do not resuscitate. . . ." After a moment the large woman began to snore gently into the pillow.

Rachel appeared from nowhere and followed Cheryl to the bathroom. "I'm jealous," she whispered. Ah, so ghostie girlie had finally deigned to grace them with her immortal presence. "Where the hell have you been?" Cheryl hissed angrily.

"Traipsing around after Bhakti," Rachel answered calmly. "That man is *really not happy*. If he's a bad boy now, he could change his eternal fate. Know what I mean? It's everything I can do to keep him on the Up escalator."

Cheryl was taken aback. "You mean you can affect your fate even after—" She halted. "I thought when you died that's when you started paying for everything."

"Only the really bad ones. Everyone else gets a few more chances."

B illy took the first room he found and lay on the bed in the dark. Man, he'd seen some messed up things in his life, but Mr. Washington's last walk to the maple tree with a Jesus statue in his pants—

A figure stood in his open bedroom doorway. Mr. Washington tugged his bathrobe around his shoulders but didn't look angry, just tired, lonely, and cold. "You could have stopped me," the figure said. "Why didn't you?"

Did they let Mr. Washington die? A hard question.

Billy didn't know the answer. Maybe they had.

He sat up and brushed the sleep from his eyes. He'd been dreaming.

No Mr. Washington, just a shadow, a trick of the light.

Billy walked cautiously across the dark room and checked the corners just to be sure. No, no Mr. Washington. The camera light in this room blinked on too, following him on his little walkabout. Billy glanced at the nosy thing.

"We'll see you tomorrow, bright and early," Billy told it.

G uy took the mousy spinster's room and wished he hadn't. The place was infused with air freshener the lung-cougher seemed to use on everything—a cloying scent that reminded him of lavender hospitality soap. The only good thing about this room, the video camera was dead as a doornail. Outside, a landscape light shone up a tree trunk, the branches throwing shadows onto the ceiling, stick fingers groping in the wind. He couldn't get Mr. Washington out of his mind either, walking over to the trees, falling under the claws of—

Guy tried to squelch the vision, bundled a quilt behind him, and spooned into Corky and Peaches, who had wedged themselves onto the bed, all eight paws in the air. Most times a dog whiffed sleepily and Guy would be sawing along too, but tonight was different. The snow brushing the windowpanes made the long-fingered shadows snatch at the ceiling. Manic hands come to claim him. Hands that never gave up.

L auren and Eleanor took first watch with Alice in the empty parlor. The women needed only to shout to rouse the house. The two sisters dimmed the lamplights as the snow flew past the windows gathering thickly beyond the eaves of the porch. When the wind sighed around the dark corners of the roof, a nameless chill seeped into Lauren's bones.

It began to feel like the outside world no longer really existed—the mailbox empty, the curbside trash waiting for a pickup that would never come. Everyone turned into milk-carton kids. *Have you seen us?* When the gabbing, texting, Tweeting finally died, a silence reigned over the world, an overwhelming solitude that no one had felt for over a century.

The only one who didn't seem affected was young Alice, but maybe because she wasn't from this time. No, Alice came from a time when it took three months to contact San Francisco, when whale-oil lamps burned at night, and the most faraway thing you ever heard was thunder in the distance. But the young lady was as human and frail as everyone else; not wanting to sleep upstairs alone, she curled up on the couch with her head in Lauren's lap.

After a seemingly endless spell of silence, Lauren finally asked that question she had been meaning to ask her sister: the question about Auntie Whitcomb.

"Eleanor," she asked softly, "do you remember if it was Auntie Whitcomb or Great-Auntie Whitcomb who disappeared for a while and suddenly, unexpectedly, returned? Some sort of family scandal, wasn't it?"

Eleanor petted Janet's metallic urn as if reluctant to answer.

"You mean when Great-Auntie Whitcomb was kidnapped by elves?"

The statement hung in the air, an awkward thought. What do you say to that? Eleanor put aside the silver urn and picked up young Alice's Horse Friends diary. The young girl hadn't locked it. "Think she'll mind if we look?"

"It's okay," a voice said from Lauren's lap.

The two women nearly jumped out of their skins. Young Alice scrunched up in the afghan and looked at the sisters with Bambi eyes.

"I drew them for you."

"For us?" Lauren asked.

Eleanor turned up the reading lamp by her elbow and opened the diary young Alice had worked on so diligently. She flipped to one page, then another, and another, becoming more and more anxious with each passing page. Eleanor shut the diary with shaking hands. "How do you know this?" she demanded. "Tell me how!"

Lauren feared her sister might do something to their young friend—a cold, brittle light burned in her sister's eyes—but suddenly Eleanor flopped back into her armchair, all the fire gone. Lauren picked the diary off the coffee table and looked for herself—

"God save us."

The child's pictures told a strange and yet familiar story.

The weird and incoherent tale Eleanor blurted about the Ant Colony, in one broken account or another, the drawings crude and yet expressive. First, a factory—the Whiteside sign under a row of dirty brick smokestacks. An old service door in the side of the building under the light of a naked bulb. All manner of repellent insects were scribbled over the pages, crawling down underground tunnels, on top of desks and chairs. The ants go marching one by one, Hurrah.

Maggots, grubs.

Rolpens. Rolpens had taken over the facility complex known as πr^2.

"That's what I ripped out of me," Eleanor choked. "That's what they're making—millions of them."

"You can't let them breed," Alice explained. "They're giving birth down there. You can't let them leave. And soon they'll be big enough to get out."

39

The Last Mind Glide

The data on Jasper's laptop glided in and out of focus. Lattimore could not concentrate any longer; it had been a day since the preppy kid's call, since the youngsters in Room 3327 begged him to find some kind of killer malware to inject into that depraved government research lab. Lattimore had been working the problem, searching for a wormhole into the digital body of the Hillsboro facility to the exclusion of everything else.

So far, total failure.

He glanced at the time: 3:45 a.m. Perhaps he was not the man to breach the fortress of the Pi R Squared complex.

He considered going down to the subbasement one more time to employ the power towers. Maybe later. He noticed Mildred was up, sitting on the edge of his bed with the drink she'd poured from the decanter in the library. Odd time of night, but after age fifty nobody slept normal hours anymore. She rolled the liquor around in the glass but did not drink it. That should have been a tip-off.

Mildred licked her lips, breathed heavily, and looked nervously about. She got up off the bed, fluffed her hair, and made for the elevator.

"I'm going down to the café, Mr. Lattimore," she said over her shoulder. "I think there's some produce I forgot to put away. I won't be long. Let me back up, all right?"

The boss glanced at the clock on Jasper's laptop again: 3:47 a.m.

"Sure," Lattimore said. Mildred disappeared into the penthouse elevator.

Ten minutes later, when she hadn't returned from the Cosmos Café, he went down to look for her. Mildred had entered the refrigerated food locker, where she hovered over the body of Security Chief Nash. The cold body was now uncovered, shirt open; Mildred had taken a large meat cleaver to him, opened his chest with a Y incision like a coroner, and cleanly emptied the chest cavity and his intestines into a large plastic five-gallon bucket. She layered the empty chest cavity with extra-wide Saran Wrap.

As Lattimore quietly stared at her, Mildred began to repack Security Chief Nash's empty chest cavity with shrink-wrapped kilo bricks of Dalekto rainbow powder. The chest could manage about twenty of them. The Cosmos Café cashier had laid away an extra supply for a rainy day. She looked up, mildly startled.

"He was right. I had some. I had some all along."

Mildred had been snorting Dalekto while she worked; she wiped a trace of rainbow dust from her upper lip, slightly ashamed. "I just couldn't sleep."

"Sure," Lattimore replied quietly. "Me, neither."

"I won't let it interfere with whatever we have to do," Mildred reassured him. She was trying. Hooked, lost, hands in a cadaver, but she was trying.

"I'm going down to the basement server farm for a while, Mildred," Lattimore said as nonjudgmentally as possible. "Call me on Nash's radio if you need me. Think you can get upstairs okay? Got enough of that for tonight?"

Mildred wiped her forehead with the back of her arm; it was quite a struggle getting the wads of dope into Nash's chest. She looked at the sweat on her forearm from her forehead. It had a tinge of rainbow to it.

"Yes, thank you, Mr. Lattimore. I think so."

Lattimore left her and went downstairs.

The pod-bay blast door let him into the lead-lined sub-basement.

He chose a metal chair to block the heavy barrier just in case it decided to close on its own or the power went. Backup generators were supposed to automatically come on, but why chance it? No point in getting trapped in the server farm with a hophead doing rainbow dust in the penthouse.

Sitting in front of the screens, Lattimore tasked Jasper's PC into the server farm. Now what?

The more he researched servo-corrupting software the more hopeless it became. You needed the manufacturer's digital certificates on doors and locks just to get the Pi R Squared computers to trust you. You needed the specs on the locking devices, keypad codes, every entrance and egress point, the air filtration systems. . . . You could do it, but someone would have to physically walk it inside to plug the malware into a terminal.

Use the electric bots to kill the worms.

A fortune-teller girl who'd channeled one of the Takers was asking him to do the impossible. The task became harder every time he grappled with it. Why set him about a hopeless task—what point in that? Maybe no one realized the task's impossibility, not even the one called the Light Tesla. Lattimore stared stupidly at the large flat-screens. The only way he'd ever gotten inside that bloody place was on a mind glide, and what of his other mind glides?

Lattimore did not know what to believe. Perhaps his visions were not meant to be understood. *That floating cities fought a war for mankind's genetic future, good angels nuking bad angels so mankind could reach for the stars.* Perhaps some questions were not meant to be answered. *The dark possibility his father might have tattooed blue numbers on his arm in order to escape punishment one such question.*

Lattimore stopped mooning.

An image had come to Jasper's laptop and across the server screens. Lattimore's own personal past gazed out at him like some kind of time window. The multiple screens showed the tree house his father had built in the backyard, and the dappled yellow leaves of late autumn. As he peered closer it seemed like a living photograph, and Lattimore saw some movement in the tree house window. Young Clem stared out, youthful face golden from the yellow leaves, and the man staring back almost called out.

Is this how a person cracked up under stress?

You entered an old 1960s' *Outer Limits* episode?

There is nothing wrong with your television set. Do not attempt to adjust the picture. We will control the horizontal. We will control the vertical.

A new image appeared. The living room inside his parent's house. His father sat in the armchair reading a book. His father stopped reading. He closed *Ship of Fools,* marking his place, and then stared out the window, sitting there calmly.

Expectant.

The light from the living room window changed from autumn gold to silver and then silvery blue. A shaft of brilliant light poured down on the sitting man. Mother came in from another room and stood by his father, putting her arm around his shoulder. The light embraced them, a living caress.

A few moments later the chair sat empty, his mother and father gone. So this was how it happened when young Clem came into the house to find them missing. Clem Lattimore suddenly realized this was no abduction, no local crop-circle episode, and not some hushed-up mission to secure downed UFOs in rural Bucks County. His parents had not returned psychotic or confused, but wonderstruck.

They'd gone up on a mind glide of their own.

What had they seen up there?

He remembered them as they came in from the rain, wet and naked. Sitting huddled on the couch with haunted eyes, a little distance apart. Mom and Pop had seen something incredible, and not cirrus clouds from the window of a flying doughnut. Their eyes had been opened.

What had the Takers shown them? What could his parents have seen?

Lattimore's mind whirled with possibilities, dwelling mostly on the Fate of Man and his troubled existence. Perhaps his parents had seen humanity's past and then its future. Its entire history from beginning to end. . . .

Perhaps they'd seen how the far-seeing Long Souls, the "benevolent" ones, had altered Man for the better, nurtured his nascent nobility, instilled compassion, mercy, courage, resolve—rejecting the dominance of the three-fingered Grays, rejecting the insect collective.

Perhaps they saw how the Long Souls helped the knuckle men evolve, allowed the species to refine itself so that their descendants might distinguish right from wrong and good from bad?

Perhaps his parents had been shown how the Progenitors of Man rejected selective breeding for the seemingly random forethought of infinite design. Worshipping free will, individuality, and a great voice from a burning incandescence: *I Am That I Am*—

His parents' stunned faces reached out to Lattimore through time and space as his mother and father desperately tried to cope with what they saw. Out of the distant past, Clem quietly heard his father say, "Yes, I know. I know we have to call everyone. I'll do it in a minute."

That meant the authorities, the friends and neighbors who had stepped in to help take care of Clem. Mom murmured a question like, "What are you going to say? What are you going to tell them?"

"I don't know what to say just yet," Father replied quietly. "Maybe the truth."

Then the long pause Clem remembered so well from his perch on the stairs. His father finally settled on no answer at all.

"No, I don't think they'll believe it. Would you?"

Clem Lattimore realized once and for all that his father had not faked *anything* in life; that some of the details of his own mind glides had been manipulated inside out. The Pied Piper floated into his mind wearing Bhakti's skin, grinning at Lattimore through the Punjabi scientist's eyes. *Glad we finally met. . . .*

His parents' faces on the screens began to fade, and Lattimore felt his head nodding to the keys of Jasper's laptop. The Takers were going to take him one more time. *Fine, let's go somewhere nice. . . .* Alas, no luck.

The familiar landscape of the Alaskan plain stretched to the horizon.

Mountains in the distance, but not verdant green like before, or soaked under lashing rain—now all white. A white blanket covered everything from horizon to horizon under a fierce gray sky.

The prickly forest of the High Frequency Active Auroral Research Program, the HAARP radio antenna array, was nowhere to be seen. No antennae, no signals getting out. Soon winter's night would come, freezing this place in ice and snow till August.

The military's force multipliers had done their work too well, and now the storm was living on its own. Overhead, a huge coriolis of cloud twisted slowly toward the south. And Lattimore went to follow it, the mind glide letting him ride General Winter across the globe.

Deep snow stretched from Anchorage to Prudhoe Bay.

The big storm reached as far south as Baja; while across the Atlantic in Europe and Eurasia masses of clouds buried everything from London to Moscow, and lesser storms spun off into the Indian Ocean. General Winter marched across the face of the world, and no one could stop him.

Across the planet, once-blessed lands lay in ruins, crops under snow or swept away by whirlwinds. Cities crumbled as tectonic plates shifted four feet here or eight feet there; fires burned out of control. And endless lines of people, refugees from the great urban centers, streamed from the chaos, a step ahead of galloping catastrophe. Everywhere Lattimore looked people were struggling or dying. Some begged a deaf god with both hands raised to the sky, while others ended their lives in despair.

In places yet to be snowed under, along the mighty rivers—the Mississippi, the Nile, the Yangtze—hordes of dead locusts, beetles, and especially mosquitoes covered the water like pond scum. The flying insects fell like volcanic ash, clogging tributaries and deltas, while legions and legions of birds came to feed on their carcasses. The birds died too after gorging themselves, and covered the ground.

At last, the Takers dropped him where there was no snow: Florida, but as cold a day as ever recorded. A harsh wind whipped the dune grass, over patches of cracked and partially frozen sand. Lattimore stood on the shore of a sandy beach on the shore of the Atlantic, and being a rocketeer the man knew his exact position on the global grid and the significance of this parcel of beachfront real estate.

The ground zero of Florida's Space Coast, the Merritt Island National Wildlife Refuge: half a mile north of the Cape Canaveral Air Force station and a couple of thousand feet south of the JFK Space Center's launching pads A and B and their towering gantries.

Lattimore looked inland from the beach. A huge wave must have swept up from the Atlantic Ocean, pushing sand and dune grass back from the shore, and a large container ship with it. The ship had landed in a lake of brackish water, salt marsh, and mangrove swamp called the Devil's Elbow—part of the wide wetlands that surrounded the space facilities. The immense vessel lay on its side in the semifrozen muck, broken in half, disgorging its cargo of containers onto the grassy tidal flats.

The container ship *Anja* had finally reappeared.

When Lattimore looked closer at the beached ship he saw container after container spilled out onto the marshy ground, a hundred hues of blue metal and red metal, orange, yellow, and purple—as though an enormous ship piñata had emptied its guts from its split hull. Footsteps pockmarked the mudflats, traipsing off across the dunes; apparently some of the crew had survived the wreck and walked away.

But one container stood out among the riotous colors.

A silver tractor-trailer shipping container. The Tea House of the Hidden Moon.

The plain stainless-steel container with L1/5 etched on its side lay farthest out from the ship, landing on an apron of marshy grass. As Lattimore drew closer for a better look, the curious designation etched on the metal morphed as it had before, deep in the ship's hold, L1/5 changing to the simpler L2.

L1/5 or L2?

Make up your mind!

The swing doors of the container had broken open, releasing the contents of the Tea House onto the ground. Lattimore looked in dismay at what had once been that bit of heaven òn Earth. The rice paper windows, the tile roof, the fire pit stones, and chuckling stream thrown pell-mell like the scattered pieces of a child's dollhouse onto the mud. Two koi fish lay frozen on the ground, the little Japanese bridge shattered. The red miniature maples and the bulrushes were torn apart as though a whirlwind had blasted them out of the box. The Tea House of the Hidden Moon a total ruin.

Lattimore's heart sank in despair at this perfect shadow box coming to such a bad end. A refuge no more, this tiny bit of heaven gone with everything else.

Then a curious thing caught his eye. Two rabbits bunny-hopped from within the silver box and sat for a moment, looking out on the marsh. They twitched their noses at the big wide world, looked at Lattimore with pink eyes, dismissed him, and hopped off into the marshy muck. Then two butterflies danced about the spears of elephant grass, got caught up in the wind, and vanished from sight. A bluebird appeared on the roof of the container, ruffled its feathers, and chirped once.

Back on the ground the rabbits had vanished. Their bunny paws left tracks on softer patches of mud and stretched across the flats. That's when Lattimore noticed more rabbit tracks going this way and that. Even bird footprints. Apparently quite a number of critters had come out of the Tea House.

The tracks seemed to march off across Merritt Island toward the marshy lagoon surrounding the NASA space center. And that sparked a queer bit of knowledge about this place, an arcane factoid. This lagoon system linked to estuaries and thence to the Intracoastal Waterway, dozens of inlets with names like Ponce de Leon and Mosquito—a winding ribbon of water that stretched from Key West to Boston and connected every major river in the United States east of the Mississippi.

Lattimore felt sure there was a greater significance to this that he didn't quite grasp, feeling himself on the cusp of understanding. In all these frozen flats there was something eternally hopeful about the tracks in the snow, across the icy swamp. The contents of the Tea House emptied on the ground, life returning after hibernation. Wild and untamed *life*, set free to roam the world, making its irrevocable impact on whatever it touched. A Noah's Ark moment.

The bluebird chirped one more time, dipped off the steel container.

The bird swooped over the marsh grass.

Lattimore pulled his head off the workstation desk, things much clearer now. He wasn't the savior of the big world, great protector against all that was bad. The struggle wasn't down here searching for computer worms to kill a sicko government breeding program. There were matters much closer to home to deal with. He'd left Mildred alone far too long.

In the few minutes he'd been away she could've been overdosing, naked in a bathtub with rainbow dust rimed around her nostrils—no, he'd never forgive himself. The last mind glide message was very simple. Take care of what you can, and let the big bad world take care of itself.

40

※

Granny Sparrow

Y *ou can't let them breed.*
  You can't let them leave.

Everyone from the bedrooms upstairs had come down
to the parlor at the sound of agitated voices. The crude pictures of the factory, the grubs, and the "Rolpens" in young
Alice's diary got passed around from woman to woman,
then man to man. First Cheryl looked at the pictures, passed
the diary to Beatrice, who passed it to Guy, and finally to
Billy.

Their faces growing darker as they touched the ugly
pages.

Eleanor's mind slowly smoldered. . . . Husband gone,
daughter gone. No Bhakti, no Janet, not even her friends,
Kay or Mr. Washington. Eleanor's last connection to this
broken world was her sister Lauren. So *now* what?

Go back to Fairfield crammed in the SUV with two dogs
and their *Alice in Wonderland* girl? Drive back to Texas?
Clean out the refrigerator, change the bedsheets, wipe the
lipstick graffiti from the bathroom wall?

What then?

Turn on the TV and crawl into bed? To do *what* exactly?
Get up in the morning? Look up and down the gentrified
ticky-tacky street in the Van Horn subdivision, knowing
her friends and neighbors were never coming back? Dutifully pick up where she'd left off at the frozen smoke lab?

The πr^2 complex floated to the troubled surface of her
mind: the overgrown fenced parking lot, the battered metal
door under the bare lightbulb, the dirty tunnel descending

to the glass-enclosed workstations and operating theater. Her mind's eye glided by the trimester rooms with their huge sucking fans, to the recycling section, the final black tunnel, all the way out the slimy crack in the earth.

She knew the way in; she knew the way out.

Those government insects had lured the innocent victims from Van Horn—Mrs. Biedermeier, Mrs. Stanton, Mrs. Perkins, Mrs. Quaid—impregnated them and then watched them die of one grotesque disease or another—orange mold, neuralgia, paralysis.

Time to exterminate the red ants. Every damn one.

For a second she paused. What did she know about extermination? Enough. Put gasoline in a jar and throw it. Eleanor glanced around the room at her companions and spoke with great gravity.

"The ants go marching one by one. Hurrah. Hurrah."

One look at Eleanor and the unspoken powwow that goes on between females came together, like fingers closing on a mental fist. Nobody needed a vote. The women in the gabled house knew exactly what to do. Drive hell for leather to Hillsboro, go down the hole, burn the place down, kill every damn Rolpen and every creep in a lab coat they could lay their hands on. When Eleanor saw the reckoning in their eyes, she nodded her head.

"We're doing the ant dance now."

Except for Lauren.

She wasn't about to leave young Alice; while Guy had no intention of leaving his two ladies alone, not with hungry inmates lurking on the grounds. Not to mention he was sick. Guy had managed to pick up a wicked cold, laced with bronchitis. It came on fast and hard in the few hours he slept, and by dawn, the grippe owned him body and soul. He sat on the couch shivering and sweating and shivering again with Mr. Washington's afghan around his shoulders.

Cheryl put the stethoscope away and dug into the found medical bag to see what she could do to fix him up. Too late for a flu vaccination, but she gave him one anyway, and a big shot of antibiotics. She also shook some pill bottles in his face—a week's worth of penicillin for the bronchitis and Theraflu for the cough.

"Don't forget to take those acidophilus pills," the lady cop told him. "I shot you full of enough bread mold to kill off half your stomach lining."

"I'll remember," Guy croaked.

The women decided on the yellow Blue Bird school bus with the big red plow parked in maintenance. The antique ran on diesel; a sixty-gallon tank might get them almost there, six hundred miles without refueling. Nevertheless, they planned to fill as many five-gallon fuel containers as they could scrounge with extra juice so they could top off along the way. Still, it would be close.

It fell to Cheryl and Beatrice to get the diesel into the bus' fuel tank. On a nice warm day in June no problem; drive around the corner to maintenance, stick the nozzle in the tank. But at the crack of dawn on half a night's sleep, the job turned three kinds of nasty. The garage pump was a snowman with a frozen lock on it. The wind picked up, gusts to 15 mph then 20 mph that almost peeled the skin off your face. You couldn't see past the edge of the maintenance garage. A white squall.

Big Bea got growly quick when Cheryl had trouble working the key to the pump lock and discovered the slot jammed with ice. No point in banging the thing. Cheryl found some antifreeze in the garage, dipped the key in that, and after a bit of jiggling got it open. By that time Beatrice, downright snarly, sagged on her bad leg, and her face had gone gray.

"Go inside and sit down," Cheryl told her over the wind.

"Sure," Bea grumped back at her as she stumped into maintenance. "Let's see if that clunker starts. Where'd you say the bus key was at?"

Beatrice found it in the adjoining security office; apparently those silent watchers became scarce when people with guns showed up. She made a mental note to leave Guy and Lauren a pistola and plenty of ammo.

After two tries the Blue Bird bus turned over with a throaty roar. Beatrice found an ancient garage door clicker tucked behind the windshield flap and pressed the button. The massive electric door at the end of the bay rumbled upward. A single figure stood in the white light. Billy Shadow in his overalls and fur-trimmed parka, the only things missing were a fish spear and a kayak. She gunned the Blue Bird and it lurched forward. She yanked the hydraulic passenger door lever to let Nanook of the North climb inside.

"Let's get the chains on this baby, the tank topped off, and on the road," Billy said. He brushed white crystals off his eyebrows. "And drop that cowcatcher a notch or two; there has to be half a foot out there already."

Beatrice pulled up to where the tire chains hung on the garage bay wall. Thank God they didn't have to put the chains on outside. She glanced at Billy and again at the chains on the wall. Smiling wryly, "I love a man around the house."

Snow flew past the steamy bus windows; Billy hovered between sleep and waking. Through half-closed eyes, he watched the endless stretch of Interstate 84 West. From Connecticut to the Newburgh-Beacon Bridge, they'd seen no traffic of any kind. The bus cruised past the empty eastbound tollbooths on rattling tire chains, while the wind whipped snow over the span and into the Hudson below, the river black as sin.

Beatrice roused Billy for a spell and he took the wheel through Pennsylvania. The land rose and fell over rolling hills, then wound toward the sharp granite cleft of blue-collar Wilkes-Barre. Only a few days ago fires had lit dark forest and a darker sky. This time the hills were an endless white wasteland where nothing moved. The roar of the bus drummed into his head; the sharp plow split the snow like the prow of a ship. Billy pushed the bus to 55 and 60 mph, the chains clacking away underneath him. Frost glazed the windshield, making him peer into the thick air as though through fogged eyeglasses, and the vehicle's antenna sang as the wind played it like a harp. Every twenty miles Billy pulled over, scraped the ice off the windshield, and then climbed back inside.

In normal weather going from Connecticut to Ohio took about twelve hours, but in a snowstorm the trip took longer. Sixteen hours all told, including potty stops in snowbound rest areas. Billy, Big Bea, or Cheryl stood guard outside the stalls while they each took turns, but they need not have bothered. No one was around.

The blizzard seemed to come and go; during the whiteouts the bus crawled. When the wind eased, they used the plow to push abandoned vehicles or wrecks out of the way. A miracle they hadn't broken down or slammed into a guardrail.

For the last couple of hours, Eleanor sat in the rear with the urn of Janet's ashes wedged in beside her; she'd found her own pad and pencil, her own little diary, and grimly sat there muttering to herself and drawing that same M. C. Escher creature again, just like young Alice. Only in Eleanor's case she kept going over and over the pencil lines, making the little armored worms darker and darker until her pencil wore through the paper and onto the next page.

Eleanor had almost reverted to the manic state of months ago when she woke up after Pi R Squared robot surgery and crawled out the meat seam. When she'd driven off into the rain and pulled into a Dairy Queen to work on herself with a plastic spoon. Now the time had come to rip something living from Pi R's uterus. Her fingers frittered away, scribble-scribble, conversing all the while with her poor dead husband.

"Yes, Bhakti, I understand. I know why they want the children. I understand why they want Lila Chen."

A pause.

"You want me to repeat it all again?" Eleanor sighed. "All right, stop interrupting. Through Lila Chen they can enhance our physiological profile, make überhumans through gene mutation. With the little fortune-teller girl they can sharpen the species with combined clairvoyance and remote viewing. But not for everyone, just the chosen few. While millions of slaves serve the Celestials. The Anointed. Am I right?"

She seemed to listen, finally replying, "No, I don't expect you to fix it all yourself."

A longer pause, then:

"I miss you too." Then whispering so no one could hear, "It's so good to see you again."

Finally, the pencil point snapped on the overworked paper. Eleanor looked around the bus, agitated, annoyed. "Are we there yet?"

Was the poor lady going cuckoo the closer they got to Ohio? From another part of the bus, Cheryl's voice rose over the clanking tire chains.

"Yes, Eleanor. Almost there."

Rachel's ghostie reclined nearby, lounging over a couple of seats like a teenager who won't sit up straight. Cheryl's bestest girlie gazed dismally at half-mad Eleanor, shrugged, and gazed blankly at the snow streaming past the window. No doubt she could see Bhakti well enough herself.

"Since your pal Bhakti got his knickers in a twist everything's haywire," Rachel remarked to Cheryl offhand. "I kept after him for a while, making sure he didn't do anything too crazy, but now he's blocking me. And I'm stuck. Stuck right here with you." She paused, absorbing the dreary surroundings of the bus again. "I don't know why

I'm hanging around. I don't know why I can't just go. I'm dead, and I haven't a clue what God wants." Rachel looked down at her skimpy hospital gown. "And I *still* don't have anything good to wear."

Cheryl cleared her throat but said nothing. Wise enough to know you could never soothe a woman who felt ill-dressed for an occasion.

The bus bumped like an angry bronco, and Beatrice dropped into a nearby seat. The large woman reached over and touched Cheryl's wrist. Bea was only trying to reach across the last few inches that separated them. Silently, Cheryl nodded back at her friend and pressed her wrist too, as if to say, *Yeah, I understand.* Rachel stared from her seat, going from envy to loneliness to sympathy all in a few moments.

"Well, I'm just glad you're here," Cheryl said to both.

D usk came, and then nightfall; they crossed the Susque-hanna, another black river.

By then Cheryl was driving and Billy's eyes had rolled into his head again.

H e stood on the path to Granny Sparrow's trailer.

Instead of curled in bed sick and afraid, Granny waited for him on the top of those creaky wooden steps. An inch of snow had fallen on the ground, and more descended in peaceful spirals. Billy looked at Granny's wrinkled paw as it emerged from the ghost dancer shirt. He took her hand and let her lead him through the buffalo grass into the Black Hills, dusted in white.

They stood overlooking a rocky hollow. In an arena of stone, Lakota braves had made a teepee fire by a stunted cottonwood tree. A medicine man with a face older than

Granny's beat time on a drum with feathered drumsticks as the snow fell in lazy spirals. The fire burned brightly. The warriors, naked to the waist, circled the drummer's fire. Their chests were painted yellow and blue; porcupine quills hung from their stamping knees, clacking to their chant. Billy heard them indistinctly, but sensed they sang of pain and loss as their words vanished into the air on puffs of breath and smoke. He watched as the spirits, the ghosts of the Ghost Dancers, chanted out of the long past as if their bones still cried from the earth, while the buffalo grass shivered in the wind.

"They're calling the rabbits to save the People," Granny Sparrow said into Billy's ear. "For every rabbit that thumps its bunny paw another baby lives."

Billy looked into the old woman's wrinkled face.

"That can't be right, Granny. We never had a Rabbit Chant. That's something you made up. Come on, tell me the truth."

Her kind, wrinkled face smiled kindly back at him; she stroked his wrist with her soft fingers:

"I always tell you the truth, Wakanisha. You're my little Easter Bunny, my little Bunny Thumper." Billy knew that word. *Wakanisha* meant "Sacredness," but Bunny Thumper? He almost laughed. A pale white face floated into his silly dream. Big Bea hovered over him in the clanking bus, her meaty hand on his shoulder. He glanced out the streaked window and listened to the rumble of plowed snow sluicing past.

"Wake up. We're getting close now. Your turn to drive again."

The three women silently watched the back of Billy's head as he lowered himself into the driver's seat. With both hands on the wheel he stared straight out, concentrating on the dangerous icy road—alert, but not tense. You could tell he'd handled a lot of different vehicles; no white-knuckle driver. The bus headlights pierced the night, and the white snow swirled in every direction. On this last stretch the wipers flashed *whap-whap-whap,* leaving streaks on the windshield. As the snow increased the closer they got to the meatpacking plant, Billy's fingers tensed on the wheel, then relaxed, then tensed again.

There was something about this guy.... Maybe it was his quiet command. Billy Shadow could make you think everything was going to turn out all right. Something most men never did. People talk about animal magnetism; this guy had animal courage.

The bus swayed and rocked them against the cold window.

Billy's shoulders were hunched a little, tense now. As they closed in on the Whiteside Meatpacking Plant, they climbed a switchback toward the factory. Everyone in the bus saw a faint light thrown against the smokestacks. One more twist of the switchback and the top of the battered chain link came into view, snow-laden vines coiled over barbed wire. A few compound lights on the high stanchions cast a pale glow.

Which is when the tire chains lost it.

Pong and the bus shimmied sideways. The wheels spun into the icy muck, and the bus slowly slid backwards. Eyes scared wide, everyone cried, "No!"

Headlight beams glanced strangely off the switchback walls as the Blue Bird skidded down the slope. Helpless at the wheel, Billy stared at his white knuckles. The bus was going to pop over a switchback, roll all the way to the bottom. They all knew it; they all felt it. The sound of metal grinding on rock shrieked like giant fingernails against a blackboard. The Blue Bird bus jerked to a halt, flinging its riders like rag dolls in their seats. What the—?

That big red cowcatcher plow had dug its way into the slope and caught an edge, wedging the bus into the hillside.

"Are we there yet?" Eleanor repeated; then soberly, to the metallic urn wedged in beside her, "I think we're here, Janet. Don't you go anywhere. I'll be right back." She paused, waiting for Janet's ashes to answer.

"Or do you want to come along?"

41

❧

You Really Don't Want to Know

Under the factory smokestacks, the shabby side door under the bare lightbulb stood ajar. The group had slogged up from the last switchback with as much gear as they could carry: Billy with a rifle, the gals with handguns, gas cans, and bottles. Molotov cocktail fixings.

"Follow me," Eleanor said in a normal tone of voice, leading the others into the tunnel.

"Y'know, maybe we weren't thinking straight," Billy said. "A sophisticated facility like this must have some kind of Halon fire-control system, some kind of automatic spray." He let that sink in for a moment. "Gasoline might be totally useless."

Beatrice realized how unprepared they were. "Maybe we should have raided a National Guard armory," she growled. "Or a construction site."

"Well," Cheryl remarked. "There's nothing here—"

Click-Click. Everyone fell silent.

They weren't alone.

Again: *Click-Click*.

Flashlight beams crossed like shining sabers. The tunnel roof:

Click—

Their first Rolpen.

The creature was only about eight inches long, its pearl-colored exoskeleton segmented into that familiar nautilus armor plating. The hybrid clung to the ceiling upside down and stared incuriously at them with glassy emerald eyes. Unlike the funky M. C. Escher lithograph, a pair of tiny emaciated human hands clung to the tunnel roof, while toward the tail elongated human vulture toes did the same. The parrot beak went *Click-Click* again. Cheryl drew her weapon, took a step back, and aimed point-blank at the tunnel roof.

"Don't let 'em know we're coming," Beatrice said quietly.

Cheryl hesitated and lowered her pistol. She looked from Bea to Eleanor and then to Billy. Nobody spoke, and Eleanor wasn't paying attention, withdrawn again, petting Janet's metal urn. The half-mad woman looked vaguely at the Rolpen, then down the long tunnel, the caged lightbulbs marching off into the distance.

The Rolpen went *Click* for the last time and dropped from the ceiling with a flat thud. Everyone leapt away. Billy banged the worm once for good measure with his rifle butt. The creature's armor cracked and oozed grayish red-veined goo like a squashed centipede. It writhed once and went very still. The glimmer died from its green glassy eyes.

"Are we there yet?" Cheryl asked, and everyone almost laughed.

Except for Eleanor, who said deadpan, "Yes. We're almost there."

The half-mad woman led them down the tunnel. After a hundred steps, they came upon clusters of sick or dead Rolpens who had fallen off the walls. A handful struggled to move, but Billy crushed them as before. Stepping on them took some grit; you went for the head, breaking the casing around the neck. If anyone wondered why the creatures were sick and dying, they didn't say. Difficult enough just killing them.

They emerged from the grimy tunnel into the operational areas: the Hatchery Observation Unit with its battery of screens and groupings of clean desks, the Antenatal Chambers, with their abandoned, empty beds. Farther on they passed the sealed labs, the surgery theaters; the complex was far larger than anyone had imagined or Eleanor remembered. Not all of the Rolpens were dead. Some still crawled around dark corners, lying on desks or keyboards, but what everyone noticed first was the lack of people. The people were missing—the lab technicians, the scientists, the staff. Ominously, jackets, pants, pantsuits, watches, and jewelry lay about in discarded heaps.

A Rolpen crawled out of a sport coat sleeve hanging on the back of a chair. Cheryl leapt away. "Oh, God." Everyone realized more or less at once that the Homo sapiens who ran the Pi R Squared complex might have been eaten by these humanoid caterpillars; food for slugs.

"What the hell are they?" Beatrice demanded, meaning the Rolpens.

"Who knows?" Billy said. He examined a dead one under a desk lamp, one with weirder hands in the odd shape of lobster claws—flesh-colored lobster claws, with human bone and tissue, not hard shell. A test model? A carnivorous worm.

As if to answer everyone, a voice came out of the public address system.

"We call them Rebreeders, Major Howahkan. A quickly evolving species, with a nearly instant reproductive cycle, a short lifespan, each one a piece of the larger puzzle; we take what we need from them and ignore the rest. They live for a while like fruit flies and then die out."

They looked around for the source of the voice, but all they saw were empty desks and dark screens. "After we caught our dear Webster talking out of school, we went to some trouble to find out who each of you were," the voice explained with some pride. "You see, we're the area of a circle. Everything *is* inside. We possess the machinery to vaccinate, inoculate, repopulate the world. Remake humanity. How could anyone really stop us? But we had to be sure."

At the far end of the operations bay, a wall of black glass gently changed shades; dim lights revealed an office. The group cautiously gravitated to it past dark screens and workstations.

The professor sat with his back to the glass at a long governor panel, overseeing the complex's operations. "We've found any number of useful improvements," he said. "But human flesh lobster claws weren't one of them."

There was something very strange about the professor's hands; they emerged from his white lab coat and moved across the control panels as he typed some kind of instructions on a keyboard. Then they noticed the change; his hands were not human hands anymore, now just three elongated fingers and an opposing thumb. No superfluous pinkie.

Satisfied, the professor turned from his operations panel and faced the window. His head had lost all the white fuzz, that halo of white hair, and seemed swollen, as though his body was trying to grow a bigger brain. His eye sockets seemed to have enlarged as well; a large pair of Hollywood sunglasses partially covered them. A repellent look, eyes larger than the frames; he tapped the dark lenses with his perfectly tapered new fingers:

"Forgive me; my new eyes simply refuse to adjust to the light."

He paused for a moment, considering the people staring at him through the shaded glass.

"You are welcome to stay and evolve along with the rest of us."

Everyone looked up and down the empty operations room. Who were *us*? Gauging their initial reticence through the transparency, the professor licked his lips.

"We're expecting an outside advisor very soon." A short pale tongue darted in and out. "A specialist is flying in from New York for additional consultation, bringing enhanced genetic material from multiple donors. I think you know who they are. Then we can go from prototype to production. Of all the people outside the circle, you managed to find us. So consider yourself invited to join the Celestials. The Anointed. The not-so-meek who shall inherit the Earth. Survival of the fittest on a molecular level."

Stunned to silence, no one spoke, but the desire to burn this wormhole into the ground, leave it a smoking ruin, was overpowering. Billy, Big Bea, and Cheryl scanned the ceiling for nozzles, sprinklers—signs of a fire-control system. To their disappointment they found them; dozens of circular pucker holes no bigger than fisheyes. They had to get onto that operations control panel, disable the system. There had to be a plug to pull. Beatrice's voice brought them back to the immediate present.

"You killed Webster," she said to the thing behind the transparency. "You killed my brother and never thought twice. If that's how the fittest survive, I don't want it."

The mutation turned away from the glass, returning to his keyboard and his panel of screens, losing interest in them. His weary explanation:

"Killed him? Not really, Big Sis. A genetic deficiency killed him. He lacked the protein suppressor that keeps your average human being from turning into Model-A, then to Model-B, then to Model-C, and so on. Once isolated, we learned to manipulate, to direct the protean protein suppressor so the Wild Three comet dust could do its work. Making us all open to the change. Pretty soon everyone will be walking around with big heads and three fingers. There's something to this progressive evolution that's quite liberating—lose a useless digit on one hand, gain virtual immortality on the other—"

Without waiting for an invitation, Cheryl drew her gun.

She'd heard more than enough. A gunshot wracked the underground room. A bullet appeared right at the back of the professor's head, stuck in the transparency, flattened out like a button. The professor didn't even bother turning around, saying merely, "There's really no such thing as death down here. When the snow lifts, we will send Rebreeders out to breed on their own, to devour and recycle every cadaver from California to the New York Island, from the redwood forest to the Gulf Stream waters. This land was made for you and me."

He fell silent, kept working. They'd been dismissed.

A movement caught their eyes; a figure gliding along a glass-walled hallway beside the operations center. An elegant, tall figure in a tattered, white lab coat loped along with the gait of a gymnast on stilts, then vanished beyond the edge of the glass wall toward the trimester rooms.

Beatrice turned and stumped across the operations center; the others followed, knocking over chairs. They rocked down the metal-floored hallway. Trimester One—nothing but empty plastic jars. No embryos, no tadpoles, just spilled amniotic fluid. Trimester Two—nothing there either, not even one little preemie waving from the safety of its fluid. They caught up with the tall loping figure inside Trimester Three—the tufts of blond hair gave him away, which meant you didn't have to read the name stitched on the worn and dingy lab coat. *No such thing as death around here. . . .*

Beatrice backed away from the glass wall, hand pressed to her mouth, strangling a scream, and stared at her brother. For a moment it looked like she wanted to touch Webster; she put her hand to the transparency. Then drew it away, leaving a foggy five-fingered outline; gray-faced, she closed her fist. The enhancement that had once been Webster Chargrove, PhD, paid no attention to the gawkers gaping through the glass wall.

At some point the eggheads must have decided to allow Mother Nature to take a hand—no more incubators, no more feeding tubes. Automated indifference had been eliminated in favor of real mothering with real mothers. Now four women sat up in four hospital beds nursing their children while the reconstituted Webster in his white lab coat tended to their every wish and need. A fifth hospital bed lay empty, as if the Celestials expected another woman to return and occupy it.

It slowly sank into everyone on the other side of the glass that all those women from the subdivision had also cheated death, and now the women of Van Horn breast-fed their hungry young 'uns. Last time Eleanor saw Mrs. Biedermeier she was a bloated whale, but she'd lost some weight— now merely an average overweight American woman. A healthy baby suckled at her breast, and she smiled contentedly down at it.

As for the skinny Mrs. Stanton, she was no longer skeletal. She had filled out; put on twenty healthy pounds for good measure. Her complexion pink and her infant just as hearty as Mrs. B's. The child cradled to her breast slept with eyes squeezed shut, its face pressed against the gold cross hanging from her neck.

The shy Mrs. Perkins seemed to have beaten back the flesh-eating orange mold that had covered her body; she showed no sign of her previous condition whatsoever. Here again, the woman held a fat healthy baby, gently suckling. The only peculiar aspect, the infant's peach fuzz on its crown gave off a distinct orange glow.

None of the women acknowledged the faces staring at them through the glass wall. At least one of them should have recognized Eleanor, but so far, none did. The women were apparently content to breast-feed their babies, staring into a middle distance like glassy-eyed cows totally at peace with their lot in life.

Except for the widow, Mrs. Quaid.

The silver-haired Mrs. Quaid seemed very much the same—the nerve thing, whole-body paralysis; her mouth twisted into a rictus of a smile. As before, her eyes zinged back and forth in her head. For a second she zeroed in on Eleanor behind the transparent wall; sentience and intelligence blazed inside the woman.

Along with an emotion: pure hate.

Damning Eleanor for leaving her in this helpless condition, all this time, while the maniacs in the white coats spread her legs and inseminated her; brought her to term and placed a squalid baby on her tit. Her arms lay useless by her sides, not even a finger twitch.

Here, the ever-useful ex-Webster Chargrove, PhD, justified his existence. The mantis-thin arms carefully held Mrs. Quaid's baby to her breast, cradling the head so it could suck. He'd finally grown a bigger brain all right; the exposed portion looked like an emerging grapefruit from his skull, with a thin, protective layer of leathery epidermis covering its folds. A mop of blond hair flopped across it as he moved. An extra bit of brain, but it didn't seem to make him any smarter; perhaps he hadn't really put it to use yet. He didn't seem to recognize anyone beyond the glass; or perhaps ex-Webster simply didn't care about them anymore. He gazed blankly at Big Sis Beatrice for some moments, then the Model-A turned his attention to the baby at Mrs. Quaid's breast. Unlike the other children, Mrs. Quaid's little Rebreeder paused sucking to stare curiously at those watching from the glass wall, bright glassy green eyes in its little head darting from one face to the next. Then back to the teat.

Smart little bugger.

The child finished feeding; ex-Webster Chargrove, PhD, removed the infant from Mrs. Quaid. As his long arms lifted the child from her bosom, the creature clung to her pap, sucking so hard as to lift the whole bag. Finally, the udder snapped free, but with a chunk of flesh missing at the nozzle. Mrs. Quaid's breast began to bleed, and the infant's moist mouth went *Click*. Behind pert pink lips, the child had a parrot beak. Glassy green eyeballs, pert lips, and a bird's beak. A nipple biter.

The faces at the transparent wall looked away in revulsion, but an irresistible hand pulled them back again. The *new and improved* Webster in the frayed white lab coat carefully patted the bleeding nipple with a gauze pad. In a few moments, the wound had stopped bleeding. In a few more moments, it scabbed over, and those watching knew what would happen in the next few moments after that. The scab would flake away. Accelerated epidermis regeneration. Skin was the largest organ in the body, a natural choice for enhancement, and the female nipple—a muscle, a nerve, a glandular cluster—would grow back in moments every time.

Webster patted Mrs. Quaid's breast clean, then tossed the gauze into an overflowing wastebasket stuffed with hundreds and hundreds of used, dirty pads. In a few more moments, the missing chunk of skin had completely filled in, and Mrs. Quaid's eyes were leaping out of her head.

The hate had evaporated; instead, her frantic eyes implored everyone standing behind the glass, pleading for anyone to come inside. The helpless woman was begging for her life—no, for someone, anyone, to come and kill her. Mrs. Quaid had not changed; same message as before. *Don't leave before you kill me. Just kill me.*

Then reality came full circle. The enhancement with the protruding gray matter in the dirty lab coat, the thing that used to be Webster Chargrove, PhD, quietly glided to the transparent reinforced door of Trimester Three, put his three-fingered hand to the palm reader for clearance, and opened the door. The door obeyed him, and he looked at Eleanor as if inviting her in. No one knew what to say or even do. The creature was inviting Eleanor back inside to occupy her old bed again. To maybe have a little Rolpen inserted in her, to become a mommy once more.

Eleanor stroked the metallic urn in her arms; the woman's

eyes flitted from one companion to the next. Cheryl's cocoa skin had become quite green. Billy's too. Beatrice could barely look at the thing that had once been her brother; the big woman's eyes falling to the ground.

Eleanor took a step to the waiting door.

Cheryl lunged to stop the crazy lady, but Beatrice restrained her friend with a hand on her arm. Nothing good here. Yet everyone felt the same thing at once. *No, Eleanor, don't go in there. Stay.* While the Webster enhancement held open the door, silently bidding her to enter. What was there to keep Eleanor from going through? Husband dead, child gone. Nothing left of life worth living. Beatrice unclipped the safety strap to her weapon—to use on the Webster creature, to stop Eleanor? Big Sis didn't know herself.

Eleanor's eyes drifted to the gun. Her face stoic and calm, as though resigned to her fate, as though contemplating one last duty to perform. She looked lovingly down at the metal urn cradled in her arms. Janet, poor Janet, what was she going to do with her? Reluctantly she offered her daughter's ashes. "Janet wouldn't like it here," she said to Cheryl. "She'll be comfortable with you. She doesn't belong here."

The metal urn with her daughter's ashes made the last long trip hand to hand, woman to woman. Cheryl cradled it in her arms just as the other had done. Eleanor dwelled on the unfastened gun in Beatrice's holster.

"May I borrow that?"

As if in a dream, as if she didn't even own the damn thing, Beatrice slowly handed her sidearm over. The gun found its way into Eleanor's hands. Everyone stared silently, too paralyzed to move. Eleanor took it gingerly, now oddly calm, weighing the weapon for a moment. Satisfied, she tucked it in her waistband. "Don't worry," she reassured everyone. "I'm from Texas." After a moment adding, "I think you're going to have to let me finish this." She meant the women in the room, especially the desperate Mrs. Quaid. "Something I should have done before I left. I'm just waiting for Bhakti; he promised to help, and he'll be along shortly."

Eleanor entered Trimester Three.

The security door automatically closed behind her.

Had the poor woman lost her mind for good? Obviously. Suddenly Billy and Beatrice snapped out of it, clamoring to the glass wall. But Cheryl shrank back, clutching Janet's ashes, knowing in her gut it was too late for a sane outcome.

Eleanor ignored the thumpers at the glass. She hobbled over to the waiting hospital bed and hoisted herself on it. Pushing up against the pillows, letting her legs dangle over the side. She looked at the big gun in her hand, popped the clip, and counted the rounds.

"Don't let my Janet get lonely."

On the far side of the transparency, her companions could hear the infants crying for their mothers' teats again through the open intercom in the wall. Feeding time came often with such marvelous enhancements. The elongated ex-Webster began his helpful rounds once more; if he saw the gun it made no impression. His sole concern was the women in the beds. Sounds of contented suckling filled the room.

Eleanor stared at the weapon, contemplating what she had to do. Kill babies; babies with fragrant, moist, healthy human skin and green eyes and parrot beaks where their pink gums should be. No abomination worse in the world than to slaughter innocents, and it took Eleanor a little time to get her mind around it. You had to tell yourself these were monsters in baby-skin. Making the decision point clearer and clearer, this was not sacred life—not human, not human life at all. They had come too late to the battle for human life, and now you had to murder to keep things human. These were the by-products, the excrescence of men, men like the pathological three-fingered professor, men who had taken Janet from her, who had taken her husband—taken everything.

Even her sanity.

Eleanor slapped the clip back into Big Bea's large black gun, then looked at Mrs. Quaid and nodded gently. The panicked woman's eyes finally relaxed—all this wouldn't matter soon. She knew what was coming. Long overdue.

Eleanor spoke to the glass wall. "I'm going to take the chance that the professor behind the bulletproof glass is exaggerating when he says there's no such thing as death in this place." She glanced at the four women in bed cradling their infants, then gazed with cold eyes at the grotesque remnant of Big Bea's brother. Model-A wasn't going to leave Trimester Three either. Webster stared back at her with open, uncomprehending eyes. His job was to help the mothers feed their babies. That was all.

"So if it's all right with you, I'll stay here."

The onlookers crept back from the glass resigned, letting go.

Eleanor glanced down at her thighs hanging uselessly over the mattress edge. Whatever they did to her had finally worn off. She massaged the muscle as though by kneading a wad of flesh she could bring her legs back to life. You could see in her face the certain realization her legs would never return. She gently kneaded her thigh with her free hand. Nothing.

Legs gone for good now.

"I can't get up."

42

Looking Glass Girl

L auren stood on the porch of the gabled house overlooking the snowbound hospital grounds. Under the eaves, beyond reach of the swirling snow, she watched Billy Shadow and the women leave in the bus. The rumbling yellow dragon drove out toward the main gate, the chains clanking and the cowcatcher plow spraying white frozen slush.

Two desperate inmates dashed out from the trees as the bus reached the main entrance. They must have survived the night somewhere on the grounds. One fell facedown into the snow, but the other grasped onto the cowcatcher plow and tried crawling onto the hood. The bus didn't slow for a second, took a heavy bounce and bumped the clinger loose; in a blink of the eye he got sucked under the wheels. A faint shriek as the bus rumbled out of sight.

The engine faded into the distance, and the snow fell thickly. A quiet hush returned, under the forsaken weight of a woman on her own. Make that, with a child, a sick man to care for, and snooping security cameras. A woman alone.

Young Alice came outside and gently took Lauren's hand.

"We better go inside," the girl said. "There may be more."

Lauren yielded; she locked the gabled house door firmly behind them. Guy, on the couch, stared with dark fevered eyes. He was shivering again, and the two dogs had managed to wedge themselves into the warmest spot on the couch. He tucked the pistol Beatrice left them safely into the crack of the cushions. Better than a holster.

"I've been thinking," Guy said, his teeth chattering a little.

"Well, don't strain yourself, darling," Lauren replied. "I'll get you another cup of tea."

"No, listen."

Lauren and Alice indulged him, taking up parlor chairs.

"Did you ever wonder how Alice came here?" Guy asked. "Or why? Now just think about it for a moment." He paused, tugging the blanket under his chin.

"There has to be a gateway, doesn't there, Alice? A portal. Somewhere in our house, the Finn House back in Fairfield. I'd guess it works on the stairs where I first saw you. Maybe the ice storm opened it up and you slipped through. Maybe it only opens at certain times, like the time we walked into the past through the old Keeping Room and you couldn't see us. Maybe as things got crazier and crazier in the real world, the past and the present—our time, your time—got all mixed up. Sort of like a Jacob's ladder with the angels climbing up and the angels climbing down."

Guy took a ragged breath.

"Except now you're always with us. Which makes me think that since we've been away from Fairfield you can't go back. That the gateway or portal, whatever it is—is actually part of the house. And I'll bet we have to get back there for you to go home again." Alice stared back at him and squirmed in her chair.

"Don't you want to go home?" Lauren asked.

The girl avoided their eyes. Apparently, Alice wasn't in such a hurry to go anywhere. Which meant that whatever awaited her back at home might be worse than here and now. Maybe Yellow Jack was worse; the dead laden in carts, the sorrowful, smoky torches. Maybe that's why the little girl ran away. The only thing waiting at home were mom and dad dressed in their Sunday best posing for their death photos.

Guy stared at the puddle of dissolved sugar at the bottom of his tea mug.

"This is where the whole thing starts to get weird. The *why*. Maybe you were supposed to come here, Alice. Maybe if you'd stayed in your own time, Yellow Jack would have claimed you too."

Guy put the mug aside. "If young Alice dies in an epidemic of yellow fever in the nineteenth century she has no children. She has no grandchildren. No Granny Whitcomb, no Auntie Whitcomb. Maybe you're not even born, Lauren; we don't get to live in the Finn House and so we never see young Alice on the stairs."

He paused to clear his throat, trying not to cough.

"If Alice dies in a yellow fever epidemic she doesn't join us. If she doesn't come into the future, Eleanor never sees the drawings, never returns to Hillsboro. Everything hinges on getting Alice back to Fairfield. If she stays here, she'll die here; she will have never existed. A time traveler who dies in the future never gets to live out his life in the past—"

This ended in a fit of coughing.

Guy recovered and took another deep, ragged breath:

"God works in mysterious ways, right? Occasionally he has to bend time and open doors and close them. Sometimes he needs the same soul in two different worlds. So Alice came ahead and she warned us, and that's good. And the gang went to kill as many worm-people as they can, and that's good, but the young lady can't stay here. She's gotta get back, live a life, have some children who have children. Leave the Finn House to her descendants so she can come visit us. You see, this is where the *why* gets more complicated. She came here to tell us about the Rolpen disease, so the others could kill the little monsters. How did she *know*? How'd she get the idea? I'm curious how she knew to draw insects and fossils. How did you know, Alice?"

Alice looked down in her lap, almost embarrassed. Very softly, she explained, "When the yellow sickness came, I hid in the root cellar. Whenever things got bad, that's where I went. When I thought it was safe again I came upstairs. But all the stairs in that house are funny. The cellar stairs or the Keeping Room stairs took me away. Away to where the world was different. Cleaner. Nicer. But the longer I stay here with you—the bigger a fuss there'll be when I go back. They'll miss me."

She paused, looking side to side as if afraid she'd be overheard. Her voice dropped; she whispered confidentially, "Down in the cellar there are thousands of dead worms everywhere, even in the foundation of the house, even in the stone. And in Mama's diary I saw the place in Ohio where the worms come from, where the worms go to be born. They go home to Thanksgiving."

For the first time, Lauren spoke, trying to get her mind around all this, repeating incredulously:

"You learned about Ohio and the worms in the cellar at home on Thanksgiving?" But Lauren never finished the sentence.

In the upper corner of the parlor, the security camera whirred softly and the dish towel slipped from the lens. Guy instantly regretted not smashing the thing back when he was feeling better. The camera panned across the room and stopped, the video Cyclops staring at Lauren and the young lady.

"They're much hungrier now," Alice whispered.

Guy looked at Lauren in alarm, and the two dogs Corky and Peaches snapped their heads to the locked door as if sensing something outside. The doorknob rattled, and both dogs leapt off the couch, dragging poor Guy's covers.

Several things happened at once. A white-haired man appeared from the kitchen—Gramps, a man about seventy, with white unshaved whiskers, blood from his last meal still around his mouth. *Could they have been so stupid they forgot to lock the back door?*

Then the front door banged open. Lauren got the fleeting impression of a scruffy teenager with lots of studs, lip piercings—and a pouch-faced sad sack of a woman. These were no horror show zombies, but fairly healthy people. The teenager and the woman went directly for Guy on the couch. The two brave dogs snarled and snapped. Gramps went for Alice, who shrieked.

Lauren grabbed the closest thing at hand—a table lamp—and swung it as hard as she could. Unlike stage props in cowboy movies, this didn't fly into pieces. The lamp base connected with the back of the teenager's skull, denting it in a good inch. He dropped like a stone.

Guy fumbled over Big Bea's gun in the cushion crack while the pouch-faced woman tore at his stocking feet. The gun finally went *bang,* barely missing Guy's toes, and took off most of the woman's face.

Gramps had cornered young Alice by the kitchen door; she struggled wildly as he tried to get a grip on her wriggling arm. Too many flailing limbs for a gunshot; Lauren used the lamp again, *whang,* and stove in his white-haired dome.

The place went quiet. Alice shivered up against the wall. The two adults caught their breath, and snow from outside flew into the parlor. Corky and Peaches stopped tearing at the scruffy teen. After a few moments, Lauren staggered to the front door. The inmates had used an extra key card from security. She took the key card out of the lock, shut the door, and came back to deal with the mess inside.

"Jesus."

Guy looked three kinds of pale and almost managed to rise from the couch. "Let me help you clean up."

Lauren just shook her head. "Stay where you are."

The two dogs pressed into Alice by the wall, nosing her

over and over, trying to get her to pet them. She stopped shivering for a moment and took both animals' heads in her hands. Tears and fear now.

"I want to go home. Take me home."

Lauren shared a glance with her husband. How in hell were they going to do that? Guy was so sick he could barely move. There was three feet of snow in every direction. Would there even be any power back in Fairfield? At least here, they had some juice going, hot water, food, and medicine. Lauren really wanted to get out, go home—she really did—but there was no way either she or poor Guy shivering on the couch were going anywhere right now.

"As soon as we can," Lauren said. "As soon as we can."

43

Eye of the Storm

Mr. P. gazed out the window of the Gulfstream jet as it rose through a patch of open gray sky into a dark wintry dawn. The lights of LaGuardia airport retreated below. Parts of New York seemed blacked out, curious puzzle pieces dotted with building fires, while other parts were brightly lit, the houses of northern Queens, no rhyme or reason.

The plane climbed, hit·a bump of air, but plowed through as the heavens opened. The gaunt man realized with a pang of bitterness that this was probably as close as he'd ever come to using his wings again, sitting in a flying metal tube. How barbaric.

Mr. P.'s head throbbed just like after he'd raptured those

hicks in Nebraska; the gritty sparkles of light swam behind his closed eyes. His effort at weather control, clearing a hole in the clouds so the Gulfstream could take off, had taken him all night. Usually he could do it by staring at a television, just like when he rewrote rerun episodes or made a little snowstorm in Utah via the Weather Channel. But every minute he sat in the cabin of the jet seemed to weaken him, as if the Light Tesla and the specter of the angry Punjabi scientist were sapping his powers. And the outside world wasn't cooperating either. The jet's TV couldn't pick up any local weather, and radio signals crackled incoherently.

Finally, he used the lad's iPad to find a weather satellite beaming info down to all the flight controllers nodding over their screens at LaGuardia Tower. Slowly and steadily and with excruciating effort he cleared a hole through the clouds like the eye of a hurricane, large enough to get a jet off the ground.

And just in time, as the not-so-special locator guys had finally located a ground crew asleep in a warm corner of the airport, bribed them at gunpoint to gas up the plane and skim off the runway. Mr. P. waved a fond farewell through the airplane window to his useful idiots as the jet taxied off, leaving the soldiers on the snowy tarmac. No need to control them anymore; he could rest at last. The Gulfstream ascended to the heavens, the Piper's head throbbed, and blessed sleep took him away.

Kid stared at the Piper as the gaunt man began to snore.

Dead Bhakti kept watch too; the uninvited specter of the Punjabi scientist ran a hand gently through the gaunt man's hair with ghostly fingers. The Pied Piper stirred but did not wake, and Kid could feel the tall man's mind simmering away.

The Piper had so many evil things planned. Once in the underground labs they'd rip the girls apart molecule by molecule. Mixing cells and blood and sperm and eggs;

enhancing certain chosen mantises from suckle-servants like Webster into a completely new human species—though not the kind who made for a better world. No. Rather creating a select few silver-haired floating-city dwellers and many, many slaves to service the lucky ones as they looked down from on high. While the women from Van Horn— Mrs. This and Mrs. That—and Mr. P.'s female children constantly produced offspring, bearing one perfect creature after another.

Lila, Maria, and the Van Horn women were to raise the enlightened. Masters of the Change who would command the legions of instant Rebreeders, the malformed Rolpens. Who in turn would dispose of every mistaken experiment, eat the meat seam clean, and crawl outside through the crack in the Recycling Cavern to fertilize the grass. Then all of Mr. P.'s brand-new little worthies would march out to repopulate the world, one by one and two by two.

Kid saw it all. For Lila Chen, endless motherhood as Mr. P. used her like a cow to breed a greater race. And if the Chen girl was going to be hooked to a birthing machine, Maria's future was even worse. Wire the child for sight and sound and touch; screw hundred-watt lightbulbs into her eyes and solder her finger bones to electrodes. Expose her brains in order to find that perfect strand of protein, the look-see molecules, and reproducing them in überangels, allowing the anointed to see the future so they would never fall again.

Kid saw his own future as well. Mr. P. would forgive him every trespass and betrayal; Kid would become exalted again, the man's right hand. He would learn all about molecular-genetic engineering, ovarian implantation, and artificial insemination. Unlike that amateur scientist Webster Chargrove, PhD, Kid's brain would not explode but respond to the off-world Wild 3 glycine by geometrically enhancing neural synapse density. Instead of an estimated hundred billion neurons and hundred trillion synapses, the young man's brain would grow a trillion neurons and a quadrillion synapses, putting him far above any creature that ever crawled the earth. Kid would oversee the manufacture and care of a new generation of Celestials. Even learn the secret of growing wings so he could fly with Mr. P. to the floating silver city they would build together, any time he wished. As if dreaming the same delicious dream the gaunt man smiled in his sleep. . . .

Kid reclined in the jet's plush banquette. He'd seen all these tricks before. An angelic Michael Jackson standing at his apartment door back on Avenue A. Lobster and cognac, the national sport of Turkey. No more Room Time.

Fuggedaboutit. No more lies; take nothing from that man anymore. Kid gazed calmly at the two girls, the older and the younger, who had held his hand, who had brought him back from devil worship and love of a false idol.

"Leave it to me," he told them softly. He knew what he would do. He donned the poker face one more time. Kid's voice clanked into the gaunt man's head.

"Hey, we're over Ohio, but the Columbus Tower isn't answering. Hillsboro in five minutes."

The Pied Piper rubbed his eyes. Silently, he unfolded off the banquette and went forward to the cockpit. As he approached, the cockpit door swung back and forth, an empty, lonely movement.

"Oh, Stewardish," the Piper called, and stuck his head into the cockpit. No one replied, but the pilot's seat wasn't empty, just unoccupied. The drunken airline pilot, who wanted out of New York, had finally been called to the good lord's bosom. Mr. P. nodded in approval as the Gulfstream's trim flaps and fly-by-wire autopilot kept them stable; the dead man's hands frozen at the wheel gently steered on puppet strings.

"Thanks for flying Piper Airways."

His eye caught the Bhakti ghost glowering at him from a bank of blinking lights.

"You can stay with him if you want. Or come with us. I don't care. But when I'm done down below, I think I'm going to turn your immortal spirit into a hemorrhoid on a rat's anus for a few thousand years. Whattaya say?"

The ghost said nothing.

"Fine. Stay here," the gaunt man grunted.

Back in the cabin the Kid had opened the hatches to the two Lattimore Aerospace escape pods in the belly of the jet. Mr. P. grinned as if to give himself a gold star for leasing this model Gulfstream, the one with the lifeboats. The EZ-access panels to each cocoon stood open like the open petals of a plastic flower; within the capsules plush couches with padded leg cushions and full-body crash belts waited for their occupants.

The pods' Vision III Topography screen showed their present course and designated landing site from glide path to touchdown. Ground zero, the factory parking lot blinked *Whiteside, longitude-latitude*. A wide red touch panel on the screen read *SEAL AND RELEASE*. All you had to do was push the button, the escape capsule would seal the double hatch and then drop from under the jet. Ten minutes later, you'd be on the ground.

Lila looked doubtfully down into the tight, double-berth tube. Little Maria cowered in the older girl's arms; both reluctant to slide into the lifeboat. Or maybe just reluctant to leave Kid behind. He tried to reassure them.

"It's all right. It's preset. We're going to the same place." Lila's eyes looked darkly at him, doubt and suspicion. "This is the best way. Honest. I'll see you in a little while."

The two girls slid into their cushioned pod; the crash-couch material automatically cleaved to them like living gel. Lila looked back up the hatch, her dark eyes even darker now. She touched the red touch panel to seal and release.

"See you."

Kid nodded as the inner and outer hatches slid shut. The

jet jumped a tad as it discharged the tube, but then automatically righted itself. Mr. P. came down the aisle and slung himself into the other escape capsule.

"Just you and me?"

"Girls with girls and boys with boys," the Kid answered. "Better open up another eye of the storm, Daddy-O, and make it snappy. This crate isn't going to fly forever."

The Gulfstream jet lurched as the second lifeboat fell away.

Inside the empty cabin, the grim ghost of the Punjabi scientist stared at the recently deceased pilot sitting in the cockpit. A large blood vessel in the man's head burst somewhere over western Pennsylvania; he'd seen a flash of light and then nothing else. And since the plane was on autopilot, nobody in the cabin had noticed. Not even him.

"Hey! Wake up!" Bhakti said. "I know you're in there somewhere." His ghostly hand slapped the dead man's face, leaving barely a ripple of wind; but the man stirred.

"C'mon! Stop fooling around."

The pilot grunted and opened his eyes. Extremely sober now, he glanced at the Sikh gentleman staring at him—a man with several large gunshot wounds to the chest. The pilot blinked his eyes.

"That's right," Bhakti told him. "You've had a stroke. You're talking to another dead man. Now listen carefully. You're on your way to the big airline in the sky. They're going to offer you a contract to fly with the fleet—but while we have these few moments together, there's something you have to do for me. Now don't argue. It's not going to hurt—"

The pilot didn't argue. He looked down to his hands, clasping the steering yoke. One hand regrasped the yoke, then two. Dead man flying.

"Okay," the pilot replied. "Where to?"

* * *

The escape pod's porthole by Lila's head showed next to nothing. Dark gray mist, clouds; a razor-thin line of red dawn so distant it hardly counted. The escape capsule felt like a falling stone; her heart leapt into her throat and her ears clogged; her head stuffed with cotton. They were falling, all right—angels without wings. More interesting to her was the Vision III Topography screen over their heads; the land below, like Google Earth, zoomed closer and closer.

At about 20,000 feet Lila could pick out roads and streets; the Vision III system gave the landscape below a white sheen, miles and miles of snow, but you could still see lines of trees demarking fields, the dots of farmhouses and silos. A square spider's web of gray buildings grew closer; the words HILLSBORO, OH appeared over a section of the ground below. A quadrant of the growing picture started to flash WHITESIDE MEATPACKING PLANT: PARKING LOT.

The snow-covered trees below began looking larger. Altitude: 13,000 to 12,000 feet. The flight display flashed again: DROGUE PARACHUTES DEPLOYED. EXPECT JOLT.

The parachutes blossomed; the cords snapped taut. Heavy crosswinds buffeted the craft and rocked the two girls inside their cushioned tube. On the vision screen the ground approached in that dreamy way between hovering and sliding. The escape capsule caught an updraft and the altitude counter rose several hundred feet, then returned to a jumpy, chaotic descent. This kept up for some while, threatening to blow them past the touchdown point—until they shot into the bull's-eye of Mr. P.'s calm-weather hole. Down to 5000 feet, the parachutes cut loose. The Vision screen flashed GLIDE PATH MODE, and they fell through the eye of the storm.

Out the tiny viewing port, they saw the escape vehicle's long glider wings deploy, their delicate airfoil ailerons compensating and correcting the tumult around them. The craft began large descending circles. A long slow cork-screw plotted to drop them according to plan. Lila felt a wave of nausea in the confined space, and tried not to retch. Maria's pale face looked back with alarmed eyes.

"Kid's right behind us," Maria gasped heavily. "Mr. P. is changing form, shape after shape, but Kid won't let him go. Kid has him by the tail. Now he's got him by the throat—"

44

The Reckoning

Eleanor sat on the bed, useless legs dangling, gun in her lap. The Webster drone quietly attended to his charges, oblivious to everything else. Eleanor glanced coolly through the glass, but Cheryl was unable to meet the woman's eye. The others turned from the transparent wall, helpless; nothing they could do for their friend now except leave.

Had they come all this way for nothing?

They shared a creeping sense of failure, deflated, all the fight knocked out of them. Maybe it was the endless road trip, the slog up the hill, then down into this evil place. . . . Sure, they'd go kill as many of the Rolpens as they could, but who knows how many were left? Would the three-fingered professor in his Hollywood shades even care?

Cheryl clutched Janet's canister close, turned away, and retreated after the others. Cheryl's only thought was to obey a mother's last wish to keep her daughter's ashes safe. A dozen yards up the ant tunnel, they all heard a pistol shot down below. Then a second shot echoed off the stone walls. No one paused or turned back.

Eleanor looked at the smoking gun in her hand.

She'd only fired it twice.

Once to get rid of the Webster enhancement, and once more for Mrs. Quaid trapped in her body. The three-fingered mutant in the dingy lab coat lay slumped against the wall. Poor Mrs. Quaid looked peaceful for once, her eyes shut, her infant asleep on her chest. Relief had finally arrived, and Mrs. Quaid seemed grateful; but as for the others, the other women and their infants . . . The gun lay helplessly in her lap.

She glanced up to the glass wall. Bhakti stared at her from the other side. He put his hand up to the transparency and mouthed the words, "I love you, Eleanor." And she started to choke on tears, burbling and sobbing, just glad to see him but crushed at her own weakness.

"I can't do it, Bhakti. I can't do it. I thought I could, but I can't do the others; they just look too real. I think that was the point. Make them look like us and nobody would want to hurt them. Like killing puppies or kittens," she despaired. "I'm sorry, Bhakti."

His voice penetrated the glass. "It's all right, Eleanor," he reassured her. "I'll take care of it soon. I'm almost there."

The survivors of the Pi R Squared complex emerged from the rusty side door of the Whiteside Meatpacking Plant and into the parking lot under orange glowing floodlights. Overhead more snow danced out of a gray sky, and jet engines whined, sometimes closer, sometimes farther away. . . . Billy Shadow and Cheryl and Beatrice waded into the snow. Three- and four-foot drifts sloughed up against the fencing and buried a few parked cars. The approaching dawn lit the slowly swirling mass of clouds in the eye of the storm.

The two escape pods from the Gulfstream jet had landed close to where programmed, on a postage stamp–sized drop zone beside an abandoned factory in the middle of nowhere. However, the two rescue cylinders had come to completely different ends. One landed intact, its emergency beacon/locator strobe flashing blue-red, its long delicate parasail wings bringing it gently home. The wasp-nosed missile sat on the snow like a winterized dragonfly, bristling with pitot tubes, the lifeboat body-hatch open to the sky.

The other silver cylinder hadn't been so lucky. The second escape pod skimmed in over the factory roof, buffeted by crosswinds, and clipped a smokestack; you could see the wing embedded in the brick of the stack tower where it had torn clean off the lifeboat. The needle-nosed craft had dropped like a broken toy Concorde airliner. The shiny tube had crushed several vehicles, finally skewering a parked car. The silver skin of the craft seemed burnt, the stainless-steel cylinder scorched, a telltale rainbow hue as though superheated from within.

The Chen girl and Little Maria had climbed out of their undamaged pod and stood beside the burned lifeboat looking down into the crashed craft's cushioned interior. The fur trim on the girls' parka hoods fluttered around their faces. The three survivors who came out of the complex struggled across the parking lot and stood silently in a rough semicircle without so much as saying hello. The searchers for Lila Chen and Little Maria had finally found their girls. Finally.

The snow began to whip again as the eye of the storm started to close.

For long moments, everyone silently stared at the destroyed craft. Mostly everything had been burned to cinders: the foam crash couches, the crash belts, very little left. The interior burned clean except for the remains of the two occupants: Kid's fire-washed bones and those of the Pied Piper, all their flesh consumed.

The young man's skeleton lay on top, dismembered. His bones actually blown apart, but with nowhere to go they lay about the interior of the capsule in essentially correct order. Kid's white skeletal hands encircled Mr. P.'s bird-like neck and had snapped it in two.

The remains of the Pied Piper were another matter altogether. What lay in the scorched interior no longer looked like a man. More like the bones of an ancient flying reptile with a long name, out of the Jurassic or Cretaceous periods—millions and millions of years ago. The sharp snapping beak; the backward pointing skull crest; a flying creature as bizarre as any that ever flew.

The slender skeletal bird body lay in the incinerated crash couch, most of its bones intact, with the exception of its tapered wings. Only the faintest mark of folded quills, the curved struts, remained; fire so intense it burned the thinner bones, leaving a white powdery line on the capsule's interior.

Quietly it dawned on everyone that once upon a time Mr. P. had lived in the skin of a lizard, a flying reptile. As he fought for life, he had returned to one of his earlier life-forms. If the capsule had broken open, way up in the air, he'd have been able to fly.

"*Pteranodon longiceps,*" Beatrice murmured. The others stared at her, questions in their eyes. Big Bea shrugged. "I almost became a paleontologist. He's a male. Young. You can tell by the crest—it's not really long or tubular yet, but getting there. He's from the late Cretaceous period. Like a hundred million years ago. Fairly recent in dinosaur time."

"As God made him," Billy said.

The wind picked up and stiffened while the five people stood around the broken glider, each of them wondering how it had all come down to this. A burnt husk of an escape pod, a broken skeleton of a young man, and the flame-whitened remains of a long-extinct flying lizard . . .

In the mass of swirling gray clouds above their heads,

they all heard the whine of the Gulfstream jet as it flew slowly through the sky. It passed over the factory, the sound fading, and then grew again as it slowly circled back overhead. Looking for a place to land? The five glanced at the iron sky, the whine of the jet fading once more. Lots of luck.

Maria shivered and pulled her hood closer over her face. "Did you kill all the krill and the grubs and the Daddy Long Leggers?"

"What about the women from Van Horn?" Lila persisted.

Nobody knew exactly what to say, having come all this way, only to admit the complex had beaten them. No, and they hadn't eliminated all the Rolpens or Daddy Long Legs. Webster wasn't the only hybrid; many more fled like frightened deer, vanishing into the metal labyrinth of the facility. As for the segmented Rolpen worms, they squashed as many as they could, but stepped over and under hundreds more crawling up the walls or across the ceilings—while Webster's mutated siblings loped away down the halls. What about the women from Van Horn abandoned to Eleanor? Two bullets spent; and it was anyone's guess where the bullets went.

They even discovered the function of those holes in the ceiling, but it made no difference. Not fire control, but a web of polyethylene piping connected to tanks of hydrofluoric acid; an automatic system capable of spraying everything with a fine, corrosive mist.

Living things absorbing the mist through the skin or exoskeleton liquefied from the inside out. And when the acid came in contact with metal—metal hallways, metal doors—it released hydrogen gas. Turning the whole complex into a fuel air bomb; a single spark from a wall switch or a thermostat and the facility would go up like the Hindenburg.

A brilliant self-destruct fail-safe. The only catch—the operating system had been permanently disabled. The professor had no intention of letting his creations turn into protein napalm and had sealed off the large acid tanks. Yes, the complex had beaten them through and through.

More snow began to fall over the Whiteside parking lot, and the jet whistle cut through the wind. Cheryl looked down at the canister of ashes she held in her arms; Rachel stood next to her now, bare legs calf-deep, her hospital gown flapping. Her bestest ghostie spoke urgently in her ear, "Cheryl, we have to go," Rachel warned. "Don't wait here!"

But Cheryl seemed frozen in place. Mesmerized, eyes turned inward. The Piper wasn't through with her yet, even though they'd never met face to face. The father of lies reached into her mind from beyond death, and now Cheryl could actually see him taunting her from beneath his human skin—paralyzing her with the worst he could dredge up, the worst of her past:

Back to old Poughkeepsie; Cheryl stood in her parents' grimy apartment in her plaid Catholic school skirt. Fourteen years old? Fifteen? Oh, yeah, this was why she fled all the way to California. California wasn't far enough. The moon wasn't far enough. Stepdaddy Ronald, out of work again, sat in the beaten armchair in front of the blurry TV. His white gut and hairy belly button smiled at her from under his T-shirt. He waved her over. "C'mere Cherry darling. Let Ronny show you how much he loves you. Hey, where you going? Hey, don't you give me that sassy look!"

Rachel hissed into her face, "Don't listen to him!"

Cheryl snapped to the present; the cold ran through her. Not summer in Poughkeepsie, winter in a Midwest parking lot. In the few moments Mr. P.'s forked tongue whispered in her ears, she'd pried the cover from Janet's ashes and poked her fingers through the plastic liner, into the whitish dust. The gray Nambe metal cover lay at her feet. Horrified, she snatched it off the snow and crammed it back in place, a plume of Janet's ashes flying into the wind.

Rachel's eyes were anxious and urgent: *"We have to go now, Cheryl—get everyone to go, just get out."* The whine of the jet engines crossed over their heads. Close enough to make the fillings in your teeth vibrate. The jet was too damn close.

"Get out of here!" Rachel cried.

"We have to get out of here!" Cheryl shouted to the rest. How far was the bus?

The snow clung around their calves and knees, turning the slipping and sliding trudge down the switchback slopes into an eternity. They slogged down one length of road, then made the turn, falling, getting up, and doing it again. The snow came down so hard you could barely see twenty feet ahead. Beatrice slid to her knees half a dozen times on the way down. She suppressed the urge to curse, instead whispering *thank you, thank you,* every time Cheryl got her on her feet again.

So where was the bus?

The yellow Blue Bird with the big red cowcatcher plow wasn't where they had left it.

But big tire marks showed where the old bus had slid backward down a length of switchback; its rear wedged against an embankment, at the hairpin turn. Nose and plow positioned to skid down to the bottom. They all clamored to get inside, bunching up at the door. As they clambered aboard, the bus slid on its own again a few more feet. Bea, with her bum leg, stumbled, blocking the entrance. Cheryl pushed her through.

Jet engines roared overhead, ear-splitting, head-crushing loud. The turbines reached screaming decibels. A shuddering crash echoed out of the gray swirling sky. The Gulfstream jet had finally reached its mark, crash landing in the abandoned Whiteside Meatpacking Plant, burying itself in the complex below. Cheryl turned from the bus door; the others plastered their faces to the window.

Fierce red-and-yellow firelight leapt into the sky. The

snow itself seemed to pause, inhale, a great gasp, a moment's pause. Then an even greater roar—

The aircraft found the hydrofluoric acid tanks and lots of hydrogen gas.

The ground shuddered as the underground complex began to implode. Eleanor didn't have to kill green-eyed babies after all. Everyone in the bus pressed their faces to the glass; now each one of them got the strong impression of an underground inferno, as if they had X-ray vision. Metal-walled tunnels bent in the fantastic heat, plastic keyboards and monitors erupting in flame, the recycling area with its huge processing machines breaking apart, the meat seam slithering and writhing as the Rolpens burned.

Finally, the lonely impression of the professor's lean, precise face; the man stared out from his operation console with a look of mild surprise. The bulletproof glass melted; his sunglasses caught on fire, but he was too confused even to scream.

A wave of heat blossomed in every direction. On the switchback slope a great billowing blister of searing air surged toward the bus. The snow on the vehicle's metal roof began to melt, the roadway turning to slush. Cheryl stood in the open passenger-well door and wiped her eyes. Her eyelashes were singed, the fur on her trimmed hood shriveled. She tasted a strong bitter taste on her tongue. Like alum, only worse, and in a flash, Cheryl knew—*she knew* before anyone else. Some of that hydrofluoric acid from the tanks within the complex had reached out and touched her.

Just a lick, just enough.

She said nothing. Instead, she gripped the hand railings and backed inside. Cheryl spat onto her sleeve and wiped her mouth. Blood. Billy hit the accelerator, turned the engine over, and the bus roared to life.

* * *

Billy and Big Bea's faces looked stricken; not something a sick person ever wants to see. "Don't worry, it's not contagious," Cheryl told them. They had left the burning ruin behind. At an abandoned Mobil station, they pulled over to recuperate.

Along the exterior of the Blue Bird, a waft of acid discharge had blistered one side of the curved metal skin. No one else had been affected, only Cheryl. Almost too much to bear as everyone in the bus wanted to "be there" for her; the two grim adult faces, the two grim younger ones, the concern, the tears, but there was no overcoming the fact that Cheryl had reached the end.

Now Cheryl just wanted to crawl off by herself.

Beatrice found a couple of chairs in a corner of the Mobil station convenience store and sat with Cheryl for a while. Neither woman wanted to think how it would go. The acid absorbed through Cheryl's face didn't feel like much at first; but pretty soon the flesh and bone would start to dissolve. Beatrice's pained eyes floated in and out of view.

"Are you sure you don't want to sit in the bus with us? Billy's got a shot for the pain in his first-aid kit."

"Give me one now. I'm starting to hurt." Cheryl paused. She coughed, and a thread of blood came up her mouth. Her face was blistered. "You make another syringe with whatever you need to finish it off. And you give it to me, Beatrice. Only you, Bea."

The heavenly host of morphine warmed her cold limbs for a spell, and Cheryl wondered whether they'd take her to a church, let her sit in the pew and stare at the stained glass. Sure they would. But would she make it? She coughed again. More blood, which she wiped off with some lemon-scented disinfectant wipes. No, she wouldn't make it to church.

Beatrice's voice floated over her.

"Hey there, Gorgeous . . ."

"Hey, yourself."

Tough to see the older woman's face now; it sort of sparkled. Cheryl's eyes were tearing badly, streams of tears flowing down her cheeks, but Cheryl didn't feel like she was crying. When Cheryl touched her face she felt blisters; blisters from forehead to chin. She feared that if they cracked all her life would seep away. Maybe Big Bea was doing all the crying and that's why her face sparkled, with pings of light in blue and yellow.

"I had plans," Cheryl said to the angelic face in front of her. "They weren't big plans, but they were my plans. I thought maybe you and me—" She hacked a little, covering her mouth. No more plans. A few more words slurred up Cheryl's throat. One last request. Very slowly and deliberately the words came out:

"Could you give me the extra shot now? The pain is coming back. And I don't want to scream so anyone hears."

"I understand," Bea said to her. "I understand."

Cheryl saw the needle shimmering on the edge of sight. Suddenly wishing she could have done it herself and not made Beatrice do it. Regretting that so deeply. *Sorry, sorry, so sorry . . .*

Inside the bus Maria hid behind a seat, huddling as if there was no shred of doubt, no hope. With every fiber of her being the little girl tried to see the future. What to do? *What to do?* There must be something they could do— but her mind was filled with clouds, just like the sky outside.

Billy and Lila crouched with Maria, trying to comfort her. Lila held the little girl's hands and stroked her arms, grateful the child didn't have to watch Cheryl pass away. Not good for a child to see something like that; Maria had been through enough of that sort of thing. But as Lila touched the child's face she felt the silvery lightness—a kind of soft tingle at the tips of her fingers. And then Billy Shadow felt it too, like the trill of that tin wolf whistle making the hairs on the back of his neck stand up.

"Can't we be blood brothers?" the little girl asked.

Was she really suggesting what they thought she was? Would that really work? A child's notion, that if you held hands, one person's blood flowing into the next, Cheryl wouldn't die, that they could somehow heal her. Blood brothers, like at a ceremony?

"We could do it," Maria insisted. "Make a cut, make a chain, hold hands, take the poison away." Billy and Lila didn't know what to say. "Then when we're done rub ashes in the cuts to make the bleeding stop." Perhaps this was just exhaustion talking. But what was there to lose? Nothing. Hope and one last chance . . .

Cut your hand, press palm to palm—

"Everyone should do it," Maria whispered. "But Lila first. Lila's the strongest." Billy Shadow understood. They'd all survived the wandering sickness. They were all strong. It was worth a shot.

Nothing to lose but the dying.

Seconds later, Lila, Billy, and Maria half slogged, half ran across the Mobil station, appearing in the convenience store doorway. Billy held Maria in his arms, carrying her over the four-foot drifts. They stumbled in, dragging a wave of snow with them. Beatrice was weeping silently, face in her hands, the syringe trembling in the other.

"Put down the needle!" Lila said. "Maria showed us. Billy and me."

"What?" Beatrice demanded.

Billy Shadow opened his penknife. "Give me your hand," he said.

Big Bea looked at him in alarm.

"Do you care if we're wrong?" Lila asked.

* * *

Outside the abandoned convenience store an onlooker would have seen the strangest thing: three women, a child, and a man holding hands in a line; just holding hands as though they were praying. Heads bowed, letting their life force flow between them, a transfusion of cells and blood, bone marrow, and molecules. Like that old, musty, antique fossil of a rhyme:

> *Six little Injuns all alive,*
> *One kicked the bucket and then there were five;*
> *Five little Injuns on a cellar door,*
> *One tumbled in and then there were four.*

Except this one wasn't going to die. Blood to blood and hand to hand, filtering Cheryl's essence from one person to the next—from Cheryl to Lila, to Maria, to Beatrice and, finally, Billy. . . .

Lila Chen, the first to hold the sick woman's hand, grew very pale, her breath coming in shallow gasps, and as the poison passed from one person to the next, each grew sick in turn. Until at last it came to Billy; he felt the burning sensation flowing outward from Big Bea. Holding his free hand over the convenience store sink, a last cut from his penknife let drops of blood drip down the drain. And as each drop of tainted blood flowed away, slowly the life returned to Cheryl's honey-brown skin, then to Lila, and so on down the line. . . . In the end the color returned to each of their faces.

Before they were done they took a pinch of Janet's ashes and rubbed them in their wounds. The cuts coagulated, and hardened. The blisters on Cheryl's once-smooth cheeks cracked, leaked, and shrank. Finally healed—but the scars would remain for the rest of her life.

The final syringe lay forgotten on the counter. Beatrice squeezed the dose down the drain along with everything else. Cheryl struggled to stand; then glanced about the abandoned convenience store. Eyes darting, she looked for Rachel, her bestest girlie.

Then found her.

"I hoped you'd be here if I came back from the dead."

"I guess I just wanted to make sure you were okay," Rachel whispered into Cheryl's ear. She touched the hem of her hospital gown. "They're having a special in Eternity Wear. I think I can go now." Rachel kissed her cheek, but Cheryl couldn't feel it. Exhausted, wrung out, yes, dead tired, she couldn't feel anything. Rachel's ghost breezed through the plate-glass store window, then across the drifts, bare feet, no prints. Outside, the snow slowed to faint spirals; the clouds broke; a shaft of sun lit the empty ground.

I know your face better than my own.

G uy and Lauren spent the longest night of their lives waiting out the storm in the gabled house back in Middletown. No one dared sleep. Guy hacked away, sweating and shivering all at the same time. Alice brought him endless cups of tea, with lemon juice and plenty of sugar. The two greyhounds came to lie with him on the couch, canine hot-water bottles. The hours crawled on their hands and knees as the snow flew sideways across the porch.

Snow, Guy thought. God, what did people do in the good ol' days? Wind drifts and ice fog—you couldn't see beyond your hand. Guess in olden times people snuggled inside until the weather broke and the sun came out; then shoveled a lot. The first few inches weren't so bad, but as it started to accumulate—half a foot, a foot, when it grew to two feet—the harder it became to get out of your way. He'd read somewhere that horses pulled rollers and sledges to pack down the roads. Guy remembered watching plows work the Albany airport some years ago; 2 a.m. and the maintenance crews were still pushing mounds around under the runway floodlights. By dawn, Guy had stopped hacking long enough to drift off.

A bar of feeble daylight crossed the carpet. Lauren opened her eyes. The snow had stopped. The first thing she noticed—two bold rabbits sitting on the windowsill on the other side of the glass. Corky and Peaches perked up their ears, twitching inquisitive noses. In one bound they leapt over Guy's snoring body.

The rabbits vanished.

Lauren cautiously padded across the floor. The dogs' noses had steamed the lower panes of the frosted window. The rabbit tracks stretched back to the edge of the trees. The world was covered in snow.

Lauren sighed and looked away. But her eyes snapped back to the window at the grumble of a large engine driving around the hospital grounds. The forgotten and yet familiar sound of road surface being plowed; the rhythmic rumble and thump of a plow pushing snow. In a few moments the vehicle came into view. Lauren ran to get her boots and parka and the revolver. To Alice she said, "Stay with Guy and the dogs."

The vehicle turned out to be the Kubota front loader with one of the maintenance guys driving. A cheerful fellow about sixty in a dark blue snowmobile suit; he pushed a mound of snow deftly past the line of parked vehicles— Mr. Washington's car, the white minivan, the yellow 4Runner. Then pulled up by the porch and leaned out the transparent plastic cab.

At once Lauren thought of him as the Good Samaritan, coming out of nowhere to rescue her and Alice and Guy marooned in the snow.

"Saw some tracks leading up here and just checking to see if everyone is okay."

He glanced at the bodies stacked on the porch completely covered in snow. The Good Samaritan wagged his head in dismay. "Lot of that going around. But it seems to be tapering off. Are you hurt?"

Lauren shook her head no, then finally remembered to say something. "Can I get you something. Tea or cocoa? Would you like to come inside and get warm?"

"No, I'm all set," the man replied. "I'm the only one who showed to work today, but that's better than nothing." He saw Lauren's confused expression.

"There seem to be a lot of people waking up," he explained. "People you thought were gone for good. Believe it or not, they opened up the minimart back in Middletown this morning." He chuckled. "Cold cuts but no bread."

Then Lauren noticed an animal moving by the Good Samaritan's boots. A bunny stared out the bottom of the plastic see-through cab. The man stared down at the creature and laughed again. "He just hopped in and likes plowing. Go figure. Anyway, he makes me feel better."

Lauren didn't know what to say.

The rabbit wrinkled its nose and cocked his ears. And somehow that made Lauren feel better too.

EPILOGUE

American Gothic

Happy the man, and happy he alone,
He who can call to-day his own;
He who, secure within, can say,
To-morrow, do thy worst, for I have liv'd to-day.

—John Dryden (1631–1700),
Imitation of Horace, Book III, Ode 29, Line 65–68

45

Tea House of the Hidden Moon

Lattimore stood at the bronze window of his library and stared out across Sioux Falls. The setting sun shone across miles of white snow. Outside the aerospace building, Lila Chen and Little Maria were decorating the trees on the sidewalk with Christmas lights. The two girls unwound the sparkling strings from a large roll the company kept in the basement—handing the pretty lights off to Billy Shadow, who passed them on up a tall double-sided ladder to Cheryl and Big Bea. Strangely, or not so strangely, the large woman didn't seem to need her leg brace any longer, her knee miraculously healed. And Cheryl was just happy to be alive.

Several lit trees gave off an air of sugarplums and fairy magic. A few weeks ago, you wouldn't have thought it possible. A few weeks ago, the aerospace boss wouldn't have thought much of anything was possible.

When Lattimore returned from the server farm he found Mildred facedown on the bed, OD'd, a rime of rainbow dust around her lips and nose. That night—a very long walk about the apartment, keeping her on her feet until the drugs relented. Then there were the days of detox after Lattimore got rid of her stash, Mildred snarling, *"Clem! Clem, you bastard, get me one more touch. One more touch. . . ."*

For several days, Lattimore changed soaked sheets, poured endless cups of tea down Mildred's throat, and mopped her brow every time the devils leapt out of the walls. During the quieter moments of hand-holding, a deep silence reigned over the world, and Clem began to wonder whether they were the only two people left.

No one knew the real numbers on the dead. Some thought one in three, others thought one in four. Lattimore guessed one in five. Twenty percent; this meant fifty or sixty million people in the USA alone. The lucky ones hid like peasants in the Dark Ages until it was safe to come out. The cities took it the hardest; most metropolitan areas—Chicago, New York, Los Angeles—cracked open on the pavement, like ancient Rome abandoned to corrupt officials, scavengers, and cutthroats. For a time it felt as though the cockroaches had finally inherited the Earth.

One small blessing; as winter had come, the massed dead in the North could be stored outside and eventually carted off to landfills as rail freight and trucking limped back to life. In the South, they made bonfires, and this process, if you could call it a process, replicated itself around the globe.

In Sioux Falls, those first few weeks were no fun. North-Western Energy and Black Hills Power faded every couple of hours; people huddled around fireplaces and woodstoves, scrounging gas or oil for their generators. Word got around that Lattimore, Inc., still had supplies of food; scores of frightened, famished people with nowhere to go lined up outside the aerospace building. Nothing to do but open the doors of the Cosmos Café . . . until the food ran out. At least the company generators kept people warm, and the empty frozen body of Security Chief Nash got taken outside for good.

However, just as the point of no return approached, the deliveries that people took for granted, and lost all hope of ever seeing again, miraculously started up. In a few weeks people discovered extra stores of goods, allowing the employees of big box outlets to distribute staples. Food banks were set up with regular collection times, and finally the rail depots on the edges of towns started seeing more freight. Foodstuffs were getting in—not much in the way of fresh, but plenty of frozen vegetables, and flour and rice, along with mountains of canned meat—enough to keep people going. Americans lived in a very rich country; you couldn't eat everything at once even if you tried. South Dakotans, along with the heartland and huge hunks of the South and Southwest, had avoided total annihilation.

No, not every grocery store was stocked with milk and cookies. Not everyone was a Good Samaritan, but mankind had shaken off a crazy bit of itself and somehow emerged a little freer, a little stronger. As if a silent power had exhorted every person to *Be Good and Do What You Can*. People rallied and somehow scrambled back from the abyss.

Was it because of mankind's inner decency, or because mankind had a little help?

Maybe both.

After the crisis abated, an explanation appeared on Lattimore's desk in the form of a large manila envelope, perhaps the best answer anyone was ever going to get. Lost in the company mailroom, then suddenly found again, the envelope explained a lot.

Originally posted from Belgrade, it arrived at Lattimore Aerospace headquarters over a year ago, and was misplaced on its trip from the mailroom to the boss' inbox. Mildred found it wedged underneath the reception counter. Fallen on the floor, slid under a crack, and overlooked at about the time everybody and his or her aunt were getting high on rainbow dust.

"I just found this downstairs," Mildred told him quietly. The flap was already open, the clasp broken.

"God, this thing's been here for months," Lattimore remarked. The envelope was marred with stuck crumbs and the smudge of a footprint, the way things look when they live under a desk.

The cover letter:

Office of the Curator
Nikola Tesla Museum
Krunska 51, 11000
   Belgrade, Serbia
Tel. + 381 11 24 33 886
Fax. + 381 11 24 36 408

Mr. Wen Chen
Vice President
Lattimore Aerospace

Dear Mr. Chen:

  The curator has reconsidered your request. Please find copies of all our materials regarding Lagrange Points in our files. We assume they were mistakenly included in Nikolai Tesla's materials by person or persons unknown. These have been catalogued as "Miscellaneous." The museum has no record as to the circumstances of their inclusion, their authenticity, chain of title, and no recorded source of origin.

  We assume the photographic materials and hand-written notations to be frauds or hoaxes of some kind, and are prepared to say so publicly.

Yours Sincerely—

The contents were a series of photographs and some foolscap, the photos too strange for words, nearly impossible for anyone to have actually taken, though Lattimore recognized one physical snapshot immediately.

An old Polaroid print from one of those big plastic Polaroid Swinger 3000 land cameras. *His father's Polaroid.* Raindrops dotted the picture where Pop had brought it in from outside. On the back of Dad's Polaroid picture his old man had written, *Dear Curator—for your Tesla files.*

So this is where my father sent the pictures after he and

my mother disappeared and just as suddenly returned, wet and naked. Squirreled away, safe and sound. Buried the evidence in a sheaf of another man's work in a foreign country. Send them to Belgrade. Nobody'd find them there.

What of the photo itself?

Pop Lattimore's abduction Polaroid showed another image of a silver Tea House trailer; this one in the blackness of space and lit up with sunlight. In the background Earth looked like it did from the moon, only a little bigger, a fat, blue, cloud-swirled planet about the size of a half dollar. No way a Lattimore Aerospace satellite took *that*.

Is this where Mom and Dad went, Light Teslas whisking their physical bodies off on a little trip? How else could they have taken Polaroid photos? Well, why not? Any entity that could stick you on the deck of a lost container ship or drop you in Alaska to chase a flying cafeteria tray could take you into space for a photo shoot and bring you back.

The designation *L1* was strikingly visible on the trailer's metal skin, but instead of merely etched on the outside of the container, the designation seemed to be glowing from the inside of the Tea House, as though this picture captured some kind of radiation. Not just a label on the skin of the trailer, but an internal signature, and damned if Lattimore knew what made it glow.

Moreover, the Tea House looked broken; a meteor had struck it amidships, leaving a dirty black hole. Colored gas vented into the space, the remnants of whatever was housed inside—bulrushes, blue birds, koi fish, and fire pits?

Finally, it hit Lattimore—*L* stood for Lagrange. *L1* would be Lagrange Point Number One. He didn't recognize it at once because it almost always appeared

$$L_1$$

With the numeral dropped a half space.

Of course, *Lagrange Points.* The Mind Gliders, the Light

Teslas, had taken Mom and Pop to Lagrange Points to show them all the Tea Houses.

Lattimore clicked into Jasper's laptop to find an image:

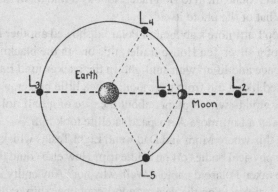

Those static gravitational points near any massive pair of objects where a third object can be stationary. At five points between the Earth and the Sun (1 through 5) gravitational balance allowed yet another object, in this case *a silver shipping container,* to remain in a "fixed" position. Stick the Tea House in the proper Lagrange area and it would follow Earth around for eternity. I mean, if you needed to hide something in plain sight—a needle in a haystack, a speck of sand on a beach—what better place to put it? Stick it in space.

How could Lattimore *the satellite manufacturer* miss something so obvious as L1/5? It beggared belief.

L1/5 would mean Lagrange Points Number 1 through Number 5. Maybe if the silver Tea House trailer sprouted solar panels and beacon antennae, or even appeared as a black monolith hanging in space, he might have made the connection. But in a plain silver wrapper, so to speak—a plain silver box stuffed with living goodies, pretty blue birds, lazy carp—his mind had seen what he wanted to see, a busy stream and cute bunny rabbits, and overlooked the rest. Of course! There had to be more than one Tea House.

Five, at least.

Obviously, the silver trailer in the container ship *Anja* beached in a Floridian swamp was the one from L_2, Lagrange Point 2, the point on the far side of the moon, at a mere 932,000 miles. Nothing much out there but a couple of big government radio telescopes: the Advanced Composition Explorer, the Wilkinson Microwave Probe. Lattimore saw the logic of it. If the closest Tea House at L_1 was rendered a smoking hulk from an asteroid hit, might as well go to the second-closest Tea House at L_2.

How the damn trailer from Point L_2 got down to Earth and into the hold of a ship was anybody's guess. But any "Taker" who let a rocket scientist from Pennsylvania take a pic of Tea House L_1 could probably arrange for Tea House L_2 to land on Earth without too much trouble. Even hide a whole Norwegian container ship in a fog bank so no vigilant Coast Guard inspectors investigated a curious heat bloom. Once among the earthlings, that silver tractor-trailer would vanish among the millions of other containers sitting around the globe in warehouses and industrial parks and docksides.

Then came the last photo. A sixth Tea House of the Hidden Moon.

Not one of his father's Polaroids. The final impossible photo was a black-and-white glossy of a moon crater. A caption on the photo read *Тесле*. And its moon coordinates: *38.5 N 124.7 E.* And over the whole image appeared the words *Совершенно секретно* in red. Lattimore guessed the red letters said what they said in every government office on the planet: *Top Secret.*

A crater on the dark side of the moon. The dark side being a misnomer as it got just as much sun as the light side; you just couldn't see it from Earth. The crater was called

Tesla, and since the name was written in Cyrillic, obviously the photo had been taken in Soviet's *Luna 3* flybys in the late 1950s. NASA did comprehensive mapping in the 1960s, but you had to wonder if America's space administration had bothered to enlarge the image as the Russians had. The depth of the 31-kilometer-wide Tesla crater was still unknown to this day, but there in the center the Ruskies had managed to capture the clean angles of yet another silver Tea House trailer. This one half-buried in moon dust; visible on its roof, that same peculiar metal etching process, the words:

Кратер Тесле Луна

A Soviet State secret? Hell, the Central Committee wouldn't know what to make of this any more than NASA would. Ignore it. Bury it in the Tesla archives. Lattimore was tempted to pop the Cyrillic letters into a Russian-English translator. Not necessary, he had a good idea what the Russian words etched on the Tea House meant: Crater Tesla Moon.

Make that, Tesla Moon Crater.

The real question was, so how did the silver trailer know to display its name in Cyrillic? The Ruskies didn't go down to the moon and write it there. And why not English or Chinese Oracle Bone script? In a stab of insight, the answer stared him in the face. The designation changed as the position of the Tea House changed—and most importantly, depending on *who looked at it*. When a Tea House was in the bowels of a ship off the coast of Florida, it showed in English, the simple message revealing its origin: L1/5 now L2.

Make up your mind.

Actually, it did it for you. Full English Translation:

This is one of the five Tea Houses, this one from Lagrange Point 2.

When another silver Tea House was photographed from a Russian spacecraft, it told its point of origin in Russian. If you found one off the coast of Bombay, the curious etching would present in Hindi. Cleverly and conveniently, it told you a little bit about itself in whatever language was most accessible to the reader.

Then a dangerous thought struck Lattimore even harder. The Tea House of the Hidden Moon *reacted*. The thing was sentient. Perhaps it could change its appearance at will to suit its background like a lizard or a frog. In a ten-story stack of containers waiting to be loaded aboard a ship maybe it was red or blue. To be hidden or discovered at its own discretion, hiding in plain sight until desiring to reveal its presence. That turned coincidence into intelligent design.

Tea House of the Hidden Moon—how had that name *even come to him*? It fit okay; and it still fit. Five Tea Houses hidden at Lagrange Points, making them the extra and "hidden" moons of Earth. A sixth on the moon itself, hidden on the far side. But the phrase had just popped into his head as if the thing was trying to tell him its name. A Tea House *hidden* in space, a Tea House *hidden* on the Moon . . .

Tea House of the Hidden Moon.

Of course . . . Why explain something one way when three or four ways will do even better?

Redundancy, the drum of cognition.

The Rosetta Stone Principle. Very wise.

Lattimore put the Russian crater photo aside.

The last item in the envelope from the Tesla Museum was photocopied foolscap. Pop Lattimore seemed to have written a few notes from his space trip. Halting, fragmented words as if to confirm every one of his son's assumptions and conclusions.

They showed me a box, and then showed me inside. They told me its name. Tea House of the Hidden Moon.

As Lattimore held the photocopy of his father's scribbling he felt himself standing in the bowels of the ship again, overcome by the same warm rush of heaven on

Earth—the rice-paper windows, the stone fire pit. The steaming teakettle and the càrp staring lazily from the pond. The sound of falling water over river stones, and the scent of cherry trees in blossom filled his head. A wise old cricket stroked his wings as if to say, *Remember?*

Of course he remembered.

Was the silver Tea House its own little world? Yes and no, Lattimore realized, and he sensed it was something much, much bigger in the scheme of things, especially if you took the long view. Lattimore shuddered and grasped the purpose of the hidden Tea House. The Tea House of the Hidden Moon was existence distilled. The essence of all you saw. When half the world died, you could bring it back to life, back from the dead.

Pop Lattimore had scribbled a few more lines. Hypothesis confirmed.

It is my conjecture that even the weight of the container does not reflect its true size. Its mass many times heavier than what appears. A drop of water equal to an ocean.

Ah, the nub of it. The Ancestors of Existence had planned their project well. In the fluttering heart of a single bluebird, the muscle mass of every breathing animal, beating away at the same time. In the iron kettle, the tonnage of every mountain in every range across the planet. Within the fire in the fire pit, the molten core of the planet itself.

If a great asteroid blasted away Earth's atmosphere, if supervolcanoes exploded the planet from within, if a magnetic reversal tore the oceans from their beds, *if the devil himself came down to lead us into hell*—that wouldn't be the final word. That wouldn't be the end. The Tea House of the Hidden Moon ensured survival. The endurance of all things:

A *Lifeseed.*

Lattimore paused at the pure genius of it.

His father's final note: *Over the centuries, the Tea House may have had many names. The Hebrews called it the Guf, the Hall of Souls; the Moslems, the Well of Souls. Others*

*called it Shangri-La, or the Fountain of Youth. A waiting
seed when the face of Earth goes barren.*

*Lots of dangers in the cosmos—but God seems to like
us. The Tea House of the Hidden Moon is his smile in the
face of catastrophe. For who else could make such a thing
but Him? The Master of the First Thought.*

Was that it? Bits of myth and religious tales floated to the
surface of Lattimore's mind. A voice from a burning bush.
A pillar of fire. A Law Giver bringing tablets down from a
mountain. Noah's great-grandfather, Enoch, brought before
the face of the Lord. Fallen Angels who mated with the
beautiful women of mankind, their offspring the Nephilim,
a race of demigods. A blue-skinned floating Shiva, Destroyer of Worlds. Zeus hurling thunderbolts and spreading
his seed with every shepherdess and princess he could find.
Leda mating with a swan to make Helen of Troy and Castor
and Pollux. Call them Star Children. Call them Lila Chen
and Little Maria's great-great-great grandparents.

Every ancient tale was magic. Every ancient tale a story
of cross-breeding or visitations from above. Great beings,
Long Souls who floated down from the skies, changing
mankind for better or ill. Who dragged men up from their
hovels, to wander across mountaintops, to worship the won-
ders of heaven. Who fought wars for the possession of Earth.

Bad ones like the Piper and better ones who smiled upon
mankind, who walked on water and made blind men see.
The same who gave us fire and foresight and forgiveness—
and ten rules to live by. God made *them* too.

The Tea House was Pandora's Box. The primordial soup
with a pleasing appearance, the tree of life. The immortal
flicker of sacred, animate existence. Once opened on a Floridian mudflat the Tea House flowed everywhere, all life
spilling from its open container doors. Well, he'd seen it
reach landfall—the silver trailer from Lagrange Point 2
broken open in a swamp with its guts spilled out, its living
contents hopping off across the grassy waterway.

Lattimore almost laughed. They'd seen the answer all along, every place they went. A tiny, shy creature, savior of one and all.

Rabbits.

Rabbits going everywhere; invaders from space, breeding with their earthly rabbit kin. How perfect. Innocuous. Hiding in plain sight. What superlative little creatures. Lived anywhere, worked for nothing, asked nothing in return—just to breathe and breed. The real rebreeders. Magic rabbits from the magic Tea House bringing harmony and balance out of ruin.

They didn't need claws or fangs or tuxedos or top hats; they only had to keep out of sight, eat a leaf, hide in a hole. Come out when the coast was clear, when things needed to be brought back from the end.

Magic rabbits. The good aliens.

Maybe what the innocent creatures gave was as simple as hope. That you could pick yourself off the ground. Do it all over again. Hope and another chance.

Why not? In all his wisdom God had improved on Angels, both good and bad.

He'd turned them into rabbits.

46

American Gothic

Cheryl and Big Bea had gone off Christmas shopping in a nearly empty Empire Mall. Billy tagged along to hold their shopping bags. He didn't complain. After a few weeks with those two, he'd gotten "Yes, Dear," down pretty good. As had the other two, who now knew it was okay to touch.

Back at the aerospace building the Christmas lights on the trees below glistened up from the street. Lila Chen sat on the couch in the library with her nose in a large hardbound illustrated book—*The Collected Works of Buck Rogers in the 25th Century*—that she'd found on the shelves. Another book, *Applied Physics,* sat nearby along with, *Biochemical Calculations: How to Solve Mathematical Problems in General Biochemistry.* A legal pad with scribbles showed where she'd been working a problem. The two textbook tomes momentarily put aside for Buck Rogers; she needed a break. Buck was much better than biochem.

Maria sat in an armchair, watching the library's large TV, slumped so low in the cushions you could barely see her head. A local station had started running cartoons; Elmer Fudd in his sporty hunting outfit had finally cornered Bugs Bunny. While Bugs—dressed as a very shapely girl, in a skirt, blond wig, and lipstick—employed deception. Elmer Fudd, no fool, pointed his shotgun at the wily wabbit.

Maria, from the armchair, did a fair rendition of Mel Blanc's flat, nasal tone: *"Okay wabbit, I see through that disguise, say your pwayers!"*

Mildred came in from the kitchen where she'd been making the children lunch: canned tuna on white with Miracle Whip. She stood mesmerized for a few moments, quietly awed. "My God, the TV is back. When did that come on?"

Lila looked up from Buck Rogers. She rubbed the side of her head. Her missing ear wasn't missing anymore, but starting to grow back, an attractive, scalloped shell. *"Shhh,"* the older girl told Mildred. *"Be vewy, vewy quiet. There's something awfwy scwewy going on awound here."*

Billy unpacked the Kargo Kooler and weighed the dingy baggie in his hand, a burnt ear for goodness sake—*Lila's ear* with the hematite earring still attached; and the match Bhakti found on her dresser. All those bits had served them faithfully; first as a compass, then later as some kind of prophylaxis against the wandering sickness. But the magic baggie long ago past its expiration date.

"Get rid of it," Beatrice said.

"We'll *buy* her earrings," Cheryl added.

But still, the women felt they had to do something for poor Eleanor; at the very least find a resting place for Janet's ashes in the silver Nambe urn. *She'll be comfortable with you.* Right from the beginning it had always been Cheryl. Cheryl who found Janet in the back of that orange Chevy, who brought the body to the funeral home, ridden with her farthest, first with Bhakti, then alone. It seemed fitting that Cheryl should take Janet to her final resting place.

As for Billy Shadow, he needed to perform one last rite—pay his final respects to Granny Sparrow. Nobody had told him, but somehow he knew the old woman was dead. Since the troubles there had been no word in or out of the rez; cell service and phone lines still down. In any case he had to see for himself.

The two women decided to go along with him—one last road trip.

They made time over nearly three hundred miles west on I-90 to Pine Ridge, having to pump gas out of the ground only once at a service station. When the three got out of the car on the reservation, Granny's trailer no longer stood in the high weeds at the end of the gravel path. Instead, a bare spot greeted them. The grass tramped down, wheel marks and footprints crisscrossing the snowy ground; Granny's trailer towed away.

Billy hadn't seen this coming, but it made sense. With the old woman gone there'd be no reason to leave a trailer there; any used car dealership would pay good money for it.

A few paces off, Billy's people had laid Granny Sparrow's body on a burial platform. The platform stood about seven feet off the ground, held up at four corners by stout poles. The old ways. Granny wore her feather war bonnet and her ghost dancer shirt. Nobody had pinched or taken those. Nobody would dare. Granny did not look like she had been gone long. Days, a week maybe. . . . In the cold she'd hardly changed.

The better part of her body covered in the flag that used to hang over her bed, tucked around her like a blanket. An inch of snow had fallen since she passed. Some of it blown by the wind, exposing her face, thinner than Billy ever remembered: deeply sunken cheeks, gray lifeless skin. Under her hand he saw a metal object. Her claw-like fingers kept it from dropping to the ground or blowing away. The silver wolf whistle. Cautiously Billy lifted Granny's finger and finally took the whistle back.

Cheryl gently tucked Janet's ashes in the Nambe urn under Granny Sparrow's withered hand, half expecting her to grasp it, but Granny's fingers didn't move.

"Do you want to say anything?" Cheryl asked him.

Ashes to ashes?

Billy shook his head. "No, I don't think so."

Another month exposed to the sky, all manner of creatures would come, returning Granny to the earth, leaving only the bones. For a few moments Billy lowered his head, bending all his will to Skin Walk one more time. The paw prints of various critters dappled the snow, padding off in a dozen directions. For a few fleeting moments, his mind crept along the ground beside the burial platform. Then he saw. . . .

A wise old hare sat in the brush sniffing the air and flicking his whiskers. Nearby, three cautious mice stared through the thickets, not daring to emerge from their hole. A few paces away, a sly old badger bided his time; thinking hard about whether to have the three skittish mice for breakfast or chase the stringy old hare. A bright yellow warbler clung to a stalk and twirled a long, sweet solo.

Billy put his old wolf whistle to his lips in answer. The sound of *Whoop! Whoop! Whoop!* rose into the sky. The wise old hare bolted into his hole, the badger waddled off, and the three mice vanished into the ground. But the warbler clung to his stalk, swaying back and forth. The whooping faded away, and silence cloaked the prairie like a final prayer.

Beatrice gazed up at the overcast sky, the clouds breaking across slashes of blue.

"Looks like things are clearing up."

G uy and Lauren slowly drove down their street in Fairfield. Guy sneezed; he still had a bit of a cold. Young Alice sat silently in the backseat with the greyhounds curled in the cargo well for most of the ride. The only sound was her giggling as Corky or Peaches snuffed her ear.

Not much had changed on their street except that Mr. Fenniman's body had vanished. Oh no, not quite—Lauren glimpsed bone sticking out of a pair of pants and a loose shoe. The body dragged farther under the shrubs by his house. Coyote work. Snow covered most of the rest, but she could see gnawed ribs shining whitely, picked clean. No one felt like unpacking; instead piling their stuff just inside the Finn House door.

A terrible melancholy overcame Lauren, and she saw as much in Guy's eyes. The unnatural quiet of their street hung in the air, their footsteps in the snow the only ones. Nobody had been around; nobody had broken into the place.

Most of all, neither of them wanted to see young Alice leave. They both felt like they'd almost go with her if she asked. Appear in the 1800s, bring the dogs, and start over. Now that it came to it, Alice seemed reluctant too. She sat at the base of the stairs, the very way Guy saw her so long ago. Her hand touched the railing, as though she was thinking about ascending, but couldn't work up the courage to move.

Lauren spoke, but her voice felt strange, and forced.

"Can I get you anything? Cinnamon toast?"

Alice silently shook her head. Suddenly the girl rushed to Guy and threw her arms around him. He held her for a moment, and Lauren pressed herself in with them. She inhaled the clean fragrance of Alice's skin. The dogs came too, wedging their heads and noses everywhere. *Pet Me! Pet Me!*

As Alice broke away, Lauren tucked her fingers under the dogs' collars.

You two stay.

Softly, the front door creaked open, pushed open by the wind. A sparrow darted into the house. The bird flitted about the Keeping Room, into the kitchen, back out again, finally settling on the stair rail. It preened a little and chirped as if to say, *C'mon!*

Had the sparrow come with Alice out of her past? Or was it the one Guy saw stunned on the front steps when he rushed home in a fright all those months ago? Who could say?

Stoically, the girl mounted the stairs, passing the bird on the way up. "Well, c'mon yourself."

She climbed the steps, the bird fluttered along with her, one step after another. Alice looked back. She steeled herself and pressed on, gliding up to the upstairs landing, where the darkness engulfed her. The sparrow fluttered once more and was gone.

Guy and Lauren waited silently below, knowing in their hearts that if they followed the girl's footsteps, if they walked up there now—there'd be no Alice. No bird. Then Lauren realized to her shock Alice had worn her store-bought modern winter parka, her heavy shoes, even carried her kid's backpack. Oh good Lord, unless she ditched them before appearing in public, people were bound to ask questions.

Suddenly Corky and Peaches broke from Lauren's grip. They bounded up the stairs four steps at a time and paced back and forth. But of course, there was nothing to find. The two good dogs whined, terribly frustrated. Lauren couldn't bring herself to fetch them back. "Guy, please, will you get them?"

Guy went upstairs. "C'mon Corky. C'mon Peaches. C'mon you two." He plucked a tiny sparrow feather off Peaches' nose where she snuffed it off the floor.

"Let's go downstairs, gang. Maybe we've got some cookies."

Nevertheless, young Alice's fortunes in the past or the present did not quite end on the stairs. Ever since their stay at the gabled house, something bothered Lauren about Alice's repetitive drawing in her diary. Not that the little girl drew pictures—drawing by itself was normal enough. Considering everything the girl had seen—her parents' death by yellow fever, the wandering sickness—you'd expect her to draw strange things. But why Rolpens? Why a fanciful creation from an artist, M. C. Escher, whose books and prints and art had yet to be created or published in the girl's own time?

How the heck did Alice know? The girl started drawing in the car before they ever reached the sanitarium or the gabled house. And how did she know about the factory in Ohio? Another mystery. Somehow, Alice knew all about the meatpacking plant and the Rolpens and came ahead to warn them.

Lauren found the answer the very day their Wonderland girl vanished on the landing; in the cellar downstairs with a flashlight, right where Alice said it would be. *Worms in the cellar—worms in the stone.* Fossilized trilobites dotted every granite foundation block. The flashlight lanced from one chiseled block to the next. On every slab some species of fossilized animal flashed back at you: nautilus, prehistoric shrimp, every ancient creature petrified, curled nose to tail in eternal extinction. So Alice's words were true. *They were everywhere, even in the foundation of the house.*

Guy's voice came down the stairs, "Honey, what are you doing down there?"

"Hunting Rolpens," Lauren called up. Guy growled faintly, "What?"

Lauren only laughed. Back in the Keeping Room she got out that moldy old diary they'd discovered in the antique writing desk, the journal with the cyanotypes. Not that there was anything more to learn from it—she and Guy had gone over the relic pretty thoroughly—but fresh eyes couldn't hurt. Bits and pieces still troubled her. The factory, for one; what in the heck made young Alice think of a factory in Ohio?

Lauren felt almost the fool, desperately trying to understand the inexplicable. She laid the leather-bound volume on the kitchen counter and touched the fragile pages. Lauren dwelled again over the lines:

They put an X on the front door. We haven't been outside in a week. Pastor Simmons has been very kind and brought us food. We leave the money on the stoop—

Lauren stopped cold. Her hands began to tremble. Behind some pointless scraps, the torn cover of Alice's contemporary Horse Friends diary appeared. Very old, very dingy as if it had been hidden away in that leather book forever. So easy to miss when you weren't looking for it. Another entry appeared on a fragment of yellowed paper, something she'd missed the first time around. Young Alice writing:

Mama and Papa were sick. Then they died. After Yellow Jack nobody missed me. I went to the new house again today to escape the fever. I like the people, I like the dogs. But I have to go back.

Then the final entry:

*Grammy wasn't too angry when I came back. She
missed me. But she didn't want anyone seeing the new
clothes. Or my memory book.*

Lauren turned the last page. At the very back she found a
newspaper clipping; a tiny notice really, about three inches
square:

KIDNAPPED BY ELVES
ORPHAN RETURNS WITH PIXIE DUST

Miss Alice Whitcomb, 12, missing since early November, returned to her family today after an absence of
several weeks, claiming she had been kidnapped by
elves. As proof of her abduction, the little girl
produced curious sugar treats called Pixie Stix that
have been sent to New York for composition testing.
Throughout the summer months the little girl had gone
missing for spells at a time, but in late October—

The rest of the article had disintegrated. That made Lauren laugh; clever girl, she had to say something. Then a
red waxy wrapper of a Tootsie Pop fluttered out from behind the news clipping; brought back a hundred and fifty
years and saved in the pocket of her pinafore. Lauren
touched it, remembering that day in the supermarket
how Alice looked in amazement at the shelves. Lauren
almost took the silly red wrapper to keep in her jewelry
box; she almost cried and pressed it to her lips. But with
great reserve she put it back in its place. She'd show Guy
later.

Lauren closed the book, and then turned it over. On the
back cover, an image caught her eye. As was often com-
monplace with diaries, the leather-bound book carried an
advertisement on the back, like appointment calendars

from insurance companies did today. Once again, easy to overlook, as it didn't mean much at the time. Now the advertisement meant something. The picture showed a version of the Currier and Ives print *Home to Thanksgiving*:

Whiteside's Purveyor's, Hillsboro, Ohio

HOME TO THANKSGIVING.

Whiteside's Purveyor's, Hillsboro—Serving the Heartland and Points East.
Featuring Our Cured Bacon and Dutch Meat Rollades.
"From Our Smokehouse to Your Long House"

The address of the meatpacking plant had faded from view, but Lauren had seen enough. A dank cellar with extinct creatures embedded in the walls. An old advertisement for Dutch Meat Rollades. Rolpens from a meatpacking plant. *Where the worms go to be born. They go home to Thanksgiving.*

She understood now. Young Alice's vision and leaps of intuition were happy accidents fueled by happenstance. An exceptionally clever girl with an exceptionally vivid imagination, who fit the bits and pieces of reality together—past, present, and future—any which way she could. Rendering coherence and reason from pure coincidence—God's way of remaining anonymous, even inside young Alice's head.

Guy came into the kitchen, up from the cellar. "I think some of the pipes busted," he informed her rather nonchalantly. "I guess the power went on and off while we were away. A couple of times, maybe."

"Well, if that's the worst of it, we got lucky."

Lauren held the old, worn diary to her chest like the most precious thing in the world. Guy wasn't about to take it from her. "Admit it, you tortured your dolls as a little girl. Didn't you?" Guy teased her. "Only you didn't have a toy guillotine."

Lauren loosened her grip on the book and smiled a little.

"You married me anyway."

Late that afternoon neither Guy nor Lauren could stand being in the house any longer. In any event, they wouldn't get the water pipes fixed today. Maybe there'd be a plumber answering his phone tomorrow. The lights flickered, but hung on. Guy had left a big stack of cut wood before they left, so they'd use the Keeping Room fireplace if the power died.

Curious about the big wide world, Lauren decided to take the dogs for a walk into town. Might as well see how bad things were. Reading his wife's mind, Guy put the leashes on the dogs before Lauren found their coats. The ten-minute walk took twenty uneventful minutes through half-plowed streets and six inches of slush. A couple of their neighbors came to their windows, peeking cautiously through the curtains.

The late-afternoon sun began to sink toward the horizon as dusk settled onto the snow-bound houses of Fairfield. Guy noticed two bright stars rising over the rooftops, and from the two bright pinpricks in the eastern sky a spray of shooting stars leapt out at him. Flash and then vanish, the shower of meteors pulsed out of the heavens. An old nursery rhyme popped into his head. *Star light, star bright, the first star I see tonight. . . .* Now there were dozens. What wish should Guy wish tonight? Escaping the end of the world with Lauren and the dogs and a roof over their heads—what sane man could want anything more?

Days later, he found an old paperback on a shelf in the Keeping Room, a Golden Nature Guide called *Stars,* and discovered he'd been looking at Castor and Pollux, the brightest stars in Gemini, and the shooting sparks were the Geminid meteor shower. But at the time all he saw was that bright light in the east shooting stars toward his face.

And it struck him hard, how unknowable and immense that great well of creation. Too much to see, too much to grasp, a vast ocean; while Earth, its humans and human struggle, were just bits of microscopic plankton in the baleen of a cosmic whale. Two hundred billion stars in the Milky Way? Four hundred billion? No one knew. . . . But one thing was certain. No one on this busy little planet would ever be really alone in this crowded universe.

Guy returned to Earth. In the village, a few good things had returned to life. The Community Movie Theatre's marquee was lit up; a comforting kind of light. At the start of the troubles the theatre had booked that Broderick Fallows flick; a few disjointed letters from its last booking clung to the theatre's promo windows: *In-x-plc . . .*

That afternoon the marquee boasted a new attraction:

Now Showing:
Health Clinic/Dentistry—Mon/Wed/Fri. Board Certified.
IOUs Accepted

Also, the Firehouse Deli had reopened. The brightly painted fire-engine red building decorated for Christmas; stringed lights, pretty glass balls, and boughs of holly hung from every corner. The establishment had swept their camp tables clean; a large heated dispenser served Swiss Miss hot chocolate. The toppings free of charge; Reddi-wip, a huge jar of maraschino cherries, and cinnamon candy hearts. A few hardy souls sat outside with their steaming drinks, talking and laughing.

"Want a hot chocolate?" Guy asked.

"I wonder if they take money." Lauren laughed.

In the alley around the corner of the delicatessen, a curious figure came into view, and Lauren's smile faded from her lips. A dumpy, chubby homeless man sat in front of the deli's dark green Dumpster on a camp chair. He wore dark slacks and black rubber galoshes and a dirty black raincoat tied with a belt. Beside him sat a ventriloquist's dummy on a barstool, Charlie McCarthy with his cocky top hat and tails and trademark monocle. The whole scene was somehow unbecoming, unsettling, and awkward.

So who was this fellow, the mad scion of Edgar Bergen?

Moreover, the lone figure seemed strangely familiar. Though they had never set eyes on the man, Guy and Lauren felt like they were *supposed to know him.*

To make matters more bizarre, the plump ventriloquist arranged the Dumpster like a stage front, propping leftover letters from the theatre marquee against the open metal lid:

Bck by Poplr Demd—Musik!

He turned the handle on an antique Victor Victrola portable hand-crank phonograph that sat on a camp table and got a scratchy record playing. An old Negro Spiritual. Guy didn't recognize the song, but he could clearly read the title on the 1920s faded record label, as it spun around: "Jubilee."

What is the matter with the mourners?
O, my Lord!
The Devil's in the Amen corner,
my Lord!
Jubilee, Jubilee!

With his hand up the Charlie McCarthy's back the queer fellow made his dummy sing along:

> *You better stop, you fooling sinner man*
> *O, my Lord!*
> *Jubilee, Jubilee!*

But before Charlie McCarthy could sing any more, the old Victrola sputtered to a stop. The chubby fellow took his hand out from Charlie McCarthy's back and cranked the record player's handle a few turns. No use, the thing wouldn't play. The raggedy man suddenly spied Guy and Lauren watching him.

At once, he abandoned the Victrola, picked a battered black leather attaché off the ground, and placed it on his knees. He opened it up like a street vendor's case and began to rummage through his knickknacks. After a moment, the chubby fellow looked over the top of the attaché and measured Guy.

Damned, if he could only place this chubby oddball—

The fellow cocked his head sideways, as though forgiving Guy for his slip of memory. "It's not important," Mr. Chubbs said quietly.

What an ominous and yet pathetic figure—prompting Lauren to say, "Oh for God's sakes, Guy, give him something."

Nevertheless, even as she said it, she found she did not want her husband *to give him anything.* Corky and Peaches bristled, and she held the dogs close. Guy felt for a few crumpled bills in his parka, a five and a ten. The smart-aleck ventriloquist's dummy grinned under that cocky top hat with the spiffy monocle in his eye, daring Guy to fork over the money.

"You don't expect my Charlie McCarthy to speak by himself, do you?" Mr. Chubbs asked, as if explaining to a simpleton, *No Virginia, there is no Santa Claus.*

"He's just a wooden dummy."

The fellow glanced coolly at the rumpled paper in Guy's hand.

"I'm sorry." Guy felt suddenly ashamed. "That's all I have."

"Well, that's not going to get you very far in this world. But let's see if I've got anything you can afford."

Guy, taken aback, almost laughed out loud. He hadn't expected to *buy* anything. The chubby man in the dirty black raincoat pawed through the open attaché case. With a quiet sense of satisfaction, he repeated a bit of that Negro spiritual—"*The devil's in the amen corner*"—and chuckled to himself as if it were a private joke. "*Oh my Lord, Oh my lord . . .*"

Then he said to Guy, "Perhaps one of these will fit."

From out of the attaché, he drew two Halloween masks. The first mask was a pullover rubber Red Devil; Lucifer with the familiar leering grin, the horns and pointed ears. Smiling Satan come to make you a deal.

"What do you think?" Mr. Chubbs asked.

Guy was not amused.

"No, not your style?" The chubby man paused for effect. "Ah, maybe this is more to your liking." The second mask was made of thin plastic, the benevolent face of an Angel.

An Angel or the Devil?

"I don't think I can afford them both," Guy said.

The plump ventriloquist waved aside his concern:

Irrelevant. Immaterial. Money wasn't an issue.

"No honest man has just one face, *Mr. Poole*. Jubilee. Jubilee. I'll take your IOU."